Praise for S.C. Stephens' Thoughtless:

...possible to p...
York Times bestselling author

...ve, beautifully written, and uniquely captivating'
...ey Garvis-Graves, *New York Times* bestselling author

'What happens when you find your soul mate at the worst
possible time, in the least expected place? What if being with that
person means doing the most wrong thing you've ever done?
[It] leaves you thinking about these questions, the characters and
their choices for days if not weeks after reading.'
Tammara Webber, *New York Times* bestselling author

'This book has climbed right to the top of my list of favourites this
summer and made itself cosy there.'
A Turn of Page

'Really addictive. Could not put it down! This is my kind of
guilty pleasure.'
FashionandSarcasm.Blogspot.com

'I felt like after Thoughtless I was climbing off of the longest,
curviest, craziest roller coaster that I have ever virtually been on.
Let me tell you, that is absolutely not a bad thing!'
The Indie Bookshelf Blog

S.C. Stephens is a *New York Times* #1 bestselling author who spends her every free moment creating stories that are packed with emotion and heavy on romance. In addition to writing, she enjoys spending lazy afternoons in the sun reading, listening to music, watching movies, and spending time with her friends and family. She lives in Washington State with her two children.

Thoughtful

S. C. STEPHENS

SPHERE

First published in the United States in 2015 by Grand Central
First published in Great Britain in 2015 by Sphere

A CIP catalogue record for this book
is available from the British Library.

ISBN 978-0-7515-6043-5

Printed and bound in Great Britain by Clays Ltd, St Ives plc

Papers used by Sphere are from well-managed forests
and other responsible sources.

MIX
Paper from
responsible sources
FSC® C104740

Sphere
An imprint of
Little, Brown Book Group
100 Victoria Embankment
London EC4Y 0DY

An Hachette UK Company
www.hachette.co.uk

www.littlebrown.co.uk

I would not be where I am today without the love and support of my fans, so I'm dedicating this one to you. Thank you for coming out to see me, sometimes from thousands of miles away— your shirts, scrapbooks, jewelry, and considerate gifts completely blow my mind! Thank you for loving me enough to memorize my work; hearing it repeated back to me is a thrill that will never go away. Thank you for your passion, your devotion ... and your tattoos. I'm awed and humbled whenever I see one that was inspired by my life. And lastly, thank you for loving me despite my many flaws. I'm aware that there are quite a few, but you choose to see beyond them and love me for me, and I appreciate that more than you know.

Always in my heart,

Kellan Kyle

Chapter 1

All in a Day's Work

I'd been playing the guitar since I was six. While I'd been with the D-Bags for a few years now, I'd been in one band or another since high school. My childhood hadn't been the easiest, and music had been my saving grace. From the first time I'd held my guitar, I'd been hooked. It was the feel of the wood beneath my fingers, smooth, cool. It was the toughness of the strings, the reverberation deep inside the instrument. Even when I had been too young to really understand the impact music would have on my life, playing the guitar had spoken to me. There was something meaningful in that simple instrument that was dying to come out. There was something meaningful inside of *me* that was dying to come out.

My parents had given the instrument to me as a gift, but even back then I'd known it was more for them than for me. It was a convenient way to keep me occupied and out of their hair so they didn't have to be around me as much. My conception had been an unwanted accident, and my parents had never warmed up to me, never accepted me. I was a mistake that had forever changed their lives, and they'd never let me forget it. Whatever. The guitar kept me out of their way and I loved playing it, so it was a decent present, regardless of the ulterior motives behind it.

They hadn't bothered getting me lessons though, so I'd taught

1

myself. It had taken forever on my own, but being an only child with no close friends and parents who didn't want to have anything to do with me had afforded me a healthy amount of free time. My dad had liked to have the radio on whenever he was home. He would generally listen to talk radio, NPR and such, but when he put on music, it was almost always classic rock. I loved trying to mimic the songs, and once I'd mastered the basic chords, I'd played along with every song I could. It had irritated the hell out of Dad. He'd turn the radio up and order me to my room. "If you want to cause permanent ear damage with your god-awful racket, then do it alone so only you have to suffer," he'd say.

I'd go upstairs, but I'd leave my door cracked open so I could still hear the music. We had a big house when I was growing up, but if I strummed really softly, I could follow along with whatever was playing. For the next several years, "Stairway to Heaven" was my favorite song, but, then again, I think that's everybody's favorite song when they're learning.

For the first time in my young life, I'd found something that gave me complete and total peace, something I connected with, something with similar wants and desires. The guitar *needed* to be played. I *needed* to play it. It was a mutual, beautiful, symbiotic relationship, and for a long time, it was the only real relationship I had.

Grabbing my beloved instrument, I closed the door to my house. "Home" was a term I used lightly when I was describing my place. Truly, it was my parents' house, but they'd died a couple years ago and left it to me. I stayed there because it was a building with four walls and a roof, but I had no emotional attachment to it. It was nothing but wood, brick, glass, nails, glue, and cement.

While I'd been living in Los Angeles, my parents had sold my childhood home and moved to a much smaller house. I didn't know about it until they died. When I came back, I soon realized that they'd tossed everything of mine. It was confusing. They'd tried to scrub out my existence, but they'd still left me the house, the stocks, the retirement funds—everything. Sometimes I had a hard time understanding why they'd done that. Maybe they'd had a change of heart about me? Or maybe not.

I turned away from their house to see my gorgeous black-and-chrome Chevelle Malibu shining in the late-afternoon sun. I'd gotten her dirt cheap in L.A., and I'd spent a decent chunk of my summer fixing her up. She was a thing of beauty, my baby, and no one drove her but me.

Setting the guitar in the trunk, I headed to meet the guys for rehearsal. After easing my way onto the freeway, my eyes, as always, drifted to the unique cityscape of the Seattle skyline as it blossomed into view.

I've had a dichotomous relationship with the Emerald City over the years, both loving and hating it at times. Bad memories lurked around every corner—the loneliness of my childhood, the rejection, the biting remarks, the constant put-downs, the daily reminders of how much of an undesirable burden I was. The emotional poison my parents had injected into me had left its mark, but I had a good thing going here now, and the band was a large reason for my changed attitude toward the city.

Evan Wilder and I had formed the D-Bags together. With only my guitar on my back, a few dollars in my pocket, and dreams of a better life in my head, I'd left Seattle right after my high school graduation ceremony. Hitchhiking a ride wherever I could get one, I soon found myself at a bar on the Oregon coast. I'd stopped in for a drink and found Evan trying to convince the bartender that he was old enough to have a beer. He wasn't. Neither was I, but I managed to wink my way into a pitcher. I'd shared it with him, and we'd bonded over our mutual love of beer and music.

After spending a little time with Evan's family, the two of us had headed south, to L.A., City of Angels, to pick up some more band members. We'd found Matt and Griffin Hancock in the unlikeliest of places. A strip club. Well, maybe that wasn't so unlikely. Evan and I were horny, fresh-out-of-high-school teenagers after all.

The four of us had worked well together, even from the beginning, and were soon rocking bars and clubs in L.A. We'd probably

3

still be there, except I'd dropped everything and rushed back to Seattle after my parents died. Surprising the shit out of me, the guys had followed, and we'd been playing here ever since.

Traffic thickened as I neared downtown. We always rehearsed at Evan's place, since he technically didn't live in a residential area, so our noise wasn't an issue. His studio was above an auto body shop. That came in handy when my baby needed servicing. Roxie was my favorite mechanic there. She loved my car almost as much as I did, and would often take a look at her while I was upstairs with the guys.

Roxie was laughing with a coworker when I pulled up, but she still shot me a wave the second she saw me. Or, more accurately, my Chevelle; the girl only had eyes for my car. "Hey, Roxie. How's it going?"

Running a dirty hand through her short hair, she answered, "Good. I'm thinking of writing a children's book about a monkey wrench who helps animals that are in trouble. I might have him drive a Chevelle." She winked.

"Sounds awesome." I laughed. "Good luck."

"Thanks!" She grinned. As I headed for the stairs with my guitar, she shouted, "Let me know if the Chevelle needs anything! You know I'd make house calls for her, right?"

"Yep! I know," I shouted back.

Griffin was in the kitchen, rummaging through Evan's food, when I walked in. Playing always gave him the munchies. His pale eyes shifted my way, and smiling, I tossed him the box of Froot Loops I'd brought along with me. I'd picked them up while grocery shopping on an empty stomach, but they really didn't sound that great, and I knew they'd never get eaten at my house.

Griffin's expression brightened as he caught the box. "Sweet!" he muttered, immediately ripping it open. He reached into the bag, grabbed a handful of the sugary cereal, and was loudly crunching on it before I'd even made it into the living room area of the one-room loft.

Matt looked up when I set my guitar case on the couch beside

4

him. He'd been staring at something on his cell phone that sort of looked like a website. I wasn't entirely sure, I didn't even own a cell phone, and probably never would. Technology kind of mystified me, and I just didn't care enough to figure it out. I liked what I liked, regardless of whether it was out of date or not. My car still had a tape deck in it, for God's sake, which Griffin continuously chided me about, but as long as it still worked, I was happy with what I had.

"I think we should start playing festivals and fairs, and not just bars. It's too late to get into Bumbershoot this year, but I think we need to do it next year. I think we're ready." With slim features, blond hair, and blue eyes, Matt and Griffin were physically a lot alike. Personality-wise, though, the cousins couldn't have been more different.

"Yeah? Think so?" I asked, not too surprised that Matt was contemplating our future. He often did.

Behind him, I could see Evan wading through the rehearsal equipment that the band kept here at his place. His warm brown eyes were smiling at me beneath his close-cut dark hair as he approached the couch. "Definitely, we're as ready as we'll ever be, Kell. It's time to step it up a notch. With your lyrics and my rhythms… we're golden." While Matt was one of the most talented guitarists I'd ever seen, Evan was the one who arranged most of our pieces.

Matt glanced back at Evan with an eager nod. Looking between the two, I pondered whether we were ready. I supposed they were right, we were. We had more than enough songs, and probably enough fans. It could be a big step for the band, or it could be a giant waste of time.

When Evan got to the back of the couch, he crossed his arms over his chest. All of my bandmates were littered with random tattoos—Griffin's were a bit on the obscene side, naked girls and stuff, and Matt's were classier, with meaning behind every twist and symbol. Evan's though, his were like a living, breathing work of art. His arms alone were a museum-worthy masterpiece of fire, water, and everything in between.

5

While Matt and Griffin were both on the skinny side, Evan was bulkier. My body type was middle of the road, not too bulky, not too lean, and in terms of body art, I was a virgin. I just couldn't think of one thing I loved well enough to permanently scratch it into my skin. Nothing in life was permanent, so why pretend it was by immortalizing it? Seemed pointless to me.

I grinned at my two eager bandmates. "Let's do it then. Make it happen, Matt."

Smiling, Matt went back to his phone. Griffin walked up and tossed an arm around me. "Awesome! What are we doing?" Some stray pieces of cereal fell from his mouth after he asked.

"Nothing yet," I answered, smacking his chest.

He made an *oomph* sound, and even more of the brightly colored circles fell from his cheeks. I swear Griffin had the largest mouth of anyone I knew.

After a couple of hours of rehearsal, we called it a night. Piling into our cars, we headed over to Pete's Bar. The bar was our home base, where we played at least once a week, if not more, but we always seemed to end up there, even on nights we didn't play there. It was like the day didn't feel complete until we'd stepped through the double doors, however briefly. Everyone knew us there, and we knew just about everyone. Our stuff was there, our friends were there, our life was there.

I pulled the Chevelle into my unofficial parking spot. As usual, it was empty, waiting for me. When I shut the car off, the sounds of Fleetwood Mac died midchorus. I briefly considered turning the car back on to finish listening to the song, but I'd heard it a million times, and I really wanted to go sit down and have a nice cold, refreshing beer. That sounded fantastic right now.

Evan was getting out of his vehicle at almost the same time I was getting out of mine. He clapped me on the shoulder when I met him at the back of my car. I looked around for Matt and Griffin, but I didn't see Griffin's Vanagon anywhere. "Uh, where are Tweedledee and Tweedledum?" I asked Evan.

He raised a corner of his lip. "Jackass said he needed to run

6

home because he forgot Traci's shorts, and she needs them for work."

Picturing those two, I shook my head. Traci was a waitress at Pete's. She and Griffin had been messing around lately, which wasn't really a problem, except for the fact that Traci was starting to get attached, and she wasn't the type to be okay with keeping things casual forever. And that made her the exact opposite of Griffin.

The warm light of the bar's neon signs washed over me as I pushed open the doors to my haven. I inhaled a deep breath as I walked in, and unknown anxieties leached from my muscles. Everything about this place relaxed me. The noise, the smells, the music, and the people. If ever I could say I was truly content, it was here.

From my left, a husky voice let out a coarse "Hey there, Kellan."

Looking over, I saw the bartender, Rita, studying me. She had an expression on her face akin to a man who was dying of thirst, staring at a pitcher of water. I was used to that look on her though. I'd slept with her once, and by the way she looked at me, once wasn't enough. "Hey, Rita." I nodded my head up in greeting and her eyes fluttered closed with a soft groan.

"Jesus," she murmured as she ran a sharp, painted nail along her plunging neckline. "So fucking hot…"

After waving a greeting to the regulars, Evan and I made our way over to our table. Well, I suppose technically it wasn't ours, but, like my parking space outside, it had become known as the band's by our frequent visitations.

Leaning back in my chair, I propped my feet up on the end of the table. Just as I was debating whether I wanted chicken strips or a burger, my feet were unceremoniously dumped to the floor. I lurched forward a bit in my seat as my body weight shifted. A cute blonde wearing a tight red Pete's Bar shirt was standing at the end of the table with her hand on her hip. Her full lips were pursed in displeasure. "Don't put your feet on the table, Kellan. People eat there."

7

An amused smile curled my lips. "Sorry, Jenny. Just getting comfortable."

Jenny's mouth expanded into a charming smile. "A beer is what will make you comfortable. Two or four?" Her pale eyes shifted between Evan, me, and the empty chairs at our table.

Evan interpreted her question about our missing bandmates and raised four fingers. "They're on their way."

Jenny's smile turned playful as she reached out and scratched Evan's head. He closed his eyes and started thumping his leg on the floor like a dog getting its belly rubbed. Jenny giggled, and her eyes lit up in a way that was exceedingly attractive. I liked Jenny. She had a good heart, and she never openly judged me for the promiscuous nature of my life.

I'd discovered sex at a really young age, completely by happenstance, and like music, it had touched a nerve with me. I still craved that feeling, that closeness, and I sought it out as often as I could. I wasn't picky about who I slept with—older, younger, attractive, homely, mothers, girlfriends, wives. Who they were didn't matter to me, I only cared that they were interested. That probably wasn't the best thing to admit, but it was the truth. Sex was a release for me. It made me feel like a part of something bigger than myself, made me feel connected to the world around me. And I *needed* to feel that way. My life was full of empty spaces.

I'd tried pretty hard to date Jenny when she'd first started working here, but she'd point-blank turned me down. She said she didn't want to be anybody's fling. She hadn't turned away from our friendship though, and that meant a lot to me. I wouldn't say no if she changed her mind and wanted to go a round or two, but I wasn't going to push it again. I liked where we were, even if it wasn't sexual.

As Jenny started walking away, I called out, "I'll take a burger too! With bacon!" She lifted her thumb in the air, so I knew she'd heard me.

As I shifted my eyes from Jenny's backside, Evan poked me in the ribs. "Hey, Kell," he asked, "what do you think about Brooke? I was thinking about asking her to go out with me. I don't know, but I think she could be the one, man. I mean, have you seen the dimples on her?"

Evan grinned and I couldn't help but smile at him. "Yeah, I think she's great. Go for it." Evan found a new "one" every other month, it seemed. Might as well give it a go with Brooke. It could be the best month and a half of his life. My input given, I returned my feet to the table and waited for my food, my drink, and the rest of my bandmates to arrive.

"Oh my God. You're Kellan Kyle…"

I turned at hearing my name. Thanks to my occupation, I got recognized from time to time, especially here at the bar. At the table across from me, a petite young woman with hair so blond it was almost silver was staring my way. Framed in thick black mascara, the girl's irises were a turquoise shade of blue, like calm tropical water. There was no denying she was cute, and she seemed to know who I was, so I gave her a genuinely warm smile as I responded to her statement.

"At your service," I said, tipping a hat I wasn't wearing. She giggled, and the sound was oddly innocent, considering how she was eyeing me. The truth was plain though; this girl was no angel. Neither was I, so already we were a good match.

She asked if she could sit at my table and I shrugged. Sure, why not. After she pulled up a chair, she gushed, "I saw you play a couple of weeks ago in Pioneer Square." Her hand came up and her fingers touched my chest, then trailed down my stomach. "You…were amazing."

My lips parted as I stared her down, and her eyes tracked the movement. Just that brief touch sparked something in me…desire, longing. I wasn't sure why, but there was something about human touch that spoke to my soul. A clap on the back from a friend could completely alter my mood, while a girl running her hand up my thigh could instantly put me *in* the mood. It was a potent and unexplainable connection that I shared with people when they crossed into my personal space, whether they realized the significance of it

9

or not. And right now, this strange woman caressing me was opening me up to something wanton and lustful.

I was putty in her hands right now. I'd do anything...all she needed to do was ask. *So ask, Ms. Ocean Eyes, and I'll be anything you want me to be.*

And at the end of the night, she finally did ask, in a roundabout way. "How about we go to your place for a drink? Where do you live?"

Eagerness rushed through me at what I knew was about to happen, but I kept my expression casual and carefree. "Not far."

It took less than fifteen minutes to get to my house; my "date" followed me in her car. With her almost on my heels, I walked up to the front door and opened it. Stepping into the entryway, I flung my keys onto the half-moon table underneath a row of coat hooks. Over my shoulder, I asked her, "So, what kind of drink would you like?"

The front door slammed, and then fierce fingers grabbed my arm and spun me around. Hands pulled me down, and before I knew it, the blonde's mouth was all over mine. I guess she'd changed her mind about the drink. Reaching down, I grabbed her ass and lifted her up. Like a python, she wrapped her legs around my waist and squeezed. It made it slightly uncomfortable to carry her, but I managed to make my way up the stairs.

The blonde was tearing off my clothes the second I set her down in my bedroom. Once my jacket and shirt were in a heap on the floor, she raked her fingernails over my stomach. My muscles clenched in response and she groaned. "Holy shit, you have hot abs. I just wanna lick 'em."

She pushed me onto the bed and started to do just what she'd said. My eyes fluttered closed as the light flicks of her tongue sent shock waves of desire to my groin. Exercise was another release for me, something I did to clear my mind, shake out the cobwebs of bad memories that sometimes clung to the corners, refusing to leave me. As a result, I worked out quite a bit, and my body was lean and defined. Women loved that, so I was grateful for the sculpting side effects of my release.

10

When the blonde got to my pants, she didn't even hesitate. She unzipped them, pulled them down, and kept right on going with her mouth. Sucking in a breath, I grabbed a fistful of her hair when she got to the sweet spot. Some girls didn't like it when I held them in place. Some went nuts. The blonde moaned, sending stimulating vibrations down my cock.

When she was done tasting me, she pulled back. I opened my eyes to see her peering up at me with an expression full of passion, lust, and playfulness. For a brief second, I wondered what she really thought about me. Did she know anything about me besides my name and that I was in a band? Did she realize I screamed my heart out in my lyrics? Did she understand that my life left me feeling vacant inside? That I was so fucking lonely I almost couldn't stand myself? Would she want to know any of that? Or was the fact that I was a "rock star" enough for her? Like it was for all the other girls I'd slept with.

What felt like five seconds later, we were both completely bare and I was exploring her body with my tongue. Feeling aggressive, my date rolled me over and took the top. That was fine; her hands on my body felt wonderful. Relaxing, I slowly gave myself over to the feeling of being physically attached to someone. I loved this part. The girl's lips traveled down my body and her almost-silver hair tickled my skin; I loved that too. Without any rhyme or reason, she switched from flicking her tongue into my belly button to taking me into her mouth. Groaning, I grabbed a handful of the sheet as pure pleasure ignited me. My mind shut off, and I really started getting into this. When I could feel the buildup reaching an almost painful point, the girl stopped. I snapped my head up to stare at her. *God, now she becomes a tease?*

Eyes hooded, she licked her lips. "You are so fucking hot. I want you inside me. I want you to fuck me, right now. Hard and fast."

Direct and to the point. Okay. I was wound up enough that I could do both of those things. Pushing her over, I climbed on top of her. When I tried to pull away so I could grab a condom, she wrapped her legs around my hips, like she was going to work

11

her way onto me. *Geez, patience.* I unwrapped her legs and she frowned; there was even a hint of a glare in her eyes.

While she squirmed and begged for me to hurry up, I opened a drawer on my nightstand. Condoms were one thing I was a stickler for. I'd rather not catch something, and I'd really like to avoid getting anyone pregnant. My very existence was the result of my mother cheating on my father, one of the many reasons why he'd detested me. Why Mom had hated me too. One bastard branch on my family tree was enough, so I always wrapped it up.

Grabbing one of the many square packages in there, I opened it and rolled the condom on before my date could complain too much more about my absence. When I drove into her, she wasn't as tight as I liked, but she felt good... *really* good. When I entered her, she screamed my name. Literally. My ears rang. She was so ready for me that moving inside of her was a piece of cake. I gave her a deep thrust, sinking in as far as I could, and cringed as she screamed again. Was I really satisfying her so much that she couldn't stifle the screaming?

"Yes, Kellan! Harder! Faster!"

She said it so loud I was sure everyone on my block could hear her. Maybe that was the point. As I pumped into her again and again, she wrapped her arms and legs around me. Feeling something even nicer than my impending climax, I buried my head into the crook of her neck. Her hand came up to gently tangle into my hair, and I finally felt it. *That.* That connection. That bond. That was what I wanted, what I liked, and I desperately tried to hold on to it. *Let me feel this for just another minute...*

"Harder, Kellan! Oh, God, you're amazing! Fuck me! Yes, fuck me!"

The connection died away as her screams intensified. I tried to hold on to that intimate feeling, but I couldn't; the moment was gone. Grunting, I dug in deeper and harder. Might as well get this over with. Her cries and moans turned almost theatrical, but I felt her walls tightening around me, so I knew she wasn't completely faking. The tightness finally pushed me over the edge too.

"God, yes," I murmured as I started coming. *Fuck.* For a split second as I released, I felt great. Everything about my life was perfect, all was right in the world. Then my orgasm ended, the feeling faded, and a darker emotion started filling the void.

Pulling out, I rolled over to my back. She was panting beside me, a satisfied expression on her face. "God, you're just as amazing as they say."

I glanced over at her. *They say I'm amazing? Who are they exactly?* "I'll be right back."

Standing up, I left my room, walked into the bathroom, and took off the condom. I knew I should feel amazing right now, but I felt strange. More incomplete. It was getting to be a familiar feeling, right after sex. Like waking up with a hangover, I always felt slightly crappier than I had before.

While I stared at myself in the mirror and debated my confusion, I heard my date stirring in my room. A second later, she popped out into the hallway, fully dressed. With a wistful sigh, she gazed at my lean, naked body. "God, if I had time, I would stay and totally do that again with you." She shrugged. "I've got to get going though." Stepping into the bathroom, she tossed her arms around me and gave me a hug. "I had a lot of fun. Thanks!" She kissed my shoulder, then swatted my bare bottom. "See you around, Kellan." Giggling, she added, "I can't believe I just had sex with Kellan Kyle."

Turning, she practically skipped down the hall to the stairs. The front door opened and shut a minute later, and then a car started and pulled away. Still staring out the bathroom door, I whispered, "Bye," into my empty hallway.

Returning my eyes to the mirror, I inhaled a deep breath. Disappointment flooded me; I should feel better than this. When I was younger, the euphoria from sex had stayed with me for a long time. Sometimes for days. Now, though...it faded almost instantly. Something was missing. I felt hollow and even lonelier than before the sex...and I had no idea what to do to change that.

13

Chapter 2

An Unexpected Request

The walls of Evan's loft reverberated with the power of our amplified instruments. Cymbals crashed while the snare drum tapped out a measured beat. Matt's guitar squealed an intricate melody while Griffin's bass provided a steady backdrop for us to paint our musical masterpiece upon.

Not holding back one ounce of my ability, I sang the intense chorus at a pitch that was at the upper crest of my range. I nailed it though. My voice harmonizing with the various rhythms circling our small stage gave me goose bumps. Near the end, the song reached an apex. All instruments were going full bore, hard and intense. Then it suddenly dropped off to complete silence. This was the hardest part of the song. For me at least. I had two lines to sing in that pin-dropping silence. There was no music to mask any potential flaws in my voice. No chance for a redo when I performed this live. It was just me, my voice, and hundreds of ears analyzing it. But I wasn't worried in the slightest. There were very few things I was certain of in my life, and this was one of them. My voice wouldn't let me down. It never did.

In the quiet of Evan's loft, I sang my heart out. After the second line, Evan came back in with the drums. Easy at first, almost unnoticeable, but then building into a crescendo that complemented the intensity of my voice. As I ripped out the last of the four lines, the guys sang with me. Then every instrument kicked in again, even my acoustic guitar. The hairs were standing up on my arms as we finished the powerful song, and I was grinning ear to ear as the last note faded away. The fans were going to go crazy for this. It would definitely be on our set list for a long time to come.

Wondering if the guys felt the same, I twisted around to meet Matt's and Evan's faces. Matt was grinning just as widely as I was. Evan let out a low whistle. "Shit, man. That was awesome. I think it's ready. We should play it Friday."

I nodded in agreement. That was just what I'd been thinking. Removing his guitar, Matt set it on its stand and walked over to me. Eyeing me like a doctor observing a patient, he asked, "How's your throat? That one too high for you? Too intense? We could drop it down a notch and I think it would still work."

Testing the waters, I massaged my throat and swallowed a couple of times. "No, I feel fine."

Matt squinted like he didn't believe me. "We're going to be singing this song hundreds of times. If you can't recreate it perfectly *each* time, then we should modify it so you can. Consistency is what's important. It doesn't do us any good if this song fries you."

My mouth blossomed into a smile at Matt's equal concern for my well-being and the band's sound. If it wasn't for his tenacity, I had no doubt that we wouldn't be half as good as we were. "I know that, Matt. Trust me, if I couldn't do this, I would tell you. I know my voice; this song isn't a problem."

Seemingly satisfied, Matt finally smiled. "Good. 'Cause that seriously kicked ass." He laughed, and I couldn't help but laugh with him.

Gathering up my guitar, I headed for its case resting on Evan's couch. Thinking of my melancholy mood last night, and remembering one of my reasons for it, I said over my shoulder, "Oh, hey, Joey moved out, so if you guys know anyone looking for a room, my place is open again." My passionate ex-roommate had moved out a few nights ago, and the house had been really quiet ever since. I hated the oppressive silence.

Griffin had been busy pretending to play his bass to a horde of adoring fans. In between headbanging, he was throwing out devil horns, tongue waggles, and pelvic thrusts. As usual after rehearsal, all of us had been ignoring his over-the-top, I'm-a-rock-star, look-at-me antics, choosing to let him live out his fantasies in peace. He usually ignored our comments too, since they were usually all music related. My last one got his attention though.

His face fell as he set down his guitar. "Joey's gone? Fuck. Really? What happened?"

I didn't feel like going into details, so I gave him as vague of an answer as possible. "She got mad, moved out." Truth was, she'd caught me in bed with another woman and flipped out. Joey and I had fooled around on occasion, but I hadn't realized how possessive she was until a few nights ago, when she'd practically ripped my nuts off and chased my date down the street. She'd had more than a few choice words for me, but the phrase "You're going to be alone for the rest of your life, because you're a worthless piece of shit" was the one that rang in my ears most often.

Griffin saw right through my hazy answer. Thin lips pursed in annoyance, he crossed his arms over his chest. "You nailed her, didn't you?" I made no response to that. I didn't even blink. Griffin huffed out an irritated breath. "Goddammit, Kellan. I was supposed to bang her first."

Even though his argument was absurd and idiotic, I had to smile at him. I hadn't realized there was a waiting list for my ex-roommate. Matt scoffed at his cousin. "You wanted him to wait sixty years until Joey finally got bored enough to give you the time of day? Nobody has that kind of patience, man."

Griffin glared daggers into Matt while Evan laughed at his comment. "I'm pretty sure I wasn't talking to you, asswipe."

Matt wasn't dissuaded by Griffin's thought-provoking comeback. Instead of minding his own business, like Griffin had implied, Matt countered with, "And why would Kellan want your seconds anyway? He could catch something. They make after-school specials about crap like that, you know?"

Fire lit up Griffin's light eyes. "I have to get his seconds all the goddamn time. Why shouldn't he get mine every once in a while? Seems fair to me."

Evan started laughing so hard he had to swipe a finger under his eye. Seeing him start to lose it made me laugh too. Matt tried to keep a straight face while he answered Griffin's inane question, but he struggled. Voice choppy with chuckles, Matt told him, "Kell's got options. You don't, cuz. You have to take whatever you can get."

Not amused, Griffin eyed each one of us in turn. "Fuck you, and you, and you." With that, he stormed off, the front door banging closed behind him.

Matt sighed as the last of his laughter left him. "I suppose I should go pacify him. We do need his van for the gig tonight." I thumped his shoulder as he walked by. *Good luck.*

Two weeks later, I was still living alone in my parents' empty house when the phone in my kitchen rang.

"Hello?" I asked, picking it up. Leaning back on the counter, I played with a section of the cord while I waited for a response. It was quick in coming.

"Hey, Kellan?"

My lips broadened into a wide smile as recognition hit me. I knew the accent on the other end of the line. I'd know it anywhere. "Denny?"

Just hearing his voice again made me feel lighter, like my worries were already fading. Denny Harris had been one of the brightest spots of my childhood, perhaps the only one. In order to look like freaking saints to their friends, my parents had decided to participate in hosting a sixteen-year-old exchange student when I was fourteen. They hadn't asked my opinion, of course, but I'd been fine with the arrangement. I'd always wanted a brother, and the idea of having a friend at home for an entire year had sounded amazing.

I'd counted down the days until his arrival, and when the time finally came, I'd bounded down the stairs to meet him.

When I'd rushed into the entryway, a tan, dark-haired teen had been standing between my parents, looking around our home with interested eyes. A polite smile was on his lips as he raised his hand in greeting; his eyes were just as dark as his close-cropped hair. I'd returned his gesture with a crooked grin. I had been the only family member smiling.

Mom's lips had been pursed in disapproval. Dad had been scowling, but that was nothing new. Dad had always scowled at me.

In a prudish voice, Mom had said, "It's rude to keep your guests waiting, Kellan. You should have been waiting at the door, or met us at the car so you could help unload the bags."

Dad barked, "What the hell took you so long?"

I'd wanted to say that I *should* have been waiting at the airport with them, but that was an argument I couldn't win, so I hadn't bothered bringing it up. I'd asked to go, but they'd made me stay home. Mom had said I would just "get in the way," like I was a toddler and still underfoot or something. Dad had simply said, "No. Stay here."

I'd been upstairs playing my guitar when I'd heard the front door open. It had taken me all of thirty seconds to set it down and run out there. But, knowing nothing I said would have mattered, I'd merely widened my smile and given them an answer that I knew they would, at the very least, agree with. "I'm just slow, I guess."

Impatience and irritation had been brimming in Dad's eyes, also nothing new. "Isn't that the truth," he'd murmured. His eyes narrowed as he examined me. He'd wanted me to dress nicely for the new arrival, and I think he'd been expecting a suit and tie. Fat chance. I'd been wearing frayed jeans, sneakers, and a T-shirt from a local bar.

Catching me off guard, Dad had reached up and snatched a handful of my hair. He fisted his hand close to my scalp, stinging me with pinpricks of pain. Knowing any movement was going to make it even more unpleasant, I'd held very still. Yanking on my hair, Dad had jerked my head back and snarled, "I told you to cut this crap off. You look like a no-good degenerate. I'm going to buzz you in your sleep one day." Mom and Dad had always hated my shaggy, unkempt style. Maybe that was why I'd kept it for so long.

Out of the corner of my eye, I had watched the dark-haired stranger taking in what was happening with wide, shocked eyes. By the way he glanced between my dad and me, uneasily shifting his weight back and forth, it was pretty obvious that he was uncomfortable witnessing the confrontation. I didn't blame him. It wasn't exactly a great welcome-to-the-neighborhood moment.

Through clenched teeth, I'd asked my dad, "You gonna introduce me to our guest, or are you gonna try and scalp me with your bare hands?"

Dad had snapped his gaze to the stranger among us and immediately dropped his hold on me. Mom, in all her maternal glory, had let out a beleaguered sigh. "Don't be so dramatic, Kellan. It's not like he hurt you by 'touching' your hair." From her tone of voice, it had sounded like Dad was only playfully ruffling my hair. Strangely enough though, her words had made me feel like I was overreacting.

Puffing his chest out, Dad finally introduced us. "Kellan, this is Denny Harris. He's joining us all the way from Australia. Denny, this is Kellan...my son." That last part had been added with clear reluctance.

With an affable smile, Denny had stuck his hand out. "Nice to meet you."

Touched by his sincerity, I grabbed his hand and said, "Nice to meet you too."

After that, Denny's bags had been thrust into my face, and I'd been ordered to be the house butler while my parents showed him around. My parents expected obedience from me, so no kind words had followed their demand, but Denny had thanked me for my assistance as I'd taken his stuff. That had instantly made me like him. His simple gratitude was more heartwarming than anything Mom and Dad had ever said to me.

My moment of warmth hadn't lasted long though. The second Denny disappeared with Mom, Dad had grabbed my arm and sneered, "Don't push me, Kellan. You need to be on your best behavior while Denny is here. I won't put up with any of your crap. You step out of line, I'll whoop you so hard, it'll be a week before you can stand up straight. Two before you can sit properly. You understand me?"

Dad had shoved his finger into my chest for an emphasis that I hadn't needed. I'd understood him completely. Unlike some parents, Dad hadn't been giving me an empty threat to keep me in line. No, he had meant every word he'd just said. He would ignore my cries and pleading for him to stop. He'd leave me raw, just on the verge of bleeding. Because he was in charge, and he wanted me to know that. I was nothing to him. Absolutely nothing.

Reminding myself that my father's threats didn't matter anymore, I pushed the memory to the far recesses of my brain and focused on Denny. I was thrilled to be hearing from my old friend. It had been ages since we'd last talked. That was unfortunate, since he was living stateside again and keeping in contact should have theoretically been easier now. Denny was frequently in my thoughts though, and I often wondered how he was doing with college.

Denny chuckled. "Yeah, it's me. Long time, no hear, huh, mate?"

My smile grew. "Yeah, way too long. I think we're due for a reunion."

"Well, actually... that's kind of why I was calling. I'm moving out to Seattle when I graduate in a couple of weeks, and I was hoping you knew of a place I could stay. Well, a place my girlfriend and I could stay. Preferably someplace that's not too expensive. Things are kind of tight right now."

I blinked in disbelief. He was moving back here? For good? Excitement danced up my spine. I couldn't wait to see him again. "You're coming here? Seriously? That's great, man. And your timing is perfect! I have a room free. Fully furnished too, since my last roommate left a lot of her stuff. I'll rent it to you for whatever you can afford." I would have told him he could stay for free, but Denny wasn't one for handouts, and I knew he'd never accept that offer. This offer though, there was no way he could say no.

There was a pause on the other end that dampened my spirits some. Hadn't I just told him great news? Shouldn't he be ecstatic? "Denny, did you hear me?"

"Ah, yeah, I just hadn't expected… You sure you're okay with us staying with you?" His accent thickened with what sounded like concern. Was he concerned for me? Did he feel like he was imposing? That couldn't be farther from the truth.

I tried to reassure him with my tone and my words. "Of course, man, why wouldn't I be? I'm stoked about this. Aren't you?"

Another oddly long pause met my ear, then a heavy sigh. "Yeah, yeah I am. This will be great. And Kiera and I won't be any problem for you, I promise."

A soft laugh escaped me. Denny was never a problem. He was the easiest person in the world to get along with. In fact, I couldn't think of one person who didn't like him. "Don't even worry about it. My place is your place." After a pause, I teasingly added, "So, you finally got yourself a girl, huh?"

Denny had infamously refused every girl's advances in high school. He'd said he hadn't wanted to get involved with someone when he knew he wasn't going to be around long. His constant refusal to date had sort of been a longstanding joke between us. But I thought it was great that Denny had finally found a girl to commit to. The odds were good that he was no longer the virgin he'd been in high school. *Good job, mate.*

"Kiera, was it?" I asked. "What's she like?"

I swear his laugh was strained, like he was suddenly nervous. "She's… she's great. The love of my life. I don't know what I would do without her."

He stressed the words, like he was warning me about something. I furrowed my brow, not understanding. Shaking my head, I decided I was just misreading him. It had been a long time since we'd spoken, after all. There was bound to be some awkwardness until we got caught up with each other. "Well, good. I'm glad to hear it. You deserve happiness."

After another pause, Denny softly told me, "So do you, Kellan." An uncomfortable feeling settled over me as his words brought the silence of this house crashing down around me. He'd said something similar when he'd left to go back home when we were teenagers.

"Um, thanks," I whispered, incapable of saying more.

Denny cleared his throat like he was wiping away the past. "No worries. I'll call you again when it's closer to our time to leave. And...thank you, Kellan. This means a lot to me."

"You're welcome." *It means a lot to me too.*

When I set the phone back in the cradle, a feeling of rightness flooded into me. Denny was coming back. I honestly never thought he'd return. It had never even occurred to me that he might. Even though Denny and I had only lived together for a year, he felt like family to me. A brother.

He'd ended up somewhat saving me that summer, when I had unintentionally pushed my father too far. Dad had been reining in his temper whenever Denny was around, but anger management had never been one of his strong points.

"Kellan, get your ass in here!"

Wondering what I had done to make my dad sound so incensed, I'd swallowed a deep breath and hesitated. I hadn't wanted to join him in the kitchen. I'd sort of wanted to run. But Denny had put a calming hand on my shoulder and said, "I'll go with you, mate." That had made me relax. If Denny was with me, Dad probably wouldn't do anything other than yell, and I could handle that.

Putting on a brave face even though my insides were twisting, I'd stepped into the kitchen with Denny just a few steps behind me. Either Dad hadn't known Denny was with me, or he'd been too worked up to care. Grabbing my shoulders, he'd jerked me into him, shifted direction, then shoved me into the wall. The sudden movement had caught me off guard, and I'd smacked my skull against the plaster.

My vision had hazed as a jolt of pain wrapped around my head. In case Dad wasn't done with me, I'd instinctively raised my hands. He'd only yelled though. "I told you to make sure the lids on the garbage were tight! You did a half-ass job, and now there is garbage strewn all over the backyard! Go fix it. Now!"

I remembered my anger that that was what he'd been mad about. *The fucking garbage?* It still incensed me.

Denny had stepped to my side then. "We'll go clean it up together, Mr. Kyle."

Stepping forward, I'd put a hand on Denny's shoulder to silence him. I hadn't been sure how worked up Dad was, and Denny didn't deserve any of his wrath. Not wanting him to become a part of our argument, I had shaken my head and told him, "No, you go upstairs. I got this."

Impatient, Dad had shoved my shoulder back. I'd lost my balance, stumbled, and fallen on my ass. My wrist had wrenched as I'd landed on it, and I remember gasping in pain. Dad hadn't cared. Glaring down at me, he'd snipped, "Quit wasting time and go clean up that mess you made before the neighbors see the pigsty you've let our house become."

Irritated and hurt, I'd barked something at him that I never should have. "If you'd leave me the hell alone, I could go fix your precious fucking lawn!"

All the blood had drained from my face the second I'd realized I'd said that out loud. I'd talked back to Dad, *and* I'd sworn. Staring up at my father, I clearly saw the restraint slipping away from him, and I had known, without a doubt, that Denny being a witness didn't matter anymore. My insolence had gone too far, and Dad was going to do his worst.

While I had gingerly risen to my feet, Dad had balled his hands into fists. I recalled closing my eyes, knowing what was coming. *Go ahead, Dad. I'm ready* echoed through my memories. Surprisingly, it had been Denny's voice that had interrupted the ominous silence. "No, wait—"

There was a sickening crunch, then Denny's body had collided with mine. I'd recovered in time to catch him as he'd started to fall, and when he'd looked up at me, there had been blood trickling down his split lip. He'd stepped in front of the hit for me, taken my pain. Dazed and disoriented, I had helped Denny sit on the floor, then squatted beside him.

Dad had just stood there, staring at us like we'd both spontaneously combusted. Then he'd shifted his gaze to his hands and murmured, "Jesus." Without another word to us, he'd darted out of the kitchen like he was fleeing a crime scene.

I remembered shivering as I'd squatted beside Denny. I'd been so sure that Dad was going to turn on me after hitting Denny, punish me for unintentionally cracking the façade. At the time, I had been positive that he still would, once I was alone. That was when Denny had put his hand on my knee and said, "It's okay. I'm okay."

When I had looked over at him, his lip had been bloody and swollen, but he hadn't seemed the least bit afraid as he met my eye. Shaking his head, he'd soothingly repeated, "It's okay."

Scared, I'd started shaking my head like I had a nervous tic. My entire body was vibrating, like I was suffering from hypothermia. I couldn't calm down. I was certain my dad would never let it go. He would get me. He would teach me a lesson. He would make me suffer.

Sitting up a little straighter, Denny had put a comforting hand on my shoulder and spoken words that no one had spoken to me before. "Everything is going to be okay. I'm here for you, Kellan. I'll always be here for you."

My fear had started diminishing as I stared into his calm eyes. He had seemed so sure...It had given me hope. And he'd been right. My dad had been so afraid of Denny telling someone what he'd done that he hadn't laid a hand on me for the rest of the time Denny had stayed with us. It had been the best year of my life.

Waiting for Denny and his girlfriend to get here was a painstaking exercise in the art of patience. I tried to let time flow as naturally as possible, but there were moments when I literally stared at the clock and willed the hours to surge forward. But nothing helped, and every day seemed to be more sluggish than the last. I thought the anticipation of his arrival would make a blood vessel burst in my brain before he got here. Wouldn't that be poetic?

I was really excited for Denny to hear my band. That was probably because he was the reason I'd started a band in the first place. Normally, my parents never would have agreed to let me do something like that, but after Dad had inadvertently slugged Denny, he was a lot more agreeable; in an effort to keep Denny happy so he'd keep quiet, I don't think there was anything Dad would have denied him.

Denny had always been fascinated by my ability to play and sing, and he'd always pushed me to use it. "You have God-given talent," he'd say. "Not doing anything with it would be a waste." When he'd found out that our school was having local bands play junior prom instead of hiring a DJ, he'd urged me to put a group together, and had even cleared it with my father.

Not only had Denny been a bright spot in my past, he had unknowingly given direction to my otherwise meaningless life. He'd set the mold for my future, and I would do just about anything to return the favor.

I was whistling when I walked into Pete's that Friday night. Jenny gave me a look that clearly said, *What's with all the joy?* I shrugged. "It's Friday. TGIF."

Jenny laughed at my answer, her blond ponytail bouncing around her shoulders. Leaving her, I walked over to Sam, the bouncer at the bar. Stretching out my hand, I showed him my spare house key. His brows bunched together and his lips compressed. "We moving in together? You're great and all, Kellan, but I like living on my own." His voice was deep, husky, and perfectly matched his absurdly large muscles. I swear the man's biceps were as large as my skull, and I wasn't sure how it was physically possible, but he had no neck whatsoever.

Chuckling, I shook my head. "Denny's coming in tonight. I'll probably be onstage. Will you give him this for me?" Denny and

Sam had been in the same grade during high school, and the three of us had hung out a lot while Denny had been here. As soon as Denny had called me about a room, I'd told Sam.

His huge fist closed around the shiny metal. "Sure thing," he gruffed, shoving the key into his pocket.

"Thanks!" Clapping him on the shoulder, I turned and headed toward my table.

Evan and Matt were already there. Griffin was having a conversation with Traci near the bar. And by conversation, I mean Traci was rapidly telling him something while he blinked with a dumbfounded, confused expression on his face. Matt watched Griffin with a smirk on his lips while Evan cuddled with Brooke. I guess she'd said yes when he asked her out. Well good, that should make him happy for a bit.

Two seconds after I sat down, two girls approached me. Pulling chairs in so they were on either side of me, they spoke at almost the same time. "Kellan Kyle! We love your music!"

Their eyes were darting over my face and body, and I wondered if they meant what they'd just said. As courteously as I could, I replied, "Thank you. That means a lot to me."

Both girls feverishly flirted with me until it was time to go onstage. I was certain I could go on a date with either one of them, if I wanted. Maybe both, if they were up for it. I didn't ask though; my mind was other places. Denny would be here soon.

When it was time for us to go play, a familiar feeling washed over me—anxiousness mixed with peace. As I walked up the steps to the stage worn with use, I felt the remnants of who I was melting off me. Onstage, none of my worries touched me. It was like I was a different person. Like I was acting, and yet I was being more truthful than I ever was off the stage. I bled my heart out while I was performing, not that many people truly noticed; they were too busy enjoying the showmanship to dig beneath the surface of the words. There was safety in the scrutiny, anonymity in the spotlight. I felt invincible up there. Just me and my guitar.

Behind me was the coolest backdrop of any stage I'd been on to date. The wall was pitch-black, and covered with old guitars in every shape, size, and model you could think of. None of them held a candle to my simple acoustic instrument though. Sometimes the most beautiful things in the world were overlooked because of their flashier counterparts. I preferred quiet beauty.

As I gripped the microphone stand, I shifted my gaze out in front of me. Ear-splitting screams blended into one giant wall of sound. Girls of every race, age, and size were jockeying for position in front of my feet. I smiled down at them with an expression that was as much encouragement as it was a come-on. They ate it up, jumping and waving their hands so I'd notice them. I lifted my eyes to take in the crowd farther back from the stage. Clumps of people surrounded the various tables. The bar was packed. Good. I liked playing to a full house.

"Evenin', Seattle," I murmured into the microphone.

The girls right in front of the stage started shrieking again. One of them to the left of me slumped like she was fainting. Luckily one of her friends caught her and helped her to her feet; I'd hate to be the cause of someone getting seriously injured.

"Everybody doing okay tonight?" I asked while Matt, Griffin, and Evan got situated. There was a flurry of answers from the bar, most of them of a positive nature. I glanced at my bandmates, saw that they were settled and ready, and turned my attention back to the crowd. "Let's get this party started then!"

I pointed behind me to Evan. He took my cue and began the first song on our set list. A hard, driving beat filled the bar, and I lost myself to the rhythm. Matt and Griffin joined in for their parts, and then I joined in for mine. The girls near me went crazy. I played with them, flirted a little, made each and every one of them feel like I was anxious to meet up with her later tonight. I wasn't going to, not tonight anyway, but what harm did it do to make them believe that? Everyone wanted a little fantasy in their life.

Throughout our set, I kept one eye on the doors for Denny. He should be showing up any time. I wondered if he'd look the same—unruly dark hair that stuck up everywhere; short, skinny frame. I

27

wondered what his girlfriend looked like. I kept picturing her as a petite blond thing for some reason.

The song we were singing was a fan favorite, and everywhere I looked people were singing along. I focused in on the group in front of me. Propping a foot up on a speaker, I leaned out into the crowd, letting them touch me. It was complete mayhem, but the way they grinned made me smile. It was nice to be able to make people happy, even if it was for a really strange reason.

I was suggestively running my hand down my body when I felt something. It was the oddest sensation I'd ever felt, like lightning was about to strike and the air was charged with static electricity; even though it was warm in the bar, my skin was pebbled with goose bumps. I kept the majority of my attention on the girls clamoring for me to notice them, but I lifted my eyes to the doors.

There was a girl being led into the bar. Whoever was with her was weaving her through the packed crowd. I couldn't see the person in the lead at all, and was only catching glimpses of the mystery woman, but it was enough. I saw hundreds of girls every night, some plain, some beautiful enough to be highly sought-after cover models, but this girl… even seeing her through a crowd, there was something about her that sang to me. It nearly stopped me in my tracks. Mentally, at least. I was having difficulty getting the right words to come out of my mouth. I was sure I'd said those last two lines completely wrong.

It was almost like I'd been punched in the gut. My breath felt strained, and I was getting sort of light-headed. What was it about her that affected me so much? I didn't entirely know, and it freaked me out. She was studying the band as I discreetly studied her, and from what I could see of her expression, she didn't seem overly thrilled with us. I wondered why.

Wavy brown hair bounced along her shoulder blades as she walked through my field of vision. It was hard to clearly make her out with the space and bodies between us, but I saw long legs under her jean shorts; they seemed to go on forever. And she was wearing a tight shirt that highlighted her small, perky breasts. The light yellow fabric almost reached her waistline, and the thin band of skin around her middle showcased her trim stomach in a classy but tantalizing way. She was long and lean like she was a runner, like me. I wondered if we had that in common. Then I wondered what else we had in common. Blue eyes? A love of music? An almost debilitating need to never be alone?

I wanted to keep covertly staring at her all night long, but I couldn't let this odd, overwhelming sensation of attraction distract me from the fans. I had a job to do, after all. I dropped my eyes to my girls and gave them all of my gyrating, teasing attention as I tempted them with my voice and my body. Whoever this random woman was, I'd probably never see her after tonight. And if I was going to meet her at all, it would have to be after our gig. There was no need to fixate on her now.

Even still, I couldn't resist a peek, and I again shifted my eyes to take her in. Oddly, she and the person she was with, who I could now see was a guy, were talking to Sam against the far wall. Sam seemed happy to be talking with the pair. Sam rarely looked that way at work, especially on a night when the bar was jam-packed full of people. Or potential problems, as he liked to call them. But he was smiling. He even reached out and gave the guy a hug. That was when it hit me. The guy was Denny. The girl I was instantly attracted to, even from the massive distance between us…was Denny's girlfriend.

Well, of course she was.

I instantly locked my eyes onto the fans in front of me and amped up my seduction of them. I even reached out to touch a few of them, since they were safe. Denny's girlfriend was *not* safe. I could not be having thoughts about her. It was inappropriate on so many levels. I may on occasion have slept with girls who were in committed relationships, because who was I to judge what someone decided to do with their body, but I wouldn't do that to Denny. He was my brother. My *family*. The only real family I had in this world, besides my band.

Missing my long-gone friend, I looked up to make eye contact with him. I wanted to make sure he got his key, make sure he was settled, maybe even give him a quick wave, even though I was still singing. I spotted him clutching the girl's hand, and a smile broke out through my words. Denny looked older, for sure, but he still had that youthfulness about him that made me want to reach out and give him a noogie. The innocence on his face, in his smile, warmed my heart. *I'd do anything for this guy.* Give my life for him if necessary.

Denny's girlfriend—Kiera, if I remembered correctly—was gazing up at him like he was the moon and stars to her. I let go of my initial attraction and smiled over their relationship. He was clearly happy with her, and it was obvious they were in love. I pushed back my own desires and only let my happiness for him shine through. I gave him a small wave as the song ended, and he lifted his chin and raised his key to let me know he had it.

Hating to break eye contact with the friend I was itching to catch up with, I quickly glanced at Matt and gave him the okay to start the next song. The job came first, especially when I was onstage. The song Matt started playing was one of my favorites. It was also one of the most painful songs for me. I had written it about my parents. It was sort of my plea for them to love me. *Too little. Too late.* They never had, and now that they were gone, they never would. I still sang it almost every night though. Hopeless as it was, I couldn't stop trying to win their affection.

For a moment, I was so lost in the words and the painful memories that everything else faded into the background. Then I found my gaze wandering to Kiera. She was leaving the bar with Denny. She glanced back at me at the last minute though. Lips parted, her expression was awed as she watched me cut open my heart and bleed out all over the stage. Maybe it was the lights, but I could have sworn her eyes were watering, like she understood that this song was painful for me. That I had to fight against my throat constricting with every syllable. That the only reason I could sing it at all was because of endless rehearsals and performances. For the first time in a long time, I was looking at someone who saw me. Not the rock star, not the playboy, but *me*. The real me. And for the first time in a long time, terror crawled up my spine. Kiera shivered, like she also shared my fear, then she disappeared with Denny.

This girl... she'd already made an impression, and I hadn't even been introduced to her yet. The three of us all living together could be an incredible, eye-opening experience. Or it could be a living nightmare. Either way, it was definitely going to be interesting.

Chapter 3

Glad You're Back

The sun was blinding, and a surge of panic raced through me. It was morning. Denny was leaving.

Feeling dread circling around me, I rushed to Denny's bedroom. His door was closed. Was he still asleep? He didn't answer when I lightly rapped on it, so I knocked harder. "Denny?" When he didn't respond, I cracked his door open. "Denny?" The room was completely empty, and my voice echoed back to me. He was gone? But I hadn't said goodbye…

I ran down the stairs, yelling at my parents to wait for me. No one was there though, and nothing but silence answered me. I checked every room in the house, but I was completely alone. In a daze, I stared at the front door. *They'd left without me.* My parents had stolen my final goodbye to the best friend I'd ever had. Those fucking assholes. Hot tears stung my eyes. That was just like them to steal any moment of happiness from me that they could. I was probably never going to see Denny again.

Just as that thought pounded through my brain, I heard a car pull into the driveway. Overwhelmed with guilt and anger, I screamed at my father when he stepped through the front door. "How could you leave without letting me say goodbye!"

When I stepped within range, the back of Dad's hand lashed out and bashed my jaw. I tasted blood in my mouth, and it surprised me so much I fell to the ground. I'd gotten used to Dad backing off with Denny around. I'd grown complacent...comfortable. But Denny wasn't around anymore. I was on my own.

When I peered up at Dad, he had a look on his face that bordered on happiness. "Do you know how long I've been waiting to do that?" he asked, his voice gruff.

Beginning to tremble, I scooted back until my spine was against the wall. "I'm sorry," I immediately sputtered. *How could I forget what he was really like so quickly?*

Dad narrowed his eyes, then slowly and methodically removed his belt. I felt like I was going to be sick as I watched him, and knowing that I couldn't run, that I had nowhere to go, nowhere to hide, made tears haze my vision.

While Mom stood behind Dad with apathetic eyes, he calmly said, "It seems to me that you got off easy while we had company. You flaunted our leniency...tested us, abused our kindness. You made us look like fools." His voice heated and his face darkened. When the belt was free of his slacks, he folded it in two. Grabbing each end, he snapped the leather, making a horrible crack that I knew was going to hurt like hell.

Shaking my head, I murmured, "I'm sorry."

He ignored me. Stepping right in front of me, he bit out, "Did you think we'd let you get away with that kind of insolence forever? Did you think there wouldn't be a price to pay for your actions? There's *always* a price, Kellan. And it's high time you learned that."

I woke up with a start, my chest heaving, my heart racing. With shaking fingers, I raked a hand through my hair. You would think the nightmares would stop once the people who had inspired them were dead, but that wasn't the case. I frequently had bad dreams, some based on reality, some founded in fantasy. The one that had just startled me to alertness was real. It had happened just like that. My parents had taken Denny away while I'd been sleeping, and when I'd chewed Dad out when they'd returned, Dad had made up

33

for all the times he hadn't hit me that year. He'd left me bruised and bloody; just breathing had hurt.

That was the day I'd decided to run away the minute I graduated. I'd decided to run away and never look back. Only, I had. I'd looked back, and I'd come back, because in the end, regardless of how they'd treated me while they were alive, they were still my parents, and I couldn't *not* say goodbye to them.

Feeling slow and sort of dazed as I shook off the remnants of my dream, I climbed out of bed. I needed water. I pulled open my slightly cracked door, and there in front of me was a sight that made all thoughts of my nightmare evaporate.

Denny's girlfriend, Kiera, was exiting the bathroom that was tucked between the two bedrooms. She'd apparently just taken a shower, and she had one of my thin, tiny towels wrapped around her body. The scant material didn't leave a whole lot to the imagination. She had it tight around her chest, but there was a gap between the bottom edges of the towel that ran right up to above her hip bone. And it was quite possibly the sexiest hip bone I'd ever seen.

Scratching a sudden itch on my chest, I let out a lazy yawn and forcefully shoved that thought to the far corners of my mind. *Nope, not this girl.*

She seemed shocked to see me. Or maybe it was *how* she was seeing me that was shocking to her. My presence shouldn't be surprising. I did live here, after all. Her eyes were wide as they took me in, starting at my messy head of sandy-brown hair and lingering on my exposed abs. It took a lot of willpower, but I stopped myself from becoming even the tiniest bit aroused by her inspection. Denny would not like the idea of his girlfriend giving me a woody, although I didn't think he could fault me for being human.

Now that she was so close to me, I could see she had hazel eyes. Beautiful eyes. I'd never seen a pair quite that color; they seemed alive, shifting and changing in the light. I had the strongest desire to take her outside so I could watch the browns and greens flux and deepen in the sunlight. I supposed that wouldn't be appropriate at the moment though, especially given the fact that we hadn't even been introduced yet. Well, that was something I could rectify.

Tilting my head, I said, "You must be Kiera."

I was about to tell her my name was Kellan when she awkwardly extended her hand, like she wanted me to shake it. "Yes…hi," she mumbled. Her attempt to be formal while wearing only a towel made me want to laugh, but she seemed really embarrassed about the situation, so I only gave her a small smile as I took her hand. Her palm was warm, soft with moisture from her recent shower. The contact was so pleasant, I could have held on to her for a lot longer, but I let go.

Her chest flushed with color and she shifted her weight like she really wanted to turn around and run. Instead of fleeing, she said, "You're Kellan?" I could almost see her mentally kicking herself for asking me that. Process of elimination would tell her who I was. She was awkward, shy, adorable, and beautiful. A deadly combination. Denny was a lucky man.

"Mmmm…" I answered her, distracted. There was something about the way she said my name that was mesmerizing. It was the way her lips moved when she spoke. She had amazing lips, full, with a slight curve to the corners that I bet gave her an incredible smile. It was probably inappropriate for me to think it, but I wanted to see a bright, carefree, un-self-conscious smile.

Kiera seemed uncomfortable under my scrutiny, but instead of telling me to go away or stop leering at her, she apologized. "Sorry about the water. I think I used all of the hot side."

She turned and put her hand on the doorknob of her room, clearly using this moment as a chance to escape. I had to smile at her polite consideration of any potential problems she may have caused. It wasn't an issue though. A shower wasn't really what I wanted just now. Although, just by talking to her, the horror attached to the memory of my dream was fading. I should thank her for the distraction.

With genuine sincerity, I told her, "No problem. I'll just use it tonight, before I leave."

35

She mumbled, "See you later then," before dashing into her room, almost slamming the door in her haste to get away. A small chuckle escaped me. God, she was cute. And sweet. A good match for Denny.

No longer needing water, I made a quick visit to the bathroom and then returned to my room for a few push-ups and crunches to get me going. Lyrics flashed through my brain while I exercised. Not wanting to lose the thoughts floating through my mind, I stopped my routine early and grabbed a notebook from my drawer. I had a ton of them spread throughout my house. It really wasn't the best way to organize my thoughts, especially since lyrics for one song could be inside four or five books, all in different rooms. If anything ever happened to me, Matt and Evan would have a bitch of a time compiling my thoughts into a coherent song.

I could hear sounds of passion coming from Denny and Kiera's room while I jotted down some random verses. I paused to listen for a second, then with a shake of my head and a chuckle, I blocked them out and continued working. Hearing people have sex through the walls was nothing new to me. Hell, I'd been at parties before where the couple was getting busy in the same room as me. I didn't care. People were free to do what they wanted. And really, every morning should start off with a little nookie.

After immortalizing a few surprisingly peppy lines, I pulled on a shirt and some shorts, fixed my messy hair as best I could, and headed downstairs to make some coffee.

While it brewed, I went to the living room to find the newspaper. Thinking Denny might like to know what was going on locally, since he'd been gone for so long, I'd started picking them up. I heard Denny and Kiera walking down the stairs. Folding up the paper, I started heading toward the kitchen to meet them. Maybe they'd like to have coffee with me?

The article on the front page caught my attention, and I was busy reading about the future of Green Lake when I heard Denny's voice. "Hey, man."

I looked up, my grin uncontainable. It had been a long time since I'd heard that voice in person, and I'd missed it. And him. I was so happy he was back. "Hey, glad you guys made it!" I clasped Denny's shoulder in a quick hug. A few steps behind him, Kiera was watching us with a small smile on her face, like she found us cute. Her tiny grin was captivating.

Denny looked back at her once we broke apart. "You already met Kiera, I hear."

Her smile instantly left her at the memory of our scantily clad encounter. A small pout formed on those perfect lips, and I knew I was not going to be able to resist teasing this woman.

"Yes," I murmured, imagining all the ways I could potentially make her blush. No, I wouldn't. "But nice to see you again," I said, as politely as possible. Resisting a laugh, I moved to the cupboard to get some mugs. "Coffee?"

Denny was making a face when I glanced at him. "Not for me, no. I don't see how you guys can drink that stuff. Kiera loves it though."

I looked over at Kiera as I set two cups on the counter. She was giving Denny the full, loving smile that I'd been hoping to see. Just as I'd predicted, she had an incredible smile. Just…beautiful. I could only imagine how it made Denny feel to have that smile directed at him. He must constantly feel like a million bucks.

"Hungry?" he asked her, his voice soft with caring. "I think there's still some food in the car."

"Starving," she replied, biting her lip. She gave him a light kiss, then playfully rapped her fingers against his stomach. It was a quiet yet sensual display of affection. I couldn't help but grin while I watched them.

Denny gave her a peck, said, "Okay, be right back," then left the kitchen.

Kiera stared after Denny like she could somehow watch him through the walls. Did she miss him already? He was still inside the house, grabbing his keys. She was definitely attached to him. Shaking my head in delighted amusement, I walked over to the fridge and grabbed some creamer. I didn't know how Kiera liked her coffee, but she seemed like the sweet-and-creamy type to me.

I prepared our cups, mine black, hers toffee-colored, while Kiera finally blinked out of her trance and sat down at the table. I stirred her cup, put the spoon in the sink, then walked over to join her. Might as well learn something about my new roommate, aside from the fact that she had absorbing eyes that took in everything around her and an unbelievable smile that probably dropped men to their knees. And a solid relationship with my friend. That might be my favorite thing about her so far.

I set the creamy cup in front of her, and her small smile shifted to a frown. Hmm, maybe she preferred it black. Well, she could have mine. I didn't care. I'd drink any form of coffee there was. In offer, I told her, "I brought mine black. I can switch you, if you don't like cream."

"No, actually I do like it this way." She gave me a mischievous smile as I sat down. It was charming. "I thought maybe you could read minds or something."

I had to chuckle at her sense of humor. "I wish," I said, taking a sip of coffee. That would be a handy superpower. I could have avoided the whole Joey mess. Although, I wasn't sure if I wanted to know what people really thought about me. On second thought, ignorance was bliss.

Kiera raised her cup. "Well, thank you." She took a sip. Her eyes fluttered closed and a small pleased noise escaped her throat, like she was having a mini-orgasm. Looked like she enjoyed coffee just as much as I did, maybe more. I liked that we had something in common. It was easier to live with people who had similar tastes.

Curiosity overwhelmed me as her expressive eyes reopened. I knew why Denny was here—a new job with pretty amazing potential—but I was still a little mystified as to why Kiera was. All her family and friends were back East. She'd left school and everything she'd ever known to follow a guy she was seeing. Why? I'd never met a woman who would give up everything like that. I knew

Denny thought the world of her, and she seemed to think the world of him too, but from all I'd seen in my short life, couples in our age range didn't stay together long.

Tilting my head, I asked her, "So, Ohio, huh? Buckeyes and fireflies, right?"

That was about all I knew of Ohio. Kiera seemed to be suppressing a laugh, like she realized my knowledge was limited. "Yep, that's about it."

"Do you miss it?" I asked, wondering if I'd ever have a girl who would give up her entire life for me. I doubted it. Girls wanted sex from me. Nothing more.

"Well, I miss my parents and my sister, of course. But I don't know...a place is just a place." She paused, then sighed. "Besides, it's not like I won't ever see it again."

She gave me a smile laced with sadness, and the green in her eyes darkened to a deep jade. I just didn't get it. She was clearly suffering from some small amount of homesickness. She missed her family, her friends, her life. The curiosity became too much for me, and even though I knew it would sound incredibly rude, I had to ask what the hell she'd given it all up for. "Don't take this the wrong way, but why did you come all the way out here?"

She seemed a little annoyed by my question, but she still answered it. "Denny."

Denny's name rang with reverence. She really had changed her entire life just for him. To remain together as long as possible, even if it was a futile attempt. Or maybe it wasn't. The way they looked at each other, the respect they showed one another...I'd never seen a relationship like that before.

"Huh" was all I said in response. There wasn't much else I could say. *Good luck with that* seemed a little asshole-ish.

She blurted out her next question while I sipped on my coffee. "Why do you sing like that?" Her cheeks flushed with color, like she hadn't meant to say what she'd just said. I narrowed my eyes, wondering what she meant. I only knew one way to sing. Open your mouth and let it pour out. Was she saying I sucked? Ouch.

That wasn't something I was used to hearing. Most people liked my voice.

"What do you mean?" I asked slowly, bracing myself for a bad review of my abilities.

She took forever to answer me. I didn't take that as a good sign. She must have hated it. For some reason that thought really bothered me. I could have sworn there had been a moment last night when she'd understood me. Completely got where I was coming from. It had really freaked me out at the time, but maybe I'd misjudged her expression. Maybe she didn't get me at all.

Swallowing her sip of coffee, she sputtered, "You were great. But sometimes you were just so..." She paused, and I could sense her apprehension. Her criticism of my performance came out in a whisper: "Sexual."

Relief hit me—*she liked it*. The surge of good feelings was immediately followed by a good helping of humor. I started laughing. I couldn't help it. The look on her face while saying a word as innocent as "sexual" was killing me. God, she might be the cutest thing I'd ever seen.

Kiera's expression darkened and her face turned bright red. I could tell she was mortified as she stared into her coffee, and I did my best to stop laughing. I didn't want her to think I was making fun of her. I wasn't. Not really. "Sorry...It's just, that's not what I thought you were going to say." Thinking over my aggressive flirting onstage last night, I shrugged. "I don't know. People just tend to respond to it."

By the look on her face, I was pretty sure she knew that by "people," I meant "women." I couldn't resist going in for a little dig. "Did I offend you?"

"Nooo." She glared at me and I had to bite my lip to not laugh. She needed to work on her stern face, if that was supposed to intimidate me in any way. "It just seemed excessive. Besides, you don't need it—your songs are great."

There was no sarcasm or hidden meaning in her words. She was just giving me her honest feedback. I sat back in my chair and simply stared at her in appreciation. It had been a long time since a girl had given me an honest critique. All I usually heard was fluffed-up crap designed to get me out of my pants. Her one small suggestion was refreshing.

She was staring at the table again, maybe embarrassed about her comment. "Thank you. I'll try to keep that in mind." She looked up at hearing the sincerity in my voice. Wondering what had happened to Denny outside, I asked her, "How did you and Denny meet?"

A beautiful smile spread over her face as she reminisced about her boyfriend. It made me wish someone would smile over me like that. "College. He was a teaching assistant in one of my classes. It was my first year, his third. I thought he was the most beautiful person I had ever seen." Her complexion turned rosy as she gushed over Denny. I kept my smile even, not wanting her to be too uncomfortable to continue. I wanted her to feel okay talking to me. I had a feeling she'd be easy to talk to. The thought was mildly unsettling. I didn't talk a whole lot. Not about important stuff.

"Anyway, we just hit it off and have been together ever since." Her smile widened into a bright, carefree grin. Stunning. With a questioning expression, she asked me, "What about you? How did you meet Denny?"

My grin grew as wide as hers as I recalled it. "Well, my parents thought it would be a good idea to host an exchange student. I think their friends were impressed with that." My mind froze and my smile faltered as my parents' pompous expressions entered my head. They got that look whenever anyone asked them about Denny. A look that clearly said, *See how great we are? How warm and welcoming? Aren't we wonderful people?*

Shaking the memory away, I returned myself to the present and fixed my smile. "But Denny and I hit it off right away too. He's a cool guy." I hadn't been able to shake off the past as well as I'd hoped, and my dream flooded over me again. I had to turn my head away from Kiera. She didn't need to see my pain. She wouldn't understand it anyway. No one did. My father's voice boomed

41

through my ears as I wallowed in the murkiness of my past. *There's always a price, Kellan. And it's high time you learned that.*

Almost in a trance, I whispered, "I owe him a lot." Denny had given me hope. Clinging to that hope now, I made myself smile and return my gaze to Kiera. I could tell she wanted to question me further. Hopefully she didn't. Shrugging, I acted as casual as I could. "Anyway, I'd do anything for the guy, so when he called and said he needed a place to stay, it was the least I could do."

"Oh." She opened her mouth like she wanted to say more, but then she closed it again, giving me space. I sent her a silent thanks for that. I didn't want her to ask.

Denny came back into the kitchen with snacks from the car—chips and pretzels. After the pair ate their junk food, Kiera called her parents while Denny and I caught up. Tapping his arm, I asked him about the little bit of the show he'd caught last night at Pete's. "What did you think of the band? Quite a step up from the Washington Wildcats, huh?" That had been the unfortunate name that my band in high school had chosen. They'd thought it oozed school spirit. I'd thought it sucked.

My heart rate actually increased while I waited for Denny's response. If he hadn't liked our sound...I'd have to admit, I would be a little disheartened. He smiled though. "Oh yeah, you've come a long way since junior prom, mate. You were amazing."

Pride swelled in my chest, but I pushed it back. I wasn't the only reason the D-Bags were good. Remembering my old band and that high school dance, my first major gig, made me laugh. "Do you remember Spaz? My...third drummer, I think?"

Denny laughed with me as he nodded. "That guy earned his name...he was nuts. I wonder what he's doing now..."

Seeing an opportunity to tease him, I tossed out, "Maybe he married Sheri. Do you remember her?"

Flashing a glance at Kiera, Denny murmured, "Yeah...nice girl."

Laughter overcame me. "Nice girl? She was your one high school hookup, if I remember correctly."

Denny frowned. "You're not remembering it correctly. You liter-

42

ally threw her at me at prom, and we spent the night *dancing*. That was it."

Memories of being onstage and watching the crowd filtered through my mind. He'd done a bit more than dance with her. It was the only time I'd seen him with a girl while he was here. "Dancing? Is that what they call tonsil hockey in Australia?" Even though they'd only kissed that night, I still felt like I'd successfully gotten him to date. Sort of. *You were stubborn as hell, but I won, mate.*

Looking over at Kiera again, Denny shook his head. "Are you trying to get me in trouble?" he asked. Before I could answer, his expression smoothed into a smile. "Besides...if *I* remember correctly...you were the one who hooked up with her. And her twin."

I shrugged in answer and he laughed. After the levity passed, he shook his head and said, "It always impressed me that you were never nervous onstage. I suppose you're still not?" Shrugging again, I shook my head. Performing didn't bother me. I felt more comfortable in the spotlight than I felt being alone. Denny smiled. "It's just like I told you back then...you're meant for this life, Kellan. It's in your blood."

"Yeah..." I said, feeling uncomfortable.

In the silence, Denny added, "I also remember what your dad said when we got home after prom."

Denny didn't repeat what he'd said, and he didn't need to. I remembered it all too well. After Denny had commended us on our playing, Dad had turned to me and said, "I've heard the crap kids listen to these days. A trained goat would probably be considered good music to them." He'd then proceeded to berate me on my outfit, my hairstyle, and the fact that we were ten minutes past curfew. It had been a monumental night for me, and Dad couldn't even throw me a bone by giving me *one* compliment. Story of my life.

Clearing my throat to clear away the memory, I clapped Denny's shoulder. "In case I never said it, thank you for making that night happen. For making a lot of great nights happen. I owe you more than you know."

43

Even though my voice was edged with seriousness, Denny swished his hand at me, like it didn't matter. "You make too big of a deal out of it. I really didn't do much." *Yes, you did.*

Before I could say that though, Denny moved on to another topic, and our conversation drifted to lighthearted memories. It felt good to revisit them. Sometimes the darker moments had a tendency to overshadow the good ones. And Denny and I had had a lot of good times together.

Once Kiera was off the phone with her family, she and Denny went about settling themselves at my place. I asked Denny if I could give him a hand, but with a cringe he told me, "You've done so much for us already, letting us stay here for next to nothing. I wouldn't feel good about it." I opened my mouth to argue, but he quickly added, "No worries, mate. We've only got a few boxes."

With a laugh, I clapped him on the shoulder and left him to it. And he was right, of course. The pair of them got all of their boxes to their room in two trips. When they came back downstairs, Denny asked how to get to Pike Place from here. I told him where the market was, and he and Kiera prepared to leave.

"Thanks. See ya later this arvo," Denny said, grabbing Kiera's hand.

Kiera smirked at Denny, then turned to me. "That means afternoon."

I laughed and shook my head. "Yeah, I figured." Our eyes locked as we smiled at each other, and for a second, I felt trapped. Something stirred in my chest, speeding my heart. I almost felt like I'd gone for a run and hit my stride. I just felt…good…and all I was doing was looking at her. Sharing a moment. Sharing a connection. It was strange, but pleasant.

It took a lot of willpower to toss my hand up in a wave and casually turn around and head toward the kitchen, but I made myself do it. I shouldn't be having connections with Kiera, no matter how nice it felt. Some pleasures I'd just have to deny myself.

Finding a notebook in the junk drawer of the kitchen, I pulled it out, sat at the table, and started writing down lyrics. Phrases and phrases about kaleidoscope eyes were tumbling through my mind. I thought I could write an entire song about Kiera's ever-shifting eye color. That would be highly inappropriate though. Maybe I'd change it to another color in the final draft. No. Even as I thought it, I knew I'd never change the color. Can't change perfect.

When I heard the front door open, I glanced at the clock. Denny and Kiera had been gone a long time. They were laughing when they entered the kitchen, arms full of bags. After setting down their things, Denny wrapped his arms around Kiera and she kissed his neck. I knew it was wrong and kind of creepy, but I just couldn't stop watching them. It was wonderful seeing two people so content and happy. It was also painful, stirring things in me that I'd long buried. Hopes. Dreams. But that life wasn't meant for me. Hookups were what I had. I'd accepted that a long time ago, and I was fine with it. I had to be.

Giving them privacy, I forced myself to resume studying my notebook. After a few quiet departing words, Kiera left the room, and I looked over at Denny. Laughing a little, I told him, "I know you're going to say no, but I'd be a dick if I didn't offer, so…can I help?"

Over his shoulder, Denny met my eye and smiled. "No, mate, you can't." He put a few things in the fridge, then shut the door. Turning to face me, he said, "I'm done though. Want to find a game to watch?"

I suddenly remembered something else about Denny. He liked sports a heck of a lot more than I did. Probably why Dad had connected with him more than he had me. Well, one of many reasons why. But I didn't have anything better to do since there was no rehearsal today, so I shrugged and told him, "Sure." I could sit through sports to hang out with him.

Denny grinned like I'd given him the best news ever. I laughed again and stood up to put my notebook back in the junk drawer. I probably should tuck that one away in my bedroom so Kiera or Denny didn't find it, but thousands of people had hazel eyes. I could be singing about anybody. Or nobody. Not every song was based on reality.

I listened for Kiera upstairs more than I watched the sports highlights on TV. That was far more interesting. I could hear her clunking around her room, and I even heard her drop something and swear. That made me snort. Her innocent face seemed incapable of saying a bad word.

When she finally came downstairs, I gave her a polite smile. I wasn't sure if she saw me though; her eyes were only on Denny. When she saw him sprawled across the couch, a blissful smile graced her lips. She crawled on top of him, then wiggled her way between him and the couch. Denny's arm went around her waist while Kiera tossed her leg over his and laid her head on his chest. Denny sighed, kissing her head, and Kiera's content expression never left her. If anything, she became even more at peace.

An ache vibrated through my chest as I watched them. It was like seeing warmth and love personified. No one had ever touched me like that. Not in a nonsexual way. Not for purely the joy of contact, with no other plan or agenda. Watching what they had together was almost too much to bear, but I couldn't turn my eyes away either. Was that the way love was supposed to look? Calm, happy, peaceful? I'd never seen it that way. Not really. I'd seen anger, jealousy, bitterness, and resentment. Love equaled pain in my world. And I generally tried to avoid pain.

Kiera's eyes shifted over to me. There was a question in the brownish-green depths. A question I didn't want her to ask, because somehow, I knew I would eventually answer her, and it would hurt like hell when I did. Thankfully, she closed her eyes and remained silent. Then, surrounded in her sea of serenity, she drifted off to sleep. For a moment, I wasn't sure who I was more envious of: Kiera, for the peace she was experiencing, or Denny, because he'd found someone amazing to share it with.

Chapter 4

Burned Out

While Denny rested and Kiera snoozed, I trudged upstairs to get ready for my night. After showering and shaving, I picked out a red long-sleeved shirt to wear, tossed on some deodorant that I thought smelled pretty good, and worked some product through my hair.

My guitar was still in the car from last night's performance, so I grabbed my wallet and headed downstairs to let Denny know I was leaving. When I got to the bottom of the stairs though, I could see he was busy. Kiera was awake now, and she'd apparently woken up horny. Denny was massaging her butt while she squirmed on his lap. I couldn't tell where her head was, but I could bet she was licking his neck or something. I chuckled as I walked toward the coat hooks in the entryway. Living with these two was going to be like living with honeymooners, I could already tell.

Kiera must have heard me laugh. She sat straight up on Denny's lap like I'd just poked her with a cattle prod. She had a flush from her cheeks to her chest, and her eyes were wide like she was mortified. For kissing? Was she that shy? Thinking of how different she was from the girls I knew made me laugh even harder.

"Sorry," I chuckled, grabbing my coat. "I'll be out of your hair in a minute…if you want to wait." I paused, considering. "Or don't. It really doesn't bother me." I already knew that Kiera wasn't the type

47

to ever be okay with having sex right in front of me, and I knew I shouldn't make her any more embarrassed than she already was, but she was so damn cute, it was hard not to tease her.

She immediately hopped off Denny, sitting as far on the other end of the couch as possible. She looked over at Denny with bunched brows and pursed lips. He must have had the same amused expression as I did, because her mood didn't change any. Looking flustered as well as embarrassed, she glanced up at me and barked out, "Where are you going?"

Her tone of voice surprised me a little, but I figured it was mainly from being teased. She seemed to immediately realize she was being rough, and I could see her calming herself as I answered. "Pete's. We've got another gig there tonight."

"Oh." Her eyes drifted over my hair and my clothes, like she was finally noticing that I was dressed differently. The inspection made my breath quicken.

Wanting to cover that reaction, I asked, "Do you guys want to go...?" I couldn't resist another tease, so I gave them a playful smile and finished with "...Or stay here?"

Once again, Kiera seemed to answer before thinking. A gut reaction. "No, we'll go. Sure."

"Really?" Denny said, sounding a little disappointed. He must have been looking forward to me leaving them alone for the night. Oops. Didn't mean to cock-block him. I did like the idea of Denny listening to a full set though, so he could really hear how much I'd grown, in the musical sense.

Kiera fiddled with a strand of her hair, like she was thinking of an explanation for her assertive statement. Interesting. To Denny, she timidly said, "Yeah, they sounded really good last night. I was hoping to hear a little more."

"All right. I'll get my keys." Denny sighed, slowly sitting up on the couch.

I couldn't help but wonder if Kiera really meant what she'd just said about the band. She'd seemed sincere when we'd been talking earlier today, but she hadn't seemed sincere when she'd told Denny she wanted to go. Which one was it? I wasn't sure. She glanced up at me while Denny stood, and I suddenly saw the truth in her eyes and her shy smile. She may have unthinkingly blurted out something she might or might not have wanted to do tonight, but what she'd just said was true. She did want to hear more. I tried not to read too much into that. It was the music she liked.

Shaking my head at the idea that I'd actually coerced her into going to Pete's by embarrassing her, I told them, "Okay, I'll see you there then."

I thought about Kiera on the way to the bar. Sometimes she was easy to read, sometimes she was impossible to gauge. But nothing I'd seen so far was mean or malicious. She was kind and sweet, easily embarrassed and unnecessarily shy, innocent and naïve, yet seductive and playful too. Even though I was sure we were roughly the same age, I felt like I was a million years older than her. It made me want to protect her, even though that was truly Denny's job, since he was her boyfriend. Well, I could play a big brother role in her life. A friend. Someone for her to lean on. I had a feeling she'd need that, living so far away from her home and family.

There were a couple of beers in front of each of my bandmates when I got to Pete's; they'd been here for a while. I had some catching up to do. After grabbing a beer from Rita, I took a seat by Griffin. "Want to hear what I did last night?" he said, looking over at me.

Matt, across from me, sighed. "If he says no, will you actually keep your mouth shut?"

Griffin tossed a look Matt's way. "Suck it." He returned his eyes to mine and started in on his story without even waiting for my answer. "So, there were these two blond chicks at the show last night...Melody, Harmony, Cadence, Tempo...I don't know, their names were something musical..."

I glanced at Evan sitting beside Matt and he mouthed, *Tempo?* I tried not to laugh as I took a sip of my beer and returned my attention to Griffin. "Anyway," he said, waving his hand, "they were on fire for me, like practically humping me in the parking lot."

49

Against my will, an image of Griffin being mauled leaped into my head. "They invited me to this afterparty, right. A bunch of people were playing drinking games in the kitchen, so me and one of the blondes sat down to play…"

Griffin smacked my shoulder and raised his eyebrows, like I wouldn't believe what happened next. While I wasn't sure what might have gone down during the game, I had a pretty good idea how his story ended. I'd heard variations of this before.

Leaning in, Griffin told me, "She eye-fucked me for a good twenty minutes. I was hard as a fucking rock!" He closed his eyes like he was remembering…or he was getting hard thinking about it. I seriously hoped not. Opening his eyes, he told us, "This girl, damn, she had the best rack I've ever seen." About a foot and a half away from his chest, he mimed boobs with his hands. "And the shortest skirt too. Everybody around us was completely wasted, so I ducked under the table and shoved that skirt as high as it would go. Then I grabbed my beer bottle and stuck—"

Out of the corner of my eye, I happened to notice people approaching the table. I instinctively smacked Griffin across the chest to get him to shut up. His stories usually weren't safe for mixed company, especially with what I was sure he'd done with that bottle.

While Griffin looked confused, I glanced over to see Denny and Kiera standing at the end of the table. Kiera was bright red and looked like she wanted to be anywhere but here. She'd definitely heard him then.

"Dude…I'm getting to the good part, hold on."

He looked like he was about to resume his story, so I quickly interrupted. "Griff…" I pointed at our new arrivals. "My new roommates are here."

"Oh yeah…roommates." Griffin gave them a cursory glance, then turned back to me with a pout. "I miss Joey, man…She was hot! Seriously, why did you have to tap that? Not that I blame you, but—"

I quickly cut him off with a hard rap on the chest. Griffin could get exceedingly graphic if left unchecked. And I didn't really want

50

Kiera to know what happened with Joey. She wouldn't understand. She'd think I was a pig. *Wait, what?* It shouldn't matter what she thought of me. With a surprising amount of effort, I shoved that thought out of my mind.

Ignoring Griffin's annoyance, I pointed up at my roommates. "Guys, this is my friend Denny and his girlfriend, Kiera."

I looked around for more chairs while Denny and Kiera said their hellos. Spotting some at the table across from us, I stood up and walked over to where a couple of girls were staring our way. Both women started getting a little frantic as I approached, so I figured they were fans. With a disarming smile on my lips, I walked over to the girl beside the two empty chairs I needed. I leaned over the back of her chair so I could talk directly into her ear; it was pretty noisy in here.

She was shaking as I tucked a strand of hair behind her ear. "Sorry to intrude, but would it be all right with you if I took a couple of your chairs for my friends?" She nodded that it was okay, and her friend giggled. I thanked her, straightened, then grabbed the two chairs for Kiera and Denny. There was a lot of tittering behind me as I walked away.

Kiera was watching me as I set the chairs at the end of the table. She seemed a little uncomfortable with the friendly flirting I'd done to get the chairs. "Here, have a seat." Kiera frowned as she took a seat, and I had to stop myself from laughing. She was even cuter when she was uneasy.

When I caught Rita looking my way, I motioned to her to send two more beers to the table. She gave me an *Anything for you* smile, grabbed some beers, and handed them to Jenny. I turned to Denny while Jenny worked her way over to us. "So, what are you going to be doing at your new job anyway?" I asked him.

Denny gave me an amused smile. "A little bit of everything." He started going into the specifics of what he'd be doing for the advertising company, and I could hear both the nervousness and excitement in his voice. Since Kiera was sitting between us at the table, she was in my line of sight as I listened to Denny. It seemed like she'd heard his story before, so she was checking out the bar. Her eyes drifted over the front windows, plastered with neon bar signs, to the darkened stage, waiting for us to play. Then she shifted her attention to the bar at the other end of the room, where Rita was busy keeping everyone refreshed.

Jenny approached with the beers while Kiera was looking around. Jenny seemed rushed, and I understood why. Like it usually did before our set, the bar was quickly filling up with customers; the band was good for business. She handed Denny and Kiera their beers, then hurried off to the kitchen.

Sipping on her drink, Kiera started taking in the other half of the bar. Her curiosity was as endearing as her awkwardness. Thinking I was spending too much time eyeing Denny's girlfriend, I did my best to tune her out and concentrate on having a conversation with Denny about why some commercials had absolutely nothing to do with the products they were selling.

Evan was asking Denny, "But why are there bathtubs in every commercial? I don't get it." Before Denny could answer, someone approached our table. Looking over, I saw it was Pete, the owner of the bar. While he looked professional in his Pete's polo and crisp khakis, he also looked worn out, like the stress of life was getting to him. Pete had been really good to me, so I hoped he was okay.

"Guys ready? You're up in five." Pete let out a big sigh that did nothing to alleviate the stress on his face.

"You all right, Pete?" I asked, concerned.

"No... Traci quit over the phone, she's not coming back. I had to have Kate pull a double so we were covered tonight." His gray eyes narrowed to pinpricks as he glared at me. His expression clearly said, *What the hell did you do to my waitress?* But I wasn't to blame for this one. No, the jackass to my left was the instigator this time.

I rolled my head around to glare at Griffin. Traci must have found out that Griffin had slept with her sister, and she was appropriately pissed. Griffin should have known better. Unless they were both in on it and okay with it, you didn't mess with sisters. Everybody knew that.

And apparently Griffin did know that, for he looked genuinely sheepish as he took a long draw off his beer. "Sorry, Pete."

Pete could only shake his head in response, 'cause what else could he do? As aggravating as it must be to have us interfering with his staff, Pete needed us. It was kind of a catch-22, and I felt bad for him. I made a mental note to talk to Griffin later. Maybe it was time to make a new band rule—no dating Pete's employees.

Kiera spoke up then. "I was a waitress. I need to get a job, and working nights would be perfect when school starts." By the look on her face, she had said it as much to help Pete out as herself. She cared about others. I liked that. More than I should.

Pete gave me a questioning glance. Wanting to help Kiera get the job, I introduced her and Denny so Pete would know they weren't complete strangers. My stamp of approval wouldn't go too far, but hopefully it would go far enough. They both needed this.

Pete gave Kiera an appraising glance, but I could tell he was relieved that he'd found someone so fast. "You twenty-one?"

Curious how old she was, I paid attention to her answer. She seemed nervous to give it, or maybe she was just nervous about her impromptu interview. She'd sort of spoken without thinking again. "Yeah, since May." I smiled. That made her my age. I liked that too.

Pete seemed satisfied with her answer. And I was 99 percent sure she was telling the truth. She just didn't seem like the type to lie. "All right," Pete said, a small smile gracing his lips. "I could use the help, and soon. Can you start Monday, six p.m.?"

Kiera glanced at Denny, like she was silently asking for his permission. I figured she was purely being polite. I couldn't imagine Denny not letting her do whatever she wanted. When he gave her a brief nod and a warm smile, Kiera returned her eyes to Pete. "Yeah, that would be fine. Thank you."

Pete left just a bit lighter, like some of the weight had been lifted from his shoulders. It made me glad to see it. Turning to Kiera, I told her, "Welcome to the family. Guess we'll be seeing a lot of each other now that you're working at my home away from home." I gave her a playful smile. "Hopefully you don't get too sick of me."

Kiera's cheeks turned rosy and she quickly brought her beer bottle to her mouth. "Yeah," she muttered before taking a few long gulps. I laughed at the look on her face, then noticed Denny behind her giving me a slight frown. He fixed his face so fast that I almost thought I'd imagined it. Must have imagined it. Denny and I were tight.

Pete turned on the stage lights and the bar erupted into shrieks. Kiera's eyes widened at the noise. Standing up, I told her, "Just wait, it's about to get even louder."

Evan and Matt scooted away from the table and were making their way toward the stage. Griffin was still sitting, chugging his beer. I flicked his ear, making him jump; a few rivers of alcohol leaked from his mouth to wet his shirt. "Let's go," I told him when he glared up at me.

He took another second to finish his bottle, let out a belch that was almost louder than the crowd, then stood up. "Patience, dude. The pipes have to be primed."

I had to raise an eyebrow at that. Griffin sang backup, true, but he didn't do *that* much singing. He was facing the bar and raising his fists in the air like Rocky, so I left him to it and made my way to the stairs. The volume increased with every step I took toward the stage. Matt was prepping the equipment. I clapped his shoulder, then made my way to my microphone. Grabbing the stand, I pulled it up to my mouth. "This thing on?" I murmured in an intentionally low voice.

The corresponding screams were so loud my ears started ringing. Smiling, I scanned the fans starting to crowd around the stage. Kiera and Denny were still at the table, but they both had ear-to-ear grins. "How the fuck are you, Seattle?"

The girls closest to me started jumping and hollering in response. From the side of the room, I could see Griffin taking his damn sweet time getting to the stage. Frowning, I said into the microphone, "We seem to be down a D-Bag. If any of you can play bass, please feel free to hop up here and join me."

About a half dozen girls wasted no time in scrambling onstage with me. Sam was on them in an instant, pulling them back into the crowd. It made me laugh, but Sam shot me more than one irritated glance. Griffin did too. He ran onto the stage so fast you'd think a naked girl was up here. Grabbing his bass, he looked my way and shouted, "Bite me, asshole."

Matt and Evan laughed with me as Griffin hurried to get himself ready. Giving him time, I addressed the crowd again. "Sorry about that. Looks like we're all here after all." Kiera and Denny were laughing, along with a good section of the back of the bar. The girls closest were still shrieking their heads off, oblivious to the humor. "Any requests?" I asked them.

"You!" A couple people shouted that, and from different sections of the room. I scanned the bar, but I couldn't tell who'd said it.

Laughing, I responded with, "Maybe later. If you're real nice." Whistles and catcalls followed that remark, and I wondered if anyone would try to take me up on the offer. I looked back at Evan, and he gave me a thumbs-up. Everyone was ready. Twisting back to the bar, I said into the microphone, "We've got newbies here tonight, so how about an old one?"

Without looking, I pointed back at Evan, cuing him to start the song. He tapped it out, then started the intro. Matt came in a few beats later. Biting my lip, I kept time by swaying my body while I waited for my turn. Griffin came in a half beat behind me, and then we really took off.

I loved starting off with this song, because I got to curse in the chorus. Not only was it fun, but it loosened up the crowd, made them go nuts—not that this crowd had a problem with that; they were used to us here, and were always ready for a good time. It helped in new bars though. Watching Kiera's reaction to it was outstanding.

"*You knocked me down, you fucked me up. I'm holding still, waiting for you to do it again. Call me crazy, but I can't get enough.*"

She was gaping when she first heard the line, then she was laughing, then she buried her head in Denny's shoulder. Her being entertained by one of my songs gave me a weird sense of satisfaction. It was a perfect way to start the night.

We played quite a few songs after that, the crowd laughing, screaming, and dancing, wholeheartedly enjoying themselves. Denny and Kiera spent most of the time on the fringes of the crowd, dancing along to the music together. When I grabbed my guitar and slowed the set down with a mellower song, they started slow dancing. It gave me a huge smile to see Denny so happy. He looked satisfied, like everything in his life was just the way he wanted it. Seeing him that way, my mood started mirroring his. All of us living together was going to be great—almost like a family of sorts.

They were softly kissing with their arms tight around each other, a picture of perfect peace. Kiera laid her head on Denny's shoulder. Her head was facing toward me, and I gave her a warm, friendly smile. Then I winked at her, 'cause I just couldn't resist making her blush. She was clearly surprised by my friendly move, and I laughed and looked away. Some of the fans right in front of me started fanning themselves like I was making them overheat. That made me laugh too.

We played one more fast song, a fan favorite, to close out the night. Knowing it was the end, some of the girls started screaming for an encore; they did that sometimes, which seemed weird to me. We were here every weekend. If they really wanted more, they knew where to find us.

I spoke into the microphone, and they quieted to hear me. "Thank you for coming out tonight." I waited for the brief burst of screams to diminish, then raised a finger. "I want to take a second to introduce you all to my new roommates." Not able to resist the temptation to make Kiera's face fill with color, I pointed at her and Denny. She looked like she wanted to either kill me or melt into the floor. Maybe both. Denny moving to her side was probably the only thing keeping her upright. And in the bar.

"Ladies, the tall, dark, and handsome one would be Denny. Don't get too attached though, that hottie beside him would be his girlfriend, Kiera." Kiera hid her face in Denny's shoulder, mortified. Wondering if she'd convince Denny to move out before the morning, I playfully told the crowd, "Now, you'll all be happy to know that Kiera is joining the happy little family here at Pete's, starting Monday night."

Kiera peeked up and glared at me with a delightful set of evil eyes and bright red cheeks. If I were close enough, I'd probably get a firm smack too. I laughed at the look on her face. Too bad she was too far away...and I had a microphone. No matter how hard she glared at me, she couldn't stop me from teasing her.

Getting to the point of my speech, I told the crowd, "I want you all to be nice to her." I turned my eyes to Griffin, who was mentally having his way with Kiera. "Especially you, Griffin."

Griffin turned to me and gave me an *Oh, yeah* smile. I shook my head at him, told the crowd good night, then sat down on the stage to rest for a bit. It got hot under the lights. The girls below me didn't seem to care that I was sweaty. They hopped up on the stage to be near me. Since the set was over with, Sam let them approach me.

One handed me a beer, which I gratefully accepted. Another started playing with my hair, sending shivers down my spine. I loved the feeling of fingers against my scalp. One aggressive girl made herself quite comfortable on my lap. Laughing, I let her. "You're sweaty," she said with a giggle, then she leaned in to lick a bead off my neck. I'll admit, it turned me on, and I was in such a good mood, I welcomed the affection.

I looked over at Denny and Kiera; they both looked exhausted. I doubted we'd be doing any more roommate bonding tonight. They were probably just going to go home and crash. As I watched, Kiera yawned, confirming my suspicions. Denny said something to her, then turned my direction. Spotting me in the clump of women near the stage, he lifted his hand in a wave. I raised my beer in goodbye. Yeah, I'd hang out with them later. I was enjoying a pretty good performance buzz right now, and I kind of wanted to keep it going.

The girl on my lap was working her way toward my ear. My cock was quickly hardening, and by the way she squirmed her hips, I knew she knew it. When she got to my ear, she whispered, "I think you're enjoying this."

I gave her a smooth smile. "A gorgeous woman licking my neck? What's not to enjoy?"

She bit her lip as I took a swig of my beer. "Want to get out of here?" she asked, a grin full of promise on her lips.

I considered that as I swallowed the beer in my mouth. Did I want to leave with her? Denny and Kiera were on their way home, my band was currently hooking up with friends or fans and heading out, I was feeling amazing from an awesome show, and I wasn't the least bit tired. Why the hell not spend the evening wrapped around a woman? And besides, it felt nice having her in my arms.

"Sure. What did you have in mind?" I was pretty sure I knew what she wanted, but it was always good to double check. I wouldn't want to assume and look like an asshole.

"I have an apartment on Capitol Hill," she said, and giggled again.

"Sounds great," I told her. Wrapping my hands around the girl's hips, I eased her onto the floor. She played with a long strand of pitch-black hair while she waited for me to join her. I carefully extracted myself from the group of girls around me, making them groan, whine, and toss nasty insults at my date. She didn't say anything, just gave them a vindictive smile. "Play nice, ladies," I told all of them before hopping down to join her.

She wrapped her arms around my waist the minute she was able to. I put my arm around her shoulder and started leading her toward the doors. The crowds were thinner now than before the show, but the bar was still pretty full, and women reached out to stroke me as I weaved us toward the exit.

I led the girl to my car and opened the door for her. She slid in and moved all the way over to my side on the bench seat. When I sat down behind the steering wheel, there was hardly enough room for me. Her hand was instantly on my inner thigh, her mouth once again on my neck. Her tongue flicked against the vein in my throat and I suppressed a groan. This was going to be a long car ride if she kept this up. "Where to?" I asked.

Nibbling on my ear, she told me which way to go. When we

reached her place, my date grabbed my hand and rushed me up the steps to her apartment. We dashed inside, and she immediately led me to the bedroom. I wasn't quite sure why she was in such a hurry. I certainly wasn't going anywhere for a while.

Once we were inside her room, she closed the door, wrapped her arms around my neck, and forcefully pulled me over to her bed. It was almost like she was afraid I would disappear if she didn't get me under the covers as soon as possible. "This is going to be so much fun," she purred before ripping my shirt off.

About twenty minutes later, when we were both spent, I lay back on her bed and stared at the ceiling. She was already fast asleep, her naked body sprawled across her side of the mattress. I felt strange. She'd been right, that had been a lot of fun, but there was something missing. All I had been able to think of as I'd plunged into her was Denny and Kiera, which was a weird thought to be having at the time. But their tenderness and gentle touches were kind of what I'd been hoping for tonight. My date hadn't given me that though. She'd wanted it hard, rough, and athletic. And noisy. I'd gotten the job done, and I'd had a pretty good climax, but I wouldn't say I'd enjoyed it. Liked it, maybe.

Feeling ready to leave, I quietly got up, found my clothes from where they were strewn about the room, and got dressed. After tugging on my boots, I opened the door and left her apartment. Feeling unsatisfied, I walked to my car with my head down.

I wasn't sure what I wanted, but I knew I wanted more than this. Maybe it was time I took a break from sex. Maybe I was just burned out.

Chapter 5

Roommates and D-Bags

I felt better after a few hours of sleep. Perky, even. I didn't have anything to do until rehearsal later and was looking forward to a lazy day with my roommates. I just felt like hanging out with Denny and getting to know Kiera a little better. I was continually surprised by her. She was different from most girls I knew. Different in a good way. And she had the most amazing smile...

I was sipping on my coffee and finishing the newspaper article I'd started earlier when she ambled into the kitchen. Her hair was a mass of snarls from sleep, and she shuffled instead of walked. She obviously wasn't a morning person. She glanced at me sitting at the table, dressed and ready for the day, and I swear irritation darkened her eyes and tightened her mouth. It was hard to tell if it was directed at me though. She could have just as easily been cursing the sun for rising.

"Mornin'," I cheerily told her.

She made a grunting noise that sounded like "Uh."

I figured some coffee would cheer her up, so I returned my eyes to my paper and left her to it. I waited until she was seated and had a sip in her before I asked the question I'd been dying to ask her since our set ended last night. "Well, what did you think?" I couldn't help my cocky grin. I knew from her face while she was dancing that she'd enjoyed herself.

She struggled with her expression, like she was going to try to pull one over on me, but I wasn't buying it. Her joy hadn't been faked. "You guys were amazing. Really, it was unbelievable."

I nodded, sipping my coffee. *I knew it.* "Thanks, I'll tell the guys you liked it." Curious how she'd respond, I peeked up and asked, "Less offensive?"

Her face flashed with remembered embarrassment, but then a small smile lightened her features. Her eyes were more of a brown color today, a shade of warm honey that hinted at the caring nature of the soul behind them. Sensuality surrounded by a crisp green line of determination. Remarkable. "Yes, much better…thank you."

I laughed at her response, then we nursed our coffees in comfortable silence. Well, it was silent until Kiera blurted out, "Joey was the roommate before us?"

I slowly set down my mug as tension seeped into the room. Would she judge me for what happened with my ex-roommate? Chalk me up as a womanizer, a player, a self-absorbed asshole? It was really disappointing to think she might see me that way. Damn. Why the hell did Griffin always have to open his big-ass mouth at the most inopportune time? "Yeah…she left a while before Denny called about the room." *Let's just leave it at that.*

The intelligence in Kiera's eyes flared as she examined me. She was curious, but did she really want to know? I hoped not. She'd think the worst of me. "She left a lot of her stuff here. Is she going to come back for it?"

I held my breath as I looked down. This was more because of Joey than me, but either way, it wasn't going to sound good. Returning my eyes to her, I bluntly said, "No…I'm pretty sure she left town." *She was a drama queen, a control freak, and possibly mentally unstable, which…makes it seem even worse that I slept with her, so I'll just keep that to myself. Please don't ask what happened.*

"What happened?" she asked, ignoring my mental plea. *Damn it.*

I paused, searching for a way to describe the situation with Joey

61

without making either one of us look bad. "A...misunderstanding" was what I came up with.

Kiera seemed to understand by my guarded tone that I didn't want to talk about Joey. That was a lose-lose conversation for me. Thankfully, Kiera didn't press the issue. She gave me a sympathetic smile, then concentrated on her coffee.

When Denny came down a while later, Kiera got up and gave him a monstrous hug, like he was returning from the war, not the shower. It made me smile. Denny closed his eyes as he returned her hug. His embrace was just as all-encompassing. I'd never seen two people who hugged with their entire souls. And again, I found myself envious of both of them.

Pulling apart, Denny asked Kiera, "It's our last day of complete freedom. What would you like to do?"

Kiera bit her lip while she thought about it. "Veg?" She shrugged.

Denny laughed and rubbed her arm. "I can veg." He looked over at me. "What about you, Kellan. Want to veg with us for a while?"

"Sounds great," I told him.

Kiera was nervous about starting her new job at Pete's, so Denny and I spent the next hour or so prepping her. We ran through every drink we could think of. There was no way she was going to remember them all, but we had a good time with it. We even made up a few drinks, just to get her extra prepared.

When I left the house later in the evening, Kiera finally seemed comfortable about her new job, and Denny was the one starting to lose it. I considered canceling rehearsal to stay home and have a drink with him or something, but by the look Kiera was giving him, I was sure she had a better way to relax him. With a chuckle and a wave, I left her to it.

The next morning Denny looked pale, but calmer. I was drinking my coffee and reading the paper when Kiera walked into the kitchen. She took one look at my T-shirt and started laughing. I was wearing one of the many band shirts that Griffin had made. DOUCHEBAGS was proudly splashed across the front in large white letters.

I teasingly told her I could get her one, and with a good-natured grin, she gave me an enthusiastic nod. When Denny came down a little later, in a snazzy pressed shirt and pleated pants, he also commented on my shirt. I made a mental note to grab a couple from Griffin.

Kiera and I bolstered Denny's spirits for his first day of work. She told him he was hot; I teasingly agreed. She gave him a goodbye kiss; I playfully gave him a peck on the cheek. He was laughing as he left, and I knew that even though he was still a little nervous, he'd kill it at work. Denny was a smart guy. Always had been.

After that, I was completely alone with Kiera for the first time since she'd arrived. It was strangely nice to have just the two of us in the house. She filled the home with a peaceful energy. Warm, sweet...innocent. Just being around her made me feel better.

I worked on lyrics at the table while she watched a little TV in the living room. I could see her watching me from the couch, and wondering if she'd be open to helping me, I asked her, "What do you think about these lines: *Silent eyes shout in the dark, begging for an end. Cold words fall from closed mouths, cutting to the quick. We bleed out, two hearts pumping, but timeless, endless, the pain carries on.*"

She blinked at me, wordless. For a moment, I thought maybe I shouldn't have shared that verse with her. Maybe I should have picked a more benign one, something light and peppy. But this was what I was working on right now, and by asking for her opinion, I could share myself without really sharing myself. So long as she didn't ask me to explain the lyrics, I was safe.

Swallowing, she inhaled a deep breath and said, "Well, I'm not that great at music, but maybe if you came up with something in the second line that rhymed with 'end,' it would flow better?" She shrugged, and her face skewed into an apologetic expression.

I smiled at her, letting her know I wasn't in any way offended by her suggestion. Most people just said, "Sounds great," and didn't bother giving one. I appreciated her honest attempt to try to make the song better.

"Thanks, I think you're right. I'll work on that." Her eyes lit up when she realized I was genuinely grateful for her assistance.

As I went back to work, a feeling started in my chest and crept over all of my muscles, until I was coated with the warm sensation. I wasn't sure if it was contentment, comfortableness, happiness, or something more, but it was wonderful, and I soaked it up like a sponge.

Kiera disappeared a couple of hours before her shift to get ready. I wondered if she really needed that long. She didn't seem the type to primp and preen for an ungodly amount of time. Her beauty was natural; she didn't need to do anything to improve upon it. But when she came downstairs and asked me for a bus schedule, I understood why she was getting ready so early.

Shaking my head, I told her I would take her. She stared at me from the entryway, jacket in hand. "No, no. You don't have to do that."

I could tell she just didn't want to trouble me. It was no trouble though, and besides, I practically lived at Pete's. Driving over there was no more trouble than walking to the fridge. "No problem. I'll grab a beer, chat with Sam. I'll be your first customer."

I gave her as charming a smile as I could, but she didn't look heartened by my comment. If anything, she looked even more apprehensive. Walking into the living room, she told me, "Okay. Thanks."

She sat beside me on the couch and stared at the TV while she played with the zipper on her jacket. She reminded me of Denny, a bundle of nerves while she waited for her new situation. I'd been mindlessly watching some old sitcoms. Not really caring what was on the TV, I handed Kiera the remote. "Here, I wasn't really watching anything."

"Oh, thanks." She seemed touched by my gesture as she flipped through the channels.

I wondered what she would stop on, and was mildly surprised when she paused on a scene with two people going at it. She asked me about the premium channels, like she wasn't really aware of just

64

what she'd stopped on. I contained my laughter as I waited for her to realize what she was seeing. I had a feeling she'd be embarrassed watching soft-core porn right next to an almost complete stranger.

When Kiera finally caught on to what was playing, her cheeks flamed bright red and she fumbled the remote in her attempt to change the channel. She turned it back to my sitcoms and nearly tossed the remote at me in her haste. I managed to only lightly laugh at her, and I was pretty proud of myself for my restraint.

When there was about twenty minutes left before her shift, I shut the TV off and asked her if she was ready to go. Even though she was a little green, she told me, "Sure."

I told her she'd be fine, then we grabbed our coats and headed out the door.

While Kiera seemed to enjoy riding in my muscle car—and who wouldn't?—she still looked like she was about to be sick; she stared out the window, taking deep breaths in through her nose and out through her mouth. I thought about pulling over and letting her get some air, but I figured just getting there and getting it over with would be the best thing for her nerves.

I had the oddest desire to hold her hand when we arrived at Pete's, just to be supportive and to help stop her racing mind, but it seemed inappropriate, so I didn't. She stared at the building like the double doors were going to grow teeth and bite her. I wanted to reassure her again that everything would be fine, but I held my tongue. At some point, the encouragement might sound patronizing.

When we stepped through the doors, Kiera unconsciously stepped toward me. For a moment, I thought she was going to clutch me like a lifeline. I'd have let her, even though that would have been just as inappropriate as holding hands. Whatever she needed to get through this. Jenny bounded our way though. With a bright smile on her lips, she stuck her hand out. "Kiera, right? I'm Jenny. I'll get you situated."

With a wave to me, Jenny grabbed Kiera's hand and started leading her to the back room. Kiera looked back at me with an expression that said both *Help me* and *Thank you*. It made me laugh. Rita instantly honed in on my humor. "Hey, sexy. I love hearing that chuckle. Almost as much as I love hearing other sounds you make."

Knowing what she meant, I raised a corner of my mouth. She bit her lip as her eyes locked onto my mouth. "Jesus, those lips…" She groaned, then reached down and grabbed me a beer. "Drink this," she stated, setting the bottle down in front of me. "I need a distraction before I pull you over the bar and have my way with you. Again."

She winked and I laughed. "Um, thanks." I handed her some money for the beer, and a little extra for anything else I might owe the bar. I didn't always remember to pay. Pete was used to it though. He kept a tab for the band under the register, and took it from our pay if we owed anything at the end of the month.

When Kiera reappeared from the hallway, I couldn't help but smile at her. She looked great in her red Pete's shirt. Amazing, actually. Sensual. The bright color brought out the pink undertones in her skin, making her look a little flushed, like she'd just had sex. Her messy ponytail highlighted her slim neck, emphasizing the illusion. I knew I shouldn't be looking at her that way, but I wasn't dead. I noticed attractiveness same as any other man, and Kiera was extremely attractive. She was going to do very well here. Even if she didn't feel it yet, she looked as if she'd always been here.

She was frowning though when she returned to my side. I wasn't sure why until I realized she was looking at the beer in my hand. That's when I remembered that I was supposed to have been her first customer. Oops. "Sorry, Rita beat you to it. Next time."

Jenny took Kiera away after that, showing her the ropes. I watched Jenny teaching Kiera for a while. Longer than I should have. But eventually it came to the point where I *had* to go, so I made my way over to Kiera to say goodbye. I handed her a tip for my beer, the one she missed getting for me. Her brows were bunched as she took it. "For my beer," I explained. She looked about to reject it, but I held my hand up to stop her. She needed it. I didn't.

"I have a gig at another bar. I gotta go meet the guys...give them a hand with all our stuff."

Her eyes softened as she looked me over. "Thank you so much for the ride, Kellan."

I smiled down at her, my earlier contentment nothing compared to what I was feeling now. Just as I was about to comment, Kiera reached up on her toes and placed a light kiss on my cheek. She seemed embarrassed for doing it after she pulled away, and my skin was warmer where her lips had touched me. I wanted her to do it again, and yet, at the same time, I knew I shouldn't want that. Kissing was something she did with Denny, and it should absolutely stay that way. They were great together. But it was just on the cheek...It didn't mean anything. I mean, *I* kissed Denny on the cheek this morning. It was no big deal.

I looked down, almost feeling embarrassed myself. "Don't mention it," I muttered, trying to think straight. Pulling myself together, I said goodbye to the others, then headed for the doors. I tossed Kiera a "Have fun" right before I left. By the way she smiled at me, I was sure she would.

The next night, the band decided to go to Pete's after rehearsal. Well, I don't think it was really a decision, it was more like, "See you at the bar, right? Yep, I'll be there," as we were finishing.

Denny pulled into the parking lot right as I was shutting off the engine of the Chevelle, and I waited for him at the back of my car. He was dressed in his work clothes, a big smile on his face as he made his way over to me. "Hey, mate, fancy meeting you here," he told me.

I clapped him on the shoulder and asked him how his job was going. By his answer, you'd think he'd just unlocked one of the secrets of the universe. A content smile was on my face as we walked toward the front doors of Pete's. Both of my roommates were finding their way here. I liked that. And I was thrilled Denny was happy with his new job. They say you should do what you love, and he definitely seemed to love it.

Matt, Griffin, and Evan walked in a few steps ahead of Denny and me. Like she could sense us, Kiera's head swiveled in our direction. I was too far away to know for sure, but she seemed to inhale a deep breath, composing herself, like she was nervous to wait on us. Were the D-Bags intimidating? I really didn't think we were. We were playful. Fun. We might tease her some, but we only teased the people we liked.

She seemed to relax when she saw that Denny was with us. He tossed her a wave, and she curled her fingers in response. Quietly to me, he said, "Is it just me, or does she look a little frightened?"

I laughed as I looked over at him. "It's Griffin. He frightens everybody." Almost as if on cue, Kiera's eyes swung to Griffin and she immediately looked away, her cheeks clearly red even from a distance.

Denny and I shared a laugh as we all made our way to my favorite table. When Kiera approached us, Evan scooped her up into a hug, making her laugh. Griffin squeezed her butt while she was helpless in Evan's arms. She shot him a nasty glare that promised physical violence, but he was already sitting at the table, out of her reach. Matt held up his hand in greeting, and I gave her a brief nod. When Evan set her down Denny immediately took his place. Denny and Kiera wrapped their arms around each other, sharing a warm, peaceful kiss.

No matter what individual fears they had, they found strength and comfort in each other. They were a team. That moved me, and I found myself continually wondering what it would be like to have something even moderately close to that.

For the first time ever, my house was consistently warm, peaceful, and happy. Kiera and I hung out during the day; Denny and I hung out at night, usually at Pete's, so he could see Kiera for a little bit. We got right back into our easy friendship, and after a while, it didn't even seem like he'd ever left Seattle.

Jenny commented on my good mood one evening while I watched Kiera work; Kiera was humming while she cleaned off a table, and I was pretty sure she was humming one of my songs. That made me insanely happy. "Hey, Kellan. How's it going at your place? Everybody seems happy so far."

I tipped back my beer before I answered her. "It's great. We all get along really well. Denny and Kiera are...good people." My eyes drifted back to Kiera when I said her name. Hanging out with her was surprisingly refreshing. She wasn't melodramatic, psychotic, or using me to fulfill some rock star fantasy. I could just be *me* with her.

Jenny looked back at Kiera with me. Returning her eyes to mine, she narrowed them. I kept my expression even. *I was just looking, no harm in that.* "Yeah, she and Denny are adorable together."

I got the feeling that she was subtly telling me to leave Kiera alone. No warnings needed. I was solidly on the Denny/Kiera team. Giving Jenny a playful smile, I told her, "Not half as adorable as you and Evan."

She rolled her eyes at me as she glanced over at Evan sitting on the stage, flirting with a group of girls. I happened to know that he was currently in between love interests. If Jenny wanted a turn, now was the time to get in line. "Please, we're just friends, Kellan."

"Yeah, but I saw you two cuddling on the Fourth, and you looked awful cozy."

She gave me a placating smile. "And I saw you with red, white, and blue what's-her-name. Doesn't mean anything." She gave me a bright smile like she'd just won the argument. With a laugh, I let her.

Holding my hands up, I said, "Okay. You got me. I was just throwing it out there." Lowering my hands, I playfully added, "But when you two end up together, just remember...I called it."

She shook her head with an amused smile on her lips. "All right, Nostradamus, whatever you say." I leaned back in my chair, chuckling to myself as she walked away.

Matt and Griffin were nearby, showing Sam their new tattoos. Matt's was the Chinese symbol for determination. Griffin's was a girl getting it on with a snake; Griff loved suggestive tattoos. Having already seen their artwork, I tuned out my friends and watched Kiera as she bounced between her tables. She had taken to waitressing easily enough, and like Denny at his job and me at mine, she seemed to enjoy it.

Kiera noticed me watching her just about the time my beer was empty. I motioned her over to get another one. "Hey. Beer?" she asked.

I nodded, loving that she could anticipate my needs now. "Yeah, thanks, Kiera."

Her eyes flicked behind me a couple of times, and I would almost bet money that she was wishing Griffin would put his clothes back on. As she tucked a loose strand of dark hair behind her ear, her face suddenly flushed with color and she wouldn't meet my eyes. She usually only turned that shade when I was teasing her, but I hadn't said anything, so she must be thinking of something that she found embarrassing. Curiosity drove me to find out what it was.

"What?" I asked, already amused.

"Do you have one?" She pointed over at Griffin.

I looked back at him. He was flexing his arm for a group of fans. They squealed as they touched him. "Tattoo?" I asked, turning back around. Shaking my head, I told her, "No, I can't think of anything I'd want permanently etched on my skin." Wondering if she had any markings hidden anywhere, I smiled and asked, "You?"

She seemed a little flustered as she answered. "Nope...virgin skin here." Apparently, she hadn't meant to say that, for she turned bright red. I had to laugh at the unhappy expression on her face as she muttered, "I'll be right back with your beer..."

She sped away from me like a bullet from a gun. Shaking my head, I kept chuckling. I wasn't sure why she was so easily embarrassed; there was certainly nothing about her or her personality that needed to feel that way, but watching the inner struggle was amusing. And yet, at the same time, I hoped that she felt comfortable and confident in her own skin one day. She should feel that way. She was wonderful.

While I watched, Denny burst through the doors, nearly colliding with her. He grabbed her shoulders, his face alight with what could only be good news. Kiera smiled, obviously happy to see him and eager to hear his news. Then her face fell. I frowned, wondering what was going on. Denny shrugged as he said something to her, and her mouth dropped open like he'd slugged her in the gut. I wished I was closer and could hear what they were saying, but I knew the conversation was none of my business, so I stayed put.

Kiera looked upset while she rattled something off to Denny. Denny looked confused while he explained something to her. Then she suddenly exclaimed, "What?" People throughout the bar started turning to look at the couple, who were obviously starting to argue. I stood from my chair, concerned. Denny and Kiera didn't argue. Ever. Or if they did, it certainly wasn't in a public place like this.

Denny looked around at the curious eyes, grabbed Kiera's arm, and pulled her outside. I took a step, wanting to follow, but this had nothing to do with me. I couldn't intrude. I had a really bad feeling though.

Keeping my eyes on the doors, I walked to the bar to get a beer. While I sipped on it, I stared at the doors and willed Denny and Kiera to come back through them their normal, happy, all-is-right-with-the-world selves. I sort of had the feeling that they were breaking up, and it filled me with dread. What would happen to our makeshift family if they split? Why the hell would Denny break up with her anyway? She was warm, sweet, funny, real...beautiful. She was as close to perfect as a girl could get.

When the doors finally reopened, Kiera was alone. I didn't take that as a good sign. She was trying to put on a brave face, that much I could tell, but when she swiped her fingers under her eyes, I knew she was on the verge of failing. Something was wrong.

Frowning, I walked over to her. "Are you okay?"

Her eyes were red and shimmering as she avoided eye contact

71

and looked over my shoulder. She'd been crying, and she was about to do it again. "Yep."

It didn't take a genius to see she was lying. "Kiera…" *Talk to me.*

I put a hand on her arm, hoping she'd open up. She raised her eyes to mine, and the floodgates released. I immediately pulled her into my arms. Protectiveness surged through me as I held her tight to my chest. *How dare Denny hurt her!* Even as I thought that, I knew I couldn't judge what I didn't understand, so I did my best to push that feeling aside. Resting my cheek against her head, I rubbed her back, soothing her as best I could while she sobbed. People around us stared, but I didn't care. She needed me, and I was going to be there for her.

I was mildly surprised at how natural holding her felt. She fit into my body perfectly, like we'd been molded for each other. And comforting her was stirring things inside me. Besides wanting to protect her, save her, something else was growing… friendship, or maybe something even deeper than that. I wasn't sure. All I knew was I didn't want to let go.

I wasn't sure how long we stood there embracing, but eventually Sam came up to me. I knew what he was going to say before he even said it. The band was on, it was time to go play. I shook my head at him, warning him to give me a minute. Kiera peeked up at me, disrupting our contact. She was mostly under control now, just a few sad tears escaping that she swiped from her cheeks. "I'm fine. Thank you. Go, go be a rock star."

Concerned, I asked, "Are you sure? These guys can wait a few more minutes." *If you need me, I'm here for you.*

She smiled, touched by my offer even as she rejected it. "No, really, I'm fine. I should get back to work anyway. I missed getting you your beer again."

I didn't want to, but I released her. With a chuckle, I told her, "Next time."

I rubbed her arm, wishing she was as fine as she was pretending to be, cursing the fact that I had to leave her to go onstage, and wondering why the silkiness of her skin made my heart beat faster.

Shaking that irrelevant thought aside, I let her get back to work. Maybe she'd feel okay enough after the show to open up to me. I really hoped so. I wanted her to talk to me, wanted her to trust me. I would never do anything to hurt or betray her, and I wanted her to see that. She meant a lot to me.

Chapter 6

I'm Here for You

Evan was eyeing me strangely when I walked onto the stage. *Relax, I'm not going to do anything with Kiera.* I wouldn't charm her, hit on her, or be inappropriate in any way with her. She was Denny's.

I watched her throughout the set, trying to gauge her mood. I'd run off the stage and collect her in my arms if she needed me to again. She just had to give me a sign that she was breaking down. She didn't though; she just gave me reassuring smiles whenever she caught me looking.

But when her shift was over, she sat backward in a chair and looked for all the world like she didn't want to go home. She even wiped away some more tears, like she was starting to cry again. Hoping she'd finally open up to me, I sat in a chair beside her. "Hey," I said when she peeked over at me. "Want to talk about it?"

She looked over to where the rest of the band was still lingering. She hesitated to answer me, and I figured they were the reason why. When she shook her head, I was sure of it. Instead of pressuring her to talk to me in front of them, I asked, "Want a ride home?" I understood the need for privacy, and I also understood the reluctance to talk. I wouldn't press her.

She looked back at me with a grateful smile and nodded. "Yes, thank you."

"Sure, just let me get my stuff and we'll head out."

I gave her a warm smile of assurance. Like she was embarrassed, her cheeks mildly tinted. Maybe she felt bad, like she was inconveniencing me. She shouldn't feel that way though. It's not like I wasn't going in her direction anyway; we did live together. I headed back over to the guys to get my stuff. Griffin had a look on his face like he knew something. I was sure he had an assortment of kinky imagery of Kiera and me in his head. Awesome.

Sam was there with them. He had a glass of something in his hand, and raised it to me when I got close enough. "Want to have a drink with us?" He narrowed his eyes. "Just one, mind you. I don't need to babysit your drunken ass again."

I laughed at his comment. It had been a while, but Sam had had to give me a ride home on more than one occasion. It was an aspect of his job that he didn't enjoy. He only did it at all because we were coworkers. And friends. "No thanks. Kiera needs a ride, so I'm gonna take her home." Griffin pursed his lips and poked Matt in the ribs while he nodded. Obviously, he thought he was onto something.

I shook my head at his incorrect assumption and grabbed my guitar. As I turned to leave, Evan grabbed my elbow. Leaning in close he said, "I saw you two earlier. Anything going on there?"

Irritation prickled my spine that Evan's mind was running in line with Griffin's. He should have a little more faith in me than that. "No. Something happened earlier with Denny, I'm not sure what...and she's upset. I'm being a friend, because she needs one. But that's it."

Evan accepted my answer and let go of my arm. And he should accept it; I was telling the truth. Letting the encounter roll off my back, I returned to Kiera. "Ready?" I asked her.

Standing, she nodded, and we left the bar together. She was silent for a while, and I let her be. If she wanted to talk, she would. If she didn't want to, I couldn't force her. The soundlessness between us wasn't oppressive though. There was no tension, no apprehension. Just comfortable friendship.

When I was sure the silence would last the entire trip home, Kiera quietly said, "Denny is leaving."

I couldn't have been more shocked by her words. *No...I just got him back, and they've been so happy together here. What could have possibly happened? Why would he want to leave? Did I do something...?* "But...?"

Her face scrunched like she was mad at herself. "No, just for a few months...just for his job."

I relaxed as I realized Denny's departure was only temporary. Our relationship was still intact, then, and so was theirs. Adding long distance to it would be trying, but I was certain they could do it. "Oh, I thought maybe..." *You were over.*

She interrupted me with a sigh before I could finish my thought. "No, I'm just overreacting. Everything is fine. It's just..." She paused, like even the act of saying the words would hurt her.

"You've never been apart," I guessed.

Glancing over, I saw her lips curve into a small smile of relief. Relief that I understood, and relief that I hadn't judged her. "Yeah. I mean, we have, but not for that long. I guess I'm just used to seeing him every day, and, well...we waited so long to live together, and things have been going so perfectly, and now..."

"Now he's leaving."

"Yeah."

I could feel her eyes studying me while I studied the road. I tried to imagine what that would feel like, waiting so long to be with someone, and then having it snatched away the moment you had it.

"What are you thinking about?" Kiera murmured that in a far-away voice, almost like she wasn't talking to me.

"Nothing..." I looked over at her and her eyes were wide, like she hadn't realized she'd asked me a question. I ignored her startled expression as I thought over what I'd been wishing for. "I was just hoping things work out for you guys. You're both..." *Incredible people, an inspiration, my hope for the future...important to me.*

Silence settled over the car again, but it was grateful silence this time. I was glad that Kiera had opened up to me, and happy that her problem seemed short-term.

When we got to the house, Denny's car was in the drive. Kiera inhaled a deep breath at seeing it. She was smiling though, like she was happy he was home. I hoped she always felt that way. Turning to me, she said, "Thank you...for everything."

I had a sudden desire for her to kiss my cheek again, and I looked down. If I were more like her, that thought would have had me blushing. "Not a problem, Kiera."

We got out of the car and made our way into the house. Kiera paused at her bedroom door, and I paused at mine. I watched her staring at the closed wood, her hand clenching the metal knob instead of turning it. She seemed nervous, like she was afraid of what lay on the other side.

"It will be fine, Kiera," I whispered into the darkness. She looked back at me, warmth and gratitude in her eyes.

"Good night," she told me, her eyes never leaving mine. Then she steeled herself and opened the door into her bedroom with Denny.

Alone in the hallway, I stared at their closed door for several minutes. The remembered feel of Kiera in my arms returned to me, the smell of her hair, the warmth in her eyes, the comfort of her body pressed against mine. For a split second I wondered what it would be like if Denny left and never came back. Would Kiera see me as anything other than a playboy rock star if we were alone in the house? Would I want her to see me as more?

Shaking my head, I opened my bedroom door and walked inside. It didn't matter if she would have developed an interest in me or not. That wasn't what was happening here. Denny wasn't leaving her, he was just going away for a couple of months. No big deal. They were fine, absolutely fine, and for some weird reason, that thought made me a little sad.

Denny and Kiera were attached at the hip while they counted down the minutes until he left, but I managed to get Denny alone. "Hey, can I talk to you?"

"Of course. What is it?"

I had no idea how to say what I wanted to say without sounding rude...so I just said it. "I saw how upset Kiera was when you told her you were leaving. Are you sure about this?"

Denny frowned, like he thought I'd overstepped my bounds. Maybe I had. "It's just a few months." His expression shifted to excitement. "You don't understand what this could mean for me, Kellan. This could be the beginning of something great."

I held my tongue, but all I could think was *It could also be the end of something even better*.

On the day Denny had to leave, I offered to drive him to the airport, since I didn't know what else I could do. Kiera's eyes were only on Denny as we made our way to Sea-Tac. Denny's eyes, however, were locked on me the entire drive there.

Inside the airport, I gave my two friends some space to say their goodbyes. It was an emotional moment, and I found it hard to watch Kiera's obvious struggle. Her devotion...I'd never seen anyone care that much. Certainly no one had ever cared that much about me.

They broke apart after a passionate kiss. Denny said something that had to be goodbye, kissed her cheek, and then made his way over to me. He smiled as I said goodbye, then he glanced back at Kiera. When he returned his attention to me, his face was completely different. Hard, almost. Leaning in, he whispered, "I need your word that you won't touch her while I'm gone. That you'll look out for her, but you'll stay as far away as possible. You understand what I'm saying?" He pulled back, his expression deadly serious.

Shocked, I flicked a quick glance at Kiera watching us. Was he seriously warning me not to sleep with his girlfriend? Did he really think I would? Yes, I liked Kiera...I cared about her a lot, actually...but she was his, and I respected that. I respected him. I would never...

Denny stuck his hand out. I nodded once, dumbfounded, then reached out and clenched his hand. Somehow shaking hands felt more like we were making a pact than saying our goodbyes. "I won't... I would never do anything to hurt you like that, Denny."

Denny gave me a brief smile in response to my oath, then turned and blew Kiera a kiss before he headed to security. It took me a minute to process everything that had just happened. I always thought Denny saw the best in me... but he must not trust me as much as I thought if he believed I'd do something like that while he was gone. Even Evan thought he had to warn me... Was that the person people saw when they looked at me? Was that who I was?

Kiera was staring at the space Denny had just left, and tears were starting to form in her eyes. I figured she was about fifteen seconds away from a meltdown, and I also figured she didn't want to do that in the middle of the airport, so I quickly ushered her back to the car.

She held it together until we hit the freeway, then she completely fell apart. I'd never seen someone so torn before, like her soul had been shredded into pieces. Her pain made me ache, and I found it really hard to understand why Denny would put her through this. I wanted to fix her, wanted to take away all of her pain, wanted to protect her from ever feeling that way again. I realized I couldn't do any of those things though, so I simply drove her home, set her up on the couch with some water and a box of tissues, and sat in the chair beside her to keep her company.

Hoping it would take her mind off things, I found something funny on the TV for us to watch. It seemed to work. After a few chuckles, her complexion was brighter and she wasn't going through nearly as many tissues. I watched Kiera more than the movie. Her eyes were greener in her pain, and she chewed on her lip while she watched the ridiculous movie. I suddenly wished I could sit beside her on the couch, maybe wrap an arm around her, give her my shoulder to cry on, but I'd promised Denny I'd keep my distance.

Eventually her tears dried up. I could see the exhaustion on her face when she lay down on the couch, and it didn't surprise me at all when she fell asleep before the movie was over. She probably hadn't slept at all last night. I found a light blanket and laid it over her curled body. She stirred a little and smiled, like she knew I'd done that for her.

I stood over her, watching her for the longest time. A strand of hair had fallen over her cheek and across her lips. Her light breath was making the ends flutter, and I was positive that any second, it would tickle her awake. Careful to be slow and gentle, I lifted the strand from her face and tucked it behind her ear; it was silky between my fingers.

Kiera didn't move, so I figured she was still asleep. I knew I shouldn't, but her exposed cheek was calling to me. My breath sped in anticipation and my lips parted. She really was incredibly beautiful. Even emotionally drained, with light circles under her eyes, she was stunning. The pad of my thumb brushed against her cheekbone. Her skin was so soft, I wanted to cup it in my palm, feel more of it beneath my fingers. I wanted to rub my cheek against hers, brush my lips across it. But I was already crossing the line right now, and I wouldn't cross it any farther. Kiera and I had the foundation of a really nice friendship. It seemed too simple when put in those terms, but it was the only way I could describe us, and I wasn't going to do anything to jeopardize our relationship, or mine and Denny's, even if he didn't fully trust me.

I did my best over the next few days to make Kiera comfortable with her situation. Mainly I tried to keep her mind off it by filling up all of her free time. She unfortunately had a lot of time on her hands since she hadn't started school yet.

The more time we spent together, the more I enjoyed her company. She was smart, funny, insightful, and a pleasure to look at, especially when I could make her cheeks flush bright red. She was also silly and playful when she broke out of her shell, a fun fact I discovered when I successfully got her to dance and sing with me at the grocery store. I was supposed to be getting *her* mind off *her* loneliness, but she was actually getting my mind off mine.

Sure, I flirted with girls on occasion, because a woman's touch wasn't something I was ready to give up just now, but I couldn't even recall the last time I'd slept with someone. It felt like forever, but I rarely thought about sex anymore. Well, I rarely thought about sex with girls I didn't know anymore. I did on occasion have steamy, and really inappropriate, thoughts about Kiera. And dreams. Sweet Jesus, the dreams. Some of the ones I had about her had me hard enough to cut glass when I woke up. But I didn't let that affect our friendship, or my promise to Denny. Both people meant too much to me.

I was having a rather inappropriate thought about what she might look like soaking wet when I heard her knock on my door one evening. I'd just gotten out of the shower and was a little soaked myself when I told her she could come in.

Shoving away the image of water dripping between her breasts, I threw on a bright, friendly smile as she pushed the door open. "What's up?"

She was standing in the doorway, staring at me with her mouth open. She probably hadn't expected me to be only half dressed. She closed her mouth, attempted to compose herself, then started stammering. It was a cute reaction, and one I wasn't used to. Maybe she thought about me naked too? No, no way.

"Um...I was wondering...if I could go with you...to Razors... listen to the band..."

"Really?" I grabbed my shirt off my bed, surprised. Razors was a small bar that we were playing at tonight. Kiera heard the band so often at Pete's that hearing us there would be a little monotonous. If that was what she wanted though, I'd love her company. "You're not sick of listening to me yet?" I winked as I put on my shirt. She had to be a little over it.

She swallowed, like she was still taken aback by my body. Hmmm, on second thought, maybe I *should* be half-naked in front of her more often. Her distraction was alluring.

Friends. Just friends.

"No...not yet," she said. Almost as an afterthought, she added, "It will give me something to do, anyway."

I laughed at her comment. It always came back to Denny, and the perpetual waiting game she was playing. Finished getting dressed, I went to my dresser to get the styling product I used on my hair and tousled up the mess into ordered chaos.

When I looked back at Kiera, she was engrossed with watching me. "Sure, I'm almost ready to go." I sat down to pull on my boots and patted the bed so Kiera would join me. When she did, I found that I liked having her beside me; her clean fresh scent wrapped around me, and even without touching her, I somehow felt a warmth I'd never had before. But I knew I shouldn't think stuff like that.

The show turned out really nice, and I was glad that Kiera had a chance to see it. Once the set was over and our stuff was packed up, I made sure to thank the employees for having us, and the patrons for coming down to see us, or at least putting up with us, if they hadn't known we were playing. As I was hugging the bartender goodbye, a forward girl put her hand on my back pocket and squeezed my ass. When I looked over my shoulder at her, she said, "Have any plans tonight?"

My eyes darted from her to Kiera, standing by the doors, watching. Not too long ago, I would have agreed to go anywhere this woman wanted me to go, but things were different now, and I didn't want to go anywhere with her. And besides, I couldn't. I actually did have plans.

"Sorry, I do." She frowned, so I gave her a kiss on the cheek. Hopefully it was enough to make her happy.

Kiera was in a great mood on the ride home. She was staring at me like she was mesmerized. I wasn't sure why, until I realized I was quietly singing the last song we'd played.

"I love that one," she told me. I nodded. I already knew that. No matter what she was doing, she always stopped and listened to "Remember Me" whenever we played it at Pete's.

"It seems important to you," she asked, suddenly inquisitive. "Does it mean something?"

She almost seemed embarrassed for asking, like she'd done it without thinking again. Her question caught me off guard, as did her insight. And her concern. Most girls didn't notice my lyrics when they were around me. "Huh," was all I could come up with to say.

Of course, that wasn't enough for her. "What?" she asked, her voice timid.

In that one simple word, I could almost hear her begging me to open up to her. The idea of her knowing what that song meant to me, what I was *really* singing about, didn't scare me like it had when I'd first watched her reaction to it. I felt very comfortable with her. I wasn't comfortable enough to open up and tell her every sob story I had inside me, but I was comfortable enough to not be afraid of confiding small pieces of myself to her. So long as she didn't ask for too much, and she didn't push when I didn't want her to.

With a warm, carefree smile, I told her, "No one's ever asked me that before. Well, no one outside the band, that is." I paused, wondering if I wanted to crack open the confession door just yet. "Yes..." I murmured, looking over at her. She blinked and turned my way, her eyes wide with some emotion I couldn't even begin to place. Losing myself in the shape of her mouth, the shine in her eyes, I let a section of my heart spill out. "It means a lot to me..."

What I've hoped all my life to have. What my parents could never give me. What I know I'm not worthy of...someone's love. That's what it means to me.

A slice of unexpected pain jarred my heart. I didn't want to tell Kiera any more, didn't want more pain to seep out, so I tightened my mental defenses and studied the lines on the road, hoping she would get the hint. Thankfully she didn't ask me to elaborate. Kiera always seemed to understand when she was pressing on a scar, and I was grateful that she backed off before she tore it open.

I contemplated heading over to Evan's or Matt's when we got home, anything to take my mind off the last several minutes, but Kiera's smile was so warm and inviting when she thanked me for the fun evening that she melted the ice around my heart that had been chilling me. That was what it felt like, anyway. And like she was the sun, I just wanted to be near her, so I stayed.

Having Kiera around was brightening my life in ways I hadn't anticipated. Like one afternoon, when I came home to find my place completely transformed. It amused me at first. I even laughed when I caught Jenny and Kiera putting up pictures in the kitchen. But as I walked from room to room, I was struck by what they'd done. The odd baskets, art, and photos made the home seem lived in. All of a sudden, it wasn't just four walls and a roof anymore. It had personality, and the personality belonged to Kiera. The house felt like her.

Even my bedroom.

Stopping in my doorway, I stared into my room, amazed. Hanging on my wall was a Ramones poster. I loved the Ramones. I tried to think back through all of our conversations, but I couldn't recall ever mentioning that to her. The fact that she saw something while she was out, thought of me, and bought it...well, that was sort of incomprehensible.

I couldn't remember the last time someone had done something for me out of the blue like that. It wasn't a holiday, wasn't a special occasion. It was just Sunday. Sitting on my bed, I stared at the poster, mystified, overwhelmed, and deeply touched.

I heard Jenny say goodbye, and I yelled a goodbye back. Staring at my floor, I thought about how barren my house had looked before Kiera spruced it up. I'd never felt so unimportant in all my life as the day I'd raced back to Seattle and discovered that my parents had basically eradicated me from their life: All my things were gone, no pictures were on the walls, and no mementos were on the shelves. Seeing the effacement was ten times worse than all the times Dad had subtly, and not so subtly, implied how meaningless I was to him; words cut deep, but this cut deeper. There was no way to misinterpret what they'd done.

Seeing how they'd cut me out of their existence had been a bigger hit to the gut than every kick from Dad's steel-toed boot. I'd wanted to cry, I'd wanted to vomit. What I'd ended up doing was putting every piece of furniture they'd owned on the side of the road with a FREE sign on it. By the time I was done removing any trace of them, the house had been as empty as I was.

I heard a knock on my door and looked up to see Kiera standing there. Pushing aside my dark memories, I waved her in.

She cringed a little when she spoke, which made a cute wrinkle form on the top of her nose. "Hey...sorry about the stuff. If you don't like it, I can take it down."

She looked so apologetic as she sat down beside me, like she'd truly done something wrong. But all she'd done was add a little... life...to my life. "No, it's fine. I guess it was a little...empty." *To say the least.* I pointed over at the Ramones picture behind me. "I do like that...thanks." *I more than like it. And thanks isn't enough, but it's all I can give you.*

"Yeah, I thought you might...you're welcome." Her beautiful smile shifted to a frown. "You okay?" she asked, her brows bunched like she was actually worried about me.

Was she concerned over me? All she'd seen was me staring at the floor for a second. *What did she think she saw?* "Yeah, I'm fine...why?"

Again, she seemed embarrassed, like she was infringing on my privacy. "Nothing, you just looked...nothing, sorry."

Remembering all the times she hadn't pried when she could have, remembering how opening up to her just a small fraction had felt nice before it had hurt, I considered telling her what I was thinking about when she'd walked in. There was no way I could though. It wasn't something simple that could be explained with a line or two. No, to explain just how much what she'd done meant to me, I'd have to explain *everything*. And I couldn't. It wasn't a story I told people about.

Instead of telling her what I was sure she wanted to hear, I smiled and asked, "Hungry? How about Pete's?" Amused, I added, "It's been so long since we've been there."

Once we were at Pete's we settled down at the band's table and placed our order with Jenny. People were staring at the pair of us together, but I ignored them. I was having a meal with my roommate. That was all.

Kiera was usually fine when it was the two of us, but sometimes she could slip into funks. "Denny depressions," I called them. While we waited for our food to arrive, I watched the perkiness on her face shift to sullenness. She was missing him.

Even though I knew what was wrong with her, I asked if she was all right. She shrugged it off, shaking her head and sitting up taller as she said she was fine, but I could see that it was all for show. Her heart was aching, and she was lonely. I could understand loneliness. I wished there were more I could do for her, but I wasn't the one she was yearning for, so my help was limited. I was a patch, something to help suppress the sadness. That was okay. At least I was useful.

Chapter 7

Promise Made, Promise Almost Kept

It had been several weeks since Denny had left Seattle, but the time had flown by. For me, anyway. One thing I'd begun to notice was the fact that Denny was calling less and less frequently. I didn't mention my concerns to Kiera, but it was starting to bother me. Mainly because it bothered her. I saw the disappointment on her face. It was like watching a sculpture getting chipped apart piece by piece. If Denny didn't shape up soon, he was going to have a problem on his hands that had nothing to do with his unfounded fears about me.

I talked to him sometimes, when he'd call the house while Kiera was gone. "So, how is Tucson treating you?" I asked him one afternoon.

He laughed. "It's a hell of a lot hotter than Seattle, but I like it. How are things there?"

"Good. No worries here." *I'm keeping my promise.*

He let out an exhale that was saturated with relief. "That's good. I'd hate for there to be…problems…while I wasn't around."

My jaw clenched, wondering if that was a vague warning to me. He had nothing to worry about, seriously. Kiera wasn't even interested in me. All she ever thought about was Denny.

Clearing my throat, I redirected my thoughts. "I've noticed you haven't been calling as much. Any *problems* on your end?" *See, I can ask vague questions with hidden meanings too.*

Denny was silent for several seconds. He was a smart guy, so I knew he understood what I was really asking. He was either shocked that I would go there, or he was debating how to answer me. My stomach churned at the idea of Denny possibly straying on Kiera. Would I tell her if he had? I already knew I would. Withholding the truth from Kiera wasn't something I ever wanted to do.

"No...no problems here. Just...a lot of work, and not a lot of downtime." He sighed, like he was suddenly exhausted. "I'm doing the best I can, mate."

From the tone of his voice, I knew he was telling the truth. I gave him some encouraging words, then dropped it. I was their roommate, not their counselor.

Concern over hearing from Denny was slipping from Kiera's list of stresses as school neared. I could almost see the tension building in her each day. She was more anxious about the first day of school than she had been about anything else so far, and I was sure Denny not being here for it was only making the feeling ten times worse.

Kiera's apprehension exploded in an eruption of stress one afternoon. It was a theatrical blowup that I probably wasn't supposed to see, but I'd walked into the kitchen at just the right time. She let out a loud "Fuck" and knocked all of her school brochures onto the floor.

I had to laugh at the over-the-top display. "I can't wait to tell Griff about that one."

She flushed with color once she realized I was there, then she groaned when my words sank in. I nodded at the mess on the floor while she recovered from her embarrassment. "School starting, huh?"

She bent down to pick up the fallen papers, and I did my best to ignore how good she looked bent over. "Yeah," she said with a sigh, "and I still haven't really been on the campus. I have no idea where everything is." She straightened, and a forlorn look of Denny-sickness was on her face. "I just...Denny was supposed to be here for this." She frowned, either irritated at herself or irritated at Denny. Maybe a bit of both. "He's been gone almost a month," she murmured.

I studied her, noting the sadness mixed with anger and embarrassment on her face. I think she wanted to be strong and independent, but for some reason, she lacked the confidence. I couldn't figure out why. She was beautiful, smart, funny, sweet…She had nothing to be afraid of. But I also understood needing someone else around to make you feel complete. I understood all too well.

Kiera looked away from my scrutiny, and in a soft voice, I told her, "The D-Bags play the campus every once in a while." Her eyes returned to mine, and I smirked at her. "I actually know it pretty well. I can show you around if you like."

Her instant relief was almost palpable. "Oh, please, yes." Suddenly looking mortified, she cleared her throat and shifted her feet. "I mean, if you don't mind."

Her hazel eyes were a tranquil shade of green in this light, alive with warmth, caring, and hopefulness. How could I possibly say no to those eyes? "No, Kiera, I don't mind…" *I'd do just about anything for you. Which both makes me happy and terrifies the shit out of me.*

I took her to register for her classes the next afternoon, then took her on a tour of the campus a few days later. Wanting to impress her, I may have overdone it on the campus tour. I'd just wanted her to feel as comfortable as possible when she started there. She ate up every word I said though. Maybe that's why I really did it. I liked having her hanging on my every word. It made me feel sort of invincible.

I was showing her the building where her European Lit class was going to be when a voice broke through the quiet hallway. "Oh! My! God! Kellan Kyle!"

I knew just from the octave of the voice that it was a fan shouting at me. I cringed, wondering how this was going to play out, but ever considerate of my fans, I turned around to look. A springy-haired redhead was practically running down the hall to get to me. I really had no idea what she was going to do once she reached me.

I considered grabbing Kiera's hand and making a run for it, but I didn't have time. The tiny girl was surprisingly fast. She had her arms flung around my neck and her mouth all over mine before I even knew what hit me.

While she peppered me with fevered kisses, I racked my brain, trying to place her, but I couldn't for the life of me recall who this girl was. "I can't believe you're visiting me at school."

Okay, she went to school here, so that narrowed it down...not one single little bit. The girl glanced at Kiera beside me and I tensed. She'd better not try to start something. Luckily, the girl wasn't too interested in who Kiera was.

After flicking her eyes at her, she curved her lips into a frown and muttered, "Oh, I can see you're busy." Reaching into her purse, she scribbled something on a piece of paper, then shoved it in my front pocket. Her fingers ran along the inside of the pocket, searching for me, and I fidgeted just a bit. A girl kissing me in front of Kiera was one thing; fondling though, that was kind of awkward to have Kiera witnessing.

"Call me," she breathed before giving me one last kiss and bounding away.

Well. Okay then.

I started walking down the hallway like nothing weird had just happened. What could I say to that anyway? I could feel Kiera watching me. She had to be curious about the girl who'd practically devoured me in the hallway.

When I finally turned to look at Kiera, she still had an expression of disbelief etched on her face. "Who was that?" she asked.

I tried to bring up a name to go with those flaming red curls, but I was drawing a blank. "I really have no idea," I told her, knowing it was going to sound bad. Now that I was really thinking about it, I seemed to recall running into her before, but the details were fuzzy and her name was completely gone. Cheating, I peeked at the note she'd stuffed in my pocket. "Hmmm...that was Candy."

Oh yeah. Candy. I'd met her near a vending machine. I still found that funny. Laughing, I crumpled up the piece of paper with her name on it and tossed it in the wastebasket. I wanted more than random hookups. As we left the building, I noticed Kiera smirking, like she was pleased I'd thrown the note away. Interesting. I wondered why she cared either way about me seeing somebody. Maybe she was just looking out for me.

As the days went on, Kiera started slipping into a funk. More and more time was passing between Denny's phone calls. I wished I could help in some way, but I really didn't know how to fix what was slowly breaking them apart. Denny returning was the only solution, and that would happen soon enough. Kiera just had to get through a few more weeks without him.

When the weekend hit and she was once again on the couch in her pajamas, I knew I had to do something. The guys and I had plans for the day, but it wasn't anything that she couldn't join us for. In fact, she'd probably have a great time if she came out with us. All I had to do was get her off the damn couch. She was currently glued to its lumpy cushions, flipping through channel after channel like a person possessed.

When she let out yet another forlorn sigh, I stepped between her and the TV. "Come on," I said, extending my hand.

She looked up at me, confused. "Huh?"

"You're not spending yet another day moping on the couch. You're coming with me." I raised my hand a little higher, but she stubbornly refused to take it.

Frowning, she sulked. "And where are we going?"

I grinned, knowing that what I was about to say was going to make absolutely no sense to her. "Bumbershoot."

Like I'd just spoken a foreign language, she slowly blinked her wide eyes as she tried to comprehend just what that could be. "Bumper-what?"

I laughed at the way she mispronounced the strange name, then flashed her a bright, reassuring smile. "Bumbershoot. Don't worry, you'll love it."

The mocking smile she gave me in response made her lips curve in an extraordinarily appealing way. I did my best to ignore how attractive it was, and how amazingly soft they probably were. "But that will ruin a perfectly good day of wallowing."

"Exactly." I grinned, flexing my hand so she'd finally take it.

Still being stubborn, she let out a dramatic sigh and stood on her own. "Fine." She put on quite a show of being put out that I was making her go have fun, and I laughed at the display. She'd have to do better than stomping her feet and sticking out her lip to make me believe she was angry. Right now, she was just…cute.

When she came down later in shorts that exposed almost all of her thighs, and a tight tank top that hugged every curve like a second skin, I realized that she was something else. Sexy. Unbelievably sexy.

Collecting our things, we got in the car and made our way over to Pete's, where the guys were meeting me so we could all ride together. Still curious where we were going, Kiera made a joke out of it when we pulled into the parking lot. "Bumbershoot is at Pete's?"

I rolled my eyes as I pulled into my favorite stall. "No, the guys are at Pete's." Looking around, I could see they were already here. Evan's vehicle was next to Griffin's van.

Kiera seemed a little disappointed with my answer. "Oh, they're coming too?"

I studied her face after I put the car in park. Why did she look so sad? I thought she liked the guys. Well, maybe not Griffin, but the others at least. Frowning, I told her, "Yeah…Is that okay?" The guys would be pissed if I told them we wanted to go alone, but if that was what Kiera wanted…I'd do that for her. Actually, I kind of liked the idea of it just being the two of us.

Kiera shook her head with a sigh, like she wasn't sure why she'd said what she'd said. "No, of course that's fine. I'm intruding on your day anyway."

I suddenly had the strangest desire to touch her, to run my thumb along the faint blush of red coloring her cheek. "You're not intruding on anything, Kiera," I told her, my voice soft. *Today will be better because you're here to share it with me.* Not wanting to freak her out with my overdramatic thoughts, I kept them to my-self.

The guys came over once they saw my car. There were a few is-sues getting everyone settled, mainly because Griffin was being a pansy and didn't want to take the middle seat. Thankfully, Kiera solved the problem, although her solution was to move to the back-seat and be harassed by Griffin the entire trip, which I wasn't too excited about. It made a weird sort of protectiveness surge through me at just the idea of his hands anywhere near her. We'd have to come up with a different seating arrangement on the way back, or I just might strangle him.

When we got there, everyone piled out of my car, careful to not hit the cars beside me. It was a well-known fact that damaging the Chevelle in any way resulted in an automatic free pass to walk your ass home. A fact that, to date, only Griffin had tested, when he'd once had the audacity to hurl in my backseat. I swear I could still smell the vomit sometimes.

I waited for Kiera by the door, holding my hand out so she'd take it. As she was about to find out, Bumbershoot was a music and art festival at the Seattle Center, and it was typically jam-packed with people. I didn't want to take the risk of getting separated from her, especially since neither of us had cell phones. She'd just have to hold my hand today, an idea that made me happier than it really should have.

Evan gave me a look when he noticed our physical connection, but I ignored it. I had a valid reason for touching her. It was purely for her own safety. That was what I told myself, anyway.

Kiera's eyes were wide when she looked around the Center. Her obvious joy and wonder made me appreciate it again. I came down here so often, I'd sort of lost respect for the area. It was refreshing to see it all again through Kiera's eyes. It almost made the fact that we were constantly being bumped into by strangers unnoticeable.

There were booths everywhere, selling everything from T-shirts to cotton candy. Artists had their work on display; there were a lot of wild animal prints, landscape prints, and prints of Seattle. As we passed near the Space Needle, Kiera's eyes traveled to the observation deck at the top. Leaning in so she could hear me, I told her, "We can go up later, if you want?"

Her eyes flashed with green in the sunshine, and she gave me an eager nod. I had to laugh at her enthusiasm.

Once we got into the main part of the Center, the crowds thickened. I could hear music playing in all directions. Oddly, it blended well with the noise of the people ambling around, creating a pleasing, energizing melee of melodies. It amped me up. I was ready to check out one of the many stages, to hear some new tunes.

Matt and Griffin had the map and instantly started leading the way. Evan followed after them while Kiera and I brought up the rear. I made sure to keep a tight hold on her hand as we weaved through the packed crowds. When we got to the outdoor stage where Mischief's Muse was playing, Kiera squeezed my hand. I smiled and pulled her closer to me. I was *not* losing her in the masses.

The guys wanted the best seats in the house, and Matt wanted to check out the band's equipment, so they shoved their way toward the front of the stage. I could tell from the look on Kiera's face that she didn't want to enter the rowdy pit of people near the front, so I stopped us well near the back. We still had a good view, but we weren't being bothered. Too much. We *were* being jostled by people going around us, wanting to get closer to the stage. Kiera was pressed tight into my side, trying to get out of their way, but it still wasn't enough.

Wanting her safe as well as comfortable, I pulled her in front of me so I'd take the bulk of the hits. I slipped my arms around her waist so she'd be even more protected from the people around us. Well, and because I *wanted* to put my arms around her; it felt completely natural to hold her when she was directly in front of me like she was. Anything else would have felt awkward. It was still a poor excuse though, and I knew it. I was beginning to push on a line I shouldn't be messing with.

Kiera didn't seem to mind my arms around her. She left her hands tangled with mine around her stomach and leaned back

94

against my chest. She seemed just as comfortable as I was as she watched the band and the crowds. She turned her head to focus on something to the far right of the stage, and my gaze followed. My bandmates were over there, getting high by the looks of it. None of the guys did any hard drugs, but they did smoke pot on occasion, Griffin especially. Personally, I didn't care for the stuff; I'd rather have beer, but I didn't care if they did it.

I looked down at Kiera, wondering if she'd care. With a smile, I shrugged. She seemed reassured by my gesture, so I figured she was okay with it and returned my eyes to the show. That was when everything changed for me. Kiera let out a long exhale, like she was finally breathing for the first time in weeks. I was just thinking how glad I was that I'd made her come out with us when I felt her body shifting. At first, I thought she was just done with having a strange man's arms around her, so I let her go. But she didn't step away from me. No, she turned *into* me.

Her arms slipped around my waist, holding me tight, and her head rested on my chest. Every muscle in my body instantly locked with tension. Her fingers against my side started stroking back and forth in a calming, rhythmic pattern, and she inhaled another deep, cleansing breath. Was she just getting more comfortable? She definitely couldn't see more of the show this way, since my chest partially blocked her vision, so it had to be about comfort.

As I relaxed into her embrace, wrapping my arms tight around her, I immediately started feeling that comfort. It was a warmth brighter than the sun radiating in the sky. It was a buoyancy lighter than floating on the water.

I knew I was overstepping so many boundaries right now that it was ridiculous, but I couldn't help myself. Holding her—just *holding* her—felt better than anything I'd felt in a while. If I was going to be honest with myself, I'd wanted to hold her like this for some time now, I just hadn't had a good reason to. I knew this would hurt Denny if he could see it, and hurting him was the last thing I wanted to do, but goddamn...I needed this, and for the moment, I was going to be a selfish asshole.

95

Closing my eyes, I stroked my thumbs across her back and inhaled the heady scent of her. I'd never had anything like this feeling, and I desperately wanted to keep it going. *I'm sorry, Denny, but I can't let her go.* I kind of never wanted to let her go.

I did though. We broke apart before the guys returned to us. I didn't want any of them thinking things they shouldn't—well, anything more than they already thought about us. Holding hands in a place like this was harmless enough, and they'd already seen us do it, so I continued keeping a firm grip on her. I was anxious though, wanting to get to the next musician, not so I could hear the music but so I could feel that connection with Kiera again. So I could touch her, wrap my arms around her, feel her arms wrapped around me. It was the most unbelievable thing I'd ever known, and I never wanted it to end.

At each act, Kiera and I paused farther and farther back. I'd watch for Evan, Matt, and Griffin to disappear in the mass of gyrating bodies, then I'd smile at Kiera and wrap my arms around her. I loved having her head right over my heart, her shoulder tucked under mine. My arm wrapped around her back and my fingers brushed against her rib cage. It took every shred of willpower I had to not lean down and kiss her head. I satisfied the instinct by resting my cheek against her hair. It was heaven. Pure, painful heaven, because as nice as it was, I knew it wasn't right. *Denny wouldn't like this…*

We stayed locked together in some way the entire day, and even though half of Seattle seemed to be packed into the Center, it felt like Kiera and I were alone. We talked about the bands we'd seen. I'd only been half listening to them, but Kiera had been paying attention. Her first remark about any band I asked her about was always "Well, they're definitely not as good as you, but…" Her eyes shone when she said it too, like she really meant it. I was on cloud nine all day long.

Even the inquisitive glances Evan was giving us didn't ruin my natural buzz. I continued to ignore the innuendo in his gaze, but thankfully, after Matt passed around his "adult juice" during lunch, his meaningful looks became less frequent. I knew Evan would question me about today though; it was just a matter of time.

I didn't want to think about that, or anything, so I concentrated all of my focus on Kiera. She had my complete and total attention today. And once again, I couldn't help but think that I'd started out the day wanting to help her, but it had turned out to be *her* who was helping me. I hoped one day I could be a little less selfish around her.

After lunch we all goofed around in the amusement park for a bit. Leaving the guys at the rides, Kiera and I did our own thing. It was fun. Kiera laughed a lot and smiled even more, which made me even happier. I even managed to win her a teddy bear—that only cost me about thirty bucks—but we promptly gave it to a little girl who was having a meltdown over a ruined ice cream cone. I will never forget the look on Kiera's face when she watched me give that toy away. It was almost…adoring.

Once we rejoined the guys, we hit up some of the bigger acts. Like they had all day, the guys disappeared into the swarm of the crowd, and Kiera and I melded together once they were gone. At the last show of the night, we were near the back of the crowd, but not as close to the edge as we'd been before. It was pretty tight around us, and Kiera and I were holding each other so close, we were almost one person. I ran my fingers through her hair as her fingers swirled a pattern on my chest. My heart sped up at her nearness combined with the darkness, and I hoped she couldn't hear it.

The song blaring through the speakers was a popular song on the radio, and I sang along to it. It was a slower song, and I swayed my body a little as I sang. Kiera matched my movement, and before long, we were sort of slow dancing together. I stopped singing and just enjoyed the moment. I pulled her tight for a hug, and she returned the sentiment. It made my heart beat even harder that she'd hugged me back. *Why does touching you feel so good? And will it stop the second I drive you home?*

I didn't want it to stop, but I knew it should. What we were doing was stupid and dangerous. Someone was going to get hurt. Denny was going to get hurt. Even though I knew that, my fingers drifted from her hair down to her back, caressing her. I so badly wanted to allow them to drift farther down, to feel them curve around her backside. I wanted to feel her, all of her, but she'd probably slap me if I took it that far. And that's not what this was about anyway. This wasn't about sex, this was about our connection.

I still wanted to feel her body though. I wanted to bend down and kiss her too, but I shoved both desires aside. Dancing with her was enough. Dancing with her was amazing. Better than any sex I'd ever had.

I didn't want the song to end, I didn't want the show to end, but eventually both did. Kiera and I loosened our holds on each other as the crowd around us dispersed. Maybe I was reading too much into it, but she seemed reluctant to break apart from me, like she'd enjoyed the closeness just as much as I had.

She was clearly exhausted though. When the guys joined up with us, they were wired, practically bouncing off the walls, but Kiera could hardly walk in a straight line anymore. Still holding her hand, I led her through the thinning crowds and back to the car. I did a quick inspection of the Chevelle, but it seemed okay.

Evan and Matt got in the car, and Griffin held the door open for Kiera. He was half-lit at this point, and I could only imagine what he might try to do to her if she sat with him. I was about to tell him to switch with Evan when Kiera crawled into the front seat, between me and Evan, instead of the back. Griffin instantly pouted, and I shot him a smile as I got into the car after her. *Sorry, Griff, no fondling this trip.*

Spent, Kiera laid her head on my shoulder. She was out like a light by the time we reached the freeway. I could almost *hear* Evan looking at me; the entire right side of my face burned from his stare, but I concentrated on the road. *Nothing to see here, Evan, I swear.*

When we got to Pete's, Kiera was still sleeping, so I made sure I didn't jostle her too much when I pulled into the parking lot. I stopped my car behind Griffin's van to let everybody out. Matt and

Griffin hopped out, and Griffin started animatedly telling Matt all about how amazing it was going to be when the D-Bags ruled Bumbershoot. Matt, for once, seemed to agree with him.

Evan got out, asked Matt and Griffin a question, then turned back to me. "Hey, Kellan, we're gonna stay at Pete's. You comin'?" By the look on his face, it was clear that he wanted me to.

I looked down at Kiera asleep on my shoulder. She was wiped. Waking her up and dragging her into the bar didn't seem fair. Neither did leaving her in the car, not that I would ever leave her alone and vulnerable like that. "No, I'll pass tonight. I think I'll get her to bed."

Evan just stared at me in response. He was torn, I could see that much. He knew I was right, I needed to get her home, but he was worried about what might happen if I took off with her. I wished he wouldn't worry about stuff like that. Nothing was going to happen. Not while she was happy with Denny.

After a long pause, he finally told me, "Be careful, Kellan. You don't need another Joey and…Denny is a friend, man."

Even though I knew he was thinking it, it stung to hear him say it. I cringed as I thought over how I could possibly explain to him what Kiera and I were. What she meant to me. What Denny meant to me. That I'd never hurt either of them. It was hard to say though, because…I'd really enjoyed holding Kiera today. A lot more than I should have; I already wanted to hold her like that again.

In a soft voice, I made myself tell him, "Evan, it's not like that. I wouldn't…" *Wouldn't what? Betray Denny? Make a play for Kiera?* Hadn't I already, just by allowing today's events to happen? Feeling guilty and wanting out of this conversation, I gave Evan the response I knew he wanted to hear. "Don't worry. Yeah, maybe I'll drop in later."

By the smile on his face, I could tell he was satisfied with my answer and he fully expected to see me tonight. "All right, see ya."

He closed the door and I let out a long, cleansing exhale. I didn't like what Evan was thinking, but I could understand why he was thinking it. I hadn't always cared about other people's relationships. Since every relationship was temporary anyway, there usually wasn't a reason to let that little tidbit get in the way. But Denny and Kiera were different; they were supposed to be together. I needed to back off and just be Kiera's friend, because she really needed one right now.

My mind spun and battled while I drove us home. I wanted her friendship, I wanted her arms around me, and I wanted her and Denny to stay together and be obscenely happy. The three desires weren't compatible, even I knew that, and I also knew that if the physical side of Kiera's and my relationship continued, it could lead to more. If left unchecked, it might lead to sex, and that would destroy everything, for all three of us. Unless I was strong enough to not let it go that far. Then, maybe I could have the closeness, the connection that I'd had today, but Denny and Kiera could still be a strong couple. Maybe. But it would require a lot of willpower, and ignoring my urges was not something I'd ever been much good at.

When we pulled into the driveway, I shut the car off and looked down at Kiera sleeping on me. She seemed so comfortable, so content. I wanted to stroke her hair, cup her cheek, kiss her forehead. A surging desire was building in me to put both my arms around her and hold her tight. To tell her how much she meant to me, that no one saw me the way she did, no one cared for me the way she did. To tell her I cared about her in a way that sometimes scared the crap out of me. She was comfort and pain, wrapped up in one beautiful package...that wasn't mine.

I couldn't say any of that though, so I simply stared at her and thanked whatever fates there were for bringing her into my life.

After a moment, she yawned, stretched, and lifted her head from my shoulder. It was nice to look into her eyes again, but an ache was already shooting through me with the loss of her touch.

"Hey, sleepy," I whispered, resisting the urge to pull her in close again. "I was beginning to think I'd have to carry you." *I was hoping I would get to carry you.*

The imagery seemed to embarrass her. Her eyes were dark in the minimal light, and they flicked away from me as she apologized. "Oh...sorry."

I laughed as I pictured her cheeks flaming red. So endearing. "It's all right. I wouldn't have minded." *I actually would have loved it.* "Did you have fun?"

A wide smile broke over her face. "Yes, a lot. Thank you for inviting me."

The genuine sincerity in her eyes, in her voice was almost too much to bear. You would think I had done something spectacular from the way she was looking at me with such adoration. But I hadn't done anything. Once again, *she* was the one who had lifted *me* up. That was the best afternoon I'd had in...years. "You're welcome."

"Sorry you had to hang back with me and miss all the moshing."

She laughed as she said it, and I shared in her mirth as I looked back at her. "Don't be. I'd rather hold a beautiful girl than be all bruised tomorrow." Oops. I probably shouldn't have said that. It probably wasn't appropriate for me to call her beautiful, but...she was, and she should know it. Besides, today had been a day full of inappropriateness. What was one more incident?

Thrown off by my praise, Kiera looked down. Not wanting her to feel awkward or uncomfortable around me, I changed the subject. "Well, come on. I'll get you inside."

I turned toward my door to open it. In the edge of my vision, I saw her shaking her head. "No, you don't have to do that. I can manage. You can go on to Pete's."

My head snapped around at her comment. *How did she know about that?* She'd been sleeping when Evan and I had been talking...right? If she hadn't, if she'd heard Evan's comment and my weak-ass attempt to defend myself, she might think...well, she might think I was just some sleazy guy who was trying to get in her pants, like Evan had implied. I wasn't though. I just wanted...I just wanted to be near her. That was all. I wanted a connection with her. Sex was the last thing I wanted.

Maybe seeing my confusion, or panic, I wasn't sure, Kiera

shrugged and said, "I'm guessing that's where the other D-Bags went off to?"

She wasn't looking at me like I was a creep, so I relaxed. "Yeah, I don't have to go though. I mean, if you don't want to be alone. We could order pizza, watch a movie, or something." *Anything you want, let's just keep this going a little while longer.*

Her stomach suddenly grumbled, like it was on my side. Kiera laughed through her embarrassment. The smile on her face was incredible. "Okay, apparently my stomach votes for option two."

I grinned. I was going to have to order the best pizza in town to thank her stomach. "All right, then."

I cracked my door open, stepped out, then held it for her. She crawled out on my side, grabbing my hand as she exited. Her hand was warm and soft, and the connection was instant. Even though we'd been touching like this all day long, I couldn't get enough. It was such a small thing, really, but I was already addicted to it.

Chapter 8

Cuddling

I was worried when I woke up the next morning. Worried that Kiera would say we'd taken things too far at Bumbershoot. I wasn't sure what to expect when she came down for coffee, but giving her a warm smile, I started pouring her a cup. I wanted to hug her, put an arm around her...something, but there really was no reason for me to touch her like that. There were no crowds to keep back in my kitchen.

Then she came up to me and rested her head on my shoulder while she let out a long yawn. The tension eased from me as I wrapped an arm around her. It was almost as if she was silently asking me to hold her. She wanted this too. That amazed me.

Her arms timidly came around my waist and she snuggled into me like she was cold. I ran my fingers up and down her bare arms, warming her, and her skin pebbled where I touched it. Her cheeks turned rosier the longer we stared at each other; the flushed look was very alluring. Mixed with her wild hair and slightly askew clothes, it looked like she'd just had sex. I tried to shift my focus, but before I could, a picture of Kiera clutching my back and moaning my name popped into my head. I shoved it aside as I reached over and grabbed the coffee mug I'd poured for her. Regardless of how nice it felt to touch her, it was not okay to go there.

103

A peaceful smile on my face, I held the mug out for her. "Coffee?" I asked, knowing she would eagerly want some.

Her eyes sparkled as she let me go to gingerly take the mug I was offering. I held in a sad sigh at the fact that she was no longer touching me. But, surprisingly enough, it didn't end there. After showering and getting ready for the day, Kiera came down with a book and read beside me while I worked on lyrics. She rested her head against my shoulder as I scribbled down random thoughts. After a while, I put my free arm around her shoulders. All she did was let out a happy sigh and cuddle farther into my side. I could have died happy right then and there.

The cuddling continued throughout the week. We hugged in the morning, sometimes for as long as it took the pot to brew, and I would spend what felt like an eternity gently rocking her to the rhythm of the coffee percolating. Holding hands, we'd watch TV before her shift. Whenever we did, I had no recollection of anything we'd watched. Her fingers on my skin were my only concern. On the nights we had off together, I'd skip going out with the guys and we'd stay in, order a pizza, and watch a movie. I'd have my arm around Kiera while she sat with her legs stretched along the cushions. She'd rest her head on my shoulder and I'd close my eyes, content. As long as neither of us brought it up, we could pretend nothing was wrong with what we were doing.

While Kiera and I were pretty snuggly at home, we kept our distance at work. I didn't want people to gossip about her, and I didn't want Evan to question me about her. I didn't want people to think about us one way or the other. Plus, our intimate moments of connection were private. Nobody needed to know about them but us. The only time I even touched her more than a casual acquaintance might was when Griffin started a dance fest in the bar and made a move on her. Then I intervened.

I did feel guilty whenever Denny called; he wouldn't like what was going on behind his back. And listening to Kiera talk to him was a painful reminder that everything between Kiera and me was temporary. Things would change the minute Denny returned. She would cuddle with him, not me, and that was the way it should be. But still, every day there was a clock ticking in my brain, warning me that all of this was stopping soon, and I should end it now before I got too attached. Too late for that though; I was already addicted to being near her.

"I don't feel like going home. Let's go kick it at Kellan's."

Hearing my name, I lifted my head to stare at Griffin. He was smiling at me and nodding, like the suggestion he'd just made was the most profound statement ever spoken by a human being. We'd just played a gig downtown, and Evan and I were struggling to load Evan's drum into Griffin's van. We set it down with a grunt, and I tried my best to keep the irritation off my face. So far, Griffin's contribution to "cleaning up" had consisted of playing air guitar and signing autographs. Unsolicited autographs.

"Why my place? We have to take this crap back to Evan's, we could just hang there."

Evan clapped my shoulder in answer. "Can't. I've got a date, man."

I blinked at him in surprise. "It's two in the morning."

He shrugged as he moved some cymbals into position. "Time waits for no one, Kell."

I frowned as I considered how true that statement was. "Okay, well...Kiera will be asleep by the time we get back there, so you two will have to be quiet." I pointed at Matt and Griffin. Matt shrugged; Griffin rubbed his palms together while a maniacal smile grew on his face. I shifted my attention to just him. "If you so much as open her door, I'll kick your ass."

Griffin frowned, then pouted. "Your sense of bandmateship is skewed. Aren't we supposed to share everything?" He shrugged.

Evan, Matt, and I answered him at the same time. "No."

Evan and I laughed while Matt added, "No one wants to share anything you've got, cuz. In fact, you should probably share a little less, so that crap doesn't spread throughout *all* of Seattle."

Griffin gave Matt a dour glare. "You're so fucking funny my sides hurt."

With a completely straight face, Matt told him, "Syphilis is no laughing matter, dude."

Griffin looked around for something to toss at his cousin, but the only thing near him was his guitar. He settled on kicking a pebble on the street toward Matt's general vicinity. "I don't have that shit. I'm totally fucking clean, man. I just got tested last week." While Matt laughed at him, Griffin frowned in confusion. "And why the fuck would I have that? I drink orange juice every day."

We all stopped what we were doing and stared at him, dumbfounded. What the hell was he talking about? Matt was the one who figured it out first. Leaning over he was laughing so hard, he sputtered, "Syphilis, dumbass. Not scurvy."

Griffin still looked confused, but Evan and I were laughing hysterically at this point too. Griffin flipped us off, then stormed to the driver's seat to pout while we finished putting everything away. So much for bandmateship.

We dropped our stuff off, then headed to my place. As a precaution, I made Griffin tiptoe as he entered my house; he was generally about as quiet as a freight train. He glared at me as he exaggerated small footsteps. When those footsteps started leading him upstairs, I snapped my fingers and pointed at the ground. "I have to pee," he whispered.

I pointed down the hallway that led past my kitchen. "Use the other one."

He stood up straight. "You have another bathroom?"

Rolling my eyes, I shoved him in the right direction. Matt and I grabbed ourselves some beer from the fridge. Griffin grabbed one when he was done peeing, then made a beeline for my TV. Matt and I exchanged shrugs and followed him. We made ourselves comfortable, Matt on the chair, me on the couch, and sipped our beers while Griffin looked for something smutty to watch.

Griffin was still flipping through the channels when he suddenly twisted his head and looked back at the stairs. "Kiera! Hey, sex kitty! Nice PJs."

Turning to look, I saw Kiera stepping off the last stair. Just as

Griffin had said, she was in her pajamas, with a wild case of bed head. She looked worn, maybe a little upset too. One of us, aka Griffin, must have woken her up. Oops. She seemed a little unsure if she should continue into the living room, but it was too late at this point. Griffin had spotted her.

I gave her an apologetic smile. "Hey, sorry. We didn't mean to wake you."

She shrugged her shoulders as she slowly walked toward us. "You didn't...bad dream."

I mentally frowned, wondering what her dream had been about. Hoping she didn't want to go right back to bed, I gave her a smile and lifted my bottle. "Beer?" Even though it was late, I'd love to spend some time with her. Maybe I could take her mind off her nightmare.

"Sure."

Delighted, I headed to the kitchen to grab her one. She was still standing when I got back, so I nodded to the couch. Still irritated at his lack of good porn, Griffin sat down at the same time. He took the spot closest to the table so he could set his beer down and really concentrate on his smut surfing. Before I could even wonder if Kiera would want to sit next to him, she darted over to the far cushion. With an amused shake of my head, I took the middle seat. I could have safely bet money that Kiera wouldn't willingly sit by Griffin.

I sat down as close to her as possible. She cuddled right into my side, like she belonged there. Pulling her feet up, she angled her legs into me. Wanting to touch her and keep her warm, I wrapped an arm around her legs. I probably wouldn't have if Evan were here with us, but luckily for me, he had a date. I playfully bumped Kiera's shoulder, and she smiled before she rested her head against my shoulder. I almost sighed in contentment. Heaven.

Now that he didn't have to be quiet, Griffin broke the silence. "You know, I've been thinking."

Matt let out a *Here we go* groan and Kiera laughed; it was a beautiful sound. Griffin continued undaunted. "When this band breaks up…" Kiera lifted her head, surprised that Griffin would say that. I wasn't. I'd heard a few of his "after the band" talks. His last post-D-Bags idea had been vagina waxer, so I was kind of curious what he was dreaming about doing now.

"I think I'll do God-rock," he finished.

Kiera spat out her beer and started coughing. I'd heard worse from Griffin, but I rolled my eyes and shook my head anyway. Matt turned to Griffin with a blank expression. "God-rock…you? Really."

With his eyes still glued on the TV, Griffin smiled. "Yeah! All those hot, horny virgins. Are you kidding me?"

Griffin finally settled on something to watch while Kiera took long draws off her beer. The show Griffin had chosen was a typical Griffin choice. There was a guy ramming it into a girl who was moaning and groaning like his wild thrusting actually felt good. It must have been some space-themed porn, because they were going at it on the bridge of a starship. And for some odd reason, they were both wearing helmets that I assumed were meant to be used in outer space. Why they had them on indoors made no sense…

While I was being distracted by an inconsequential detail, Kiera beside me was staring into her beer like she'd dropped something important down the bottleneck. Wondering if she was okay with this ridiculous movie, I watched her curiously for a second.

Her cheeks were flushed with color, showing through in even the relatively dim lighting of the room. She was embarrassed, that much was clear. Had she not noticed the stupid antennas on the helmets? She wouldn't be nearly as self-conscious if she saw how silly it all was. But she obviously couldn't get past the intimacy of the sex act being performed.

Wanting to give her an out, I leaned over and asked, "Are you uncomfortable?"

She immediately shook her head. With how hard she shook it, I could tell she didn't want me to think this bothered her. I didn't know why it mattered to her what I thought about it. If she wanted to leave, I understood. Watching people have sex was odd. Hot, but odd.

I started picturing Kiera in the scene. Without the weird green people and stupid helmets though. I pictured her alone...with me. I imagined kissing her ear, licking her neck, sucking on her nipple. I imagined it was my fingers sliding inside her body, feeling how wet she was, how ready she was for me...I took a sip of my beer, ran my tongue over my lower lip, then, wishing it was Kiera touching me, I dragged my teeth over the sensitive skin. God, this stupid porn was making me hard. I should stop watching it, and I should definitely stop thinking about Kiera that way.

I heard a soft moan escape Kiera. Unlike the sounds coming from the TV, the noise she'd made was real. That was when I remembered that she was still here, beside me...and I was touching her. My eyes shifted to take her in. She was staring at me, not the movie. Her lips were parted, her breath was faster. Blood surged through my body, raising my heartbeat, quickening my breath, hardening my cock. I tried to remember why I couldn't lean over and suck her bottom lip into my mouth. I tried to remember why I couldn't reach over and feel the nipple poking through her tank top. Why I couldn't lay her down and take her. And at the moment, I couldn't recall anything but how much I loved her skin against mine.

I wanted her. *Now.*

My eyes flashed to her full lips. They were beckoning me, calling me, drawing me to them. I brushed my tongue against my lower lip again, but it was *her* tongue I wanted touching me. I bet she tasted good. I bet she felt good. I wanted to find out. I'd never wanted anything more in my life. My eyes rose to hers again, and I saw the heat there as she stared at me. She *wanted* me to kiss her. She wanted me to taste her. I'd almost say she wanted it as much as I did. My body strained against my clothes, begging me to do it. *Just do it.*

I returned my gaze to her lips and let them draw me in. *Yes...please...kiss me.* Her breath quickened the closer I came to her; I could see her chest rising and falling, could feel the air against my cheek. Her body squirmed under my touch. I bet she was wet. I bet she was ready. *For me.* But…no…she wasn't mine.

Like my skull had been slammed against a brick wall, I suddenly remembered why I couldn't touch her. *Denny.* She was Denny's, and he was my best friend. Fuck. I had to stop this. It was so hard to stop though. Everything between us felt electrified. Every point of contact between us felt on fire. Instead of pressing my lips to hers, I touched my forehead to hers and only let our noses meet. The tease I'd just given myself went straight to my groin, sending an ache of pleasure through me. Fuck, I didn't want to stop.

A whimper escaped Kiera's lips that only made it harder for me not to lower my mouth to hers. She started raising her chin, searching for me. Fuck, this was going to happen if I didn't do something soon. When I could just feel her lip brushing mine, I twisted away so my face ran along her cheek. I groaned in blissful torture. Fuck. I needed her. I needed to feel her, touch her, pleasure her, be with her. I was going to betray Denny. I was going to ruin everything, because I had no fucking willpower whatsoever.

My nose still resting along her cheek, I took two panicked breaths. I was trying to calm my body, to return to my senses. Kiera melted against me like she was losing hers. Her body shifted toward mine, her hand dropped to my thigh, her head turned toward my mouth. I knew I didn't have the strength to turn away again. If her lips made their way to mine, she would find me eager and willing. Screw Denny. Screw Matt and Griffin. I'd throw her down on the floor and we'd have sex right along with the stupid-ass movie.

And she'd never forgive me. I'd never forgive myself.

I clenched her hand on my thigh and ran my mouth to her ear. "Come with me," I whispered. My body desperately wanted her to "come" with me, but that wasn't going to happen. I wouldn't let it.

Standing, I led her to the kitchen. I knew I would need to be in complete control to do this, so I pictured everything I could to turn myself off. Denny. How good they were together, how much they belonged together. The look on his face when he'd asked me to not touch her. The look that I knew would be on his face if he knew I

110

had betrayed his trust. Denny sparing me from my parents' wrath. Denny standing up for me, taking a hit for me. Denny. My brother, by virtue if not blood. I couldn't do this to him.

I was more or less put together by the time we reached the kitchen. I could still hear that fucking movie in the background, but I ignored it. Releasing Kiera, I set down my beer, walked over to the cabinet, and started preparing a glass of water for her. She was still breathing heavily, confused and frustrated, as I took her beer and handed her the glass of water with a peaceful smile. As she took it, she seemed embarrassed too. She'd probably expected something much different to happen in here.

She took deep, calming breaths, then downed her water like she hadn't had any all day. I felt bad that she was embarrassed; that hadn't been her fault. That was mine. I'd gotten carried away, taken things too far. I shouldn't have leaned in…I shouldn't have been touching her to begin with. And I definitely shouldn't have been playing my own porno in my head, with the pair of us as the stars.

There was no good way to apologize for that though, so instead I said, "Sorry about the movie choice…" I made myself laugh when she looked back up at me. *Keep it light.* "Griffin is, well…Griffin." I shrugged. Not wanting her to say anything that might lead to a conversation I didn't want to have, I asked, "You seemed upset earlier on the stairs. You want to talk about your dream?"

I leaned back against the counter and crossed my arms over my chest, feigning casualness. When all else fails, fake it. Kiera's brows drew together as she took in my posture. She still seemed shaken, embarrassed, and really confused. "I don't remember it…just that it was bad."

"Oh." I was suddenly struck with a bout of guilt and grief. Her dream had to have been about me then. I was causing her pain, and I'd just made it worse by caving in to my desires for her. I needed her closeness, but I had to keep her at a distance. It was a fine line to walk, and I wasn't sure that I could.

Upset herself, she set down her glass and started walking past me. "I'm tired…Good night, Kellan."

It took everything in my power to not stop her and pull her in for a hug. *I'm so sorry. Please forgive me.* "Good night, Kiera," I whispered.

After she left the room, I dropped my head into my hands. *What the fuck did I just do? What the fuck did I just let happen?* I could have ruined everything. Slumping against the counter, I massaged the bridge of my nose where I could feel a massive headache forming. Maybe I already *had* ruined everything. I really wouldn't know until tomorrow, when I saw Kiera again. For the first time in a long time, I never wanted tomorrow to come.

Its arrival was inevitable though. When dawn broke through my window, my eyes were already open. I hadn't slept much, if at all. Last night had been way too close. I owed Denny more than that. So much more.

I was nervous when I went downstairs. Nerves weren't something I suffered from a lot, so when I got them, they were almost crippling. I was scared that she'd want to "talk." I didn't want to talk. I just wanted to pretend last night never happened. I wanted things to go back to normal. Well, our version of normal. I just wanted to hug her and not have it be weird. Maybe if I didn't mention it, she'd think last night was just part of her dream. God, I hoped she hadn't had a nightmare about me. I didn't want to hurt her, not even in her head.

When I heard her coming down the stairs, my hands started shaking. "Stop it," I whispered, clenching and unclenching them. She didn't need to know I was freaking out. I inhaled a deep breath, then put on my game face. I should probably thank my parents for giving me so many opportunities to perfect it.

Besides my heart rate spiking, everything was normal when Kiera stepped into the kitchen. Her cheeks reddened, so she was probably still embarrassed. I didn't give her time to dwell on it. "Mornin'. Coffee?" I extended the steaming cup in my hand to her.

She smiled as she took it. The weariness under her eyes hadn't lessened any; she must have slept about as well as I had. "Thank you."

I poured another cup for me while Kiera poured creamer into hers. We sat at the table together, and a second of sadness washed over me. We hadn't hugged. Kiera frowned, and my thought evaporated. *Fuck. She wants to talk. No, please. Let's just let it go. Some things don't ever need to be talked about. Like how much I want you, and how wrong it is to feel that way.*

"What?" I whispered, wishing I were anywhere but here.

She looked confused as she pointed to my shirt. "You never did get me one, you know."

I looked down at my T-shirt. It was the Douchebags one she'd mentioned before that she'd wanted. I'd been meaning to grab her one, but it had slipped my mind.

Relief washed through me that we weren't having the conversation from hell, the one I'd been dreading all morning. "Oh…you're right." I was brimming with good feelings now that we were past the hard part. Not wanting to deal with Griffin anytime soon and liking the idea of Kiera wearing my shirt, I stood and slipped it off. Her eyes brightened at my half-nakedness; she suddenly didn't look tired at all. The way she looked at my body made me want to be naked all the time, but that wasn't exactly a good idea. The connection between us was already difficult enough.

I fixed the shirt and looped it over her head. She just gaped at me, so I put her arms through the sleeves like she was a child. "There, you can have mine." She looked good in my shirt. I should have given it to her ages ago.

She sputtered on a response as her cheeks turned a charming shade of rose. "I didn't mean…You didn't have to…"

She couldn't seem to form any more words than that. So cute. I got the gist of what she was saying though, and I laughed as I told her, "Don't worry about it. I can get more. You wouldn't believe how many of those damn things Griffin made."

I turned to leave the room, then looked back at Kiera. She was staring at my ass. When she realized she'd been caught, her cheeks went from rosy to bright red. Most girls I knew would devour me with their eyes and not give a shit if I noticed, but Kiera was always so embarrassed. Containing my laughter, I smiled and looked down. She was so damn adorable, and even though I knew I shouldn't, I loved the way she looked at me.

"I'll be right back," I told her. I gave her another smile, then left the room to get another shirt. My grin was uncontainable as I bounded up the stairs. Thank the fucking stars up above...we weren't going to talk about it. We were going to sweep the incident under the rug, where it belonged.

While we weren't mentioning last night, I wasn't sure where we stood on...well, cuddling was probably the best way to put it. Part of me wanted it to stop; the rest of me couldn't stop. As long as she was okay with me holding her, I wanted her in my arms.

It took her most of the day to approach me, but when I settled on the couch to watch a little TV before rehearsal, she stared at me with longing. Since I needed her touch and we hadn't even hugged today, I held my arm out and patted the couch in invitation. *Please.*

She gave me a breathtaking grin and snuggled into my side. I closed my eyes, content. Nothing had changed. We could still do this. We were fine. Everything was fine.

Our routine continued like nothing strange had happened between us. I did notice a small change though. Our touches seemed more...intimate. When we hugged, my hands rested farther down her hips, her breasts pressed more firmly against my chest, her fingers ran up and down my neck, and her head was angled toward me, not away from me. I loved every second of it though, so I wasn't about to complain.

As usual, she was still asleep when I left my room the next Tuesday. I pictured her sprawled out on Joey's bed. Or maybe she was curled up into a lonely ball? I wished I could open the door to look, to watch her as she slept, but that would be weird if she caught me. Kind of creepy actually. With a sigh, I headed downstairs. There were just certain aspects of life that we'd never get to share; sleeping together was one of them.

To perk myself up, I sang while I made a pot of coffee. I started out singing a popular song on the radio, but by the time the coffee was done, I was singing a D-Bags song. It was typically a fast song, but I sang it slow, like a ballad. It actually worked really well that way. I'd have to tell Evan to add it to our acoustic playlist.

Kiera stumbled into the kitchen while I was singing. She stopped and listened like she'd never heard me sing before. I loved the way she really listened to me when I sang, like she was trying to absorb the meaning as well as the words. Most people I met didn't bother.

She was leaning against the counter in an unconsciously appealing way. It had been hours since I'd had her in my arms, and since I was still suffering from a bit of melancholy, I found I couldn't wait another moment to touch her. Reaching out, I pulled her to me for a dance. She gasped in surprise, then her face brightened. She'd been a little off this morning too. Wanting to make her smile, I twirled her away, then back to me, then dipped her. It worked, she laughed. It gave me a thrill that I could make us both a little happier.

I slipped both arms around her waist, and she let out a happy sigh as she laced her arms around my neck. There was nothing quite like dancing with her. The way our bodies moved together, the way she felt in my arms...I could have done this all day, but I knew I had to end the moment sooner or later. I didn't need a repeat of "porn night," and I had a feeling if I slow danced like this with her for too long, the urge to kiss her would overwhelm me. Good intentions or not, I was only human, after all.

I stopped moving and Kiera stopped too. We gazed at each other, and my heart started beating harder. She was so close to me, and she felt so good. Her lips would feel even better. Her fingers were threading through my hair, sending bolts of delight down my body. Did she realize how amazing that was?

As if she could hear my thoughts, she removed her fingers from my hair and rested them on my shoulders. Knowing we were heading toward dangerous territory again, I quietly began my question. "I know you'd rather have Denny here..." She stiffened in my arms and I cursed myself for bringing him up. I had to though. We both needed the reminder. "—But could I take you to school on your first day?"

She seemed flustered, by either me or my question, I didn't know which. She was at ease when she answered me though. "I guess you'll do," she said with a playful smirk.

Laughing, I squeezed her, then let her go; it was really hard to let her go. Needing a task, I stepped to the cabinet and got a mug down for her. "That's not something I'm used to women saying," I muttered, trying to keep up the lightness.

Kiera took it the wrong way though. "I'm sorry, I didn't mean—"

I laughed again as I started pouring coffee for her. Did she actually think she'd offended me? It would take a lot more than that. I glanced in her direction. "I'm just kidding, Kiera." My eyes returned to her mug. "Well, kind of." That really wasn't something I heard from women. In a twisted way, it was kind of refreshing to hear it.

When it was time, I drove Kiera to class. She was a bundle of nerves, worse than her first day at Pete's. If she could only see what I saw when I looked at her—beauty, grace, humor, intelligence—she wouldn't be nervous at all about school. She'd walk into her classroom like she owned it.

Kiera looked ill when I stopped the car. I couldn't drop her off and make her walk to class that way. She might actually throw up, and that was an embarrassment she didn't need on the first day. I was pretty sure I could keep her calm enough to at least prevent puking, so I cracked open my door and hopped out of the car.

Her expression was bewildered as she watched me walk around to her side. When I opened her door for her, she crooked a grin. "I think I can handle that." She nodded at the door as she stood from the car.

I laughed as I grabbed her hand. I knew she was able. Willing, now that was another story. Smiling, I indicated the building where her class was. "Come on."

She looked up at me, curious. "And where are you going?"

I laughed as I looked down at her. "I'm walking you to class...obviously."

Like she felt I was being unreasonable, she rolled her eyes; the gesture was clearly from embarrassment though, not irritation. "You don't have to. I can manage."

"Maybe I want to," I said, giving her hand a squeeze. We approached the building and I opened the door and held it for her. As she walked through, I added, "It's not like my mornings are earth-shatteringly busy or anything. I'd probably just be napping." *Or thinking of you.*

She laughed as she looked back at me. "Why do you get up so early then?"

I let out a wry laugh as I walked beside her down the hall. "It's not by choice...trust me." No, my dad had ingrained my sleep patterns in me long ago. Now, I usually woke up around the same time every day, and if I didn't, if I slept in for some reason, more often than not, I woke up in a panic, half expecting to see him at the foot of my bed. Even though he was long gone, the irrational fear remained. "I would rather sleep in than function on four or five hours a night."

She told me I should nap and I told her I would. And I might, actually. I could use the refresher, and it would make the time fly by. We'd reached her classroom, and I held this door open for her as well. She gave me an odd, calculating expression, and I wondered if she thought I was going to walk her to her seat. I hadn't planned on it...but I would if she wanted me to. "Would you like me to walk you in?" I asked, only half teasing.

She released my hand and pushed me back. "No," she playfully responded. She stared at me for a moment, her expression turning serious and adoring. I loved seeing that look on her. "Thank you, Kellan." Leaning over, she gave me a soft kiss on the cheek. I loved that too. It made that warmth I felt whenever she was near grow stronger.

I looked down, then peeked up at her. "You're welcome." *I'd do anything for you.* "I'll pick you up later." She started to protest, but

I quickly cut her off with a look. After she consented to me giving her a ride home, I checked out her classroom full of studious, young eager beavers. Telling her to have fun, I turned and headed out. Curious, I looked back to see if she was watching me leave. She was. That made my chest squirm, but in a good way. I held my hand up in a wave. Being at school with her wasn't so bad ... I could get used to this.

I ended up taking her to school every day that week. By Friday, I was thoroughly enjoying our new routine, and while I missed her during the day, seeing the gratitude on her face when I walked her to class in the morning and the excitement in her eyes when I picked her up in the afternoon made the time apart worth it. For a minute, I could pretend that I meant everything to her, because she was certainly starting to mean everything to me. And if you pretend something long enough, it eventually becomes real. Right?

Chapter 9

Cure for Heartache

I closed up my guitar case, eager to go home. It was Sunday, still pretty early in the evening, and Kiera wasn't working tonight. Now that rehearsal was over, we could have the entire night together. If I hurried, I could possibly make it home before she had dinner and we could eat together. Maybe I'd attempt to make something for her tonight. Spaghetti? I wasn't the greatest cook, but boiling water was something I could do.

I glanced up at Evan and Matt. "See you tomorrow." *I have a date. Well, not a date, but I have somewhere to be.*

Evan gave me such an odd look that I froze. Either he suspected something...or I was forgetting something. "What?" I asked, slowly.

Evan didn't say anything, he just tilted his head at Matt and raised his eyebrows. That was when it hit me. "Fuck. Matt. It's your birthday. I'm sorry, man, I totally forgot."

Matt's cheeks turned red as he scratched his head. "Don't worry about it, Kell. It's no big deal." He gave Evan a pointed glance. "We don't have to do anything special. Just playing with you guys was enough."

Griffin was sitting on the back of the couch. He made a disgusted noise at Matt's comment. "Screw that. We're partying. No birthday is complete until you've upchucked your dinner." He scrunched his brow in concentration. "Have we eaten yet?"

Evan smiled at Matt. "Nope, not yet. Where you wanna go, birthday boy?"

Matt's expression was bordering on irritated. He really didn't like being the center of attention. "I'm not five...please don't call me that." He sighed. "I don't know...somewhere low-key, where they don't make a big deal out of a person being one year closer to death."

Griffin raised his eyebrows. "Wow. Morbid much? How old are you again? Seventy-two?"

Matt held up both of his middle fingers. "I'm this old."

Griffin grinned. "Eleven?" His smile grew as he turned to me. "Sounds about right."

Even as I laughed at Griffin's joke, my insides felt like ash. Kiera would be home alone now, and for probably most of the night. I wouldn't get another chance to spend an evening with her alone for...well, it would feel like forever. I couldn't *not* go out with the guys tonight though.

Making myself smile, I told Griffin, "I know this place where they make everyone wear insulting hats and the staff abuses you all night long."

Griffin jumped off the couch. "Fuck yeah, let's do that! Like, what do they do to you though?" Turning around, he bent over the couch and stuck his ass in the air. "Will they spank me if I'm naughty?"

Matt pointed a finger at his cousin. "There is no way in hell I'm going anywhere where he might get spanked." Shrugging, he added, "Can we just go to Pete's?"

Holding in a sigh, I shrugged. "It's your night. Pete's it is." *Why couldn't Kiera be working tonight?* Maybe I'd call her once we got there and invite her over. I hopped in my car feeling a little irritated but willing to let it go. It wasn't like I didn't see Kiera all the time. But...I was all too aware that I was missing out on time alone with her, and I had this horrible feeling that our time together was fleeting.

I tried to sneak off to the back to make a phone call when I got to Pete's, but Griffin walked in the door with me. Grabbing my arm, he immediately pulled me to the bar. Slamming his hand down on the counter, he announced, "Round of Jäger for the band, Reets. We're getting fucked up tonight!"

Rita smirked at Griffin's nickname for her, then leaned in to kiss my cheek. Without looking like I was pulling away from her, I moved out of reach. She sighed at the near miss. "Anything for my favorite rock stars." She pursed her lips like she was kissing me in her mind. "Mm, mm, mm," she muttered as she started pouring shots.

Griffin raised his drink in the air when they were all passed out. Loud enough for the entire bar to hear, he exclaimed, "To my cousin, who finally grew pubes this year, and is hoping to touch a naked woman for the first time... Happy birthday!"

The entire bar was laughing. Evan and I were laughing too while Griffin downed his shot alone. Afterward, he stuck his tongue out, making a face, while Matt gave him a blank stare. "I really fucking hate you," he said dispassionately to Griffin.

Griffin stole his drink and downed it too. "I know," he said with a smirk when he was done. Then he grabbed Matt by the neck and gave him a noogie.

Matt eventually started laughing as he tried to get away, and just like that, the two constantly fighting cousins were best friends. Shaking my head at the pair of them, I handed Matt my shot. He gladly slung it back. Evan took his, then we set our glasses on the bar, where they were immediately refilled.

It was ages before I was finally able to slip away. I headed to the bathroom hallway and found the pay phone in the back. No one really used it anymore, and it was a little dusty when I picked up the handset. I found some change in my pocket and dialed home, but it just rang and rang. The machine didn't even pick up, which I thought was a little odd; Kiera was obsessed with making sure it was on and ready to record any calls from Denny that she might have missed.

All I could come up with was that Kiera had gone to bed. I'd missed her. An almost overwhelming sadness filled me, but I threw on a smile for my band's sake. I didn't want them asking questions when I returned to the table.

By the time the evening wrapped up, it was late. I'd stopped drinking a while ago so I could drive home, but I still felt a little off when I shut my car off in the driveway. I smiled when I noticed Denny's Honda beside my car. Kiera was home and safe in bed. I loved knowing she was here, sleeping only a few feet away from me…as soon as I could get my slow ass through the door. Maybe some water would help clear my head. Yeah. Water would be good.

Intent on hydration, I made a beeline for the kitchen when I got into the house. I tossed my keys on the counter, then came to a standstill when I realized I wasn't alone. Kiera was still up, dressed in her pajamas…and she was clearly upset. Her eyes were bloodshot, her face a little puffy, and she was downing a glass of wine like it was juice. Something was very, very wrong. My heart sped up in anticipation.

"Hey," I said, trying to sound casual.

She didn't answer me, just kept drinking her wine. I could tell from the empty bottle on the counter that she was almost at the end of her supply. There was only one thing that would make her this distraught…

"You okay?" I asked, already knowing she wasn't.

She paused in her drink to answer me. "No." I thought she'd leave it at that, but she surprised me by adding, "Denny isn't coming back…we're done."

A multitude of emotions washed over me at the same time: compassion, grief…joy…and guilt. I walked over to her, eager to wrap my arms around her and tell her I was here for her, that I'd never leave her, but it was obvious she was trying to suppress her pain. Hearing how much I cared about her probably wouldn't help her right now; I needed to let her grieve first. Instead of touching her, I leaned back against the counter. I even rested my hands behind me so I wouldn't be tempted.

Not knowing what to do for her, I watched her studying me for a minute. Then, hoping she'd say no, because I really didn't want to discuss her feelings about Denny, I asked, "You want to talk about it?"

She again paused from her drink only long enough to answer me. "No."

Relief hit me again that she didn't want to talk about him. She probably didn't want to talk about me either, but that was okay. I understood not wanting to talk. And I knew what I *would* want if I were her. I glanced at her empty wine bottle, then the glass she was finishing. "You want some tequila?" I asked.

A genuine smile spread across her lips. "Absolutely."

I opened the cupboard above the fridge and, rummaging through my alcohol stash, I grabbed the tequila. I wasn't sure if getting Kiera drunker was a good idea, but it was the only solution I could think of right now. And besides, at least she wasn't drinking alone anymore. I grabbed glasses, then salt and limes from the fridge. Setting out a cutting board, I sliced up the limes. I could feel Kiera's eyes on me the entire time.

I poured us shots, then handed hers to her with a smile. "Cure for heartache, I'm told."

She took the glass from me and our fingers briefly touched. It was enough to send heat through my body. She was single now...that changed things. Or did it? Denny was my best friend. I owed him...

Determined to stop thinking, to just go with whatever happened, I dipped my finger into my drink and wet the backs of our hands. Kiera watched every move I made as I shook some salt over our hands. When she made no move to drink her shot, I broke the ice and took mine so she'd feel more comfortable about doing this with me. My throat was numb from doing Jäger shots all night, so it didn't even burn. It burned for Kiera though.

Her tongue came out to lick the salt off her hand, her mouth opened to receive her drink, and her lips curled around the lime, squeezing its juices. It was an erotic thing to watch. Then her face twisted into a grimace. I chuckled at her reaction, then poured us another round.

The second shot went down easier for her. The third was even easier. We didn't talk, just drank. And the more alcohol she consumed, the hungrier her eyes became. She was staring at me as tenaciously as the women in the bar did. I did my best to ignore it, but it was difficult to do…I *wanted* her to look at me like that. I wanted to look at *her* like that. But I wasn't about to make any assumptions on what was going to happen tonight. We were just two friends sharing a drink. Two single friends who had almost shared a lot more recently…

By the fourth shot, the alcohol was getting to me. I spilled the tequila trying to pour it in those tiny little glasses. I laughed as I almost dropped the lime from my mouth. I was way beyond buzzing now.

On the fifth shot, everything changed. Just as I was bending down to lick the salt from my skin, Kiera took my hand and ran her tongue over the back of it. She was soft, wet, warm, and felt amazing on my sensitive body. I wanted her to keep doing it, but she pulled back to drink her tequila shot. When she placed her wedge of lime between *my* lips, my heart sped up. *Was she…?*

She was. Her mouth reached up to connect with mine. Our lips pressed together as she sucked on the lime. All I could taste was lime and her. It was an intoxicating combination. But it wasn't nearly satisfying enough. I needed more.

My breath felt strained when Kiera pulled away. Ragged. She teasingly removed the lime from her mouth and set it on the counter. When she seductively licked her fingers, my resolve evaporated. I suddenly didn't give a shit what we'd been before, or who we'd been with. I didn't care if she'd dated Denny—that seemed like a long-past memory at the moment. I didn't care about Evan's warnings, my regrettable experience with bedding roommates, my promise to Denny to stay away, or my own decision to not cross that uncrossable line. Kiera *kissed* me. She wanted me. And fuck, I wanted her too.

I took my shot of tequila straight, slammed the glass on the counter, then pulled her back to my mouth, where she belonged.

Our lips moving together felt better than I had imagined. There was so much eager, pent-up passion, I felt like we were both going to burst into flames. I couldn't get enough of her. My hand on the back of her neck tightened, drawing her in even closer. My other hand found the small of her back. Perfection.

I pushed her until she bumped against the counter, our lips still moving together with a near-frenzied intensity. Her tongue brushed against mine, teasing, searching. I groaned, needing more. My fingers roamed down her sides, slid across her ribs, down to her ass. Reaching down, I lifted her up and set her on the counter. She let out a soft, seductive noise as she wrapped her legs around me and cinched me tight. *Yes*...

Even half-drunk, I was hard. All I could think of was taking her to my room, laying her on my bed, and exploring her. I wanted to feel every curve, discover every peak, taste every inch. I wanted all of her. And I was beginning to believe that maybe I always had.

My hand drifted across her throat, and my lips followed. Her skin was sweet, like strawberries. Delicious. With a moan that went straight through my body, Kiera dropped her head back and closed her eyes. God, she was so beautiful. Her breath was as heavy as mine; we were both nearly panting. Desperate to be together.

I ran my nose up her throat to her ear and gave the skin below it a gentle lick. Kiera squirmed, and her fingers started digging into my shirt, like she was going to either take it off or rip it off. I helped her remove the obnoxious fabric. She pulled back to look, and her eyes devoured me. I loved it. I loved seeing the unabashed need on her face. It drove me crazy.

Her fingers raked down my chest, and I couldn't take it anymore. Thank God all the obstacles were gone. Thank God we could finally do this, finally cave in to what we felt for each other ... what I felt for her. I swept my arms around her and picked her up off the counter.

I was uncoordinated on my feet, my body not all the way in sync with my mind. I bumped into a wall here and there, and almost dropped Kiera before we even reached the stairs. It didn't help anything that I wasn't watching where I was going. I couldn't. All my focus was on her—my eyes, my lips, my tongue, my breath, my heart, my soul. It was all hers.

Just after the turn in the stairs, I lost all control and stumbled to the ground. I managed to catch myself before I crushed Kiera into the steps, but it was still jarring, and I was sure we'd both feel it in the morning. Nothing mattered now though, so we both laughed.

"Sorry," I muttered, running my tongue up her throat. She shivered under my touch, dug her fingers into my shoulders. I was lying on top of her now. Having her beneath me was much better than having her on the counter. I worked my way between her legs, then ground my hips into hers. She gasped when she felt how hard I was. *That's all for you. That's what you do to me. I want you…so much.*

She sucked on my earlobe, sending explosions of desire throughout my skin. Needing her warmth, needing her softness, needing to taste her again, I sought her mouth. She tangled her fingers into my hair, keeping us held together. Still needing more, I pulled at her pajama pants. Off. I needed them off.

She helped me, and when they were around her ankles, we kicked them down the stairs. Her hands went to my jeans, but her numb fingers couldn't undo the stiff buttons. She giggled as my palms explored her bare thighs, caressed her ass over her underwear. Giving up on my jeans, her hands returned to my chest, feeling the hard muscles. I sucked on her lip as my hands traveled north. I was nearly shaking with anticipation as I approached her breast. I'd wanted to feel this for so long. I cupped her in my palm, stroked my thumb over and around her rigid nipple. *Jesus, she felt so good.*

I wanted to swirl my tongue over her breast, pull it into my mouth, but I wasn't done exploring her yet. Kiera was squirming beneath me, placing light kisses along my arm, lightly biting my shoulder. It drove me wild. Throaty moans escaped her every time I touched her. She had already felt my desire for her…I wanted to feel her desire for me. As I hovered my lips over her mouth, teasing her with the tip of my tongue, I slipped my hand into her underwear. She bucked against me, eager, wanting me to touch her there. Just the thought of it made me want to come. I held it together though…I wanted this to last.

Looking down, I angled my hand so I could watch my fingers enter her. One finger slid across her slick skin and Kiera cried out. *She was so fucking wet.* My mouth dropped open as I twisted to watch her reaction. She was so fucking hot. And she wanted me. *Me.*

She was going crazy underneath me as I teased her with my hand. Her fingers traveled over my arms, my back, my shoulders. She swiveled her hips, desperate for more. "Please, Kellan…take me to your room. Please. Oh God…please," she whispered.

Fuck. Her softly begging me was the hottest thing I'd ever heard. I scooped her up, and didn't set her down again until we were in my door frame. Once she was on her feet, I tore off her underwear. Then I removed my shoes and socks and got to work on my jeans, since Kiera still couldn't do it. She laughed at her ineptitude, and I laughed with her. Her smile as she laughed was incredible. It made me want her even more. I pulled off her tank top, then bent down to finally feel that perky breast in my mouth. Kiera moaned and held my head to her body.

After a brief tease, I playfully pushed her back onto my bed. I stripped off my boxers while she sat up on her elbows and took me in. The playfulness in the room vanished as we stared at each other. There was no one in the world I wanted more than her, and she was finally here, in my bed, wanting me…

I crawled into the bed with her, and our skin collided. She was warm, and soft. She felt better than anything I'd ever known. As we stared at each other, I felt that connection between us. When we kissed, it intensified. My hands roamed her body, then my lips followed suit. The feeling of being connected, being one, grew with every place I touched her. My mouth wandered between her legs, and I tasted her desire for me. It was as amazing as the rest of her. She cried out, her hips moving against me as she murmured my name.

127

Sitting up, she ran her fingers over all of my muscles, then her mouth covered me with soft kisses. I lay down as she moved farther south. I clenched the sheets when she ran her tongue around the tip of me. I was done. I couldn't take any more. I needed to be inside her.

I flipped her over to her back, then pushed myself into her. The sensation of filling her blew me away. We were staring at each other with our mouths open, breaths in a pant, and she was cupping my face and stroking her thumb across my cheek. I'd never felt such warmth during sex. It was only when I started to move my hips that I realized I hadn't put on a condom. My cardinal rule, and I'd just broken it. I considered stopping and putting one on, but Kiera whispered my name with such adoration that I couldn't. We were finally free, and I didn't want anything between us ever again. She was mine, and I wanted to leave a part of myself with her.

We moved together so seamlessly that it was like our thousandth time, not our first. As the sensations rocketed through my body, I hoped this was the first of a thousand times. I hoped it never ended. Our movements were slow at first, more about pleasure than purpose. Then Kiera pulled at my hips, murmuring, "More." I sped up, feeling the intensity build as I did. I couldn't contain the noises coming from my mouth. I'd never felt anything this good. Kiera seemed equally overwhelmed. Her soft noises were more stimulating than any of the screamers I'd bedded; they could have learned a thing or two from her.

I felt my climax coming, and I desperately wanted it, and didn't want it. Coming inside Kiera right now would be heaven and hell. Heaven for the pure bliss of it, hell because this feeling would be over once we were spent. Kiera grabbed my head and pulled me close as her cries increased. She was close. I was close. Fuck, this was happening.

I felt my stomach clench, felt the release bursting from me as the pleasure exploded over my body. Kiera stiffened and cried out at the same time I did, and we rode out our climaxes together. I'd never come at the exact same time with a girl before. It intensified the moment for me; I felt like I came forever. When it finally started to ebb, I stared into Kiera's eyes. She stared back at me, and I was nearly overwhelmed by the emotion on her face, the emotion in my heart. I'd never experienced anything like this before. It was beyond all expectation, all reason. It changed me. I would never be the same after this. *We* would never be the same after this.

Staring at each other, we panted until our hearts slowed down. I gently removed myself from her, then wrapped her in my arms. I'd thought once that dancing with her was better than sex. I was wrong. So very, very wrong. Dancing didn't come close to sex. Not sex with her, at least.

Kiera passed out once we were relaxed. I held her tight, relishing the warmth I felt with her in my arms. I watched her sleeping for a long time. It was so nice to hold her, to feel her skin against my skin, to feel her light breath against my chest. I felt so connected with her right now, and she wasn't even conscious. Time ticked by, and then, in the silence of my room, she spoke. "Kellan..." she murmured. My heart thudded in my chest; I was sure she'd just woken up. What would I say to her? What would she say to me? I froze, terrified, but she didn't say anything else.

I slowly felt myself relaxing into the mattress. Kiera was still asleep, and she was thinking about me. *Me*. It amazed and mystified me that I was in her thoughts, and I wondered what she was dreaming about. I felt lighter than air as my heart started pounding for another reason. Her saying my name, thinking about *me* while she slept, almost gave me a bigger buzz than the sex had. And I knew, without a doubt in my head, that I could fall asleep with her in my arms every night and be completely happy. And that thought scared the crap out of me, because on the flip side, I knew I would be completely miserable without her.

So what were Kiera and I now? I had no clue. I didn't have a clue about anything anymore. All I knew was that for a long time now, I had cared about Kiera in a way I shouldn't have cared about her. And tonight, I'd done something with her that would kill my friend if he ever found out. Over or not, Kiera was off-limits to me because of him. I'd known that, and I'd screwed her anyway. I was a horrible person.

As I pondered the word "screw," my insides churned with distaste. That word wasn't right. We hadn't just gotten drunk and fucked. At least, I hadn't. My soul had been in that act. Being with her meant everything to me. *She* meant everything to me. The way she laughed, the way she smiled, the way she listened to my music, the way she looked at me with so much compassion, like she understood my pain even if she didn't know what it was. Everything about her took my breath away.

I looked down at her nestled under my arm. Her mouth was slightly open as she slept. Her eyes twitched like she was still in the midst of dreaming. I wanted her to say my name again. I wanted her to still be thinking about me. I hoped I was on her mind, since she was the only thing on mine. I wanted to protect her. I wanted to help her grow. I wanted what she had... with Denny.

Shit. Denny. Where did he fit into all of this? I'd selfishly shoved him aside so I could take what I wanted. I'd gone against his *one* request of me. A wave of guilt crashed over me while my brain settled back into reality, and I couldn't help but think of the times he'd been there for me... I was a fucking asshole. He would never forgive me for this. I was going to lose him. And for what? Did Kiera care about me at all?

Almost like she'd heard my thoughts, Kiera turned away from me. She flipped over onto her stomach, and a chill washed over me with her absence. My eyes drifted over her bare back; the skin there was smooth, creamy, and perfect. She was perfect. I considered pulling her into my arms again, but my mind had begun to spin, and now it was churning. I couldn't get a handle on the multiple jarring thoughts beating against my brain. What had I just done?

You just had sex with the woman who's been on your mind every second of every day, a woman who is in love with your best friend, a best friend who you owe everything to, a best friend who you just stabbed in the back by sleeping with "the love of his life" five seconds after they broke up. That's what you just did.

"Shut up," I muttered to myself. I didn't want to lose this high by letting reality in. All I wanted to do was dwell on this feeling pounding against my rib cage, vibrating through my head. I felt completely plastered as I lay next to Kiera, but it wasn't alcohol that was making me feel this way. No, it wasn't tequila that was making my chest light, my head giddy. Alcohol wasn't filling me with the need to smile, laugh, and clutch Kiera tight. I was completely drunk…on her.

But did that mean anything for us? Were we even an *us*? Or was it still her and me? Completely separate.

The sheet was low on Kiera, exposing most of her body. I really wanted to lean down and place kisses between her shoulder blades, rest my cheek on the small of her back, pull her close to my body. I was scared to wake her up though. What would she say when she regained consciousness? That what we'd done was a mistake? That she was still in love with Denny? That she was going to leave the house? Or…would she say the impossible? That she cared about me, and she wanted to be with me?

No, that was highly unlikely. No woman I'd ever slept with had actually cared about me. Not like that. Most likely, all that had happened was Kiera had been sad, and I had cheered her up. End of story.

But…the way she looked at me sometimes. The way she held me. The way she kissed me on the cheek, then blushed. I couldn't get it out of my head. I couldn't get *her* out of my head. Ever. She was always on my mind. God, I just wanted her to care about me. I didn't want to be the only one feeling this. I cared about her so much. I loved her so much.

Whoa. Back the fuck up. I *loved* her? Did I even know what that meant?

I hopped out of my bed like someone had just tossed a bucket of ice water on me. Thankfully, Kiera didn't move when I ripped my arm away from her. I guess she was really out of it.

I loved her? *Loved.* As in, I couldn't live without her, and I didn't want anybody else? Crap, that felt so right. But I couldn't actually be in *love* with her. Could I?

Fuck.

Stopping my incessant pacing, I turned to stare at Kiera on my bed. She looked so good sprawled over my sheets. I could feel myself starting to get aroused again just watching her. God, what I wouldn't give to slide back into bed with her. I'd wrap my arms around her and gently kiss her awake. I would give anything to have sex with her again. But sober. I'd take my time. I'd cherish every inch of her body. I'd...make love to her. God, that sounded weird, even in my own head. I wasn't even sure what that meant? *Make love?* It was all the same act. It was all the same moves. Sex was sex, so what was the difference? And why did phrasing it that way make my stomach tighten so much I felt like I was permanently messing up my insides?

Because you're in love with her, you idiot.

The moonlight filtering in through the window highlighted the ridge along her lower back. God, I loved that ridge. There was something about that spot that was insanely erotic to me. The way the light hit her skin, accentuating one area, darkening others...it was almost like the moon was caressing her. It made me jealous. I was actually freaking jealous of the freaking moon. I needed to get out of here so I could get a fucking grip.

Turning from her, I stormed over to my dresser. I tore open the top drawer and grabbed some clean boxers. After putting them on, I shut the drawer a little harder than necessary. I glanced back at Kiera, but she was still out. *Why am I so angry?*

Because you love her, and you're not good enough for her. She'll never love you, and you know it. You've been unlovable from the start.

Swallowing, I turned away and rummaged through another drawer to find some jeans. Yes, all of that was true, but...maybe I could convince her to give me a chance? She didn't have to love me in return, but maybe she could...really like me or something?

Maybe we could try to have a relationship? I knew her heart was still with Denny, obviously, since they'd just broken up, but if I told her I loved her...maybe...maybe she'd at least try me out for a while. And a while with her would be better than nothing. I almost couldn't believe Denny was really gone, that he'd actually chosen his job over her.

Zipping up my pants, I stared at her with unabashed longing. She was alone. Wouldn't being with me be better than being alone? No...she might prefer being alone to me. I wasn't exactly the easiest person to care about. But if I said I loved her and I only wanted to be with her, maybe she'd feel comfortable enough with me to say okay.

Irritated, I turned back around to find a shirt. All right, so how the fuck did I go about doing that without sounding like a complete and total fucktard? How the hell did I tell her I loved her? I could barely even think the words. Anger crept over me again as I yanked a T-shirt over my head. I didn't know how to do this. I didn't know how to be open and honest. I didn't know how to let her in. I could give myself to hundreds of girls, a different one every night, and that didn't bother me in the slightest. But actually opening myself up to *her*...scared the living shit out of me.

I had to get out of here. I couldn't think straight with her in the same room. Fuck, I couldn't think with her in the same house. I slipped on my shoes and trudged out of my bedroom. Kiera's clothes were strewn everywhere. The house was suffocating me. I needed air. Snatching my keys off the kitchen counter, I paused to stare at the evidence of our rendezvous...my shirt on the floor, an empty bottle of wine, spilled tequila, used lime wedges, empty glasses. So much had changed in so little time.

I could almost hear Kiera's moans of ecstasy as I stared into the room that had started it all. Turning, I got out of there as quickly as I could. I'd clean it up later, when I came back to tell Kiera what she meant to me. I'd clean it all up later. I'd fix this, somehow.

Fleeing from the house, I sprinted to my car. Crawling inside, I took a deep, cleansing breath. I knew I was being a coward, and

I should march myself back inside and back into bed with the woman I loved, but fuck, even thinking it made my skin itch. I couldn't really love her, could I? And could she love me? Was I brave enough to find out?

As I watched the house for signs of movement, I started my car. Nothing happened when I revved the engine. She was probably still sleeping, or more accurately, she was passed out. I should stay and make sure she was okay. She drank a lot really fast; she might be sick when she came around.

Even as I thought it, I put the car in reverse. I wanted to stay, but I couldn't. I just couldn't.

I took off down the street, not knowing where I was going, just knowing I needed to drive. I needed to think. Before I knew it, I was driving through Olympia. Maybe I'd just keep going? What was here for me? A girl I couldn't have, who I also couldn't get away from. *But maybe I could have her.* As unlikely as it seemed, I would never know if I ran away.

Grunting in frustration, I jerked the wheel at the last possible moment to get off the freeway. Then I drove around town until I found a twenty-four-hour restaurant. A girl around my age greeted me with a bright smile.

"One or two?" she asked, looking behind me to see if I was alone or not. *That's the question of the day, isn't it?*

"One," I muttered, feeling very alone as the word reverberated through my head.

"Great! Follow me." The waitress led me to a nearby table, asked if I wanted coffee, then left to get a pot when I said I did. She seemed thrilled that I was by myself. I wasn't. *I should go home.*

While I debated the odds of Kiera caring about me, the waitress returned with coffee and pie; it had a berry filling that smelled incredible. She set it down in front of me with a playful wink. "On the house." I wasn't in the mood for flirting, so I only gave her a polite "Thanks" in return.

I stayed at the restaurant for a while, drinking a bottomless cup of coffee and pushing the pie around my plate. With a hopeful smile, the waitress left when her shift was over, but I stayed. I stayed well past sunrise, then I figured it was time to go somewhere else. After paying my bill, I slowly made my way back home.

I sighed when the Seattle skyline came into view again. I knew what I needed to do. I needed to sit down with Kiera and have a heart-to-heart. I needed to tell her that over the last several weeks, when it had just been the two of us, I'd grown fond of her. I cared about her, more than I cared about anyone, and I wanted her to be mine. Because I was head-over-heels, ends-of-the-earth, till-death-do-us-part in love with her. God, I was such an idiot.

I took a freeway exit that led downtown. I wasn't ready to go home yet, and Kiera was probably still sleeping it off anyway. I'd give her a chance to wake up and recover before I bombarded her with my pathetic, unrequited feelings. Heading down to the water, I found a place to park by the pier and paid for all-day parking, just in case. Stepping out of my car, I inhaled the fresh midmorning air and decided to go for a walk. That would clear my head and calm my nerves. Then I'd be ready to face her, and my fears. I was sure of it.

I walked for hours. I covered so much ground, my feet started to hurt. But that pain was still better than having Kiera tell me she didn't feel what I felt. I couldn't stand the thought of what was between us being one-sided. The way she'd caressed me last night, kissed me...she had to care about me. She just had to.

When the sun was low in the sky, I knew it was time to man up, go home, and do this. Fuck. I wanted to pull her into my arms, hold her, kiss her, tell her I was sorry I bailed and left her alone this morning, and then tell her I loved her. That was what I wanted to do. It was also what I *didn't* want to do.

My heart was hammering when I neared my street. Fuck, I was really going to do this. I was going to lay it all out there, throw my heart at her feet, and hope she didn't tear it into tiny chunks. She could destroy me...or she could say she felt the same, and my life could completely change. It was that possibility that kept me going.

I had to breathe out of my mouth when I pulled onto my street. This was it. All or nothing.

When my house appeared, I noticed something that made my heart drop. The Honda was gone. I'd been killing myself stressing with worry, and Kiera wasn't even home. Where the hell was she? Oh, it was Monday. Of course. She'd had class today, then she'd gone to Pete's. I thought about pulling out of the drive and heading straight to the bar, but I couldn't. I couldn't pour my heart and soul out to her at a bar, with dozens of people watching. No, this needed to be just the two of us. Private. Then we'd figure everything out, and we would decide to be together. I'd be her boyfriend. She'd be my girlfriend. A tingle went through me at just the thought. *Girlfriend*. I'd never had one before. I couldn't wait for Kiera to be the first. God, I hoped she said yes.

I yawned as I climbed out of the car. I was so freaking tired. The smell of alcohol hit me the minute I stepped into the entryway. Oops. I hadn't cleaned up our mess yet. I had a smile on my face the entire time I put stuff away; last night had been amazing. The second I was done cleaning up, the phone rang. Hoping it was Kiera, I eagerly answered it. "Hello?"

"Kellan, where the hell are you?"

I furrowed my brow as I registered the irritated voice on the other end. "Matt? What do you mean, where am...." My voice trailed off as I recalled the fact that I was really late for rehearsal. Sighing, I told him, "I'll be there in twenty minutes."

"Okay" was all he said before he hung up.

I looked around my clean kitchen, then glanced upstairs with longing. I really wanted a nap, but it would have to wait. That was probably a good thing anyway. I probably wouldn't have woken up until tomorrow, and then I'd miss my chance to talk to Kiera. And I desperately wanted to talk to her today. I had a lot to tell her.

Matt and Griffin fought more than usual during rehearsal, so it took longer than usual. Every time they started getting into it, I closed my eyes. Standing by my microphone, I even nodded off a couple of times. I was mentally and physically drained. When Matt finally called it a night, and Griffin muttered, "Thank God... let's go drink," I was relieved. Until I got into my car and contemplated what to say to Kiera, that was.

I'd gone over it a thousand times in my head, but I hadn't really come up with a good way of telling her how I felt. Maybe I should write her a song? Serenade her? God, no, that was pathetic.

After the guys left for Pete's, I laid my head back on the seat and closed my eyes. I needed something good, something honest, something real, so she would know I was serious, that I wasn't playing her, messing with her mind, or trying to be the playboy people assumed I was. I just wanted to be with her.

When I opened my eyes, it was hours later. *Damn it.* I'd fallen asleep. Turning on the Chevelle, I made my way home. Oddly enough, Kiera's car was at the house. I figured she'd still be working, but this was good. I could talk to her now instead of waiting until later. But now that I was finally here, and this was finally happening, my nerves returned. I took small, uncertain steps to my front door, not sure what I was going to do or say. I had to ease into it. I had to listen to her pain over Denny, be helpful and understanding, then gently offer her an alternative to her misery. Surely she'd want an alternative?

I held my breath as I opened the front door. Quietly closing it, I let out a long exhale. I glanced into the living room and kitchen, but Kiera wasn't there. Walking over to the stairs, I opened my mouth to say her name, but I heard something odd and I froze, listening. It almost sounded like Kiera was watching TV, but…if she was, she was watching the type of movie Griffin preferred. Clear sounds of sex were floating down the stairs to me. Panting, moaning, a bed squeaking. Then I clearly heard Kiera cry out. Having heard that sound before, I knew it wasn't a TV show. It was real. She was fucking someone…right now.

Completely floored, I backed away from the stairs. I couldn't comprehend what was going on. This wasn't Kiera. She wasn't the type of girl to bring some stranger back to the house. It would have to be someone she knew. But who did she know in Seattle besides me? Maybe a guy from school? She hadn't been there long though, and I just couldn't believe she would do that to me. That she would do that to…Denny. *Fuck*. Denny.

My eyes returned to the chair in the living room. A coat was lying on the back of it; bags were sitting behind it. Denny's coat. Denny's bags. Denny was home. He was here, in my house, screwing the girl I'd just made love to. My girl. No…his girl.

She'd always been his. She was upset last night because of him. She'd let herself get drunk because of him. She'd screwed me to forget about him. Everything was all about Denny. I was nothing to her. Absolutely nothing. She'd used me, just like every other bitch had used me.

I could still hear them fucking upstairs. There was no way in hell I was staying here, listening to that. Not after I'd had her. Not after I'd figured out how much I loved her. Fuck. Pain tightened around my chest, making it hard to breathe, hard to think, hard to do anything. I loved her so much, and she didn't give a shit about me at all. She didn't want me. No one wanted me.

I needed to get out of here. I needed to stop my head from spinning. I needed to stop thinking. Heading for the kitchen, I tore open the cabinet above the refrigerator and pulled out a bottle of whiskey. I needed to get rid of this pain in my chest. I needed to lose consciousness, and this would help me do it.

I left the house, wondering if I could ever return to it. I didn't want to. I didn't want to ever see her again. Especially since her lips, her body, the moans she'd made for me were so fresh in my mind. Damn, she'd really fooled me. I had actually believed, for just one small minute, that I'd meant something to her. How stupid of me.

I kept picturing her and Denny together while I drove. I pictured their mouths pressed together, their hands on each other. I visualized him thrusting into her over and over again. And because I was a sick son of a bitch, I even pictured the looks on their faces when they climaxed together. Fuck. Denny could be coming inside her right now. My pain transformed into jealousy as I thought of his seed covering mine. By the time I arrived at my destination, Sam's house, my jealousy had shifted into anger.

That fucking bitch, whore, slut.

Grabbing my whiskey, I got out of my car and slammed the door shut. Then I reopened it and slammed it again. That little fucking cunt. She teased me for months, finally got me to fuck her, then went right back to him like it was nothing. Like we were nothing. She was the biggest fucking whore I knew. And I knew a lot of whores.

I paced Sam's walkway and started taking long pulls, two- or three-gulpers. I was going to finish this fucking bottle and slip into fucking oblivion. The rage would end. Then the jealousy would dissipate. Then the pain would stop. I gagged a couple of times but kept forcing the whiskey down. I couldn't take this ache in my chest. I couldn't handle the way every muscle in my body felt tight. I was shaking, and I felt like I might throw up. Why did I have to care about her? Why did she have to do this to me? Why couldn't she just love me the way I loved her?

I kept drinking until eventually my body rejected the alcohol. While I lay there, inhaling and exhaling deep, controlled breaths, I heard a voice say, "What the fuck is this?" Sam was home. He kicked my boot. "Kellan? That you? What the hell are you doing here? And…did you throw up on my roses? Goddammit."

Sam sighed and then helped me to his car. Not being overly gentle, he shoved me inside. I kept my eyes glued on his glove box. If I didn't move, I didn't feel quite so sick. Sam got in on his side, and I wanted to tell him not to take me home. *Take me to Evan's, take me to Matt's, just don't take me home. I was wrong about her. I was wrong about everything.*

He didn't listen to my unspoken request though, and back home is where I ended up. Sam opened my door, then helped me out. My legs felt like rubber; he had to prop me up to keep me standing. We made it to the door and Sam started pounding on it. I wondered which one of my roommates would answer. The girl I'd just fucked, or the guy she'd just fucked? Either way, *I* was fucked.

As fate would have it, Kiera opened the door. I wasn't looking at her, but I could tell it was her by her feet. And her legs. And her hips. Such luscious, sexy hips. Too bad they welcomed the whole entire world. Slut.

"I think this belongs to you," Sam stated as he started moving us inside. I wanted to protest his words. I didn't belong to her. I didn't mean anything to her. That was the problem. Sam led me to the living room, then unceremoniously dumped me into the chair. I slouched over, because it was all I could do…

I slept like shit. I tossed, turned, my stomach heaved, and I swear my body was vibrating. None of the physical pain compared to the images that flashed through my brain though. I saw Kiera and Denny in all their I-love-you-forever glory. I watched them make love a thousand times, over and over. I saw her face when he brought her to the brink. I heard them whisper their feelings for

140

each other. It was torture, but it was worse when I replayed Kiera and me together. My head ran through the entire encounter, trying to find one moment that was blatantly fake or forced. I couldn't find a second where Kiera wasn't fully and completely into it though. There was nothing about the moment that didn't feel genuine, but I knew in my heart it wasn't. She hadn't been having sex with me; she'd been putting a Band-Aid on a wound.

Giving up on the sleep that wasn't happening, I sat up in bed. My head was pounding, and my throat was completely dry. The last thing I clearly remembered was Sam driving me home…and Kiera. She'd been awake, she'd opened the door. I couldn't remember much after Sam dumped me onto my chair, but she must have helped me get upstairs and into bed. Why the fuck would she do that?

My head almost hurt too much to use it. Glancing at my floor, I saw my damp shirt, and I recalled walking into the shower fully clothed. Shit…she'd helped me shower. She'd cleaned me up, helped me to my room… *Why?*

I had one crystal clear memory then, of saying, "Don't worry. I won't tell him."

Even wasted I'd known she was just being nice to make sure I stayed silent. Well, I didn't need her fake sympathies. I wasn't going to tell him, because I had no desire to hurt him. I was inconsequential anyway. I was a tool she'd used when she'd needed something fixed. Nothing more. The hammer doesn't complain when it's put away after all the nails are driven. And the hammer doesn't squeal to the screwdriver.

I stared at my dresser, but it was much too far away, so I leaned over to grab my dirty shirt off the floor. I thought I was going to lose my stomach bending over, but that was nothing compared to straightening back up. My damp shirt clenched in my fingers, I inhaled a deep breath and let it out slowly. I needed water. And coffee.

I pulled the fabric over my head; it was cold, and stuck to my body, making me shiver. I glanced at my jeans, but there was no way in hell I could get those back on. I was staying in my boxers, and my roommates would just have to deal with it. They had bigger issues than my outfit anyway. I wasn't going to tell Denny anything, but I wondered if Kiera would. If she confessed, it would change things between Denny and me. He'd hate me. And he *should* hate me. I'd done exactly what he hadn't wanted me to do. I'd just thought... I was sure Kiera...

It didn't matter what I'd thought. Nothing mattered.

I slowly straightened. Each inch I moved brought a new ache, pain, or discomfort. I wasn't sure how I was going to make it downstairs, but what I needed was down there, so I had to try. Each step I took was slow and methodical. If I concentrated on my toes, everything else wasn't so bad. I glanced at Denny and Kiera's closed door, then returned my focus to my feet. My feet were all that existed right now. My feet would get me through the morning.

I shuffled to the kitchen, spied the table, and ached with the need to rest on it. Just for a minute. Just until the pain went away and my stomach settled. I carefully sat on a chair; I'd seen ninety-year-olds sit faster than I did, but there was a brief truce going on between my stomach and my head, and I didn't want to disrupt the alliance by moving too fast.

When I was finally down, I hunched over the table, my head in my hands, and worked on breathing. In. Out. Repeat. Coffee was on my mind, but I didn't want to move again. Not yet. Just a minute.

I wasn't sure how long I sat at the table, taking long, careful breaths, but eventually Kiera stepped into the room. Perfect.

"Are you okay?" she whispered.

Why was she shouting? "Yes," I replied. *I'm peachy.*

"Coffee?" she asked.

I flinched, then nodded. *Yes, please.* Coffee was the whole reason I'd come down here.

She started making the pot, and I had to close my eyes. Everything she did was so loud. When she was done tormenting me, she asked, "How did you know Denny was back?"

142

I sank my head to the table and groaned. My brain was throbbing against my skull. Everything hurt. Even her question. *How did I know? Because I heard you. I heard you having sex with him, right after having sex with me.* "Saw his coat," I mumbled.

"Oh." I felt my heart drop. *That's all she has to say to me? "Oh"?* Apparently it wasn't, for she quickly added, "Are you sure you're okay?"

I snapped my eyes to hers. *You fucked me, then my best friend. I love you. Nothing about this is okay, so quit fucking asking me that.* "I'm fine," I stated, my voice cold.

She seemed confused by my words and my actions. Was I really so confusing? She was the one who was hard to understand. She loved Denny, but she looked at me like I was something special. While she went about finishing the coffee, I thought about Bumbershoot. That day had been amazing. The way we'd held each other, the way she'd sought my comfort. It was almost like Denny hadn't even existed. What had changed? Or was she using me even back then? No, she'd cared... the talks we'd had, the way she listened to my music, my lyrics, the way she'd pried into my soul. She had cared. Maybe she still did. Maybe she was torn, confused, overwhelmed. Maybe she was hurting, and I just wasn't seeing it.

When the coffee was done, she grabbed two mugs from the cabinet. Heart in my hands, I risked a question that could lead to a really hard conversation. But maybe it was time we had a hard conversation. We'd never talked about us. We'd always ignored the things that had happened. I couldn't ignore this though. I needed to know if I meant anything to her.

"Are you... okay?" I asked. It was a loaded question, a stupid question. I should have just manned up and asked her what I really wanted to know. *What am I to you?*

She gave me a bright, chipper smile. "Yes, I'm great."

Her face, her words, they confirmed everything I'd already known. I didn't mean a goddamn thing to her. I felt like I was going to be sick right here at the table. I laid my arms down and buried my head in them. She was great... and I wished I'd never been

143

born. I could feel my eyes water, so I concentrated on my breathing. I was not about to give her the satisfaction of seeing my pain. My emotional pain, anyway. That was mine; she didn't have a right to it.

I could hear her pouring the cups of coffee. I needed to mellow out, shove down the feelings bubbling up, threatening to devour me. She was Denny's, I knew that. She'd used me; I was used to that. I could get over this. I had to. I needed help though. Even though I'd overdone it the last couple of nights, I needed alcohol. Twisting my head so my mouth was clear, I told Kiera, "Put a little Jack in that." She smirked at me, like she thought I was joking. Did anything about me right now seem like I was kidding? She was causing me pain; I wanted to numb it. A few shots of Jack Daniels would do the trick. A equals B. The least she could do was humor me.

I raised my head. Struggling to remain polite, I told her, "Please."

She sighed and muttered something that sounded like "Whatever," and I laid my head back down. I didn't need her to understand, I just needed her to comply.

I heard her rummaging through the liquor cabinet above the fridge. I didn't move when she found the bottle and set it in front of me. She came back a moment later with the mug and set it in front of me too. I still didn't move. After a second of my stillness, she poured some alcohol into my mug, then started to screw on the cap. I knew she wouldn't pour nearly enough in, so without even looking, I coughed to get her attention, then motioned for more. She sighed, but she did it.

I lifted my head and, out of habit, I gave her a soft, "Thank you." *Thank you for ripping my heart out. Thank you for showing me something I can never have. Thank you for looking so beautiful this morning, it makes me want to tear my eyes out. Thank you for not seeing me as anything more than a release.*

"Kellan…" she finally began. I took a long draw of coffee. *Here we go…* "The other night…" She stared at me while I stared back at her. *Yes, the other night when I touched every inch of your body, dipped my tongue inside you, pushed myself into you over and over until you came around me... that night? Or did you have a different night in mind?*

She cleared her throat, looking very uncomfortable. *If sex makes you so uneasy, Kiera, maybe you shouldn't be doing it. Especially when you don't mean it.* Finally, she murmured, "I just don't want a...misunderstanding."

I could feel my blood begin to boil as I took another long draw of coffee. Really? A misunderstanding? She was going to use my words against me? She was going to compare what we'd done to what I'd done with Joey? We'd had meaningless sex, and she was asking for nothing to change between us. She wanted us to go back to what we were before, so she and Denny could move forward with their happy ending. Nope, no misunderstanding. I meant nothing to her.

"Kiera...there are no misunderstandings between us," I told her, my voice flat. *There is nothing between us. There never was.*

Chapter 11

Holding On to Anger

Denny came down a while later, and I quickly excused myself and got out of there. I couldn't deal with Denny yet. I could barely deal with me. I kept shifting between anger, guilt, resignation, and sadness. I wasn't sure where I'd finally end up. Except alone. That was pretty much a given.

Crawling into bed, I curled into a ball and tried to get some sleep, but it was elusive and kept avoiding me. I kept picturing Denny and Kiera together downstairs, happy and laughing as they exchanged hopes, dreams, and plans for their future. They were probably picking out a wedding date and baby names. They'd probably ask me to stand up with Denny while he married the woman I loved, and then they'd make me their sweet little baby's godfather. Fuck my life.

I wondered if Kiera would tell Denny the truth before they walked down the aisle. I should find out what her intentions were, so I wasn't blindsided by anything...like Denny's fists. I should, but I didn't want to talk to Kiera. Her joy was pissing me off. She didn't have to flaunt how fucking happy she was. I got it. Denny completed her. Good for Team Australia.

I heard Denny leave the house, then heard Kiera getting ready for school. I needed some water, I needed a shower, but I didn't want to face her. Once she left me alone, then I'd attempt to take care of myself.

When I heard her shuffling around the entryway, I knew she was on her way out. School was a ways off, but Denny had their car, so Kiera would need to catch the bus. Even if my car were here, I wouldn't drive her to school today. A pang went through me that driving her around and walking her to class was over. I'd enjoyed that time together. It wasn't real though. Why keep up a pretense just because it felt good on the surface? If she didn't feel what I felt... what was the point?

I ambled downstairs when I heard the door open. On my way to the kitchen, I glanced out the window and saw Kiera standing there, staring at the empty driveway. Was she missing Denny already? He couldn't be gone for five seconds without her falling apart? God.

She turned then, and saw me in the window staring at her. She started to wave, but I left before she could finish the pointless gesture. *Don't act like you care if you don't.*

Alone with my thoughts, I began to dwell. I couldn't stop thinking about Kiera, and what we'd had, and what I'd wanted us to have in the future. I thought about Denny, our past and our friendship. One stupid, careless act had changed both relationships. If I'd just been stronger, pushed Kiera away when she'd needed comfort, none of this would be happening now. But I was weak. I'd needed her. I'd fallen for her. And now, we were all paying the price.

While I was still lounging on the couch, hoping to still my brain by filling it with images of meaningless TV shows, I heard the front door open. I didn't know if it was Kiera or Denny. It didn't really matter either. I'd called Griffin a while ago to get a ride to my car. He would be here soon, and then I could leave. Maybe I wouldn't come back.

Like nothing was different, Kiera strolled into the room and sat down in the chair opposite the couch. I glanced over at her, then returned my eyes to the TV. She looked good, her hair curled, her makeup still fresh. She was the complete opposite of me. She looked like she was on top of the world, while emotionally and physically I felt like shit.

We were both silent, and kind of ignoring each other, when Kiera suddenly blurted out, "Who do you rent this place from?"

I kept my eyes glued to the TV. *Really? That's what you want to talk about right now?* "I don't. It's mine," I told her.

I could tell the curiosity was eating away at her. "Oh. How did you afford—"

She stopped herself from asking a question that seemed completely pointless and random. *Why do you care?* I wanted to ask. I didn't though. That might open a door into a conversation about us, and I didn't want to go there. Instead, I answered her unasked question. Kiera could still get me to open up, even when I'd rather be doing anything other than talking to her. "My parents. They died in a car crash a couple years ago. Left me their...palace. Only child and all..." That still haunted me. Did they care in the end, did they feel bad, or was it just another mistake in a long line of mistakes?

"Oh...I'm so sorry," Kiera told me, genuinely looking guilty for bringing it up.

"Don't be," I told her. "It happens." *Lots of shit happens. And none of it matters.*

Kiera's curiosity still wasn't satisfied. "Why do you rent the room then? I mean, if you own the house?"

I paused before answering her. For a second, I forgot that everything had changed between us, and I opened my mouth, prepared to tell her the truth. *I don't like living in an empty house. I like the company. You and I are alike that way.* But then I remembered that things were different, and I closed my mouth. Her desire to never be alone had led her to use me as a source of comfort. I'd thought she was different, that *we* were different, but she'd used me just like all the others.

My heart hardening back up, I turned back to the TV and told her a lie. "The extra money comes in handy."

Maybe that was the wrong thing to say to her. Kiera got up and walked over to the couch. She sat down right beside me, and my body ached with her closeness. I'd give anything to hold her. I hated that I still felt that way. Why couldn't I turn this off?

Her expression apologetic, she told me, "I didn't mean to pry. I'm sorry."

Prying into my past was the least painful thing you did, Kiera. I swallowed a hard lump. "Don't worry about it." *Just leave me alone. Please.*

She didn't though. She leaned over my body, giving me a hug. I stiffened under her touch. It wasn't that long ago that I'd craved these moments. I'd gone out of my way to make them happen. But that was when I'd thought they mattered. I'd thought *I* mattered. She shouldn't be touching me like this anymore. Not now that her boyfriend was back. Not now that it hurt so much to feel what I couldn't have. *Get off me.*

She pulled back, and her eyes went wide with shock, like she suddenly comprehended that I wasn't enjoying her presence. *Leave me alone.* I stared past her so I wouldn't go off on her. There was no point in yelling, no good in getting angry, and no reason for her to ever touch me again.

Kiera let go. Her face confused, she said my name with a clear question. "Kellan...?"

I needed to get away from her. I sat up on the couch. "Excuse me." My voice was rough and hard, but at least I still managed to be polite. I wouldn't be if she kept approaching me with such indifference, like none of this bothered her at all.

She grabbed my arm before I could stand up. Fire burned through me. *Stop touching me.* "Wait... Talk to me, please."

I narrowed my eyes at her. *Get your fucking hands off me, leave me alone. Quit pretending you care. I see right through you. You don't.* "There is nothing to say." Nothing that mattered, anyway. I had plenty of things to say. Shaking my head before I snapped, I bit out, "I have to go." Brushing her hand away, I finally stood up.

"Go?" she said from the couch. She sounded confused and dejected. Was this really so incomprehensible to her? *I'm in love*

149

with you. You gave yourself to me, then ran right back to him. You. Killed. Me.

Leaving the room, I told her, "I have to get my car." *I have a life without you. You're not my entire world. You're just the part I loved the most...*

I dashed up to my room, slamming the door behind me. I leaned against the cold wood, shutting my eyes. Goddammit. Why couldn't she see how much she'd hurt me? Why couldn't she see that I loved her? Why couldn't she love me back? *Tell Denny to leave, Kiera...Stay with me. Choose me.* That was never going to happen though. I had a better shot of getting my parents to return from their graves and apologize for the decades of abuse and neglect. That would probably hurt a lot less too.

I took my time getting ready. When I figured Griffin was just about here, I trudged downstairs to get my coat. I almost wished there was a secret door that would let me escape unnoticed. I really didn't feel like another odd, painful confrontation with Kiera. Luck wasn't with me though.

"Kellan..."

There was something in her voice that made me look over at her in the living room. Sadness, panic, I wasn't sure. She stood up and walked over to me. I wanted to sigh. I wanted to beg her to let me go, tell her that all she was doing was hurting me, but I couldn't. I couldn't resist her, so I let her approach me, even though I knew I was going to get hurt by whatever it was she felt she had to say to me.

She started blushing, like she was embarrassed, and dropped her gaze to the floor. I frowned at her expression. She generally only looked that way when she felt stupid or silly. Is that how she felt around me now? I was heartbroken, and she was mortified? What was she going to say now? I really had no idea.

Not meeting my gaze, she mumbled, "I really am sorry about your parents."

She peeked up at me and I relaxed. She was still worried about that? It was nothing. Water under the bridge. They were assholes, but they were gone. The end. But my parents were something not many people talked to me about. She was still trying to get to know me, trying to understand me, trying to delve deeper. Why? *You already had me, Kiera; what more do you want?*

Softly, I told her, "It's okay, Kiera." *I'd give you everything, if you'd only take it.*

We stared at each other for long, silent seconds. I wished things were different. I wished our time together had been different. I wished I meant more to her. I wished she loved me, like I loved her. I wished my heart didn't pound when I stared into her eyes. I wished my lips didn't ache to press against her skin. But wishing didn't change anything.

After another second of silence, Kiera leaned up and kissed my cheek. It burned so much, I felt like she'd struck me. I looked away as waves of pain nearly brought me to my knees. *Jesus... please let the torture stop.*

Turning from her, I headed out the door. I needed space. And the ability to shut off my memories. That one tiny display of affection was rewinding every moment Kiera and I had had together. Holding each other, laughing, making her blush, making her happy, making her moan. It was all too much. I pinched the bridge of my nose as I felt a headache building. If I could forget, like she had apparently forgotten, then I wouldn't be in pain anymore.

Griffin pulled up, and I walked around to the passenger's side to get in. I glanced up at the house and spotted Kiera watching me from the window. Why was she watching me? Why did she keep approaching me? Why couldn't she leave me alone? Why couldn't I forget about her?

Shaking away my thoughts, I got in the car. I needed to do something before this grief consumed me.

Anger seemed my best option. When I was ticked at her, it didn't hurt as much. And being angry with her was something I was good at. It didn't take much to stoke the embers in my belly into full-on flames. I would push her away when we were alone together. Make her keep her distance, since she shouldn't be near me anyway. Then

151

I'd stay as far away from her as I was able to. Anger and avoidance. That was how I'd survive this.

When she came down for coffee the next morning, I wrapped my fury around me like armor. Let her try to find a crack. I dared her. Leaning back against the counter, I lifted my head and listened to her approach. I could do this. I could shut her out, close down my heart, push away the pain. She was nothing to me, just like I was nothing to her. All of this was nothing.

When she entered the room, I slid my eyes over to her and half smiled. *Mornin', whore. Denny know about us yet?*

"Hey," she whispered, clearly not happy with the look in my eye. Well, what the fuck did I care if she was happy?

"Mornin'," I answered, staring her down. *Like the way I look at you now? You wanted my attention... well, now you have it.*

She grabbed a mug and waited for the pot to finish brewing. Her face was speculative. Was she wondering what to say to me? She could say anything she wanted, I didn't fucking care. She could tell me to have a nice day, she could tell me to take a flying leap. None of it mattered, and none of it changed the fact that she was a cold-hearted bitch. I hated her so much. Only, I didn't. I didn't hate her at all. I didn't even blame her. I wouldn't want me either.

I shoved that nagging thought aside and focused on my ire. Anger made the pain go away. Anger was all I'd let myself feel.

When the coffee was done, I poured my mug, then held the pot out to her. "Would you like me to fill you?" I asked, meaning it in the crudest way possible. Maybe Denny wasn't getting the job done. Maybe the whore needed a good fuck this morning. I was just doing my civic duty by offering up my services. *That's all I was good for anyway, right, Kiera?* I was a walking, talking vibrator. That was all I'd ever been, that was all I would ever be.

She seemed confused and uncomfortable with my question. Her eyes were almost solid green this morning. Stunning. The beauty in them only pissed me off even more. *Take your incredible eyes and shove them. I don't need them. Or you.*

"Um... yes," she said, her mug extended.

152

As I filled up her mug, I held in a laugh. I couldn't believe she actually said yes to that. Guess she did want me to fuck her. "Cream?" I asked suggestively. *Want me to come in you again?*

"Yes," she whispered, swallowing like she was nervous.

No need to be nervous. We've done this before. I'm just your toy anyway. No need to fear a toy. I stepped over to the fridge to get the creamer for her. The creamer I only kept buying because of her. The bitch had infiltrated every aspect of my life. I really fucking hated that.

Kiera looked like she'd rather be anywhere but near me when I returned with her creamer. I held it up. "Just let me know when you're satisfied."

My eyes were locked on hers while I gave my liquids to her. *Want the real stuff? I'll give you that again too. We'll just fuck this time. No messy emotions, no misconceptions, no misunderstandings. Just a grade-A fuckapalooza. I have a feeling you'd be really good at that.*

"Stop," she told me, almost immediately.

Leaning in close, I whispered, "Are you sure you want me to stop? I thought you liked it." *I thought you liked me, but I was wrong... about so many things.*

She swallowed again and turned away from me. Her hands were shaking as she fumbled with the sugar. I laughed, even though nothing about this was funny.

I stared at her for a while, building my reserve of anger before I brought up a topic that I didn't want to talk about, but I needed an answer. I needed to know what to expect. I needed to know what our plan was. Or *her* plan, since this was her show. I was just her puppet.

"So you and Denny are... 'back on'?" I asked, clenching my stomach to get through the discomfort of speaking his name.

Kiera flushed with color. "Yes."

I felt like she'd just punched me in the gut. I even had to stop myself from hunching over. The pain started trickling in, and I had to force myself to remember how much I hated her to make it stop. *Fucking bitch.* "Just like that... No questions asked?"

She looked freaked out by my question, like she thought I was suddenly going to go run to Denny and tell him everything. *Sorry, but I actually care about hurting him, so I'm not going to say a word. I wouldn't be surprised if you did though. Whore.* "Are you going to tell him about...?" I made a crude fucking gesture with my fingers. That was all it was. No point in trying to paint it in a prettier light.

"No...of course not." She looked away from me, like I'd offended her. Was truth offensive? Yeah, I supposed sometimes it was. Returning her eyes to mine, she whispered, "Are you?"

I shrugged. I may have been drunk at the time, but I'd already answered this question, and I'd meant it. I wasn't going to be the one to hurt Denny. That was her choice. All of this was her choice. "No, I told you I wouldn't." Holding tight to my anger, I lied through my teeth. "It doesn't matter much to me anyway. I was just curious..."

"Well, no, I'm not...and thank you for not telling him...I guess." She seemed taken aback by my answer, and my indifference. Why should I care about her, if she didn't care about me? I was just leveling the playing field. Suddenly, her anger spiked. Her eyes narrowing, she spat out, "What happened to you the other night?"

Grinning wickedly, like I'd been up to nothing but scandalous debauchery, I grabbed my coffee and took a long draw. *What happened to me is none of your business, and if I have anything to say about it, you'll never know how stressed I was about telling you I loved you, or how hurt I was when you ripped the rug right out from under me. You'll never know anything real about me. That's the only way I can punish you now.*

She walked away after that, and I let her. There was nothing left to say anyway.

Once my coffee was done, I went to my room and hid out. I hated that I was hiding, but I didn't want to see Kiera any more today. I could still hear her, which was bad enough. I heard her laughing with Denny before disappearing into the bathroom to take a shower. I lay on my bed as I listened to the water running, and images of her naked body rotated through my mind. I hated the play-by-play, and wished I could shut it off. The painful memories of what I could no longer have wouldn't leave me though. I was stuck in a visual hell of my own creation.

As soon as I could slip out without either roommate noticing, because I couldn't handle talking to Denny at the moment either, I left for Evan's. I even took a few extra things with me, since I didn't plan on coming home. I just wanted to be away for a while. I wanted to be somewhere where I wouldn't have to see Denny and wouldn't have to be alone with Kiera. Being around the guys was a great escape.

When I showed up at Evan's with a duffel bag, he raised an eyebrow at me. "Care if I crash here for a couple days?" I asked.

As I expected, Evan shrugged and said, "No. Can I ask why?"

I could tell from the glint in his brown eyes that he thought it had something to do with Kiera. It did. Exactly what he'd been worried about had happened. I'd caved. I was a scumbag. But Kiera was a scumbag too, and I didn't really want to talk about her with him.

Throwing on a trouble-free smile, I said, "Denny's back. He was gone a long time, so I thought I'd give the happy couple some breathing room."

My voice was a little strained on the words "happy couple," but Evan didn't seem to notice. He was too freaking ecstatic that Denny had returned. *I know, it's great news, isn't it? Now you don't have to worry about me crossing the line with his girlfriend. Well, sorry to burst your bubble there, Evan, but Denny came back one day too late for that.*

While I managed to avoid my house for the most part, I wasn't so successful in avoiding the bar. Kiera could run me away from one place, but not both. It was easier to be around her at Pete's anyway. There was safety in numbers. It didn't hurt so much to see her when I was surrounded by my bandmates, the bar staff, and dozens of women who would love a turn with me. If only for a night. Since that was all I was good for.

I used the opportunities at Pete's to get back at Kiera in small, pathetic ways. It helped fuel my fire to pick on her, and anger was the only thing keeping me going lately. If I lost the anger...I think the pain of losing her, or more accurately, the pain of never having her, would consume me. Like an empty plastic jug tossed on a fire, I'd collapse in on myself, dissolving into nothing. So I stoked my rage to protect my sanity.

I flirted with Rita at the bar, acting like I was interested in going another round with her. I refused to let Kiera get my drinks for me, and she actually looked offended that I wouldn't let her serve me. She'd served me enough. I engaged Griffin in his sordid stories, stories that might or might not have even been true. Griffin loved getting graphic about them though. I knew Kiera hated hearing it, so I made sure she had no choice but to listen. I even dragged her into the conversations whenever I could.

She flushed with color almost every time she approached our table. Griffin loved embarrassing her, so the two of us had a great time, but I heard about it from Evan later at his loft. "Why are you picking on Kiera so much?"

Ice flashed through my veins as I looked over at him. I was lying on the couch, getting ready to go to bed; he was in his "room," reading. "I'm not picking on her."

Evan closed his book and sat up on his bed. I mentally cringed. I didn't want to have this conversation, not with him. "Yeah, you are. You're being a jackass. Why? Why are you really here, Kellan?"

I sighed in my head. I'd have to go home tomorrow, just so Evan wouldn't get suspicious. I tossed my arms out to the sides. "I'm not doing anything. I was just having a bit of fun with Griffin. I was more picking on him than anything. He's an idiot, and ninety percent of those stories are pure crap."

Evan laughed. "Yeah, that's true. I don't think Kiera realizes that though, so maybe you should ease up around her."

I gave him a bright smile as I laid my arm over my eyes. "Yeah, sure. I wasn't trying to make her uncomfortable or anything." Just miserable. Like me.

The next morning, I headed back home. As long as Kiera and I didn't look at, speak to, or get anywhere near each other, being home should be just like being at Evan's. This would be fine. Just fine.

I opened my front door and froze. Denny and Kiera were awake. They were practically going at it on my couch. While I once found that amusing, it wasn't so funny anymore. Pain leached up from my stomach, but I pushed it back. She was a fucking whore who'd used me and I hated her. *And I missed her.*

Kiera and I locked gazes. She was sitting on Denny's lap, her fingers in his hair. I remembered her fingers being in mine, and hate flowed through me. Damn her for hurting me. As I smirked at the skank, Denny finally noticed me. I quickly shifted my expression into an amiable smile. "Mornin'."

"You just gettin' home, mate?"

Denny started stroking her thighs. It reminded me of her legs wrapped around me. God, that had felt so good. She'd felt so good. But what we'd shared wasn't real. It had only been a release to her. Fucking bitch.

Only looking at Denny, I replied, "Yeah, I was…out." I shifted my gaze to Kiera on the word "out." *Take that any way you want to. I don't care.*

Kiera seemed uncomfortable and scooted off Denny's lap. He laughed as he put an arm around her. My stomach twisted as I watched them cuddling. They looked so fucking happy together, but it was just as big of a lie as the two of us had been. Denny wanted his old job back, and Kiera…well, who the fuck knew what she wanted.

"See you guys later," I muttered as I ambled up the stairs and into my room. I shut the door and lay down on my bed. My anger was only increasing with each breath I took, but I welcomed the heat. The heat kept away the pain.

Denny was at the bar when I strolled in that night. If we didn't have to play later, I would have strolled right back out; being around him was painful. Being around him and Kiera together was agony.

Like I was still drawn to her, even though it was pointless and

157

futile, my eyes locked onto Kiera. She had her hair pulled up, exposing her slim neck. Her Pete's shirt was tight to her body, and she wore these tiny black shorts that showed all of her lean legs. How good she looked was torturous.

Her full lips were parted, and if I didn't know any better, I'd swear she was holding her breath, like just seeing me affected her. But I knew it didn't. I was nothing to her. She flicked a glance over to Denny, like she didn't want to be caught staring at me. I looked too, but Denny was greeting the band and not paying any attention to us. Knowing he was going to sit at the table all night, further making my life a living hell, I walked over to Kiera. If tonight was going to be half as awkward as I thought it would be, I might as well be half-cocked for it.

When Kiera noticed me approaching her, she seemed uneasy, like she sort of wanted to run. I didn't entirely blame her for that. I hadn't exactly been nice lately. Well, I could be nice now, since Denny was watching. I could be cordial, but I wouldn't be friendly. That, I couldn't do anymore.

"Kiera," I stated dispassionately, as if I'd read her name from her nametag.

"Yes, Kellan." Her tone was guarded, and she seemed to be making herself look at me.

Liking that I made her uneasy, I smiled. "We'll have the usual. Bring one for Denny too . . . since he's a part of this." *The largest part. Much bigger than me, that's for sure.*

Some girls decided to cuddle with me before the show, and I let them. In fact, I lost myself in their feminine attention. It was better than watching Kiera and Denny make googly eyes at each other. Needing the distraction from my pain, from my guilt, I mercilessly flirted with the girls; I didn't even look Denny's way.

When it was time for the band to go onstage, a sneer was on my lips. I couldn't contain my satisfaction. I'd changed the lineup so that we were playing every *I hate you, you suck* song we had in our arsenal. I needed to vent, and I was going to do it through music to help prevent me from doing it with my mouth.

I knew the second Kiera understood that my set list was about her, in feeling, if not by the lyrics. The one we were currently playing was one fans often misinterpreted as being about one-night stands. It wasn't, but I played it up that way, so Kiera would think it was. *Yes, it's about meaningless sex. And yes, Kiera, I'm dedicating it to you, and the meaningless sex we shared.* As I sang, I flirted the hell out of the audience. *Too sexual? You haven't seen anything yet, Kiera.*

Kiera gaped at me, and I swear her eyes misted over. It hurt me some to see her in pain, but I pulled my anger tighter around me and trudged onward. She was just upset because I was calling her out, not because she cared. She'd never cared. It had all been a lie.

The next morning, I felt a little better. Sure, I was being a dick, but being an asshole was better than brooding or curling up into a fetal position because some bitch had devastated me. Fuck that. I'd survived worse.

I was reading the paper and drinking my coffee at the table when Kiera stepped into the kitchen. She looked nervous yet irritated when I glanced up at her. I watched as she closed her eyes and took a deep, calming breath. I thought she might say something to me about my performance last night, but instead, she made a cup of coffee. Liquid courage perhaps?

By the time she sat at the table, I was invested in my paper, or at least, I pretended to be invested. I'd read the same paragraph three times. I considered ignoring Kiera, but purposely not speaking to her would imply that I cared. And I didn't. We were nothing, and that was fine. Just fine.

"Mornin'," I said, not bothering to look up.

"Kellan…"

I looked up at her. *What, Kiera? What more could you possibly want from me? Because I've got nothing left for you.*

"What?" I snapped.

Avoiding eye contact, she whispered, "Why are you mad at me?"

What? Did she really not get what she'd done to me? How she'd treated me like meat, just like every other girl I'd been with? That,

159

until that moment, I'd thought we were different? I'd thought I loved her. No…I did love her. *I do love her.* But I needed to hate her right now, so I had to push all that aside.

"I'm not mad at you, Kiera. I've been exceedingly nice to you." Even though she wasn't looking at me, I gave her a snide smile. "Most women thank me for that." *And write me off, just like you did.*

Anger flashed in her eyes as she looked up at me. "You're being an ass! Ever since…"

She stopped talking. She still couldn't say it, she still couldn't talk about sex. Well, if she couldn't bring it up, then I wouldn't either. *Why should I make this any easier for her? In fact, I think I'll ignore it altogether.* I returned my attention to my article and my coffee. "I really don't know what you mean, Kiera…"

"Is it Denny? You feel guilty…?"

That irritated me, and before I could stop myself, I snapped out, "I'm not the one who cheated on him."

She flinched at my words and bit her lip, like she couldn't believe I would go there. I hadn't meant to, but her comment got to me. Of course I felt guilty. I owed Denny everything, and I'd betrayed him…for absolutely nothing. I'd risked it all, and for no damn reason, and if Denny ever found out, he would never forgive me.

"We used to be friends, Kellan," Kiera whispered, her voice warbling.

That comment got to me too. We were friends once, and then so much more. Or I thought we'd been more, but that hadn't been the case. I'd been a blanket to keep her warm when she'd been cold. Nothing more.

I began to read the article again. "Were we? I wasn't aware of that."

Pain and heat were in her voice when she responded to my callous comment. "Yes…we were, Kellan. Before we—"

Her words were opening up wounds I was trying to let scab over. I didn't want to talk about this. My eyes rose to hers, cutting her off. "Denny and I are friends. You and I are…roommates." The term was distasteful in my mouth, but it was the truth.

Her cheeks flamed with anger as she gaped at me. "You have a funny way of showing friendship then. If Denny knew what you—"

Again, I let my rage get the best of me. "But you're not telling him, are you?" I bit out. Calming myself, I resumed reading the paper. Each printed word I spoke in my mind brought my temper down a notch. But calming down let the sadness in, sadness I didn't want to feel. I mulled over the worthless feeling in the pit of my stomach. Why was I so impossible to love? I knew I needed to get angry again to shove this pain aside, I just didn't have it in me at the moment.

I studied my paper, not seeing a word of it. Being more honest than I had been in a very long while, I told her, "Besides, that's between the two of you—it had nothing to do with me. I was simply...there...for you." *I love you so much...It hurts so much... And I remember how we were together, when it was just us here, and it kills me all over again.*

Needing to be away from her, needing to be away from this house, needing to be away from my life, I sighed and looked back up at her. Her gorgeous eyes were wide, her cheeks pale, her lips full and welcoming...and not mine. "Are we done?" I asked her, my voice soft. Seemingly shell-shocked, all she could do was nod. I stood and walked from the room; I felt drained by every step I took away from her. Staying near her was worse though.

Once I got back to my room, I grabbed some stuff, then left the house and drove to Matt's. It wasn't as close as Evan's, it wasn't as quiet as Evan's, but no one would question if I stayed a couple of days. And I needed space. Guess I was weaker than I thought. So much for being able to handle anything.

After spending some time at Matt's, I managed to pull my shit together and go home. I went back to my tried-and-true method of dealing with the pain—anger and avoidance. I spent a lot of time in my room. I spent a lot of time torturing Kiera with crude comments. I spent a lot of time reminding myself why I shouldn't give a rat's ass about her. That never worked though. I still cared, I still hurt.

Denny got a new job, since he'd quit his old one when he'd rushed back to Seattle to salvage his relationship. When I finally had the strength to talk to him, he confessed that he hated it.

"Have you ever gotten the feeling that no matter what you do, you're never going to do enough?" he asked me. Pausing, I wondered if he meant Kiera. She seemed to be growing more discontented every day since Denny had returned. I wasn't sure why, but I wasn't about to ask her.

"Sometimes," I quietly answered him. *Okay, maybe every day since birth.*

Denny shook his head, and I could see regret and guilt warring in his features. "This new job...I feel like I'm butting my head against a wall. I keep trying to show my worth, but the harder I try, the more they resent me. I know I shouldn't compare, but my other job never would have...I just miss..." Sighing, he let his thoughts die.

Knowing, as a friend, I should say something to make him feel better about his sacrifice, I pushed aside my guilt and heartache and said, "At least you still have Kiera." I hoped he couldn't hear the bitterness in my voice.

With a sad smile, he murmured, "Yeah." I understood. He was suffering from remorse; I was too.

Denny's job kept sending him on more and more errands that had nothing to do with actual work, from what I could tell. It seemed like he was gone more often than not now. With every task he was sent on, Kiera became more irritable. There was a frost between them that hadn't been there before, and I found her reaction to his absence interesting. He'd left his dream job for her and she was the one getting pissy about his replacement gig? Considering what she'd done to him with me, you'd think she'd be a little more understanding. But when I came downstairs one night and she was staring out the sliding door to the backyard, face forlorn, eyes close to tears, my heart still ached to comfort her. Even after everything, I still loved her. I probably always would.

As I witnessed Denny and Kiera getting frustrated at each other more often, a part of me was happy to see a small crack in their fairy tale. Another part of me felt guilty, like maybe it was my fault. It wasn't though. I wasn't part of that equation.

Several days passed, and nothing got better. Denny was grumpy, Kiera was agitated, and I was angry. My home had become laced with sharp thorns, and everyone was on edge and griping at each other. It was hell. I'd been waiting for things to get easier, but nothing was getting easier. I was hurt, angry, lonely, and fed up. And even though it was childish and immature, I knew it would make me feel better to push Kiera's buttons, so I did.

After watching Denny storm out of the bar one night, I approached her with my lips curved into a cold smile. Like she was going to try ignoring me, she busied herself with cleaning a table. Nice try. But I wasn't about to let that happen right now. I needed to release this pent-up pain.

Coming up beside her, I pressed into her side. She couldn't ignore me if I was well inside her personal space. Being that close to her again ignited something in me, but I converted the feeling into fuel for the fire in my belly. Just like I knew she would, Kiera pulled away and glared up at me.

"Denny leave you again?" I asked. "I could find you another drinking buddy, if you're...lonely? Maybe Griffin this time?" I cringed at the thought of Griffin touching her but didn't let it show. All Kiera saw was my wicked smile.

Kiera apparently wasn't in the mood for me to pick on her. With heat in her voice, she fought back. "I don't need your crap tonight, Kellan!"

"You don't seem to be happy with him." I'd meant to say that in a snarky way that was full of innuendo, but it left my mouth as a serious statement. I dwelled on the truth of it while Kiera responded with a glare. She *wasn't* happy with him. She had been happier with *me*.

Kiera saw right through my words and spoke my thoughts. Face pinched, she snapped, "What? And I'd be happier with you?"

My heart contracted as she hit the nail on the head. *Yes, you*

163

would be happier with me. If you let yourself love me, as I love you, we could both be truly happy again. And I would make you so happy... I couldn't say any of that to her though; all I could do was smile.

My grin set her off. Leaning into me, she hissed, "You were the biggest mistake of my life, Kellan. You were right—we're not friends, never were. I wish you would just go away."

I felt like she'd just reached into my chest and squeezed my heart until it burst open in her hands. Her words hurt me more than anything I'd ever heard before, and I'd heard some pretty shitty things in my lifetime. This was worse than anything my father had ever said or done to me. It was worse than hearing her have sex with Denny five seconds after me. This...destroyed me.

My smile vanished and I brushed past her to get my stuff and get the hell out of the bar. I was the biggest mistake of her life? She wanted me to go away? Fine. Then that was exactly what I would do. I would pull a Joey and get the hell out of this godforsaken city. This town was suddenly suffocating anyway.

Chapter 12

Mates' Night Out

I fell asleep staring at that stupid Ramones poster and dreaming about the day Kiera had given it to me. *I thought you might like it.* When I woke up, I felt like I hadn't slept in weeks. I was finally clear about what I had to do though. I had to leave. As soon as I had my cup of coffee, I would pack up my car and get the hell out of here. For good. *I wish you would go away. Don't worry, Kiera, I will.*

Of course, Kiera came down while I was drinking my coffee and reading the paper. I didn't look at her, and she didn't speak to me. She filled up her cup and left. But at the last minute, she tossed an "I'm sorry, Kellan" over her shoulder.

Confusion washed over me. She was sorry she wanted me out of her life, or sorry she'd told me she wanted me out of her life? My anger evaporated as her vague apology washed over me, and nothing I did could bring it back. Now, all I felt was pain. Bone-crushing pain.

I spent the next several days wallowing in depression while I weighed my options. I hardly spoke to anyone, and when I did, everything I had to say was polite and courteous. People noticed my unnatural silence, but I smiled and waved away their concerns.

Finally, one Saturday morning, Denny called me out on my

mood. I was leaning against the counter, sipping my coffee, debating my options for tonight. Maybe a distraction was what I needed…a going-away party of sorts, if that was still my plan, and I was pretty sure it was.

When Denny walked into the kitchen, I nodded a greeting. He nodded one back as he grabbed a mug from a cabinet, but he gave me sidelong glances as he pulled it down. Empty mug in hand, he turned to face me. "You all right, mate? You've been looking a bit crook lately."

I faked a casual smile. "Never been better."

Denny frowned. He'd seen me fake a smile one too many times. Setting his mug down, he crossed his arms over his chest. Clearly, he wanted a real answer from me. "What's going on with you?"

I shook my head. Most good lies were based on fact, so I ran with what I knew to be true. "I don't know. I think it's just…there's been a lot of tension in the air lately. It's getting to me."

Denny sighed and looked up to where Kiera was. "Yeah, things have been different since I got back." He returned his eyes to me. "It's my fault. I've been miserable, and I'm bringing that misery home with me." He looked away and I briefly closed my eyes so I wouldn't have to look at his face. He thought this was his fault? Out of all of us, he had the least amount of blame.

His voice was soft when he continued. "Kiera feels guilty, because I left my job for her and I hate where I am now, but…that's my fault too. I shouldn't have accepted the position in Tucson and stranded her here in Seattle. I knew she couldn't transfer again, not without losing her scholarship, and I knew she couldn't give that up. She was stuck until she was finished with school, and I knew that…and I didn't care. I wanted the job, so I took it. And then I waited days to tell her I wasn't coming back…It's little wonder she broke it off with me. I was an ass."

I cringed internally. *No, I was the ass. I should have urged her to make amends with you. But instead, I urged her to my bed.*

Denny's frown shifted to a small smile; seeing it was like a punch to the gut. "But that's all in the past now, and I don't want to dwell

166

on it anymore. I want things to go back to how they were before, so I have an idea."

I had to swallow the lump of shame in my throat. "Yeah... what's your idea?"

His smile was bright and hopeful when he told me his master plan. "We need to all go out together and unwind. Have a little fun for once. Act our age for a change." He laughed a little. "Or maybe a few years below that."

I wanted to crawl into a deep, dark hole. I'd rather chop my limbs off than hang out with my roommates right now. But... I was at a breaking point, and I couldn't stay here anymore. Hanging out with them might be the last time I ever saw them. The more I thought about it, the better it seemed. Yes, it was time for me to go. Staying in Seattle was slowly killing me. The only option left was for me to leave. I would have this one last night with my roommates, where I would try to pretend that everything was like it used to be, and then I would pack up and head out. Greener pastures awaited. Or at least, less painful ones.

"Sounds like fun, Denny. I have a friend playing at the Shack tonight. We could go listen, if you want."

I gave him a soft smile as he clapped me on the shoulder. "Perfect."

Kiera entered the room when we were standing like that. She seemed touched that we were talking; I hadn't done much of that lately. Denny looked over at her when she approached him. "Can you get someone to trade shifts with you? We're all going out tonight—mates' night out."

A small smile tried to form on her lips, but it quickly fell off her. She didn't want to do this either. "Ohhhh, that's a great idea, honey. Where are we going?"

Meeting her eye for the first time since she'd told me to go away, I filled her in on the details. She mentioned she could trade shifts with a coworker, and just like that, everything was set in place. We'd all go out together tonight. One happy family.

"Great!" Denny exclaimed, giving her a kiss. I turned away at the display. God, I hated seeing it, hated hearing it. The affection bounced off them like heat waves rising off the concrete in the middle of summer. It made me want to vomit.

Denny excused himself to go take a shower. When I was alone with Kiera, something I typically avoided, she asked, "You okay?"

I was getting tired of people asking me that. Looking over at her, I could see she was still dressed in her pajamas, her tank top tight over her small, perfect breasts. Her hair was loose around her shoulders, caressing them. And her eyes were a deep, dark green. Incredible, beautiful, and not the least bit interested in me. "Sure," I told her. "This will be…interesting."

My words worried her. She stepped closer to me as her brows furrowed. "Are you sure? This doesn't have to happen. Denny and I can go alone."

Studying her face, I watched her eyes slightly shift color in the sunlight. I loved the way they did that sometimes. Like everything else about her, I committed it to memory. Even though it was painful to remember, I didn't want to forget anything about her. "I'm fine, and I'd like to spend one…night…with my roommates." *One last night. Before I leave. Forever.*

I turned and left her then, because staying hurt too much, and tonight would be painful enough. No need to prolong the agony.

When I got to the Shack later that night, Denny's car wasn't there. I was kind of happy I'd gotten there first. It gave me a chance to prepare myself. I ordered a pitcher with three glasses, then made my way outside. The beer garden was a large fenced-in area, with a stage at one end and tables and chairs at the other. I found an empty table near a gate that led to the parking lot. I had a feeling I might need to make a quick escape later, if this got to be too much.

While I waited for Denny and Kiera, I shifted my attention to the stage, where the band was setting up. The drummer, Kelsey, was a friend of mine. The music scene in Seattle was small; everybody knew everybody. And everybody had slept with everybody. For the most part. Walking over, I raised my hand to her, and she waved back. "Hey, Kellan. How's life treating you?"

Oh God... where to begin? "Fine. You?"

Kelsey shrugged. "It's all right. Can't complain."

The singer came over. I knew him too. We'd done a few shows together when he'd been with another band. "Hey, Brendon. Good to see you again."

I stuck my hand out, and Brendon reached down and grabbed it. "Excellent. Glad you're here. It's gonna be a good show tonight."

Even though I didn't feel it, I gave him a carefree smile. "Yeah, I'm glad too."

Brendon straightened back up with a smile. "We need to do another show together soon."

I nodded, then looked over to the doors. Kiera and Denny had arrived, and I motioned to where the beer was waiting for us. They raised a hand in thanks and made their way over to the table. *And it begins...*

I looked back up at Brendon. "Yeah, let's do that." I felt slightly guilty for saying it. I was leaving after tonight. It was easier to just say yes though.

I said my goodbyes, then grudgingly returned to my table. Denny and Kiera were kissing as I approached. It was like a knife in my gut, twisting and turning. I only had to put up with it for one more night though, then I'd be free. Somehow, that thought didn't make me any happier. Sitting down, I started pouring beers. I needed a drink; surely they needed one too.

"When does your friend go on?" Denny asked me, his voice bright and chipper.

I glanced his way and tried to push aside the fact that he was diddling the woman I loved. "Another twenty minutes or so."

I took a long, much-needed drink from my beer. A girl walked past the table. Stopping, she stared at me like she expected me to leap up and ask her out. I really didn't feel like it. She stalked off when I didn't give her the time of day, and Denny noticed. "She was cute."

"Yep." I took a swig of beer and avoided any eye contact.

"Not your type?" Denny asked. Kiera fidgeted in her seat, but I ignored it.

"Nope," I answered, my beer close to my face.

There was a moment of silence, then Denny again tried to strike up a conversation with me. "How's the band going?"

"Good," I replied. Did we have to talk? Couldn't we just sit here, silently, until it was time to go home?

Denny asked a few more questions, then gave up. I could tell Kiera was annoyed at me, but I didn't care. Sitting here with them sucked ass. I was doing the best I could. Eventually the band started up, which alleviated some of the stress at the table. After a while, Denny pulled Kiera onto the dance floor. Even though I wanted to ignore them, I watched them relentlessly. They moved together perfectly, and it was obvious that dancing was something Kiera loved to do. Her flirty black skirt swirled around her body, her loose hair blew in the slight breeze. Her cheeks flushed a rosy pink that almost matched the shirt underneath her sweater-jacket. She was breathtaking, and watching her with another man was excruciating.

Girls asked me to dance, but I turned them all down. There was only one girl I wanted my hands on, and she was currently being twirled around by my best friend. Our night was just beginning, and I already wanted it over with. I couldn't do this. It was too hard.

It was getting colder outside, and I was getting colder inside. This was hell for me, and nobody seemed to notice or care. I was utterly and completely alone. I should just leave right now. Drive off with only the clothes on my back and the guitar in my car. What else did I need? Nothing.

Kiera and Denny came back from dancing, breathless and happy. I stared at my empty glass, wishing I could stick my head in it and disappear. I could feel Kiera's disapproving eyes on me, but I didn't care. *So I can't fake happiness anymore. Sue me.*

I was just thinking of excusing myself for the evening when Denny's cell phone suddenly rang. Denny answered it while I discreetly peeked up at Kiera. She hated that damn phone. More often than not, when it rang, Denny left. Kiera was frowning at Denny while trying to make it look like she wasn't upset. After a second, Denny swore and shut his phone. "Battery died." He met eyes with Kiera. Hers narrowed. "Sorry, I really need to call Max back. I'm gonna check inside, see if I can use their phone."

I returned my attention to my glass. If he was leaving, I should too. Kiera told him, "No problem, we'll be here." I could tell that she was trying not to sound agitated, and I could also tell that she was. I'd heard them arguing about Denny's boss before. Denny was doing anything he could to impress the man, and that included being his errand boy. Frowning, I wondered if I should wait for him to come back, like Kiera said, or just get up and walk out right now. What did it matter if I was gone?

Denny stood up and kissed Kiera before he left. I sighed and tried to get comfortable in my chair. It was impossible for me to feel anything other than uncomfortable though. I shouldn't be here, listening to them make out right in front of me. I was so sick of hearing their lips smacking all the time. That was another thing I wouldn't miss.

Once Denny was gone, Kiera turned her attention to me. "You said you were fine with this. What is with you?"

I met her eyes. Battling my churning emotions, I told her, "I'm having a fabulous time. What could you possibly mean?" *Watching you and Denny fawn all over each other is awesome. Just plain awesome.*

Kiera looked away, and I could tell she was struggling with her emotions as well. She looked about ready to slug someone. "Nothing, I guess."

My patience snapped. *Exactly. Nothing. I was nothing. I am nothing. And staying here and pretending nothing happened is fucking insane. Something did happen, and it meant something to me. You mean something to me, so seeing you play house with Denny while you pretend I don't exist is no picnic. It fucking sucks.*

Setting down my glass, I stood up. Staying was pointless, I was out of here. "Tell Denny that I was feeling ill…" I considered adding on to the lie, but I didn't even have it in me to do that. Let him think what he wanted. With a shake of my head, I told her, "I'm done." *I'm absolutely, completely, 100 percent done with this shit.*

As if she understood that I wasn't talking about merely hanging out tonight, that I was done with all the chaos of my life, Kiera slowly rose from the table. I narrowed my eyes as I watched her, daring her to speak. *Go ahead, call me out. I don't fucking care.* When she didn't say anything, I turned and headed out the gate. It figured that she had nothing to say.

I was halfway to my car in the parking lot when I heard the gate crash closed and heard Kiera yell my name. "Kellan! Please, wait."

There was panic in her voice, and it shot straight to my heart. *I can't wait for you when I never had you...*

Slowing, I looked over my shoulder and sighed. She was practically running to catch up to me. Why? What did she care if I left?

"What are you doing here, Kiera?" *What are you doing out here, what are you doing with me? What the fuck am I to you?*

She grabbed my arm, turning me toward her. "Wait, please stay."

I batted her arm away. She didn't have the right to touch me. She shouldn't touch me. She only cared about Denny. I saw that every time they spoke, every time they kissed. She loved him. I stared at the sky before meeting her eyes. I felt like I was losing my mind. "I can't do this anymore." *I'm going insane, because I love you, and you don't give a shit. So why are you here, staring at me like that?*

Her wide eyes searched mine. She looked scared. "Can't do what...stay? You know Denny would want to say goodbye to you." Her voice trailed off, like she knew this wasn't about Denny. Not really.

Pain gnawed at my stomach. I couldn't lie. I couldn't give her a snide response. I couldn't even laugh it off. I was drowning in pain, and truth was my only outlet. "I can't stay here...in Seattle. I'm leaving."

Just saying the words tore me apart. I didn't want to go, but staying here with her wasn't an option anymore. It would be like willingly dunking myself in boiling water. Impossible.

Tears sprang into Kiera's eyes. She grabbed my arm again and

172

held on with a fierceness I'd never seen from her before. "No, please, don't leave! Stay…stay here with…with us. Just don't go…"

She started to sob, and the tears ran down her cheeks like rivers. I'd only ever seen her this upset about Denny. When he left she'd cried like this. Why was she crying for me? No one ever cried for me. No one. "I…why are you…? You said…" I swallowed back the confusing emotions that were making speech impossible. Why was she crying? What did this mean? I didn't want to hope, but a trace amount of the feeling was bubbling up through the despair. Did she care about me? Honestly care?

I stared past her. I couldn't watch the confusing tears anymore. "You don't…you and me aren't…" *You don't care about me. I know you don't. Do you?* "I thought you…" *You love him. I was a mistake. I'm the only one who cares here, that's why it hurts so much.*

Exhaling a steadying breath, I met her eyes again. "I'm sorry. I'm sorry I've been cold, but I can't stay, Kiera. I can't watch it anymore. I *need* to leave…" My voice trailed off in a whisper as horror flashed through me. I'd told her the truth. I'd put my heart out there, and she could cut me. Again.

She looked shocked by my confession, but that was her only reaction. Grief welled in me. No, she didn't care. I turned to leave, but she yanked my body into hers and yelled, "No! Please, tell me this isn't because of me, because of you and me…"

"Kiera…" *Yes, that's exactly what this is about.*

She brought a hand to my chest and stepped closer to me. The tenderness and proximity sent a shock of desire through me. I still wanted her. I still loved her. It eased the pain, but not the confusion. "No, don't leave because I was stupid. You had a good thing here before I…"

I retreated from her by a half step. It was the farthest I could push her away, because I didn't want to push her away. I wanted her closer…so much closer. "It's not…it's not you. You didn't do anything wrong. You belong to Denny. I never should have…" I sighed as the truth hit me like a ton of bricks. This was never her fault. All this time I'd been angry at her, and I was the one to blame. I had known she loved Denny. I had known she was masking her pain with me. But she hadn't known that I loved her. She hadn't known she meant anything to me at all, so how could she possibly have known that she'd hurt me? I'd vanished right afterward, then grown cold, then grown distant. She was never mine to take. She was Denny's, and I was a bastard for ever going there. "You…you and Denny are both…"

Tears still streaming down her face, she stepped closer and pressed her body against mine. Her touch burned like fire…and I was so cold. "Both what?" she asked.

I couldn't move; I could barely breathe. I wanted her more than I'd ever wanted anyone, but this wasn't right. We weren't meant to be…but I needed her so much. "You're both…important to me," I whispered, meaning every syllable.

She brought her lips so close to mine, I could feel her breath on my face. My heart started racing. She was so close. Another inch…and she'd be mine. "Important…how?"

Say it. Just say it. Tell her that you love her. Tell her that she's all you think about, and every bad mood or dick comment you've ever made was because she hurt you. Confess, goddammit.

Why? She's with Denny. It won't change anything.

I shook my head and stepped back again. "Kiera…let me go. You don't want this…" *You don't want me.* "Go back inside, go back to Denny." *Where you belong.*

I moved my hand to pull her off me, but she batted my arm away. "Stay," she commanded.

Warmth and pain battled within me. No one had ever asked me to stay before. No one had ever shed tears over me before. She did care. She had to. But she cared about him too…and I didn't know what to do about that. "Please, Kiera, go." *Before we both get hurt even more…go.*

Her beautiful eyes were a deep emerald green in the semidarkness. They searched mine as she spoke. "Stay…please. Stay with me…don't leave *me*."

Her voice broke as she begged for herself, not for Denny. This

174

no longer had anything to do with Denny. This was about her and me. A tear rolled down my cheek, and I did nothing to stop it. She wanted me to stay with her. She cared about me. She wanted me. *Me.*

But as much as I wanted to pretend it was just the two of us in this parking lot, I knew we weren't alone. And I couldn't do that to him. He meant a lot to me. But I'd never had this... I'd never had anyone want *me.* I'd never been wanted at all. Warring with myself, I muttered, "Don't. I don't want..." *I don't want to hurt him. I don't want to hurt you. I don't want to get hurt. So what do I want?*

Her palm touched my face then, and her thumb brushed away the track of my tear. Her warmth seared me. It traveled all the way down my body, igniting me. My breath stopped as my eyes locked onto hers. I wanted her. Now. But I still couldn't do this.

Her other hand reached up to grab my neck. She pulled me until our lips brushed together. I almost crumpled to my knees, it felt so good. She closed her eyes and pressed her lips against mine again. I stiffened, but moved my lips with hers. Jesus, I'd missed this so much. I'd missed her so much. I wanted her so much. I loved her so much. But still...

"Don't do this," I whispered to myself between our hungry lips. *This will only hurt us... all three of us. Be strong enough to walk away. Stop this.* Her lips pressed harder against mine. Even as pain leached out of my throat in a whimper, my willpower dissolved. "What are you doing, Kiera?" *What am I doing?*

She paused with her lips brushing mine. "I don't know... just don't leave me, please don't leave me." The truth and pain in her voice were undeniable—*she wanted me.*

Her eyes were shut, so she couldn't see the smile on my face. *I won't. I won't ever leave you.* "Kiera... please..." *I'm yours... take me.* My resistance faded away with a shudder, and I sought her mouth. I needed her. I'd always needed her. And she wanted me to stay... she wanted me with her... she wanted me. And I was hers.

My lips parted and my tongue brushed against hers. She moaned in my mouth and feverishly tasted me again. She wanted more. I wanted more. Now that we were chucking all common sense out the window and going for this, desperation was driving us. The needy energy bouncing between us electrified me. I wanted to rip her clothes off and drive inside her. I wanted her body clutched around me. I want to feel her skin dampen with sweat, wanted to taste every inch of her, wanted her to cry out my name as she came. My body was ready for her. My heart was ready for her too.

She wanted me...

I pulled us backward as our mouths frantically moved together. There was an espresso stand in this parking lot. I'd seen it on the way to my car. Kiera and I needed privacy to keep going with this, and there was no way in hell I was stopping now. I loved her, I needed her, nothing else mattered. No one else mattered.

My back hit the door of the espresso stand. Kiera pressed me into it, her body squeezing into mine. Fire spread throughout my body, and my breath quickened as my cock hardened. I needed her so much. I slipped my hands under her shirt to feel the smooth, soft skin of her lower back. I wanted to feel more. We needed to be more alone than this.

I reached behind me to open the door. If this fucking thing wasn't open, I was going to bust the goddamn door down. One way or another, I was getting inside. Luckily, the knob twisted under my grasp. Thank God for careless employees.

Pushing away from the door, I shoved it open. Kiera and I locked eyes as our mouths broke apart. There was so much passion and desire in her gaze...it tore me. And I swear...I swear I saw something else there too. Something deeper. Something that made risking everything we were about to risk worth it. I replayed every kind word and gentle touch that she had given me. She cared. She was worth it. She was worth anything.

My body was aching. I needed to be with her. I slid my hands down her back, clutched her thighs, and picked her up. Once we were inside the dark stand, I released her and closed the door. We stood there for a moment, panting. The electricity between us grew as the darkness amplified our senses. Her arms were tight around my neck, my arm was cinched around her waist. I couldn't believe we were here, together, wanting the same thing from each other...needing the same thing.

I love you, Kiera. So much. Let me show you how much, in the only way I know how.

Holding her tight to my body, I sank us to our knees. As soon as we were steady on the floor, Kiera started attacking me, ripping clothes off my body. My chest was bare in seconds. Her fingers drifted across my body, over my nipples, along my ribs, tracing the deep lines that led all the way down to my groin. God, I wanted her hand wrapped around me. I wanted those soft, firm fingers to squeeze me, stroke me. *Please... touch me.*

A deep groan broke free from my lips, then I sucked in a quick breath. I felt like my head was spinning, like I was drunk, dizzy, overwhelmed. I'd never needed anyone so much in my life. Kiera let out an impassioned moan when I dropped my mouth to her neck. I trailed kisses across her sensitive skin while I slipped her jacket off her shoulders. She started squirming in impatience when I unbuttoned her shirt.

Even though I was doing it as quickly as I could, it wasn't fast enough for her. She ripped her shirt off and I caressed her with my eyes. God, she was perfect. Shapely, seductive, sexy as hell. I ran my palm down her skin, over her breast, down to her waist. A loud, arousing exhale broke the stillness of the air. It sent shock waves straight down my fully erect cock. *Yes...*

I ran my hand back up her skin, teasing her nipple underneath her bra. She arched into me, sought my mouth again. God, I bet she was so wet...for me...

Reaching out, I lowered her to the ground. We were in the storage area of the espresso stand. Bags of coffee beans on the shelves and along the ground made the entire place smell like our favorite morning drink. Something we shared almost every day. It seemed only fitting that we would cave in to our desire for each other here. Our relationship had practically started over coffee.

Once we were resting on the dirty floor, Kiera raked her nails along my back. I moaned my delight. *God, yes, that felt good.* She pushed my hips away so she could unbutton and unzip my jeans. We were both breathing so hard, I thought we might pass out soon. While her fingers worked, I groaned and inhaled through my teeth. *God, yes, please touch me, Kiera. Please.*

She shoved my pants down my hips, then just stared at me, straining against my underwear, desperate to be with her. *This is all for you...please, touch me.*

Then, like she'd heard my silent plea, her fingers trailed down the length of me. I dropped my forehead to hers, gasping. *God, yes...more.* Her hand curled around me, lightly pushing and pulling. *Oh God, yes...I need you. I love you.*

My lips pressed against hers, frantic. My hands scrunched up her loose skirt, then I ripped off her underwear. I needed to be inside her. Now. In my ear, she moaned, "Oh, God...please, Kellan..." She wanted me. Me. She loved me. She had to.

I shoved my underwear down, out of the way, then pushed into her. Kiera whimpered as she bit my shoulder. I buried my head in her neck, needing a minute to recover from the wet warmth throbbing around me. *Jesus...fuck...so good. You feel so good. This feels so right. I love you so much...*

Kiera raised her hips, moving me into her. Waves of pleasure rippled down me, and I pressed hard inside her, needing more. So much more. "Harder," she groaned. Grabbing her hips, I drove into her again and again. I'd never felt anything like it. The pent-up desire, the sadness, the desperation, the loneliness, the passion, it was all culminating in the best sexual experience I'd ever had. I never wanted it to end, and yet I couldn't wait to come with her.

"God, Kiera..." I murmured as our bodies rocked together. "God...yes...God, I love you..." I whispered, the sound getting lost in her skin.

She moaned and pulled me tighter. Our movements became faster, deeper, harder. I gripped her tight, knowing I was probably hurting her, but I was too close to exploding to care. Kiera thrashed underneath me, crying out again and again as the pleasure built up to an uncontainable level. Lost in the moment, I cried out too. I'd never felt a climax so strong. Every nerve ending was on fire, tingling, building up with tension that needed releasing. Kiera started moaning in an escalating rhythm. *God, yes, please, come for me... come now.*

I felt her walls constrict around me as she let out a stuttering cry. Then I felt her nails clawing down my back so hard, my skin felt wet. I inhaled a quick, pain-filled breath. The slight agony mixed with the profound pleasure drove me over the edge. I let out a deep moan and tightened my fingers around Kiera's thigh as hard as I could while my body exploded in bursts of glorious release.

My hips slowed as the euphoria lessened. For a few seconds, I felt nothing but peaceful satisfaction. I loved her. She loved me. We'd made love to each other, and it had been better than anything I'd ever felt before. I wanted to curl up in her arms, feel her stroke my hair, whisper that I loved her and that I'd never leave her. I'd stay here with her, because this was where my heart was. She was my heart.

Then I felt Kiera start to cry. No, not cry. She was sobbing. Pain-filled, remorseful sobs that screamed *Why did I just do that?*

My happiness disintegrated as I pulled back from her. I fixed my clothes, then sat back on my heels. Grabbing my shirt, I held it in my hands since I couldn't put it on yet. My back was bloody, I could feel it. She'd cut me with how badly she'd wanted me, and now she looked like she might vomit. I'd just had the most profound physical connection that I'd ever had with someone, and she looked like she was going to throw up. Because... she didn't love me. This was a mistake. Again. All I would ever be to her was a mistake. Fuck. I'd told her I loved her, and she looked like her world had just ended.

While Kiera put her underwear back on, my body shook with a cold that had nothing to do with the temperature. She dressed herself one-handed while she used her other hand to clamp her mouth shut, like if she let go, she'd immediately get sick. Anger brewed within me as I watched her put her shirt back on. God, was I so disgusting to her? Was what we'd done so repulsive?

179

When she was dressed, she sniffled and said my name. "Kellan…?"

I hadn't moved, hadn't helped her, hadn't lifted my gaze from the floor. I couldn't. I was shocked by her reaction. And angry. *She'd duped me again.* I looked up when she said my name. My eyes were wet, but I didn't care. I'd risked everything for her…my friendship with Denny, my sanity. I'd put it all on the line, because I'd believed I'd actually found someone in this world who cared about me. And here she was, devastated. She didn't care. She *still* didn't care, not like I needed her to. It killed me that I'd betrayed Denny again, for nothing. I should have gotten in my car and driven away. I could have been out of the city by now. That had been my plan; why hadn't I stuck to it?

"I tried to do the right thing. Why couldn't you just let me leave?" *Why aren't I strong enough to walk away? Why am I so fucking selfish? Why am I still in love with her?*

She started crying again. Grabbing her jacket, she stood and prepared to leave. I stared at the floor again, wishing I could crawl through it. I wanted nothing more than to disappear. Suddenly, I heard Kiera gasp. She made a move toward me, and I understood why; I could feel the blood dripping down my back. She'd just realized what she'd done to me. *Yes, Kiera. You tore me, so much deeper than you realize.*

Not looking up, I told her, "Don't. Just go. Denny has probably noticed your absence by now." *And he's the one you want to be with, right? I don't need your sympathy. I need your love. But that, you'll never give me.*

Kiera turned and fled the stand, and then I was alone. Again.

Chapter 13

Stay or Go?

I stayed in that espresso stand for what felt like hours. I heard people come and go, and had to assume that one of the cars leaving the lot had Kiera and Denny inside it. My skin stung as my shirt brushed against my cuts when I put it back on, but I welcomed the pain. It was a reminder that I was an idiot. I deserved to have my heart bashed in. Stupid, stupid, stupid.

As I walked to my car, I recalled the moments before Kiera and I had caved. She'd begged me to stay. The first girl in my life who'd asked me to stick around. The first person *ever*. Even my own parents had never asked me to come back when I'd run away. No, instead they'd sold the house, moved, and tossed all my shit. They'd thrown me away, and that was what I expected from everyone else. But Kiera...she'd cried for me. Sobbed. Her tears had been genuine...she couldn't fake emotion like that.

I stumbled to my car, disoriented by my conflicting thoughts. I hated her. I loved her. She didn't give a shit about me. She cared so much, she'd cried. *Okay...so what the fuck do I do with all of that?* And did any of it matter? She was still Denny's girl. He'd still been the one to take her home. He'd won, and a part of me wanted it that way; after what I'd done behind his back, he deserved to have it all—the career and the girl.

Climbing inside my car, I started it, then pulled out of the parking lot. I wasn't sure where to go. My options were endless, but the results were all the same. Anywhere I took off to, I would be completely alone. That really only left one option.

A set of watery hazel eyes filled my vision. *Don't leave me, please don't leave me.* She'd begged for me to stay. She'd given herself to me, even though Denny had been less than a hundred yards away. That had to mean something…and I would never know what if I left. She might very well be the first person to ever have feelings for me. She might just be confused, because she had feelings for Denny too. We'd had a real moment together tonight. We'd spoken real emotions, real fears. She wasn't playing me, she wasn't faking. She wasn't a whore or a bitch. She was confused, hurting, and scared…just like me.

My heart softening, I relaxed into my seat. What if we were more alike than I realized? What if she was only with Denny because she didn't like being alone and she didn't know any other way? Or what if she loved him, but she felt something for me too? Could I share her with him? Would that be better than nothing, better than being empty and alone? Denny could have the majority of her, but I would get small, tiny fragments…like tonight, when she'd asked me to stay. Could I live with just that much?

I wasn't sure, but I knew one thing. I couldn't leave. The pull to her was too strong now. I'd missed my window of opportunity. I was here for good now, to see this through, one way or another. And I knew it would hurt. It would probably be the death of me. But…life was overrated anyway, and a second with her was better than decades on my own. If my life was destined to be a sea of emptiness without her, then I was glad to give it up.

I headed for home through the side streets. I wanted time to think before I got there. I wanted to make sure I could do what I was planning on doing. I couldn't go back to the angry, painful dance Kiera and I had been engaged in since Denny had returned. No, if I was going to go home and stay with her, then we were going to have a *relationship*—a mutually agreed-upon one. I needed closeness. I needed to hold her, and I needed to be held by her. If she pushed me out again, this wouldn't work.

By the time I got back to the house, it was so late, it was almost time to get up. I was giddy when I walked through the front doors. Oddly, I felt completely at peace. Kiera liked me. She wanted me to be here, and so here I was. And we would all be happy and joyous again. So long as no one found out that Kiera and I had feelings for each other.

Denny woke up and ambled downstairs. A smidge of guilt seeped into me, but I pushed it aside. What I had with Kiera was more than I'd ever had in my life with anyone. I didn't want to hurt him, but I couldn't let it go. It didn't really have anything to do with him anyway.

I made a pot of coffee while Denny prepared himself a mug of tea, and we talked about random things that had nothing to do with what was happening between Kiera and me right underneath his nose. While I was sitting at the table, sipping my coffee, I heard someone running down the stairs. Denny didn't seem to notice the commotion; he was leaning against the counter, sipping his tea, and watching the TV in the living room.

Knowing that Kiera was about to step into the room any second, I glued my eyes to the entryway leading into the kitchen. Like a goddess descending from heaven, she stepped into a shaft of light as she rounded the corner. Then she stopped and stared at the odd image of Denny and I getting along like nothing had changed.

I wanted to give her a warm smile, maybe even kiss her cheek, but she was staring at me with such shock that a surge of annoyance flashed through me. She'd asked me to stay; why was she now surprised that I had? Had she changed her mind? Was she not even going to give me a chance? I smiled at her as I tried to push back the anger. I'd been holding on to that pain for so long now, but it was time to let it go. It was time to let her in. I needed to relax.

Denny turned to Kiera when he noticed her. "Good morning, sleepy. Feeling any better?"

It took her a second to peel her eyes away from me long enough so that she could answer him. That made my smile grow. At least I had her attention. "Yes, much better," she told him. I was curious what they were talking about, but then figured faking a sickness had been her excuse to get away from the bar last night.

My eyes followed her as she walked past Denny to sit at the table opposite me. She hadn't even touched him. Interesting. She studied him though, once she was seated at the table, and her face was somber and full of guilt. It was clear that she was torn, saddened by betraying him and opening herself to me. I hated that she looked that way, and it made a surge of jealousy and guilt flood through me. *No… Let it go… This isn't about Denny.*

When she was finished with Denny, she swung her eyes my way and started studying me. She didn't look happy about what she saw, and her mournful expression shifted to one of anger. Was she angry at me? Why? I hadn't forced her. In fact, she was the one who had begged me to do it, so if anyone should be feeling anger here, it should be me. Mirroring her expression, I narrowed my eyes as I studied her.

I turned away just as Denny turned to Kiera. Denny caught her sneering at me, and I couldn't contain my smile. Served her right. She could be a lot of things this morning, but angry with me wasn't one of them.

"Do you want me to make you anything to eat?" Denny asked her, genuinely concerned that she was still ill. She wasn't.

"No, that's all right. I'm really not feeling up to food yet."

I wanted to move past this awkwardness. I wanted what we'd had back. And I wanted more. She looked so damn good this morning, I was starting to get aroused just watching her. I would love to take her upstairs and put her back into bed. *My* bed.

"Coffee?" Denny asked her, pointing to the pot beside him.

Kiera's face paled as she whispered, "No." I knew she was remembering what I'd been remembering all morning—my hands on her, her hands on me, moans, groans, thrusting into her, feeling her come around me, releasing inside her. Heaven and hell. The smell of coffee was permanently linked with sex now.

Denny set down his mug and walked over to her. My heart started beating harder as he got closer. I knew what he was going to do even before he did it, and it bothered me. Leaning down, Denny tenderly kissed her forehead. I didn't want to watch, but I couldn't stop myself, and I struggled to control my emotions. All I wanted to do was growl at him to get away from her, but I had to stay silent. If Denny knew about Kiera and me, his joy wouldn't be the only thing that would be destroyed. Our friendship would be too.

"All right. Let me know when you do get hungry. I'll make you whatever you want," Denny said with a smile before heading to the living room and plopping down in front of the TV. I wanted to sigh in relief that he was gone, but my stomach was in knots. Would Kiera join him, or stay with me?

Surprising me, she stayed at the table. From the way she had her head down though, I thought maybe that was purely out of guilt. Sadly enough, I would take it. I cleared my throat, and Kiera startled like she'd forgotten I was there. That hurt. I looked over at Denny, peacefully oblivious, and that hurt too. I was the worst sort of person. I really didn't want to hurt him... I just wanted her so much. I loved her, and all I wanted was for her to love me too. Just a little bit. A fraction of her feelings for him... that was all I wanted. That wasn't too much to ask, was it?

When I returned my eyes to hers, she was studying me again. She was examining my shirt, like she was picturing me naked. Maybe she was remembering raking her nails down my skin. Maybe she wanted to do it again. I'd certainly let her. Whatever she wanted to give me, no matter how big or how small. My body was reacting to just the thought of her hands on me, and I kind of wished she could see what she was doing to me. *That's how much I want you.*

A crooked smile lifted my lips, and now that Denny was out of the room, I finally felt the jealousy and guilt slipping away. It helped to be alone with her. When it was just the two of us together, I let myself imagine for a few moments that we were the only two people concerned. Kiera's cheeks flushed with color and she looked away from me. She *had* been thinking about it then. Right now, she was thinking about being with me. She *wanted* to be with me. And damn... I wanted to take her again... regardless of what that would do to Denny. And if she was thinking about it... maybe she wanted that too.

"A little late for modesty, don't you think?" I whispered, teasing her. *If you let me, I'll tease you in a different way.*

"Have you lost your freaking mind?" she hissed, trying to be quiet but failing. I smiled a little wider. *Yes, it's quite possible I have. Love does that.* Calming herself, she asked, "What are you doing here?"

I tilted my head to the side as I played with her. What I wouldn't give to *really* play with her. "I live here... remember?" *You can have me every night, if you want.*

Kiera almost looked like she wanted to slug me. She laced her fingers together though. "No, you were leaving... remember? Big, brooding, dramatic exit... ringing any bells?"

Her tone was so sarcastic, I couldn't help but laugh. She was so cute when she was irritated. I could calm her down if she'd just go upstairs with me. "Things changed. I was very compellingly asked to stay." Smiling, I bit my lip. *Ask me to stay right now, Kiera. Let's go in the other room, and I can show you again how much I want to be with you.*

She closed her eyes and held her breath. Her face right at that second reminded me of last night, when she'd been overwhelmed with need for me. *I could scratch your itch, Kiera. I'm ready. Are you?*

"No. No, there are no reasons for you to be here." She opened her eyes, took in my smile, then glanced behind her at Denny, still oblivious in the other room.

As much fun as playing with her was, I knew I needed to let her know that I was serious. That I was staying, because she'd asked. That I needed her, and I knew she needed me too. She was just too damn stubborn to admit it. Leaning in, I told her, "I was wrong before. Maybe you do want this. It's worth it to me to stay and find out." *You're worth everything to me. Everything. If it came down to it, even my friendship with Denny.*

She sputtered for something to say, like I'd just told her I was an alien or something. "No!" was all she came up with. After a second, she gathered herself and added, "You were right. I want Denny. I choose Denny."

She was pleading, but I really couldn't tell if she was pleading with me or with herself. And if there was a grain of doubt in her mind, then I couldn't walk away. Doubt inside her was hope inside me.

Smiling, I reached out, touched her cheek, and traced a line across her succulent mouth. Almost instantly she reacted to me. Her breath quickened, her eyes half closed, and her lips parted when I brushed against them. I knew if I continued exploring her body, I'd find her just as ready for me as I was for her.

With a great deal of willpower, I stopped myself. I had to chuckle at her reaction. *Be as stubborn as you want, your body doesn't lie.* "We'll see," I said, forcing my hand to return to *my* lap, when all it wanted to do was explore hers.

Irritated, Kiera jerked her head Denny's way. "And him?"

My vision sank to the table. Yes… Denny. No matter how I spun the situation, I was betraying Denny. Hurting him wasn't something I wanted to do, which was why I was okay with keeping this a secret, keeping it just between us. If Denny didn't know what we were doing, Kiera could keep him. If she chose. Whatever she wanted to do with her boyfriend was up to her.

Hating what I had to say, I told her, "I had a lot of time to think last night." I peeked back up at her. "I won't hurt him unnecessarily. I won't tell him, if you don't want me to." *I'll keep quiet about this forever, if you never want him to know that you share your life with both of us. Whatever will make this easier for you. Whatever you want. So long as I get a part of you, no matter how small, I'll be happy.*

Her answer was immediate. "No, I don't want him to know." She looked pained by that admission. I understood. I hated that Denny was a part of this at all, but unfortunately he was. But their relationship would be separate from ours, and I was… trying to be okay with that. Kiera didn't appear to share my acceptance. She looked torn and confused. "What do you mean... unnecessarily? What do you think we are now?" she asked.

My smile came back to me as I reached across the table to hold her hand. It felt so nice to hold her again. Once she got over the shock and the guilt, she'd remember how great it felt to touch me, how amazing the connection we had was.

She flinched and tried to pull her hand away, but I securely held it as I stroked her fingers. She needed to remember how easy it was to hold me. That was the only way we could return to how we were. "Well... right now, we are friends." I ran my eyes up and down her body, wishing we were completely alone again. "Good friends." *And so much more. Let me in, and I can be your everything.*

She gaped at me, then she got angry. "You said we weren't friends. Just roommates, remember?"

I knew I couldn't explain everything that I was feeling to her, not when she was still clouded with guilt, so I playfully told her, "You changed my mind. You can be very... persuasive." Not able to resist, I lowered my voice and asked her, "Would you like to persuade me again sometime?" *Maybe right now? I would love to run my hands over your body again, hear you pant my name, feel you clench around my body. I'd love to make love to you. I'd love to take care of you. Just give me a chance.*

She stood up so fast she scraped the chair against the floor. I let go of her hand, but I wasn't about to let go of her. She'd have to forcefully send me away this time, and I knew she wouldn't. Not anymore.

Her abrupt movement got Denny's attention. "You okay?"

Looking flustered and embarrassed, Kiera called back, "Yes. Just going upstairs to take a shower. I have to get ready for work... for Emily's shift."

I immediately pictured her soaking wet—her dark hair slicked back, soapy bubbles sliding between her breasts. My jeans started getting uncomfortable as I let my fantasy run away with me. While she glanced back at Denny, who had already turned back to the TV,

I quietly asked her, "Would you like me to join you? We could continue our... conversation."

She glared at me, so I took her response to my playful suggestion as a no.

While she went upstairs and took a shower, I sipped on my coffee. My every thought swirled around her as I absentmindedly watched the TV show Denny was watching. I pictured her undressing, I pictured her turning on the water, I imagined her stepping inside, goose bumps on her skin until the searing water soothed them. I pictured her hands running over every curve. With that lewd movie playing in my head, sitting still at the kitchen table was difficult; all I wanted to do was go upstairs and join her. I could tease her with soft caresses, gentle kisses. Rile her up until she begged me to take her again. I'd love to do that... but not while Denny was here. That felt too far over the line, and I'd already stepped farther than I'd ever intended. It was too late to go back now though, so all I could do was be as good as I could be when he was around, and a charming but devilish bastard whenever he wasn't.

Addicted

Once things calmed down around the house, I relaxed, but I had the hardest time stopping myself from relentlessly flirting with Kiera at every opportunity. I couldn't help it. Even if Denny was around I did it, which always made me feel a little guilty afterward.

I touched her in intimate places, kissed the back of her neck and shoulders, and mentally undressed her with my eyes. I just wanted her to touch me back...kiss me...make love to me again. It was all I thought about. I had Kiera on the brain twenty-four/seven.

And I knew Kiera felt the same, even though she resisted, even though she pushed me away. Her body reacted to every place I touched her. Just running my fingers across her shoulder blades nearly gave her an orgasm. It was fun to watch, and it made the anticipation that much stronger. I knew, with the passion between us, that the next time we were together, it would be explosive. I was addicted to Kiera, plain and simple, and I couldn't get enough.

She called me out on my change of behavior. Shivering under my caress one morning, she pushed me away, and with an irritated tone of voice, said, "You are so...moody. I can't keep up with you."

She had a cute glare on her face. It quickly slipped off though, like she was afraid she'd angered me. I supposed I did seem moody to her. I had been icy cold after our first time, and now I was fiery hot. But I'd loved her the entire time, and she'd been very misleading with her feelings, so if I was moody, it was only because she made me that way. Smiling, I playfully told her, "I'm an artist...not moody."

Her lips pursed into a perfect pout. I wanted to suck on them. "Well, then you're a moody artist." Under her breath, she added, "You're practically a girl."

Amused by her comment, I backed her into the counter and pressed my body against hers. It felt so good to be so close to her. It reminded me of our first time. My half mast hardened in an instant, and grabbing her leg, I hitched it around my hip so she could feel me. Running my hand up her back, I pulled her flush against me. In her ear, I breathed, "I assure you...I am not."

My lips trailed down her neck, tasting her, teasing her. She pushed against me, but it was a weak attempt, with no real effort behind it. She wanted this. "Please...stop..." she whimpered.

Even as she said it, she minutely exposed her neck to me, begging for one last kiss. I fulfilled her unconscious request, sucking hard on the skin I loved to touch. Then I pulled away with a sigh. Her eyes were slightly unfocused as she gazed at me. "All right," I told her. "But only because you begged. I love it when you do that."

It sprinkled a few days later, and I knew Kiera wasn't big on rain, no matter how light it was, so I decided to do the gentlemanly thing, and I showed up at her school to offer her a ride home. But honestly, being a gentleman wasn't the real reason why I drove out there with a huge smile on my face. I'd missed giving her rides. It was a part of our old routine that I wanted to start up again.

When she spotted me, her breath caught. I didn't know if that was because she was happy to see me, since I hadn't been here for a while, or if she was upset. I hoped it wasn't the latter. I wanted to tease her, to break down the wall of resistance between us, but I didn't want to hurt her.

She rolled her eyes after I smiled, so I figured she wasn't as happy to see me as I was her. I hoped she would accept my invitation instead of being obstinate. It wasn't like I was going to shove her in my car, lay her down on the seat, and have my way with her. Unless she wanted me to, of course.

Kiera walked over to my car like she was trudging through a swampy mire. I took it as a good sign that at least she was headed my way. Pearls of dew lined the hair around her face and small beads had collected on her eyelashes and lips. She was gorgeous.

When her inquisitive eyes looked up at me, I said in a smooth voice, "I thought you might want a ride."

"Sure, thanks. I'm going to Pete's." Her tone was light and breezy, but nothing else about her was. She was breathing faster and she kept staring at my lips and hands, like she was debating which one she wanted on her first.

I had to smile at her body's betraying actions, and at her choice of destination. Her shift wasn't for a few hours. It was pretty clear that she was only going there to make sure she wasn't alone in the house with me.

After opening her door with dramatic flair, I walked around to my side. Kiera was staring at me as I sat down. She tensed up when we pulled away from school, and I couldn't help but wonder what she thought we would do along the way. I'd do anything she asked.

She suddenly glanced at the backseat and her cheeks filled with color. Was she picturing us back there? There was plenty of room, and I could make her very comfortable, if she wanted me to. Curious what she would say, I laughingly asked her, "You okay?"

She faced the front and squeaked out, "Yep." *Sure. Liar.*

"Good," I said, letting her lie go.

We stopped at a red light and I looked over to give her a friendly smile. She started breathing so hard she was almost panting. I was certain she wanted me to touch her, she was nearly bursting at the seams for it. It turned me on, but I resisted. I didn't want her to know when it was coming. I wanted to catch her unaware so I could drive her over the edge, so she'd stop this charade and let me in.

When the light turned green, Kiera turned to stare out the window. She seemed like she was deep in thought. I wondered if she was thinking about me. Since now seemed like a good time for it, I put my hand on her knee and slid it midway up her inner thigh. She closed her eyes, and I felt fire coursing through me as my desire for her kicked into overdrive.

Her breaths became long, slow, like she was forcing herself to calm down. She kept her eyes closed the entire trip; they were still closed when I parked the car. There was so much I wanted to do to her. I wanted to kiss her. I wanted to lay her down. I wanted to make her cry out with need. I wanted to whisper how much she meant to me, how much I loved her. I wanted everything.

I unbuckled my seat belt and slid across the seat to her. The sides of our bodies pressed together, and her slow breaths increased. She was so ready for me. I was ready for her too. I shifted my hand so that it was all the way up her thigh, my pinkie resting against the inner seam of her jeans—so close to where I wanted to be. A lascivious sigh escaped her as her mouth dropped open. God, she wanted me, but she was still resisting this. She had to accept us before we could make love again. I'd have to settle for just teasing her right now.

I ran my cheek along her jaw. I could feel her struggling to not cave in to me, to not turn her head and find my lips. I kissed the very corner of her jaw, then lightly ran my tongue up to her ear. She was trembling, I was throbbing. I nibbled on her ear, wishing it were her nipple. "Ready?" I breathed.

Her eyes flashed open and locked on mine. Her breath was heavy with desire, but she was clearly panicked by my question. Her gaze lowered to my mouth as she turned her face to mine. Mere inches separated our lips now. It took a tremendous amount of willpower, but I made myself not kiss her. I needed her to cave before I kissed her, but God, not doing it was difficult.

Shifting my focus, I unbuckled her seat belt. Knowing this was nowhere near what she expected, a playful laugh escaped me as I pulled away. Sure enough, my tease frustrated her. Irritated, she shoved open her door, then slammed it closed. I couldn't help but grin at the annoyed, embarrassed look on her face before she stormed off toward the bar.

Sorry, Kiera, but if you want more, you have to ask for it. And this time, you have to mean it.

Kiera practically attacked me the next morning, but not in the way I wanted her to. She cut off my cheerful greeting by ramming her finger in my chest. Having her initiate contact between us made me smile as I returned the coffeepot to its base.

"You need to back off!" she demanded, her face a mixture of desire and irritation.

Grabbing her hand, I pulled her into my arms, where she belonged. "I haven't done anything to you... recently." *But I'd love to, if you'd just let me.*

She made a show of trying to get away from me, but it wasn't enough to break my grasp. She'd have to try a lot harder to push me away. I wasn't going anywhere anymore. Her lips pursed in an expression of annoyance, she glanced at her arms trapped under mine. "Uhhh...this?"

A small laugh left me as I kissed her jaw and nuzzled against her. She felt so good in my arms. Amazing. "We do this all the time. Sometimes we do more..." *We could do more now. I could take you upstairs, undress you, ravish you. I could make you happy.*

Kiera wasn't on the same page as me. Flustered, she sputtered, "The car?"

I laughed harder at that response. "That was all you. You were getting all...excited on me, just sitting there." Squatting down, I met her gorgeous hazel eyes. "Was I supposed to just ignore that?" *How could I possibly ignore you?*

Her face filled with color, and she turned away from me with a sigh. She knew I was right. She knew she wanted me. She kept avoiding the truth, but that didn't make it go away.

I knew I should be honest with her, tell her everything in my heart, but I couldn't go there. Just the thought of opening up, letting her in, made my insides twist into painful knots. I'd rather stick

194

myself in the eye with a dozen needles. No, teasing her was all I was comfortable with, so that was what I did.

"Hmmm...do you want me to stop?" I traced a line from her hair to her cheek, down her neck, right between her breasts, and down to her hips. Like a flower turning toward the sun, her body opened under my touch. It was so subtle, she probably wasn't even aware she was arching toward me, but I knew women. I could read their body language better than my own. And Kiera's was screaming *Take me*.

Her eyes closed as her breath quickened. "Yes," she breathed. *Exactly, Kiera. Say yes to me.*

In a low voice, I told her, "You don't seem so sure...do I make you uncomfortable?"

I ran my finger along the inside of her waistband and watched her face while she struggled to not let me see how much she enjoyed it. I was sure she was ready for me. I'd just have to move my hand a bit and I'd feel it. God, I wanted to. I wanted her so much.

"Yes," she whispered. Her voice was almost pleading more than rejecting.

Leaning in, I whispered in her ear, "Do you want me inside you again?"

Her answer was instant. And surprising. "Yes..."

Her eyes snapped open as she came out of the mini-trance I'd coaxed her into. Her eyes were wide, like she was terrified I'd take her up on her suggestion without giving her a second to reconsider. "No! I meant no!"

I couldn't help but smile at the expression on her face. She was flushed, from either embarrassment or desire. I tried not to laugh at her, but when anger flooded her face and she repeated, "I meant no, Kellan," one brief laugh escaped me.

"Yes, I know—I know exactly what you meant." *You want to say yes, but you're not ready.*

When I saw Kiera again that afternoon, when she got back from school, she seemed spent. She was sitting on the couch, staring at the TV, but she obviously wasn't watching it. She didn't seem to no-

195

tice me standing at the edge of the room, staring at her. Definitely tired then. She usually knew the instant I was looking at her. As I approached the couch, I wondered if I was to blame for her exhaustion. I hoped not.

Without looking, she started to stand when she felt the cushion compress beside her, like she knew it was me and she didn't want to be anywhere near me. Her reluctance combined with her stubbornness was amusing. Grabbing her arm, I pulled her back down. Things wouldn't move forward between us if she ignored me.

She looked my way with narrowed eyes, obviously unhappy that I was forcing us to spend time together. She crossed her arms over her chest, further letting me know just how put out she was. Did she realize how cute she was right now? She looked away from my adoring smile. Shaking my head, I wrapped an arm around her shoulders. She immediately stiffened but didn't pull away. Until I started pulling her toward my lap—then she jerked away like I'd poured ice water down her back.

I startled at her sudden movement and icy glare. I just wanted her to rest on me, like she used to. I wasn't sure why she was having such a violent reaction until I understood what she thought I'd been implying. I started laughing, even more amused.

Pointing to my lap, I assured her that I meant nothing sordid by the gesture. "Lie down...you look tired." Not able to help myself, I playfully added, "But if you wanted to, I wouldn't stop you."

Frowning, she elbowed me in the ribs. At least she realized I was joking. I grunted at the minor pain, then pulled her back to my lap. "So stubborn," I muttered as she finally let me lay her down.

She twisted to her back, and I gazed at her and stroked her dark hair. She was so beautiful, and so unaware of it. She was unaware of a lot of things. Like how much she meant to me, how different she was from every other girl I'd ever met, how I'd do absolutely anything for her. Even leave, if she changed her mind and asked me to. I hoped she never asked me to.

"See...that wasn't so bad, was it?" I asked her. *We could have this every day again, if you'd just let me back in...*

196

Kiera studied me while I stared at her with open longing. Did she see how much I wanted this? Was it apparent on my face? Would she understand if she saw it? She was so naïve, so inexperienced. It made me believe that Denny was the only person she'd been with, the only person she'd opened up to. Maybe she really had no idea what she was doing, how much she affected me. Even though I knew I had no right to ask, curiosity compelled me to.

"Can I ask you something, without you getting angry?"

I was sure she'd say no, but surprisingly, she nodded. I couldn't meet her eye as I asked my horrible, invasive question. I studied my fingers running through her hair instead. "Was Denny the only man you'd been with?"

By her voice, I could tell she was annoyed that I'd asked her that. I didn't blame her. It was none of my business. "Kellan, I don't see how that's—"

I interrupted her with another jackass request. "Just answer the question." *Please. I know I have no right to ask, but I need to know... are Denny and I the only two people you've been with? Is that why you can't let him go?*

She seemed confused as she looked me over. I felt a little pathetic, so I was sure I looked it too. "Yes... until you, yes. He was my first..."

I nodded. I knew that. He was her first love, her first time, her first... everything. That's why she was so deeply bound to him, why sharing her affections with me was so difficult for her, why just the thought of him leaving her sent her into near-hysterics. He was a part of her, down to her core. How could I possibly compete with that kind of history? I couldn't. And I didn't need to. I didn't need to have *all* of her... just a tiny bit would do. A fraction of her warmth, a fraction of her love. I could be happy with that...

Kiera's soft voice broke my train of thought. "Why would you want to know that?"

My hand in her hair paused as I stared at her. Keeping my smile plastered in place, I considered telling her the real reason why. *I love you, but I know Denny has your heart. Most of it, anyway. I was just curious if there was a chance for you to love me more than him. But there isn't. And that's okay. So long as I have this much, it's okay if he has the rest.*

I couldn't say that, so I said nothing and continued stroking her hair. Like she sometimes did, Kiera seemed to know that I couldn't answer her, so she didn't press me. She relaxed against me, and my mind started spinning as we stared at each other. I wanted so much to be the one and only in her eyes, but that wasn't going to happen. Even if she and Denny did separate, that wouldn't happen. He was too much a part of her. But she cared about me... we had *something*, and I would cling to that for as long as I possibly could.

While I watched, Kiera's eyes filled to the brim with tears. The green depths shimmered at me, and the pain behind them was unmistakable. I frowned as I wiped away a tear that had rolled down her cheek. Why was she crying? "Am I hurting you?" I asked, hoping that I wasn't; I didn't ever want to cause her pain.

"Daily," she whispered.

And there it was. My flirting with her, teasing her, playing with her... trying to kindle the fire between us so she'd accept us... was hurting her. I was a bastard, yet again. "I'm not trying to hurt you. I'm sorry."

Her brows scrunched together as she snapped, "Then why are you? Why don't you leave me alone?"

My heart felt like she'd just tightened a vise around it. *You begged me to stay. You cried for me. You made love to me. How can I possibly leave you alone after that? When I love you more than anything else in this world? I just want a part of you, is that too much to ask?* I frowned, hoping she wouldn't tell me it was over... completely over. "Don't you like this... being with me? Even... just a little?" *Please say yes. I can't handle it if you say no.*

She hesitated, like she wasn't sure what to say, then her entire expression relaxed, as if she'd accepted the truth. Finally. "Yes, I do... but I can't. I shouldn't. It's not right... to Denny."

Even though I was relieved by her answer, I didn't feel happy. *Denny.* Yes, she was right about that. It wasn't fair to him. None of this was. "True..." I said, nodding. I could only truly share her with him if he agreed too, and he never would. What sort of man would say yes to something like that? *What sort of asshole would ask his best friend and the girl of his dreams to enter into a twisted relationship like that?* My fingers paused in her hair. "I don't want to hurt you... either of you." *You both mean so much to me...*

We watched each other for several long minutes. I wasn't sure what she was thinking as she watched me studying her. My mind was a jumble. Denny was innocent in all of this, and he deserved better, but I couldn't give up my true love. Not entirely.

Kiera and I could still have an intimate relationship, but it would be purely emotional, not sexual. I would sacrifice the sexual aspect and wouldn't push her to sleep with me. I would respect that part of her and Denny's relationship, and Kiera and I would go back to the nonsexual contact that we'd had while Denny was gone. Then I would get to keep the closeness that I really needed from her. And if we weren't being sexual, then we wouldn't have to feel guilty anymore. This could work.

Or it could backfire... and we'd all lose.

"I'll leave it at this. Just flirting. I'll try not to be inappropriate with you. Just friendly flirting, like we used to..."

She seemed surprised by my suggestion. And I suppose it was absurd, but... I needed her to agree to it. I needed this. "Kellan, I don't think we should even... not since that night. Not since we've..."

I smiled that she still couldn't say it. The memories of our intimacies flooded through me, but I let them flow right out. I could give that up, if it meant I got to keep her. I stroked her cheek, wishing it was more, but knowing it never could be. "I need to be close to you, Kiera. This is the best compromise I can offer you." A burst of wickedness flashed through me, and the words escaped my mouth before I could stop them. "Or I could just take you right here on the couch."

Stiffening on my lap, it was clear she didn't find my suggestion funny. "I'm joking, Kiera." I sighed.

199

She shook her head. "No, no you're not, Kellan. That's the problem. If I said okay…"

I smiled as the thought of making love to her again clouded my senses. "I would do whatever you asked." *Anything. Everything. Just say yes.*

She looked away from me, exposing her neck. I trailed my finger along her cheek, down to her collarbone, and then to her waist again. She was so beautiful…Kiera looked back at me with a sharp glare, and I gave her a sheepish grin. This was going to be harder than I thought. Much harder.

"Oops…sorry. I *will* try." *I promise. Just give me a chance. Things were so good between us before. I want that back. No, I need it. Please, Kiera.*

She didn't say yes, but she didn't object anymore either. I took that as a sign that she was considering it. I hoped so. I resumed stroking her hair, and eventually the repetitive motion lulled her to sleep. I smiled as I watched her eyes close. As much fun as it was to rile her up, to leave her squirming with desire and panting for breath, having her like this, calm and peaceful, was nice too, in a different way. I wanted to experience every emotion with her. Well, all the good ones at least.

When it was clear she was deeply asleep, I shifted her off my lap and stood up. She was still sleeping, but she had a frown on her face, like she missed me. I wondered if she'd dream about me. The thought made me incredibly happy. I wanted to invade her subconscious, just like she'd invaded mine. Leaning down, I scooped her up. She sighed in contentment and nuzzled her face against my chest. I closed my eyes and savored the moment. We could be so great together, if she'd just let me in. And maybe now she would begin to. Really, that was all I could ask of her.

I tucked her into her bed, then stared at her for the longest time. If she woke up and found me watching her like this, she'd probably think I was mentally disturbed. I wasn't. Just in love. It felt good to admit that. If only I could admit it to her, then maybe she'd have an easier time believing that I wasn't using her, or only interested in sex. It went so much deeper than that. But I couldn't say those things. The words just wouldn't come.

I left her sleeping in her room and headed out to go meet up with the guys. We had a gig tonight at Razors, and I was actually looking forward to it. I felt hopeful, for the first time in a while, and it lightened my heart, and my mood. I was joking around with Matt when Evan asked me about it. "You seem different. Not as melancholy as you were a while ago," he said. "Something happen?"

Shrugging, I nodded over at Griffin. He'd just taken a drum off the van, and he was looking around like he had no idea what to do with it now. "Yeah. Clueless over there is actually lending a hand for once. That's a modern-day miracle. Who knows what could happen next? World peace. The end of hunger. The Huskies and the Cougars getting along. Anything is possible. Except maybe that last one."

I laughed as I pulled a guitar out of the van. Evan narrowed his eyes but didn't ask me anything else. I kind of felt bad for avoiding his question, but I couldn't tell him the truth. I was in love with Kiera. She *saw* me. She understood me. Well, she understood the parts of me I let her see. She meant everything to me, and wrong as it was, I couldn't wait to see her again.

The next morning, Kiera came downstairs while the coffee was brewing. She hadn't done that in a while. She'd been avoiding being alone with me, and as far as I knew, she hadn't had coffee since the espresso stand; I still couldn't think of coffee without thinking of her moaning beneath me. It was a damn shame that was over with.

I turned to greet her when I heard her enter the room. Her hair was messy and disheveled from sleeping, and she was still wearing her pajamas—lounge pants and a tank top. As usual, she wasn't wearing a bra with it, and her firm breasts were clearly outlined beneath the tight fabric; her nipples were rigid peaks in the early morning chill. She was breathtaking. And completely oblivious to that fact, which made her even more enchanting.

"Mornin'. Coffee?" I asked, pointing to the pot.

She gave me a dazzling smile that made my heart skip a beat, then she slipped her arms around my waist, making my heart beat harder. Her touch surprised me so much, I stiffened before I relaxed into her embrace. God, it felt amazing to have her arms around me again. I never wanted to let her go.

Her gorgeous eyes were a tranquil green this morning when she looked up at me. "Good morning. Yes, please." She indicated the coffeepot with her head.

Peace washed through me as I gazed down at her. *Yes, this was what I really wanted.* "You aren't going to fight me on this?" I asked, pulling her closer.

She gave me a smile that matched the calmness I was feeling. "No…I missed this."

I leaned in to place a soft kiss on her neck, but she gently pushed me back. "We do need ground rules though…"

I laughed, wondering what rules she'd come up with. Besides no sex. That one was a given. "Okay…fire away."

She pointed out the one I was thinking about first. "Well, besides the obvious one, that you and I aren't ever…" She blushed, unable to complete her thought. So cute.

Unable to resist, I teasingly drawled out, "Having…hot…sweaty…sex? Are you sure you don't want to rethink that? We're pretty amazing—"

She thumped me on the chest in answer. With a bewitching glare she told me, "Besides that obvious one, no more kissing…ever."

My smile dropped. Well, that sucked. I liked kissing her, liked tasting her skin. Even if it wasn't on the lips, it was incredibly enjoyable for me. And as long as it wasn't on the mouth, I really didn't see the problem with it. Maybe I could get her to see it my way. "What if I just stay away from your lips? Friends kiss."

She frowned, then shivered. "Not like you do."

I sighed, hating that she was taking that away, but too happy that we were finally on the same page to really care. At least I'd still get to hold her every morning. "Fine…anything else?"

With a saucy smile, she stepped away from me. Like her body was a game show prize, she showcased her breasts and her hips.

That was a game I wouldn't mind playing. "Off-limits...don't touch," she told me, a playful but serious note to her voice.

I could have guessed that much, and it was unfortunate, but I exaggerated my disappointment as I told her, "God, you're sucking all the fun out of our friendship." I reversed my expression into a smile, so she'd know I was playing with her. "Okay...any other rules I should know about?"

I opened my arms and she stepped right into them. Heaven. Her eyes searched my face. "This stays innocent, Kellan. If you can't do that, we end this."

I could tell she was looking for some sign that I couldn't handle this. I could. If it was this or nothing, I could handle anything. I pulled her head to my shoulder and hugged her tight. "Okay, Kiera." *I love you. So much. Whatever you're willing to give, I'll take.*

Pulling back, I playfully pushed her away from me and said, "That goes for you too, you know." I pointed to my lips, then pointed to my crotch. "Don't touch." She rapped me on the chest again and I added with a laugh, "Unless you really, really want to..."

When she smacked me again, I pulled her in for a hug. Sharing this with her was amazing. Being with her was amazing. She was amazing. I would take a lifetime of pain if I knew I'd get moments like this. *This* made it all worth it.

Kiera was relaxed in my arms, accepting our connection. However strange it was, it worked for us. She jerked to alertness when the phone rang though. She looked up at the ceiling before dashing over to pick up the receiver, and I knew why. Denny. The cloud of potential pain and guilt literally hovering above our heads. We could only have this closeness and intimacy when he was asleep, or gone. I knew why it had to be that way, but still, it stung. As much as I loved and respected Denny, a part of me would always want what he had.

Kiera bent over the counter when she picked up the phone. Her ass on full display for me was too much. A small laugh escaped me as I thought about all the things I could do to her in that position. I knew I shouldn't think those thoughts about her, since we were keeping this "innocent," but she was perfection. Dirty thoughts were hard to keep out.

Straightening, Kiera spun around. She put a hand on her hip as she pouted. The expression did nothing to realign my indecent thoughts, but I made a swift halo over my head. *I may think dirty things about you, but I won't act on them. I'll be as much of a gentleman as humanly possible.*

Kiera smiled as she leaned back on the counter. "Hi, Anna." I started preparing our coffees while Kiera spoke to her sister.

"Isn't it a little early for phone calls?" Kiera said into the phone. She was silent while I poured some creamer into her cup, then she said, "No, I'm up."

I stirred Kiera's coffee while she laughed at something her sister said. "No, hot-bod is awake too." I looked over in time to see Kiera cringe and look my way. Hot-bod? Really? Did she mean me? Raising an eyebrow, I mouthed the word as I pointed to myself. Rolling her eyes, Kiera nodded. I had to laugh at the nickname, and wondered who had come up with it first—Kiera or her sister?

My eyes glued on Kiera, I took a sip of coffee. A playful grin grew on her lips, and I wondered what she was thinking about. Nonchalantly, she told her sister, "We were screwing on the table, waiting for the coffee to brew."

I nearly choked to death on my coffee as I spat it back into the cup. I could not believe she'd just said that. I was becoming a bad influence on her. Or a really, really good one, depending on how you looked at it. My dirty thoughts instantly returned, and Kiera turned her face away from my grin; her cheeks were flushed.

"Geez, Anna, I'm just joking. I would never touch him like that. You should hear about all the girls he's been with. Ugh, he's disgusting…and Denny is asleep upstairs, you know."

She looked up at the ceiling, up to Denny, and my eyes drifted to the floor. *He's disgusting.* So…that was what she really thought of me? My lifestyle repulsed her. I repulsed her. On some level, I was dirty and disgusting to her. I knew she had to think that. I was, after all, completely unworthy of her. She should run back to Denny and never give me the time of day again. That would be the smart thing for her to do.

Setting down my coffee, I started to leave, but Kiera reached out and grabbed my arm. Feeling sad and defeated, I looked her way. *You should just let me go.* Staring intently into my eyes, she said into the phone, "Everything is fine." I knew by her tone she wasn't just answering some random question her sister had asked, she was letting me know that she hadn't meant what she'd said.

She pulled my arm around her waist, and I needed her too much to resist her. Even if she thought I was a hideous beast, it didn't change the fact that I needed the connection I felt when I was with her.

Relaxing, I smiled and held her tight against me as we both leaned against the counter. A bright red stain highlighted her cheeks while she stared at me. I wanted to know why, but didn't ask her since she was on the phone. I'd like to think that she'd thought something about me though, something good.

I tried not to listen as Kiera finished up her phone call, but from what I did catch, the sisters were making plans to meet up. And Kiera wasn't entirely thrilled about it. She cursed when she finally hung up the phone.

When she asked me not to share her swear with Griffin, I shrugged. I never actually told Griffin things about Kiera anyway. "What's wrong?" I asked, smiling.

In a forlorn voice, she told me, "My sister. She wants to visit."

I scrunched my brows. I'd pieced that together, but not the reason for her reluctance. "Okay...and, you don't like her?"

Rubbing my arms, she shook her head. "No, no I do. I love her, dearly, but..."

She averted her eyes and I tried to regain contact with her. "But what?"

With a defeated expression, she looked at me again. "You're kind of man-flavored candy to my sister."

205

I laughed. Guess her sister was interested. And by Kiera's description, her sister was far more aggressive than she was. Well, it didn't matter much to me. Kiera was the only woman around in my eyes. "Ahhh...so I'm pretty much going to be attacked, right?" I laughed again, picturing having to keep Kiera's sister at bay. This would be interesting.

Kiera wasn't as amused as I was. "It's not funny, Kellan."

I gave her a warm smile. "It kind of is, Kiera." The sister I wanted couldn't give all of herself to me, but the one I wasn't interested in was already willing to rip her panties off. I found that highly amusing, in a twisted way.

Kiera seemed to sadden more and more. Even though she looked away, I saw tears forming in her eyes. I still had no idea why she was so upset. What did it matter if her sister came out here? What did it matter if she was all over me? My heart was Kiera's alone. Fully and completely.

Tucking a strand of hair behind her ear, I murmured, "Hey..." Gently grabbing her chin, I made her look at me. "What do you want me to do?" *I'll do whatever you want. Just ask.*

She looked like she was fighting with herself, wrestling with whether or not to be honest with me. I wanted her to. I wanted to understand the problem here. I couldn't do the right thing in her eyes if I didn't know what it was. "I want you to not '*do*' her. I don't want you to even touch her."

She glared at me, and I began to understand. She was jealous. She thought I'd sleep with her sister, since I couldn't sleep with her. As if I would want a pale imitation of the real thing. As if I could stomach being with anyone else, when Kiera was all that existed to me. I wasn't sure how long I could go without sex...but I *knew* how long I could go without Kiera. And it wasn't very long. I wasn't going to do anything that might push her away. Touching her sister... wasn't even a thought in my brain.

"Okay, Kiera," I said, brushing her cheek.

Not understanding the depth of my agreement, her eyes filled with tears. "Promise me, Kellan."

206

I gave her as reassuring a smile as I could. "I promise, Kiera. I won't sleep with her, okay?" *You're the only one I want.* It took her a moment, but she finally nodded and let me pull her in for a hug.

You're the only one I'll ever want.

Chapter 15

Heaven and Hell

The last several days with Kiera had been amazing. It was just like it had been before, but different. Before, we'd flirted, but we'd never acknowledged the flirting. We'd never even talked about it. Now though, there was innuendo in the air, and I was able to hold her, flirt with her, and tease her about it. It changed things, amplified our relationship. There was nothing innocent about our flirting now, but Kiera seemed comfortable with it, so I didn't point out to her that there was enough sexual tension between us to power a small city. She had to know anyway, she just didn't want to admit it.

Staring at my ceiling, I replayed the dream I'd just awoken from. Kiera had been in the kitchen, making me a lunch before I went off to work. After handing me the bag, she'd looked deep into my eyes and told me, *"I love you so much, Kellan. I don't know what I would do without you."*

I wanted her to say that to me for real, so badly. Smiling into the darkness, I whispered, "I love you too, Kiera. More than you know."

It was really early in the morning, and I hadn't had much sleep anyway, but when I closed my eyes, all I saw was Kiera. Anxious to see her again, I couldn't get back to sleep. When I finally gave up trying, I headed downstairs and got to work making a pot of coffee.

My smile widened as the dark brown liquid began to fill the carafe. Seeing it, smelling it, reminded me of her. It reminded me of making love to her, reminded me of my dream. Such a nice fantasy...I wished it were real.

The pot was nearly to the top when warm arms wrapped around my waist. I inhaled a deep breath, taking her in, then twisted to face her. She gave me a tired but happy smile.

"Mornin'."

Her smile grew at hearing my greeting. "Good morning." She pressed her head to my chest and I pulled her into me. Closing my eyes, I savored her—her scent, her softness, her warmth. I wanted to remember everything, just in case this was a dream too.

We didn't pull apart until we heard the shower running upstairs. With a small sigh, Kiera pulled back. There was a slight mar on her forehead. Guilt. I wished she didn't feel that way, but I understood why she did. A part of me did too. We were both bastards, playing this game, sneaking around behind Denny's back, skirting near a line we'd already crossed and shouldn't cross again. We should both stop what we were doing...but I already knew I couldn't. I was in too deep.

While I prepared mugs for us, Kiera started making tea for Denny. It was sweet of her, but it was a cruel reminder that my dream was just that—a dream. Watching her stabbed like a knife, so I focused on our drinks instead.

Moments later, Denny came downstairs. I gave him a friendly smile and greeting as I sat at the table with my coffee. Kiera was leaning against the counter, drinking hers. She was keeping her distance from me so Denny wouldn't be suspicious. She handed him his tea, and he told her, "Thanks, babe," as he leaned in for a kiss.

The look on her face as she gazed up at him wrenched me, but I couldn't stop staring. There was love in her eyes for him; there was no question who had her heart. But when he angled his head to playfully nuzzle her neck, her eyes turned to me, and oddly enough, her expression didn't change. Well, maybe her smile slipped some, and troubled sadness filled her eyes. She looked sorry, but I wasn't sure if she was feeling that toward me or Denny, or both of us. It was confusing, painful. I gave her a brief *Don't worry about me* smile, then concentrated on my coffee.

As Kiera sat down, Denny told her, "I may have to work really late tonight. Max has a *job* that he needs my help with." Denny said the word "job" oddly and Kiera frowned, like she was sure the task was something trivial, something beneath Denny's skills. Stuff like that really irritated her. Seeing her expression, Denny quickly added, "You'll be working anyway, so I didn't think you'd mind if I said I'd help him … right?"

Kiera opened her mouth, seeming like she wanted to object, but she had no real reason to. After flashing a glance at me, she murmured, "Right … sounds good." She seemed guilty again after she said it, and I resisted the urge to hold her hand.

I was all smiles as she slid into my car later. Driving her to and from school was almost my favorite part of the day. I loved seeing her across the seat from me. It felt so right. She smiled as she closed the door, equally happy. As I started the car, I asked her, "Do I get to walk with you today?" She'd made me stay behind the last time I drove her.

She pursed her lips in thought, then shook her head. "No, I think it would be better if you stayed in the car."

I sighed, but left it at that. She had her reasons, I guess. But I really enjoyed walking with her, and it was innocent, like she wanted. I'd keep trying. I dropped her off with a "Have fun. I'll see you later," then headed to the grocery store for supplies.

When I was done shopping, I went home to work for a little bit. There was a song Evan and I were working on that was nearly finished. Evan was busy arranging the music for it, and a couple of the lines I'd had didn't fit now. His melodies were better than my lyrics though, so I was switching it up to fit his stuff.

I worked at the kitchen table until my vision started going in and out and I started nodding off. Guess three hours of sleep wasn't enough. Putting away my notebook, I shuffled over to the couch. I had a little time to rest before picking up Kiera. After turning on the TV, I stretched out on the cushions. My lumpy beast wasn't the most comfortable couch in the world, but it got the job done.

Just as I was starting to fall asleep, the front door opened and surprise washed through me. Kiera was home; she shouldn't be done with school yet. "Hey, you're back early. I was going to pick you up," I said as she walked into the living room.

She stepped over to the couch, and I sat up and patted the space between my legs so she'd sit close to me. "You look tired," she commented. "Everything okay?" She nestled herself between my legs and leaned her back against my chest. *Yes, I'm more than okay. I'm in heaven.*

Holding her tight, I played with her hair. "I'm fine…just a late night, didn't sleep well."

Turning her head around, she gave me a playful grin. "Oh. Feeling guilty about something?"

I laughed at her remark, and gave her a squeeze. "About you? Every day."

I sighed. There was too much truth in that statement, and I didn't want to think about it. Intent on changing our focus, I pushed her forward a little bit. She resisted, saying my name and turning to face me, but I clamped my hands on her shoulders and made her face straight. I needed her back for what I wanted to do.

I kneaded my fingers into her muscles, and she stopped trying to protest. In fact, she melted like warm butter under my hands. "Hmmmm…I could get used to this flirting thing," she murmured as she relaxed in my embrace. As I laughed at her comment, she asked, "Did you have a bad dream?"

Remembering my dream made me smile as I moved my hands along her shoulder blades. "No…I had a good one, actually."

"Hmmmm…what about?" Her voice had a slightly distant sound to it, like my fingers were completely distracting her.

I moved my hands down her spine and she made a soft, satisfied noise in her throat. I kept my fingers there while I answered her. "You." I dug my fingers in deeper and the noise she made intensified.

"Hmmmm...nothing naughty, I hope. We *are* keeping this innocent, right?"

My fingers moved down to her lower back and she let out a deep exhale full of pleasure. Remembering my sweet, thoughtful dream version of her, I laughed. "No...nothing even remotely scandalous, I promise."

I started returning my fingers up her back, loosening knots, feeling the rigid muscles turn to Jell-O. Kiera let out a low moan as I worked on a spot holding a lot of tension. "Hmmm...good, I don't need you thinking about me that way," she mumbled.

A small pang went through me at the wall between us that was keeping us physically apart, but at least I had this much of her. It would have to do. We didn't talk any more after that. Kiera seemed too relaxed to keep up a conversation, but I was fine with comfortable silence.

I reveled in the feel of her body under my hands, the smell of her shampoo tickling my nose, the satisfied noises she let out whenever I relieved an ache from her body. As I headed south again, reaching out to get more of her rib cage, she started letting out noises that were darn near indecent. It was captivating to listen to her, and I paused wherever she made a sound. If I closed my eyes, I could pretend that I was making love to her...the sounds coming from her fit perfectly. It made desire rocket through my body. I could feel myself hardening and bit my lip to contain a groan of my own. God, I wanted her.

As her sensual noises continued, my body shifted into readiness. I needed her. When my hands got down to her hips, I shifted my position and pulled her against me. She teasingly just brushed against my jeans. I needed more. I needed to rub against her. I needed to lay her down, pull her clothes off, and thrust inside her. I needed to hear more of her intoxicating sounds. I needed to hear her come.

Thinking I was finished with my massage, Kiera leaned against my chest with a contented sigh. That's when she seemed to notice that I wasn't calm and peaceful anymore. I was aching with need and ready for action. I wanted her. That was the only thought in my mind.

I ran my hands up her inner thighs, pulling her into my body, and she spun in my arms. Swallowing back the need coursing through me, I slowly opened my eyes to gaze at her. Her eyes were wide with alarm, and her lips were parted; I wanted to taste them. I could tell by her reaction that she saw the desire on my face. *Yes, I want you.* I brought my hand to her cheek, and started pulling her into me. *I need you.*

It looked like it took some effort on her part, but she shook her head. "No... Kellan."

Hearing that word from her returned a small amount of reason to me. Closing my eyes, I pushed her away. I needed space if I was going to let this pass through me. If I even could. I was so ready for her, my unyielding denims were a little uncomfortable. I focused on the slight pain in my groin instead of the massive amount of pleasure. "I'm sorry. Just give me a minute..."

I felt Kiera move away from me, and I pulled my legs up and locked my elbows around them. I took three calming breaths while I thought about things that were in no way sexy: war, disease... my parents. When I felt more in control—no longer feeling like I needed to throw her on the floor and take her—I opened my eyes. She was intently watching me with a worried expression on her face.

Trying to ease her concern, I smiled. "Sorry... I am trying. But, maybe next time, you could not... uh, make those noises?"

Not realizing she'd been mimicking sex with her groans of pleasure, she blushed bright red and looked away. It was enchanting, and I had to chuckle at her reaction. God, what was I going to do with this woman?

Sometimes I really wasn't sure, but as long as I could be around her, touch her, feel connected with her, I could handle anything. Even her having sex with another man.

"Will it bother you if Denny and I sleep together?"

Kiera and I were fully engaged in our morning routine—sharing a cuddle while we waited for the coffee to finish brewing. Denny was upstairs, sleeping. Kiera had her arms around my neck and was looking up at me with an expression of regret, pain, and curiosity. Her question cut right to the quick. I really wasn't sure how I felt about them being together. I was certain they had been—Denny had been home for over a month—but I hadn't seen or heard anything since that one time, so it was easy enough for me to pretend it wasn't happening. The thought of them being together churned my stomach. It was making me feel ill right now, with her safely in my arms.

Not really wanting to answer her painful question, I smiled and said, "You sleep with him every night."

My jackass response earned me a poke in the ribs. "You know what I mean," she whispered, her cheeks turning a delightful shade of pink.

Being blunt, I rephrased her question. She really needed to get comfortable talking about sex, especially given our…complicated relationship. "Will it bother me if you have sex with your boyfriend?"

The rose color on her face deepened as she nodded. I kept my smile plastered to my face, but didn't say anything else. How could I? What could I possibly tell her? *Yes, I love you with all of my heart, so the thought of you being with him…when I can't…kills me.*

Raising her eyebrow, she gave me a *gotcha* smile as she said, "Just answer the question."

I laughed that she'd turned my words against me. Looking away, I sighed and decided to be honest. Somewhat. "Yes, yes it will bother me…but I understand." I looked back at her, my heart in my eyes. "You're not mine." *But I'm yours…*

Her eyes moistened as she stared at me. I wasn't sure what she was feeling, but it seemed to be difficult for her. She started to pull away from me, and I clutched at her. I didn't want her to go. "Just a minute…" she whispered.

Recognizing the words I'd used when I'd been too riled up to be near her, I released her. "I'm fine, Kiera." *You don't need to pull away from me.*

214

She met my eyes and she looked sad. I hated to see her sad. "*I need a minute, Kellan.*"

That surprised me. She was worked up enough to want to attack me? Because she felt guilty. It hurt that she felt that way, and at the same time, it warmed me. *She wanted me.*

We prepared our coffees in silence, then leaned against opposite counters as we sipped them. All the while I wondered what the hell I was doing with her. I should end this before Denny got hurt. But then her voice surged through my brain—*Stay. Don't leave me. Please*—and I knew I couldn't let go. She couldn't release him, I couldn't release her. We were all fucked.

I begged Kiera to let me walk to her class, and this time she conceded. I had a feeling it was because she still felt guilty over this morning, but I'd take her pity if it meant I got to spend a little more time with her.

Walking with her felt just like old times, and I savored every second. We talked about inconsequential things—her life, her parents—and I held her hand the entire way. It was bliss. After dropping her off, I went home and sat down to work. My phone rang while I was struggling to come up with a lyric that wasn't sunshine and happiness. The song I was working on was dark, but Kiera filled me with light, and all I felt at the moment was amazing.

"Yeah?" I said, after picking up the phone.

"Hey, Kell, it's Matt. Just reminding you about tonight."

I rolled my eyes. "I know. We're playing up north. Everett, right?"

"Yep. So you need to be here earlier than usual, so we have time to get up there."

I was used to Matt calling me, reminding me about stuff, but I swear, sometimes he talked to me like I was five. Or Griffin. "Not a problem. I'll see you in a few hours." Shaking my head, I added, "Why did you book a show that far north anyway? Aren't there plenty of places around here?"

Matt let out a small sigh, like he'd already explained this a couple

215

of times today. "I book the shows wherever I can get them. Pete's is great, but we need to keep expanding our fan base if we're ever going to get bigger. That might mean traveling from time to time."

I shrugged. It didn't really matter to me if we got huge or not. I just wanted to keep doing this for a while. As long as we could, really. The music was what mattered to me, not all the extra crap. "Okay, you're the boss."

Matt laughed at that. "Damn straight, I am. Don't be late."

He hung up the phone and I shook my head again. "Okay," I muttered to the empty room. Matt needed to chill out. Maybe Evan and I could find a girl to hook him up with tonight. Matt tended to be on the shyer side and sometimes needed a little help coming out of his shell. Or a shove. Maybe some feminine attention was just what he needed to mellow out.

I spent the remainder of my time alone thinking of what I could do for Kiera, since I wouldn't get to see her tonight. I came up with espresso, which seemed like the right call. When she saw me in the hallway outside of her class, holding a drink in my hand for her, she squealed like a little girl.

I hated to leave her once we were content and snuggly at the house, but eventually I had to go meet up with the band. Matt would have my head if I wasn't there on time. With a long sigh, I fingered a loose strand of Kiera's hair. She was doing homework on the couch while I kept her company. There were books spread out everywhere, and she was scribbling down some notes for a paper she was writing. She looked up at the sound of my exhale. A smile was on her lips as she studied me instead of her textbooks.

She watched my fingers playing with her hair, then returned her eyes to mine. A strange expression passed over her—guilt mixed with sadness. "You're probably really bored watching me do homework, aren't you?"

I smiled and the guilt on her face evaporated. "No. I could watch you do this all day." I frowned. "But I can't. I have to go meet the guys. We have a show tonight."

Kiera frowned with me. It made me happy that she did. Maybe

she was going to miss me just as much as I was going to miss her? "Oh...okay," she said.

I wanted to lean in and kiss her, just on the cheek, but I knew that was off-limits, so I simply ran a finger down her skin instead. "I'll be late, but I'll see you in the morning."

Her smile returned as she nodded. "Okay."

I stared at her a moment, memorizing every beautiful detail about her, then I got up to gather my things and leave. Work beckoned, and I had no choice but to obey. Even though I didn't want to.

A few hours later, I was helping the guys unload the van at the venue. We were behind the place, in the alley, so that no one attending the show tonight would see us. All fifteen of them; this place was tiny. Matt was talking to the owner of the bar, getting a feel for where to set up, since we'd never been here before. I took his moment of distraction to step over to Griffin, leaning against the side of the van.

"Hey, Griff," I casually said.

Griffin immediately frowned. "I already told Matt I'd help bring shit in, so no need to get on my case about it."

I shook my head. "I wasn't going to. I was just thinking... Matt's a little high-strung lately, right?"

Griffin turned to me. "Abso-fucking-lutely. Son of a bitch has been pissing me off left and right. He's got a stick shoved up his ass so far, his eyes are turning brown."

I blinked at Griffin's turn of phrase, then smiled and suggested, "Maybe he needs a distraction?"

Griffin gave me a blank stare. "Huh?" I was about to respond when the lights clicked on and he added, "Oh, you mean a chick? Fuck yeah, let's get him laid." A slow smile spread over his face and he patted my shoulder. Before I could agree or disagree, he told me, "Don't worry. I got this."

I was frowning as he walked away. Putting Griffin in charge of anything was usually a bad idea. Seeing my expression, Evan walked over. "What's up?"

I jerked my thumb at where Griffin was disappearing around the side of the building. So much for helping us bring shit in. "I think I just made a tactical error. I thought maybe Matt could use some company of the female persuasion, and now Griffin is on a mission to find him a girl."

Evan looked over at where Griffin had disappeared. He was silent a moment, then said, "You know that's going to end badly, don't you?"

I gave him a half smile in answer. Yep. I did. Matt was going to kill me.

Matt was fine throughout the set, no different than he usually was, so I thought maybe Griffin had failed. I should have known better. Matt was gone when Evan and I began tearing down the instruments; Griffin was whistling. That right there should have clued me in to an upcoming problem. I was clueless though, and didn't think anything of it until Evan and I were wrestling his drum set into the van.

Completely red in the face, Matt came storming out the back door. Evan and I paused as we watched him. It had started to drizzle, and I swear the raindrops around Matt were evaporating in his anger. "Who the hell did that?" he shouted into the alley.

Evan and I exchanged a glance while Griffin sniggered. Great. What the hell did Griffin do now? Setting the drum down on the concrete, I took a tentative step forward. "Did what? What's wrong?"

Matt clenched his fists, furious. "Hired a hooker for me," he seethed.

My jaw dropped, and I flashed a look at Griffin. He was full-on laughing now. Pointing a finger at me, he said, "Kell told me to."

I immediately held my palms up in supplication. "No, I didn't."

Matt ignored Griffin and glared at me. "What the hell?"

I shook my head, wondering how I was going to get out of this one. Fucking Griffin. I knew I should have been supervising him better. "All I said was maybe you could use some company…" I shut my mouth. That didn't sound any better than hiring him a prostitute.

Matt started vibrating. "A whore? That's what you thought I needed?"

I shook my head again. "No! Griffin took it the wrong way. I just—"

Matt cut me off with a wave of his hand. "I'm done with you fuckers. I'm taking a cab back."

I gave Matt a look of disbelief. Taking a cab this distance would cost him more than we made tonight. It was stupid. "Look, if you don't want to ride with Griffin and the instruments, I understand, but you can at least ride back with me." There really wasn't enough room for everyone and all our stuff, so I almost always drove my car to gigs.

Matt raised a pale eyebrow. "I said I'm taking a cab." With that, he turned and headed back into the bar.

"Matt! You're being ridiculous. It's not like you slept with her!" I yelled. Pausing, I reconsidered. "Did you sleep with her?" He *was* gone a long time.

Griffin was practically rolling on the ground in laughter now. I started to go after Matt, but Evan grabbed my arm. "I think I better handle this one," he told me. Shaking his head at Griffin, he headed into the bar after Matt.

I looked back at Griffin with my brows bunched. "You're an idiot."

Griffin wiped tears from his eyes. "Do you think he nailed her?" He started laughing again and I sighed. This was going to be a very long night.

It took Evan two hours to convince Matt to get into my car. Even though I apologized more than a half dozen times, he didn't say a word to me on the drive home. I'd have to make it up to him somehow. I dropped him off at Evan's, since he didn't want to be alone with Griffin, then I made my way home. I was exhausted as I trudged up the stairs, but I paused at Kiera's door with a stupid smile on my face. I couldn't wait to see her. And since it was so incredibly late, I'd only have to wait a few hours. One small benefit of staying out almost all night.

My body had other plans though. I woke up much later than I usually did. Guess I was more tired than I thought. That happened on occasion. My body rebelled against my schedule and I'd sleep for twelve hours straight. Fortunately, it wasn't that bad this time.

Once my mind cleared to alertness, I sat up and started doing some push-ups. That woke me up even better than coffee. I heard the water running while I worked out, and figured Denny was getting ready for work. That probably meant Kiera was downstairs, waiting for me. I paused in a plank position, then sprang to my feet. I wanted to see her more than I wanted to keep my muscles trim.

Quick as a rabbit, I slipped on some pants and a clean shirt. Opening my door, I was just about to start humming to myself when I noticed an odd sound coming from the bathroom. There were banging noises, like someone was moving around in the shower, and under that…there were moans and groans. Someone was having sex in the shower. My stomach twisted into a giant knot while I listened to the unmistakable sound of Kiera in ecstasy. From the way her moans were increasing, I'd say she was well on her way to climaxing. With Denny. He was inside her right now. Pushing into her. Making her cry out with how much she wanted it. Wanted him. She wanted *him*…

I looked over to their bedroom door, hoping, praying, that Kiera would step through it. That somehow, some way, Denny was screwing a different woman right now. But Kiera didn't step out of her room, because she *was* the other woman. No. I was the other man in this situation. And if I was going to keep having any sort of relationship with Kiera, dealing with this was just something I would have to do. I couldn't freak out on her like before. I had to keep things light, easy. That was the only way I could keep her.

My vision hazed and the knot in my stomach traveled up my throat. I was going to be sick…I just knew it. I headed downstairs as quickly as I could, but I wasn't quick enough. I tried not to listen, but I clearly heard Kiera's final cry as she came…with another man.

I bypassed the kitchen and headed for the downstairs bathroom. I made it just in time to be sick in the toilet instead of the hallway.

220

Luckily there really wasn't anything in my stomach. I flushed the bile away, then sat back on my heels. Tears stung my eyes, but I fought them down. I had known this would happen. I had to let it happen. *I can share her. I can share her. I can do this...*

Standing, I walked to the sink and ducked down to rinse out my mouth. When I was more or less put back together, I stumbled into the kitchen and prepared some coffee. Today was just a normal day. No need to let this affect me. The sound of Kiera coming rang through my ears as I poured my cup though. Hers was still sitting on the counter, cold. She'd come downstairs first, and I hadn't been here...and Denny had swept her away.

I put her mug in the microwave, then sat down at the table and made myself drink. My hands were shaking. I heard the love-birds coming downstairs before I saw them. With a deep inhale, I prepared myself for nonchalance. Denny was all smiles when he walked into the room. Well, of course. He'd just had a mind-blowing orgasm with a beautiful woman. I'd be smiling too. "G'day, mate."

"Mornin'...mate." I did my best to not have any bitterness in my voice. This wasn't Denny's fault. This wasn't anyone's fault. It just...was.

Kiera didn't look quite as happy as Denny. She looked uncomfortable. Guilty. Her wet hair was a painful reminder of what she'd just done, so I concentrated on my coffee. I heard Denny kiss her, then he said, "Now I'm going to be late. You're worth it though." I knew what he meant by that, and my stomach churned again. I forced it to settle down. I did not want to have to run to the bathroom again.

After Denny said goodbye and left, quietness blanketed the kitchen. I broke it first. "I put your coffee in the microwave. It was cold..."

She walked over to the microwave, started it, then said my name. "Kellan...I'm—"

"Don't," I said, interrupting her. I didn't want to hear an excuse. I didn't need one, and she didn't owe me one.

"But…"

Standing up, I walked over to her. I paused well away from her. I just couldn't be near her right now. Not yet. "You don't owe me an explanation…" I stared at the floor, unable to look at her. "And you definitely don't owe me an apology." I raised my eyes to hers. "So just…don't say anything, please."

Sympathetic pain flashed over her face, and tears pricked her eyes as she held her arms open for me. "Come here."

I hesitated, torn. I wanted to hold her, more than anything, but the sounds of her and Denny weren't leaving me. I felt like I'd just been electrocuted, and the residual jolts were still crashing through my body, frying me from the inside. I needed her though. She was my greatest pain, and my only salvation. She was the only one who could heal this hole in my heart, a hole she'd torn open.

Slipping my arms around her waist, I buried my head in her neck. I could do this. I could love her and let her go, all at the same time. She rubbed my back as she held me. It hurt, because those hands had just been caressing Denny, but it was soothing too.

"I'm sorry," she whispered, her voice full of regret and pain; this was hard for her too. She didn't like to hurt people, intentionally or otherwise.

Her words were simple, but they worked. A small Band-Aid of love was placed over the gaping wound of hurt. It didn't completely heal the void, but it at least kept me from bleeding out. I exhaled a cleansing breath and nodded against her shoulder.

I love you, and you don't need to apologize, because there is nothing to forgive. You're not mine…

222

I drove Kiera to class like normal, but things didn't entirely feel normal between us. The wall separating us had gotten just a little larger. But I had the power to fix this, to let the hurt go; I just had to be strong enough to do it. I made myself be funny, made myself be light and carefree. Once Kiera was safely tucked into her classroom, I felt exhausted from the effort. Even though I'd slept in today, I wanted to take a nap. I couldn't though. I had to start mending things with Matt, and now seemed as good a time as any. I didn't want to let this sit and fester too.

I headed over to Evan's, since that was where Matt had crashed. Surprisingly, Griffin's van was parked there. After the way things had ended, I'd kind of assumed Matt would have a restraining order against Griffin. Roxie approached me as I crossed the street. Wiping her hands clean on a rag, she said, "Hey, Kell. Miss the sleepover?" She indicated Griffin's van with a tilt of her head.

I laughed at the look on her face. "Yeah, apparently, I did." And I kind of wished I hadn't. My morning would have gone a lot differently if I'd woken up over here.

Evan's door was locked when I tried to open it, so I knocked and patiently waited for someone to unlock it. When no one did, I knocked harder. There was a gruff sound of mumbled voices, followed by a curse or two, then the door unlocked and cracked open. A pale blue eye framed by long strands of dirty-blond hair stared at me through the open space. "Kellan? You're about a hundred years early for practice. Unless you're here to make breakfast, go away and let us sleep."

Griffin started to close the door, but I stopped it with my palm. "I was checking on Matt. He still mad at us?"

Griffin scoffed, like I'd said something funny. Opening the door wider, he pointed to a confusing pile of blankets and pillows on the floor near the couch. "Nah, he's fine. We got him wasted to the point where he told us he loved us all." Scratching his head, he let out a low laugh. "He even told Roxie he wanted to marry her when she showed up this morning."

My eyes widened at that news. If they'd been partying late enough to see her, then they'd just recently gone to bed. No wonder Griffin's eyes were bloodshot and he was wobbling on his feet. I glanced at Evan's mattress in the corner; he was snoring so loud, I could hear it over the shop noise downstairs. Matt was quiet, but the mountain of blankets moved up and down in a rhythmic fashion. He was sleeping too.

Clapping Griffin's shoulder, I told him, "Good. I didn't want him mad at me for something *you* did."

Griffin looked offended for a fraction of a second, then smiled. "Fucker's always mad at me for something. You get used to it after a while."

He yawned and I shook my head. "All right. I'll let you guys get back to your nap then. You look like you need it."

Reaching down, Griffin grabbed his junk and gave it a squeeze. "What I need is for Lola to drive down here and give me a freebie. Hooker or not, that chick was hot!"

I pulled the door closed while he was preoccupied with himself. "Night, Griffin."

Since things with Matt were sorted out quicker than I thought they would be, I had some time on my hands. When I got home, I decided to pull out my guitar. I sat on the couch and played random rhythms. I used to do that when I was younger. Just play whatever came to mind, with no meaning or direction behind it. It was freeing, and it cleared my head. There was no drama, there was no pain, there was only music. In its own way, this filled me with as much contentment as being with Kiera. Almost.

I was lost in my impromptu song when the front door opened and Kiera walked through the doors. I checked my mental clock when I looked over at her, and knew she was very early. She must have skipped a class. I didn't like that I was becoming a bad influence on her, but it did thrill me that she'd come home early just to spend time with me.

Pausing my fingers on the fret board, I shifted the guitar so I could set it down. Walking over, Kiera sat beside me on the couch. "No, don't stop. It's beautiful."

I shifted my gaze to the floor, and even though I wasn't looking at her, Kiera's large, expressive eyes filled my vision. *No, you're beautiful; that was just me messing around.* I set the instrument on her lap. "Here...try again." I had tried teaching her before, but it hadn't gone over too well. The sounds that she had produced from the instrument had been anything but soothing.

When I glanced over, I saw her grimace. "It's beautiful when you play it. Something seems to happen to it when I try."

Laughing, I twisted her on the couch so I could put my hands over hers. It was a happy bonus that I also got to hold her. "You just need to hold it right," I whispered in her ear. I saw a shiver run through her body, and peeking at her face, I saw that her eyes were closed.

It made me smile that being close to me affected her so much. When our fingers were in the right position, I told her, "Okay." Seeing that her eyes were still closed, I nudged her shoulder with a short laugh. "Hey." Her eyes flashed to mine and her cheeks heated in embarrassment. It was such an endearing expression, I laughed again. "Here...your fingers are perfect, right under mine." *Right where they belong.* I held up a pick in my other hand. "Now, lightly strum it like this..." I stroked the strings and they sang for me.

225

Kiera made a face, like she was sure she'd never be able to do what I'd just done. She took the pick when I placed it in her fingers though. She did what I did against the strings, but the sound was anything but beautiful. She just had a knack for being really bad at this. That was a skill in and of itself. I locked our fingers together and strummed our connected hands against the instrument. It sang again, with me doing most of the work.

Kiera relaxed into my body, and playing the song blind, I smiled at her. "This really isn't so hard. I learned this one when I was six." It was one of the first songs I had learned on the guitar, back when I'd taught myself to play.

I gave her a playful wink and her cheeks softened with color. "Well…you're just more talented with your fingers," she replied.

I froze as my mind instantly went into the gutter. When I laughed, she rolled her eyes and laughed too. "You have such a dirty mind. You and Griffin are a lot alike."

I grimaced as I remembered Griffin talking about a hooker while he fondled himself. God, I hoped we weren't *that* much alike. "I can't help it if I think that way around you." Wishing I could do more than just think things about her, I removed my hands from the guitar. "You try."

To her credit, she didn't give up until she'd made a noise that was somewhat melodic. I smiled when she giggled in delight at her accomplishment. I loved seeing the way her eyes glowed when she was happy, the way the corners compressed into warm wrinkles.

Once she had that basic chord down, I showed her another one. After a few attempts, she had that one down too, and then she could sort of play the song I'd taught her. She played for a while, but then she started flexing her hand, and I knew she was done for the day.

I set the guitar on the ground, pulled her into my chest, and started massaging her fingers. "You have to build up the strength for it," I told her.

Perfectly content, her only reply was, "Hmmmm…"

I couldn't help but notice she didn't make any pleased noises this time. She was trying to make this easier for me, and I appreciated it. After a time, I stopped and simply held her. It was peaceful and wonderful, but I still wanted more. "Can we try something?" I quietly asked her.

She automatically stiffened, her eyes suspicious when she looked back at me. "What?"

I laughed at her reluctant expression. By her eyes, she thought I was going to ask her for something sordid and risqué. It amused me that I wasn't the only one with a dirty mind. "It's innocent...I promise."

Lying back on the couch, I opened my arms wide in invitation. Her reluctance shifted to confusion, but she eventually nestled herself into the space between me and the couch. A happy sigh escaped me as I wrapped my arms around her. *Yes, this is what I needed.*

The fruity scent of her shampoo was all around me as I held her close. Her skin was soft and her body was warm. I felt whole and complete as I lay with her, and for the first time today, I was truly happy.

Still seemingly confused, Kiera lifted her head and looked down at me. "This is what you wanted to do?" Was she surprised that my request wasn't sexual? I'd told her I'd be good. I'd meant it.

I shrugged. "Yeah, it looked...nice...when you did this with Denny..."

She nodded, looking slightly overwhelmed, then she rested her head on my chest, her eyes facing me, and wrapped her arm and leg around me. I nearly purred, it was so wonderful. Why had I never done this before? Because I'd never had anyone who cared about me before, that was why.

Sighing, I leaned my head against hers. I wished this never had to end. "Is this okay with you?" I whispered into her hair.

I felt her muscles release all of their tension and I smiled wider. She was relaxing with me. She was enjoying this. "Yeah...it's nice. Are you okay?"

I felt her tracing a circle on my chest and I laughed. I'd never been more okay in all my life. "I'm fine, Kiera." *I'm wonderful.* I rubbed her back and she clutched me tight. I firmed up my hold on her, savoring the moment. I *really* didn't want this to end.

I felt Kiera nuzzle into my neck, then her hold on me relaxed. Her breath washed against my skin in a slow, even pattern. "Kiera," I whispered. "Are you asleep?" I waited several seconds, but she didn't respond; she didn't even grunt like she was partially awake. She just kept lightly breathing. Smiling that I'd made her comfortable enough to pass out, I gave her a small squeeze. "Thank you for doing this." After a long pause, I found some courage and breathed the words, "I love you...so much."

My throat closed up on me and I couldn't say any more. I was a little surprised I'd even gotten that much out. Speaking my feelings was difficult. Even when I was saying it at a nearly inaudible level, even knowing that she couldn't hear me because she was fast asleep didn't make it any easier. Judging by how hard that was, I was beginning to think that I was incapable of ever telling her how much I cared. I'd just have to show her, and hope that she could correctly interpret my actions.

I held her for an eternity while she napped. Then my arm started falling asleep, and I knew I needed to move. We had time before Denny was due home, so I didn't want to wake her yet. I shifted my position as carefully as I could. Flexing my hand, I tried to regain blood flow. The brief movement was too much though, and Kiera stirred in my arms. "Sorry...I didn't mean to wake you," I murmured when it was clear she was awake.

She startled at my words and sat bolt upright. Staring at the front door, she whispered, "Denny." She seemed terrified as she glanced down at me.

Sitting up, I hooked some loose strands of hair around her ear. "You weren't asleep long. It's still early. He won't be home for an hour or so." Hurt that our moment was over, that Denny was occupying her thoughts again, I looked away. I understood her reaction though. I didn't want Denny to see this either. He wouldn't understand. I barely did. "I wouldn't let him..." I met her eyes again. "I won't let him see this, if you don't want him to." *But if you do want to be with me, openly, we could come clean to him.*

She shook her head no, and even though I nodded at her, a slice of pain ran across my heart. No, she didn't want to be with me. No more than the brief, "innocent" connections we had. I knew that. It was stupid to assume she wanted more just because I did.

Kiera seemed a little overwhelmed by the intense way I was staring at her. I didn't mean to make her uncomfortable, I just couldn't turn away from the sight of her. She blurted out a question, like it had just come to her. "Where did you go when you used to disappear? When you didn't come home all night?" She settled down beside me, and we sat side by side. Remembering all the times I'd run away from her, hiding, I smiled, but didn't answer. She took my silence to mean something scandalous. "If you were… if you *are* seeing someone, you should just tell me."

I cocked my head to the side, surprised by her assumption. "Is that what you think? That when I'm not with you, I'm with a woman?" I suppose that would explain some of her frosty attitude toward me, if she thought I was stepping out on her all the time. Not that we were together or anything…

Kiera cringed. She knew she had no right to feel jealous, since she was the one who *was* actually seeing someone. "You're *not* with me; you have every right… to date."

She'd grabbed my hand while she'd said that, and I stroked her fingers. "I know." *But what woman on this earth could give me what you give me? There is no one else for me.* "Would it bother you if I was seeing someone?" I asked, insanely curious whether she would have the same reaction I did when it came to her and Denny.

Clearly not wanting to answer, she turned her head and swallowed. Surprisingly, she did answer me though. "Yes," she whispered.

With a sigh, I stared at the floor. So we were both going to be miserable with certain aspects of each other's lives then. Great. What did I do with that information? I didn't want to hurt her, far from it; I wanted to love her. But what she was saying was that I

229

would be largely alone as long as we were "together." I would sleep alone while she slept with Denny, never be able to show her affection in public, and never be able to tell the world that I cared about her. And I would never have sex with her while we were in our pseudo-relationship. I didn't want it with anyone else, but it made me feel really lonely to think of being celibate for the rest of my life. Could I live like that? What choice did I have?

"What?" Kiera tentatively asked.

Putting an arm around her waist, I rubbed her back. "Nothing." *Don't worry about me. I can do this…*

She melted into my side. "I'm not being fair, am I? I'm with Denny. You and I are…just friends. I can't ask you to never…"

She again cut herself off before saying the word, and a small laugh escaped me. The word "friends" hurt though, and I suddenly wished this painful conversation were over. "Well, we could solve this little problem if you relaxed your rules." Even though I was somewhat serious, I gave her a playful grin. "Especially that first one." *Let me make love to you again…*

She didn't share my humor, so I stopped laughing. Nothing about this topic was really that funny anyway, I just preferred laughter to hard conversations. Her face straight, she told me, "I'll understand. I won't like it, any more than you probably like me with Denny…but I'll understand. Just don't hide it. Don't sneak around on me. We shouldn't have secrets…"

I was dumbstruck for a second. She was giving me permission to sleep around, so long as she knew about it. I found it difficult to wrap my head around that one. Would she really be okay with me having sex with someone else? I was sure that she cared about me, a lot, but maybe it wasn't as much as I'd thought. I mean, if she wasn't affected by the idea…But maybe it *did* bother her as much as it bothered me, just like she'd said, but she was going to allow it to happen anyway, because we could never be a couple. There would always be a Denny-sized wall between us, and she didn't want to deny me intimate contact…because she was in love with me. She *had* to be in love with me.

I felt full of sadness as I nodded at her. *I wish it were you that I could date.*

"So, where do you go?" she asked.

I smiled, welcoming the change of subject. "Where do I go? Well, it depends. Sometimes it's Matt and Griffin's place, sometimes it's Evan's. Sometimes I drink myself into oblivion on Sam's doorstep." I had to laugh at that one. Sam was still mad at me for throwing up on his roses.

"Oh…" She seemed genuinely surprised that my answer was so simple. She must have thought some very nasty thoughts about what I'd been doing. And, at one point in my life, she would have been right. I would have forgotten my problems by flitting from bed to bed. But ever since she had entered the picture, things had changed. I'd changed. And random sex with strangers wasn't as satisfying as it had once been. It wasn't even appealing anymore.

Reaching up, she stroked my cheek. The contact sent a thrill straight through me. Why did I need sex when just her touch did that to me? "Where did you go after our first time? I didn't see you all day, all night. And you came home…"

Shit-faced? Well, I was wandering the city, dreaming up ways to tell you how much I love you, then I came home to hear you screwing my best friend. That's what happened.

Not able to say any of that, I stood up and held out my hand. "Come on. I'll give you a ride to Pete's."

She took my hand and let me help her up. She wasn't about to let the conversation die though. "Kellan, you can tell me, I won't…"

I made myself smile, even though I didn't feel it. I did *not* want to talk about this. There was no point. I'd been hoping for a future back then, when we'd made love the first time, but that was a fantasy. I knew the reality, and I physically couldn't talk to her about this. I couldn't get the words past my lips. I could barely do it when she was incoherent. Having her stare at me, completely alert, was too much. It was too hard.

"You don't want to be late," I told her. *Take the hint, this topic is closed.* She pursed her lips, annoyed. She hadn't wanted secrets between us, but there was going to be at least one. Until I was able, until I was positive that saying the words wouldn't put me in an early grave, I would protect myself the only way I could, the only way I knew how. I'd stay silent and keep my feelings to myself.

Boasting her independence, Kiera told me, "You don't have to give me a ride everywhere, you know." When I gave her a playful smirk, she pouted. "I managed just fine without you." I didn't let her see, but her words sent a chill through me. *I know you did.*

I stayed with Kiera at the bar instead of heading to Evan's for practice. I was sure Matt would be irritated when I didn't show up, which would only make him angry at me again. But maybe not. He was probably really hungover. Maybe he wanted a night off. I thought about calling him and finding out for sure, but I was afraid he'd tell me to get my butt over there. And I didn't want to be there. I wanted to be here, laughing with Kiera and teaching her how to play pool. Sort of.

Griffin and Evan came in while I had Kiera bent over the pool table, helping her line up her shot, even though I had no idea what I was doing. I felt a little strange about having the guys see me in that position with her, but I acted like it was no big deal. Two friends playing a friendly game. Nothing to see here. Smiling, Griffin immediately grabbed a stick and started chalking up the tip, like he was playing the winner. Kiera and I were tied...we each still had most of our balls on the table. Pool just wasn't my game. Kiera's either. She was the first person I'd ever played who was just as bad as me. It was refreshing to actually have a chance for once.

After Kiera's attempt missed, I tried my hand. I couldn't see anything on the table worth hitting, so I just smacked one of the closest balls and hoped for the best. When I scratched, Griffin snorted and Evan patted my back. "You've got to look a few shots ahead, Kellan. Blindly hitting balls won't get you anywhere."

I gave Evan a sour expression. "Seeing a few shots ahead would require premonition. And if I could see into the future, I wouldn't waste the superpower on a stupid pool game."

Evan laughed, then asked, "What would you do with it?"

I looked past Evan to Jenny. She was walking from a table near the stage to the bar with a bright smile on her face, like today was the greatest day of her life. She almost always looked like that. "I would help out my friends, of course."

Evan turned to look at what I was looking at, then he rolled his eyes. "I can't believe you're still on that. Give it a rest already."

I shrugged as a laugh escaped me. Teasing Evan and Jenny about their soul mate potential was one of my favorite pastimes. "I only call 'em as I see 'em."

Evan shook his head, then glanced over at Kiera. His deep brown eyes grew inquisitive. "And what about you? Any new developments?"

My smile dropped a smidge. If he wanted me to ease up on his love life, then he needed to ease up on mine too. "Nope, nothing new." I turned to watch Kiera miraculously sink a ball. She seemed shocked that she had, and snapped her eyes to mine. She let out a little squeal of happiness and did a little jig. It was adorable, and all I wanted to do was wrap my arms around her. Returning my attention to Evan, I quickly changed the subject. "Where's Matt? Was he mad I didn't show?"

Evan cringed. "No...he's...um...not feeling so hot. He spent most of the afternoon alternating between lying down and throwing up. Griffin and I finally took him home before coming out here." He scratched his shaved head. "We may have gone a little overboard on cheering him up last night."

I shook my head, grateful that at least I hadn't made him mad again. "Poor guy. Next time he should just accept the prostitute with a smile."

Evan laughed and we both looked over at Griffin. He was leaning over a woman sitting on a stool, chatting with her friend. It was clear from his stance that he was trying to see down the girl's shirt. Just as I was thinking it, Evan muttered, "Jackass."

I was laughing with him when Kiera approached me. Seeing my smile made her beam. Her eyes were a pale shade of green tonight.

233

Mesmerizing. "My break is over. You'll have to finish the game with someone else."

Leaning against my stick, I dramatized scanning the room. "Hmmm...whom to lose to?"

Kiera laughed, then placed her fingers on my shoulder. My skin tingled where she was touching me. "You shouldn't go into it thinking you're going to lose. You should always think you're going to win." She squeezed my shoulder, then turned and left. Conscious of Evan's eyes on me, I watched her leave. Her words floated around my brain on a never-ending loop: *Always think you're going to win.*

But the only thing I really want to win, Kiera, is you.

Matt was right as rain the next day. I showed up to practice extra early, just to make up for the last couple of nights. He seemed surprised to see me on time. He seemed even more surprised when I gave him and Evan a new song to start working on. As much as Matt loved perfecting the old stuff, he loved new tunes even more. "We need to stay fresh, keep moving forward," he often told us.

I loved watching the way his pale eyes lit up as he read through new lyrics. He was bobbing his head to a beat only he could hear as he instantly created a song in his mind. He peeked up at me before flipping the page. "This is good. Really good."

His eyes returned to the paper, so he missed seeing me shrug. "It's all right." The lyrics he was looking at were pretty peppy, upbeat...almost sappy. It wasn't like the stuff we typically sang about. It was...romantic, I guess. It was about finding that person who completed you, and discovering that you completed them too. It was wishful thinking on my part. I didn't make Kiera whole. Denny did.

After rehearsal, we all went to Pete's. Evan and Matt busied themselves over a melody for the new song, while Griffin busied himself with dancing on the table to "Baby Got Back." Eventually his antics got Pete's attention, and he was thankfully ordered off the table, but not before we all had a good laugh. The smile on Kiera's face was intoxicating to watch, and my eyes didn't leave her for very long.

It was only because of my incessant need to watch her every move that I saw something disturbing. Some asshole in her section reached up her skirt and grabbed her leg. Sometimes the drunker customers would try to hit on the staff. Not the regulars, but the drop-ins. I had never seen the guy currently accosting Kiera before, but I was about to get up close and personal with him and his friend. I started to stand, but Kiera had already moved away from him. I settled back in my seat, watching the guy. If he touched her again, he was dead.

Evan noticed that I was glaring at the guy. Kiera was avoiding him for the most part, but whenever she came near enough, his fingers reached out for her. I wanted to chop those fingers off and stuff them down his throat. "Who are we mentally burning alive?" Evan asked me.

I nodded over to the seedy guy and his equally seedy friend. "That guy groped Kiera. I'm making sure he doesn't do it again."

Evan glanced over at the scumbag I was staring at. "Hmmm, Sam's off today, isn't he? Well, Kiera's a big girl, I'm sure she can handle him."

"She shouldn't have to," I seethed.

Evan eyed me, then nodded. "Okay, we'll keep an eye on him then."

It wasn't five minutes later that Kiera grudgingly walked over to the guy to hand him his bill. I tensed, then sprang to my feet. He hadn't made a move toward her, but I was already striding over to him. Evan got the other guys' attention and I heard their chairs squeak as they all followed me. I didn't particularly care for violence, but I wasn't about to let this guy touch *my* girl again.

Oblivious to what was coming his way, the jerk-off grabbed her ass, pulled her tight to his body, then put his other hand on her breast. *Oh no, he did not just fucking do that.* Kiera knocked his hand off her chest, but she couldn't push him away. Unaware that I was about to kill him, the man laughed. Kiera looked around for help, but help was already on the way.

Maybe seeing that I was going to rip the guy's arms off, Evan beat me to him. Coming up behind the asshole, he yanked his hands off Kiera and pinned them to his sides. The man seemed stunned, like he truly hadn't expected anyone to intervene. *Sorry, buddy. You don't get to attack someone on our home turf and just get away with it. No way. Especially not when it's the woman I love that you're molesting.*

Restraining myself from pummeling this man into an unrecognizable mess, I seethed, "Not a good idea." His teeth were yellow and his breath smelled like he'd been on a three-day booze fest with no time for basic hygiene, like showering. The smell didn't keep me out of the guy's face though.

From somewhere behind me, I heard Griffin say, "Yeah, this ass is ours." I had to assume he was standing by Kiera.

Shaking off Evan, the man shoved me back. He was strong, and I retreated a step. "Piss off, pretty boy."

Grabbing his shirt, I stepped right in his face again. "Try it…please…" *I'd love to have an excuse to punch your lights out. Not that I don't already have one…you touched the wrong girl.*

We stared at each other for long seconds, neither of us backing down. My adrenaline slowed while I watched him. I knew I couldn't hit him unprovoked, not after the amount of time that had gone by. I really didn't want anyone questioning why I was defending Kiera, so I made myself calm down. True, I would defend any of the waitresses here, but defending and completely coming unglued were two different things. I needed to be calm, reasonable, and rational.

I released him with a warning. "I suggest you leave now. I wouldn't come back if I were you."

His friend grabbed his shoulder, urging the man to do what I said. "Come on, man. She's not worth it."

Wrong. Kiera was worth anything. Asshole gave me a derisive sniff, eyed me up and down, then had the audacity to wink at Kiera. I wanted to smash his teeth in, but I let that one go. He turned to leave the bar and I relaxed and looked back at Kiera. Griffin had his arm around her shoulder. Her eyes were wide as she flicked her gaze between the man and me. She looked really freaked out. I wanted to take Griffin's place, wrap my arms around her, but we'd need to go someplace private first. Just when I was about to ask her if she was okay, her eyes opened even wider and she yelled my name in warning.

I instantly followed her gaze and returned my attention to the man I'd thought was leaving. Turned out he wasn't. He lunged at me, and I saw light glinting off of a knife in his hand. I managed to spin away before we collided, but a sharp pain exploding along my side let me know I hadn't been quite quick enough. I was momentarily shocked that the fucker had a weapon. Chaos erupted around me. All at the same time, I saw Griffin pull Kiera back as she made a move for me, Matt shove the asshole's friend aside, keeping him out of the fight, and Evan make a move for the knife in the guy's hand. I had the better position though. Pulling my arm back, I swung just as hard as my dad would have; he might have even been proud.

After my fist connected with his jaw, the man went to the ground and the knife skittered under a table. I went for the guy, eager to finish this, but he scrambled away from me. Without a glance back, he fled the bar; his friend quickly followed him. Pete's was deathly quiet for a long time, then noises slowly started up again.

Flexing my aching hand, I turned to find Kiera. "You okay?" I finally asked her.

As I watched, the tension seemed to melt right off her. "Yeah, thank you, Kellan...guys." She looked over all of us, then her eyes settled on Griffin, still standing at her side. "You can get your hand off my butt now, Griffin."

I felt a little light-headed as I laughed at my opportunistic bandmate. A playful smile on his face, he pulled his hand back and held it in the air. "Sorry. Mind of its own." He winked at her, then drifted over to Matt. Talking about the incident, the pair walked back to our table.

Evan stayed near Kiera and me. I kind of wanted him to leave so I could make sure Kiera was fine. He was eyeing me with concern though. "You okay, Kell? Did he get you?"

Cringing, I turned my body toward Kiera. She seemed even more concerned than Evan was. She must not have noticed that he'd nicked me. I put my hand under my shirt, feeling the point of pain along my ribs. I felt the wetness on my fingertips, and wasn't surprised in the slightest when there was blood on my fingers when I pulled them back.

Kiera flipped out at the sight though. "Oh, God..." She grabbed my hand, examining the red, then lifted up my shirt to inspect the damage. I had a pretty decent-sized slice along my ribs. It was bleeding quite a bit, but I didn't think it was very deep. It would close on its own. Kiera didn't seem to think so. "Kellan, you should go to the hospital."

"He barely got me. I'm fine." I smiled and raised an eyebrow at the fact that she was still holding my shirt up. She let it drop, then grabbed my hand again.

"Come on," she said, pulling me away.

She led me through the swarm of curious onlookers, then to the back room. She got some first aid supplies from there, then we headed back out to the hallway. Ordering me to stay put, she ducked into the women's room to make sure it was empty. I was patiently leaning against the wall, waiting for her when she returned.

"This isn't necessary. I'm fine," I said, as she grabbed my hand and led me into the bathroom.

Once the door closed behind us, Kiera scowled at my stubbornness. "Shirt off."

I smiled. Maybe this wouldn't be so bad after all. "Yes, ma'am."

I took my shirt off, then held it in my hand as I waited by the sink for her to fix me. The thought of her fingers on my bare skin gave me a chill, although I wasn't looking forward to the pain she was about to cause me. Just the fabric of my shirt touching the cut had sucked. I could take it though. It would be worth it to have her caress me.

She turned on the water and soaked a towel. When she brought the rag to my wound, I sucked in a sharp breath; it was cold, and it stung. Kiera actually grinned at my reaction, which I found amusing. "You're such a sadist," I muttered. She didn't like that. She gave me an appealing put-out expression that she probably thought was a nasty glare. I laughed.

Her ministrations more gentle, she asked in a disbelieving voice, "What were you thinking, going up against a guy with a knife?"

I struggled through the searing ache at my side. I hoped she finished soon, or I might start whimpering, and that would be really embarrassing. "Well, obviously, I didn't know he had a knife." Kiera pressed the towel firmly into my side, trying to stanch the blood. "I wasn't about to let him keep touching you like that." Anger flooded through me as I remembered his hands on her. Bastard. He should be the one with his side split open. Hopefully he at least had a headache.

Kiera and I locked gazes and all the anger left me. She was so beautiful, so caring, so warm and tender. She was amazing. She pulled the towel away, and a satisfied smile touched her lips. I looked down and saw that the bleeding had stopped. Good. I hated hospitals.

As she opened the bandage, I couldn't help teasing her. "He can't touch you like that if I don't get to. It's against the rules." I laughed and Kiera slapped the bandage on my side. A flash of pain seared through me, and I made a mental note to not irritate a woman when she was patching me up. Words to live by.

Remorse crossed Kiera's face and she gently stroked her fingers over the cover, flattening the edges. "Well, it was stupid—you could have been seriously hurt, Kellan." She swallowed a hard lump in her throat, and I clearly saw how much the idea bothered her. She'd miss me if I was dead and gone. No, she'd mourn me. That was surprisingly comforting.

Grabbing her fingers, I held her hand to my chest. "Better me than you, Kiera." I couldn't picture mourning her. I couldn't picture her being gone. I didn't even want to. We locked eyes again; hers were a deep, thoughtful green with specks of brown around the edges. I could easily get lost in them. "Thank you...for watching out for me." I wished I could kiss her. That seemed the only way to truly thank her. But she didn't want that, and I'd respect her wishes.

Her breath caught, then she averted her eyes and her cheeks flushed with color. "You can put your shirt back on now," she muttered.

She stared at the ruined remains of my T-shirt after I put it on. Her eyes started to tear up, and I could tell she was thinking about losing me again. Needing her close, I pulled her in for a hug. She squeezed me back, hard, and I inhaled as a sharp pain wrenched my side. Realizing she was hurting me, Kiera eased up. "Sorry. You really should get that looked at."

Knowing I wouldn't go see a doctor unless I was bleeding out, I nodded and held her close again. She sighed and relaxed into my arms...and that was when the door opened. "Oops," Jenny said. "Just checking to see how your patient was doing."

Kiera quickly moved away from me. The loss of her touch hurt worse than my side. "We were just...he's fine," she stammered.

Amused by her flustered response, and also not wanting Jenny to think anything of us holding each other, I laughed and walked into the hallway. Turning back, I said, "Thank you, Kiera," then I nodded at Jenny. "I should probably get that knife from Griffin now."

Jenny's pale eyes looked confused for a moment. "Griffin has it?" I raised an eyebrow in answer. Jenny knew Griffin just as well as I did. If anyone in the bar had nabbed it, it had been him. And Griffin was the type of person who should never be armed. It was safer for all mankind that way. Jenny rolled her eyes, understanding. "Griffin...yeah, you should go get it."

I looked back at Kiera, masked my longing with a casual laugh, then walked down the hall. I heard Jenny ask Kiera if she was coming, and heard Kiera tell her that she needed a minute. Was that because of me? How upset was she over the thought of forever losing me? Maybe this would change things for her. Or maybe not. Regardless of Kiera's "think you'll win" attitude, I couldn't count on things working out my way. Hope was too painful.

Chapter 17

Sleeping with a Beautiful Woman

A week went by, and Kiera and I got even closer, while Kiera and Denny drifted farther apart. I felt bad about that, I really did, but being with Kiera felt too good to try to stop it. I wanted more of her, not less. And as close as we were, it wasn't enough.

The passion between us simmered under the surface, slowly boiling away. We dipped into it on occasion, when a touch drifted into an off-limits area or a gaze turned smoldering. We were playing with fire. I was fully aware of that. Our "innocent" flirting was complete and utter bullshit. Nothing we were doing was innocent. Maybe it wasn't quite so bad as a full-on affair, but it was damn close. We were both emotionally cheating on Denny. Of that, I was certain.

Looking him in the eye was getting harder and harder to do. Sometimes I caught myself staring at him before he left for work, willing him to decide he hated it here and he was moving back home. It tore me that I wanted him to leave. He was a significant part of my childhood, the closest thing I'd ever had to a brother, and all I wanted was for him to leave me and his girlfriend alone together so we could stop sneaking around behind his back. I was one twisted son of a bitch.

"You all right, mate?" he asked me one evening.

Tired, I'd come home from Pete's early. Kiera was still there working, and Denny was home alone. Usually, if Kiera was at the bar, I tended to stay until her shift was over. But I was the only D-Bag left at the bar, and the multiple yawns coming from me had Jenny asking why I was hanging around. I couldn't tell her I was staying to watch Kiera work. No, I'd had to leave so Jenny wouldn't catch on to the fact that Kiera was my entire world.

Throwing on a smile, I walked into the living room and sat in my comfortable chair. "Of course. Why wouldn't I be?"

My heart started beating a bit harder as Denny tilted his head and gave me a penetrating stare. "Well, for starters, it's only ten o'clock. You're usually gone a lot later than that."

I laughed at his statement. "Yeah, I suppose so. I was beat though, so I decided to call it a night." Unfortunately. I wondered what Kiera was doing right at this moment…

Denny leaned back on the misshapen couch. "Alone? Call me crazy, but I haven't noticed any sheilas hanging around since we've been here. From what I remember of your…activities…that's kind of strange. You switch sides, mate?"

I raised an eyebrow at his question and he laughed. Shaking my head, I told him, "I've just been…keeping things quiet, I guess."

With an amused smile, Denny told me, "I hope that's not for our sake. Kiera and I don't care if you have girls over. It's your house."

My smile felt tight to me, but I kept it plastered on my face. I wouldn't let my expression clue him in to just how wrong he was. Kiera would care. She would care a lot.

Denny went back to watching his TV show. Some cop drama where all the employees were dressed like they were heading out to a fashion show and not a crime scene. I was just thinking of heading upstairs to attempt to drift off to sleep with visions of Kiera in my mind when Denny let out a long sigh. Examining his face, I saw a weary haggardness that hadn't been there when he'd first arrived. He hated the situation he was currently in, but didn't know how to change it. I sympathized.

"You okay?" I asked him.

242

He looked over at me, and for a second his expression was guarded. Then he sighed again, and he looked more tired than I felt. "It's just work. I've been trying to focus on the good parts, but it's hard to do. I still hate it there, and…I know it's wrong, but I get mad at Kiera for it sometimes."

I flinched when he said her name, but worked hard to keep my face neutral. "Well, that's understandable, I suppose." I replayed dark looks I'd seen from Denny toward Kiera, arguments behind closed doors. They weren't outright fighting, but there was still tension in the relationship.

Denny looked back to the TV. "No, it's not. It's a dick move. She didn't ask me to quit my job and come back here. If I'd just given her time, she would have cooled down and we would have worked through it. I just…panicked. I felt like…I felt like I had to come back, or it would be too late…" He glanced back at me. "I'm not sure why I felt that way."

When he returned his eyes to the TV, I closed mine and swallowed a lump in my throat. He felt that way because of me. Because he had known I would fuck his girl if he left her alone and single with me. That was *my* dick move. And it was one I constantly kicked myself about.

When Denny sighed again, I opened my eyes. He was luckily staring at the TV still, and hadn't seen the guilt that had overwhelmed me. "It will all work out," I told him, hating myself even more. My intention was a good one, but the assurance was an empty one. If they worked out, Kiera and I wouldn't, and as much as I cared about Denny, I wanted her. More than anything. But Denny and I had a history, and I wanted him to be happier too. "Is there something I can do? Help you find a new job? Maybe stay at someone else's place…so you and Kiera can have some time alone…" God, I hoped he didn't take me up on that last one.

A small smile lightened Denny's expression, but he shook his head. "Unless you know some higher-ups in the advertising world, there's not much you can do for me, mate." He paused for a moment, then added, "Thank you, though. It's nice of you to offer."

I schooled my expression, but the dagger of guilt in my gut was being twisted with every word he said. He shouldn't thank me for anything.

With a frown on his face, Denny added, "As for Kiera and me having alone time…maybe that's a good idea, but I don't know. She's busy, I'm busy. Time is against us. I actually have to head out of town again tomorrow. And do you want to hear something really weird? I told Kiera I was going, and she didn't seem bothered at all. Considering how she acted the last time I left, I think that's strange."

My heart surged in my chest. He was leaving? Had my silent prayers been answered? It was almost too much to hope for. To keep up appearances, I frowned and told him a truth wrapped in a lie. "Maybe she feels guilty about what happened last time, so she's trying to handle it better." I was certain she did feel guilty about last time, but I wasn't sure how she felt about him leaving again. Was she as excited as me? We could have quality alone time…maybe we could get away for a while, go somewhere where we didn't have to hide anything. The possibilities were endless, and my heart started beating with adrenaline instead of fear.

Denny shrugged as he looked me over. "Yeah…maybe."

Not liking how he was examining me, I asked, "How long are you gone for?"

A sheepish look passed his face. "Just one night. But it feels like a thousand, you know?"

I smiled, but didn't say anything. It probably felt that long to him because he didn't trust her. And he didn't trust her because of me. Because I was a horrible human being.

He didn't say anything after that, and silence fell between us. I let it linger, because I didn't know what to say to him anymore. There was a certain amount of dark humor to the fact that we had nothing to say. You'd think we'd have a lot to talk about now, since we were both in love with the same woman.

Once I was away from Denny and the never-ending guilt of what I was doing to him, I began to get excited about the idea of him being far away again. So much had changed between Kiera and me since the first time he'd gone. I wanted to strengthen our connection, without completely betraying Denny. Impossible as that sounded.

It took me a long time to fall asleep once I finally went to bed. And when I did, only one thing was on my mind. I wanted to fall asleep with Kiera in my arms. I'd never wanted anything so badly.

The next morning, while Kiera and I held hands and sipped our morning coffees, I decided to broach the topic with her. "So, Denny's gone tonight?"

She was instantly suspicious of what I was about to ask. "Yes...he's in Portland until tomorrow night. Why?"

I looked down, wondering if she would see my heart on my sleeve; I desperately wanted to be with her tonight. Keeping my gaze on the table, I said, "Stay with me tonight."

"I stay here with you every night," she replied.

Amused by the confusion in her voice, I peeked up at her. "No...sleep with me tonight."

She seemed shocked by my suggestion. "Kellan! That is not going to—"

I had to laugh. Her mind was in the gutter, just as often as mine was. I hadn't meant it in a sexual way though. "I meant literally... fall asleep with me on my bed."

Embarrassed by what she'd assumed I meant, she looked away. When she finally returned her gaze to me, she said, "I don't think that's such a good idea, Kellan."

I gave her a carefree smile. This didn't have to be a big deal if we didn't let it. I just wanted to sleep with my arms around her...no harm in that. "Why not? Completely innocent—I won't even get under the covers."

Considering it, she raised an eyebrow in question. "Completely dressed too?"

Ecstatic that she was maybe going to say yes, I laughed and stroked her fingers with my thumb. "Sure. If that is what you'd prefer."

She laughed, then smiled. The way her lips curled up made my heart skip a beat. "It is." Euphoria burst through me. She was saying yes. My high didn't diminish at all when she frowned. "You'll let me know the moment it gets too hard."

I couldn't believe that she'd just said something so suggestive. I turned away, trying to be mature and not laugh. The sexual tension between us was so thick that I often walked around a little hard.

"You know what I mean," she whispered, embarrassment in her voice.

A laugh escaped me as I looked back at her. "Yes, I know what you mean...and yes, I will." Happiness flooded me as I gazed into her tranquil hazel eyes. "You really are adorable...do you know that?"

With a smile on her lips, she looked away from me. "Okay... we'll try it," she told me in a soft voice.

As I beamed at her, a strange sadness washed over her face. I knew she was worried she was making a mistake with me, that she would cross her self-imposed line of restraint and cave in to the lust that swirled around us. I hated seeing the guilt on her; it was a reflection of my own.

I don't want to hurt him either, Kiera. I care, just as much as you do, which is why nothing will happen tonight. I promise.

Since it was Friday, the D-Bags were playing at Pete's. Before we began the set, I told Evan we were adding in the song "Until You." He looked at me funny, then nodded. "Until You" was the sappiest song in our catalog, and Evan was usually the one to request it. In fact, I think he had requested it every time he was swooning over some girl; Matt and Griffin had nicknamed the song "Evan's Whipped Again." Evan had written the bulk of it—it was one of the very few D-Bags songs written by anyone other than me—so I guess it made sense that it was his go-to romance song. It was weird for me to ask for it, but I couldn't help it. Kiera had changed my life, given me something to live for, hope for, and as discreetly as possible, I wanted to let the world know.

246

I tried not to look at Kiera while I sang it, but I somehow hoped she knew the song was for her. Everything was for her. I spied her talking to Jenny during the song, but I couldn't tell if she was listening to the lyrics, if she was somehow understanding the hidden meaning behind my words. *I love you, and only you.*

When we got to the last song of our set, I let the crowd know there wouldn't be an encore tonight. I had a mattress to lie on and a sexy-as-hell girl to hold. I got the eager crowd's attention by holding my hand up. "Ladies…and you guys, of course." I paused for the screams and shouts. "Thank you for coming out tonight. We got one more for you; then we're baggin'." I peeked over to where Kiera was watching me. "Plans and all."

It was hot under the lights, and sweat covered my forehead and dribbled down my cheeks. With the hem of my shirt, I wiped some of the wetness off my face. The fans watching my every move went nuts, and from somewhere in the back of the bar, I heard Rita yell, "Take it off! Woooooo!"

Amused, I grinned at her, then looked over at Kiera standing in front of her. Kiera seemed both embarrassed and intrigued by the thought of me stripping down. Laughing at the idea, I looked around at the guys to see if they had any objections to it. They seemed fine with it; whatever amped up the masses.

Since I was high on life, I decided to give the fans what they were craving. Reaching down, I grabbed the edge of my shirt and pulled it up. The sound in the bar grew deafening as more of my skin was exposed. It made me laugh. When it came to visual stimulus, men and women were more alike than they cared to admit.

Tucking my shirt into the back of my jeans, I turned to Evan. He eyed my half-naked body with an amused raised eyebrow. I shrugged and told him, "Could be worse. I could be in chaps."

While Evan laughed, I told him the name of our closing song, "All You Want." I signaled him to go and he immediately started the intro. Facing the front of the stage again, I gripped the microphone and ran a hand through my hair. The fans were in a frenzy. It was chaos, excitement, noise, and adrenaline. It gave me a rush, and I was already buzzing just thinking of my upcoming slumber party.

While I played with the crowd, stretching out to make contact with the ones near the front, I glanced toward the bar. The entire staff was back there watching me...even Kiera. She was boring holes into me, like she couldn't get enough, and it turned me on to have her hungry eyes staring at me like that.

When the song was over, I took a small bow to thunderous applause. The crowd tonight had been very vocal. Maybe I should be half-naked more often. After I slipped my shirt back on, some of the girls started booing. I shook my head as I laughed. No, in some ways, girls weren't that far off from boys. Kiera was still watching me at the bar, and I gave her a huge grin. I loved having her eyes glued on me. I loved that we were going to cuddle later...all night long. For once, I wasn't going to wake up alone. I found that thought exceptionally comforting.

When Kiera's shift was finally over, I felt giddy. I couldn't stop smiling. Did love turn everyone into an idiot? Or was that just me? When she was ready to go, I led her out of the bar with my hand on the small of her back. It felt so natural to be touching her that for the moment, I didn't even care if anyone saw.

Once we were outside, I grabbed Kiera's fingers and started singing "All You Want" again. I thought she would enjoy hearing me sing it to her, but she frowned. "What?" I asked, perplexed.

She pouted, but I could tell it was a forced expression; she wasn't really upset. "Didn't we have a conversation once, about the nature of your singing?"

I laughed and gave her innocent eyes. "What was wrong with that?" Pointing back to the bar, I told her, "I was fully dressed for *nearly* all of the set."

She tried to poke me with her elbow, but I scooted away from her. Then, because I was in such a damn good mood, I ran up behind her and picked her up. She squealed in surprise and tried to get away, but I had her tight. When I finally set her down, I kept a firm hold on her. *You're not going anywhere. Not tonight. Tonight...you're mine.*

As we walked toward my car, locked together, I told her, "I did that for Pete."

She stopped moving and I ran into her back. She turned around to look at me and her eyes were wide with shock. "Oh...OH!"

I had no idea why she looked so startled. I ran through my words, trying to hear what she'd heard, and then it hit me. She'd thought I'd stripped for Pete. Literally.

Releasing her, I backed away. I had to clutch my stomach, I was laughing so hard. The image of Pete fawning over me was just too much. Priceless. "Oh my God, Kiera! No, that's not what I meant." I was tearing up now, and had to wipe my eyes dry. My natural high was making this moment even funnier than it normally would have been. If I'd been on cloud nine before, she'd just lifted me to cloud ten. "God, I can't wait to tell Griffin about that."

Kiera didn't find the moment as funny as I did. Her cheeks were flaming red, and I realized I was embarrassing her by laughing so much. I tried to control myself; it was difficult. "Ahhh...and you think *I* have a dirty mind." *Sorry, babe, but you're just as freaky as I am.*

I slipped my arms around her and let out a slow, steady, calming breath. When I felt like the uncontrollable urge to laugh had subsided, I said, "Didn't you hear the response when I did that? You watch, tomorrow the bar will be twice as full. He'll have to turn people away. I did it to help him, Kiera." Shrugging, I rocked her back and forth, savoring the connection I felt between us.

Her expression shifted from annoyance to understanding. "Oh...well, I guess that makes sense. You bring in more people, he makes more money, you get more exposure, and I'm assuming more money as well..."

I really didn't give a rat's ass about the money I made, but she had the basic idea down. "Something like that."

Her lip curled into the sexiest half smile I'd ever seen. My breath caught in my throat. I wanted to taste her skin, feel her softness, lose myself in kissing her...

"I guess I'll just have to allow it then," she told me. Then she leaned over and kissed my cheek.

Warmth burst across my face where she'd touched me. Not wasting a second, I kissed her cheek in return. She blinked, surprised, and a euphoria-filled smirk curved my lips. "If you get to break a rule...so do I."

I gave her a wink, then started pushing her toward the Chevelle. I was ready for the cuddling portion of our evening to begin. I was ready for a lot of things to begin.

As we got into the car, Kiera commented, "You're awful perky tonight."

I couldn't contain my smile. "It's not every night that I get to sleep with a beautiful woman." Honestly, I couldn't even remember the last time I'd slept all night with a girl. I was pretty sure I never had. If a girl came over for sex, she left soon afterward. If I went somewhere for sex, I left afterward. Cuddling had never even been suggested before. Kiera didn't know it, but tonight was a first for me.

As I started the car, I noticed that she seemed a little uneasy about my remark; she'd taken it as dirty again. She also seemed a bit...sad. To ease her mind that we weren't doing anything overly wrong, I told her, "Hey, I said sleep, not fu—"

Her tone was sharp as she interrupted my coarse language. "Kellan!"

Her displeased expression was so distracting that I had a little trouble thinking up a different term to use. I sifted through *F* words until I found one that was slightly more savory. "Fu... or...ni...cate?" She had to give me props for trying.

Laughing, she scooted across the seat until she was pressed into my side, then she laid her head on my shoulder. Heaven.

When we got home, Kiera disappeared into her bedroom. For a moment, I thought she was going to back out of our arrangement. Disappointment instantly surged over me. I wanted this so much it hurt. It took her twenty minutes, but she eventually stepped out of her room, fully dressed. She was even wearing a sweater. I laughed as I looked her over. All that was missing was a set of gloves, a hat, and maybe a hazmat suit, and she'd be as protected from me as she could be.

As she stepped into the bathroom to brush her teeth, I playfully asked her, "Are you sure you'll be warm enough in that?" She rolled her eyes as she shut the door, and I laughed. *This is happening.*

When she was finished, I changed places with her. As I stared at myself in the mirror, I heard her walk into my bedroom. She was in my room. Closing my eyes, I exhaled a slow breath. I could do this. I could keep it light, carefree, casual. I wouldn't mess up and scare her away by going too far. Even though I wanted nothing more than to kiss every inch of her body, I would be good. The connection was what mattered, not the physical stuff. When I reopened my eyes, I glanced at my reflection. I still had sort of a glow about me, thanks to the layer of dried sweat on my face. I ran the water, made it as warm as I could tolerate, then rinsed my face. When I was done, I patted myself dry and looked again. I still seemed to be radiating. Maybe it was Kiera giving me the glow. With a shake of my head, I brushed my teeth. I was hopeless. Absolutely hopeless.

When I got back to my room, Kiera was standing in the middle of it, staring at the bed, her expression torn. I considered asking her what she was thinking about, but then she might want to talk about us. I wasn't ready for that. There was safety in silence.

I indicated the bed, which she seemed reluctant to get into. "Go ahead. It won't bite you." With a laugh, I added, "I won't either." *Keep it light, keep it playful.*

She looked back at me with an amused smile, then took a deep breath and crawled under the covers. Like I told her I would, I lay down on top of the covers. It was an odd way to sleep, and I was pretty sure I was going to freeze my butt off, but I'd put up with anything to be with her. Accepting my chilly fate, I rolled over onto my side to face her. I slung my leg over hers and draped an arm over her stomach. Even through the blankets between us, it felt amazing to be next to her. It felt right, like I belonged beside her.

Stretching across her, I turned off the light on my nightstand. Darkness blinded me, but my other senses sharpened. I could smell the flowery fragrance of her shampoo as I laid my head down beside her and pulled her close. I could hear her soft breathing. My heart pounded in my chest, and I was instantly aware of every section of my body that was touching hers. What I wouldn't give to be under the covers with her. To have nothing between us, no sheets, no clothes…no secrets, no walls.

"Kellan…" Her voice sounded a little strained, like she was struggling.

"Yeah?"

"Could you please turn the light back on?"

A soft laugh escaped me at her question. My closeness *was* getting to her. That made me happy. I wanted to get under her skin.

Reaching across her again, I flipped the light back on. I blinked in the harshness, and immediately missed the intimacy of the dark. Without light on us, it was easier to pretend that we weren't doing anything wrong…that we weren't skirting around a very dangerous cliff, where only pain and suffering were waiting for us if we fell.

Shaking off my morose thoughts, I lightly asked her, "Better?" Settling back down on the pillows, I propped myself up on an elbow so I could look down at her. Her eyes were more golden than green tonight. Honey, with emerald flakes. Gorgeous.

She seemed mesmerized as we stared at each other. Then all of a sudden, she blurted out, "Who was your first time?"

Her random question caught me off guard. "What? Why?"

Looking embarrassed, she swallowed. "Well, you asked about Denny and me. It's only fair."

Now I was embarrassed, and I studied my sheets. I shouldn't have gone there, shouldn't have asked her that. Damn curiosity. "I guess I did, didn't I?" I peeked up at her. "Sorry about that…that really wasn't any of my business."

She gave me a victorious smile. "Just answer the question."

I laughed as she used my line against me. Touché. Thinking back through my numerous dalliances, I tried to recall the details about the girl who'd taken my virginity. Bright blue eyes, platinum-blond hair, and a smile that promised a good time instantly filled my mind. I couldn't remember her name...I'd always called her Marilyn in my mind. Marilyn Monroe. Classy, curvy, and kind of slutty.

While I recalled the past, a funny expression formed on Kiera's face, like she couldn't believe I had to think about it. I suppose it was a lot easier for her; she was still dating her first time. I laughed at her look, then told her, "Well...she was a girl from the neighborhood, sixteen, I think...very pretty. She seemed to like me..." Remembering just how much she'd liked me, I smiled. "It was just a couple of times one summer."

Her expression changed and her voice came out quiet, like she was afraid her question would hurt me. "Oh...why, what happened?"

She seemed so serious about it that I couldn't resist teasing her, and a part of me was curious if she'd believe me if I said something outlandish. Running my fingers through her hair, I murmured, "I got her pregnant and she had to move in with her aunt to have the baby."

She immediately flipped to her side to face me. "What!"

Laughing, I poked her nose. "I'm just kidding, Kiera."

With a grunt, she pushed me away. "That's not nice."

I sat up on my elbow again. "You bought it though. You must think the worst of me." By her tone, I could tell she hadn't doubted my story...because deep down, she thought I was the kind of person who would just abandon someone in that situation. She thought I would run if things were too hard. And I almost did run from Kiera. Was that why she didn't trust me? Was I trustworthy? Look at what I'd done to Denny. "I'm not a monster, Kiera." I may have broken Denny's trust, but I'd never break hers.

Kiera propped herself up on her elbow and faced me. "You're no angel either, Kyle." She grinned at me in such an appealing way that I had no choice but to return her smile. I supposed she had a point. "So, what really did happen to the girl?" she asked.

I shrugged. The real story wasn't all that interesting. "Nothing so dramatic. She went to her school, I went to mine. Different paths..."

Confusion passed over Kiera's eyes. "I thought you said she was a neighbor. Why were you in different schools?"

My face went blank as I realized my mistake. I couldn't tell her the truth, that I was incredibly young. Illegal young. Kiera wouldn't understand what I'd been going through, what my life had been like, how sex had been my only comfort from endless torture. No, all she would see was my age. She'd be disgusted, think horrible thoughts about me. I didn't want Kiera to think I was a sex-addicted monster. And I didn't want her to think I was broken, messed up... so lonely I could barely stand myself. I didn't want her to see the dark spots inside me. I wasn't ready to open up like that. Just the thought made me nauseous, so I gave her the vaguest answer I could think of. "We weren't in the same grade."

I could see the gears in Kiera's head turning, and I knew I needed to shift the conversation. "But she was sixteen... How old were you?"

It was the exact question I didn't want to answer. But somehow, before I could stop myself, a portion of it slipped out anyway. "Not sixteen..." *No... I was twelve years old. Clueless. A child. But you wouldn't understand...*

Kiera still looked confused. "But—"

Angry at myself for letting way too much out, I firmly told her, "You should get some sleep, Kiera... it's late." *And I'm not going to talk about this anymore.*

I thought she would fight for more information, but instead, she seemed to sense that I wasn't ready, and she let it go. She brought her hand out from under the covers, and smiling, grateful, I held it. We both settled back on the pillows, and I reached out to her and pulled her onto my chest. With her head above my heart, I began stroking her hair and rubbing her back. Peace replaced all the anxiety that I'd felt about her finding out about my past. None of that mattered anyway. Only right now, with her in my arms, mattered.

She nestled into my body and I instinctually kissed her head. It happened before I could stop it, but she didn't push me away, didn't storm from the room. She didn't do anything. She just lay on me, enjoying my comfort as much as I was enjoying hers.

While we lay together, her fingers started tracing my body. She began near the cut along my ribs, the knife wound I'd gotten for her. She then ran her fingers up my chest, and my heart started beating heavier. It felt so nice to have her touch me. Sighing softly, I squeezed her tight.

She noticed that she was affecting me, and I watched as she pushed herself up to look at me. Tiredness was in her eyes, but it only made them more intoxicating. "Kellan, maybe we shouldn't—"

No, I don't want this to end. Ever. "I'm fine, Kiera... Get some sleep."

She lay back down, but shifted to rest in the crook of my shoulder. That was fine; it felt nice too. She reached over to grab my hand and lace our fingers together. She brought our entwined fingers under her cheek, then rested her head on them. I sighed in happiness; I'd never felt such a warm connection with anyone before. I thought the world could end right now, and I'd still be completely at peace.

I kissed her head again and she whispered, "Kellan...?"

Knowing she was concerned that this was becoming too much for me, I reassured her. "Really, I'm fine, Kiera..."

She peeked up at my face. "No, I was just wondering... why do you want to do this with me? I mean, you know it's not going anywhere... why waste your time?"

A slice of pain cut through my perfect moment, but I buried it as best I could. I would take whatever she could give me. "No time with you is wasted, Kiera. If this is all..." I couldn't confess all my desperation, so I left it at that.

For the first time, she seemed to understand that this wasn't about sex for me. That she meant something to me, and I was struggling to handle the fact that she didn't want to be with me. As she gazed at my face, I knew she was seeing me... *really* seeing me. It hurt, but I didn't pull away, change the conversation, or alter my expression. This was me, laid bare.

Her eyes were battling some inner confusion as she released my hand and stroked my cheek. It amplified the pain. I'd never have her. Not fully. Brief glimpses of happiness would be all that I had with her, because tomorrow night, she'd be back in her bed, with Denny by her side, and I'd be alone. Always alone.

Now that I knew how amazing this felt, I hated the thought of never getting to feel it again. I didn't want to be alone anymore. I didn't want to be without her anymore. I didn't want to share her anymore. Selfishly, I wanted every section, every piece, every corner. I knew I was pushing against a line I'd sworn to never cross again, but Denny didn't appreciate what he had. I did. I cherished every second I had with her, and I wanted our connection to be deeper. I wanted more.

Losing myself, I leaned over and kissed her, but just the very corner of her lips. I was shocked at myself for making a move that was clearly going too far, but Kiera was surprised too, and she didn't push me away. I left my head there, breathing softly on her warm skin, and she did nothing. Nothing but hold her breath and continue to stroke my cheek.

As her thumb brushed my skin, subconsciously urging me onward, my resolve weakened. I wanted her so much. I needed her so much. I lowered my lips to her jaw and placed a light kiss there, then a light kiss under her jaw. She still did nothing, and she tasted so sweet...I needed more. My hands ducked under the covers and slid up to her waist, pulling her into me. My breath grew heavier, and with a soft groan, I trailed kisses down her throat. *Yes. More.*

My fingers clenched and unclenched around her hip. I wanted to rip the covers off, rip her clothes off, remove all the barriers between us. Breaths coming fast and shallow now, I pulled my lips away from her skin and rested my forehead against hers. I wanted her mouth on mine.

"Kiera..." *I need you. Kiss me...or stop me.*

I stared down at her, willing her to kiss me, praying that she didn't. *Would another taste drive me mad?* She wasn't saying anything, but her expression was a mixture of conflicting desires.

There was a connection between us, something beyond just physical attraction...I was sure of it. I saw the way she cared about me in her shy smile, felt it in the casual way she laid her head on my shoulder when she was tired, heard it in her laugh during the brief carefree moments when neither one of us felt guilty about what we were doing. Kiera was struggling under the weight of maintaining the barrier between friend and lover. She was torn, same as me, but I couldn't stop myself anymore...

As my lips started lowering toward hers, her fingers on my cheek shifted over to cover my mouth, feebly trying to stop me. Groaning, loving the feeling of her skin against mine, I ignored her gentle rejection and closed my eyes. She didn't move her fingers or try to stop me from kissing her, so I pressed my lips against hers, even though her hand was still between us. Pretending her hand wasn't separating our lips, I kissed her fingers. Kissing them wasn't enough though, and I started pulling her fingers away from my lips.

"I want to feel you..."

When her top lip was exposed, I pressed mine against it. Kiera acted as if I'd dumped ice water down her back. With a sharp inhale, she shoved me away and scrambled out of bed. That was when I truly realized what I'd just done, and what it might have cost me. Kiera didn't want this with me; she'd said so a hundred times.

Out of breath and feeling panicked, I quickly sat up. "Kiera, I'm so sorry. I won't..." I swallowed a few times, trying to calm down. *Please don't tell me this is over.*

Kiera was struggling to breathe normally as she stared at me with wide eyes. "No, Kellan...this was a really bad idea. I'm going to go to my room. Alone."

She pointed at me, and I felt like her finger was a dagger in my heart. *No, don't leave me.* I struggled to move my body. I felt like my hands and feet had turned to lead. "Wait...I'm fine, just give me a minute. It will pass..." *Please don't go.*

She put both arms up to stop me. "No...please stay here. I

can't... I can't do this. That was too close, Kellan. This is too hard." She backed up to the door.

No... please don't say goodbye. I'll be good. "Wait, Kiera... I'll do better. Don't... don't end this..."

She paused as she took in my stricken face. I felt like my world was shattering as my utopia crumbled around me. I was an idiot for thinking tonight would be anything other than a gigantic mistake. I should let her go, I just couldn't.

Her expression softened as sympathy washed through her. "I need to be alone tonight. We'll talk tomorrow, okay?"

I couldn't speak anymore, so I nodded and watched her leave. Like me, she was going to be alone tonight. Her torment would end tomorrow though, while mine would continue. But at least I'd had a moment of pure peace with her. Even though my heart was cracking and I was terrified she'd change her mind and stop this thing we were doing, I would hold on to the feeling of holding her in my arms. I'd hold on to it forever.

I love you, Kiera. And I'm sorry.

Much to my surprise, Kiera didn't end things the next morning. Exhausted from a sleepless night of thinking about her, and about what she might say to me after the incident on my bed, I'd gone to her room as early as I'd felt I could. As painful as the prospect of losing her was, I needed to know if she was going to kick me to the curb or give me another chance. When she only gave me a brief reprimand, telling me to not take it that far again, a surge of relief washed through me. Right or wrong, she didn't want to end this yet either.

The bar was hopping later that evening, bursting at the seams with people, thanks to my little half monty the night before, but I wasn't into it. Holding Kiera in my bed was the only thing on my mind. Last night might have been the last time that happened. It made me a little sad to think about it. I felt like a gong was going off in my brain—a constant reminder of Kiera and Denny reuniting. It almost made me want to ask Denny to leave again. Or make him leave. I couldn't though; he wasn't to blame for any of this. I'd created this mess by allowing it to happen. I never should have wanted something that wasn't mine.

A couple of days later, I picked up Kiera from school and we headed over to our favorite place in a park nearby. It was near the school, within walking distance, and we came here sometimes when we wanted to enjoy the day, and nature, and each other. The first time I'd come across Kiera here, I'd accused her of stalking me, since I stopped here to exercise sometimes when I went for a run. We'd laughed, joked around, and had nearly kissed that day. We seemed to be nearly kissing a lot lately. Being around her was incredible, but difficult too. Pain and pleasure twisted together so thoroughly that it was sometimes hard to separate the two.

With an espresso in one hand, I grabbed a blanket from my trunk with the other. It was sunny out, but crisp and cold. Winter was fast approaching. Kiera was bundled up in a puffy purple jacket, but her nose was still pink. I had the oddest desire to rub my nose against hers—pink against pink—but I didn't know if that would be crossing a line or not, so I didn't.

We found a spot to lay the blanket down, near a field where a few people were running around, trying to stay warm. Setting my coffee in the grass, I snapped the blanket, then let it float to the ground. Careful to not spill her own coffee, Kiera settled onto her hip, then smiled up at me. The joy on her face stole my breath. Even though Denny was back, Kiera beamed at me whenever she saw me. And maybe I was wishing it to be true, but…she didn't seem to be smiling as widely for Denny. Or as often. In fact, they didn't seem to be spending much time together at all. Just the other day, Denny had skipped out on Kiera right before they were supposed to go see a movie together—it was at least the second time he had left her dateless. She'd been mad at him for it, but then she'd invited me to go with her instead, and we'd had a great night together. I tried not to feel bad about Denny's dwindling connection with her. Or happy either. Their relationship was separate from ours, or so I convinced myself. I would be whatever Kiera needed me to be.

We sipped our coffees in a comfortable silence. As much as the liquid coursing down my throat warmed me, it was nothing compared to sitting beside Kiera. She heated me from the very center of my core. Thawed cold, dark places that I hadn't even been aware of before. Just being around her made everything better.

When our drinks were finished, we put the empty cups on the grass, and I grabbed her fingers. They were still warm from holding her hot drink. Kiera interrupted the quiet with a question that I was surprised to hear her ask. "That song the other weekend, the kind of intense one... it's not really about a woman, is it?"

I knew exactly what song she was referring to. It was called "I Know," and like she'd said, I'd played it a while back. The song was about a woman in an abusive relationship. Hiding behind that lie was as close to my past as I could get. I hadn't realized she'd been listening to the words so intently, and I hadn't known that she'd have enough insight into me that she'd be able to see right through the lyrics. How the hell did she know?

Seeing the unasked question on my face, she supplied an answer, one I hadn't considered. "Denny. He told me what happened, while he was staying with your family. The song was about you, wasn't it? You and your dad?"

I turned away from her and gazed out over the park. Denny. I should have guessed that he would tell her. It kind of hurt that he'd told her something so private, but on the other hand, I was kind of glad she knew. I didn't want to talk about it though. I nodded, but didn't say anything.

"Do you want to talk about it?" she quietly asked.

"No." I didn't ever want to talk about it. There was no point in even thinking about it, much less discussing it. It was what it was.

"Will you anyway?" she asked, pain and compassion in her voice.

With a sniff, I looked down at the grass. Grabbing a blade, I twirled it in my fingers. I kind of felt like that ribbon of grass, being spun around against my will. What would the grass say, if it could talk? *Do what you will with me, I'm already torn open.*

When I peeked up at her, my father's condemning eyes clouded my vision. "There's nothing to talk about, Kiera." *He beat me up because he hated me, and everything I represented. Mom allowed him to do whatever he wanted to me because I ruined her life. I ruin everything; just look what I did to you and Denny...* "If Denny told

261

you what he saw, what he did for me, then you know as much as anyone."

"Not as much as you." Her voice was firm, but full of empathy. Ice ran down my spine. She wasn't going to drop it this time; she was going to pull, pry, and try to unearth my secrets. I wasn't ready to tell them; I didn't think I'd ever be ready. And yet... I didn't want to stop.

Looking like she was sorry for asking, she said, "Did he hit you often?"

So many memories bombarded me that I couldn't separate them all. Cringing under his heavy fists, screaming as his belt bit into the flesh of my bare thighs. Crying. Begging for him to stop...

My heart pounded in my chest, and my throat completely closed. I couldn't speak now if I wanted to. With a hard swallow, I nodded, just once. It was a weak, pathetic way to answer a question, but it was the hardest admission I'd ever made in my life. *Yes, he beat me all the time. Every goddamn night he found a reason to hurt me. I couldn't do anything right. And I tried. I tried so hard to be good.*

"Very badly?" Kiera asked, clearly struggling with her own emotions.

I didn't want to answer her, I desperately wanted to change the subject, but her eyes held me, and after a long time, I finally nodded again, just once. There were times I couldn't sit, and times I couldn't stand. Broken bones, bruised ribs, concussions... I'd had it all.

"Since you were little?"

I nodded again, and my vision grew hazy as tears stung my eyes. *For as long as I can remember.*

Kiera swallowed, and I could tell she didn't want to ask any more painful questions, but she couldn't stop herself now either. She'd already ripped off the bandage; now she had to clean the wound before she could re-dress it. "Didn't your mom ever try to stop him... help you?"

It was clear that all of this was unfathomable to her. Understandable. From what I could tell, Kiera's parents were warm, loving, good. Mine...were not. I shook my head no, and a tear in my eye rolled down my cheek as I remembered Mom watching me with disdain, like everything being done to me had been my fault. "You brought this on yourself, Kellan," was her frequent response.

I could see the horror on Kiera's face even more clearly once the watery obstruction in my vision was gone. I wasn't sure if that was a good thing or not. Seeing the look on her face brought even more memories rushing to the surface. They pummeled me relentlessly.

Her eyes as watery as mine, Kiera asked, "Did it end when Denny left?"

My mind shifted to the months of abuse after Denny had gone back home. My dad was furious that he'd gotten caught, that I'd made him look bad, that there had been a crack in the façade... that I had begun to grow a backbone. He and Mom wanted to look like the perfect family. Appearances had been everything to them. Much more important than me.

Swallowing the knot in my throat, I shook my head again. "It got worse...so much worse." I was surprised I could tell her that. I was surprised I could speak at all.

Again looking like she couldn't picture such cruelty, she whispered, "Why?"

Because there is nothing about me worth loving, a fact proven by what I have done to you and my best friend.

"You'd have to ask them," I whispered.

She started crying in earnest now, but I only felt numb inside, scoured raw by the memories. I impassively watched her tears falling, then watched as she put her arms around my neck and held me close. "I'm so sorry, Kellan," she whispered in my ear.

I loosely brought my arms around her; pain was beginning to seep through the edges of the numbness, all the more intense because I was rubbed raw. "It's okay, Kiera. It was years ago. They haven't hurt me in a long time." *This shouldn't still hurt so much. I should be over it.*

She held me tight, and it all became too much. I couldn't contain the anguish, couldn't reconstruct the wall she'd torn down. A lifetime of pain ricocheted around my body, bouncing from one corner to the other. Each hit left me bruised and battered, and I shook as silent tears coursed down my cheeks.

After several minutes, Kiera pulled back to gaze at me. She said nothing about the moisture on my skin, the redness in my tired eyes. She just brought her hands to my cheeks, wiping them dry as she held me. One last tear fell from my eye as I gazed at her beautiful, loving face. *Why can't you love me like I love you? Why can't anyone? How awful am I?*

Kiera leaned over and kissed my tear away. Her warmth seared me to the core. *I need you…so much.* As she pulled away, I turned toward her mouth. I didn't mean to; it was an instinct driven by pure need. *I need the pain to end…this is the only way I know how to end it.*

Our lips brushed together, but neither one of us moved. Afraid to move, afraid to break this connection that was second by second depleting my grief, I held my breath. I wasn't sure how long we sat that way, our lips pressed together, Kiera's hands on my cheeks, but eventually I needed air. I needed to breathe, and she was the best thing I could think to inhale. Surely she'd fill the void in my chest better than oxygen ever could.

I opened my lips to suck in air…and Kiera kissed me.

Her lips moved against mine, and the tears nearly returned to my eyes…it felt so good. I returned her kiss immediately, and we softly moved against each other. I couldn't believe she was letting me do this, and by the way she was trembling, I thought she couldn't believe it either. The movement was warm, tender, full of depth and meaning, but it stoked a fire within me, and it wasn't long before I wanted more…so much more. I wanted to feel her all over, kiss her all over, love her all over. I wanted all of her.

Grabbing her neck, I pulled her in for a deeper kiss. Our tongues brushed together and she groaned, then pushed me away. I instantly realized my error. I'd let it happen again, broken her rule about how close we could and couldn't get. She was going to freak out on me, leave me. She'd be gone. I'd be alone. I couldn't handle that, especially right now, when I still felt so vulnerable.

"I'm sorry, I'm so sorry. I thought you'd changed your mind." *Please don't change your mind. Please don't go.*

Kiera's face was a mixture of confusion, guilt, sadness, and desire. "No...that was my fault. I'm sorry, Kellan. This isn't working."

All of my fears were wrapped up in that one sentence. She couldn't end this. I didn't know what I'd do without her. Leaning forward, I grabbed her arm. "No, please. I'll do better, I'll be stronger. Please don't end this. Please don't leave me..." *Don't ever leave me. I love you. I can't live without you.*

Kiera bit her lip, clearly troubled by my passionate plea. "Kellan..."

I couldn't lose her. "Please," I begged, searching her face for some sign of hope. *Don't leave me.*

A tear ran down her cheek and she choked on her words. "This isn't fair. This isn't fair to Denny. This isn't fair to you." Her voice trembled. "I'm being cruel to you."

Sitting up on my knees, I grabbed both of her hands. "No...no you're not. You're giving me more than...Just don't stop this." *Please...I've never had anything even close to this. I love you so much. Don't go...*

She was dumbfounded by my response. "What *is* this to you, Kellan?"

I looked down. I couldn't tell her. I didn't know what she'd do if she knew the truth. If she knew what she *really* meant to me, she'd run away. She'd definitely end this. I needed to bring back the carefree, casual playfulness that we'd had before. I just didn't know how to do that at the moment. "Please," I murmured, hoping it would be enough.

She let out a sigh heavy with disquiet. "Okay...okay, Kellan."

I looked up at her, relieved. I'd get to keep her. At least for today, I'd get to keep her.

The week continued on peacefully after the park incident. Kiera and I didn't talk about it again, and I was grateful for that. We also didn't talk about how things were surely and slowly escalating between us. I was torn on that problem. I wanted us to go back to friendship; I wanted us to steamroll right into a sexual relationship. I wanted both sides of the coin with her—passion *and* companionship. But she already had a partner on the flip side of her coin. A partner who was growing increasingly aware of his girlfriend's distracted attitude.

I was in the kitchen with Denny one morning, finishing my coffee while Kiera was upstairs taking a shower. Denny glanced up at the ceiling, then back down at me. "I can't wait anymore. I have to go…Will you tell Kiera goodbye for me?"

I froze with my mug to my lips. Denny looked sad, and wary, and…worn. I instantly felt a tidal wave of guilt building in my chest. Setting my cup on the table, I nodded. "Sure, no problem."

He nodded in return, his eyes distant. "She used to always walk me out, no matter what was going on between us. I know I've been working a lot, but…it's like she's not even trying anymore, like she doesn't care that we're drifting…." he muttered, clearly talking to himself. I clenched my jaw as Denny's comment cut right to the quick. Yes, Denny's unyielding commitment to his subpar job *was* a kink in their relationship, but I was pretty sure *I* was the real reason Kiera wasn't as attentive as she used to be. I was causing him pain by taking away a part of the person he loved the most. I hated myself for that. He didn't deserve any of this, but I was incapable of changing anything; I needed her too much.

"She's probably just preoccupied with school…work." *Me.*

Denny looked over at me like he'd forgotten I was there. Guess he hadn't meant to say all of that out loud. He rarely aired their problems directly to me. I wasn't sure if that was out of respect for Kiera, or out of fear that I might somehow take advantage of the chinks in their armor. Normally I would tell him that I'd never go there, I'd never hurt him like that…but I already had. I'd already fucked everything up, so I didn't offer him any meaningless assurances. It was the least I could do.

Giving me a smile that still looked sad, he said, "Yeah, well, I'll be glad when her sister gets here. Maybe hanging out with family will help."

I could only nod. God, I was such a bastard. I should stop hanging out with Kiera. I should stop testing the limits of our relationship. I should stop dreaming about her, thinking about her, hoping for a future with her. There was no future there. Stealing her away, which I would never actually be able to do, would kill Denny. And I loved him too.

Not knowing what to tell him, I said, "Yeah, we picked a dance club to take her to. It should be fun."

Denny tilted his head and his dark eyes narrowed. "We? Kiera told me that *she* found a spot she thought Anna would like. You helped?"

I could see the unasked question in his eyes and I immediately started backpedaling. I should never have lumped Kiera and me together. We weren't a "we." "I was standing there when she asked Griffin." That was almost true. *I* had asked Griffin where we should take Anna, but Denny didn't need to know that. I gave him a playful, mischievous smile. "You don't want to know where he first suggested taking her."

The suspicion softened in his eyes as he smiled. "I can only imagine." He laughed. With one last glance upstairs, he sighed and said, "I'm gonna be late. Catch ya later, mate."

"Bye, Denny." I laid my head on the table after he left. *I am a horrible, horrible person.*

When Kiera came back downstairs, I was in the living room, looking at a program running on the TV but not really seeing it. Kiera laughed as she joined me on the couch. Pointing to the TV, she said, "Sienna Sexton? I didn't realize you were a fan."

I finally tuned in to what was playing—a documentary on the biggest pop star on the planet. Finding the remote, I shut it off. "I'm not," I told her with a smile. My grin slipped as guilt washed over me. "You missed Denny leaving. He told me to tell you goodbye."

Kiera's expression went from amused to horrified. "Oh…" She

looked down, and seemed unsure what to do with that information. *Join the club.*

She was a good person, and the paradox bothered her, which made me feel even worse. Even when I tried to do the right thing, I hurt her. All of this was so strange, complicated, and painful. I wished I could have her and avoid all the tangled bits, but that wasn't my reality. I grabbed her hand and interlaced our fingers, reaffirming our profound connection. *This* was our reality, and I would hold on to it. Kicking and screaming if I had to.

We held each other after that, until finally it was time for us to begin our day. The afternoon went normally enough; I took her to school, picked her up afterward, took her home, and then helped her study. I took her to work, then met up with the guys for rehearsal. After fine-tuning some of our songs, the lot of us descended on Pete's for some liquid refreshments. A pretty typical day.

Leaning back in my chair, I listened as Matt told me about how his grandpa wanted to come up for the holidays, but he hated to fly. Pointing over at Griffin, Matt said, "The rocket scientist over there told him he should drive."

I shrugged. That didn't sound completely unreasonable to me, but by the smirk on Matt's face, there was a catch. "Let me guess, he doesn't own a car?"

Matt's smile grew. "Oh no, he does. It's parked in his garage. In his house. On Maui."

Griffin scowled as Matt and I started laughing. "What? There's gotta be a ferry or some shit like that that he could take. Hawaii isn't *that* far away." Griffin grinned. "Maybe he could sign up for a singles cruise. Get lei'd while he's getting laid."

Matt made a disgusted face while I laughed even more. Griffin might actually be onto something with that last suggestion. Well, minus the getting laid, of course. Unless his grandpa wanted to. He was related to Griffin as well as Matt, so he could be randy as all get out. The thought gave me a shiver and I looked around the bar to clear the image of Griffin's personality in an old man's body.

My gaze passed over a table of women giggling and staring my way, obviously trying to get my attention. I continued on past them until I found Kiera. She was frowning when our eyes met. She quickly fixed her face, but too late; I'd already seen the sadness. Was she still sad about this morning, or was something else bothering her? She wasn't having second thoughts about us—was she?

I slowly got up and walked over to her. My heart started thudding as I approached where she was wiping down a table. If she ended this, I had no idea what I would do. When I was right beside her, I rested my hand on the table, close enough to hers that our fingers touched. "Hey."

"Hi." She looked up at me with a shy smile that made her even more incredibly beautiful. My heart squeezed. *Don't end this yet. I need you.* Almost like she could hear me, she straightened and stepped closer, until our bodies were touching.

We were really close together, closer than friends would stand. Even though the bar was busy, our proximity was odd. I didn't care though. I needed to know what she'd been thinking about. We were close enough for me to discreetly stroke her pant leg with my finger. "You looked like you were thinking of something… unpleasant. Anything you want to talk about?"

Please, let it be anything other than you changing your mind. Don't leave me.

She opened her mouth to answer, but stopped when Griffin walked over and clasped my shoulder. I could have turned around and slugged him. Instead, I stepped away from Kiera so he wouldn't notice that he'd interrupted a moment. Not that Griffin ever paid close attention to things that didn't involve him.

"Oh, man, you have got to see this little hottie at the bar," he said, biting his knuckle. "She totally wants me… Think I could nail her in the back room?"

I glanced back at the girl that had Griffin in a tizzy. A pretty woman with long, straight brown hair was sitting on a bar stool, facing the crowd. She had on a tight, short dress, and with her legs crossed, she was showing a lot of thigh. Her eyes locked on me once I turned around and met her gaze. Biting her lip, she shifted in her seat like she was so turned on she couldn't stand it. I wasn't sure if she was interested in Griffin or not, but *somebody* could probably nail her in the back room; she was definitely primed and ready to go.

Eyes glued on me, the woman never once looked Griffin's way. That seemed to clue him in that maybe it wasn't *him* she was interested in. "Oh fuck, man! Did you already bang her? God, I hate getting your seconds. They never shut up about—"

I was officially going to kill Griffin. Kiera hearing about the two of us sharing women was the last thing I wanted to happen. She'd be disgusted. *I* was disgusted. I knew it had probably happened before…but I really didn't want to think about it, and I definitely didn't want to talk about it. There were some things that were better left unspoken.

I smacked him in the chest to cut him off. "Griff!"

He didn't seem to get the hint. But of course, he wouldn't. "Dude, what?"

Irritated that Griffin didn't have more brain cells floating around his head, and that he found it impossible to think about anyone other than himself, I flung my hands at Kiera. She did *not* want to hear about his exploits. Or mine.

Griffin blinked as he looked at Kiera, like he hadn't even realized that she was there. Focused on possibly scoring tonight, he probably hadn't noticed her. Griffin gave new meaning to the phrase "one-track mind." "Oh, hey, Kiera."

Thankfully, the cock magnet at the bar drew Griffin away from us. I had no idea what to say to Kiera. She seemed bothered by the conversation, and I didn't blame her. I was a little disturbed too. Knowing there was nothing I could say in a bar packed with eavesdroppers, I turned and went back to the table. I'd talk to her later, when we were alone. I needed to clear up this mess, and I needed to know why she'd looked upset before. I needed to know what she was thinking, what she was planning. If my heart would soon be breaking.

Kiera seemed off as she continued her shift. I wasn't sure why, and it worried me. I offered to stay and give her a ride home, but she turned me down. She did that sometimes, if she thought I was tired, or if she didn't want to raise too much suspicion. I wasn't sure what her reason was tonight, and that worried me too.

I couldn't sleep when I got home. My mind was spinning with doubt. When I heard the front door unlock and crack open, I sat up on my bed. Kiera's light footsteps started coming up the stairs and I walked to my door. Opening it, I waited in the dark recess of my room until she walked by. When I spotted her, I playfully grabbed her, pulled her inside, then shut the door and backed her into it. With my palms against the door on either side of her body, I leaned in and trapped her in place. No one to bother us now.

With our lips just inches apart, I whispered, "Sorry about Griffin. He can be...kind of, well, an ass." I smiled, hoping she wasn't still bothered by that little fiasco. When she didn't say anything, I asked her, "What were you thinking about earlier?" *Please don't tell me it was about stopping this...*

In the dim light of my moonlit room, I could see her lips parting, but no words came out. She seemed frozen, and not just because I was holding her against the door. Her breath quickened and her gaze flicked over my face like she couldn't get enough of what she was seeing. And as I watched, desire filled her eyes. *She wanted me.*

"Kiera, what are you thinking about, right now?" She still didn't answer me, only fluttered her eyes as a shiver passed through her. "Kiera?" *Tell me you want me.*

My eyes roamed down the sensuous body I was longing to touch. I was suddenly, instantly aware of how close together we were, how dark and intimate my room was. My body hardened in response.

Before I knew what I was doing, I pressed my chest firmly against hers. It felt so right, but so wrong too; we were too close, too intimate. We were crossing a line, but my reasons to stay away—the friend who was closer to me than family, the look on his face as he discussed his fears about his love life, the long-ago promise I'd made him to stay away from his girlfriend—all of those memories were fading as the bond between Kiera and me ignited. My hands left the hard wood of the door and found the softness of her body. My fingers ran down her shoulders to her waist. I stopped at her hips. I wanted to feel the smooth skin there, just underneath her jeans. If I unbuttoned them, I could slip my hands inside. She'd feel so good...

Stopping myself, I stared deep into her eyes. "Kiera...say something." *I don't know what's right anymore. Help me. Guide me. Love me.*

She still didn't speak, but I saw the hungry debate in her eyes, the way she tracked my every movement, the way her chest was heaving against mine. Her reasons were slipping away just as surely as mine were, and the question *Why can't we have this?* was screaming around us in the silence. The unasked question bounced off the walls, reverberated in our souls, and I didn't have a good answer this time, a reason worthy of pulling away. Kiera didn't seem to have one either.

Our pent-up desires had shifted into overdrive. Kiera was so riled up, so ready for me, I could almost taste it. I wanted to taste her. I wanted to lay her down and feel every inch of her under my skin. I wanted to slip inside her, hear her cry my name, watch her face when she fell apart, tell her I loved her. My control left me, and I brought my forehead to hers. So close. I could feel her breath washing over my face. Her lips were right there...beckoning me to find them. I slid my knee between hers, closing all the gaps between us. Having her so close made me throb with need. She moaned when our hips connected and I almost lost it. I couldn't take much more of this. If either one of us was going to stop this, it needed to be now.

I couldn't take the teasing anymore. I needed more. I needed to act, or I was going to explode. With a low groan, I bit my lip and started running my fingers up her shirt. She was so soft, so warm, she smelled so good. *Yes.*

"Please...say something. Do you...? Do you want me to—"

272

She still hadn't said anything, and I was at the end of my rope. I couldn't stop myself anymore, and the uncrossable line evaporated. A shaky exhale left me as I angled my mouth so I could reach hers. I needed a taste. Just a taste. I ran my tongue along the inside of her upper lip. Oh God…she tasted so good. *More. Yes.*

My fingers traveled over her bra, and her nipples were rigid, ready. I wanted to taste them too. I continued along her bra strap until I got to her back. That perfect, sexy back. I wanted to run my tongue down it.

Kiera let out a ragged sigh and closed her eyes. She wasn't saying no; she wanted me to do this. A groan escaped me as I kissed her upper lip. My tongue darted inside the warmth of her mouth. *God yes, I've missed this. I've dreamed of this. I've wanted to have this again, so much. Yes, let me love you.*

An erotic gasp left Kiera's lips. It was a plea for more. She finally wanted more. One of my hands found her neck, and I pulled her into me for a kiss full of passion and promise. *Yes, let me worship your body. Let me in…don't push me away.*

But that was exactly what she did. With both hands against my chest, she shoved me as far away from her as she could. No, she didn't want this. And right after I'd promised her I'd do better. She was going to end this now. I'd gone too far.

I held my hands up, pleading. "I'm sorry. I thought…"

She stormed over to me, put one hand on my chest, one around my neck, and pulled me into her. Not sure what she was doing, I stopped talking and backed up a step. She pulled me into her again and stared me down. Her face was pure passion and desire. She wasn't pushing me away. She wasn't rejecting me. This was happening. We were going to be together again. We were going to make love again. Fuck, I wanted her so bad.

She ran her hands down to my pants and pulled on the loops of my jeans until our hips touched. Her body sent ripples of desire through mine. *Yes.* We were going to be together soon. We'd be tangled up in each other's arms, naked, electrified. Her lips would be on mine, her tongue would trace the outline of my abs. My hands would feel every soft inch of her. My fingers would feel her wetness. And I would taste her before I entered her. I was going to take her, right here, right now...with Denny right next door.

Fuck.

"Kiera...?" I couldn't say it. I could only glance toward her bedroom and hope she knew what I meant. *Do you want to do this, when he's right there, only a few feet away?*

My actions broke through her fog of desire. I could see the indecision on her face, the instant pain and confusion, and I immediately wanted to take the question back. I wanted to wrap my arms around her, pull her onto my bed...do all the things I'd dreamed of doing with her, and forget all the reasons why we couldn't. Reality could wait, I just wanted a moment of bliss to physically deepen our connection. But I'd already ruined it by ripping apart the illusion we'd constructed and allowing reality to crash down upon us, drowning us. There was no going back now.

Determination filled Kiera's face, like she was fortifying herself. Before she even said the words, I knew she was finally putting a stop to this. Leaning into me, she breathed, "Don't touch me again. I'm not yours." Her eyes watered after she said it, like it cut her to be so blunt with me. But her resolve was firm, and after shoving me onto the bed, she fled from the room.

Stunned, crushed, and still hard with desire, I lay there on my mattress and grieved. I'd had her. For the briefest of seconds, I'd had her, then I'd lost her. She was gone, and we were over. She hadn't said the words, but I knew...the innocence had been lost, and it couldn't be returned, no matter how hard we tried. This farce was over.

Chapter 19

Jealousy

I didn't sleep much. I kept thinking about Kiera and wondering what she was going to say the next time I saw her. I already knew what I would say—*I'm sorry. I'll do better.* It was the only response I could think to give her, but I already knew it wouldn't be enough.

When I couldn't stand it anymore, I got up and went downstairs to make some coffee. My stomach was in knots, and I felt like I was going to be sick. What would she say? Would she end this?

When Kiera finally appeared, I instantly put a hand on her arm. "Kiera, I'm sorry. I went too far. I'll be good."

She brushed me away, and I knew it was the beginning of the end for us. "No, Kellan. We went way past innocent flirting a long time ago. We can't go back to that time. We're not those people anymore. It was a stupid idea to try."

I was aware of that, but hearing her say it made a jolt of pain rip through me. It might not be innocent, it might not have ever been innocent, but I still wanted it. Right or wrong, she was all I could think about. "But...don't end this, please."

She looked pained and conflicted, but her answer was firm. "I have to, Kellan. Denny knows something's not right. I don't think he suspects what...or you...but he knows I've been distracted." Biting her lip, she looked down. I could tell she didn't want to say any of this, but she felt like she had no choice. "Denny and I haven't…done anything…in a long time and he's hurt. I'm hurting him."

Grief and relief hit me at the same time. Denny was hurting… but they hadn't been sleeping together every night. I looked down so she wouldn't see that their abstinence pleased me. I had no right to be happy that Denny was miserable. "You don't have to. I've never asked you to not…be with him. I know you two are going to…I told you, I understand."

I hated this conversation. I really wanted to tell her that I was glad they weren't doing anything. I didn't want her touching Denny. But she wasn't mine, and I had no right to put any stipulations on her. Whatever small part of herself she was willing to give to me was fine, so long as I got something.

My answer made her worn eyes even sadder; it was clear she'd slept about as little as I had. "I know, Kellan, but I've been so pre-occupied, wrapped up in you…" She let out a heavy sigh. "I'm ignoring him."

A surge of hope went through me, and it burned as it radiated around my heart. Grabbing her arms, I pulled her in close. I searched her eyes, looking for a glimpse of the love that I some-times felt from her. "You're wrapped up in me. What does that say, Kiera? You want to be with me. You want to be more than friends. Some part of you wants me too." *I know you have feelings for me. I know there's something here between us. You begged me to stay.*

Shutting me out, she closed her eyes. "Please, Kellan, you're tear-ing me in two. I can't…I can't do this anymore."

She was pushing me away, and it was hurting her; she didn't really want to do this. She wanted me, and she didn't want to end this any more than I wanted her to. "Kiera, look at me…please." If she'd only open her eyes, see the sincerity on my face, then she wouldn't end this. *I love you. Don't leave me.*

Her eyes compressed so tightly together that her eyelashes inter-laced. "No, I can't, okay? This isn't right, it doesn't feel right. You don't feel right. Just don't, please don't touch me anymore."

She was lying. I knew she was. Nothing on earth felt more right than when we held each other. We were meant to be together. "Kiera, I know you don't really feel that way." Holding her to me, feeling that rightness wrap around me, I whispered in her ear, "I know you feel something here..." *It just has to be love that you feel for me. It has to be... You cried for me.*

She opened her eyes, but didn't look at me. Gaze focused on my chest, she firmly pushed herself away from me. "No. I don't want you. I want to be with him. I'm in love with *him*."

Every word she spoke was like a chunk being torn out of my heart. I didn't want to hear it, I didn't want to believe it, but...I knew she was telling the truth. I'd always known Denny was her choice. I couldn't compete with him. I didn't stand a chance.

Kiera finally looked up at me then. She had to see the agony on my face, but that didn't stop her. With compassionate eyes, she finished ripping my heart to pieces. "I'm attracted to you...but I feel nothing for you, Kellan."

I feel nothing for you? Nothing? So, she didn't love me after all. There was nothing I could say to that, so I let her go and left the kitchen.

I couldn't be in the house with her. Hearing her, seeing her...smelling her...it hurt too much. I felt numb, and I couldn't believe that it was over. It was actually over. A part of me didn't want to let go. I wanted to keep teasing her, riling her up, making her remember what we had together. But if she didn't feel *anything* for me, what was the point? I didn't just want to be a good time to her, I wanted her to care. I thought she'd cared. I'd been so sure, but I was wrong.

Climbing into my car, I debated leaving again. I could run away, try to forget her. I knew I never would though. She would always be in my mind. From now until the day I died, I would be in love with her.

I went to Evan's for rehearsal, then stayed there when everyone went to Pete's afterward. I didn't want to see Kiera. I couldn't. Not yet. I was still processing everything she'd said. It seemed off somehow, and I couldn't quite wrap my mind around it. With her heart and soul in her eyes, she'd asked me not to leave her. Her begging me to stay in that parking lot hadn't been because she was merely attracted to me. There had been more going on. There had to have been. She wouldn't risk her relationship with Denny over a charming smile.

I was staring up at Evan's ceiling, pondering that, when I heard his door open. "Kell, you still here? What happened? I thought you said you'd be right behind us?"

Evan walked into his apartment with a naturally confused expression. Faking a yawn, I blinked and sat up on his couch. "What time is it?" I asked, my voice groggy. "I must have fallen asleep."

When the guys had packed up their stuff and headed out to the bar, I'd told them I wanted to jot down some lyrics I'd just thought up, and I'd join them when I was done. Not wanting to mess with my creative process, they'd all given me the space I'd needed—no questions asked. I hadn't written down a damn thing though; my mind was spinning way too fast for any decent lyric to pop out. I felt kind of bad about lying to the guys, but I couldn't tell them I was avoiding Kiera. I couldn't tell them anything.

Evan came over to the couch while I stretched out. "It's pretty late. We ended up closing Pete's." He crooked a smile at me. "You missed Griffin getting shot down by a hot blonde. It was... amazing." He laughed, then pointed to a notebook on the couch beside me. Yes, I'd brought props into my lie. "You finish what you were working on?"

Grabbing the notebook, I curled my fingers around it. "Yeah, almost."

"Can I read it?" Evan seemed genuinely curious about a potential new song to start putting together, but I hadn't written down anything.

With a frown, I lifted the notebook, but didn't ease my grip on it. "It's nowhere near ready. Soon though. I promise."

Evan only nodded at my answer. He respected my process enough to not badger me about it. I appreciated that, and felt even

278

guiltier. I'd have to scrap together a song soon so I wouldn't be a complete and total liar.

Running a hand through my hair, I let out another yawn. "I'm beat. I better go home and get to bed."

Clapping me on the shoulder, Evan let out a yawn as well. "Yeah, me too. Laughing my ass off was tiring." He shook his head and started chuckling. "You should have been there, man. You missed out."

Even though I didn't feel like it, I made myself smile. "Yeah, sounds like I did." I felt like I'd missed out on a lot of things. "Night, Evan."

"Night."

I took my time heading home. I stopped to get gas and picked up some groceries at a twenty-four-hour store. I even debated going back to that diner in Olympia. I didn't though. Eventually, I sucked it up and went back home. Kiera and Denny were asleep when I got there. Not wanting to wake anyone, and being careful to avoid the couple of spots that always creaked, I put away my things and then tiptoed up the stairs. I couldn't make sense of my life anymore. What seemed up was down, what seemed right was wrong. When did the world get so confusing? Or had it always been this way, and I was only now catching up?

Sleep was difficult. I kept seeing Kiera repeating over and over, "I'm attracted to you... but I feel nothing..." Then my father would appear. He'd laugh at me, then say, "I told you she was too good for you."

I woke up after only a few hours and decided to get up. Having Kiera and my father reject me wasn't exactly restful. I'd rather be tired.

When Kiera entered the kitchen, I was already at the table, sipping my coffee. She seemed relieved to see me, and guilty too. I wondered what exactly she felt guilty about—leading me on, or telling me the truth. Then I decided it didn't matter. What was done was done. I'd never expected this to last anyway.

I watched her as she sat down across from me. She seemed ner-

279

vous, like she wasn't sure how I'd react to her. I didn't blame her for feeling unsure. I'd been all over the place with her. Way up, and way down. Right now…I was just numb.

"Hey," she whispered.

"Hey," I said back. I set down my coffee cup, and an ache filled me to touch her. I just wanted to hold her fingers, stroke them. It had only been a day since she'd ended things, but I already missed her.

Neither one of us spoke again and tension filled the room. It was like we were both suffering from the stress of restraint. Or maybe I was just hoping that it was killing her not to touch me. Maybe she was fine, and I was the only one struggling. She seemed stressed though.

Suddenly, she blurted out, "My sister is coming in tomorrow. Denny and I are going to pick her up from the airport in the morning."

I blinked, then nodded. I'd almost forgotten about her sister's visit. "Oh…right." Not wanting anyone to be inconvenienced by my presence, I told her, "I can crash at Matt's. She can stay in my room." *Then you won't have to feel guilty when you look at me.*

"No…you don't have to do that. It's not necessary." She paused, and her eyes grew heavy with sadness. "Kellan, I hate how we left things."

I couldn't keep watching her eyes, so I shifted my gaze to the table. "Yeah…me too."

"I don't want this…weirdness…between us. Can we…can we still be friends? Truly, just friends?"

Dark humor on my lips, I looked up at her then. "Are you really giving me the 'let's be friends' speech?"

She grinned, and my heart ached a little. She was so beautiful, and so out of reach. "Yeah…I guess I am."

Could I be friends with her again? What did that entail anyway? Weren't we friends before she'd pulled the plug on us? No, we were never really friends. We were always slightly above that. And now, any sort of friendship was buried so far in our past, there was no way to retrieve it. I couldn't be her friend when she was my entire world, it would hurt too much, but...what choice did I have? I'd take anything she'd give me. Anything. Even this.

I was gathering my courage to tell her that we could be whatever she wanted us to be when she interrupted. "I should probably warn you about my sister."

The sudden shift in the conversation derailed my train of thought. I tried to understand what she meant by her comment, then I remembered what she'd said about her sister a few weeks ago. Pointing to myself, I said, "I remember...man-flavored candy." According to Kiera, her sister was pretty much going to attack me. Well, she couldn't be much worse than the aggressive fans at the bar. I was sure I could handle her.

Kiera shook her head. "No...I mean yes, but that's not what I was thinking of."

"Oh?" I asked, curious what else there could be.

Looking away, Kiera's cheeks tinted pink, like she was embarrassed to be telling this to me. "She's kind of...well...She's very beautiful," she said with a sigh.

No surprise there. "I figured she was." Kiera's eyes snapped to mine, and I quietly added, "She's related to you...right?"

She gave me a put-out sigh. "Kellan..."

"I know. Friends." I had to accept that friendship was all she could give me. The thought made my soul ache though.

Kiera's eyes were sympathetic. She didn't want to hurt me, and I knew that. "Are you still coming with us to the club?"

Why? What purpose would that serve? "You still want me to?" I asked, averting my eyes.

"Yes, of course. We're still friends, Kellan, and my sister expects..."

Understanding hit me and I looked back at her. Of course. I couldn't forget about the charade we had going on. "Right, we wouldn't want her asking the wrong questions," I said, my voice rough. So there it was, the real reason Kiera was smoothing things over with me right now. Not because she felt bad that she'd hurt me, but because she didn't want her sister suspicious. Because then her sister might talk to Denny, and that was the last thing Kiera wanted. I should have known. It always circled back to Denny.

"Kellan—"

"I'll be there, Kiera." *Don't you worry about it. I don't want Denny to know either.*

Finishing my coffee, I stood up. There was nothing more to talk about here. I started to leave, but Kiera harshly snapped my name and I turned to look at her. What could she possibly be mad about?

"Remember your promise," she said, her voice hot.

My promise? That I wouldn't sleep with her sister? Why would I want to sleep with the girl who was nothing to me but a poor substitute of the person I really wanted to be with? Why would I torture myself like that? And what did it really matter to her anyway, since she didn't have any feelings for me?

I thought about biting her head off with some asshole comment, but I didn't have it in me. I didn't want to fight anymore. I wasn't sure if I really wanted anything anymore, besides her, of course. Memories of holding Kiera in my arms flooded me. I'd never felt such peace in all my life. And now it was gone. My warmth had been ripped away and my insides felt ice cold. Shaking my head, I told her, "I haven't forgotten anything, Kiera."

The day dragged by with a slowness that was aggravating. Kiera and I were being cordial, but there was distance between us, and sadness. I'd spent most of the day in a zombielike state of numbness—not angry, not sad. Truly, I think I was in denial. I couldn't face reality yet, so I let a veil of melancholy blanket me. It was hard to feel bad when I wasn't letting myself feel anything at all.

The group of us were at Pete's, preparing for our gig. I was wishing it was over already so I could be alone in my room, brooding, when, just like that, the night suddenly got a lot more interesting.

With a smack to Matt's chest, Griffin muttered, "Oh...holy... fuck. Dude, I'm in love. Look at that piece of ass!"

My back was to the door, so I couldn't tell who Griffin was talking about. I didn't really care either. Kiera was handing out another round of beers and watching me out of the corner of her eye. I watched her too. Wistfully. I couldn't help it. I didn't want us to be over. I didn't want to just be casual friends with her.

Griffin sat up straight, a huge grin on his face, just as a leggy brunette walked right up behind Kiera and covered her eyes. "Guess who?" the woman asked.

Kiera yanked down the hands over her eyes and spun around. "Anna?" she said, stupefied. She pulled her in for a hug, exclaiming, "Oh my God! We were supposed to pick you up from the airport tomorrow! What are you doing here?"

Anna's eyes slid over to me. "I couldn't wait...hopped an earlier flight."

Kiera had warned me that her older sister, Anna, was pretty, but I had to admit, her looks took me by surprise. She was taller than Kiera, curvier, and definitely flashier. She had on a tight red dress that left nothing to the imagination, and her plump lips were painted in the exact same electric shade as her outfit. Her eyes were an emerald green, and were highlighted by thick eyelashes lengthened by meticulously applied mascara. Anna's hair was darker than Kiera's, straighter and shinier. She'd pulled some of it up into a clip, and there were bright red strands peeking through the pieces falling around her shoulders. This was a person who wanted the world to notice her. I'd say she probably *needed* the world's attention. Behind the primping and preening, behind the makeup, manicured nails, salon-perfect hair, and top-notch clothes, was a person who was actually very insecure about herself. I could understand that.

With fondness on her face, Kiera examined her sister. Then she picked up a bright red strand of hair. "This is new. I like it."

Anna's eyes were still taking me in. She wasn't even trying to camouflage her interest. I had a feeling she was a lot more forward than Kiera. That went along with the attention-seeking. "I dated a hairdresser," she answered. Switching her gaze to Kiera, she playfully added, "For like, an hour."

Griffin groaned, and I watched as he bit his knuckle like he was in pain. I almost laughed at his expression. If he could pick and choose female parts and slap them onto one person, that person would look like Anna. She was the stuff his pornographic dreams were made of. And she hadn't even noticed him yet. Poor guy.

I couldn't help but watch Kiera as she took in her sister. There was an emotion there that I couldn't quite read. Kiera loved her, I was certain, but she was...sad, or self-conscious...like she was comparing herself to Anna, and in her head, she was losing. But that was ridiculous. Yes, Anna was gorgeous, but with her it was...forced. Manufactured. Kiera didn't have to try that hard. She effortlessly radiated beauty. She didn't have to be bended, twisted, and arranged into a masterpiece. She was already a work of art.

Finally, Kiera inhaled a deep breath. "Guys, this is my sister—"

Interrupting Kiera, Anna held her hand out to me. "Anna," she finished, her smile warm and inviting.

"Kellan."

I was shaking her hand when Griffin stood up and yanked it away from me. *Smooth.* "Griffin...hey." He had such a way with words, it was almost magical. Anna giggled though, as she said hello.

I watched Kiera while Anna introduced herself to the guys. Kiera seemed a little uncomfortable that Anna didn't need her help. Maybe she was wishing that she could be that bold. She could be, if she really wanted to. The only thing holding her back was her.

Griffin, determined to impress Anna into his bed, grabbed a chair nearby. That chair unfortunately had someone sitting on it, but Griffin didn't care much about that. With a "Get off, fucker," he yanked the seat away and set it beside himself. While the ousted customer flipped him the bird and stormed off to go complain to Sam, who I'm sure wouldn't do anything about it, Griffin patted the cushion and beckoned his newfound love to join him.

Anna smiled, said, "Thank you," then grabbed the chair and hefted it over to my end of the table. Matt and Evan laughed at her maneuver. Griffin scowled. Surprisingly, Kiera did too. Interesting.

Was she jealous of Anna and me? Even though I'd promised her I wouldn't do anything with Anna? She sure looked that way when Anna sat down.

Testing this theory, I gave Anna a friendly grin when she sat so close to me our sides touched. I could almost see the smoke coming out of Kiera's ears as she watched us. Very interesting.

"Well, I've got to get back to work. I'll bring you a drink, Anna."

Anna's eyes never left mine as she answered. "Okay." As an afterthought, she added, "Oh, some guy named Sam put my jacket and bags in the back room."

Kiera sighed, like she couldn't believe what Anna could get men to do for her. I wanted to tell Kiera that was the power of pussy, but I didn't think she'd appreciate that comment, so I kept quiet. "Okay, I'll call Denny. He can give you a ride home."

Anna finally looked back at Kiera. "I think I can manage." I knew she meant me, and my grin widened. Anna was making this so damn easy. All I had to do was smile, let her do her thing, and watch Kiera go green with envy. I knew I probably shouldn't be playing this game, but making Kiera jealous felt a hell of a lot better than wallowing in sadness over what I couldn't ever have with her. And besides, this was what Kiera wanted. She had to know there would be a price to pay for letting me go.

Anna's eyes returned to mine. They were sparkling, playful, and easy to read—*I want you.* "So...you're a singer, huh?" She scanned my body so seductively, she may as well have reached over, shoved her hand down my pants, and started fondling my cock. "What else can you do?" she asked. Very forward.

While Anna laughed and I grinned, Kiera fled. She apparently didn't want to be anywhere near us, but she didn't want to leave us alone either. This visit was going to be so much fun.

After Kiera disappeared, her sister turned on the charm. "So, Kellan Kyle, tell me all about yourself, every little detail." With a crooked smile, she told me, "I want to know you inside and out."

I bet she did. I didn't open up like that though. She'd have to settle for the basics. "I spent some time in L.A., but I was born and raised here." *And will probably die here.* "You already know all about the band, so there's not much else to tell."

She leaned in. "Girlfriend?"

Griffin, eavesdropping, sniggered, "That asshole doesn't do girlfriends. Me, on the other hand..." He opened up his arms in invitation.

Anna glanced at him, then returned her eyes to me. "No girlfriend. Good to know." She gave me a heart-stopping smile, and I gave her a devilish grin. This was so easy, it was almost too easy.

"Okay, I told you about me, now tell me about you." I lifted an eyebrow and waited for her to start speaking. Once she did, she didn't stop, and I didn't interrupt her. The more she opened up about herself, the less I had to open up about me. I preferred to listen.

Kiera came over when Anna was discussing her years at school. She'd gone to the same college Kiera had started out in. She'd been a cheerleader. I wasn't too surprised. Kiera put a reddish drink in front of her sister, and Anna paused long enough to toss her a "Thanks" before resuming our conversation. Well, her conversation *at* me.

I peeked up at Kiera. She was frowning at us. It was entrancing, and some sick part of me really enjoyed making her jealous.

Now that Anna was around to make things entertaining, the night sped up. While Anna told me all about her life, hopes, and dreams, she flirted. And she was good at flirting. If I wasn't interested in somebody else, I'd definitely be raring to go after her little display. She touched my face, my shoulder, my leg. She ran her hands over herself, subtly outlining her curves. It was erotic, I'd give her that. And even though I was only allowing it to continue to irritate Kiera, she was an attractive woman; I didn't mind the show.

Her hand inched its way up my thigh all night. If she affected me the way Kiera did, I'd be uncomfortably straining against my jeans by now. Anna wasn't my real focus though, so it was easy to ignore the fact that her fingernail was running up and down the inner seam of my pants. When Kiera reluctantly approached the table, she noticed exactly where her sister's hand was. In fact, her eyes laser beamed onto the spot. And Kiera's eyes washing over my lap did so much more to excite me than Anna's fingers. What I wouldn't give for *her* to touch me like that.

"Time's up, Kellan," Kiera snapped. I had to smile at how angry she was getting. *It sucks seeing someone else cozying up to what you want, doesn't it? Welcome to my world.*

Anna seemed confused by Kiera's statement and she turned to look at her. Kiera slapped on a smile as she answered the question on her face. The grin was clearly forced. "They need to go onstage and play now."

Anna was overjoyed by the news. "Oh...great!" By Kiera's expression, she was done with her sister's visit already. A part of me hoped Anna never went home. Maybe if I made her jealous enough, Kiera would come back to me. We could try again.

While the guys and I took our places, Anna jockeyed into position—front and center; she clearly didn't want to miss a thing. I gave her an encouraging smile, then looked up to see Kiera stalking off to help some customers. This was seriously getting to her, and it was childish of me, but I loved every second of her ire.

I put on a show for the record books. I sang my heart out. I strutted, played with the crowd, gave every girl in the front *You're the only girl for me* eyes, and with Anna, I pulled out all the stops. I paid her so much attention that I was a little worried that the eager girls around her might elbow her in the face or something. Anna could hold her own though. When one girl tried to take her spot by giving her a hearty shove, Anna reached over, yanked on her ponytail, and brought her face close to hers. She yelled something at her, and looking freaked out, the girl fled. Weaving her way through the crowd, she popped out the back and left the bar. No one messed with Anna after that. Damn. Hot chick was tough.

Anna was jumping up and down, having a great time, when someone came up behind her and put a hand on her shoulder. At first I thought it might be a friend of the person Anna had chased out, but then I saw it was Denny. Guess he'd finally shown up to take her home. Anna turned to look at who was touching her, recognized her sister's boyfriend, and then flung her arms around him. Denny seemed taken aback by her forcefulness. He patted her back, like he wasn't sure what to do with her.

The interaction between them made me smile. Then I glanced up to find Kiera in the crowd. I wondered if she'd be as jealous of Denny and Anna as she seemed to be over Anna and me. Kiera wasn't even watching them though. She was watching me. She stared at me the entire time Denny and Anna were together by the stage; apparently she wasn't worried about them at all. Kiera continued to stare at me as Denny left Anna's side to return to her. Her hazel eyes were trapped in my gaze until Denny walked over and touched her shoulder. Then she startled back to awareness.

Denny took a seat at the bar, and Anna stayed where she was in the crowd, so I figured she'd refused to go home with him. I'd been expecting that. She was way too interested in me to give up now. She wouldn't stop until she was in my car or in my bed. Not that I would let that last one happen. I'd made a promise.

When our set was over, Anna was glued to my side again. She brought me a beer and a towel and scared away the other women with a glance. *He's mine, back off* practically shimmered off her in waves. Griffin was as irritated about the whole thing as Kiera was. I just found it funny. And not a whole lot had been funny lately.

When the bar was winding down and it was time to go home, Anna and I walked through the front doors arm in arm. Even Rita frowned at us. I had to smile that I was pissing off so many people in such a short amount of time. It had to be some kind of record. Once we got outside though, Griffin decided I'd hogged Anna long enough.

Sidling up beside her, he asked, "So, how'd you like the show?"

Her arm still wrapped around mine, Anna looked up at me and smiled. "It was amazing." From her tone, it was clear that what she really meant was *He was amazing*.

Griffin glared at me, like I'd made her say it. Shaking my head, I looked away from his annoyed face. I couldn't control who she fawned over. Grabbing Anna's hand, Griffin yanked her away from me. Again, smooth. She stumbled a little, but laughed. "I gotta show you something," he said.

When I looked back, the pair were hustling over to Griffin's van. Matt was standing on the other side of me. With a snort, he said, "Think he's whipping it out for her?" Smirking, he shook his head. "I'm not so sure that will impress her."

A laugh escaped me as I watched Griffin slide open his van and dig around inside. It took him a minute or so, but eventually he popped back out with a black thing in his hand. I laughed a little more. *Our band shirt? That's what he had to show her?*

With a flourish, he snapped open the Douchebags shirt in his hand. Anna squealed and made a grab for it. Griffin held it back in one hand and raised a finger with the other. "You don't just get these for free," he said. "You have to earn 'em."

I wanted to drop my head into my hands. *Jackass.* As I watched though, Anna smirked, then pressed Griffin against the van. Her knee went between his, and her hands circled his wrists, pinning them beside his head, like she was arresting him. While Griffin closed his eyes and dropped his mouth open, Anna rubbed her body against him. She ran her nose up his throat, then over to his ear. She whispered something, and I watched Griffin melt. He released his hold on the shirt, and Anna instantly snatched it up. When she stepped away, he had a glazed look on his face.

Breathing heavier, he said, "Fuck me. Now."

Anna giggled as she held the shirt to her chest. She touched a finger to his nose and laughed. "You're so cute. Thank you for the shirt."

"Thank you for the raging boner," he replied.

Spinning on her heel, Anna walked back to me with a satisfied smile. Griffin was still leaning against his van, clearly dazed. I shook my head at her. "What did you say to him?"

Biting her lip, she suggestively raised her eyebrows. "If you play nice, maybe you'll find out." Laughing, she started walking away. "Shall we go home?"

I looked back at Griffin. He had his eyes closed, and he was cupping himself, like his unsatisfied hard-on had just given him a stomachache. I didn't want to sleep with Anna, but I was insanely curious what she could have possibly said to reduce Griffin to a pathetic pile of horniness.

Kiera was just exiting the bar as Anna slid into my seat. Even with the distance between us, I could tell Kiera was pissed Anna was leaving with me. I had a huge grin on my face as I got into my car. Tormenting Kiera was too much fun.

When we got to the house, I showed Anna to the living room. Spotting the couch, she immediately grabbed my hand and made me sit down with her. Her hand instantly found its home next to my crotch.

I heard the door open and turned to see Kiera storming into the house. She looked like she wanted to rip somebody's head off. She couldn't though. She couldn't do a damn thing…because we were trying to be inconspicuous.

Denny came in a few moments later. He slipped an arm around Kiera, and *my* jealousy spiked a tad. It was fun making someone else feel it, but it sucked being the recipient. Luckily, I had a distraction. Anna looked over at me with an alluring smile. "So…where am I sleeping tonight?" she asked.

I knew what she was really asking me was *So…what position do you want to try first?* With a half smile, I started answering her, but Kiera beat me to it.

"You're sleeping with me, Anna." Her tone clearly said *Do not argue with me.* I contained my laughter while Kiera looked over at Denny. "Do you mind sleeping on the couch?" she asked him.

Denny did not look happy about that, and I didn't blame him. This monstrosity wasn't comfortable. "The couch? Really?"

Kiera's eyes sharpened to points. She was so pissed…I loved it. "Well, if you prefer, you can sleep with Kellan." The way she said it was final. *You have option A or option B. There is no C.*

I couldn't hold in my laughter anymore. While Denny raised an eyebrow at Kiera, I told him, "I'm just warning you now—I kick."

Looking miserable, Denny grumbled, "Couch it is," then headed upstairs for blankets.

Pushing her boobs into my side, Anna sprightly said, "You know, I could sleep with—"

Faster than a blink, Kiera had Anna on her feet. "Come on," she said as she dragged her sister toward the stairs.

Well, well, well. Kiera had a jealous streak in her about a mile wide. Watching her reaction to Anna and me was outrageously entertaining. I bet Kiera didn't sleep at all tonight. She'd be on full alert, all night long, making sure her sister didn't leave the room.

Oh man, this must be how kids felt waiting for Christmas morning. I might not sleep tonight either. I couldn't wait until tomorrow.

Chapter 20

Double Date from Hell

I woke up feeling better than I had in a while. I wondered if it made me a little sadistic that I was enjoying causing Kiera pain. Although she wasn't really pained, just jealous. She didn't want to share me with her sister. If I didn't find the whole thing so entertaining, I might be offended. Kiera had made her choice, and what I did shouldn't matter to her. I'd made a promise though, and I was planning on honoring this one.

After doing a handful of push-ups and sit-ups, I dressed and headed downstairs to make coffee. Kiera must have had an ear out for me, because she joined me a few minutes later. I wasn't too surprised that she was awake. Wondering if Anna was going to sneak into my room at any second had probably kept Kiera up all night. She looked worn, with baggy eyes and crazy hair. Even still, her natural good looks put her sister's manicured perfection to shame.

I gave her a cheery smile as I poured some water into the coffee-pot. "Mornin'. Sleep okay?"

Her expression was blank as she answered me. "I slept fine. You?"

Done with the machine, I turned around and leaned against the counter. *Go ahead and lie to me, Kiera, it's okay. I already know you slept like crap.* "Like a baby." She gave me a forced smile as she sat at the table, and I suppressed a laugh. She was so cute when she was fuming. "Your sister is…interesting," I said, intentionally leaving my sentence vague and open to interpretation.

She frowned as she debated what I meant by that. When she finally responded, her cheeks were a beautiful shade of embarrassed pink. "Yes…she is."

I found it amusing that Kiera's answer was also vague. Guess neither one of us was going to go into specifics. When the coffee was done, I prepared our cups and set hers down in front of her. I leaned back in my chair, perfectly content as I drank mine. Kiera hunched over her cup like she was freezing and it was the only source of warmth in the room. I knew her reaction wasn't from the cold though, and knowing that made my smile even wider. *Jealousy is a bitch, isn't it, Kiera?*

I left Kiera in the kitchen not long after we finished our coffee. I thought it might be best if we didn't talk too much. Well, I thought I could keep the jealousy going if we didn't talk too much. I wasn't sure why I wanted to goad her. Retribution? Proving a theory? This wouldn't bother her so much if she didn't have some feelings for me. She said she didn't, but…she just had to. *Please.*

I went for a long run to clear my head, but everywhere I turned, something reminded me of Kiera. Making her jealous only eased the pain so much. When I got back home, Anna and Kiera were gone, and Denny was watching TV. He seemed happy as a clam sitting in *my* favorite chair, watching *my* TV, and most likely thinking about *my* ex-lover. For a moment, I hated him for his happiness. But then I remembered what I'd done to him, and all of my hatred faded. Denny wasn't the bad guy. Quite the opposite. He was a *really* good guy.

Denny turned his head when he saw me. With a smirk, he jerked his thumb at the TV. "I know you're not a big fan, but want to watch the game with me?"

I glanced up at what was playing, and a small smile snuck onto my lips. Hockey. Denny loved sports, and he had always been watching some game or another when he'd stayed with me in high school. He'd tried in vain to get me invested in the various games, but after Dad had shut me down when I'd tried to bond with him over some of his favorite sports, I'd developed an almost spiteful feeling toward them, and intentionally never paid attention.

Not feeling very sociable after that memory, I politely shook my head at Denny. "No thanks." He laughed at my answer, like he wasn't too surprised that I didn't want to watch.

After taking a quick shower, I stayed in my room for most of the afternoon, writing lyrics that would never make it into an actual song. The writing process helped me cope though. There was something freeing about releasing all of my problems onto the page. I could write about how lonely I was, how empty I felt, how worthless I saw myself and how much Kiera meant to me, and no one would ever see it. It was a way for me to purge my problems while still hiding them away from the world, and hiding was something I was really good at. Unfortunately.

Anna and Kiera came back in the early evening. Even though I'd been practicing melodies on my guitar, I heard them when they walked through the door. It was like my ears went on instant alert the second Kiera was around me; they strained to hear every word, every laugh, every inhale and exhale of her breath. The constant deluge of her was wearing, but it was better than the alternative. Never hearing those sounds again would kill me, I was sure.

As I paused to listen, the sisters' footsteps trudged up the stairs. I didn't need to see them to know whose was whose. Kiera's steps were heavy, plodding. Anna's were light and bouncy. Kiera murmured something about getting ready, and Anna giggled as she told her how excited she was. I wasn't sure if she was excited to go out dancing, or excited to hang out with me all night, since I suppose I was sort of her date for the evening. Kiera grumbled an answer I couldn't hear, and Anna giggled again.

When I heard Anna leaving Kiera's room, saying goodbye as she headed downstairs, I cracked open my door and looked out into the hallway. Denny passed by my field of vision. Striding to his room, he opened the door and walked inside. In the brief time that the door was open, I saw Kiera standing in the room, looking lost. Denny closed the door behind him, but didn't latch it. Opening my own door, I quietly stepped over to theirs. I couldn't see anything, but I could clearly hear them talking.

"What's wrong?" Denny asked.

"I have nothing to wear tonight. Absolutely nothing." She sighed, and I could easily picture the forlorn expression on her face.

"Why don't you wear that pink dress you have? Or the skirt? Or shorts? It will probably get hot in there."

Kiera didn't answer him, and I could almost hear her annoyance in the silence. I pictured her in the skirt she'd worn when we'd caved in to lust inside the espresso stand. I pictured the shorts she sometimes wore to work. I visualized her in the jeans she wore to school. And I imagined her in the baggy lounge pants that she wore to bed. With a sad smile, I ran my fingers down her door. "It doesn't matter what you wear...you'll be stunning. As much as you want to, you can't hide your beauty, Kiera."

I'd whispered that so quietly that even I barely heard me, but I still startled when a voice to my left exclaimed, "Kellan! There you are."

I spun around and held my breath. Had Anna heard me? Had she seen me practically caressing the door? Knowing distraction was the best defensive maneuver I had, I gave her a crooked smile while slowly letting my gaze sweep over her from head to toe. "You look...amazing."

She had on a tight dress that looked like a long tank top. It hugged every curve and barely covered her ass. If Anna was wondering what I was doing spying on Denny and her sister, she didn't ask. Instead, she gave me a once-over and said, "So do you." I was wearing all black, same as her. In between my melancholy lyric writing, I'd gotten dressed for tonight. The dark color had seemed fitting at the time, but now that Anna and I looked like twins, I wasn't so sure. Anna seemed to enjoy that we matched though. With a seductive smile of approval, she sauntered my way. "I need your help."

Feeling my racing heart return to normal, I asked her, "With what?"

She stepped right in front of me, so close her chest touched mine. "Well, I thought if you did me, I could do you?"

I raised an eyebrow, wondering what she was actually suggesting under the obvious innuendo. Anna laughed at my expression. Grabbing a red lock of hair, she explained. "Hair. If you help me curl mine, I'll help you do something funky with yours."

I really didn't care what my hair looked like, but I saw an opportunity here, so I took it. "Sure. Why not?"

I'd never curled a girl's hair before, but Anna was a good teacher. We finished pretty quickly, but Kiera still hadn't emerged from her room. I wanted to tell Kiera not to stress about her looks, but it wasn't my place to say anything. That was Denny's job, and I had to let him do it. When Anna was satisfied that her face was flawless, she grabbed a container, then my hand, and pulled me downstairs. "This will be easier if we're sitting," she explained, a playful gleam in her eyes.

"Okay," I said, not really caring.

When we got downstairs, she sat me on the couch, then climbed around behind me. I had to smile at her aggressiveness. If this were any other situation, I would have twisted her around so she was straddling me, ripped off her panties, and screwed her with her dress still on...but things were different now, and the desire for meaningless sex with people I didn't know just wasn't in me. The connection wasn't strong enough that way. It was paltry and pathetic compared to what it was like with Kiera.

Anna started running her fingers through my hair. I had no idea what she was doing to me, but it seemed like she was sticking my hair straight up. Great, I was going to look like a pincushion. Oh well. Didn't matter.

Denny had left the TV on, and I idly watched it while Anna worked. It almost made me laugh that she was taking the opportunity to squish her breasts into my back. Kiera came down while Anna was messing with my hair. I heard Anna greet her, tell her

296

she looked great, and I twisted my head around to look. Anna was right…she looked incredible. She had on a sexy pair of black jeans that, without looking trashy, hugged her like a second skin. Her hair was pulled up, exposing her neck and the tops of her shoulders. Her shirt was a low-cut, fiery red, thin-strapped tank top that did more to accentuate her body than Anna's clingy outfit ever could. And from what I could tell, she wasn't wearing a bra. Just looking at her made a surge of desire shoot through me. Jesus, did she wear that just to tease me? How the hell was I going to get through this?

Denny came down the steps behind her, whispered something in her ear, then kissed her neck. Watching the affection was like having a dagger shoved into my gut. She was so intoxicating though, I couldn't turn away. *God, she's beautiful.*

Denny stepped down to stand beside Kiera, and I instantly caught the fact that out of all of us, Denny was the only one wearing white. How appropriate. He had a mystified look on his face, and I swear I heard him ask Kiera, "She's not going to do that to me, is she?"

He was studying my hair as he asked, so I figured he wasn't impressed with Anna's handiwork. I wondered if I was going to look like a porcupine once she was through. Denny and Kiera walked into the living room. Denny sat on the chair, then patted his lap. Kiera glanced at me, but then she joined him. I swallowed the pain working its way up my throat and made my expression stay even. *It doesn't bother me, it doesn't bother me, it doesn't bother me…*

With forced casualness, Kiera asked her sister, "What are you doing, Anna?"

"Doesn't he have the best fuck-me hair! Don't you just want to…? Uh!" Anna grabbed handfuls of my hair and pulled. The sting made me flinch, but the comment made me smile. *Yeah, Kiera, don't you want to?*

Anna's fingers continued in my hair. It felt nice, but nowhere near as nice as Kiera's touch. "He's letting me clubify it. He's going to be the hottest thing in there. No offense or anything."

I peeked up to see Denny laugh. "None taken, Anna."

Silence filled the room. While everyone watched Anna, I watched Kiera. Her face was a mixture of interest and irritation. I had a feeling she didn't like Anna doing something so intimate to me. Well, considering the fact that I didn't like Kiera making herself at home on Denny's lap, I figured we were even.

When Kiera's cheeks turned even rosier and she looked away, I couldn't help but ask her opinion. "What do you think?"

Denny was the one who answered me though. "Uhhh...looks great, man," he said with a laugh.

Anna seemed offended that he didn't love it. "Oh, you just don't understand girls, Denny. They'll go nuts for this. Right, Kiera?"

I had to laugh at Anna dragging Kiera back into the conversation. I bet this was a question she was thrilled to answer too. Looking embarrassed and unsure what to say, she muttered, "Yeah, sure, Anna. He'll be—"

Unable to stop myself, I interjected with the term Kiera had used once before to describe me. "Man-candy?"

Anna squealed and slipped her arms around me. "Oohhh...I like that!"

Kiera didn't. Eyes narrowed, she spat out, "Are we ready to go?"

Nodding, I stood up. I wasn't sure exactly how I was going to get through this, but I was definitely ready to get it over with.

Not wanting to be stuck in a car all night with Denny and Kiera, I suggested to Denny that we take separate cars. I figured then, if it got too hard to handle, I could bail without leaving everyone else high and dry. Anna, of course, climbed in with me, while Kiera naturally rode with her boyfriend. Once we arrived at the place Griffin had suggested, a dance club comically named Spanks, I made sure we all got inside, then took off to buy everyone the first round.

The line for drinks was thick, but as I approached, the bartender motioned me forward. Knowing Kiera was going to hate it, I ordered tequila. After the bartender eagerly filled four shot glasses, I carefully pinched them together with my fingers. Grabbing the salt and the container of limes in my other hand, I bumped and slid my way around people to get to the table. Kiera looked surprised to see me return so fast. I watched her look over at the bar, then frown. The bartender must still be staring my way then; she'd been eye-fucking me the entire time I'd placed the order. *Well, sorry, Kiera, it's not like I can help how people react to me.*

After I passed out the drinks, Kiera returned her attention to our table. Picking up her shot glass, she sniffed it. I knew my grin was childish, but I couldn't help it. The look on her face was priceless. I could almost hear her thoughts. *Tequila? Are you kidding me? No, Kiera, I'm not. We have a history, one you begged for. You cried for me, pleaded with me to stay. You're jealous of the attention I'm giving your sister, because you care about me. Like it or not, you do care. I'm sure of it.*

While she stared at me with disbelieving eyes, I set down the limes and salt. Anna and Denny started preparing their drinks, but Kiera seemed like she was going to outright refuse to do it. When she set her jaw and stubbornly started prepping her shot, a laugh escaped me. Teasing her was almost as much fun as making her jealous.

When I started making my drink, Kiera closed her eyes. I wondered if she was being flooded with memories…just like me. *Please, Kellan…take me to your room…* It was almost too much for me to take, and I almost stopped this charade right now, but Denny leaned over and said something to Kiera that broke me out of the sadness of the past. I wasn't sure what he asked her, but her answer was directed at me. With icy eyes, she said, "Yeah…I'm just not a big fan of tequila."

Considering what I'd just been reminiscing about, I found that amusing. "Really? You struck me as the type that would…love it."

While Kiera frowned, I laughed and Anna offered up her opinion of the drink. "Well, I love it…Cheers!"

I raised my glass to hers and Anna and I did our shots together. It burned going down, and I thought that was appropriate too. Everything with Kiera burned a little, sometimes in a good way, sometimes not so much.

Denny raised his glass to Kiera, and the two of them copied Anna and me. Except for the last step. With a barely noticeable peek at me, Kiera took Denny's lime from his mouth, then she stayed there in a long, lingering, fuck-you-and-your-tequila kiss. My sudden humor about the situation vanished.

While Denny kissed the woman I loved, Anna shouted her approval. "Wooo…there's my girl!" I felt ill watching them make out. But when they pulled apart and Kiera shot me a glance, I felt even worse. So, she wanted to play mean, huh? Well, I could do mean.

Focusing my attention on Anna, I extended my hand and nodded toward the dance floor. "Want to?" I asked her. Anna enthusiastically agreed. After she practically leaped into my arms, I escorted her toward the floor with my hand almost on her ass. I glanced at Kiera before Anna and I were swallowed up by the crowd; she looked furious, and I was glad about it. I was a little upset myself. *Yes, I'm taking off with your sister. Yes, my hands will be all over her body. And yes…every second that goes by, I'll wish she were you.*

Anna and I melted onto the dance floor, near the back corner of the room. Her arms instantly slipped around my neck, pulling me tight to her. She ground her body against mine, clearly trying to rev me up. I was already churning with emotions, but none of them were what Anna wanted from me. In my mind, as I looked down on Anna, all I saw was Kiera. Her full lips, her colorful eyes, her soulful smile. I couldn't escape her. The music was rattling my chest, but I didn't hear a word of it. Kiera filled my mind.

I could feel Anna pulling on my neck, trying to get my mouth closer to hers. I kept a rigid, unyielding posture that gave her no leeway though. With a small frown, she switched tactics. She ran her hands down my chest, then down my arms. My hands were resting on her sides, like how self-conscious preteens danced. Anna clearly wanted more. Grabbing my hands, she shifted them behind her, to her ass. "You can touch me," she yelled above the music.

Flashing her a quick smile, I shifted my hands to her upper back. *I know exactly what I can do to you. You're just not the one I want.*

Anna seemed perturbed by my refusal to ravish her. She turned around and started rubbing her ass into my lap. I took a step back, but she followed me. Eventually, I ran into a speaker. Anna shot me a victorious smile as she trapped me against it with her voluptuous body. Unless I was going to push her away, I was stuck with her grinding against me.

Knowing I needed to take control of the situation, I spun her around and pulled her to me. If we were facing each other, I could at least keep some space between us. I ran my hand over her hip, urging her to straddle my leg. She did, and I moved against her in time to the music. I looked down on her, staring intensely into her eyes, and she held my gaze like she was captivated by me. Her mouth dropped open, and she adjusted her shoulders so more of her chest was exposed to me. Knowing I needed to give her something, I teasingly ran my hand up her side, my thumb brushing the edge of her breast. She closed her eyes and melted against me.

I urged her head onto my shoulder, rubbing my hands along her back as I did. It was as much innocent seduction as I could do with her. With Anna's face no longer near mine, I looked out over the crowds. Like she was a magnet, I spotted Kiera instantly. She was with Denny, near the center of the crowd. They were laughing as they danced, and even though Kiera's arms were around his neck, and his were around her waist, I couldn't help thinking that they danced like friends would.

I watched Denny and Kiera the entire time I danced with Anna. Eventually, after what felt like an eternity, Anna leaned up to my ear and told me she had to use the ladies' room. I nodded, and watched as she sashayed through the crowd. When I glanced back at Kiera, she was alone. My heart leaped into my throat as I looked around for Denny. He'd just left her side; he seemed to be headed for the bar, or maybe going to step outside for some fresh air. It was hot in here. A horrible idea surged through my brain, and I was pushing my way through the crowd before I could stop it. I'd been torturing myself all night watching Kiera, and I just wanted my arms around her. I just wanted *one* dance...that was it.

Her back was to me when I finally broke through the crowd. I glanced back at Denny, but he'd already rounded the corner and was out of sight. I knew this was stupid. I knew we could easily get caught, but I also knew I couldn't stop myself. I needed her.

Immersed in the song, Kiera was oblivious to my presence. She knew it was me the instant I touched her though. Still behind her, I stepped close and ran my hand up her shirt until my palm was on her stomach. She was warm and soft and smelled amazing. I could feel her muscles contract as she stiffened under my touch; she didn't pull away though. I pulled her back into my hip, and moved our bodies together. It felt so right, so natural, but so wrong too. If Denny or Anna saw us like this…it would be the end of everything.

A bead of sweat formed on her skin and ran down her shoulder blades. I wanted it. I wanted to taste her skin, have my mouth upon her sweetness. I shouldn't, but then again, I did a lot that I shouldn't, and I couldn't resist her anymore. Brushing some stray hair aside, I bent down and touched my tongue to her heated skin. She shuddered, and I dragged my tongue up her spine to the back of her neck. Wanting more, I gently scraped my teeth against her skin in a playful bite. It sent shock waves of desire through me. It seemed to do the same to Kiera. She melted against me. One of her hands covered mine, the other wrapped around to touch my hip. Her back rested against my chest, and her head dropped back. She wanted this.

My hand on her stomach moved down to her jeans. I wished I could undo them, feel the soft skin underneath. Kiera interlaced our fingers and clenched my hand, like she wanted that too. My breath increased as we moved together. She felt so good in my arms. I wanted her…so much. *Please Kiera, let me do this. Let me love you.*

When her hand on my hip ran down my thigh and her head started turning toward me, I almost thought she could hear my mental urging. *Yes, please. Kiss me. Now.* Not able to take her slow, teasing movements, I grabbed her chin and pulled her mouth to mine. I was sure she was going to pull away the moment we touched. I was sure she was going to haul off and slap me. But...she didn't. Her lips attacked mine with a voraciousness that betrayed how much she'd missed me. I whimpered with how much I needed her, needed this. I didn't even care who might be watching anymore. Her body was all that mattered. This connection was all that existed.

Our lips parted and my tongue felt her mouth. She spun in my arms, tossed her hands into my hair, and clung to me with every inch of her. God, I'd never felt such passion and desire. It was even more intense than our time together in the espresso stand. I wanted to lay her down, wanted to explore every inch of her, but there was no room here.

I was nearly gasping for breath as I ran my hands up her shirt. Her bare skin under my fingertips was heaven. Pure, blissful heaven. I needed more, so much more. My body was hard, straining. I wanted her to feel it, wanted her to know what she did to me. Our kiss still fast and frantic, I ran my hand down her backside, around to her thigh. I lifted her leg around my hip so she could feel me as our sensitive parts lined up. Groaning, she pulled apart from me. I thought she might leave now, but she didn't. Resting her head against mine, she panted as she stared at me. Then...she started unbuttoning my shirt.

Holy fuck. She was undressing me in the middle of a packed crowd of strangers. *Yes, let's do it here, in front of everyone. Let's let the world see how much we need each other. Let's let everyone see us...Anna...Denny. No...we can't, but God, yes, I want to do this. Where can we go? Somewhere...anywhere...*

As she continued to undress me, I crashed my mouth back down to hers. *Yes, take me...I'm yours. We'll go somewhere private and I'll make you happy. I'll make you beg, I'll make you scream. I'll make you forget everything but me. You're all I want. Let me...*

In my fog of desire, I opened my eyes and scanned the room. Women dancing nearby were watching us, but I didn't care about them. I needed a closet, a bathroom, a coatroom...somewhere with a door that I could close behind us. That was when I spotted Denny weaving his way through the crowd. *Fuck. No. Not now. What the hell do I do?* Pull Kiera away with me? He'd notice if she was gone. He'd wonder. He'd find out. But I couldn't stay here any longer.

Not knowing what else to do, I pushed Kiera back and twisted to blend into the bumping and gyrating crowd. My lips burned with the loss of her, my body ached, but Denny couldn't see this. He couldn't catch us. I wouldn't let that happen. He deserved so much better than walking in on us.

I found a nearby spot in the jam-packed crowd where I could watch Kiera without her seeing me. Her cheeks were flushed, her breath fast, her eyes blazing with desire. For me. But was that enough for her to leave him? For her to choose me? Hands brushed over my back as girls giggled in my ear, asking me to dance, but I ignored them as I watched the confusion blossom over Kiera's face. She honestly had no idea why I'd shoved her away from me. She didn't know what I knew.

She figured it out two seconds later when Denny approached her from behind. She spun to face him and I held my breath. This was it, the moment of truth. She was either going to fess up to him right now and tell him she had feelings for me, or she was going to brush aside what had happened between us. Again. And I would know, without a doubt, that I really didn't mean as much to her as she meant to me.

I was almost too scared to watch what she would do, but I couldn't turn away either. *Please tell him you want me. Please come find me. Please choose me, Kiera. Please.* Mere seconds passed before she acted, but within those seconds, a lifetime of hope blossomed within me. I'd gotten through to her. She was going to do it.

The brief hope evaporated the moment her hands grabbed Denny's face and pulled his lips down to hers. I felt like I'd been socked in the gut with a concrete two-by-four. Multiple times. I couldn't breathe as I watched her attack him. He seemed startled by her assault at first, but he eagerly returned her affections once he recovered. I didn't blame him. She was kissing him with no reservations, no inhibitions, just pure, undiluted desire. It was the same way she'd been kissing me just a few minutes ago. How could she do that to me? How could she switch gears so fast? Or had she? Was she still kissing me right now, in her head? Had I just turned her on, then handed her to my best friend? *Oh... God...*

Much to my continued horror, they broke apart for a split second, but only so she could lean up and whisper something into his ear. Whatever it was, by the look on Denny's face, it was something he wanted. He wrapped his arm around her waist, flashed his eyes around the club, then started leading her through the crowds. Fuck, were they leaving? Did she ask him to take her home? To... to...

I couldn't even finish that thought.

As she stepped away from me, I stepped toward her. No. No, this wasn't what was supposed to happen. We'd had such a profound connection on that dance floor. She was supposed to have an epiphany, realize how much she loved me, leave him... and go home with me. She was supposed to choose me. Why did she never choose me?

They were hurrying out of my sight. Panic made me continue to weave through the crowd, following them. They couldn't go home together. They couldn't... not while she was so riled up. Over me. I'd turned her on to the point where she was bursting. She'd nearly stripped me on the dance floor, she'd wanted me so much. That had to mean something. But she was still leaving with him. Why the hell was she still leaving with him? I wanted to shout her name, tell her to come back, but I was just too afraid to open my mouth. I might be sick if I did.

"Kellan, there you are!"

Hands clamped around my arm, holding me in place in the sea of reveling dancers. I looked down at Anna beside me. She was giving me an expression I knew very well—*Take me somewhere, anywhere, and I'll do things to you that you didn't even know were possible*. But Anna wasn't the one I wanted exploring my body, my soul, and I just didn't have it in me to return her seductive gaze.

Keeping my face blank, I leaned down to her ear. "I want to leave. You ready?"

Her eyes blazed with interest as she nodded. She probably took my question as an invitation, but it wasn't. I just couldn't stay in this thumping, pounding, sweaty mess of people anymore. I needed space; I needed to sit somewhere and quietly fall apart.

"Should we tell Denny and Kiera goodbye?" she asked above the music.

I shook my head, to answer her and to clear the horrid visual of Kiera kissing Denny from my mind. "They just left."

"Without saying goodbye to me? Interesting." Anna gave me a knowing smirk, like she knew exactly why her sister had taken off without even finding her first. Her smile made me even more nauseous.

Needing out of that damn club, I grabbed her hand and pulled her through the throngs of people. I purposely avoided following the same path Denny and Kiera had used. I just couldn't take it. When we got outside, I inhaled deep breaths. It didn't help clear my head much. I still felt really sick, and there was an ache in my chest that wouldn't go away. I felt like I was slowly losing my mind.

From beside me, Anna giggled. I looked over at her, wondering if she could sense the despair emanating from me. She didn't seem to. Her emerald eyes were fixated on my chest; my shirt was still almost completely unbuttoned. A chill went through me that had nothing to do with the icy wind on my skin. "You get hot in there?" she asked with a playful smile.

Dropping her hand, I hastily redid the buttons. I didn't want to be reminded of Kiera's fingers on my body. Or on Denny's body, which was probably where they were right now. God, I was going to throw up.

"Something like that," I told her as I hurried toward my car; Anna had to run to catch up to me. I noticed the absence of

Denny's car, and I had to hold my hand against my stomach so I didn't lose it all over the concrete.

Anna was panting a little when she stepped up to the passenger's side of my Chevelle. "Where'd you go anyway? When I got back from the bathrooms, you were just…gone."

I glanced at her over the top of the car and she shrugged. The image of rubbing up against Kiera's back leaped uninvited into my head, quickly followed by the image of her mouth all over Denny's. "Needed a drink," I muttered, opening the car door.

Anna's brow furrowed as I darted inside the safety of my vehicle. I did not want to think about what happened tonight. I did not want to think about what was happening right now. I did not want to think. Period. Anna got into the car while I debated what to do, where to go. We definitely couldn't go home. I didn't think I'd ever be able to go back home. Anna looked at where Denny's car had been parked earlier. She opened her mouth like she was going to make a comment. Knowing it would be something suggestive about Kiera and Denny, I beat her to the punch.

"Denny and Kiera need…alone time…so how about I take you to a friend's house…so they can have some privacy?" I was pretty proud of myself for saying it; my voice had only moderately cracked on Kiera's name.

Anna was one of those girls who were up for absolutely anything and would easily roll with life's little changes, so she eagerly nodded as she stretched her long legs out in front of her. Devouring me with her eyes, she stated, "Anything you want to do is fine with me."

I paused with my hands on the wheel and looked over at her. She resembled Kiera so much it was painful. Same thick brown hair, same expressive eyes, same curving smile. She was biting on her plump bottom lip, slightly squirming in her seat as she gave me *I want you to fuck me* eyes. I could have her if I wanted. I could probably take her right here in this crowded parking lot. I could shove the image of Kiera and Denny from my mind by wrapping myself around another woman. I could forget. I just didn't want to.

And...I'd promised Kiera I wouldn't. I wasn't sure if I still owed Kiera anything or not...but, well, I had promised her, and I was going to keep that promise.

Turning my gaze to the windshield, I muttered, "We'll go to Matt and Griffin's house. They won't mind if we just show up."

Anna let out an excited giggle as I pulled the car away from the club.

308

Chapter 21

Avoidance

Anna spent the car ride either flirting with me or talking about how great Denny and Kiera were. And because I couldn't ask her not to talk about them, I had to nod and agree with her. By the time we arrived at Matt's, I was done with my evening.

I knocked on the front door after seeing both Matt's and Griffin's cars in the driveway. I didn't know what they'd been doing tonight, but hopefully they were coherent enough to help me entertain Anna. She shifted her weight and rubbed her arms while she waited. I wasn't sure if she was actually cold or if she wanted me to put an arm around her like I had earlier when I'd escorted her into the dance club. I wasn't in the mood to be gentlemanly though, so I simply stared at the door and left her to her own devices.

It cracked open a heartbeat later and Matt's face appeared in the opening. He didn't seem surprised to see me; I often showed up with no warning. He simply said, "Hey," and opened the door all the way. As Anna and I stepped through, Matt raised his hand in greeting to her. He looked around for Kiera and Denny, but not seeing anyone else, he shut the door.

"You have any beer?" I asked him.

He nodded toward the kitchen in answer. I turned to leave, then looked back at Anna. I supposed I should be cordial. "You want one?"

Anna was busy taking in Matt and Griffin's home, but she paused to look at me when I asked my question. "I'd love one," she responded, her eyes trailing down my body. I resisted the urge to sigh. I just did not feel like being checked out right now.

Matt extended his hand to the living room for Anna while I headed into the kitchen. While I was walking, I heard Griffin's voice floating down the hallway. "Who the hell is here? And when the hell are we going to that party at Rain's? We shoulda just headed straight there from Pete's, like Evan did. But, no, pissy boy needed to come home and change. Pansy. It's not like I knocked that beer into your lap on purpose!"

I smirked, knowing Griffin wouldn't leave the house again once he realized Anna was here. He probably wouldn't leave her lap. Opening Matt's fridge, I found a pack of beer that I liked and grabbed a couple of bottles for Anna and me. Popping open the tops, I headed back out to the living room. As predicted, Griffin was all over Anna. Standing well inside her personal space, he was smiling down at her and playing with a strand of her bright red hair.

Not really wanting to interrupt them, I handed Anna her bottle as casually as I could. She still turned and looked at me though. "Thank you, Kellan."

She winked at me and Griffin frowned. If he didn't get into her pants tonight, I'd never hear the end of it. And if he *did* get into her pants tonight, I'd never hear the end of it. I was fucked either way. And I really didn't give a shit. Wanting alone time with my bottle, I collapsed on the far end of the couch.

Matt looked at me, then at Griffin. "We were just about to head out. You guys want to come?"

I shook my head—I did not want to go hang out with a bunch of random drunk people. I wanted to stay here, sipping on my beer in solitude. Or as close to solitude as I could currently get.

Before I could vocalize my objection, Griffin piped up. "Nah,

310

let's bag that shit. Here's cool." His eyes returned to Anna's chest. Anna looked over at me, maybe for guidance, since we were kind of together tonight, but I ignored her and stared at the condensation droplets on my sweaty bottle. Was Kiera sweaty right now? Oh God…why did I have to think that?

When Anna spoke, she didn't seem bothered in the slightest that I was being an uncommunicative date. "Sounds like fun. I'd love to keep dancing though. Can you turn on some music?"

I watched Matt shrug and grab the remote to his sound system. Thumping bass hit me a minute later and I almost put my hands over my ears. God, I never wanted to listen to club music again.

Matt turned on the TV to some sports recap, minus the sound, and sat back into his chair. His foot on his knee rocking with the music, he alternated between halfheartedly watching the television and watching Anna and Griffin. Anna laughed and giggled, drinking her beer and bumping her hip into Griffin's. She extended her hand to me a few times, like she wanted me to join them, but I always dropped my eyes. *Not tonight.*

She stopped trying after a while and fully gave herself over to the D-Bag desperately trying to get her attention. When I was halfway through my second beer, they were halfway down each other's throats. Still laughing and giggling, Anna scratched and clawed at Griffin in a way that only amplified my pain. That had been Kiera earlier, when she'd been ardently attacking me. Undressing me. Wanting me. God, why did she go home with *him*?

Inevitably, Griffin pulled Anna toward the hallway, toward his bedroom. She went willingly, with a huge smile on her face. She didn't even look my way when she took off to be with another man. Wasn't that fitting? Everybody else in the world was having sex tonight but me. And Matt. But he didn't seem as pissed about that as I was.

The minute Griffin and Anna were gone, I motioned to the music. "I think they're done with that now."

Matt clicked it off, then turned the volume on the TV up. As best we could, we tried to drown out the sound of light banging and

311

laughter that was coming from Griffin's room with sports stats and kitschy theme music. I didn't care about what we were watching, but I kept my eyes glued to the screen. I didn't want Griffin's and Anna's noises to remind me of Kiera and Denny, and how Denny was probably driving into Kiera right now. Jesus.

"You okay, Kell?" Matt asked from the chair.

I finished my beer and looked over at him. "Yeah, why?"

He indicated the hallway leading to the bedrooms with a lop-sided grin on his face. "You don't usually let Griffin get the girl."

Even though Griffin had music playing in his room, I could hear Anna saying, "Oh my fucking God, yes…fuck yes!" I did not want to think about what he was doing to make her say that. But thinking about Griffin getting off was better than thinking about Denny getting off, so I actually smiled at Matt.

"Every dog has his day," I told him.

Matt snorted, then leaned over and bumped fists with me. As I got up to get another beer, he said, "I'm gonna need a drink for this. Grab me one, will ya?"

I nodded as I headed for the other room. Anna's groans grew more pronounced the farther from the TV I got. "Oh God, Griffin. Fuck…me…yes!"

I quickly grabbed Matt and me some beers. When I got back to the living room, I saw that Matt had changed the TV to *The Matrix*. It was blaring now, but I could still hear muffled moans and groans from down the hall. I ignored them and focused on the movie, and on my beer. I really didn't care what the fuck Anna and Griffin did, or about the fact that it took them over two hours to do it.

When the movie ended, they were still finishing up. "Holy Jesus, fuck yes, don't fucking stop, so fucking good, oh my God, God, yes, yes, fuck yes, right there!" The sounds after that were highly complimentary, and then, blessed silence. *Thank God.*

Matt looked over at me with disgust on his face. "Jesus. Think we ought to get him an ice pack?"

A small laugh escaped me, which was saying something, considering how crappy I felt. Glancing at all the beer bottles on Matt's coffee table, I told him, "I don't think my date is leaving anytime soon, and I don't think I can drive. Mind if we crash here tonight?"

Yawning, Matt stood and clapped my shoulder. "Of course not, man. Me *casa* is *su casa*, you know that."

I raised my bottle to him. "Thanks."

He idly scratched his chest as he set down his empty beer. "Now that the jackrabbits are done humping, I'm going to bed. See ya in the morning."

Nodding, I watched him walk away. More giggling started up from Griffin's room. I groaned as I finished my beer. This was going to be the longest fucking night on earth.

I awoke sometime the next morning with a knot in my back like I'd slept on a rock. Much to my dismay, I woke up to the sound of people screwing. *Are you fucking kidding me?* Were they still going at it, or did they wake up early to start again? I put the couch pillow over my head. It was way too fucking early for this crap.

From down the hall, I heard Matt yell, "Will you two shut the fuck up!" Guess I wasn't the only one irritated.

Deciding now was as good a time as any to get up, I slunk off the couch and schlepped to the kitchen to make some coffee. At least that was one thing I could look forward to today. As I poured water into the machine, I wondered if I could go back to my house. I knew I had to, I had to take Anna back there, but the thought of walking through the doors and seeing Denny and Kiera beaming at each other as they remembered their epic night of cosmic orgasms was enough to make my stomach clench. I didn't want to see their dopey, love-filled smiles. Especially knowing that I had primed Kiera for their night. I got her ready. I got her all hot and bothered. I practically gift-wrapped her for him. Fuck, that pissed me off.

Making the coffee extra strong, since I was feeling sluggish, I decided to not go back into my house today. I'd do a drive-by. From down the hall, Anna agreed with my decision. She was shouting, "Yes, yes, yes!" with absolute abandon. Good. My mind was made up then. I wasn't going home today.

By the time Griffin and Anna were done "getting to know each

313

other," it was close to lunchtime. Griffin's room stank like sex when they walked out of it. Both of them were disheveled, blurry-eyed, and walking a little funny. I wasn't surprised. Marathon sex did that to you.

Not really wanting to leave, I waited for Anna at the front door. She was still dressed in her club clothes, and Griffin had his hand up her short dress as he hugged her goodbye. When she pulled back, he cupped her face and kissed her, hard. "I wish you were in town another night," he told her. That shocked me. Griffin wasn't one to do repeat performances. Not that I was one to talk. I didn't very often either. Guess all the "Fuck me harder" screams had made an impression on him.

Breathless, Anna murmured, "I know, me too. I'd love to fucking do that again."

Griffin tilted his head toward his bedroom. "So let's go do it again."

Biting her lip, Anna sighed and shook her head. "Can't. I have a flight today, and I really should spend some time with my sister while I'm here." Smiling, she added, "But I'll send you pictures for your spank bank when I get home."

Griffin groaned and dove in for her mouth again. "I'm going to be jerking off for the next three days straight thinking about you."

I rolled my eyes. I hated to break up this love fest, but I really didn't want to hear about Griffin masturbating anymore. "Ready, Anna?"

Reluctance clear on her features, she looked back at me with a sigh. That was a far cry from yesterday, when she was practically licking me with her eyes. "Yeah, I guess so."

Finally able to get some sleep, Matt was snoring as we left the house. Griffin was scratching his junk, or prepping himself for a marathon solo session. Okay, now I *did* want to get out of here. Griffin met eyes with me after Anna walked through the door and mouthed, *Un-fucking-believable.* Then he flashed ten fingers. *Yeah, thanks, genius. I already figured out that she was pretty spectacular from the massive amount of expletives coming from your room.*

I sniffed as I followed Anna to my car. Where the hell was I going to go? What the hell was I going to do? And how long could I avoid my home? Unfortunately, not nearly long enough. But I could at least avoid it today. I could at least avoid the afterglow. Kiera's, that was. Anna's was impossible to ignore. She was fanning herself when I climbed into the car. Even though I was not having a good morning, I smiled at her. "Have fun last night?"

Rubbing her legs together, she let out a long groan. "Oh my fucking God, Kellan. I have not come that hard, that many times... ever." Eyes blazing with residual desire, she said, "Griffin's dick is pierced. You ever had sex with someone with a piercing?"

I couldn't help but smirk. She was so different from Kiera in so many ways. "Not with a guy, no, but, uh...yeah, I've done piercings."

She raised a knowing eyebrow at me. "Then you know exactly how I feel right now."

I shook my head at her as I started the car. No, I was pretty sure I didn't know *exactly* how she felt right now—the subject in question was Griffin, after all—but I could imagine she felt pretty great. Me, on the other hand, I felt like shit. And I felt like even deeper shit the closer we got to my house. When we got to my street, I seriously thought I might roll down the window, lean over, and vomit. I couldn't stand being here, especially with the sounds of Anna's epic fuck fest last night echoing through my head. Had Kiera and Denny filled my home with similar sounds? Maybe one of my helpful neighbors would comment about how "happy" my house had sounded. God, I couldn't even handle that thought, let alone that actual conversation.

When we got to my driveway, I didn't pull in. Instead, I pulled up to the curb. Staring at Denny's car in the drive, I told Anna, "I have to meet a friend. I forgot I told him I'd swing by."

Anna frowned as she rolled her head my direction. "Oh, okay. Well, have fun." Sitting up, she winked at me. "But not as much fun as I'd have."

Leaning over the steering wheel, I gave her a genuine smile. "I doubt I could, Anna. Have a safe flight back home."

Her pout returned as she flung her arms around my neck. "I'm going to miss it here. But I'll be back, I'm sure." After she pulled away, she poked her finger into my chest and said with a stern expression, "You be good to my sister, okay?"

My smile froze as ice shot through my veins. What did she mean by that? Did she suspect something? *Fuck, what do I say to her?* Playing it cool, even though my heart was cracking wide open and spilling all over my leather seats, I coyly told her, "I'm good to everybody."

She smacked my thigh. "Yeah, that's what I hear. Bye, Kellan."

"Goodbye, Anna," I said as she gave me a light kiss on the cheek. Behind her, the house my parents had left me loomed in my vision. Even though it seemed bright and cheery, it wasn't. It was deceitfully cold, bitter, heartbreaking. No love lived there. Not for me.

I waited two seconds for Anna to get out of the car, then I punched it and stormed off down the tight street. I couldn't handle looking at my house anymore.

I drove to Evan's. I didn't even think about it. I just hopped on the freeway and that's where I ended up. When I pulled up to his loft above the auto body shop, his car was in his parking space. He cracked open his door a few seconds after I rapped on it. "Hey, man. Whatcha up to?"

With a shrug, I walked through his door. "Nothing much. Want to go over melodies for that new bit we're working on?"

Evan instantly perked up. "I was just talking to Rain about that last night. I think I came up with something that really works with that last batch of lyrics you gave me. Here, have a listen."

Before I knew it, it was well past ten o'clock. That was one of the great things about hanging out at Evan's—time flew by as we got ourselves wrapped up in the music that grounded our lives, gave us each meaning. Purpose. And Evan was right, the new beat he'd dreamt up matched my moody lyrics perfectly. He certainly had a gift, one he didn't get enough credit for. That was an unfortunate side effect of being the lead singer—everyone tended to focus on me and ignore the others. But they were just as important. Sometimes I wished I could turn my spotlight on them, but I knew I had a role to play. And I played it well.

When things were winding down for the night, I remembered the horror that awaited me back home—Mr. and Mrs. Perfect Fucking Relationship. I still wasn't ready to face them. Hating myself for being a coward, but needing an excuse to stay at Evan's, I purposely knocked my beer to the floor. I forced myself to laugh. "Sorry, man, guess I had more than I thought."

With a laugh of his own, Evan told me to stay and sleep it off. Even though I'd been in the same outfit for a day and I still had spikes in my hair, I took him up on his offer. God, I was pathetic.

I fell asleep with the memory of Kiera's breath on my skin.

When I woke up in the morning, I'd had enough of couch surfing. I needed an actual bed. And a shower. And clean clothes. I felt like I hadn't slept at all the last two nights. I was pretty sure I could have added up the total hours I'd slept decently on one hand. My nerves spiked as I approached my house. I didn't want Kiera to be there. She had school today though, so she should be gone. I hoped. Sort of.

The driveway was empty when I got there, but that was to be expected. Denny was at work. I approached the home with tentative steps. I really hated how Kiera could make me reluctant to enter my own house. She had kept me away on more occasions than I cared to admit. I needed to stop letting her run my life. But I might as well ask to stop breathing. She was the lead ball in this Newton's cradle—the cause. I was the effect. I had no choice but to react to her.

My hand was shaking as I reached for the knob. I immediately pulled it back and clenched it into a fist to get the blood properly circulating. This was nothing. No big deal. If she was here...so what? We'd ignore each other, ignore all the hurt, pain, and heat between us until it blew up in our faces again. God, we needed to break this cycle. Even I knew that.

Annoyed, I pulled out my keys and unlocked the door. A familiar smell hit me the moment I opened it. I paused as I absorbed the

317

fragrance. I wasn't sure exactly when it had happened, but at some point during her stay, her scent had permeated everything in my home. Or maybe that was all in my head. Who the fuck knew?

Shutting the door, I darted upstairs for the quickest shower known to man. I wanted out of this house. I purposely avoided looking at Denny and Kiera's room. I didn't think I'd be able to look at it again. What she'd done to him in there, while she had pretended he was me, was going to dig and fester inside my brain like an incurable disease. Fuck, I didn't want to be here. Heading to my room, I stripped bare and then shuffled to the bathroom.

Once I was dressed and refreshed, I headed back to Evan's place for rehearsal. Afterward, when the guys wanted to go to Pete's, I was torn. I wanted to say no, wanted to bow out, but a large part of me wanted to go, and that part eventually won out. As painful as it was going to be, I missed Kiera, and I knew I couldn't go another night without seeing her.

My heart was heavy on the ride over. I had no idea how she'd react to seeing me after how we'd parted ways. After parking, I sat and stared at the bar in the rearview mirror. I wasn't sure what I was waiting for, I just knew I couldn't go in there yet. The night at the club flashed through my mind—her fast breath, her eager mouth, her hands fisting in my hair. So much passion had been between us, we'd nearly ignited on the dance floor. That couldn't have *all* been fake.

A bang on my window knocked my memories from my head. Griffin was standing at my door, and Matt and Evan were a few feet behind him, waiting for me. Smirking, Griffin gestured at the mirror I'd been staring into. "You look great, princess. Get the fuck out of the car."

Rolling my eyes, I cracked open my door. I could do this. I slugged Griffin in the arm for his comment, and he backed away from me with a scowl. "Ease up, pissy pants. It's not my fault you didn't get laid the other night."

Grinning in a self-satisfied way, he splayed his fingers as he walked backward. "Five, dude."

Forcing my gaze away from the front doors I was dreading, I met Griffin's eyes. "What?"

"That's how many times she made me come! And that doesn't include the two times I jizzed the next morning." Stumbling over a rock in the lot, he almost fell on his ass. Klutz.

Grimacing, I walked around him. "Awesome," I muttered. I'd already had a color commentary *during* the act, I didn't need a play-by-play of it afterward.

Still wanting to brag, Griffin fell into step behind me. "It was unbelievable. The things that girl can do ... It's too bad for you that she chose me, man. Not that I blame her, but you seriously missed out."

Matt snorted. "Are you serious? She totally wanted Kellan, but he turned her down. You were runner-up, dude."

I looked back just in time to see Griffin's dumbstruck expression. "You smoking crack there, cuz? She was all over me, hot to trot. She even told me that she'd been wet for me since the first time we met."

A knowing smile on his lips, Matt flicked a glance at me. "When you first met? You mean, when she was practically giving Kellan a lap dance, and she barely acknowledged your existence? *That* first time?"

Griffin barged past me. "You don't know what the fuck you're talking about."

Matt was laughing as he hurried to catch up to him. "Wait, Griff! Tell me again how much she wanted you! Was that before or after she was practically palming Kellan's junk at the table?"

I shook my head at the pair of them as Evan laughed. Griffin walked through the front door first and the noise of the bar filtered out to me in the lot. Bending down, I pretended I was tying my shoelace. That was what I'd been reduced to: lame-ass stalling techniques. Fuck. Was I ready to see her?

Evan paused, waiting for me. "You okay?" he asked.

I mentally double-checked my features, but I wasn't making any strange, pain-filled expression as I retied my shoe. All of my turmoil was internal. "Yeah," I replied, standing. "Why wouldn't I be?" As far as Evan knew, this was just another night at Pete's.

Evan studied my face. "I don't know. You just seem…off." He crooked a grin. "Maybe you're still hungover from last night? You did get pretty shitfaced."

I made myself smile. "Yeah, maybe that's it. I do feel a little worn." Emotionally worn. Physically I felt fine.

Determined to prove that this was no big deal and I could be in a room with Kiera without it tearing me in two, I opened the door and walked into the bar. I tried not to look, but my eyes automatically scoped her out. She was back in the band's section, but her eyes were glued to the door, like she was waiting for me. *Goddamn, she was beautiful.* Her Pete's shirt hugged her in ways that showed off every lean asset I loved, and her jeans sat low on her hips, teasing me with just an inch of skin. Her hair was pulled back into a messy ponytail that just about undid me every time I saw it. It reminded me of sex—wild, unrestrained, passionate sex. It made me want to yank the band out, grab a fistful, and pull her into me.

But no, that wasn't what we were. She was Denny's. She'd made that clear the other night. Our friendship would never cross that line again. We really were over.

My stomach throbbed, but I forced the feeling down. It was just the way it was, no need to get an ulcer about it. My heart was pounding as we stared at each other. I couldn't read her emotions. Knowing she couldn't read mine either, I gave her a small nod and a smile. *See, Kiera, I can play nice, even if you did rip my heart out. We can still have a friendship, although just being friends with you kills me a little.*

I thought Kiera would smile in return, maybe look relieved that I wasn't angry or hurt, but instead, she frowned at me and stormed away. What the hell? I knew I'd crossed the line, but it's not like she hadn't eagerly met me on the other side of it. After all, wasn't she the one who undressed me?

Irritation bloomed in me the longer I watched Kiera working. She completely ignored me. And not in an aloof way like she just didn't care. No, every look she *wasn't* giving me was very deliberate. She wanted me to know she was fuming. I just had no idea why she was so angry. She wouldn't even approach our table, which was probably a good thing, since Griffin was regaling some random guy next to us with sex stories about Anna. God, he was going to repeat that night to people for the next six months, I just knew it.

After twenty minutes of absolutely no service, Evan finally managed to flag Kiera down. She looked over at our table, blatantly ignoring me sitting at it, then rolled her eyes and headed up to the bar to get our drinks. She wouldn't even take our order? Why the hell was she so mad at me? A little mad, sure, completely understandable, but this seemed over the top, even for her.

A few minutes later, she stormed to our table. Without a word, she slammed down a bottle of beer in front of each of us; a bit of foam frothed from the top of mine thanks to the force of the impact. I was a little surprised the bottle hadn't broken. Still silent, she then twisted on her heel and strode away from the table as quickly as she possibly could.

Matt looked at Evan after she left. "What's her problem today?" Both men then turned to look at me, like I was suddenly the keeper of Kiera's mood swings.

I shrugged and grabbed my beer. "Don't ask me. I'm not her boyfriend." I didn't mean to say it harshly, but it came out a little rough. While Evan frowned at me, I took a swig of my beer. Grimacing, I pulled it away from my lips and looked at the bottle. Lite beer? Really? I fumed in silence for a few seconds while the other guys drank their perfectly normal, calorie-laden alcohol. What. The. Hell.

A few minutes later, I noticed Kiera disappearing down the back hallway. Not able to stand her silent treatment for another second, I stood up with a screech and followed her. I was going to get my answers, and I was going to get them now. I caught up with her as she was coming out of the bathroom. By the look of shock and irritation on her face when she spotted me, it seemed like she wanted to dart inside the back room and hide. Fat chance I'd let that happen though. Wherever she went right now, I was just going to follow her. I wasn't leaving until she talked to me.

Maybe seeing that hiding was futile, she exhaled a frustrated sigh and tried to stalk past me. I grabbed her elbow. "Kiera…" Her hazel eyes burned when she looked up at me. The heat in her glare stole my breath for a second. She jerked her arm away while her eyes continued drilling holes into my head. "We should talk…"

"Nothing to talk about, Kellan!" she bit out.

Wondering what the hell I had done to make her so mad at me, wondering why she hated me so much and loved *him* so much, and wondering why just the sound of her voice made my knees weak, I quietly told her, "I disagree."

Leaning into me, she sneered, "Well…you can apparently *do* whatever you want!"

Her snotty attitude mixed with my pain and frustration. Even I could hear the sharpness in my voice as I responded to her. "What's that supposed to mean?"

"It means we have nothing to talk about," she snipped, bumping into my shoulder as she brushed past me.

I let her go, more confused than ever. What the hell was that about?

Chapter 22

I Only Wanted to Help You

At the end of the night, Kiera was still doing her damnedest to ignore me. Equally amused and irritated by her avoidance, I didn't try approaching her again. Maybe she just needed another day to cool off.

People started filtering out as the bar started shutting down. Eventually, there were just a couple of regulars left, Kiera, Griffin, Evan, and me, and Evan was heading out the door with Cassie, the cute blonde who had been hitting on him all night. I leaned against a table with my arms folded across my chest, watching Kiera as she realized that she didn't have a ride home. Guess in her pissy mood, she'd forgotten to line one up. I would take her, of course, if she wanted me to.

Kiera sighed as she noticed the rain splattering on the sidewalk through the closing front door. She didn't like being in the rain, so I knew she wouldn't want to walk home. I wasn't sure what she was going to do about her predicament. She glanced my way, but didn't make a move toward me. No, instead, she shocked the living hell out of me by approaching my bassist. I couldn't stop the grin that spread over my face. *Really? You'd rather ride home with Griffin than me?*

This should be interesting.

Kiera went for the casual approach. "Hi, Griffin."

It immediately put Griffin on guard. Their relationship wasn't exactly cordial. "Yeah? What do you want?" He smiled in a way that clearly said he was positive Kiera was about to ask if she could go down on him.

Kiera grimaced, but managed to remain polite. "I was hoping maybe you could give me a ride home?"

I barely contained my snigger. Oh God. You couldn't ask Griffin something like that and not expect him to take it in the dirtiest way possible. Griffin's brain had a permanent residence in the gutter. "Well, Kiera...I never thought you'd ask," he cooed as he undressed her with his eyes. "I'd love to give you a ride...all the way home."

And there it was. Typical Griffin answer. Kiera smiled with tight lips. "I literally meant a car ride to my house, Griffin."

Fuck, my stomach was going to cramp from holding in the laughter. Why did she have to be so damn adorable? Griffin didn't find her nearly as amusing. "No sex?" he asked, disappointed.

Kiera shook her head so hard, I thought she might give herself whiplash. "No." I could almost hear her brain adding *Ewwwwwww!* It brightened my spirits some. Here, at least, was one man I would never have to worry about.

Offended, Griffin sniffed. "Well then...no. Get your no-sex ride with Kyle."

I couldn't stop the laugh then. Yeah...no sex. Kiera glanced my way again, then looked around the bar like she was searching for an escape. I approached her while she debated what to do. My heart started beating harder with every step. Even when I was hurt by her, she affected me.

"Would you like me to give you a ride?" I asked. I meant more with that simple question than she really understood. *Choose me.*

She viciously shook her head, crossed her arms over her chest, and fled out the front doors. I guess I had my answer. She left in such a hurry, she forgot her jacket and her bag. Was I so awful to her that she had to run from me? I debated hurrying after her like some lovesick idiot, but what good would that do but get me soaking wet too? I couldn't let her walk all the way home though; it wasn't safe. And it was raining. She hated rain. I didn't want her to suffer through it because of me. Damn it. I was going to have to collect her, and she probably wasn't going to like that.

Sighing, I headed to the back room to get her stuff. Might as well get this over with.

By the time I was in my car and heading after Kiera, the rain was really starting to come down. I frowned as I searched the streets for her. She couldn't walk home in this. She'd catch her death. Hopefully she hadn't made it too far. God, I hoped she was all right.

Luckily, I spotted her right away; she was only about a block from the bar. She looked like she was freezing as she clutched her arms to her chest, and she was already soaked. Was she really going to walk all the way home in this? Now she was just being ridiculous. She could ignore me in the car; at least she'd be dry. Why the hell was she so mad at me?

Pulling over to the curb, I kept pace with her on the sidewalk. Disbelieving her stubbornness, I leaned over and rolled down the window. "Get in the car, Kiera."

She impaled me with her eyes. "No, Kellan."

Gritting my jaw, I looked up. *Lord, grant me patience to deal with this clearly unhinged woman.* Looking back at her, I, as calmly as I could, said, "It's pouring. Get in the car."

"No."

God. She was going to be difficult about this then. Well, I could be just as difficult if necessary. There was no way in hell I was leaving her out here all alone. "I'm just going to follow you like this all the way home." *Go ahead, Kiera, call my bluff. 'Cause I'm not bluffing.*

She seemed to realize that. With a huff, she stopped. "Go home, Kellan. I'll be fine."

I stopped the car and leaned on the steering wheel. Was she seriously going to be so pigheaded that she would risk her life to avoid me? This wasn't exactly the best part of town. "You're not walking all the way home by yourself. It's not safe."

Rolling her eyes, she started walking again. "I'll be fine," she repeated.

I watched her slim, shaking body walking away from me. Irritation clouded my concern. Fuck this shit. I'd drag her ass into the car if she wouldn't go willingly. Grunting, I stepped on the gas and tore away from her. "Fucking stubborn-ass woman," I muttered as I jerked the car hard around a corner. Murmuring similar obscenities, I parked along the curb, shut off the car, rolled up the window, and got out.

Kiera gaped at me as I stormed toward her. Was she really surprised that I wasn't going to let her either die of pneumonia or be assaulted by some lowlife? What kind of unfeeling asshole did she think I was?

Even though I had my jacket on, I was drenched by the time I made it to where she was standing and staring at me. My anger rose with every step I took. Being stubborn for the sake of being stubborn was just stupid. It's not like I was going to do anything to her if she got in the car. She'd made her choice quite clear at the club. She'd gone home with him. She wanted him. I got it.

"Get in the damn car, Kiera," I growled.

She yelled, "No!" then she actually shoved me away from her.

Fine. If she wanted to be difficult and immature, then I would do exactly what I'd planned on doing anyway. I'd drag her freaking screaming ass to the car. Grabbing her elbow, I yanked her toward the Chevelle. Of course, she fought me. "No, Kellan...stop it!"

She tried to pull away from me, but I wasn't about to let her go. I clamped on tight and pulled her to the passenger's side. I could tell she was furious that I was manhandling her, but I was getting a little ticked off too. Enough was enough. When I reached down and opened the car door, she managed to yank her arm away from me. Instead of being reasonable and getting into the warm, dry car, she started walking away from me. *Jesus Christ, woman!* Not letting her escape me, I looped my arm around her waist and held her to my chest. She kicked and squirmed as I lifted her off the ground, but she couldn't get away from me. Her lean, wet body rubbing against mine did things to me, took me to a place that I did not want to go tonight. Why couldn't I turn off what I felt for her? It would make my life so much easier.

I set her down near the open door, trapping her with my body so she couldn't get away. "Stop it, Kiera—just get in the goddamn car!"

Her hazel eyes were alive with hatred as she glared at me. Hatred, and something else. Her chest was heaving; her Pete's shirt clung to her body. The loose tendrils of her ponytail were dripping with heavy drops of rain; some of the lucky strands were glued to her flushed cheeks, her slender neck. My breath sped up as I watched this fiery, erotic beauty in front of me. Her passion brought me to my knees. I wanted her so much. Why couldn't she just want me back? Why couldn't she love me?

Before I could truly comprehend what she was doing, she suddenly grabbed me. Twisting her fingers into my damp hair, she pulled my face down to hers. Her aggressiveness hurt some, but I was too intoxicated by her lips being a whisper apart from mine to care. *God, yes…kiss me. Now. Please. I need it. I need you.*

As if she could hear my silent plea, she attacked me with her mouth. *Oh…God…yes.* Just as I started to return her fevered kiss, she pulled away from me. Then, less than a heartbeat later, she slapped me.

My wet cheek stung with the force she'd used; my ear rang. Acting out of pure, reflexive shock, I pushed her against the car as anger burned through my cold body. *What the fuck?*

For a second, the only sound was our fast breaths and the rain pounding all around us. Kiera stared at me with angry lust in her eyes. She wanted me, I knew she did. I could feel the desire coming off her in waves. I wanted her too. More than anything I wanted her. I was nearly hard already. I wanted to lay her down on my seat, strip those wet clothes off her damp body, and hear her scream my name as I drove into her. And she would. She would scream it over and over again as I kept her on the edge of climaxing. Maybe that was how I would punish her for hurting me, physically and emotionally—I wouldn't let her finish.

My decision made, I grabbed her and slowly forced her into the front seat. She offered no real resistance. She tried to deny it, but she wanted me inside of her. Not giving her a chance to escape me, I climbed in after her. While I closed the door behind us, she started scooting up the bench seat, away from me, like she was actually going to leave. I don't think so. Twisting back around, I grabbed her legs and pulled her back to me. Needing my body tangled up in hers, I forced her to her back on the seat as I crawled over the top of her. She pushed at my chest like she wanted me off her, but her fingers had my shirt clutched in them and I knew she was full of shit. She wanted me.

"Get off me," she snipped, her breath heavy, her eyes begging me to do the opposite.

Angry at her mixed signals, I wondered if her words and actions would ever come together. She wanted me... didn't she? "No," I told her.

Her hand reached out and grabbed my neck. She pulled me in while her words pushed me away. "I hate you..."

The look on her face made a throb pulse through my lower body. Fuck, I needed her. I needed to show her what she did to me, show her how much I wanted her. Maybe then she would stop denying this. I was rock hard now as desire, lust, and love waged war within me. I wrapped her legs around me and rubbed myself against her jeans. *This is for you. Only you. This is what you do to me. What do I do to you? Show me... Take me... I'm yours, only yours. Why can't you fucking see that?*

Her eyes rolled back into her head as she gasped, panted. She wanted this so much. I knew she did. Bitterness surged through me. I was so tired of this cycle of denial. "That's not hate you feel..." I sneered as she did her best to give me a cool glare. With a cruel smirk, I added, "And that's not friendship either." No, we'd passed friendship a long time ago.

"Stop it..." Still fighting this, she wiggled her hips under me. It only made me want her more. Using her body for purchase so she could feel how intense this would be, I slowly and deliberately rocked against her again. She cried out, arching her back as she looked at the door above her head. No, she needed to watch me. She needed to see what she was doing to me. I grabbed her cheek, forcing her head down, forcing her to look me in the eye. She didn't like that.

"This was supposed to be innocent, Kellan!" she bit out, furious.

"We were never innocent, Kiera. How naïve are you?" I matched her tone. She couldn't keep lying to herself.

Tears of frustration in her eyes, she whispered, "God, I hate you…"

God, she was stubborn. Whatever was between us, it wasn't born from hate. "No, you don't…"

I rocked against her faster. I bit my lip as a deep moan escaped me. I needed her. God, I needed her. *Say yes, Kiera. Let me in.* Even as a tear rolled down her cheek, she watched my reaction to her with intent eyes. "Yes I do…I hate you…" She could barely get the words out, she was breathing so hard.

I pushed against her again, cringing as the sensation sent shock waves through my body. *Yes. God…yes.* "No…you want me…" Her passion ignited a memory in me. The club. Her unrestrained need as we danced. That had been for me. Even she couldn't deny it. "I saw you. I felt you…at the club, you wanted me." I brought my mouth right over hers, inhaling her scent, her rapid breaths… sharing my own. It was only the beginning of what I was about to share with her. I could feel how much it excited her as she squirmed beneath me.

"God, Kiera…you were undressing me." I grinned at the re-membered feel of her fingers down my skin. I wanted them on me now. "You wanted me, right there in front of everyone." Needing to taste her, I dragged my tongue along her jaw to her ear. "God, I wanted you too…" I moaned in her ear.

Her hands flew up to my hair, yanking me away from her. I hissed in a breath as my lower body begged to be set free. I rocked against her again, not sure how much more I could take. *Stop fighting. Say yes.*

"No, I chose Denny." Ignoring her, I rubbed against her again. Harder. Faster. *God, yes. Again. More.* "I went home with him..." *Oh God, Kiera, yes, fuck...yes.* "Who did you choose?" she asked.

The vileness in her tone silenced my head, completely stilled my hips. A warning flashed in my brain. A warning, and a clue. What the hell did she mean by that? "What?"

She hit my chest with every ounce of pent-up rage inside of her. "My sister, you asshole! How could you sleep with her? You promised me!"

In a microsecond everything snapped into place for me. That was why she was pissed? Not because I'd crossed the line again. Not because she'd caved and given in to what she wanted. Not because I'd stayed away for days. No, because she thought I'd slept with Anna. Well, fuck me. She didn't get to be angry about that. Not when she left the fucking club with Denny. All bets were off the moment she tore my heart out and ripped it into bloody confetti. If I wanted to fuck Anna all night long, then I had every right to.

Truly furious now, I said something rash, and horribly misleading. "You can't be mad at me for that. You left to go screw *him*! You left me there...ready, wanting you...with her." Further digging the knife into her back, I ran my hands in an intimate way up her hips and whispered, "And she was all too willing. It was so easy to take her...to slip inside her." If she was going to be a bitch, then I would be her bastard.

The fury on her face was instant. And satisfying. I'd hurt her. Good. Now she truly knew how I felt, because she sure as fuck hurt me. She tried to smack me, but I'd anticipated that, and held her down. "You son of a bitch," she snarled.

She was so mad, I thought the raindrops falling from my hair would sizzle when they touched her skin. It amped me up, excited me. The way her cheeks filled with color, the way her eyes danced— her jealousy was intoxicating. Smiling in a way that I knew would piss her off, I told her, "I know who I screwed, but tell me"—my mind spinning with heat, desire, and passion, I lowered my lips to her ear—"who did you fuck that night?" I rocked against her as I said it, reminding her of our heated moment at the club and emphasizing the fire between us right now. She groaned, sucked in a strained breath.

"Was he better…as me?" I continued. Returning my mouth to above hers, I flicked my tongue over her sweet, rain-dampened lip. "There is no substitute for the real thing. I'll be even better…"

Fuck…say yes…

She didn't. Instead, she spat, "I hate what you do to me."

I watched her churning eyes. She was lying. At least in part. But I understood what she meant. I hated what she did to me sometimes too. But more than I hated it, I loved it. And I knew she felt the same. "You love what I do to you." Remembering being inside of her, making her scream, I ran my tongue up her throat. "You ache for it." *I ache for it. I need you.* "It's me you want, not him." *Choose me. Love me. Show me. Right now.*

I pressed my ache against her, needing her more than ever. She threaded her fingers through my hair…then rocked her hips in rhythm with mine. Oh. My. God…yes. I cried out in the same way she did. We needed this. We needed each other. *Please, Kiera. Say yes.* She moved in time with me. Our breaths picked up, our intensity picked up, the windows steamed up, and the car started gently rocking back and forth with our movements. *God, yes, now, more.*

Her fingers clawed at my jacket, wanting it off. I helped her remove it. *Fuck yes. All of these layers between us need to come off. I want to be naked with you. I want to be bare.* Her mouth came up to touch mine but I pulled away. It shot liquid fire down my groin to tease her. Fuck, yes. I wanted to tease her. Then satisfy her. She tried again but with her tongue, and I pulled away again. I thought I was going to explode. I couldn't tease her for long.

Kiera didn't want to be teased right now. Frustrated, she raked her nails down my back. Fuck, it was the same way she had scratched me in the espresso stand, when she'd been coming. I nearly came as I remembered it. I dropped my head to her shoulder, digging into her with abandon. *Yes. God, more, Kiera. Yes.* She cried out as we worked against each other, grabbing my back pockets and wrapping her legs around me in a near frenzy.

Clutching me tight as she moved against me, she moaned, "No, I want him."

Bullshit. I guarantee she had never felt anything like this with him. "No, you want me…" I said into her neck.

"No, he would never touch my sister! You promised, you *promised*, Kellan!" She stiffened beneath me. The loss of our escalating rhythm nearly drove me mad.

"That's already done with. I can't change it." She tried to push me away, but I grabbed her hands, pinned them beside her head. I ground my hips into hers, and she made a noise that let me know the momentary pause had nearly killed her too. "But this… Stop fighting, Kiera. Just say you want this. Tell me you want me, like I want you." My mouth returned to above hers. "I already know you do."

I was done teasing. I was done playing games. I needed her. Right now. We couldn't stop this. Not anymore. I lowered my lips to hers. She groaned when our mouths met and my stomach clenched in preparation. *Yes… God, Kiera, yes.*

Our kiss was hungry and passionate, with each side wanting more. I was right, I knew I was right. She wanted this just as badly as I did. I released her hands and she immediately returned them to my hair. Her fingers felt marvelous running over my scalp. I wanted to feel her long locks, see them spread across my leather seat. I ripped the hair band out and tossed it to the floor. Even wet, her hair felt amazing between my fingers.

Kiera's dual messages didn't stop now that our tongues were sliding together. Murmuring that she hated me, she ran her hands down my back and pulled on the pockets of my jeans, asking for more, deeper, harder. I obliged her physical request while I told her that she didn't hate me.

My hands traveled over every curve I could reach on her—the angle of her jaw, the swell of her breast, the tiny hills of her ribs, the curve of her hip, the roundness of her ass. Her small hands ran under my shirt, feeling my bare skin. Her flesh-against-flesh touch sent a bolt of electricity straight down my body. It was only mildly hampered by her words.

"This is wrong," she groaned into the passion-laden air.

A tiny bit of my buzz faded; she was right, of course, this was wrong. It also felt better than anything I'd ever experienced before, and it was too late—I couldn't stop touching her. My thumb brushed over a rigid nipple straining against her shirt through her thin bra. I wanted it in my mouth so bad. "I know...but, God, you feel so good."

No, she felt incredible. We melded against each other with no more words, just wild, uncontrollable desire. I could hear Kiera's breathing fall into a familiar rhythm, the throaty moans repeating in a pattern that was steadily getting louder, more desperate, more distinct. She was getting close. My own body had reached the tipping point ages ago—it was sheer willpower that kept me from an earth-shattering release. But I wouldn't finish this without her. No, I was going to finish this inside of her. And possibly with her. Yes, I wanted her to come with me. I wanted it more than anything.

I broke apart from her anxious mouth. She leaned up to suck on my lip, and my eyes rolled back. I pulled farther away. Since her clothes were so damp, I would need space to undress her. And I *was* going to undress her. I needed to see that pale white flesh quivering under my fingertips. She gasped when she realized what I was doing. Her hungry eyes watched mine, and all I saw was affirmation—*Yes, do it. Take me. I'm yours.*

I glared as I watched her heated eyes drinking me in. I knew she wanted this. The night at the club was the real mistake. *I* was the one she wanted, she just hadn't had the guts to leave with me that night. But this moment, right now, was right. And while I was going to regret betraying Denny tomorrow, I didn't fucking care anymore. I *was* going to have her tonight.

When I had one more button left to go on her jeans, she grabbed my wrists and jerked my hands up and over her head, holding them tight. Our body parts lined up again, and a throb went through me. I was so close to what I needed that it was painful. *Tease.*

"Stop it, Kiera!" I snapped. I was aggravated, turned on, and now, in a little bit of pain; I needed to come, badly. "I need you. Let me do this. I can make you forget him." Desperate, I added, "I can make you forget *you*."

She shivered beneath me; she knew I was right. What we were going to experience right now was going to be more powerful than anything either of us had ever felt before. I knew that for a fact. And I needed it to happen, now, before I spontaneously combusted. I easily pulled a hand free from her grasp, stroking her body on the way back to her jeans. She responded everywhere I touched her. *See, Kiera, you know I'm right.* "God, I want inside you."

"Stop it, Kellan!"

Irritated that she was still refusing this, I paused with my lips on her neck. "Why? It's what you want, what you beg for!" She couldn't deny that, not after all the times she'd said please. To prove my point, I shoved my hands into her jeans, over her underwear. She was going to say it first. She was going to beg me. Then both of us could stop this frustrating game.

Even though I wasn't directly touching her, she fell apart underneath me. The wanton cry she let out amplified the pleasure and pain I was feeling. She grabbed my neck and pulled my face to hers. I groaned with need. I couldn't do this much longer. I needed to be thrusting inside her. I needed release. I needed to hear her scream. I needed to feel her coming. But I needed to hear her say that she wanted me first.

But still she refused. "No…I don't want you to." My finger traced the edge of her underwear and her sentence fractured in two. She was still lying. She did want me. She was soaked with her desire for me. One small slip of my finger and I could feel it. A few tugs on her jeans and I could taste it. Oh God, I wanted to taste her…

Banishing that image from my mind, I struggled to stay in control. I needed her to say it. *Give me permission, Kiera.* But she still fought me; her hand released my neck to feebly attempt to dislodge my probing fingers. I was stronger though, and her heart really wasn't in it.

"I can feel how much you do want me to, Kiera." My voice sounded strained to me, but then again, everything about me was straining right now. I couldn't handle the intensity, the ache, the throbbing. I needed this to end. A tight, pain-filled groan escaped me. "I want you...*now*. I can't take any more," I panted. I felt like I would lose my mind if I didn't plunge inside her soon. I ripped my other hand free from her grasp and started tugging on her wet denims. "God, Kiera, I need this."

I was seconds away from begging *her* to take *me* when she blurted out, "Wait! Kellan...stop! I...I need a minute. Please...I just need a minute."

My hands froze as I stared at her. Did she seriously just say that to me? Our "safe word," so to speak. As if she was reading my mind, she repeated herself, "I need a minute."

Well, fuck.

I couldn't move while I processed what the fuck had just happened. She panted underneath me while I stared her down. She'd done it to me again. She'd riled me up to the breaking point, then told me no. And, unless I was going to keep going with this and force her to relent to me, to us, I had no choice but to let her go. Shit.

"Shit!"

She flinched at my unexpected exclamation. I sat up, raking my hands through my hair while I tried to calm down. It wasn't working. Every second I glared at her sprawled across my seat made me even more ticked off. What the fuck was she trying to do to me?

"Shit!" I snapped, smacking the door behind me as hard as I could.

She sat up nervously, refastening her jeans. Goddamn, we'd been so close. She wanted me, I knew she did. Why was she constantly tormenting me with something I couldn't have? Because she was a fucking bitch. A teasing whore...that was why. "You...are..."

I shut my mouth before my temper could get the best of me. She wasn't a bitch. She wasn't a whore. She was in love with another man, a man I cared about. I couldn't forget that. But, fucking hell,

335

this hurt. The heated air in the car became stagnant, foul with pain, tension, betrayal. I couldn't breathe. I needed out of this goddamn fucking car.

Opening the car door, I immediately stepped outside. The icy rain was a balm, but it didn't squelch my anger. I could almost feel the drops sizzling on my infuriated skin. I redirected my ire to my car's tire. I would need a stronger outlet, or I was going to turn my tongue on her. Bitch.

I kicked the tire as hard as I could. "Fuck!" It relieved some of the pent-up tension, so I did it again. "Shit! Motherfucking piece of fuck shit! God fucking damn it to fucking hell shit!" I knew Kiera was watching my nonsensical ranting, but I was too far gone to care. Fuck my fucking life. Walking away from the car, I clenched my fists and screamed my rage and frustration into the empty street. "FUUUUCK!!"

Fuck, I was yelling obscenities on the street corner like some fucking drama queen. I needed to calm the fuck down. I raked my fingers through my hair again, resisting the urge to pull chunks of it out of my scalp. Tilting my head up to the sky, I tried redirecting my focus. *Only think about the raindrops. Only listen to the sound of the rain pelting the earth. Only feel the chill. Don't think about her. Don't think about her lips. Don't think about her body. Her smile. Her laugh. Her eyes... the way she looks at you. The way she looks at* him. *Fuck.*

I lowered my hands but kept my palms up, absorbing every drop. *Only think of the rain. There's just the freezing, ice-cold rain. You. The rain. Nothing else.*

"Kellan?"

Fucking-A.

My brief moment of zen vanished at hearing her voice. *You ripped my heart out twice in the span of forty-eight hours. The least you could do is give me a fucking moment of silence to get my shit together!* I raised my finger to her, hoping she took the hint and left me the fuck alone. She didn't.

"It's freezing... please come back to the car."

336

You've got to be fucking kidding me. Five minutes? I only get five fucking minutes without her in my fucking head? *Rain. Rain. Just rain. Calm down.* Still not able to look at her, still not able to speak, I shook my head. *Take the fucking hint, Kiera. I don't want to be anywhere near you right now, but I still can't leave you alone out here, so I'm fucking stuck with you in my car, my home, and my fucking heart!*

Rain. Just rain...

"I'm sorry, please come back," she called out from the car.

Oh my fucking God, please let her shut the fuck up before I completely lose my fucking mind. Rain...rain...rain...

I heard her mutter, "Damn it," then I heard her getting out of the car.

Un. Fucking. Believable. She couldn't even give me this? What a fucking bitch. Opening my eyes, I glared at her as she approached me. I wondered if I looked as ticked as I felt. I must have, because her steps were small, tentative. "Get back in the car, Kiera." In my attempt to remain civil, I spat each word out between clenched teeth.

She looked nervous as she swallowed, but she shook her head. "Not without you."

Still so fucking stubborn. All peaceful thoughts of raindrops on sidewalks fizzled from my brain. Rage pounded through every muscle, vibrating them with tension. "Get in the damn car! For once, just listen to me!" I yelled that so loudly, my throat ached. I was going to be raspy for the concert tomorrow night. Great. One more fucking problem she'd caused me.

My temper sparked hers. Her chin lifted, she snapped back, "No! Talk to me. Don't hide out here, talk to me!"

Talk to her? What the fuck could she possibly want to talk about? How much she loved Denny, and how little she thought of me? No thanks, I didn't want to fucking hear that. I took a step toward her; we were both soaked now. "What do you want me to say?"

Her jaw quivered and her voice was thick with anger. "Why

337

won't you leave me alone? Tell me that! I told you before that it was over, that I wanted Denny. But you still torment me…"

"Torment you?"

Was she joking? She was the one who teased me on a near-constant basis. Just the way she looked at me would be enough to have most men begging on their knees. And the way she kissed me was an invitation for sex in most men's books.

"You're the one who—"

I stopped myself in the nick of time. I wouldn't give her the satisfaction of knowing just what she did to me. How much I wanted her. How much I fucking loved her. How much it fucking hurt that I would never be good enough for her. How much I wished I didn't give a shit about her. How much it killed me when she brought me to the brink. How much I wished we hadn't stopped tonight.

"The one who what?" she yelled into the sudden silence.

I looked back at her. Really? She just couldn't let anything go, could she? I was trying to not go off on her, but I couldn't hold my tongue another fucking minute. If she wanted the truth, then fine, I would give her the fucking truth, in the simplest, crudest way I could give it to her. Maybe then she'd fucking understand just how not-innocent her innocent flirting was.

I gave her a smile as dark as my shattered heart. "Do you really want to know what I'm thinking right now?" I took a step toward her; she backed away. "I'm thinking…that you…are a fucking tease, and I should have just fucked you anyway!"

Pure venom running through my veins, I took another step, putting me toe-to-toe with her. I could grab her, shove her into the car, and finish this, right now. Knowing I should step away and calm down, but also knowing it was too late, words left my mouth that I instantly regretted. "I should fuck you right now, like the whore you really—"

Her hand connected with my cheek before the words finished leaving my foul mouth. The hit was twice as hard as her earlier smack; I was sure I had red marks. I was really tired of being fucking hit! I shoved her against the car. "You started this. All of this!

Where did you think our 'innocent' flirting was heading? How long did you think you could lead me on?" I cinched my fingers around her arm; I wasn't even conscious of what I was saying anymore. "Do I still...torment you? Do you still want me?"

Tears streamed down her cheeks as she answered my question. "No...now I really do hate you!"

I felt like she'd reached inside and hollowed out my soul. Only residual anger kept me standing. "Good! Then get in the fucking car!"

Not knowing what the fuck I was doing, I shoved her into the open car door. When her feet were clear, I slammed the door shut. I wanted to open it again and slam it even harder, but I couldn't function enough to do that. Oh God. What the fuck did I just do? Why the fuck would I say those things to her? And her face...genuine hatred had been on her face. And now she was crying. Fuck, fuck, fuck. I had just fucked everything. It was bad before, but now...I'd burned a bridge, I knew it. Jesus Christ. I'd just lost her forever.

I paced in front of my car. *What do I do now? What the fuck do I do now? How the fuck do I take that back? How do I fix this? Can I fix this?*

Not knowing what else to do, I stalked over to the driver's-side door. If I'd just gone to my side in the first place, none of this would have happened. If I'd left her alone at the club, none of this would have happened. If I'd left Seattle, none of this would have happened.

Irritated, frustrated, scared, I got in the car and slammed my door shut. The silence in the car was oppressive. The very air between us was different. Everything was different now, because of my big fucking mouth. "Damn it!" I snapped, slamming my hand on the wheel. It was never supposed to be this way. "Damn it, damn it, damn it, Kiera."

I beat the shit out of my steering wheel, then lowered my head to the tight leather. "Damn it, I never should have stayed here..."

When I lifted my head, I felt empty, alone, and freezing cold. I pinched the bridge of my nose to try to relieve the pressure headache that was building, but nothing was helping. I was fucked. And alone. Completely alone. Again.

Needing warmth, needing escape, I started the car and turned up the heater. I couldn't leave this godforsaken place until I apologized. I had to at least try to right the wrong. While she cried beside me, I told her, "I'm sorry, Kiera. I shouldn't have said that to you. None of that should have happened."

She didn't say anything, only kept crying. I sighed. This wasn't what I wanted tonight. This wasn't why I followed her. I just... wanted to help her. I just wanted to return her stuff and give her a ride home so I'd know she was safe. I just wanted her safe. And happy.

Seeing her shivering, I reached behind me and grabbed her jacket from the backseat. My jacket was back there too, but I didn't want it. I deserved to be cold.

I quietly handed it to her and she quietly put it on. There were no words left to say. We were as done as two people could possibly be. She was as unobtainable to me now as my dead parents, her love just as unreachable. But this time, I deserved it. I was a bastard, in every sense of the word. She was better off without me.

As I drove her home in silence, despair washed over me. I'd touched love with her, I was certain of it. Maybe temporarily, or maybe just a friendship kind of love. I wasn't sure. But whatever it was that she'd been giving to me, it had been the best thing I'd ever felt in my entire life. And it was gone now. I'd never know it again. I was going to be alone, never knowing that kind of comfort again. And now that I'd had it, I couldn't go back to not having it. The ache would kill me now more than ever. How did I live without love now? How did I live without her?

I could feel the breakdown coming as we pulled up to the house—my empty, meaningless house, where nothing of me existed until *she* put it there. I shut the car off and immediately got out. I didn't want her to see me fall apart. And I was going to fall apart... it was coming. I was a heartbeat away from sobbing.

Tears were rolling down my cheeks as I unlocked the front door.

My throat hitched as I walked into the entryway. I held it in as I sprinted up the stairs. *Not yet. Don't lose it yet.* I closed my door behind me and paused with my hand on the wood, then I let go of my hold on the wall of crushing grief and let the sob escape me. Walking backward, I collapsed onto my bed. Bringing my dirty shoes onto the mattress, I cried into my knees.

Friend. Lover. Companion. Family. Whatever she could have been to me…I'd just lost her for the rest of my life. I had no idea how I would go on from here.

I heard the door open, but I couldn't stop the tears from coming. She'd obviously already heard them anyway. Kiera sat beside me, but I didn't move. I couldn't. All I could do was cry, cry for everything I'd lost, and for everything I'd never had. I was alone. Forsaken. Unlovable. I couldn't even comprehend why she was sitting next to me.

And then, beyond all expectation, hope, or reason, Kiera put her arm around my shoulder. Her simple act of comfort broke me. *I can't lose her. Please, God, don't let me lose her. I need her. I'll do anything. We'll end this charade, we'll go back to being purely just friends. Just don't take her away from me tonight.*

A pain-filled sob escaped me as I wrapped my arms around her and laid my head on her lap. *I'm sorry. I'm so sorry. Please don't leave me. Please don't hate me.* The final remnants of my emotional sanity vanished as I completely lost control and bawled. It felt like hours. I emotionally released everything built up inside of me, from the pain of not having Kiera's love to the pain of never having my parents'. I cried for hurting Kiera. I cried for betraying Denny. I cried for my nonexistent childhood. I even cried for the mountain of meaningless encounters I'd had over my lifetime, because meaningless encounters were probably all I would ever have now.

Kiera didn't run away from my breakdown. She held me, cradled me, rubbed my back, even pulled a blanket over my shivering body and used her heat to warm me. I'd never felt so much love and comfort from another human being. Ever. Her tenderness eventually eased my sorrow, dried my tears. In a silence that was once again comforting, she held me, gently rocking me like I suppose most mothers would rock their troubled children. I wouldn't know. My mother never had. Nobody ever had. It soothed me, and I felt sleep rushing in to fill the void left by my explosion of pain.

As I lingered in a state somewhere between awake and asleep, I started to dream. In my dream, Kiera was leaving me. I reached out for her, told her, "No," but…she still left me. In the end, she still left me.

Chapter 23

Fantasy Is Better Than Nothing

My vision was hazy, the lights in the room too bright, but through the disorientation, I saw my father standing beside the bed. His mouth was twisted in displeasure, like it usually was. "Wake up, lazy ass. We're not raising you to be slothful."

I looked to the window and it was still pitch-black outside. The sun wasn't even up yet. "It's barely morning…" I mumbled.

My dad shook his head. "You were supposed to be up an hour ago, starting your chores, but look at you, wasting away the day… pathetic," he told me in a condescending voice that I knew all too well.

Beside him, my mother was watching me with impassive eyes. "Why do you make everything so difficult, Kellan? We don't expect very much from you, but you still never fail to let us down." Her lip twisted with disappointment. I was all too familiar with that too.

My father sighed and I swung my eyes back to him. "I've already accepted that you won't ever amount to much in life, but did you honestly think you'd be good enough for her, Kellan?"

I woke up with a start, panting, my heart racing. I scanned my room, trying to understand where I was, what was happening. I had a headache, a stomachache, and a sore throat. For a confused second, I thought my parents really were in my room with me, be-

343

littling me. I even looked around for them. But then I remembered last night, remembered the rain, remembered yelling at Kiera, remembered crying in her arms. I closed my eyes as the grief swept over me. *Damn it.* For once, I wished my nightmare was the reality, and my reality was the dream.

I'd called Kiera a whore. I'd considered screwing her in my car, whether she'd wanted it or not. God. I felt like I was going to throw up. My parents were right. I could never have her, because I didn't deserve her.

I was still dressed in the clothes I'd been wearing last night, and Kiera was gone. I wasn't too surprised about that. It wasn't as if she could stay and comfort me all night. My boots were still on, and my bed was filthy. I felt filthy, but I didn't want to change. Not yet. I needed to talk to Kiera. I needed to apologize for last night. I needed to clear the air between us, tell her the truth about her sister, beg for her forgiveness.

You're not good enough for her…

No, I supposed I wouldn't ever be good enough for her, but I could at least stop hurting her. I could end this. I could let her go. What happened last night would never happen again. I wouldn't let it.

By the time I got my bereaved body out of bed, Kiera was already in the kitchen. Like she usually was when we had coffee, she was still dressed in her pajamas. She looked worn; last night had been hard for her too.

I stopped in the doorway, and Kiera looked me over with questioning eyes, like she wasn't sure how I'd treat her this morning. I didn't blame her for not knowing. She'd once teasingly called me moody, and on more than one occasion I'd proven her right. When it came to her, I *was* moody. This was just so difficult… Why did I have to love her so much?

With a heavy sigh, I joined her at the coffeepot. I needed to get this over with before I changed my mind. I held my hands up, showing her I was unarmed, physically and emotionally. "Truce?"

"Truce," she agreed, nodding.

Leaning back against the counter, I tucked my hands behind me.

I didn't want to be tempted to touch her. I couldn't meet her eyes, and I stared at the floor. "Thank you…for staying with me last night."

"Kellan—"

She started to interrupt me, but I didn't let her. "I shouldn't have said what I did; that's not who you are. I'm sorry if I scared you. I was so angry, but I wouldn't ever hurt you, Kiera…not intentionally." Finding strength in my admission, I raised my eyes to hers. "I was way out of line. I never should have put you in that position. You're not… You are in no way a…a whore." I looked away when I said that last part. God, I was a dick for calling her that.

"Kellan—"

Needing to finish my thought before all my courage left me, I cut her off again. "I never would have…I wouldn't ever force you, Kiera. That's not…I'm not…" I stopped my nonsensical jabbering and stared at the floor. Why did words fail me when I needed them the most?

Kiera's soft voice filled the emptiness between us. "I know you wouldn't." She was quiet a second, then she added, "I'm sorry. You were right. I…I led you on." Grabbing my cheek, she made me look at her. "I'm sorry for all of it, Kellan."

She was taking too much of the blame. It wasn't her fault that I'd lost control. It wasn't her fault that I'd turned into a raging ass-hole. "No…I was just mad. *I* was wrong. You didn't do anything. You don't need to apologize for—"

Her voice was low as she spoke over me. "Yes, I do. We both know I did just as much as you. I went just as far as you did."

No, she didn't. She had told me over and over that she didn't want me. I'd just refused to listen. "You clearly told me no…repeatedly. I didn't listen…repeatedly." I pulled her hand away from my face with a heart-filled exhale. I didn't deserve her kindness. "I was horrible. I went too far, much too far." Disgusted with myself, I ran a hand down my face. "I'm…I'm so sorry."

Stubborn as always, Kiera continued disagreeing with me. "Kellan…no, I wasn't being clear. I sent mixed signals."

Disbelieving her objection, I pointedly raised an eyebrow. "'No' is pretty clear, Kiera. 'Stop' is pretty damn clear."

"You're not a monster, Kellan. You never would have—"

Remembering this conversation from our earlier failed attempt to sleep in the same room together, I beat her to the punch. "I'm no angel either, Kiera...remember? And you have no idea what I'm capable of." *Just look what I did to my best friend. I'm a disappointment. I'm worthless. I'm nothing. You deserve so much more.*

Kiera pursed her lips, unconvinced. "We both messed up, Kellan." Reaching out, she touched my cheek; her fingers on my skin seared me. "But you would never force yourself on me."

No. I wouldn't. No matter how much I wanted you, if you didn't want me...I'd leave you alone. You're everything to me.

Not able to say that to her, I pulled her in for a hug instead. Kiera wrapped her arms around my neck, and for a brief moment, we felt like how we used to be. It reminded me of how far we'd come, and how much had changed. As nice as it felt to hold her, it wasn't right, and it wasn't a good idea. Space was what we needed. Distance was good.

"You were right. We have to end this, Kiera." It killed me to say it, but I knew now that it was the right thing to do. The only thing to do. I wanted something from her that she couldn't give me. It was time I respected her choice.

I pulled back to look at her and saw tears on her cheeks. I gently brushed them away. She shouldn't cry; I wasn't worth her tears. Cupping her face, I stroked her cheek with my thumb. I'd known from the beginning our friendly flirting wouldn't work, I'd just wanted her so badly...it had seemed better than letting her go.

Kiera's watery eyes locked onto mine as she whispered, "I know." She closed her eyes and more tears squeezed out. It was so hard to see her in pain. It was even harder to know I was the source of it. I was tormenting her, she said so herself. And she was tormenting me. We were toxic, and we were slowly killing each other.

It was wrong of me, but I couldn't walk away from her without one last kiss. I needed to feel her sweetness one last time, needed to securely lock it into my memory so I could retrieve it during the dark times, when I was cold and alone. Expecting her to push me away, I softly brushed my lips to hers. She didn't shy from me though; she pulled me tighter. Her lips were eager, but I kept the rhythm soft and tender, and her lips eased to match mine. I poured every ounce of love I felt into our intimate moment. Without having to say it, I wanted her to know—*I love you, more than anything.*

I could have kissed her all morning, but I knew it was time to stop. Removing my fingers from her cheek, I ran them down her hair, and then down her back. "You were right. You made your choice. I still want you," I growled, pulling her into me. "But not while you're his. Not like this, not like last night." With a wistful sigh, I loosened my hold on her.

Her eyes were brimming with new tears, and I could feel mine stinging in response. Saying goodbye was so hard. "This is over," I said, running my finger across her partly opened lips. Her tears splashed onto her cheeks, and I let out a heavy exhale. *I wish I didn't have to do this...*

"I don't seem to be very good at leaving you alone." I dropped my hand from her skin and kept it rigid at my side. Determination filled me as I swallowed a lump of pain in my throat. "I won't let last night happen again. I won't touch you again. This time... I promise."

Needing to leave, I turned and walked away from her. My dream suddenly struck me and I paused in the doorway. *You're not good enough for her...*

Before my interference, Denny and Kiera had had a consistent, comforting peace, while Kiera and I seemed to only have turbulent turmoil. Hopefully I hadn't messed them up too much. Hopefully they could work through their issues and reconnect. "You and Denny are good together. You should stay with him."

Waves of jealousy and despair crept up on me, and I stared at the floor, hoping they would pass. They didn't. I wasn't sure how I could do this, how I could let the only person who had ever shown me an ounce of tenderness go. I loved her so much, I had no choice but to release her. But not completely. I decided right then and there that I wouldn't tell her the truth about Anna. She would feel a spark of jealousy over that deception, and I would feel a spark of jealousy over her relationship with Denny. In that trivial way, we'd still be connected. Until either Anna or Griffin finally told her the truth. Then even that would be gone, but maybe that was for the best.

A tear I couldn't hold back fell onto my cheek as I looked up at her. "I'll make this right. It will be like it should be." *I won't go near you again. I won't bother you again. I won't touch you again. And maybe one day, I'll actually get over you.*

Days went by...they felt like years. I thought things with Kiera would eventually get easier. I thought that after a while, it wouldn't kill me to be around her but not touch her. I thought I would be fine seeing her loving relationship with Denny. I thought wrong. Every day my chest hurt, it was hard to breathe, and I felt like my head was imploding. I avoided Kiera at all costs. I made sure we were never alone together, and I made sure I never touched her. I spent all day in a fog of loneliness, wishing things were different, and I spent every night staring at my ceiling, willing myself to move on. But every morning when I woke up, the pain started over. I couldn't let what we had go, and nothing was getting better.

Whenever I was around Kiera, I watched her relentlessly. I ached with the need to touch her, and when I looked into her eyes, I saw the same need reflected back at me. Regardless of her heart, she wanted to be in my arms. But she needed to forget about what we'd had, and I needed to forget about how much I loved her. Things needed to change, for both our sakes.

Oddly, I found something at Pete's that I thought might help, but it wasn't alcohol. There was a girl at a table who could have been Kiera's twin, and I couldn't stop staring at her. She was so similar... it would be so easy to pretend...and pretending would help me survive this grief.

I could do this. I was good at this. It would block the pain…and that was all that mattered.

After a brief conversation and lots of playful flirting, I took the pseudo-Kiera home with me. Stepping into my house, I was bombarded by the familiar scent of the real Kiera. I closed my eyes for a second, wondering if I could go through with this. *I have to. I have to move on.* After the girl shut my front door, I grabbed her hand and pulled her into the kitchen. I needed a drink.

"Want anything?" I asked her as I opened the fridge and looked around for some beer.

She came up behind me. Leaning in, she sucked on my earlobe, then whispered, "I want you."

My mouth dropped open, and my eyes fluttered closed. Her low, husky voice made it so easy to picture Kiera. Yes…this was exactly what I needed. Keeping my eyes shut, I closed the fridge and pressed her against it. An erotic moan escaped her lips…Kiera's lips. Needing her, needing this, I found her mouth. *God Kiera, I've missed you.*

Our mouths moved together frantically, and a groan escaped me. *Kiera…yes.* I felt her tongue brush mine, and all the pain of our separation left me. We were together again. I could have her, night after night, with no guilt. Everything was fine. Everything was good again.

She wrapped her leg around my body, and I ran my hand up her skirt. *Fuck, yes. I've missed this, Kiera. I've missed you.* My body was aching in a different way now. I needed her, I needed to be inside her. I needed to hear her cry out. I needed to feel that connection between us.

Just as I was about to beg her to come upstairs with me, my fantasy crumbled. I heard soft footsteps entering the kitchen, and I knew the real Kiera had just found me. Looking toward the door, I saw that I was right. Kiera was standing in the grayness of the entryway, her eyes wide with shock. *Fuck.* No. I hadn't wanted her to see this, to see my desperation, but…I guess she should know that I was moving on. Or trying to. Maybe if she saw me moving forward with other people, she'd stop looking at me with those hazel eyes full of longing. I couldn't resist the longing. I couldn't resist her. I needed a distraction; surely she understood that.

My date hadn't noticed Kiera. She was kissing my neck, stroking my cock through my jeans. A look of horror passed over Kiera as she understood what she was seeing. *I'm sorry. I need you...and this is the only way I can be with you now.*

I knew I couldn't turn and leave Kiera without an explanation, and I also knew I couldn't give one with my date present. Turning back to the girl, I cooed, "Sweetheart...Could you wait upstairs for me? I need to speak with my roommate." She nodded and I gave her a kiss.

Breaking away, I told her, "The one on the right. I'll be up in a second." She giggled, and I contained a sigh. This wasn't what I wanted.

Silence fell over the kitchen as I watched the girl leave. I didn't know what to say to Kiera. Did I really need to explain myself? Oddly, I *did* need to.

To break the tension, I made a joke. An admittedly bad one, but I found the imagery funny, and I couldn't stop myself from saying it. "Do you think Denny would be intrigued or upset if she opened the wrong door?"

Kiera looked like she wanted to throw up. I hated seeing that expression on her, but this was for the best. For everyone. I turned to face her, to face what I could never have. Sadness threatened to overwhelm me as I stared at her. She was breathtaking in the near-darkness, a level of perfection that my fake Kiera upstairs could never come close to. I would give anything to tell that girl to leave, so that this Kiera could take her place...but that wasn't my reality. I needed to do the right thing and set us both on the paths that would forever lead us away from each other.

"You said before that you wanted to know when I was...seeing someone. Well...I guess I'm seeing someone." *Someone who I'm only interested in because she reminds me of you. Because I can't get over you, but I have to.* "I'm going to date. I told you I wouldn't keep it a secret from you, so...I'm going upstairs now, and—"

She made a face that clearly said *I don't want to hear this*, and I stopped where I was going with that. She knew what was about to happen in my room. She didn't need me glorifying any of it for her. I felt sick as I watched the conflicting emotions alter her expression. *I don't want this...I want you.* "I said I wouldn't hide it. I'm not. Full disclosure, right?"

I suddenly wanted her approval to do this. I wanted her to tell me it was okay, that I wasn't cheating on her, that I wasn't hurting her. That she wanted me to find happiness, even if it was in someone else's arms. If she was okay with this, then maybe I would be too. Maybe I could go upstairs and have sex with that woman...and not make her Kiera in my mind.

Anger darkened Kiera's features. As if she could sense my need for her acceptance, and she was in no way going to give it, she spat out, "Do you even know her name?"

Disappointment washed through me, followed strangely by relief. If she was okay with this, then she really didn't give a shit about me. Her voice was full of condemnation though, and she had no right to judge me over needing something to help me get over her. No right at all. "No, I don't need to, Kiera." *All I need is for her to remind me of you. That's it.* Kiera's expression turned even icier, and I inadvertently spoke my thoughts. "Don't judge me...and I won't judge you."

Angry, hurt, and feeling a mound of guilt over what I was about to do, I stormed out of the room. She had no right to make me feel like shit about this. I needed to get over her, I needed something to block the pain. This was the only course of action that she'd left me with.

I jerked my door open when I got to my room. My date was sprawled on top of my bed, completely naked. "I'm ready for you, Kellan," she purred, running a hand down her body.

I shut my door, then started stripping off my clothes. *I'm ready for you too...Kiera.*

351

Fifteen minutes later I was plunging inside of my date. I kept trying to hold on to the image of Kiera, but the girl I was with cried out in theatrical ways that were nothing like Kiera. It was almost as if my date was trying to wake the neighborhood. And even as my climax started building, I saw Kiera's horrified expression. My date hit her peak with an explosion of loud expletives. I couldn't come with her, I wasn't ready.

Blocking everything from my mind, I remembered making love to Kiera. The way she held me, the way she touched me. The way her moans were light in my ear. Powerful. Listening to Kiera's climax usually brought on my own. I imagined that sound as I rocked into the girl beneath me.

Kiera's voice filled my mind. *Oh God, Kellan … yes. Yes …*

I cringed in ecstasy as I felt the tension building. "Yes … Kiera, God yes … Kiera …" I felt the apex coming faster and faster. I clasped Kiera's hand, needing her to guide me through it. "Yes," I moaned in her ear. "Kiera … God, yes …"

Kiera shifted beneath me, but my free hand reached down to steady her hips. "Don't leave me, Kiera … stay with me … help me … love me …" I was murmuring nonsense now, but my climax was so close I didn't care. I gasped as I came, and in my mind, I shouted Kiera's name.

After the shuddering waves of bliss left me, I slumped against Kiera. She was tense below me, not nearly as relaxed as I was … and that's when I remembered that I wasn't actually with Kiera. My date's voice was cold as ice when she spoke. "Who … the fuck … is Kiera?"

I pulled away from her and started panicking. The only thing I could think to say was, "I thought you said your name was …"

She shoved me away from her. "No, my name is Trina, asshole." Standing, she tossed on clothes as she spotted them.

I gritted my teeth. Smooth. "Sorry." *Did she ever even tell me her name?*

It didn't matter. I'd said another girl's name in bed … repeatedly. There was no way to recover from that. Sitting up, I tried to make a peace offering. "Want me to drive you back to your car?"

She glared at me as she put her top back on. "I'll call a cab. You just stay here and get your rocks off on this Kiera chick. Fucker."

She grabbed the rest of her things, then stormed out of my room. Shaking my head, I closed my eyes and at least thanked fate that she wasn't a door slammer. Maybe Denny and Kiera were sleeping and hadn't heard her. God…I hoped they hadn't heard her. Or me. Fuck. I needed to be more careful.

Putting aside the guilt and awkwardness though, my date had actually managed to make me feel a little better. It wasn't a permanent solution to my problem, but it was certainly a start. Maybe if I distracted myself with enough women, I'd actually forget all about Kiera. Doubtful, but I had to try.

I slept a little easier than I had in a while. It might not be a good plan, but at least I had one now. That was something.

I debated how to line up more dates while I watched TV the next morning. I didn't want to be alone. My mind spun and Kiera was on constant repeat when I was alone. I thought about what I used to do before Kiera entered my life. I'd had no problems getting girls then. Honestly, I still didn't, as last night proved, but I wanted to take a more proactive approach to dating. Maybe I'd throw a party? Sure, why not. I couldn't do that without clearing it first though. Kiera would probably see right through my lame attempts to get over her, but I had to do what I had to do.

Denny and Kiera came down the stairs together, which was kind of unusual. They were already getting closer again. Yet another positive side effect of what I was doing. Turning off the TV, I joined them in the kitchen and prepared myself to ask them a question that shouldn't be a big deal, but sort of felt like a big deal.

They both looked over at me when I entered the room. Kiera looked worn, like she hadn't slept at all. God, I hoped she hadn't heard anything last night. Especially me. "Mornin'." I knew Denny wouldn't have an issue with my question, so I aimed it at him first. *I'm such a chickenshit.* "I was thinking of having a couple of friends over tonight. Would you be okay with that?"

Smiling, Denny clapped me on the shoulder. "Sure, mate, whatever... it's your place."

I looked over at Kiera. She seemed really down. I needed to know if she was all right. If my... dating... was all right. Sadly, I still needed her approval. "Are you okay... with that?"

Her cheeks filled with color and she averted her eyes. She understood my real question then. Good. I held my breath, wondering if she'd say no, if she'd make a scene right in front of Denny. "Sure... whatever." So there it was... my meager approval. I guess it was as much as I could hope for.

And who knows, maybe a party could bring us all back together. Maybe this was exactly what we needed.

The party started as soon as I got home from rehearsal. In fact, a pair of girls were waiting on my steps when I got back. One had creamy skin and strawberry-blond hair, the other had skin and hair as dark as night. I didn't know either of them, but they were obviously here for the party, so they must have gotten an invite from someone I knew.

"Ladies. You're a bit early, so you'll have to help me set up." I'd stopped by the store on my way home and picked up supplies for my shindig. With a friendly smile, I offered each of the girls a six-pack of chick beer—wine coolers. They giggled, just like my date last night, and I figured I had a shot with both of them.

My place was packed by the time Denny got home. He looked around my house in amazement; none of these people had ever come by while he'd been here. But all the people I knew here were "party friends," not friend-friends. I only ever talked to them when something was going down. With wide eyes, Denny walked into the living room after setting down his stuff upstairs. "Do you know all these people?" he asked me.

I glanced at the blonde gyrating in front of me. I still didn't know her name. "Nope, but I'll gladly kick them out the second you want me to. I don't want to be a bother." I'd done enough to be a "bother" to Denny. "Want a beer?" I asked, shifting my thoughts.

Denny smiled and shrugged. "Sure. Thanks, mate."

Just then, my dark-haired lady friend leaned over my lap. After giving me a light kiss, she playfully asked, "Need anything, love?"

"Actually, yes. A beer for me and my friend would be great. Thank you."

She laughed, then leaned in for a longer kiss; she tasted like whiskey. When she left me, I looked over at Denny. He was shaking his head in disbelief. "Do you at least know her?"

With a wide smile, I shook my head. "Nope."

Denny rolled his eyes, then laughed. "Some things never change."

I laughed with him, but a twinge of pain rippled around my insides. *Everything has changed.*

Denny and I talked, laughed, and joked around just like we used to. I asked him about his job, and he complained about his boss for a solid fifteen minutes. When he was done with his cathartic release, I said, "You know, I may not be able to get you a new job, but I bet I could get your boss removed. Maybe we could shame him into resigning? Griffin knows a few prostitutes…"

His eyes widened. "Griffin knows a few…" Shutting his mouth, he shook his head. "Yeah, that actually doesn't surprise me." Our beers arrived as we shared a laugh. Clinking bottles with me, he jokingly said, "Yes, let's do this. Call Griffin, have him call his hookers, and we'll blackmail Max. Just don't tell Kiera…She wouldn't approve of the prostitutes."

Chuckling, I sipped my beer. "I think she'd approve of them more than she would Griffin." Denny laughed so hard he snorted, and I swallowed the razorblade of pain and guilt that always sliced into me when I mentioned Kiera's name around him. When he was calmly sipping his beer again, I stupidly asked, "How are you two, by the way?" And why was I opening a door into a painful conversation that would suck regardless of his answer? Because it was the only way back to normalcy, that was why.

Denny lowered his beer from his mouth. He gave me an odd, appraising look, even as he smiled. "We're all right, I guess. Better than we've been in a while, anyway."

I nodded, feeling reaffirmed that I was doing the right thing. The void I'd created by leaving Kiera alone was being filled by Denny, and that was the way it was supposed to be. And even though my insides were cold from the loss of her, it warmed me some that at least my relationship with Denny hadn't changed much. He was still the same person he'd always been. Warm, friendly, considerate. A great friend. I was determined to be the friend he deserved to have.

I was feeling pretty good about life as the evening went on. My dark-haired date made herself comfortable on my lap and leaned in for a kiss. Even though she was completely wasted, I obliged her. Her level of sobriety didn't bother me; she could be as drunk or as sober as she wanted to be. All I cared was that she was a distraction, and if I closed my eyes, I could imagine she was Kiera.

Maybe made uncomfortable by the girl's exuberance, Denny got up from the couch. Someone instantly took his place, but I was too wrapped up in feminine attention to care who it was. Our kiss was getting pretty intense, and as I ran my hands up her thighs, Kiera's body filled my mind. God, she had a great body. Trim and athletic, but still curvy in all the right places. Amazing.

The person who'd taken Denny's spot on the couch bumped my shoulder in a clear indication that they wanted my attention. Pulling apart from the dark-haired girl, I looked over to see my strawberry-blond friend smiling at me. "Are you going to ignore me all night?" she asked; her voice had a sensuous teasing quality about it.

A smile broke out on my face as I ran my fingers through the hair of the girl sitting on my lap. "Of course not. Someone as pretty as you would be too hard to ignore for long." Keeping my smile in place, I leaned over and pressed my lips to hers; she tasted like whiskey too. The girl on my lap did nothing to stop me. In fact, she stroked my sides and nestled even more into my lap. I knew with certainty that I'd be having both of them tonight.

After a few more moments of making out, the blonde shot to her feet. "I love this song!" she exclaimed, holding her hand out for me.

My other date slid off my lap to sit where the blonde had been, and I stood up. I liked this song too, and dancing sounded like fun. A good precursor to my evening with Kiera...the way we danced together was unbelievable.

Reminiscing about dirty dancing with Kiera, I moved behind the blonde. She was grinding against my hips as I moved against her. *Kiera...I love the way we move together.* Feeling playful, I leaned down to her ear and said, "I like the way your body moves. I like the way you feel against me. I bet you'd feel even better naked."

She moaned and sagged against me. Pleased with her reaction, I glanced up into the kitchen. My heart nearly stopped. The real Kiera was home, and she was watching me with narrowed eyes. Grief washed through me. My two dates, who I was so eager to turn into multiple versions of Kiera, were nothing like her. I'd hand them over in an instant to walk into that kitchen and take her hand. But I couldn't. My fantasies, although they paled in comparison, were all I had left.

I forced myself to smile at Kiera, my *roommate*, and then gave her a brief nod of acknowledgment. Then I ignored her. I had to. The other girl came up behind me, turning me into a Kellan sandwich, and I let myself get lost in them. This was my distraction, the only thing that took the pain away, and I had to take it. Knowing Kiera was watching, I leaned back and gave the dark-haired girl a kiss. Kiera had to get used to this, just like I did.

The girls and I danced for several songs. People started leaving, and I made sure to say goodbye to each of them, but my main focus was my dates...and ignoring where Kiera was. She was just the person I lived with. I had to accept that.

Our dancing trio eventually moved back to the couch, and eventually picked up heat. As more people left the house, the three of us got friendlier. At one point, their wandering lips turned toward each other. I took that as a sign that we were all ready for this to happen. Just when I was thinking of moving this private party upstairs, I happened to catch sight of Kiera dragging Denny away. She looked pissed, or hurt. Was this too much for her? Because this was

357

what I was, and how I coped, and…it was all I had right now. I didn't want to hurt her, but I needed this release.

While my dates made out with each other, I pulled my gaze away from where Kiera had disappeared. I needed to focus on this, not worry about her. The blonde broke away from the other girl and returned to me. I kissed her eagerly, but in my mind, I was touching Kiera.

With forced playfulness, I led the girls upstairs and into my room. The dark-haired girl stripped off my shirt while the blonde ran her fingers down my back. "Damn, you're hot," she said.

The other girl heartily agreed. She unbuttoned my jeans and palmed me as she growled, "I can't wait to have you in me."

The blonde giggled, then added, "I can't wait to have you lick me. All over. I'll be your dessert."

The dark-haired girl looked over to her friend. "Great idea!" She returned her eyes to mine. "Do you have any whipped cream?"

I wanted to sigh, but I smiled instead. "Yeah. I'll be right back."

It was hard to picture Kiera with the way they talked, and it was difficult with two of them, but I was sure I could do it. I could clear my mind and feel a moment of connection with the love of my life…even if it was a fake one. Closing my door behind me, I tiptoed down the stairs and into the kitchen. Someone was still in there. Kiera. Her head was down and her back was to me; she appeared to be crying. She wasn't okay.

"Kiera?"

I saw her shoulders slump. She hadn't wanted me to find her like this. "What, Kellan?"

"Are you okay?" I asked, already knowing the answer.

She spun around to face me, then she stopped and stared. Her eyes glistened as she swallowed a lump in her throat. "What are you doing down here?" she asked, anger in her voice. "Shouldn't you be…entertaining?"

Feeling stupid, I pointed at the fridge, then opened it and found the can of whipped cream. "The girls wanted…" It was obvious what they wanted, so I left it at that. Kiera looked mortified by my actions, and I supposed they were horrifying from her perspective. I should explain myself, but how? The truth was too much for me to say; a lie…too little.

With a loud exhale, Kiera rolled her eyes and looked away. Then she closed them, and I could tell she was fighting back tears born from multiple confusing, conflicting emotions. "Kiera…" Her name came out like a caress, and I had to pause to collect myself. When she looked at me, I continued. "This is who I am. Before you got here…this is me." *Once upon a time this was me, but I'm different now…because I love you…but it does no good to tell you that, so I won't.* I pointed upstairs to Denny, the man she *should* be with. "That, that is you. This is how it's supposed to be…"

The desire to hold her overcame me, and I took a step. But then I stopped myself. If I caved now, if I touched her, we'd go back to that cycle of pain that had brought us to this point in the first place. No, I needed to keep the space between us. I needed to go upstairs and leave her. No good would come out of prolonging this agony.

I turned around to leave her, but stopped at the door. "Good night, Kiera," I whispered, then I left before she could respond. There was nothing to say anyway. As quickly as I could, I rejoined the two girls waiting for me in my room, and I made a promise to myself that I would *not* cry out Kiera's name. Not out loud anyway.

Chapter 24

Bring On the Pain

My days, afternoons, nights, and sometimes early mornings were a blur of random women. Even for me, I was exceedingly active. I was trying to stop thinking about Kiera, but she was all I ever thought about. Whenever I was with a girl, my mind drifted to her. I made love to her over and over and over again, with dozens of different bodies, but the scenario never changed in my mind.

Kiera was the one running her hands over me. Kiera was the one placing light kisses over my body. It was Kiera's mouth I was pressing against, and Kiera's tongue I was brushing with mine. And it was Kiera begging me to take her.

While my Kiera mirages were growing steadier, the real Kiera was growing icier. Every time I saw her after one of my dates, her glare practically seared my skin off. If I didn't know any better, I'd say she'd figured out that I was making love to *her* on my many dates. But there was no way she could know that; I was careful to never make a peep when I was "pretending." I couldn't risk exposing my true thoughts, which was why I didn't tell anyone what was going on. No one would understand.

My friends all sensed something was off though, and asked questions I didn't want to answer. I always brushed off their concern and expertly changed the subject. Surprising me, Denny even asked about the tension in the house. Well, he indirectly asked. One night, when Kiera was at work, he stopped me as I was about to head out to the bar. "Kellan, wait."

Adjusting my jacket, I looked back at him. He seemed uncomfortable, and I felt anxiety slipping into my calm façade. Did he know something? Scratching his head, he said, "First off, I'm cool with whatever you do here. It's your place."

I narrowed my eyes, wondering what he was getting at. He sighed and avoided looking at my face. "It's just…noisier around here than it used to be and…Kiera asked if I would…I told her it wasn't my place to say anything, and that you could do whatever you wanted with whomever you…" Stopping, he put his hands up. "You know what, I'm just going to shut up right now. It's your home, mate. You can do whatever you want. We just both really appreciate that you're letting us crash here. So, thank you. It means a lot to us." With a smile on his lips, he clapped my shoulder, then turned and walked away.

All I could do was stare after him, shocked. Kiera had asked him to…what? Talk to me about my dating habits? I knew she was being frosty, but was she really so angry with me that she'd pull Denny into this? Because she had no right to be upset. None at all.

I tried broaching the subject with her a few days later.

I gave her a polite, friendly greeting when she showed up in the kitchen for her morning coffee. She completely ignored me. "Kiera?" Still ignoring me, she grabbed a coffee cup and started pouring a mug. Well, I guess we were returning to the realm of immaturity, where we both handled things badly. "Are you…mad at me?" God, she was cute when she was being stubborn.

With a glare, she told me, "No."

"Good, because you shouldn't be." *I'm doing this for you. To make it easier for you to let go of your…infatuation, which is all I am to you.*

"Well, I'm not…" Her response was in a snotty tone of voice that really got under my skin. "Why shouldn't I be?"

Did she really not get this? Did she not remember how volatile things had become between us? How awful? Did I need to call her a whore again for her to recall why us being apart was a good thing? "We *both* ended things, when it started getting...out of hand." *Severely out of hand.*

"I know that. I was there." Her voice was pure ice. Regardless of what she said, she was mad at me. For what? For living? For moving on? How could she blame me for that?

"I'm only doing what you asked. You wanted to know if I was seeing someone." *You didn't want me, so I found something else to take away the pain. But now you want to take that too, don't you?*

"I didn't want secrets between us...but I didn't want to see it!"

So she wanted me to hide? She wanted me to sneak off to live out my fantasies so her perfect relationship wouldn't be affected by my carousing. She wanted everything to go her way. No compromises. No compassion. She was living here with *him*...and I was just supposed to deal with that...but she couldn't deal with the reverse of it? That was hypocritical bullshit.

"Where would you have me...? I have to see it...hear it. You're not exactly quiet either. Do you think I like that? That I've ever liked..." *I love you, and I constantly have to hear you with another man.* Done with this conversation, I stood up. "I try and understand. You could do the same."

The confrontation with Kiera put me in a bad mood. If I had to listen to my best friend screwing the only woman I'd ever loved, then Kiera could put up with a little pointless banging. And it was pointless. And empty. But it momentarily dulled the pain. What else was I supposed to do?

I drove around town once Kiera left for school. She'd taken the bus, just like she had ever since we'd started distancing ourselves from each other. I didn't know where to go or what to do, I just knew I needed to keep my mind busy or I was going to go nuts. I ended up driving to a convenience store. I picked up a six-pack of beer and a box of condoms; I'd been going through them like crazy lately.

A cute blonde in the checkout line recognized me and started up a conversation about the D-Bags. I could tell she was interested in me, although she camouflaged her desire behind the band. After mentioning I was working on new stuff, she said, "I'd love to take a peek at anything you'd be willing to show me." Her gaze drifted to my pants, and I knew she wasn't talking about music anymore.

With a charming grin, I told her, "How about I give you a ride back to my place? I'll show you everything." *I'll show you my body, but I'll never show you me.*

She agreed, and we were in my room not too much later. She batted my door closed while I turned on some music. "Wow… Kellan Kyle's bedroom," she said, scanning the place. "It's nice. Cozy."

Her roving eyes stopped on me. I considered telling her that she could just call me Kellan, instead of referring to me by my full name, but I didn't feel like small talk. I didn't feel like talking at all.

Finding peace in the soft music that was playing, I reached out for her. I stared at her shoulder while we danced, and in my mind, it was Kiera I was moving with. *I love the way we feel together, Kiera.*

She kissed me then, and closing my eyes, I reveled in the fantasy. *Kiera…yes, kiss me…*

Just kissing Kiera in my mind made me ready for more. By the time the girl unzipped my jeans, I was straining against them. "Jesus," she murmured. "You're so hard."

Yes, Kiera, and it's all for you.

Wanting the girl to not speak anymore, I grabbed her cheek and kissed her harder. She moaned in my mouth, then she shoved me back. "I've been wanting to do something to you for a really long time now." I wondered what she meant, and how long "really long" was. Ten minutes? Fifteen?

She pushed me back until my legs hit my bed, then she slowly pushed me down. Realizing she wanted me to sit, I complied. I was momentarily confused, until she sank to her knees in front of me…then I got it. Getting my Kiera fantasy ready, I closed my eyes. *Yes, Kiera…Kiss me there…kiss me everywhere.*

The girl rearranged my clothes so she could get to me. The air against my skin was chilly at first, but then her mouth was over me, and I was suddenly warm, wet, and insanely turned on. *Yes, Kiera...God, yes. More.* She was working against me, taking as much of me in as she could, and I could feel my climax building already. Cringing, I clutched the sheets and bit my lip. *Yes, just like that, Kiera...Don't stop. I'm so close...*

I thought I heard something, and my pseudo-Kiera started to move off me, but I was almost there...she couldn't go yet. She couldn't leave me like this. Gripping her hair, I held her in place. *Don't leave me yet, Kiera. Don't go...*

Moaning in excitement, she worked against me in a near frenzy. *Yes, I'm almost...Yes...God, Kiera, I love you...Don't stop. Don't ever stop.*

I heard an odd noise, like a door slamming, but I was too far gone. "God, yes, I'm close..." I murmured with a groan.

She moaned again, loving my words. I was almost panting now, and the pressure was building to a point where I couldn't contain it anymore. I was about to lose it, about to release, when I suddenly heard the telltale sound of my car roaring to life. *What the fuck?*

My Kiera fantasy shattered, and I tried to push my date away from me. She was too into it now though. "Stop," I firmly told her, but she only moaned as she moved against me. I heard the sound of tires squealing and panic shot through me. Did someone steal my car? Holy fucking shit! If that was the case, I was about to kill someone, but first I needed this girl to get off my cock.

"Stop!" I yelled, shoving her back. With surprise on her face, she landed on her ass.

"Hey, what gives?" she bit out, irritated at my rough treatment.

I cringed as the pleasure I'd been feeling shifted into pain at the absence of her attentive mouth. I'd abruptly stopped myself from coming, and now I was paying the price. Wincing, I tucked myself back into my jeans and dashed to the window. Sure enough, my baby was gone. Dread and hollowness filled my soul. My car...my irreplaceable car...was *gone*. She could be on her way to a chop shop right now, about to be hacked into a million pieces. Jesus. I couldn't let this happen, but what should I do? Call the cops? National Guard? "Get Jesse"?

"My car is gone. My fucking car is gone!" I knew I was freaking out, but I'd never expected this to happen to me. Or my baby.

When I looked back at my date, she had a look on her face like she was sure I was certifiable. I was certain I was losing my cool rock-star status with her, but I didn't really care. I wanted my fucking car back. I started pacing the room, wondering what to do.

"Yeah…someone came into the house and got the keys. You didn't hear that?" The girl had an incredulous expression, like it should have been as plain as day to me.

Gritting my teeth, I said, "I was a little preoccupied. Heard what? What happened?"

She shrugged and jerked her thumb at the door. "Some girl came in the house, rummaged around the next room, called your name, peeked in the door, then ran down the stairs, slammed the front door, and took off in your car." Proud of herself, she smiled. "I have pretty awesome hearing." Then she frowned. "I thought you knew she was watching, and that's why you held me down. I thought maybe you liked having an audience." She shrugged again. "I thought it was pretty hot."

I could only stare at her in disbelief as I processed everything she was saying. "She stole my car. She…*stole*…my car. No way. No fucking way."

My date only lifted her shoulders in an expression of *Oh, well, what can you do?* Narrowing my eyes, I zipped up my pants and grabbed my jacket off the floor. "We're leaving," I bit out.

She raised her hands in the air. "How? She stole your car."

Storming out of the room, I ran downstairs. Picking up the phone in the kitchen, I dialed the first person who came to mind. Luckily for me, he answered. "Yeah?"

"Matt. It's an emergency. I need your help."

"Kellan? What's going on?"

"Kiera stole my fucking car, and I need a ride to get it back."

Matt started laughing. "She...what?" I didn't share his sense of humor about the matter, and stayed silent. When I didn't return his laughter or respond in any way, he coughed and said, "Okay, yeah. I'll be there as soon as I can."

I hung up the phone without saying a word, then yanked open the fridge and grabbed a beer. Popping it open on the counter, I chugged it until it was gone. *She stole my fucking car.* I couldn't believe it.

My date came down while I was opening my second beer. "Can I have one?" she asked. Furious, I ignored her. "Okay," she muttered. "Well, I'm gonna catch a bus back if that's okay with you."

I raised my hand in a *Whatever* motion.

"Awesome. Well, thanks for...that...and I hope you get your car back." She left the room, then left my house. I felt bad for being so dismissive with her, but then I remembered that Kiera stole my baby, and all I felt was anger. Why the fuck would she do that to me?

When Matt finally showed up, I was sipping on my fourth beer, trying to calm down. It wasn't working. The minute he stepped into my entryway, I stormed toward him, beer bottle in hand. "She's at Pete's. Let's go."

Matt grabbed my arm as I stalked past him. "Wait, Kell, maybe you should calm down first. I'm sure she had a good reason?"

Yanking my arm away, I narrowed my eyes. "I'm perfectly fucking calm. Let's go."

Matt sighed but followed me out of the house. I downed the rest of my beer in his car. "You gonna be able to drive once we get your car back?" he asked.

"I'll be fine," I seethed.

"Right..."

I didn't wait for Matt to park the car; I shoved open his door while he was still pulling into the stall. "Jesus, Kellan," he was saying when I shut his door and strode over to the bar. I glanced to my right and saw my Chevelle. Thank God she was all in one piece. If Kiera had dinged her though...

I burst through the front doors of Pete's and immediately looked for Kiera. She was back in the band's typical section. Her eyes widened when she saw me, and she glanced around like she was going to run. She could try...but I wasn't leaving until I got my keys.

Matt caught up to me and put his hand on my shoulder, trying to hold me back again. "Kell, wait..."

I jerked my body away as I spun around to face him. "You said your piece, now back the fuck off."

Knowing I was at my breaking point, Matt raised his hands in the air and stepped away from me. I turned back to Kiera and focused all of my ire on her. *You did this to me. You loved me, used me, hurt me, wanted me, then rejected me. And then, on top of all of that, you stole one of the only things that matters to me.*

Kiera looked afraid at first, but then she raised her chin in defiance. God, she was attractive. I wanted to suck those plump lips she was pursing at me. I wanted to grab a fistful of her hair and pull her mouth to mine. I wanted to turn her around, bend her over the table, and take her in front of everyone. I wanted to tell her I loved her.

I couldn't do any of those things though, so all I ended up doing was anticlimactically holding my hand out. Kiera looked mildly disappointed by my reaction. Did she *want* me to bend her over the table? Would that be less disappointing?

"What?" she asked, her voice full of that snotty tone that riled me up.

"Keys," I said through clenched teeth.

"What keys?" she asked, a daring fire in her eyes.

I wanted to pull her into me so badly, my groin ached again. Matt was right, I needed to calm down. "Kiera...my car is right over there." I pointed to where it was outside. "I heard you take it—"

That got her attention. "If you heard me take it, why didn't you try to stop me?"

"I was—"

She cut me off with a finger in my chest. "You were on a 'date'?" She said the last word with air quotes.

I felt like the oxygen had been sucked from the room. In all my anger about her stealing my car ... I'd forgotten just what she'd seen. She'd walked in on a girl giving me a blow job. Yes, I'd heard several things between her and Denny that I wished I hadn't, but I'd never seen anything before. I think I'd go nuts if I did. Is that what happened to her? Well, it shouldn't matter, even if she had seen something.

My composure returning, I snapped out, "So? That gives you the right to steal my car?"

With her chin even higher, she retorted, "I borrowed. Friends borrow, right?"

Well. That was the root of our problem, wasn't it? There was always more between us than friendship. Seeing a bulge in her front pocket, I took a chance that she was holding my keys there and dived in. "Hey," she said, trying to smack me away.

It was too late though, I had them. Clenching the keys tight, I held them up to her. I didn't want to say what was tumbling through my mind, but in my anger it slipped out. "We're not friends, Kiera. We never were."

Turning, I stormed away from her. I knew she wouldn't understand what I meant by my statement, and I knew she'd probably take it in a negative way, but I was too pissed off and turned on to care. She'd gone too far.

I felt like shit after leaving the bar. But I really hadn't said anything that wasn't true. Maybe there had been a split second in our relationship when the term "friend" could have been applied to us, but the minute Denny left town, we had changed. Friendship was impossible to go back to once love entered the picture. And I loved her so much ...

When I eventually made it home, I went up to my room, shut the door, and turned on some music. I needed to think. I needed to be alone. With melancholy melodies as my backdrop, I pulled out a journal and began scribbling down lyrics. Most of them were nonsense, but a few might be usable. One in particular seared me: *You'll never know me, 'cause I'll never let you in.*

Wasn't that the truth? Why was honesty so much easier on paper?

I woke up early the next morning with my notebook still clenched in my hand. A half-finished thought was tumbling down the page in an ominous descent toward nothingness. Staring at the sloppy words in the dim light of the lamp I'd left on, I tried to recall what I'd been thinking when I'd scratched them down. The moment was lost though, the words forever forgotten. Yet another lyrical victim of my subconscious.

Sliding off the bed, I started my morning workout routine. When my abs were burning from repeated crunches, I switched to my arms. After I finished with numerous push-ups, my upper body was trembling. My mind spun. I needed to say something to Kiera. I couldn't let my harsh words linger between us. There was already too much between us.

Trudging downstairs, I tried to find the energy to start some coffee, but I didn't have enough. I sat at the table, head in my hands, and debated what to say to Kiera. A simple "I'm sorry" seemed best, but also not enough.

I heard Kiera coming into the room and peeked up. She was frowning at me, definitely unhappy. I started to speak, but Denny appeared right behind her and I shut my mouth. Kiera's lips twisted into a small smile, then she turned to face Denny. "I know you're dressed already, but do you want to run up and take a shower?"

My heart clenched at the look of innuendo on her face. I knew what she meant by that. So did Denny. I studied the table while Denny laughed and told her, "I wish I could, babe, but I can't be late today. Max is on a rampage with the holiday coming."

"Oh. It could be a quick shower?" Kiera teased. I knew she was only doing this to hurt me, and all thought of apologizing to her vanished.

Congratulations, Kiera, you got me back. If you're going to play that game, then I will too, and if you can take it, then so can I. Bring on the pain.

Chapter 25

You're Mine, I'm Yours

Things got even icier at home after Thanksgiving. Kiera openly flirted with Denny in a way she hadn't while we were "flirting," and I continued dating. There was a spark in the air though, a *How do you like this?* vibe between Kiera and me, like we were in a who-can-hurt-whom-the-most contest. I hated it, and I knew we were both being childish and immature, I just didn't know how to stop myself. Every time she caressed Denny while giving me a sly glance, it just made me want to get back at her. And when a golden opportunity to hurt her fell into my lap, I gladly took it...

I was at Pete's, hanging out with the guys, when a girl with bright red curls approached me. Confidence on her face and in her step, she walked right up to me, sat on my lap, and put her arms around my neck. "Hey, Kellan. Why haven't you called me yet?"

It took me a minute to place the petite woman nestling against my privates like she was used to being there. Her name escaped me, but I remembered running into her before—while I'd been giving Kiera a tour of the university campus. That had been mildly embarrassing at the time, but now it was kind of convenient. By the glare Kiera was giving us, I was sure she knew who the girl was. Good.

Putting my arms around the girl's waist, I shrugged and shook my head. "I washed my jeans with your note still in my pocket. I didn't have your number."

The girl giggled and pulled my face into her breasts. "Oh, well, that makes sense, I guess." I glanced over at Kiera. When our eyes met, I gave her a look that let her know I knew she knew her.

It was wrong and petty, but purely out of spite, I stayed close to the girl all night long, and when we left the bar at closing time, we went straight back to my place and indulged in some after-hours fun. I liked the fact that I knew it would drive Kiera crazy to hear us together. And the girl played her part well—she was one of the most vocal women I'd ever been with.

But even still, after my date left, I felt bad about the encounter, and even lonelier than before. Everything I was doing to try to help me forget Kiera was having the opposite effect. I was thinking about her more and more. How much longer could I keep this going?

The following Monday, Pete decided to institute Griffin's marketing suggestion to get more people into the bar during the week—two-dollar shots until midnight. At the time, I'd thought Pete was crazy for listening to any idea that came out of Griffin's mouth, but I had to hand it to my bassist, he was right about this one. The bar was packed.

Of course, the real reason behind Griffin's recommendation became apparent easily enough; the bar was bursting with buzzed college girls, Griffin's preferred dating "target," although he was having a hard time finding anyone who could live up to Anna in his eyes. Kiera's sister had raised the bar for him, and everyone else was falling short. For the first time ever, Griffin was frustrated over the lack of good poon in Seattle. His words, not mine.

He was giving it the ol' college try though. He had a pair of blond sorority types giggling in the corner. Matt and Evan were having a good time too. Evan was fawning over a girl who'd come in over the weekend, and Matt was talking to a girl so tiny, I think I could lift her in the air with one hand, possibly one finger. As for me, I was making do with the best of a bad situation the only way I knew how. I was lining up a date for the evening with a cute brunette who'd been all over me all night. She was a touch aggressive—she'd already asked me if I wanted to go down on her in the back room—but I didn't care. The more forceful the girl was, the easier it was for me to get lost.

I'd turned down her suggestion of the back room. For one, I'd go home alone if I had sex with her right now, and I didn't want to be alone tonight. And secondly, it felt wrong to do it here, in Kiera's workplace, while Kiera was here. It would be akin to taking someone on her bed. I don't know, even though things were kind of snarky between us, it just felt off-limits to me.

Kiera had been mainly ignoring me while I'd been sussing out my companion for the night, but it was clearly a forced reaction. I could tell she wanted to openly glare at me, wanted to go off on me, she just didn't have a reason to.

I was minding my own business, heading to the restroom, when Kiera finally spoke to me; these were the first direct words she'd said in a while, and after they registered, I wished she'd kept her damn mouth shut.

"Wanna try keeping it in your pants, Kyle?"

Stopping in my tracks, I turned around. Did she seriously just say that to me? Did she have any idea how hypocritical those words were, coming from her mouth? Denny's failed attempt to talk to me about my dating habits—*at Kiera's request*—flooded my mind. She had no right to talk to me that way.

"That's rich," I laughed, anger filling my veins.

"What?" Her tone was blank, but her eyes were as fiery as mine. She was ticked, and she had no right to be.

I walked over to where she was standing at an empty table. Grabbing her arm, I pulled her close to me. We hadn't been this close in a while, and my heart started beating harder. No. I would not let her affect me. I would not let her in. Kiera tensed, and I didn't know if that was because of my closeness or what I was about to say. Leaning in so I could talk in her ear, I whispered, "Is the woman with the live-in boyfriend, the one whom *I've* had sex

372

with on not fewer than two occasions, really lecturing me on abstinence?"

Kiera tried to pull away from me, but I held her tight. Frustrated anger inflamed my body, and harsh words escaped before I could stop them. Lips directly on her ear, I hissed, "If you actually marry him, will I still get to fuck you?"

I knew I'd gone too far the moment the words left my mouth. Kiera agreed. Bringing her hand around, she pulled away and slapped me. No, "slapped" is too mild sounding. She whipped my face. That was what it felt like. Staggering back a step, I inhaled a sharp breath. Stars exploded in my vision. My ears rang, and my cheek felt like she'd touched me with a hot iron. Dazed, I could only stare at her. *What the hell?*

"You stupid son of a bitch!" she screamed, seemingly unhinged.

Completely ignoring the fact that we were in a packed bar, drawing an audience with every tense second that slipped by, Kiera raised her hand to strike me again. This time, I caught her wrist and pulled it down. She winced in pain, and I realized my grip was hurting her, but I didn't let up. I knew the look in her eye—she wanted blood. My blood.

"What the hell, Kiera? What the fucking hell!" If she was going to ignore our very alert audience, then I would too. Fuck it. Fuck it all. I was too pissed to care anymore.

Her other hand twitched, and I grabbed it before she could attempt to backhand me. She still didn't fucking back down. The feisty bitch raised her leg like she was going to knee me in the balls. *Oh, I don't think so.* I shoved her to the side, away from me. She couldn't attack me if she couldn't reach me. Surprising me, she leaped after me again. She was almost like a wild animal, trying to rip me to shreds. If I weren't so angry at her, I might have been concerned.

While Evan grabbed Kiera around the waist, restraining her, Sam put a hand on my chest. It wasn't needed. I wasn't going to go anywhere near her. Jenny moved between Kiera and me, arms outstretched, like she was magically holding us apart. While my eyes were glued on Kiera, I felt Matt and Griffin step behind me. Matt was quiet, Griffin was laughing; aside from Kiera's and my heavy breaths, his laughter was the only sound in the bar. I was glad he found this amusing. It was anything but to me.

When no one seemed to know what to do with the two of us, Jenny took charge. Grabbing my hand, then Kiera's, she started pulling us away. "Come on," she told us in a tight voice. Clearly she wasn't happy about this either.

Following Jenny's lead, I ignored Kiera on the other side of her. I didn't really want to see that bitch right now. My face still felt like it was on fire. I was really tired of her smacking me. I was tired of *anyone* smacking me. I'd been smacked enough in this lifetime.

I blocked out everything and everyone as Jenny pulled us into the hallway. Evan opened the door to the back room and Jenny dragged us inside. Evan scanned the hallway for eavesdroppers, then stepped inside the room, closed the door, and guarded it, like Kiera and I were prisoners or something. The whole thing seemed ridiculous to me, and I just wanted to go home.

"Okay," Jenny began as she released our hands. "What's up?"

I started explaining what happened at the same time Kiera did. Jenny held her hands up. "One at a time."

I was done with this entire conversation, even though it technically hadn't begun yet. And what could either one of us really say right now anyway? If Kiera and I were going to discuss this, then we needed to do it alone. And I didn't feel like being alone with her.

I shifted my angry eyes to Jenny. What was the point of being here? "We don't need a mediator, Jenny," I bit out, a dark edge to my voice. *We can skirt around the problems between us just fine on our own, thank you very much.*

With a look that clearly said she wasn't bothered in the slightest by my tone, Jenny calmly said, "No? Well, I think you do. Half the people in there think you do." She indicated the bar full of witnesses we'd left behind. Her expression shifted to a frown as she eyed me with trepidation. "I happen to know a thing or two about your fights. I'm not leaving you alone with her."

Shock ran through me. She knew? If she knew about our fights...then she knew why we were fighting. She knew...everything. Kiera told her. Why in the hell would she do that?

I shifted my gaze to Kiera. "You told her...she knows?" Kiera shrugged. Her eyes flicked to Evan; he was still out of the loop. The only one in the room who didn't know the truth. "Everything?" I asked her, still disbelieving. Our secret being out in the open made it all the more real, all the more horrible. And it had been bad enough before.

Kiera only shrugged again in answer. Her nonchalant attitude about it ticked me off even more. I'd kept my mouth shut, why the fuck couldn't she? How hard was it to not tell people you were a tramp who'd screwed around on your boyfriend? Seems like that would be an easy thing to keep quiet about. Guess not.

Still stunned, I murmured, "Well...isn't that interesting. And here I thought we weren't talking about it." My eyes shifted to Evan. He was still confused, that much was clear. Well, what the fuck did it matter now if he knew or not? What did anything matter anymore?

Since none of this seemed important at the moment, I decided to fess up to all of it. "Well, since the cat's out of the bag, why don't we all get on the same page?" With a dramatic flash of my hands, I indicated Kiera while I told Evan, "I fucked Kiera...even though you warned me not to. Then, for good measure, I did it again!"

"Kellan, stop swearing," Jenny scolded, while Evan told me, "Damn it, Kellan," and Kiera screamed, "Shut the hell up!" Irritated at all of them, I glared at the room and added, "Oh...and I called her a whore!" If they were gonna be mad at me, they might as well be *really* angry.

Her hands clenching into fists, Kiera averted her eyes. "You're such a prick!"

That got under my skin. If either of us was being a prick right now, that title went to her. I stared at her until she looked my way again. "A prick? I'm a prick?" I took a step toward her and Jenny placed a hand on my chest. "You're the one who hit me! Again!" I showed her my face; I knew from the stinging there had to be a red mark on my skin.

Evan interrupted before Kiera could respond. "Jesus, man. What were you thinking...or were you?"

I snapped my eyes to him. He seemed really ticked at me. I didn't care what he was at the moment though. I didn't care about anything. Screw everyone. "She begged me; I'm only human."

Kiera made a sputtering noise, like I'd just spouted a lie or something. I hadn't. That was exactly what had happened. "You begged me, Kiera! Both times, remember?" I gestured at her and Jenny pushed me away. I felt like I was losing my mind. How did trying to do the right thing bite me in the ass so much? "All I did was what you asked. That's all I've ever done—what you've asked!" I threw my arms out to my sides, not knowing what else to do anymore. Damned if I do, damned if I don't.

"I didn't ask to be called a whore!" she seethed.

She had a point, but I was too ticked to care. "And I didn't ask to be hit again! Quit fucking hitting me!" Jenny told me to watch my language while Evan told me to calm down. I ignored them both; they weren't supposed to be involved in this anyway.

That riled Kiera up. Eyes blazing, she spat out, "You did ask for it, prick! Since we're *sharing*, why don't you tell them what you said to me!" Kiera took a step toward me, and this time, Jenny held *her* back; her petite body was the only thing standing between our mutual rage.

"If you'd given me two seconds, I was going to apologize for that. But you know what...now I don't! I'm not sorry I said it." Pointing around Jenny at her, I added, "You were out of line! You just don't like that I'm dating!"

She gave me an incredulous expression. "Dating? Screwing everything that walks isn't dating, Kellan! You don't even bother learning their names. That's not okay!" With narrowed eyes, she shook her head and spat out, "You are a dog!"

I was *what*? Was she kidding me? I was just about to rip her a new one when Evan interrupted again. "She has a point, Kellan."

Kiera and I both twisted to look at him. "What?" I felt like the blow to my head had jostled around some brain cells, and I was misunderstanding every word leaving every person's mouth. There was no way Evan had just agreed with her. By the stern look on his face though, I knew I hadn't misinterpreted anything. He thought I was a dog. Well, the truth was coming out left and right, wasn't it? "You got something else to say to me, Evan?"

I backed away from Jenny and her hand fell from my chest. Evan's expression became even harder as he stared me down. "Maybe I do. Maybe she's right. And maybe, just maybe, you know it too." I flinched at the truth in his words, and my own words froze up in my chest. Did Evan know what I was doing with all these random women? That I turned them into Kiera in my head? I didn't see how he could possibly know that, but just the thought that he might sealed my mouth shut.

When I didn't say anything, he added, "Why don't you tell her why you're so…free…with yourself? She might understand."

Anger flashed up my spine. I was tired of people commenting on my life. It was mine. No one had the right to judge me on it but me. And I knew exactly what I was. "What the fuck do you know about it?" I snapped, taking a step toward Evan.

Evan's face softened into sympathy. "More than you think I do, Kellan."

I froze in place, unable to move. He wasn't talking about Kiera. About my insane little fantasy where I turned every girl I touched into her. No…he was referring to something much deeper, much darker. I saw something in his eyes that I'd seen before…in Denny when he'd taken a blow for me. In Kiera, when I'd confessed how torturous my life had been with my parents. He knew. Fuck me, he knew. I had no idea how he'd found out…but Evan knew I sought comfort in sex because it was the only place I'd ever found it. He was calling me out, right now, but this was not something I wanted to talk about. Ever.

"Back off, Evan…I'm not asking. Back the fuck off." I was about to snap, and if he pushed me right now, I'd take him with me.

Jenny reprimanded me on my language again, Kiera wanted to know what was going on, but all of my focus was on Evan. *This is the moment, and the band is on the line. Drop it, Evan, before you ruin everything we've built.*

Evan understood everything I wasn't saying. With a sigh, he shrugged and said, "Whatever, man...your call."

With a sniff, I minutely relaxed. He was dropping it. "Damn right it is." Pointing my finger over all of them, I got us back to the topic that none of them had the right to chide me on. "How I date is none of your concern. If I want to screw this whole bar, you all—"

Kiera cut me off with a nasty screech. "You practically have!"

I matched her tone. "No! I screwed you!" In the sudden silence after my statement I heard Jenny sigh and Evan swear. My eyes never left Kiera though. Her cheeks were flushed and she was clenching her jaw so hard I could see the tension in her neck. When the room was quiet again, I told Kiera the truth. "And you feel bad about cheating on Denny." I leaned over Jenny and she brought her hand to my chest again. "You feel guilty about having an affair, but you—"

"We are *not* having an affair! We made a mistake, twice—that's it!"

My jaw dropped as I let out an exasperated exhale. Did she really believe that? "Oh, come on, Kiera! God, you *are* naïve. We may have only had sex twice, but we've most definitely been having an affair the entire time!"

She tossed her hands in the air like she really didn't get it. "That makes no sense!"

I shook my head in disbelief. "Really? Then why did you so desperately want to hide it from Denny, huh? If it really was all so harmless and innocent, then why weren't we open about our... relationship...to anyone?" I pointed at the closed door, behind which a hundred people were probably talking about us.

Kiera seemed taken aback by that. She didn't have anything co-herent to say, and stuttered on her words. I took her moment of confusion to press my point. "Why can't we touch anymore? What happens to you when I touch you, Kiera?"

Her eyes widened, but she didn't answer me. I knew I was being suggestive with my words and my tone, but I didn't care. She needed to understand what had really been going on between us. Lying to herself about it wouldn't help anything. Knowing it would embarrass the hell out of her, I decided to make it as blatant as I could.

Jenny had stepped away from me, and I used the freed space to run my hands over my body. "Your pulse races, your breath quickens." Biting my lip, I started breathing heavier. "Your body trembles, your lips part, your eyes burn." I exhaled in a soft groan, then inhaled through my teeth. Straining my voice, like I was about to come, I told her, "Your body aches...everywhere."

Closing my eyes, I let out a low moan while I tangled one hand in my hair and ran the other up my chest. Mimicking Kiera's face when she was desperate for me to be inside her, I swallowed and let out a carnal noise that was full of ecstasy. "Oh...God...please..." I drew out each word, punctuated each sound with aching desire. Then I ran my hands down to my pants...

That's when Kiera interrupted the show. "Enough!" she spat out.

I knew I had her then. There was no way I hadn't just proved my point. Opening my eyes, I stared her down. "That's what I thought! Does that sound innocent to you? To any of you?" I looked around the room. Kiera was bright red, Jenny was pale as a ghost, and Evan was shaking his head in disgust. My eyes refocused on Kiera. "You made your choice, remember? Denny. We ended...this. You had no feelings for me. You didn't want to be with me, but now you don't want anyone else to be with me, right?" Furious and feeling desolate, I shook my head. "Is that what you want? For me to be completely alone?" My voice broke on the end of my question. I was so tired of being alone.

Kiera's face tightened in anger. I was sure steam would escape from her ears if it could. "I never said that. I said if you were to see someone, I would understand...but God, Kellan, Evan's right, show some restraint!"

Quiet fell over the room after Kiera's pronouncement. Evan and

Jenny were glaring at me, clearly on her side, so I glared right back at them. After a minute of silent staredowns, Kiera shrugged and said, "Are you trying to hurt me? Do you have something to prove?"

Irritated at what was actually a good point, I looked Kiera over. "To you...? No...nothing!" *Maybe. A little.*

When I stepped away from Jenny, Kiera plunged into her. Jenny had to use both hands on her shoulders to hold her back from me. "You're not trying to purposely hurt me?"

"No." *Maybe. I don't know anymore.*

"Then what about my sister?" she snarled.

Groaning, I looked up at the ceiling. "God, not that again." I did not want a repeat of our fight in the rain, but that seemed to be exactly where we were heading.

Kiera was pushing against Jenny so hard that Evan took a step forward to help her. But Jenny glanced his way and shook her head, so Evan backed off and let her handle it. "Yes! That! Again! You promised!" she yelled, pointing at me.

Anger filled me to the brim. She had no right to say anything about anyone I'd slept with...even if I hadn't slept with them. "Obviously, I lied, Kiera! If you haven't noticed, I do that!" I tossed my hands in the air in frustration. "And what does it matter anyway? *She* wanted me, you didn't. What do you care if I—"

"Because you're mine!" she screamed.

All the blood drained from my face and collected in my stomach, where it boiled and churned into something dark and furious. When the raging fire swept back up to my mouth, the words exploded from me of their own accord. "No, no I'm not! THAT'S THE WHOLE FUCKING POINT!"

Jenny scolded me and I turned my angry eyes on her. I wasn't in the mood to be reprimanded for swearing. I wasn't in the mood for any of this shit.

Kiera didn't back down from my fierce words. Instead, she kept irritatingly goading me, prolonging the fight. Maybe she was enjoying this? "Is that why you did it? Is that why you slept with her, you son of a bitch? To prove a point?" She was so pissed off, her voice cracked.

I opened my mouth, but Jenny beat me to the punch. "He didn't, Kiera."

Turning my fury on her, I snapped, "Jenny!"

Kiera's anger started dissipating as disbelief filled her. "What?" she asked Jenny.

Seeing Kiera was calmer, Jenny dropped her hands from her shoulders. "Kellan wasn't the one who slept with her."

I made a move toward Jenny, and Evan made a move too. Knowing how Evan felt about her, I backed off. He was staying out of this for now, but if I started manhandling Jenny, Evan would be all over my ass. And I didn't feel like getting punched today. Being slapped was enough. "This doesn't concern you, Jenny, butt out!"

Jenny looked back at me, clearly irritated. "Now it does! Why are you lying to her, Kellan? Tell her the truth! For once, tell her the truth."

I knew Jenny knew about Griffin and Anna. Griffin had told the tale often enough that she had to have heard it. Honestly, I was surprised Kiera hadn't yet. Maybe I should have told Kiera what had happened a long time ago, but, well, it was the only weapon I had left against her, and I was reluctant to part with it. I couldn't speak; my mouth stayed shut and my jaw stayed clenched.

Evan and Jenny didn't like that. Kiera either. Annoyed, she shouted, "Will someone please tell me . . . something?"

Jenny's eyes shifted back to Kiera, and before she even spoke, I knew the charade was over. "Don't you ever listen to Griffin?"

Mad that my lie was crumbling, I muttered, "No, she avoids conversations with him, if she can help it." In a whisper, I added, "I counted on that."

Kiera's face scrunched in confusion, like she was having trouble connecting the dots. "Wait . . . Griffin? My sister slept with Griffin?" She said it like she couldn't believe *anyone* would sleep with Griffin, let alone her sister.

Nodding, Jenny rolled her eyes. "He hasn't shut up about it,

Kiera. He keeps telling everyone, 'Best "O" of my life!'" She skewed her face and stuck out her tongue, disgusted by the thought.

Annoyed by the details, annoyed by being back here, annoyed by my life, I bit out, "That's enough, Jenny."

Amazed by this news, Kiera shared looks with Evan and Jenny, then all eyes turned to me. "You lied to me?" Kiera whispered.

I shrugged, faking nonchalance. "You assumed. I simply… encouraged that thought."

Her expression darkened. "You lied to me!"

"I told you, I do that!"

"Why?" she demanded.

It was a fair question, and it was one I couldn't answer. I couldn't even look at her anymore, for fear she'd see right through me. "Answer her, Kellan," I heard Jenny say. I looked at her, standing between us, and she raised an eyebrow in expectation. Frowning, I stayed silent. How could I tell her? How I could I tell her anything? Opening my mouth meant opening my heart. And opening my heart meant exposing it…and she'd hurt me so much already. Another wound would kill me.

Kiera's soft voice penetrated the silence. "The whole fight in the car…the rain…all of that started because I was so angry about you and her. Why would you let me think—"

"Why would you automatically assume—" I interrupted. She'd imagined the worst of me from the beginning of Anna's visit. She'd never even given me a chance to be faithful to her. Not that I owed her that. She certainly wasn't being faithful to me. Or Denny.

"She told me. Well, she made it sound like…" Her voice drifted off as her eyes closed. When she looked at me again, her eyes were soft, apologetic. "I'm sorry I assumed…but why would you let me think that for so long?"

Her face, her voice…they melted the hardness around my heart. I loved her, even now, and I owed her some sort of explanation. Hoping it didn't hurt too badly, I confessed my sin. "I wanted to hurt you…"

"Why?" she whispered, taking a step toward me. Seeing that the storm had passed, Jenny didn't try to hold her back, didn't try to keep us apart.

Kiera's question cracked my soul. *Because I love you, but you don't want me.* Words failing me, I turned away from her. A soft hand touched my cheek and I closed my eyes at the warmth and tenderness there. It had been so long since she'd touched me. "Why, Kellan?" she repeated.

With my eyes closed, the words were easier to find. "Because you hurt me...so many times. I wanted to hurt you back."

As I reopened my eyes, I could feel the wall between us shimmering. I could feel the pain I'd been swallowing emerging. I'd missed her so much. Seeing her but not being able to touch her, hold her, love her...it was killing me. Kiera was a scar across my heart that would never fully heal, no matter how many random encounters I placed across it. My poor imitations of her were only ripping open the wound again and again. Good or bad, she was forever a part of me.

While Kiera and I gazed at each other with heartbroken eyes, Jenny and Evan left the room. When we were alone, finally, Kiera whispered, "I never wanted to hurt you, Kellan...either of you."

Kiera collapsed after her words, like they were too much to bear. Sinking to her knees, she sat there with her head down as the guilt, pain, and whatever else she was feeling settled around her. As hard as this was for me, it was equally hard for her; sometimes I forgot that.

I knelt on the ground across from her. Holding her hands in mine, I told her, "It doesn't matter now, Kiera." *Nothing matters.* "Things are how they're supposed to be. You're with Denny and I'm...I'm..." *I'm alone.*

With a shaky exhale, Kiera murmured, "I miss you."

The words coming from her lips were wonderful, and torturous. A lump caught in my throat. "Kiera..." *Don't go there...We can't do this again.*

She started crying, and whatever resolve I had vanished. I

383

couldn't let her cry in front of me without trying to comfort her, especially since it was my fault she was upset. All of this was my fault. I never should have crossed that line with her. I should have kept my promise to Denny and stayed away. Far away. We should have stayed friends, *only* friends.

Pulling her into my arms, I stroked her back. She clutched at me while she sobbed on my shoulder. It tore me in two. She was hurting just as much as I was. She'd scarred me, but I'd scarred her too. "I'm sorry, baby," I muttered. I wasn't sure if she heard me, but I felt better saying it.

Sitting back on my heels, I pulled her onto my lap. Closing my eyes, I simply enjoyed being near her. I ran my hand down her hair, wishing we could stay like this forever. We couldn't though. We didn't have much time at all, and once we left this room...nothing would change. She was still Denny's. Now was all we had. All we'd ever have.

I could sense Kiera pulling away, but I wasn't ready for her to go yet. Holding her close, I whispered, "No, please...stay."

Kiera froze on my lap and awareness flooded me. She was so close, and it had been so long since I'd held her. Even though sadness had soured my mood, desire was creeping in. Would there ever be a time when I didn't yearn for her? Probably not. As our breaths filled the still air, I slowly opened my eyes to look at her. Her cheeks were rosy and streaked with recent tears, but her eyes were hooded as she stared at me. The flame between us was mutual; she wanted me as much as I wanted her. I think that only made this harder.

Her eyes darted over my face, taking me in. "I miss you, so much."

She seemed surprised by her admission, which made it feel genuine. I rested my head against hers. *God, I've missed you too. I want you...so much.* "Kiera, I can't..." *I can't be hurt again. I won't survive it.* "This is wrong, you're not mine."

"I *am* yours." Her breath washed against my face, as intoxicating as her words.

My heart seized in my chest and a small whimper escaped me.

"Are you…?" I asked, my lungs hardly functioning anymore. When did breathing become so hard?

Looking up, I met her eyes. It was now or never. *Make a move, take a risk, or run away.* I was tired of running from her. "I want you so much…" I wanted *everything.* Our friendship. The way she looked through the bullshit and saw the person beneath it. Our walks through the campus. Our flirty banter. The way she smiled at me. The way she cared, when no else did, or had, or ever would again. She was everything to me. My reason for being.

I was expecting her to push me away again, but she didn't. Tears in her eyes, she whispered, "I want you too." She'd never admitted that to me like this, with a clear head. It stunned me, overwhelmed me, and made me love her all the more.

I repositioned us so she was lying on the floor, with me on top of her. Hovering my lips over her mouth, I debated if I could do this. Could I put my hand in the fire again, knowing I would get burned? If I took this road with her, would she follow through with me, or would she shove me away again? I had no way of knowing, and it scared the shit out of me.

Maybe seeing my uncertainty, Kiera shook her head and started opening her heart. "I've missed you so much. I've wanted to touch you for so long. I've wanted to hold you for so long. I've wanted you for so long. I do need you, Kellan…I always have."

Her words were heaven to my ears, but I still didn't know what she wanted. I couldn't go through that vicious cycle again. I searched her eyes, hoping to see just a spark of what I felt for her reflected back at me. I needed to know that if we did this, if we crossed this line again, she would still be there on the other side of it. That right or wrong, she would stand beside me as an equal participant. No blame. No guilt. "I won't…I won't be led on again, Kiera. I would rather end this than be hurt by you again. I can't…" *I can't handle another rejection.*

Her fingers reached up to grab my face. "Don't leave me. You are mine…and I'm yours. I want you…and you can have me. Just stop being with all those—"

My guard up, I pulled away. So that was what this was about? "No. I won't be with you because you're jealous."

Her hands returned to my skin, pulling my face down again. Mimicking a move that I had done on her before, she slid her tongue under and along my upper lip. I shivered in delight. She felt so good. *No. Yes.* "Kiera...no. Don't do this to me again..."

Kiera paused with her mouth almost touching mine. "I'm not, Kellan. I'm sorry I pushed you away before, but I'm not saying no anymore." Her tongue returned to my lip while my mind spun. She wasn't saying no? I could have her? Whenever I wanted? What about Denny? Could I handle sharing her with him? Yes. Not being with her was worse than any other fate I could think of.

When her tongue was only halfway along my lip, I crashed my mouth down to hers. God, she tasted good, felt good, smelled good. I'd missed this so much. A nagging thought picked at my mind as our mouths moved together. I stopped kissing her and pulled back to look at her. *What am I doing?* My breath became shallow and fast as I made a split-second decision. If she was going to do this with me, then she was going to know the truth. She was going to know how I felt about her. I couldn't let her believe this was a casual fling, that this was just sex to me. It went so much deeper than that. There was no casual here. I was all in, and she needed to know that.

Terrified of the words I'd never spoken to another human being before, I whispered, "I'm in love with you." She started interrupting me, but I didn't let her get very far. If I didn't say this now, I never would.

Bringing my hand up to her cheek, I gave her a kiss as tender as my words. "I'm so in love with you, Kiera. I've missed you so much. I'm so sorry. I'm sorry I say awful things to you. I'm sorry I lied about your sister...I never touched her. I promised you I wouldn't. I couldn't let you know...how much I adore you...how much you hurt me."

With each word I spoke, the next word was easier. Before I knew it, I was rambling in between brief, heartfelt kisses. "I love you. I'm sorry. I'm so sorry. The women...I was so scared to touch you. You didn't want me...I couldn't take the pain. I tried to get over you. Every time with them, I was with you. I'm so sorry...I love you."

I didn't know if I was getting through to her. I didn't know if I was making sense, but I needed her forgiveness. I'd done so much wrong. "Forgive me...please. I tried to forget you. It didn't work...I just wanted you more. God, I've missed you. I'm sorry I hurt you. I've never wanted anyone like I want you. Every girl is you to me. You're all I see...you're all I want. I want you so much. I want you forever. Forgive me...I love you so much."

Kiera's breath increased, and our kisses became heated, intense and passionate, just like everything about us. "God, I love you. I need you. Forgive me. Stay with me. Say you need me too. Say you want me too. Please...be mine."

Reality snapped back into me as I begged for her love. She'd been silent this entire time. She hadn't said a word in response, besides my name. What did that mean? Was she okay with what I was saying? Was she surprised how much I cared about her? Was she ambivalent? Did she care about me at all? What was she thinking...?

"Kiera...?"

She tried to speak, but no words came out. Calming herself, she closed her eyes. I could see the tears squeezing through her eyelashes, but I didn't know what that meant either. She didn't say anything for a long time, and she didn't open her eyes. I guess that was my answer. She didn't feel what I felt. She didn't love me. I'd poured my heart out for nothing. No, not for nothing. I'd opened myself up to someone, and I'd never done that before. That had to count for something.

I pulled away from her and her eyes finally opened. She grabbed my arm, stopping me. I felt my eyes stinging as I looked down at her. Was this the moment she broke my heart again? Could I stomach it? I really didn't feel like I could. A tear in my eye trickled down my skin. Kiera brushed it away, then cupped my cheek and pulled me closer. Our lips met, and my heart soared and cracked.

"Kiera…" I pulled away. I needed words from her right now, not actions.

Her eyes were as wet as mine as she stared up at me. She swallowed a harsh lump in her throat, then she finally spoke. "You were always right—we're not friends. We're so much more. I want to be with *you*, Kellan. I want to be yours. I *am* yours."

She wasn't saying it as directly as I had…but I understood. She *did* love me. She didn't want to, but she did, and she didn't want to fight it anymore. She *was* mine. Finally.

388

Chapter 26

Here's My Heart

I moved over her again, returned my mouth to hers. I kissed her with everything I had, my entire soul, but still…I held a part of me back. She could change her mind at any second. She could crush me with a word. I wanted to be prepared for her rejection; maybe then it wouldn't hurt so much.

My body trembled with restraint, and every place she touched me burned with painful need. She was everything I wanted, everything I needed, everything I hoped for. She ran her fingers down my back, then swept my shirt over my head. I ran my fingers up her skin, taking her shirt with them. I wanted us to be laid bare, no barriers between us. Not anymore. But I didn't want to spook Kiera, so I kept my movements teasingly slow.

Her fingers caressed my bare back, then swept along my side, to the scar I had along my ribs from when I had protected her. The healing wound was a small price to pay for her. I'd gladly pay it again. More if I had to. I'd give my life for her.

I felt her exposed shoulders, let the pads of my fingers run across her bra and down to her waist. I wanted so much more, but I didn't know if she was ready. I didn't know if she'd 100 percent meant what she'd said.

Shifting my weight, I brought my hands to the waistband of

her jeans. I desperately wanted this, but I couldn't handle another no. I'd explode. I needed some sort of assurance from her that this was okay. As if she heard my musings, Kiera whispered, "I'm yours...don't stop."

Her hips wriggled in a way that let me know, without a doubt, that she wanted this. She was *mine*. I had nothing to fear. There wouldn't be a rejection this time.

With a relieved exhale, I began working on her jeans in earnest. Yes, this was going to happen. We were going to give ourselves to each other. Everything was going to be fine.

Kiera unfastened my jeans while I did hers. Once hers were undone, I started pulling them off her. Adoration radiating from my chest in waves of happiness, I murmured, "Kiera, I love you," then placed a soft kiss on her neck.

As I was nuzzling against her neck, I heard her quiet voice, "Kellan, wait...just a min—"

I didn't even let her finish saying our code phrase for "back off." "Kiera..." I groaned. Disappointment warred with grief in my body as I relaxed my hold on her jeans and slumped against her. Had she really done this to me again? "Oh...my...God. Are you serious?" I rocked my head against her shoulder; at the same time I was both shocked and not surprised at all. "Please don't do this again. I can't take it."

Her voice was apologetic, but firm. "No, I'm not...but—"

Incredulous, I lifted my head to look at her. "But?" The sudden stop in the proceedings was starting to give me a stomachache. It was an ache I was getting all too familiar with when it came to Kiera. Irritation boiled a path through my disappointment. "You do realize that if you keep doing this to my body, I will never be able to have children?"

Kiera pressed her lips together, but she couldn't stop the giggle that escaped. Pulling back to look at her, I frowned. I really hadn't been kidding. "I'm glad you find that funny..."

Still laughing, humor and happiness lightening her eyes to a peaceful shade of sea-green, she ran a finger down my cheek and said, "If we are going to do this...if I'm going to be with you...it's not going to be on the floor in the back room of Pete's."

Her eyes scanned the area and I relaxed. She wasn't rejecting me, just our current location, and I could understand that. This wasn't exactly the most romantic, or comfortable, place in the world. I could wait to be with her again, but I couldn't resist a chance to tease her.

With a soft kiss, I whispered, "Now you object to being with me on a dirty floor?" Giving her a fake frown that I hoped was charming, I added, "Did you...did you just get me to pour my heart out to you...so you could get me naked again?"

Kiera laughed, then gently grabbed my face. "God, I missed you. I missed that."

Content, I stroked her stomach as I gazed at her. "Missed what?"

"You...your humor, your smile, your touch, your...everything."

There was so much tenderness in her voice, it seared me. "I missed you so much, Kiera."

I watched the emotions sliding over her face, then I leaned down and kissed her. An idea struck me and I pulled back to look at her with a playful grin. "You know...there are other options for this room besides the floor."

Her smile matched mine. She was enjoying this. "Really?" she asked.

"Yeah..." Looking around the room, I imagined all the various places and positions Kiera and I could use to discover each other. "Table...chair...shelf...wall?" My smile was devilish when I returned my gaze to her. All of those places sounded fabulous to me, and at the same time, none of them were good enough for her. I wanted to lay her down on a bed. Nothing else would do.

With a laugh and a shake of her head, Kiera murmured, "Just kiss me."

Now here was something I could do. "Yes, ma'am." Moving my lips to taste the soft skin of her neck, I muttered, "Tease."

Her response was equally playful. "Whore."

She kissed my still stinging cheek as a throaty laugh escaped me.

A light knock filtered through the room, but I wasn't about to stop what I was doing. While Kiera let out a satisfied noise, I lightly ran the tip of my tongue up her throat and over her chin. That was when the door burst open.

Startled, I lifted my head to see Evan stepping into the room. "Jesus, Evan...you scared the shit out of me!" I said with a laugh.

Evan had his hands over his eyes as he closed the door behind him. "Uh, sorry, man. I know you two are...uh, I need to talk to you, Kellan."

Evan dropped his hand and looked away. I was shielding Kiera's body with my own, so I was sure he couldn't see much, but out of respect, he wasn't looking. I appreciated that, but I didn't see what he possibly needed to talk to me about *now*. Surely it could wait.

"Your timing kind of stinks, man."

He flicked a quick glance at me before averting his eyes again. I felt Kiera clinging to me even tighter; she was embarrassed, and probably hating this exchange. Evan shook his head. "Sorry...but you're going to thank my timing in about ten seconds."

I wasn't sure what he meant by that, but I was sure he didn't need to be here. "Really, Evan, can't this wait, like ten—" Kiera nudged my ribs. When I glanced down, her cheeks were rosy, but she had a playful gleam in her eye. Looking back up at Evan, I changed my answer, "Twenty minutes?" Kiera giggled.

"Denny's here." Evan's tone was flat, ominous, and his words echoed around the room.

While Kiera whispered, "What?" I sat up. Straddling Kiera's hips, I let out a curse as I handed her her shirt. She quickly slipped it on. Why did Denny have to show up now? The one person we needed to stay away...

Evan finally looked our way, and held my gaze. "Unless you want tonight to get...even more interesting, Kiera needs to leave and you need to stay and talk to me."

Nodding, I found my shirt. He was right, of course. Denny didn't deserve to find out like this...to see us like this. Slipping my shirt on, I looked back at Evan. "Thank you..."

Evan's smile was sad. "See...I knew you'd thank me."

I stood up, then helped Kiera to her feet. She started hyperventilating while we adjusted our clothes. I knew she was freaking out. *I* was freaking out. But I put my hands on her shoulders to calm her down. He wasn't finding out today...today we were okay. "It's fine...it will be fine."

All peace and playfulness were gone from her—her eyes were wide, her breaths fast. She looked on the verge of a nervous breakdown. It reminded me how much Denny meant to her. To us. "But the whole bar...they all saw that, they'll be talking. He'll know something."

She had a point, but in her state, I couldn't let her know that. "He'll know we had a fight...that's it." I could hear Evan shifting his weight; he was antsy, ready for Kiera to leave. The longer she stayed, the better the chances were that we'd be discovered. "You should go, before he comes back here looking for you."

Kiera was reluctant, reminding me how much *I* meant to her. "Okay..."

She turned to leave and I grabbed her arm. "Kiera..." I pulled her in for a kiss that left us both breathless, then I released her.

The door shutting after Kiera felt thunderous. I wasn't sure if that was my nerves or some sort of foreshadowing. I loved Kiera, and now she knew it. She loved Denny, but she loved me too; I saw it in her eyes. She wasn't going to deny us anymore, but she wouldn't deny him either. The three of us were going to be some odd, fucked-up family. I had no idea how this could possibly end well.

Now that Evan and I were alone in the room, the air seemed to thicken. Tension settled around us. I knew he was looking at me; I could feel his eyes warming the spot on my cheek where Kiera had slapped the living hell out of me. Staring at the door and wishing Kiera would step back through it wasn't doing me any good, so with a deep inhale, I turned my head to look at Evan. He crossed his arms over his chest and lifted an eyebrow.

"What?" I asked, knowing full well exactly what his problem with me was.

393

Letting out a sigh that was heavy with disapproval, he shook his head. "What were you thinking, Kell? Denny's girl? How could you go there?"

I dropped my head, but only for an instant. He didn't know what she meant to me. He didn't know how hard I'd tried. "I fell in love. I didn't want to, trust me, but it happened anyway." I looked back to the door. "It happened, and now we're all screwed."

"What are you going to do?" he quietly asked me. That was the real question, wasn't it?

"I don't know." I looked back to his face. His expression had softened into compassion, like he really did get it, but he didn't know what I should do either. "I can't let her go, Evan. I tried. I tried to stay away, I tried to forget her. I tried to ignore what was happening between us, but it's not possible. She's with me everywhere I go, and then, when I see her…touch her…" Sighing, I scrubbed my face with my hands. "I don't know what to do."

Evan found a couple of chairs stacked along the wall and pulled them over. He sat down, then patted for me to sit beside him. He was quiet for several minutes, then he said, "You kind of screwed yourself into a corner, Kell, but…it's *Denny*. You should tell him."

Leaning over my knees, I dropped my head into my hands. "How can I tell him that I'm in love with his girlfriend? That she means more to me than…How can I tell him about any of this? He'd hate me…"

Evan let out another sigh. "And you don't think he's going to hate you when he finds out some other way? And you know it's going to get out there, don't you? You can't keep a lid on this forever, and if it doesn't come from you…" He sighed again. "It should come from you. You're the only one who can fix this."

I glanced up at him. "By breaking it?"

He lifted a corner of his lip. "It's already broken. Denny just doesn't realize it yet."

I stared at him for long moments. He was right, but I didn't want to admit it, and I didn't want to think about hurting Denny. I didn't want to think about anything. All I wanted to do was replay those magical words that Kiera had spoken to me just a few minutes ago. *I'm yours.*

Keeping the smile from my face, I stared at my hands. Evan must have seen something though. "She really makes you happy, doesn't she?"

I nodded. "And miserable, all at the same time." I peeked up at him. "Who knew a girl could do that to a person?"

Laughing, he patted me on the back. "I could have told you that. Nothing messes you up quite like a girl." Evan glanced toward the closed door, and I wondered if he was thinking about Jenny. For once, I didn't bug him about her though. I had my own problems.

"Tell me about her," he said, his face curious but nonjudgmental. "How did you get together? When did you know you loved her?"

I inhaled a deep breath, wondering if I should tell him what had happened between us, but a smile spread on my face as I thought about Kiera, and the words gushed from me as easily as water releasing from a dam. I'd been holding this in for far too long.

Evan let me talk with practically no interruptions. He asked a question every so often, and sometimes he'd frown or shake his head, but he kept most of his comments to himself. When I was finished, he knew almost everything. The only comment he made when I was done was "Why didn't you tell me earlier?"

I looked away. "I knew what you'd say. That she wasn't mine, and I couldn't go there, and...I didn't want to hear it." I flashed a glance his way. "Honestly, I still don't, but it's kind of too late now."

Evan cracked a smile. "Yeah. Cat's out of the bag, right?"

I cringed as I remembered my angry outburst. God, I could be such a dick sometimes. Evan chuckled beside me, then said, "Despite it all, I think you're a good person, Kellan, and I know you'll do the right thing."

Even though I wasn't so sure that I even knew what the right thing was, I nodded. My mind drifted to Kiera, and I focused Evan's statement on her. If I took Denny out of the equation, what would be the right thing between the two of us? That question was actually an easy one. Honesty was what we needed. The air needed to be cleared, walls needed to be torn down. I needed to show her the deepest parts of me and hope that didn't scare her off. But I'd already shown her plenty of darkness, and she was still mine, so I felt okay exposing my innermost soul to her. For the first time in my life, I wanted to open up to someone... about everything.

And I knew the perfect spot to do it. The place I'd once promised to take her—the Space Needle. Arrangements would need to be made, but luckily I knew exactly who to talk to in order to make them... the head of security was a fan of the band. I was going to owe Zeke a serious favor after this, but it was worth it. *She* was worth it.

After I was finished making preparations, I returned to Pete's and parked across the street. It was a while before Kiera was off work, but I wanted to be ready in case she was let go early. When she finally exited the bar with Jenny, I got out of my car. Wondering if she'd notice me watching her, I leaned against the door with my arms folded across my chest. Stopping in her tracks, she stared at me like she was seeing a ghost. I had to smile at her reaction. Did she really think I wouldn't give her a ride home?

After saying a few words to Kiera, Jenny gave me a wave, then headed to her car. Eager to reunite, Kiera bounded across the lot to me. Her approach warmed me in a way I couldn't articulate. It sounded completely cheesy, but she completed me.

She was grinning ear to ear when I took her hand and led her around to the other side of the car. With the radiant energy emanating from each of us, it was almost like we hadn't seen each other in days, not hours. *She missed me.*

When I slid into my side of the car, Kiera pursed her lips into an obviously fake frown, like she was put out with me. I could tell she was actually feeling playful though, so I decided to go along with it. "What? I haven't been around you for hours. What could I have possibly done?"

Even though I was giving her a lopsided smile, Kiera's expression didn't change. "I've been dwelling on something you did earlier...for hours."

Wondering which part of tonight she was referring to, I tilted my head. "I did quite a bit...can you be more specific?"

She bit back a laugh, then a genuine pout darkened her face. "Oh...God...please." Smacking my arm, she whined, "How could you mock me like that in front of Evan and Jenny? That was so embarrassing!"

Laughing, I leaned away from her attack. "Ow! Sorry. I was making a point."

"I think you made it, asshole!" After one last smack, she crossed her arms over her chest.

I laughed. "I think I'm a bad influence—you're starting to swear as much as I do."

With a smirk, Kiera cuddled up to my side, right where she belonged. I loved having her next to me. I loved teasing her too, but I did feel bad for embarrassing her. Knowing she wouldn't do it, but loving the vision of her making sensuous noises, I said, "You can mimic me sometime if you like?"

As I could have predicted, her cheeks filled with color at the idea of imitating me during sex. In a hushed voice, she commented that my performance was a good one, and I confessed that it wasn't my first time doing it. Kiera seemed surprised by my confession, and I laughed at the look on her face. Wondering if a part of her had enjoyed hearing me make intimate sounds, and wondering if I could both tease her and turn her on, I tilted my head and said, "You are right...that wasn't very fair of me. Here, I'll do me..."

Putting my arms around her, I pressed my lips against her ear and proceeded to mimic a needy groan. Breath heavy, I slowly elongated my words. "Oh...God...yes." I added a whimper on the end and Kiera spun to face me, grabbed my neck, and pulled me in for a voracious kiss. Guess I hadn't lost my touch.

I considered letting this kiss take us over, riling us up to the point where I laid her down on the seat and took her right here. But someone was waiting for us, and sex with her wasn't what I had in mind tonight. Pulling away, I gave her a playful smile. "Can we do something?"

"Yes," she moaned, reaching for my lips again.

A smirk broke over me as I avoided contact with her. "Do you need a minute?"

She wasn't happy about my amusement or my question. She smacked my arm again and her cheeks turned bright red. Then, looking a little grumpy, she asked what I had in mind while I started the car.

Finding her disappointment funny, I laughed out, "Sorry, I didn't mean to get you all...riled up." When she raised an eyebrow in disbelief, I laughed. *Yeah, you got me.* "Okay...yeah, maybe I did. But right now, I want to show you something." *Something you're going to love.*

She nodded, and I pulled away from the street.

Once Kiera figured out we were heading downtown, she asked me where we were going. "Well, I did promise you that we'd go up the Space Needle," I answered.

Her expression was blank while she processed that. "Kellan...it's two in the morning, it's closed."

With a smile and a wink, I assured her that everything was fine. I knew people, and those people were going to let us in...for a price.

I found a spot to park, then grabbed her hand and walked her over to where the iconic landmark was looming above us. It felt amazing to hold her hand again. I hadn't realized just how much I'd missed it, and just how unsatisfying all of my pseudo-Kieras had been. Nothing compared to the real thing.

Expecting our arrival, thanks to Zeke, the guard on duty met us at the base of the Needle. Reaching into my pocket, I handed him the couple of hundreds that I'd grabbed from my rainy-day fund at the house. It was a pricey trip up the Needle, but it was worth every penny. And what else did I have to use my parents' money on? It wasn't like I needed much. Just Kiera.

Satisfied, the guard led us up to the elevators. Kiera noticed the payoff. Eyes wide, she whispered, "How much did you give him?" as the elevator doors closed.

I told her not to worry about it. The house wasn't the only thing my parents had left me. There had also been life insurance policies, savings accounts, and a lifetime of abuse and neglect. There was always that.

The elevator started rising and Kiera gasped and pressed herself against the wall. The elevator's glass doors gave its riders an impressive view of the city, but it was clear from the absence of color on Kiera's face that she wasn't entirely enjoying it. Grabbing her chin, I tilted her head so she was looking at me, not the ground we were leaving behind. "You're completely safe, Kiera."

I gave her a soft kiss, which led to a deeper kiss, which led to a breathless kiss. The guard cleared his throat, and that was when I noticed that the elevator had stopped. Oops. "I guess we're here," I said with a laugh.

Patting the guard on the back, I grabbed Kiera's hands and led her out of the elevator. Her cheeks were flushed with residual embarrassment from being caught, but it only made her even more attractive. Once the elevator closed again, the room darkened. Since technically the Needle wasn't open to visitors right now, all the regular lighting was off. Only a couple of emergency lights remained on. It made the glow of the city around us seem that much brighter, and I pulled Kiera to the edge of the inner observatory.

She paused to take it all in. "Kellan...wow...it's beautiful."

Leaning against the railing, I paused to take *her* in. "Yes, it is." Opening my arms wide, I added, "Come here."

She walked over and wrapped her arms around me, and I looped mine around her. Content with her in my arms, I shifted my gaze to take in the lights of the city. It really was magnificent up here.

I could feel Kiera's eyes on me. After a moment of inspection, she whispered, "Why me?" I wasn't sure how this conversation would begin, but explaining why she'd caught my eye seemed as good a place as any.

Shifting my gaze to her, I smiled. "You have no idea how attractive you are to me. I kind of like that." It was just one of the many things about her that made her different. Kiera blushed in a beautifully modest way, and I paused as I pondered how to explain everything to her. "It was you and Denny...your relationship."

I knew that wouldn't make sense to her, so I wasn't surprised when she frowned. "What do you mean?" she asked, threading her fingers through the hair above my ear. Suddenly faced with opening my heart, I felt my nerves spring to life and I looked back over the city. I wasn't sure if I could do this. Kiera grabbed my cheek and made me look at her. She wanted me to stop hiding; she wanted an answer. "What do you mean, Kellan?"

With a sigh, I looked down. I couldn't stay quiet anymore. Not with her. I needed to open up and tell her everything. Show her everything. Hopefully it didn't hurt too much, although it couldn't hurt as much as the thought of losing her. "I can't explain this properly, without...without clarifying something Evan said."

Kiera thought for a moment, then said, "When you told him, quite rudely, by the way, to back off?"

Wishing we were already past this part and she already knew, I murmured, "Yeah."

"I don't understand—what does that have to do with me?"

I shook my head with a sad smile. "Nothing...everything."

She seemed amused by that. "Eventually you're going to start making sense, right?"

I laughed and looked out over the skyline. "Yeah...just give me a minute." Or three, or four. *I can do this...*

Respecting my wishes, Kiera put her head on my shoulder and held me tight. As I held her head in place and rubbed her back, I felt my unease dissolving. This wasn't just anyone I was opening up to. This was Kiera. She had my heart, every corner of it, so what did it matter if she knew about the darkness that surrounded me? She would love me anyway. I was sure of that. My secrets were safe with her. I was safe with her.

I began quietly, because it was the only way I could get the words

400

out. "You and Evan were right about the women. I've been...using them...for years." I'd been too angry at the time to admit it to myself when Evan had cornered me about it in the back room, but now I could clearly see what I'd been doing to women my entire life as I'd aimlessly searched for a connection with someone. Anyone. I'd used them to make myself feel better. To make myself feel worthwhile, even if it was just for a moment.

Kiera had an odd, hurt expression on her face. "For years? Not just because of me?"

Smiling, I tucked some hair behind her ear. "No...although that certainly made it worse." So much worse. I'd been completely obsessed with finding a distraction, a replacement. I'd been so stupid. There was no replacing her.

Kiera shifted her stance, a little uncomfortable. "You shouldn't use people, Kellan...for any reason."

I found that response ironic, and I called her on it. "You didn't use me, to block out Denny our first time?" I knew she had. The way she'd been drowning her sorrows in alcohol...she'd gulped me down with just as much ferocity. She'd used me to abolish Denny in her mind. Embarrassed by the truth, Kiera averted her eyes. I grabbed her chin and made her look at me again. "It's okay, Kiera. I suspected that."

Letting her go, I looked out over the water on the other side of the Needle. "It didn't stop me from believing we might have had a chance, though. I spent that whole damn day wandering around the city, trying to figure out how to tell you...how much I loved you, without sounding like an idiot."

"Kellan..."

While Kiera said my name, memories of every place I'd gone that day flooded me. I'd been so scared to tell her how I felt that I had left her alone, and probably believing that I didn't care about her at all. No wonder she'd instantly taken Denny back. She'd probably thought I was an unfeeling asshole.

Returning my eyes to her, I confessed my pain. "God...when you went right back to him, like we were nothing at all, that killed

401

me. I knew it… The minute I finally came home, and heard you two upstairs, I knew we didn't have a chance." I couldn't keep the remembered anger from my voice.

Kiera blinked when I was finished. "You heard us?" she asked, confused. I had given her some lie about seeing his jacket, if I was recalling that night correctly. I'd been pretty wasted.

Looking down, I cringed. I probably should have left that out. "Oh…yeah. I came back and heard you guys in your room, getting…reacquainted. That…pretty much sucked. I grabbed a fifth, headed to Sam's, and, well, you know how that turned out." *With me shit-faced.*

By the shock in her voice, it was clear she hadn't known any of that. "Kellan, God, I'm sorry. I didn't know."

"You didn't do anything wrong, Kiera." I glanced at her, then looked away. "I was such a dick to you afterwards. I'm sorry about that." Kiera grimaced when I gave her a sheepish smile. Apparently, she agreed with me. "I'm sorry, I tend to lose the filter on my mouth when I'm angry…and no one seems to be able to make me angrier than you." *Wasn't that the truth?*

With a humorless laugh, Kiera raised an eyebrow at me. "I've noticed that." I laughed at her comment and her expression changed. "You were always right though. And I did kind of deserve your… harshness."

Quieting, I cupped her cheek. "No, you didn't. You never deserved the things I said to you."

"I was horribly…misleading to you," she said, guilt and sadness drawing down her features.

"You didn't know I loved you," I whispered, stroking her cheek.

Her eyes were a liquid green when she looked up at me. "I knew you cared for me. I was…callous."

Callous? I suppose I could give her that much. There were times when she'd been coarse with me. And vice versa. To soften the blow of agreeing with her, I gave her a small smile and a kiss. "True. But we seem to have gotten off track. I believe we were talking about my messed-up psyche."

Shaking away the seriousness of the moment, she let out a brief laugh. "Right, your … whoring."

"Ouch." I laughed at her comment, gathered my courage, then pulled off the bandage that had been holding my splintered heart together for far too long. "I suppose I should start with the whole tortured-childhood speech …"

She tried to stop me from telling her things that she knew would bring me pain, but I needed her to know the whole story, the one I didn't tell anyone, not even Denny. I prepped her with "You're going to find it funny."

She disagreed, and I supposed she was right. It wasn't ha-ha funny, but it was interesting. For us, at least. "Well, okay, maybe not funny … coincidental, then."

When she gave me a confused expression, I slowly began my story. It was difficult, but I started peeling back the lies that were wrapped around me, started showing her the skeletons that I'd pretended my entire life weren't there. "It seems that my mother was … enamored with my father's best friend. So when dear old Dad had to leave town for several months … some family emergency thing back East … you can imagine his surprise when he came back home to find his blushing bride pregnant."

Kiera's mouth fell open, and I could tell she'd instantly spotted the similarities to our own situation. By the shock on Kiera's face, she hadn't suspected my dad wasn't my *real* dad. No one did. That was our family's greatest secret, and biggest shame, and it wasn't something we openly discussed. With anyone. And it was the main reason why neither one of them loved me.

403

Chapter 27

Preparing for Reality

I felt like a weight had been lifted when we left the Needle. There
weren't any secrets between us anymore; Kiera knew everything
about me. She knew what I'd done, and she knew why I'd done it.
She knew the real reason why my parents had treated me with such
disdain. She knew it all. A part of me still feared that Kiera would
reject me, but right now, all was right in the world.

The air was crisp and cold as Kiera and I walked back to my
car in the parking lot. The chill in the breeze was an unspoken
reminder that winter was just around the corner. I welcomed the
change though. As the temperature dropped, surely Kiera and I
would heat up. Since all the walls between us had come down, there
was nothing keeping us from each other. I might have to share her
with Denny, but at least I wasn't losing her. As sad as it sounded, as
long as I got to keep a part of her heart as my own, I was okay with
sharing her body. At least, that was what I was telling myself. Over
and over if I needed to. *I can do this.*

To shift the focus of my thoughts before they got too dark, I
looked over at Kiera with a serious expression. When we reached
the car, I stopped and said, "There is one more thing I wanted to
talk to you about."

She instantly tensed. "What?"

Shifting my intense face to a breezy grin, I told her, "I can't believe you stole my car...really?"

Kiera laughed, which I didn't find amusing, but I did find charming. Then she cringed, and I knew she was remembering the events that had led up to the carjacking. "You kind of deserved it at the time. You're lucky it came back to you in one piece," she said, poking my chest.

I knew I hadn't really done anything wrong, but I also knew how much it would have torn me up if I'd witnessed Kiera in that position with Denny. *I can do this.* Not wanting to dwell on the negative aspect of our relationship, I made myself stay in a humorous frame of mind. "Hmmmm...in the future, could you just slap me again, and leave my baby alone?"

With a playful frown, I opened her door. She placed a foot inside, then grabbed my chin. "In the future, could you not go on anymore 'dates'?"

Her voice sounded playful, but the look in her eye wasn't. She was seriously asking this of me. She wanted me to be faithful to her, while she split her love between Denny and me. Grief struck me for a moment, that I couldn't have exactly what I wanted with her, but I pushed it back. Anything was good enough.

Grinning, I gave her a light kiss. "Yes, ma'am." Shaking my head at the chaos of my life, I walked around to my side of the car.

Kiera snuggled into my side on the drive home. We held hands as she rested her head on my shoulder, and I stroked her long, slender fingers. Peaceful. That was the only word I could use to describe how I felt. Or maybe blissful, euphoric, satisfied. Except...that wasn't entirely true. Whenever I dug a little deeper, I touched a nerve of pain. *She still isn't mine...*

I wanted to feel peace right now though, so I stopped digging into my soul, stopped overthinking the situation. Delusional happiness was better than none.

When my house came into view, a pang of reality went through me. The joy we'd found tonight would be tested when we stepped through that door. I'd have to wrestle with the idea of sharing her;

Kiera would have to wrestle with the idea of willingly betraying the man she loved. And I couldn't deny that she loved Denny. Through all of this, that had never changed. For either one of us. He deserved so much better than both of us.

As we cuddled in my car parked in the driveway, I thought over everything I'd felt since Kiera had arrived—the ups, the downs, the dreams, nightmares, fantasies. She'd permeated every aspect of my life, from waking to sleeping. It was a bit remarkable to me that a person could become so entangled with another person's psyche that it was impossible to remove them. Traces of Kiera were permanently seared into the very essence of my being.

Kissing her head, I murmured, "I dream about you sometimes… about what it would have been like if Denny hadn't come back, if you were mine. Holding your hand, walking into the bar with you on my arm…not having to hide anything anymore. Telling the world that I love you."

Smiling, she looked up at me. "You mentioned that you dreamed about me once. You never said about what though." She kissed my cheek, then added, "I dream about you too sometimes."

"Really?" That surprised me, and made me really happy. I'd kind of thought that I slipped her mind the moment I was out of her sight. "Huh, we're kind of pathetic, aren't we?"

I laughed as I considered all the stolen moments we'd had with each other in our minds. What a life dream-Kellan and dream-Kiera must have already had together. "And what are your dreams about?"

She giggled with embarrassment, her cheeks flushed. "Honestly, I mostly dream about sleeping with you."

The look on her face when she spoke about sex was so damn cute, I could barely restrain myself from leaning down and sucking on her plump lip. I let out a much-needed laugh. Of the two of us, Kiera was undoubtedly the innocent one, yet she'd been having the erotic dreams, while mine had generally been on the more romantic side.

Amused, Kiera laughed with me. Grabbing her hand, I laced our fingers together. "God…is that all I am to you?" I asked.

Hoping she didn't say yes, I watched as her laughter ended and her expression grew serious. "No...no, you're so much more."

My laughter dried up as the moment grew intense. "Good, because you mean everything to me." *What would I be without her?* I didn't want to fathom it.

Kiera clutched my hand tighter as she cuddled closer to me in the car. I wished we could stay for the rest of the night, but it was already late, and if Denny woke up and found us out here...there was just no good way to explain it. There wasn't a good way to explain a lot of things between us. That slap in the bar, for instance. "What did you tell Denny?"

Kiera cringed, and I knew she didn't want to talk about this. We needed to though. I needed to know the story if I was going to back it up. "That you slept with my sister and broke her heart. That's believable. Everyone saw you at the bar together. Denny seemed to buy it."

My heart sank as I felt the ticking of time closing in around us. She'd forgotten something very important in that lie...an aspect of it that we couldn't control. "That won't work, Kiera."

Her voice sped up as she started panicking. "Yes, it will. I'll talk to Anna; she'll back me up. I've had to lie for her before. I won't tell her why, of course...and Denny probably will never ask her about it anyway."

She wasn't seeing the problem I was seeing. Of course, she didn't know the jackass like I knew the jackass, so it was easy for her to dismiss him. "I wasn't thinking of your sister. That's not why that won't work."

I saw the spark of despair in her eyes the second the realization hit her. "Oh God...Griffin."

Nodding, I agreed with her summation. "Yeah...Griffin. He really does tell everyone." Remembering her cluelessness, I smiled. "I don't know how you managed to miss that. You've gotten good at tuning him out." My humor left me as the problem loomed over us. "When Denny hears that it isn't true..." *He'll know. We'll change him...forever.*

407

Kiera looked devastated that her lie wasn't good enough. I kind of loved the fact that lying wasn't one of her specialties. I was good enough for both of us, and I wasn't proud of that fact. "What was I supposed to tell him, Kellan? I had to come up with something." She stared at her hands. "You know, it's possible that you both—"

I knew where she was going with that, and cut her off. "No. It's not possible." I smiled when she looked up at me. *I would never touch Anna. She doesn't hold a candle to you.* Remembering Griffin's explicit tales, I frowned. "Griffin is very...specific...about what he tells people. It's not just that he slept with her. It's that he slept with her, and I didn't, like he stole her away from me or something. He's got this weird competitive thing—"

"I've noticed that," she said, her lips twisting in disgust. Sighing, she laid her head back on the seat. "God, I didn't even think about that."

My sigh matched hers. *Damn Griffin.* "I can't guarantee you anything, but I could try talking to Griffin. Maybe get him to alter the story. I'll probably have to threaten to kick him out of the band. Actually, I may just do that anyway."

"No!" she yelled. Glancing at the door fearfully, she slapped a hand over her mouth.

I bunched my brows, confused. Why did she care if I kicked Griffin out? "You want me to keep him in the band?"

Dropping her hand, she gave me a faint, amused smile, then she frowned. "No, I don't want him to know—ever! He won't stay silent about that. He'd tell everyone, in horrifying detail. He'd tell Denny! Please, don't ever—"

She was really starting to freak out. In an attempt to calm her, I put my hands on her shoulders. "Okay. It's okay. I won't tell him anything, Kiera." When she let out a sigh of relief, I added, "It wouldn't matter anyway. He's told too many people already." Hating that this was hurting her, that this was going to hurt Denny, I brushed a lock of hair behind her ear. "I'm sorry, but Denny will find out that you lied to him...and then he'll start to wonder why."

She gazed up at me, like I was her saving grace. Like I had all the answers. I wished I did. "And then what? After he knows I lied, how long do you think we have?"

"How long before Denny figures out that we've slept together?" That was the question of the day, wasn't it? Interlacing our fingers again, I rested against the seat. "Well, if you stay out here with me all night, he'll probably have it figured out by morning." With a laugh, I rested my cheek on her head. I felt her relaxing against me, and knew my brief moment of humor had calmed her down some. Although, there was a lot of truth in my statement. We needed to go inside soon.

When the levity passed, I told her, "I don't know, Kiera. A few hours, maybe? A couple of days at the most."

That alarmed her. Pulling back, she sputtered, "Hours? But…he has no real proof. He couldn't possibly think…"

Her eyes were gorgeous in the moonlight—a deep, dark green surrounded by flecks of golden brown. They glistened in her fear, but behind the anxiety, I saw affection. A deeply rooted affinity… for me. It spoke volumes without saying a word. Releasing her hand, I ran the back of my finger down her cheek. "He has all the proof he needs, right here." *The eyes don't lie, and yours say you love me.*

"What do we do, Kellan?"

She peeked up at the house, like she was afraid Denny would hear my answer. Maybe he should. Maybe we should walk in there, hand in hand, wake him up…and tell him that the life he once knew was over. That we'd both betrayed him. My heart seized at just the thought of confronting him. A voice from the past drifted to me, along with a memory—Denny, his lip cut, swollen and bloody, courtesy of my father; a split lip that had been meant for me. Denny's hand on my shoulder while I shook with trepidation, afraid of how my father was going to retaliate for someone saving me. Denny hadn't been scared. Not one little bit. *I'm here for you, Kellan. I'll always be here for you.* And this is how I repaid him for his sacrifice? Crushing his relationship to irreparable pieces? No…I couldn't face him. I'd rather run…

"I can start the car, and we can be in Oregon before the sun comes up." I was such a coward.

I could almost see her contemplating it as I stared into her eyes—the two of us running into the sunset, fleeing from our problems, never looking back at the destruction we were leaving in our wake. As we gazed at each other, her breath started getting faster and shorter. Before long, she was nearly wheezing, and she started hunching over like she was going to be sick. She couldn't do it, she couldn't leave him. She wouldn't ever leave him. I was living in a fantasy...but it was so nice here...I wasn't ready to leave either.

I stroked her hair to soothe her. "Hey. Breathe, Kiera, it's okay...Breathe." Cupping her cheek, I tried to get her to focus on what was happening now, tried to get her to let go of whatever vision was rolling around her head. "Look at me. Breathe."

Her eyes locked onto mine, and her breathing slowed and deepened. Tears fell off her jaw as she shook it back and forth. "Not like that. He's too much a part of me. I need time. I can't talk about this yet."

Her reaction to just the thought of leaving him solidified the truth for me and dissolved the illusion I'd been holding on to. She cared for me, loved me even, but she wouldn't leave him. She couldn't. I knew she wasn't ready to think about making a choice yet, but I also knew that when she made her choice...it wouldn't be me.

I nodded, but I felt the fragile hold on "us" slipping. I felt time ticking faster. *I won't have long with her.* Maybe seeing my conclusion on my face, Kiera whispered, "I'm so sorry, Kellan."

I tried to smile, even though it hurt. "Don't be...Don't be sorry for loving someone." Pulling her in tight, I kissed her head. As chilly reality settled around me, I knew what I had to do. I'd started this; I had to be the one to end it. I was the only one who could. And I should do it soon, before Denny pieced this horrible puzzle together, before our secret was laid bare. And the only way to stop Denny from digging until he found the truth was to take away the need for him to dig at all. Remove the source of the suspicion, that was what I had to do.

"Don't worry, Kiera. I'll think of something. I'll fix this, I promise."

Before he finds out, I'll go, and this time I'll leave for good. Like I said before, we won't hurt him unnecessarily. He'll never know what happened here. This secret will die with us. I'll spare him the pain, and I'll spare you too. I'll carry it all. I'm used to that.

We stayed in the car until the first light of dawn turned the world pink with promise. "Promise" was such a misleading word. It suggested hope, but sometimes promise had no hope attached to it. At least, not for everyone. Sometimes, to give someone else hope, you had to cut out your own. And it was just as difficult as cutting off your own limb, but then again…if sacrifice was easy, everyone would do it.

Hating time for closing in on us, I gave Kiera a squeeze and told her what we were both thinking. "You should go inside."

She instantly locked onto the word "you," not "we." Pulling back, she looked me over with panicked eyes. "What about you? Aren't you coming?"

In the end, no, it won't be me with you. "There's something I need to do first."

"What?" she asked, confused.

Smiling, I skirted my way around the answer. I couldn't tell her yet. She'd argue, say I was wrong, but I wasn't. I knew where this was going. I saw the signs all around me. She loved me, but not enough to leave him. We'd crush Denny…for nothing. For a fantasy. I didn't want that, and I knew she didn't either.

"Go on…it will be okay." I gave her a kiss, then leaned over to unlatch the door. "I love you," I whispered as she got out. *Always.* Sliding over to her side, I leaned up so she could kiss me. We shared a brief, torturous connection, and I felt her lips trembling as we pulled apart. She had tears on her cheeks when I returned to my side of the car. This was going to be difficult for both of us.

Starting the car, I pulled away, and I swear, a piece of me ripped off when I left her behind.

411

Feeling numb inside, I drove to Evan's. He was the only one who knew what I was going through, the only one who could really help me. Parking the car, I stared up at his quiet apartment. For a moment, I let myself feel envious of Evan's life. And Matt's, and Griffin's. Looking from the outside, their lives seemed so simple, so easy. I knew that wasn't really the case though; they each had their issues. If my life had taught me anything, it was that no one's life was as simple as it appeared on the surface. Everyone had crap to deal with. That was what bonded the entire human race: pain … and love.

So Evan would hear me, I firmly knocked on his door a few times. It was so early in the morning, I really should have driven around, given him time to wake up, but … I needed him. I didn't want to be alone right now.

It took several minutes, but eventually I heard his door unlocking. A second later, it cracked open and Evan's cringing face appeared. "Kell? What are you doing here?"

"I need your help. Kiera and I …" My gaze dropped to the ground. How in the hell was I going to say goodbye to her? "We're … it's not going to last. I want to give her something, before it ends. I want to write her a song."

Evan pushed the door open and stepped away so I could enter. "Whatever you need, Kell."

I knew he wasn't thrilled about our union, but I appreciated that he was putting our friendship before his morals. Of course, I *had* just told him we were ending things. His response might have been different if I'd told him I was going to ask her to marry me.

God … now there was a thought …

One I couldn't let myself have. Marriage wasn't in our future.

Evan was yawning when I entered the living room portion of his loft. "You can go back to bed," I told him. "I'm just going to sit here and work on lyrics."

He raised his hand in acknowledgment, then walked over to his bed in the corner and collapsed on top of it. I watched the bulk of his chest rising and falling for a moment, then looked around for paper. I needed this to be good. My final song for my failed romance. I had to tell her everything I felt for her, while also telling her goodbye. It was a tricky line to walk, and one I really didn't want to be walking.

I could change my mind...ask her to pick me...fight for her. *Why?* I immediately thought after that revelation. She wouldn't choose me, and I would be asking her to destroy a man who had been like a brother to me.

No, she would leave me faster than I could blink if I forced her to choose, and that was why I had to do this...to let her know it was okay, that I understood. I wasn't good enough for her. I never was.

Sitting down on the couch with a pad of paper and a pencil, I began writing down my love, my loss, my grief, and my acceptance: *It's better to never say goodbye, to just move on, to end the lie.*

Evan woke back up a few hours later. Shuffling over to the couch, he picked up a couple of loose sheets I'd torn off and laid out. I was trying to shuffle through the painful words, find the right combination. His eyes scanned the page of one, then he peeked over at me. "Are you sure you want to do this?" he asked, his voice completely serious.

I held his gaze. "Yes."

With a sigh, he set the paper down. "Kellan, I know you're hurting, and I know this thing between you two was intense, but...if you sing this...at Pete's...everyone is going to know—"

I cut him off with a shake of my head. "This is for Kiera. I want her to hear it. I don't care about anyone else. I'll never care about anyone else," I whispered.

Evan put a hand on my shoulder. "I know this is hard, and I know it feels that way, but I promise—"

Shrugging off his hand, I stood up. "No, you don't know how this feels. She wasn't some cute blonde shaking her ass at the bar who I decided to hook up with one night because I liked the way her shirt showed off her tits. We were *friends* who fell in love. You couldn't

413

possibly know what I'm feeling right now, because you've never had a connection that deep. You fall for skanks, then you brush them aside when you get bored of them."

Brows furrowed, Evan stood up too. "Hey, not all of those girls were skanks." I raised an eyebrow at him, and Evan frowned. "Well, you don't have to be such an asshole about it."

A small laugh escaped me, and I clapped his shoulder. "Yeah, I know. I'm sorry. I just…this fucking sucks. I wish I'd fallen for a skank. I'm actually quite jealous of you."

Evan gave me a wide smile. "As you should be." His smile slowly faded as he looked back down at the paper. "Okay, I'll help you with this. But it needs to be subtler, Kellan. It needs to look like you're singing a song that could be about anyone. It needs to look fake."

I nodded. "And sound real. I know." Shaking my head, I raised my hands. "That's why I came to you."

Evan nodded and sat back down. I looked his way as I joined him. "Thank you for doing this, and I'm sure you already figured this out, but don't let the other guys know what this song is really about, please?"

Evan gave me a lopsided smile. "Don't worry about that. They'll just think I talked you into writing a song about one of my misguided love affairs with a skank." He let out a laugh, then turned and socked me in the shoulder, hard. I cringed as my shoulder started throbbing.

"Ow! What the fuck was that for?"

"Skank," he muttered, shaking his head. "You're an asshole."

Rubbing my arm, I nodded, then laughed. "Yeah, I know I am."

Writing a song took time. Sometimes, it took a lot of time. But I didn't have a lot of time. Every second, I was conscious of the fact that I was sacrificing moments with Kiera to do this. But I had to. I had to have this ready to go for when it was finally time to part ways. For good. And that could be any day now. It all depended on Denny, and how quickly he started piecing things together. The clock ticking in my brain was not helping with my creative process.

Evan stayed home with me, and we worked long into the night. I fell asleep on the couch, covered in music sheets and mutilated lyrics. The next day, I woke up early and attacked it again. My eyes ached, my fingers were sore, my brain was fried, but I kept at it until we had to leave for a show we were playing downtown. After the show, I crashed at Evan's again so I could fall asleep working on it and resume the second I woke up. The quicker I finished this, the quicker I could return to Kiera.

By Thursday afternoon, it was done and ready for the band to practice. Evan and I let out a long exhale of relief when it was completed. Looking over at me, Evan muttered, "It's been fun, but let's not ever do this again, okay?" Laughing, I nodded. No, writing a song, setting it to music, and memorizing how to perform it all in the span of a few days was not something I wanted to make a habit of. It had turned out good though. The song was well worthy of Kiera.

When Matt and Griffin came over, we began playing the song. I wanted the guys to know it well enough that we could include it in the lineup at a moment's notice. I had a feeling there wouldn't be much warning when it came time to play it. Practice went longer than usual, and Griffin was getting cranky and willful, so we called it a night. As Matt and Griffin headed out to Pete's, Evan clapped my shoulder. "You want to go tonight? Get some fresh air?"

I debated what I wanted to do. Seeing Kiera was a great option, an almost undeniable draw, but there was something else I wanted. A song was only part of my goodbye. "No, there's something else I need to do tonight. Want to help me with one last thing?"

Evan sighed, but nodded. "Sure, man. What are we doing?"

Knowing he wouldn't expect my answer, I crooked a grin. "We're going shopping."

Evan closed his eyes. "Shit." I was laughing when he cracked an eye open. "You realize how much you owe me, right?"

I clapped him on the back as I stood up. "Yes, I'm basically your bitch for the next year."

"Damn right, you are," he muttered as he stood up and grabbed his coat. "All right, let's do this." On his way out the door, he tossed out, "I'm driving the Chevelle though."

"Fuck that," I answered. Nobody drove my baby but me.

Smiling, Evan turned to me with an outstretched hand. "You owe me, remember?"

My jaw dropped. "Serious?" He made no reaction, just smiled wider. With a frown, I reached into my coat and grabbed my keys. Feeling like I was handing over my firstborn, I placed them in his palm. "We're now even," I murmured.

Evan laughed as he clenched his fingers around the keys. "Ah, Kell, we're not even close to being even yet."

He was chuckling as he sauntered down to my car. Chuckling! This was going to hurt almost as much as what I had to buy...

With white knuckles, I had Evan drive us to the mall. He groaned as he pulled into the parking garage. I groaned at how fast he was taking the corners. "You know a car could fly down the path and cream us any second, right?"

"We're in a muscle car, Kellan. I think we'd cream them." The tires screeched as he made a turn.

"Let's not find out!" I yelled, irritated.

When he pulled into a stall, he clapped my shoulder. "You're far too attached to this thing. You need to relax."

"Thing?" I yanked the car keys from the ignition. "I stay loyal to the 'things' I like. I don't change them out every six months on a whim. If you ask me, you're far too unattached."

Evan gave me a strange look. "Yeah...you might be right."

Shoving the keys back into my jacket, where they belonged, I climbed out of the car and started planning where I wanted to go first. "We need to find a jewelry store." Evan groaned again.

We searched every jewelry store in the mall, but I couldn't find what I was looking for. Eventually, Evan and I left the mall and started seeking out stores elsewhere. We were roaming the streets downtown when I finally spotted exactly what I wanted in a display case in a window. "That's it," I said, dragging him inside.

416

"Thank God," he muttered, looking like we'd been at this for days instead of hours.

The store was about to close, so I quickly found a salesperson. A tall woman, impeccably dressed, with long, straight auburn hair was locking some engagement rings into a case as a happy couple walked away from her. For a moment, as I watched the couple leave, a spike of jealousy flashed through me. The man had his arm around the girl, and she was staring at the new ring on her finger. They were getting their happily ever after, and I was preparing for lifelong misery. It didn't seem fair, but then again, when was life ever fair? Especially to me.

Pulling my gaze away, I stepped up to the woman at the counter. "Excuse me, I'd like to see something."

Pausing in locking the case, she looked up at me. Her smile widened as her eyes flicked over my face. "Oh…hello…" Pulling the rack of engagement rings back out, she said, "Are you looking for a ring to give your sweetheart?"

Wistfully, I shook my head. "No…I'm not." Raising my eyes to hers, I indicated the window with my thumb. "I'd like to see the guitar necklace, please."

Relocking the rings, she straightened and started heading over to the window. "Ah, yes, that's a lovely piece, isn't it?" Opening the display with a key, she glanced at my ring finger, then murmured, "For your…girlfriend?"

I pursed my lips, wondering if that was what Kiera was to me. "No…I don't know. We're…complicated."

With a nod, the saleswoman removed the necklace from the fabric display neckpiece. "Say no more. We see a lot of…complicated situations in here."

She handed me the necklace, and my fingers were shaking as I took it. The guitar was perfectly crafted, delicate but sturdy, and there was a large circle diamond in the center that sparkled in the lights. It was me, and it was Kiera…the perfect embodiment of what we were, or rather, what we'd never be. I couldn't think of anything better to give her to help her remember me and what we'd gone through. "I'll take it," I whispered, not even looking at the price tag.

"Excellent," the woman beamed. "I'll go ring it up for you."

While she walked away, Evan stepped up to me. "Kellan…you can't expect her to wear that. It's too obvious."

I shook my head as I stared at the glow emanating from the diamond. "I don't expect her to. I don't expect anything. But this is what I want to give her." My eyes were watering when I looked over at him. "This is how I want to say goodbye."

Evan gave me a sad, understanding nod. Not wanting to start bawling in the middle of a high-end jewelry store, I sniffed back the emotion and walked over to the register. The woman was preparing a fancy velvet-lined box. I probably wouldn't use it. I didn't want a fancy presentation, I just wanted Kiera to have it. She pressed a few buttons on her machine, then spouted out a high-four-figure total. Evan started choking and coughing simultaneously. He'd probably never paid that much for jewelry. I hadn't either, but for this…I'd gladly pay three times as much if I had to.

The saleswoman was checking me out the entire time she boxed up my purchase. After she handed it to me with my receipt, she gave me her business card. "If you ever find yourself not in a complicated relationship…call me."

She gave me a glorious smile and a playful wink. In another life, I would have taken her up on that offer. Not now though. I handed the card back to her. "I'll never be out of this relationship. Not really. She has me for life."

The saleswoman's smile fell away. "Lucky girl," she whispered.

My answering smile was faint. *Yeah, lucky girl.* Except, not all luck was good.

When we left the store, small bag in hand, Evan frowned at me. I frowned back. I figured he would be happy that we were done shopping. With a compassionate voice, he said, "I'm sorry you're going through this. I know it sucks. Well, I can imagine it sucks. I guess I don't really know."

I nodded and looked out over the streets that were starting to empty. "It sucks and it doesn't suck. It's horrible and it's amazing, all at the same time. That's what makes it so hard."

He gave me a sympathetic smile. "You're doing the right thing by walking away. If you do it early enough, Denny may not ever know."

I studied the ground. The right thing didn't always feel like the right thing. Sometimes it just felt like shit. "Yeah…" Looking back up at him, I said, "I don't feel like going to Pete's tonight. Would you mind practicing the song with me again? Just the two of us. I'll do Matt's part, and we can get through it without a bass line."

Evan's eyes were contemplative as he studied me. "Sure thing, man. Whatever you need."

Chapter 28

Making Love

I ended up staying at Evan's, perfecting my goodbye song for Kiera, until I passed out from exhaustion. Evan was still sleeping when I quietly left his place in the morning. I felt worn from the inside out when I settled into my car, but I felt ready to say goodbye. Some small part of me was still hoping I wouldn't have to... but I knew that was ridiculous. Why in the hell would she give up her perfect relationship with Denny for a broken hunk of junk like me?

Denny's car was gone from the driveway when I pulled up. I'd been gone for so long, what day it was escaped me. It must be Friday. Matt would have hunted me down by now if I'd missed our gig at the bar. The house was quiet when I stepped inside. I looked into the living room, then walked into the kitchen. When I didn't spot her, I figured Kiera was upstairs. Or gone. I hoped she wasn't gone.

Even though my clothes were clean—I'd washed and dried them, and myself, last night while working on the song with Evan—I wanted to peel them off me. I'd been wearing the same outfit for days. When I reached the top step, I heard a door opening. I looked up in time to see Kiera leaving the bathroom. She looked fresh and clean, with her long brown hair curled and bouncing around her shoulders. Her full lips shone with a rosy tint, and her cheeks were highlighted with a light peach color that hinted at the flush that crept up her skin when she was embarrassed. Everything about her was perfect...except her eyes. There was more brown than green in the wide depths this morning, and they looked as worn as I felt. As her eyes quickly filled with tears, I thought she was suffering from as much restrained pain as me. Was that a good thing, or a bad thing?

With a reassuring smile, I gave her my typical greeting. "Mornin'." I wondered if she could tell that in my head, I always added the word *beautiful* after that.

I started walking toward her, but that was too slow for Kiera. She ran to me. Tossing her arms around my neck, she buried her head in my shoulder and started to cry. That wasn't the reaction I'd been hoping for. I held her tight while she sobbed out, "I thought you left. I thought I'd never see you again."

Feeling horrible for being gone so long, I rubbed her back. "I'm sorry, Kiera. I didn't mean to hurt you. I needed...to take care of something."

She pulled away from me, then smacked me in the chest. Her eyes were fiery as she snapped, "Don't ever do that again!" Amused at how cute she was when she was angry, I put a hand on her cheek. Her anger faded as she stared at me. In a softer voice, she added, "Don't leave me like that..."

From the way she said it, it was clear she thought I *would* leave her one day. She was right, and she was wrong. I would leave her to save her. To save her relationship with the man she deserved to be with, the one she truly wanted, I would back down. But I would say goodbye first. "I wouldn't, Kiera. I wouldn't just...disappear." *I won't leave us unfinished. I'll give you closure.*

As I stroked her cheek, Kiera studied my eyes. I loved it when she looked at me. I could swim for days in her ever-shifting eyes. Out of the blue, Kiera spoke a set of words I'd been waiting a lifetime to hear...

"I love you."

The words were so simple, a barely speaking child could learn them, but they were so damn powerful...lives had been destroyed

421

because of them. And their effect on me was immediate. My eyes burned as moisture worked its way to the surface. I shut them and twin tears worked their way down my cheeks. I felt like sobbing, I felt like laughing. Joy and pain spun around within me in an agonizing dance, and I had no idea which emotion was in the lead. *She does love me. Someone loves me.*

I felt Kiera brush my tears aside. "I love you...so much."

The honesty in her voice, the sadness, the compassion, the elation...it all made me want to crumple to my knees, wrap my arms around her, and never let her go. *How can I leave the only person who has ever admitted they loved me?* More tears escaped my eyes as I opened them. "Thank you. You don't know how much I've wanted...How long I've waited..."

I could barely speak through the torrent of emotions circulating throughout my body, slicing me open and yet healing me, all at the same time. Kiera didn't let me finish. She didn't need an explanation; she knew my inner turmoil, my lifetime of pain. And right now, she wanted me to feel more than the emptiness of my lonely, disconnected existence. She wanted to show me the love she felt for me, and I wanted to let her.

Raising her lips to mine, she stopped my painful revelation with a tender kiss. I cupped her cheek with my other hand, savoring her warmth. Gently pulling on my neck, Kiera urged me to follow her. Our mouths still moving together, I did. She led us into my bedroom and stopped us beside the bed. Without a word, with our lips only momentarily pausing, we undressed. When her body was bare before me—perfectly sculpted, lean, athletic, yet soft and arousing—I pulled back to admire her.

"You are so beautiful," I whispered, running a hand through her wavy hair.

She didn't blush with my compliment this time; a warm smile was her only response. Bringing my lips back to hers, I gently eased her onto the bed. I didn't want to rush this. I wanted to know every curve of her body by heart. I wanted to hear every noise she made when I touched her, and I wanted to understand what each sound meant. I wanted to please her, give her a moment that she would never forget, because this was going to be with *me* forever.

My fingers moved against her skin as effortlessly as they moved against my guitar. And the sounds that came from her were just as wondrous as that instrument. Even though our bodies were ready, we took our time. Her hands ran along my shoulders, down my back. Mine traced the ridges of her ribs, the curve of her hip. Her mouth placed soft kisses along my jaw line, mine trailed down her neck. By the time my lips wandered down to her breasts, she was arching her back with need. A moan escaped me as I lovingly wrapped my mouth around her nipple. *I want this every day.*

When I could finally leave her chest, I traveled farther south. Kiera clutched my skin, squeezing, then smoothing, as the anticipation climbed higher. I stretched it out as long as possible, touching every part of her except the one part she really wanted. When I finally did run my tongue over the most sensitive part of her, the cry she let out was glorious. *I want her so much.*

Then I was gently pushed to my back, and Kiera explored me. She followed my cues, touching, teasing, loving me with gentle strokes. Closing my eyes, I enjoyed the sensation of her skin on mine. Nothing felt better than this. My heart and soul were connected to every move she made. And even when her tongue traveled along the deep V of my abdomen, what I felt the most was a bone-deep, life-changing love for her.

When it was clear that another teasing touch from either of us was going to drive us over the edge, I rolled her to her back and moved over the top of her. A part of me wanted to hurry up and plunge inside her, but I didn't want to rush this either. This might be it for us; I didn't want it to be over too quickly.

Locking eyes with Kiera, I slowly slid into her. I closed mine as the intensity washed over me. Every millimeter I moved was exquisite. I'd never felt anything so powerful, and for half a second, I worried that I wouldn't make it long enough to please her.

I didn't move when we were fully connected. I couldn't. I needed a minute. Kiera's fingers brushed my cheek, and her words breezed past my ear. "I love you."

Opening my eyes, I gazed down at the beautiful, incredible woman beneath me. "I love you so much."

Clenching her hand, I started to move. Bliss tore through me. "Kiera...I love you," I whispered.

Her head dropped back as her hips met mine. "I love you..."

We kept the pace slow and unhurried; even still, I could feel the pressure building. I ignored it as best I could and allowed myself to concentrate on her face, her noises, and the feeling bursting inside my chest. The emotion of the moment was dwarfing my rising climax. I never knew love could be like this...

After a long time that felt much too short, Kiera began breathing faster and her muscles started stiffening beneath me. I knew she was close. Slightly picking up my pace, I prepared myself to let go. *Let go, and love her.* Her hand in mine tightened, and her lips parted as her breath increased. She was so beautiful when she came. I could see the instant she hit her peak, and I released the precarious hold on my control. The burst of euphoria shot through me a second later, and I murmured her name as I rode it out. My name left her lips, and my bliss was twofold. *She loves me.*

The joy subsided into peaceful happiness, and after removing myself from her, I rolled onto my back. Not wanting us to be too far apart, I pulled her into my chest. She was so warm, so soft, so...wonderful. That entire experience had opened me to something I'd never known before, and I suddenly understood what the term "making love" really meant. Sex was only a small part of sex.

Wishing this moment could last forever, and knowing that wasn't possible, I held her close and listened to my heart slow down. When Kiera looked up at me, there were shiny tear trails down her cheeks and a sad smile on her lips. I understood her tears; I could feel my own eyes stinging in response. *I want to keep this. I don't want to let you go.*

"I love you," I whispered.

"I love you too," she said with a kiss.

Her words made my heart sizzle with painful joy. Unbidden, thoughts of never seeing her again entered my head. Thoughts of her and Denny entered my head. Thoughts of being alone for the rest of my life entered my head. Was that my destiny? Closing my eyes, I shut out the worries I didn't want to have right now. Kiera was in my arms, and that was all I wanted to concentrate on.

A tear leaked out when I closed my eyes though, and Kiera spotted it. "What are you thinking about?" she asked, her voice tentative.

"Nothing," I answered, keeping my eyes closed. I wanted to block out the world. Everything but her in my arms.

Kiera didn't buy my answer, even though I was being honest. I could feel her inspecting me more closely, so I opened my eyes. "I'm trying to not think about anything. It hurts too much when I think…"

Biting her lip and looking apologetic, Kiera repeated, "I love you."

I nodded as my doubts became words. "Just not enough…not enough to leave him?"

Kiera closed her eyes while I cringed. Why did I say that? I didn't mean to make this even harder on her. I just…that was the most amazing thing I'd ever experienced, and I couldn't imagine giving it up. I couldn't imagine giving her up. Couldn't picture how empty my world would be once she was gone.

While Kiera looked like she was struggling to not cry, I ran a hand down her hair. "It's okay, Kiera. I shouldn't have said that."

"Kellan, I'm so sorry…"

I put a finger on her lips to stop her from saying what I didn't want to hear right now. "Not today." Smiling, I pulled her in for a kiss. "Not today…okay?"

Kiera nodded, and we both put that painful conversation aside. There would be time for that later. Right here, right now, my arms around Kiera were all that mattered.

Breaking apart from my lips, Kiera said, "Do you think…? If we had never, that first time…would the three of us just be close friends?"

Interpreting what she meant, I smiled. "If you and I had never gotten drunk and had sex, would we all be living happily ever after right now?" She nodded while I considered that. Remembering how I felt about her back then, and how she had looked at me, I knew the answer almost immediately. "No...you and I were always more than just friends. One way or another, we would have ended up right here anyway."

Kiera nodded, then looked down to my chest. I stroked her arm and wondered what she was thinking. "Do you regret it?" I finally asked her. Was she wishing we had somehow never come to pass? That was a painful thought, but I suppose I could understand why she would have it.

She looked up at me. "I regret being horrible to Denny." I nodded and looked away. I could understand that too. I felt the same. Kiera placed a hand on my cheek and made me look at her. "I don't regret a single second that I spent with you. No time spent with you is wasted."

Hearing her repeat my line made me smile. So did her answer. She didn't regret *me*, just the circumstances surrounding me, surrounding us. I regretted those too, regretted who we were hurting in our path to each other, but I'd never regret *her*. She was everything to me.

I pulled her lips to mine, then rolled her over so her back was flush to my mattress. We had time before Denny was due home, and as long as she was mine, I was going to enjoy her.

After spending all day in bed with Kiera, it was difficult to leave her. Well, okay, it would have been difficult to leave her regardless, but our amazing afternoon together made it even harder. I wanted to freeze time so nothing between us would change. She had tears in her eyes when I said goodbye. I kissed her eyelids, assuring her that I'd see her at Pete's. It was Friday after all, and I had a show to do. Life trudged on, whether we wanted it to or not.

When I got to Evan's for rehearsal, everybody was already there. Matt looked over at me as I walked through the door. "Hey, Kell. Ready to rock?"

I nodded. We didn't always practice on the nights we played at Pete's, but I'd asked for a rehearsal tonight. "Let's run through the new song again."

Griffin slugged Evan in the shoulder. "This is 'cause of you, isn't it? Some chick break your heart again?" He shook his head in disgust. "Freaking pansy. You won't ever catch me mooning over some girl. Plenty of fish, bro. Plenty of fish."

Evan gave him an amused smile, then raised an eyebrow at me. Like he'd predicted, the guys thought he was the reason behind the song. That worked for me.

While we played the song again, I thought about being wrapped in Kiera's arms today. It was a perfect moment, and one I was afraid wouldn't ever happen again. It was hard to imagine never again feeling that connection. It was also hard to imagine sharing her with Denny. The thought of her being intimate like that with him...it made me want to throw up. I pushed that dilemma from my mind. I didn't want to deal with it yet.

After a quick rehearsal, we made our way to Pete's. Denny's Honda was in the parking lot. I was surprised to see it there, and I considered turning around and leaving. I couldn't though; I had a job to do. Even though it was sooner than I would have liked, I knew I needed to eventually face him. We did live together, after all. I guess tonight was as good a night as any.

He greeted me at the door with a genuine smile; like Kiera, he hadn't seen me much this week. "Hey, mate. You've been a ghost lately. Everything all right?"

I folded one arm around him in a brief hug. My chest was pounding with anxiety, my gut was churning with guilt, but I kept my expression warm and friendly. I could keep my feelings hidden when I needed to. "Yeah...just work stuff. It's been a little crazy." *I have been such a bastard to you...*

"Crazy is good," Denny said as he started walking toward the band's table. Heart in my throat, I followed him. "Anything in particular you're working on?" he asked.

Loving your girlfriend.

I couldn't tell if he was making small talk, or if he was curious for a different reason. Choosing to believe he was clueless about Kiera and me, I smiled and said, "Matt's trying to get us lined up for a festival next year. And, on top of that, he wants to soundproof Evan's loft so we can record a demo. It's quite a process."

Denny's eyes widened, and I was a little proud of my misdirect. *The best lies are based in truth.* Then I remembered who I was lying to, and a knot of disgust roiled in my belly. I was such an asshole. "Yeah, I can imagine," Denny said. "Sounds like you guys are on the right track. It won't be long till you hit it big."

I had to smirk at the notion of the D-Bags being "big" one day. Seemed like an amazing but improbable future to me, but it was just like Denny to believe we'd go far. He'd always supported and encouraged me. I wouldn't even be in a band today if it weren't for his interference, a fact that wasn't lost on me. It amplified the sick feeling in my stomach.

A loud noise across the bar stole Denny's attention, and I risked a peek at Kiera. She was staring my way, looking sad and full of longing, like she was forcing herself to stay put when all she really wanted to do was jump into my arms. I felt the same way. I'd been hoping for a little alone time at the bar with her, as much alone time as we got at Pete's at any rate, but it was clear Denny wasn't going anywhere. Kiera and I would both have to deal with this awkwardness.

When we were seated at the table, Denny gave me a calculating expression. It made my muscles tighten with tension. "What?" I asked, keeping my expression even.

"I know this isn't any of my business, but…" He paused, and I could see the debate in his eyes. "Kiera's sister…"

Sighing, I looked at the table. *Oh good…he wants to talk about the fake story Kiera cooked up. That, I can handle.* "Yeah…you know about that?"

Denny nodded. "Kiera told me that was why she hit you, which wasn't cool on her part, but…neither was what you did, mate." I looked up and made eye contact with him. I stayed silent, neither

428

agreeing nor disagreeing. When he saw that I wasn't going to be a dick, he added, "Kiera said you hurt Anna's feelings when you never called her. If you didn't want a relationship, you should have been honest with her from the beginning."

I bit back a dark smile. *Honest with her from the beginning?* Yeah, that was a lesson I'd learned the hard way. Maintaining eye contact, I gave him a somber nod. He clapped my shoulder. "I don't mean to scold you, it's your life, but try to keep people's feelings in mind, okay?" He lifted an eyebrow. "Trust me. I almost lost everything because I didn't do that."

He glanced over at Kiera and I forced myself to not turn and look at her. I felt like he'd just stuck a sword in my gut, then twisted it in a circle about five times. *He almost lost everything...* Had he? Only time would tell.

Since Denny was still clueless, I left the goodbye song out of the lineup. That was a last resort song—the end of the road—and Kiera and I weren't there yet. We still had time, although I was feeling that time slip between my fingers with every passing second. I cast Kiera longing glances all throughout my set. I couldn't help myself. Denny didn't notice though. He was too busy watching Kiera with concerned eyes, like he knew something was wrong, he just didn't know what it was.

Denny stayed until Kiera's shift was over. I debated heading home while they were still here. If I followed after them, I would have to endure watching them walk into their bedroom together, and that would tear me up. While I gathered myself to leave, Jenny approached me.

"Kellan...what are you doing?" she whispered. Her gaze flicked to Kiera, and I knew she wasn't talking about this exact second.

I sighed. "I don't know. And if I knew how to get out of this without hurting anyone, believe me, Jenny, I would." I raised my arms. "I honestly don't know what to do."

She frowned at my answer. "Then why get involved in the first place? She was happy with him, you shouldn't have—"

"I didn't mean to," I interrupted.

429

She gave me a stern expression. "Didn't mean to? He's one of your best friends, Kellan. That's an automatic stop sign, regardless of the circumstances. I know you don't usually care about stuff like that, but...you should have known better."

Out of the corner of my eye, I saw Denny and Kiera leaving the bar. So much for beating them home. Not having any excuse worth giving, I merely said, "I know. But I'm an asshole, and I did it anyway, so...now what do I do?"

Jenny shook her head. "Now you tell him."

My gut clenched at the thought of confronting him. How could I hurt him like that? He'd never look at me the same. *I'm here for you, Kellan. I'll always be here for you.*

I took my time going home. I drove five miles under the speed limit. I made wrong turns that took me all over town, all in the hopes that Denny and Kiera would be sound asleep when I stepped through my door. I gave new meaning to the word "avoidance."

Everything was quiet when I eventually made it home. Tiptoeing upstairs, I got ready for bed. How could we keep doing this while we all lived together? Easy...we couldn't. The friction, tension, and jealousy would tear us apart. It had already strained us. Lying under my covers, I stared at the ceiling and waited for sleep to come. It didn't...but something else did.

My bedroom door creaked open. Sitting up on my elbows, I watched Kiera slip through the crack, then shut the door behind her. What the hell was she doing here? She was resplendent in her clingy tank top and loose pajama bottoms. She seemed to glow in the silver moonlight, and her eyes were bright, with no trace of sleep in them. She'd waited up for me. Why?

Before I could question her, she slipped into my bed, wrapped her legs around mine and her arms around my neck. Her sudden weight on top of me knocked me back down to the pillows. She was with me again. "Am I dreaming?" I whispered as her lips closed the distance to mine. *If I am, please don't let me wake up.*

As our lips moved together, I ran my hands up her back, tangled

430

my fingers in her hair. "I missed you," I murmured, deepening our kiss.

"I missed you too...so much."

Her words warmed and chilled me. It felt so right to be in her arms, and so wrong. Our breaths quickly became heavy with lust, love, and desire. I was hard, aching, and I wanted her so much I almost couldn't take it. I needed more. Reading my thoughts, Kiera paused in kissing me and ripped off her tank top. A surge ran through my groin, and I struggled with controlling myself. Running my hand across her luscious breasts, I murmured, "What are you doing, Kiera?"

She pressed her chest to mine and kissed my neck in answer. Hating what I was about to say, I tried pouring reasoning-ice on the situation. "Kiera, Denny is right—"

It didn't work. She cut me off with swift, heartfelt words that were stronger than all the logic in the world. "I love you, and I missed you. Make love to me."

She pulled off the rest of her clothes. *Yes*... "Kiera..."

Her hands ran up and down my body, igniting me. She felt so good...Her fingers began pulling on my boxers, wanting the last barrier between us gone. *Yes*...

"I love you...Make love to me," she whispered in my ear.

Wishing I could let go of the guilt, I glanced at my door, then back to her face. "Are you sur—"

"I'm sure," she immediately answered, her lips attacking mine.

Against my will, Denny's face entered my mind. *I'm always here for you.* Then I saw his expression shift into one of horror, disgust...betrayal. *What have you done?* I pulled away from Kiera's intense kiss. "Wait...I can't." My breath was a fast pant, but it was my torn heart that was killing me. I couldn't betray him when he was just a few yards away, not that the distance of my backstabbing really mattered.

Kiera, adorable as ever, took my objection literally. "Oh...well, I can..." She wrapped her hand around my cock, and I just about came at her touch. What the hell was fate trying to do to me?

431

"Ah, you're killing me, Kiera." Pulling her hand away, I let out an amused laugh. At least her little stunt had replaced some of my guilt with humor. My chest felt a little looser when I clarified my comment. "That's not what I meant. I can...obviously, but I don't think we should."

Her expression both confused and hurt, she said, "But, this afternoon? That was...Didn't you...? I...Don't you want me?"

Shocked that she'd take my rejection personally when it was so obvious I wanted her, I immediately responded with "Of course, of course I do." I looked down at my body, which was hard as a rock in all the right spots, then back up at her. "You should know that." Her reciprocating smile was beautifully shy. Wanting her to know what it had meant to me, I told her, "This afternoon was the most...I've never had anything like that. I didn't even know it could be like that, which, for me, is saying a lot." I gave her a sheepish grin, and she smiled wider in return.

"Don't you want that again?" she asked, stroking my cheek.

My words echoed what was running through my mind and my heart. "More than anything." On this one point, all of me agreed.

"Then take me," she murmured, kissing me again.

I groaned as her body pressed against me. *Yes...but we shouldn't do this.* "God, Kiera. Why do you make everything so...?" *Wonderful. Painful.*

Kiera's answer was more playful than mine. "Hard?" she whispered before averting her eyes. I had to laugh at how like me she was becoming. Her face more serious, she returned her eyes to mine. "I love you, Kellan. I feel like time is slipping away from us. I don't want to miss a minute."

That was exactly how I'd been feeling. This could be our last time together, right now, and what would I regret more? Betraying Denny, yet again, or...missing out on making love to her one last time? Put in those terms, the answer was easy. I didn't want to miss a minute with her either. I didn't want to regret any moment with her that I'd wasted. She was mine, and as long as she was mine, I wanted to enjoy her. Because in the morning, this could all be over with.

I sighed in defeat, and she smiled in victory. "For the record, this is a really bad idea..." With a soft kiss, I rolled her to her back. "You will be the death of me," I whispered as she finally removed my shorts.

Our bodies slid together when I was free of my clothing. We clutched at each other's skin, quietly screaming our passion in fierce squeezes that I was sure were going to leave bruises. Soundlessly, I pushed my way inside her. It was so deliberately controlled that I almost couldn't breathe. Then we were one, and I had to clamp my mouth over hers to remain quiet. She felt... *incredible*.

Neither one of us wanted to make noise, so our movements were slow, restrained strokes that amplified every sensation. If I could, I would have cried out her name and begged for more. I would have plunged into her harder and faster, driving us both over the edge instead of teasingly skirting around it. All I could do was clamp her hand tight in mine and lose myself to the overwhelming sensations rippling through my body. The pleasure was indescribable torture.

It went on for an eternity; I was shaking with the need to release. Even though I was maintaining the slowness, I finally felt the build approaching. Kiera's was approaching too. She started moaning. It was too loud, and I clamped my hand over her mouth. She dropped her head back, tightened her legs around mine, and sank her nails into my shoulders. I could feel her walls clenching around me, and I hit the wall too. I clamped my mouth onto her shoulder as waves and waves of pleasure overtook me. It was so intense...more so, because of our restraint. I never wanted it to stop.

When it inevitably did, Kiera and I stayed close together, side by side. No words passed between us, just soft kisses and gentle strokes. I wanted nothing more than to fall asleep with her in my arms this way, but I knew that couldn't happen. The tick of time was loud in my mind.

"You should go back to your room," I whispered.

"No," she said, unflinchingly.

I was heartened by her refusal to leave, but guilt was bearing

433

down on me. We couldn't be caught like this. I couldn't do that to Denny. "It's nearly morning, Kiera."

She glanced at my clock, startled when she realized the time, then clutched me tighter. Her stubbornness made me smile, but it was time for her to go. I kissed her head. "Wait in bed an hour, then come downstairs and have coffee with me, like we always used to."

I gave her another soft kiss, then pushed her away. I'd rather be pulling her close, but she needed to go. Denny couldn't see this. It would kill him. Her clothes were at the end of my bed, almost on the verge of falling off. I handed them to her and she pouted. Shaking my head, I started dressing her. *Stubborn woman.* When she was dressed, I sat her up, then helped her stand. "Kiera...You have to go...before it's too late. We got lucky—don't push it."

I kissed her nose while she gave me a reluctant sigh. "Okay, fine. I'll see you in an hour then."

Her eyes scanned my naked body and she sighed again, wistfully this time. Then a strange expression crossed her face as she began to leave. It was a mixture of sadness, confusion, and self-loathing. She knew what we'd done wasn't right, and she felt just as bad about it as I did. We were on this slippery slope together, trying to keep each other upright, or, more truthfully, dragging each other down.

After she left my room, I sat down on my bed, then lay back on top of my covers. The chill pricked my exposed skin, but I barely noticed because remorse was rising in me like a tidal wave, and that was colder than the air could ever be. We shouldn't have done that. We shouldn't be doing any of this. I felt dirty from head to toe, and I didn't want to feel dirty about Kiera. Not when she made me feel so...alive.

You should tell him, Jenny's voice whispered to me in the gray gloom of my room. But tell him what? That his relationship was over, or that I had been a small speed bump on his path to happiness? How could I confess my sins to him if I didn't know what the future held? And if Kiera's future didn't hold me, then why tell him at all? Regardless, I needed answers, and Kiera was the only one who had them. Knowing I was about to lose her, because there was no way in hell she would ever pick me over Denny, I got dressed and made my way downstairs.

I made some coffee and watched it fill the pot. Dread filled me just as steadily as the black liquid creeping up the carafe. This was it, the all-or-nothing moment. It felt like hours later when Kiera appeared. She removed a mug full of coffee from my hand; I didn't even remember pouring one. Wishing I could be the sort of person who was fine with being a backseat lover, I looked over at her. Still in her pajamas, she looked much the same as she had when she'd left my room. Was that the last time she'd ever be in my room?

Wrapping my arms around her waist, I gave her a light kiss and pulled her in for a hug. *I don't want to say this. I don't want you to go.* "I can't believe I'm going to say this," I began. She tensed in my arms while she waited for my statement. "Last night can't happen again, Kiera."

She pulled back to look at me, and I saw the fear and confusion on her face. I hated seeing her pain, and I knew I'd be seeing a lot more of it before we were done. "I love you, and you understand what that phrase means to me. I don't say it…to anyone…ever."

Gently removing her arms from around my neck, I intertwined our fingers. "There was a time when I would have been fine with this. I would have taken any part of you that you wanted to give to me and found a way to deal with the rest…" I ran our laced fingers over her cheek. She relaxed, but she still looked scared. "I want to be the kind of man you deserve to have." She started to speak, but I stopped her with our fingers over her lips. "I want to be honorable—"

She pulled our fingers away. "You are. You are a good man, Kellan."

"I want to be the better man, Kiera…and I'm not." With a sigh, I looked up at the ceiling, where Denny was sleeping away, oblivious to the turmoil beneath him. He deserved a much better friend than me. Returning my eyes to Kiera, I said, "Last night wasn't the honorable thing to do, Kiera…not under Denny's nose like that."

435

Her jaw clenched and her eyes watered. I realized my poor choice of words instantly. "No…I didn't mean, you're not…I wasn't trying to insult you, Kiera." I held her close. Why couldn't the words ever come out the way I wanted them to? I should have written this to her in a song, that would have been easier.

"Then what are you trying to say, Kellan?"

She sniffled and I knew she was crying. I was so bad at this… and it was only going to get worse. Closing my eyes, I took a deep breath…and took the plunge. "I want you to leave him…and stay with me." Scared out of my mind, I slowly reopened my eyes. *Okay, Kiera…rip my heart out. I'm ready.*

She only stared at me in disbelief though. Maybe she never thought I'd ask her to choose. She had to know this couldn't go on forever. Feeling courageous, since she hadn't outright dismissed me, I told her, "I'm sorry. I was going to be stoic, and say nothing for as long as you wanted me, but then we made love…and I've, I've never had that…and I just can't go back to being who I was before. I want you and only you and I can't bear the thought of sharing you. I'm sorry."

I knew I was ranting, but now that I'd opened my heart, I couldn't stop. I looked down. "I want to be with you the right way— in the open. I want to walk into Pete's with you on my arm. I want to kiss you every time I see you, no matter who's looking. I want to make love to you without fear of someone finding out. I want to fall asleep with you in my arms every night. I don't want to feel guilty about something that makes me feel so…whole. I'm sorry, Kiera, but I'm asking you to choose."

Tears rolled down her cheeks as she stared at me in shock. Was it really so surprising that I wanted to be her one and only? She was *my* only…

I watched her face as she wrestled with opposing desires. Finally, she whispered, "You're asking me to destroy him, Kellan."

Grief overwhelmed me and I closed my eyes. "I know." *Why did it have to be Denny's girl I fell for?* Tears clouded my vision when I reopened them. "I know. I just…I can't share you. The thought of

436

you with him, it kills me, now more than it ever did before. I need you. All of you."

Her eyes flared with panic, and her breath sped up. I understood. I knew what I was asking of her. "What if I don't choose you, Kellan? What will you do?"

A tear escaped my eye and rolled down my cheek as I turned away. What would I do without her? "I'll leave, Kiera. I'll leave, and you and Denny can have your happily ever after." *That's how it should be anyway.* I looked back at her. "You wouldn't even need to tell him about me. Eventually, the two of you..." Anguish ripped through my throat, choking me and cracking my voice. Another tear dripped from my eye. "The two of you would get married..." *no...marry me,* "...and have children..." *no...have my children,* "...and have a great life." *How will I live without you?*

Kiera swallowed with a pained noise. Could she see my agony? "And you?" she asked. "What happens to you in that scenario?"

I die a little each day we're apart.

"I...get by. And I miss you, every day."

Every hour, every minute...every second.

A sob escaped Kiera, and she grabbed my face and kissed me hard, like she was trying to erase my painful words. I felt completely raw, scoured from the inside out. That awful future seemed far too probable. When we broke apart, we were breathless. Tears streamed from the both of us as we rested our foreheads together. *It doesn't have to be this hard, Kiera. Choose me. I'll give you everything...* "Kiera...we could be amazing together," I pleaded.

"I need more time, Kellan...please," she whispered.

Time? Asking for time wasn't saying no...not yet. I gave her a soft kiss. "Okay, Kiera. I can give you time, but not forever." *A few more days...I can give her that. I can give myself that.*

We kissed again while our breaths and tears calmed. We weren't ending today. We weren't over yet. "I don't want to hang around the house with him today. I'm going over to Evan's."

Kiera clutched me like I'd just said I was going off to war. Maybe she thought I was running away. I wasn't. Not yet. If and when I left, she would know. "I'll see you at Pete's tonight. I'll be there." *I'm not leaving today.* I gave her one more kiss, then pulled away from her.

"Wait…now? You're leaving now?" I could hear the desire in her voice for me to stay, and it tore at me, just like it always had.

Running my hands down her hair, I cupped her cheeks. "Spend the day with Denny. Think about what I said. Maybe you'll be able to…." *Decide if you really want me.*

I couldn't say it, so I gave her a final kiss instead. With a wistful smile, I turned and left the room. Everything in my body wanted to return to her, but I needed to leave now, while I could, and maybe, when I saw her again, she'd know what she wanted. Even if that wasn't me.

Chapter 29

An Inappropriate Goodbye

I started having a panic attack in the car. My heartbeat spiked; my
breath came out in sharp puffs. I felt like I was running flat-out up
a steep hill. My legs even felt like they were cramping. What had I
done? I'd given her an ultimatum. I'd basically begun the process of
shoving her away from me. Fuck, I was an idiot. Or was I finally being smart? Hard to say. There was such a fine line between wisdom
and imbecility.

I hung out with Evan until it was time to meet the guys at Pete's.
I could have avoided that and just arrived minutes before it was
time to play, but I didn't want anything to look out of the ordinary. I was the last one to arrive at the bar, the last one to enter
its doors. My eyes locked onto Kiera the second I stepped inside.
She mouthed *Hi* in such a delightful yet erotic way that my heart
skipped a beat. I nodded a greeting back to her, then took a step
toward her. I couldn't hug her in this crowd, but I could compan-
ionably sling my arm around her shoulder. Right?

She shook her head when she noticed me approaching though.
I wasn't sure why, until her gaze slid over to the band's table. I followed her line of sight and immediately understood. Denny was
here. Again. Goddammit. I'd really hoped I could avoid him to-

day. But I couldn't. Nothing out of the ordinary, that was how I was planning on getting through this.

I gave Kiera a longing look as I let myself imagine wrapping my arms around her, then I turned toward the table. *Let the charade begin.*

Matt was starting to sit down beside Denny when I approached. Denny was…beaming. He looked so stinking happy, it made my heart drop. Why was he in such a good mood?

Careful to keep my expression neutral, I sat across the table from him. "Hey, Denny. You look…chipper?"

His smile widened. "It was a beautiful day today. What's not to be happy about?"

Evan flashed me a glance that spoke a thousand words. *He wouldn't be so happy if he knew about you and Kiera.* I already knew that, so I kept my mouth shut. If Denny was having a good day, I wasn't about to burst his bubble. I had a feeling that explosion would injure me just as much as him.

Refocusing on Denny, I slapped on a breezy smile. "That's true. How about a round on me?" I pointed at his empty beer by his half-eaten plate of food.

Griffin was all over that. Standing, he whistled to Rita at the bar. "Beer wench! Five cold ones!"

Rita narrowed her eyes like she was about to chuck all five bottles at Griffin's head. Then a slow smile passed over her lips and she nodded and called Kiera over. I was pretty certain Griffin's drink was going to have some extra body fluids in it. Hopefully Kiera didn't mix up the bottles.

When Kiera approached our table, drinks in hand, she kept throwing concerned glances my way. It made her look like she had a nervous tic. I wanted to assure her that I was fine. Yeah, hanging out with Denny was awkward, and it made me feel really guilty, but I liked Denny, and if I could somehow push all of my inner turmoil aside, I didn't mind spending time with him.

Kiera passed out the beers. Griffin's was last. She watched him take a sip of his drink with clear disgust on her face. She always looked like that around him though, so it didn't seem too odd to the others. A quick peek at Rita laughing behind the bar confirmed my suspicions—Griffin's beer was...special. Rita winked at me, and with a brief smile and a tilt of my unspecial beer, I shifted my attention back to Kiera. Denny was thanking her for his drink...with his lips.

I stared into my bottle, but I could still hear them smacking. I clenched my beer and forced calmness into my body. This was temporary. I could handle it. I nearly prayed for Kiera to leave the table though, and when she did, I let out a long exhale.

"What's the matter, mate? Your day not going as well as mine?"

Oh God, how to answer that. With a smile, I took a sip of my beer. "Apparently not. I can't complain though." *Not to you at any rate.*

Griffin snorted. "He's just sore that I nailed his chick."

Knowing where Griffin was going with his statement, I pointed my beer bottle at his. "How's your beer? Taste all right?"

Griffin's brows drew together in confusion. "Yeah...why?"

He took a long draw. My stomach roiled, and I silently hoped that I had never pissed off Rita. "No reason," I said with a laugh.

Matt laughed along with me and Griffin shot him a look. "What's so funny?"

Matt shook his head. "Nothing you'd understand." Shifting the conversation, Matt asked Denny, "So, anything exciting going on, or just having a good day?"

My stomach churned again, but for an entirely different reason. I was 99 percent sure I didn't want to hear this. "I got a job offer. A great job offer." Matt and Evan congratulated him while my stomach clenched so tight, I was sure I was damaging my internal organs. "Thanks. Yeah, I'm excited about it. I thought I'd have to tell them no, because I was sure Kiera wouldn't want to move that far, but she said she wanted to go."

I felt like someone had just dropped me down a deep, dark shaft, and I was free-falling, but only for a moment. The ground was rushing up to meet me, and I would die upon impact, I just knew it. "Move...where?" I asked in a whisper.

441

Denny looked over at Kiera before shifting his eyes to me. "Back home. Australia." He gave me a small smile. "I'll be sad to leave here, I've enjoyed hanging out with you again, but this is an amazing opportunity for me, for us. This could be the start of something big, you know?" His smile warmed as he looked over at Kiera again.

Yep. I felt like I'd just smacked face-first into the bottom of that endless hole, and I was now a lifeless corpse. DOA. I heard the others telling Denny congratulations and wishing him well. I felt Evan clap me on the shoulder, in sympathy, I assumed, but it was like I was experiencing the moment outside of my body, like I was hovering in the air, looking down at Denny and the guys. External sounds were muffled, and all I could clearly hear was my heavy heartbeat.

She said she'd leave with him? Jesus...she chose him...

"Kellan...Kellan...?"

When it finally registered that Denny was speaking to me, I shook my head to snap myself out of the odd out-of-body feeling I was having. "What? Oh, uh...congratulations, man. That's...that's great news. I can see why you're so...happy."

Denny searched my face. His dark eyes were brimming with concern. "You okay? You kind of look like you're going to be sick."

Yes, I think I am going to be sick. Forcing a smile to my face, I shook my head. "I've been fighting something...but I'm okay."

His brows drew together into a suspicious point. "Oh, sorry to hear that."

Matt piped up beside him. "So, when you leaving?"

Denny started answering him. I heard the words, "When Kiera's done with school," and then I tuned him out. *She's leaving...I* looked over to where Kiera was standing beside an empty table. She was staring at me, and for a brief second, I wondered if she could see my turmoil. If she knew that I knew what she'd done today. Not lingering on her long, I pointedly looked over to the back hallway. *Meet me there, I need to talk to you. Now.*

I didn't look back at her to see if she'd understood my silent message. Instead, I finished my beer, stood up, and made my way to the bathrooms. Having to pee shouldn't raise any red flags.

Once I was in the hallway, I darted into the back room and found an OUT OF ORDER sign and some tape. I could talk to Kiera back here in the supply room, but the lock on the door wasn't working. We'd have more privacy in a broken bathroom, and right now, I needed to be alone with her. I needed answers. *She chose him...*

Figuring Kiera would be more comfortable in the ladies' room, I checked to make sure the women's bathroom was empty, then I taped the sign on the door. After I was done, I leaned against the wall in the space between the two restrooms and waited. When Kiera appeared, a smile broke over me. I couldn't help the reaction. She was so beautiful, and I'd missed her today. I hadn't even spoken to her since this morning. Reaching out for her hand, I opened the door to the women's room with my other.

She pointed at the sign as she walked by. "Did you...?"

I answered her with a smile, but it faded from me once we were in the privacy of the empty bathroom. "Are you going to Australia with Denny?" *Please say no.*

Her eyes widened. "What? Where did you hear that?"

My stomach dropped. That wasn't a denial. "Denny... he's telling everyone, Kiera. What did you tell him?" *Did you choose him? Are we over?*

Kiera closed her eyes and leaned against the wall, like this was all too much for her. "I'm sorry. He was asking the wrong questions. I just needed time."

She reopened her eyes, and they looked very apologetic. The hollow in my stomach slowly filled with fire. She hadn't made a decision yet, but she was stringing Denny along with empty promises. If she didn't follow through, he was going to be doubly crushed. I could understand being backed into a corner, but she shouldn't have done that.

"So you told him you would leave the country with him? Kiera, God! Can't you ever stop and think before you just spit things out!"

I pinched my nose, trying to ease the headache I felt coming. She'd just made this so much harder than it needed to be.

"I know it was stupid, but in the moment, it seemed like the right thing to say." Her voice was small, like she truly did realize her mistake.

Hating all of this, I sarcastically tossed out, "God, Kiera...did you agree to marry him too?" *Wouldn't that just be the topper on the cake?*

I waited for her to huff out an "Of course not," but she didn't say it. She didn't say anything. Her silence bounced around the room like the roar of a jet engine. "Did he...did he ask you?"

"I didn't say yes," she immediately whispered.

I instantly caught the problem in the way she'd worded that. "But you didn't say no." My hand dropped from my face, like all the strength had been sapped from it. The brief fire I'd felt was blown out in a puff of icy wind billowing through my chest. *She hadn't immediately said no...she was thinking about saying yes.*

"He never really asked. He just said that when we were there... we could...like, eventually, years from now..." She was clearly at a loss as to how to save me from this pain. She couldn't.

"Are you...considering it?"

She stepped toward me. "I need time, Kellan."

Again, her answer was not a denial. She *was* thinking about it. She was still thinking about a life with him, a future with him, children with him...

My next words slipped out before I could stop them. "Did you sleep with him?"

Kiera looked horrified as she froze in place. "Kellan...don't ask that."

I felt an imaginary knife plunging deep and exploding out my back. "Don't ask" meant "Yes, I did." Fuck. Me. She slept with him. The rage built inside me so fast, the room began to haze in my vision. I turned away; I couldn't look at her anymore. "So, until you decide, how exactly does this work? Should Denny and I draw up a schedule?" When I returned my eyes to her, all common sense had fled from me. Only the anger in my stomach kept me standing. "Do I get you during the week, and he gets weekends, or should we just do the week-on, week-off thing?" Wishing I could stop my mouth, I heard myself spit out, "Or how about we all fuck together? Would you prefer that?"

Calmer than I would have been, Kiera walked over and put her hand on my cheek. "Kellan... filter."

I blinked as the anger in my body dissipated. I'd hoped she wouldn't sleep with him... but he was her boyfriend, what did I expect? *I* was the outcast, the usurper, the third wheel. *I* was the bad guy here, and as much as I wanted to, I couldn't put all of my anger on her. I gave her a small, embarrassed smile. "Right... sorry. I'm just... I'm not okay with this, Kiera." *If there is no hope, cut me loose. Please.*

A tear fell onto her cheek as she kissed me. "I'm not either, Kellan. I don't want this anymore. I don't want to feel guilty. I don't want to lie. I don't want to hurt people. I just don't know how to choose."

She doesn't know which one of us she wants... There's still hope for us. I stared at her for long seconds as that thought sank into my brain. "Can I plead my case?" I whispered. Grabbing her head, I pulled her in for a deep *Choose me* kiss.

As we sought comfort in each other's embrace, a light knock sounded on the door. Wanting whoever it was to go away, I ignored it. "Guys? It's me... Jenny." Kiera and I both continued ignoring her; whatever she wanted could wait. Kiera and I didn't have much time together, and she tasted so good...

Jenny wasn't one to be ignored for long, so she opened the door and came inside. Since she knew everything anyway, Kiera and I kept right on kissing. "Uh... Kiera, sorry, but you wanted me to find you?"

Kiera nodded and I smiled, but we didn't stop kissing. I never wanted to stop kissing her. Jenny, sounding a little irritated, told us, "Uh, okay... can you guys stop doing that?"

My reply was instant. "No," I muttered around Kiera's lips.

445

Whatever she wanted, she could tell us while we kissed. And if it made her uncomfortable, she didn't have to watch.

While Kiera laughed in my mouth, Jenny sighed and said, "Okay, then. Well, two things actually. One, Kellan, you're up."

I gave her a thumbs-up, which made Kiera laugh again. I took the opportunity to stroke the roof of her mouth with my tongue. If I had more time, I would have stroked a lot more of her with my tongue...

Jenny sighed again. "Second, Denny talked to Griffin."

That got my attention. Fucking Griffin.

The moment over, Kiera and I broke apart. Looking over at Jenny, we simultaneously said, "What?"

Jenny's expression was sullen as she shrugged. "I tried to sideline Griffin, but Denny was talking about you having a hard time leaving your family." She paused to give Kiera a withering look. "Denny casually mentioned Anna, so, naturally, Griffin told him every gory detail of their time together while she was here." She cringed. Jenny had heard those details before. We all had. Except Kiera... and Denny. "Denny, of course, brought up Kellan and Anna, and the fight between you and Kellan in the bar. Griffin got all bent out of shape. He vehemently denied that Kellan had ever slept with her. That he actually took Anna out from under Kellan, and that..." She looked over at me, and seemed reluctant to finish her thought. "...Kellan was a prick for trying to... and I'm quoting here... 'nab his score.'" She cringed again, then looked over at Kiera. "I'm sorry, Kiera... but Denny knows that you lied."

So that was it. The charade was over. Oddly enough, I felt completely calm. I guess all of my preparation for this moment had paid off. Kiera couldn't choose, Denny was about to figure it out. It was time for me to go. It was time for my final goodbye. Silently wishing I'd brought the necklace with me, so I could give it to Kiera tonight, I thanked Jenny for relaying the message.

She apologized again, then left us alone. Kiera started panicking. She wasn't prepared for this moment, like I was. Clutching my shoulders so hard I could feel her nails digging into my skin, she said, "What do we do?" Searching my face, she started running though complicated scenarios that, in the end, wouldn't save us. "Okay…it's not so bad. I'll just tell him that you lied to me…and Anna lied to me…and…" Seeing the pointlessness of lies upon lies, she looked away.

"Kiera…that won't work. He'll just be even more suspicious if you start saying that everyone else is lying. No lies will work, baby."

She looked back at me, a small smile on her lips as my term of endearment warmed her. It fell off her face in an instant though. "Then what do we do?"

I say goodbye and let you have the better man, before it's too late and you lose him forever.

Sighing, I ran a finger down her cheek. "We do the only thing we can do. I go onstage, and you go back to work."

She obviously couldn't see the solution in that. "Kellan…"

"It will be fine, Kiera. I need to go. I need to talk to Evan before we start." It was time to add our new song to the mix. I hoped the crowd liked it, and I hoped Kiera understood why I had to play it. It was better to end the lie.

Kissing her head, I left her reeling in the bathroom while I sought out Evan. He was beside the stage, getting ready to go up. I stopped him with a hand on his arm. Even though I couldn't even look Denny's way, I could feel his icy eyes on my back. Denny was a smart guy, and now that the wool had been lifted from his eyes, he knew the truth. He knew I had betrayed him.

Evan's mouth was in a firm line as he looked at me. In a low voice, he said, "Kellan, we've got trouble. Griffin—"

I put my hand up to stop him. "I know. Jenny told me. Denny knows we lied. He's figuring it out, right now."

Evan looked over my shoulder, to where Denny was still seated at our table. "Yeah, and if looks could kill, you'd be sizzling right now. You should go talk to him. Fess up."

I closed my eyes. *Talk to him.* That was what a mature, responsible man in my position would do. A man who was worthy of having Kiera. But that man wasn't me…and I couldn't face Denny.

Opening my eyes, I shook my head. "I can't...I can't deal with him yet. But I want to sing the new song tonight."

Evan's jaw dropped. "Kellan...you can't sing that with him *here*, especially since he knows now. It's a neon sign—"

I shook my head again. "I don't care. It's for her. It's what I want to do. I have to...I have to say goodbye, and this is the only way..."

Evan leaned in to me. "It's not the only way." Glancing up, he scowled. He wasn't looking at Denny this time, so I had to believe Kiera had reentered the bar. Evan's expression darkened as he returned his eyes to me. "This is stupid. I don't think we should—"

I crossed my arms over my chest. I didn't often pull rank, but this was important to me. "I don't give a shit what you think. This is *my* band, and we're playing the song. End of discussion."

Feeling like the largest d-bag on the planet, I watched as Evan gave me a curt nod, glanced at Denny, then hopped onstage. The rest of the guys joined him, and Evan passed along the new lineup.

Wishing I hadn't said any of that to Evan, I risked a glance at Denny. He hadn't heard us arguing, but he'd witnessed it. The look on his face was cold...suspicious. It was an odd expression to see on him; he'd never looked at me that way before. As far as I'd seen, he'd never looked at *anyone* that way before. Kiera carefully avoided looking up at the stage, so I made myself not look her way either. Not that it really mattered now. Denny knew, or would soon. Nothing we did now would change that, so I might as well say goodbye the way I wanted to.

At the end of our set, I announced to the crowd that we had one more song for them, a new one. Evan frowned but started playing on cue. Even though Kiera was acting as if she wasn't paying attention, I hoped she heard the words...they were for her.

I tuned everything out: the crowd, Denny, Evan, Jenny, Kiera...everyone, and purely focused on the words. I wanted to bleed them from me. *"You're everything I need, but I'm nothing you need..." "You'll be all right...when he holds you tight..." "It will hurt me, it will hurt you too. But everything ends, so save your tears..."*

My heart breaking, I decided to fuck it all and sing this last part

448

directly at Kiera. She was the only one I really wanted to hear it anyway. She was standing in place, staring at me in shock, and there were tears on her cheeks. She understood. Good. Struggling to keep my pain from my voice, I sang the next lyrics clear and strong. *"It's better to never say goodbye, to just move on, to end the lie…"*

A tear ran down my cheek as the emotion overwhelmed me. Kiera's tears turned into a torrent as she continued to stare at me. *"Every single day I'll keep you with me, no matter how far from me you are…"* She put one hand over her mouth while the other clutched her stomach. It was like I was ripping her in two. I was shredding us both at the same time. It had to happen though. Surely she understood that.

While the music started building to the final crescendo, Jenny approached Kiera. She whispered something to her, then started pulling her away. Kiera looked like she was about to sink to her knees and sob. My own legs were shaking with the effort of keeping me upright. I managed to keep my voice clear, but another tear rolled down my cheek. *I'm going to miss you, so much.*

Jenny pulled her into the kitchen while I sang the last few words. *"I promise you… my love for you will never die."* You're all I will ever want. When she disappeared from my sight, the moment suddenly felt real. Horrifyingly real. My voice cracked on the final phrase, and I had to swallow the lump in my throat before I could finish it.

When the song was over, Kiera was gone, the crowd was silent, and my heart was so raw my chest hurt. The fans had no idea what to do with the emotional display they'd just witnessed. I wasn't sure if they had noticed Kiera's and my connection, but they'd certainly noticed my tears. The girls in the front were whispering to each other and pointing at me. That wasn't a reaction I was used to.

Throwing on a smile—because I still had a job to do—I raised my hand in the air and said, "Thanks for coming out to listen to us! Have a great night!" *Continue on as usual. Nothing to see here.*

The crowd finally burst into cheers and whistles, and I discreetly wiped my eyes as I slung my guitar over my shoulder. I met Evan's gaze and his face was sympathetic. I had to swallow again. *You were right…that was stupid.* I was sure Denny had just seen all of that between Kiera and me. I hadn't had the courage to look at him yet, but I could feel his eyes on me. It was just a matter of time.

Jenny was leading Kiera over to the bar when I looked back out at the crowd. She handed Kiera something in a glass that I was sure wasn't water. Kiera downed it as she collapsed onto a stool. Her eyes met with mine, and even with the distance between us, I saw the longing there. She wanted to run to me, but that was impossible; there might as well have been continents between us.

Or at least *one* continent was between us. Denny approached me when I stepped off the last stair to the stage. "Interesting song," he said, his dark eyes cold. "Write it about anyone in particular?"

My eyes accidentally drifted to Kiera at the bar, but I immediately pulled them back to Denny's face. Hopefully he hadn't noticed. Making my lips turn up into a casual smile, I shook my head and clapped Denny on the shoulder. *Nope. No one. It's just a song…a random, meaningless song.* Denny's expression was blank as he watched me put my guitar away. I knew he wanted more of an answer from me, and I should have shared my thoughts with him, but I didn't trust my voice at the moment. It might break again, and that would completely destroy any lie I gave him.

I hurried out of there, but not without one final look at Kiera. Her eyes were still watery. I wished I could go talk to her, give her the necklace I'd bought for her. But I didn't have it with me, and besides, I definitely couldn't do that with Denny watching. I'd done too much already. It was well past time to go.

Pinching my nose to stave off the headache forming, I practically ran from the bar. Once I was in the safety of my car, I laid my head on the steering wheel and let the pain out. Fat tears rolled down my cheeks, and there was nothing I could do to stop them. *It's over…*

When I was drained, physically and emotionally, I started my car and headed home. Should I leave now? Was a song a good enough goodbye? I walked through my front door, looked around at the emptiness before me, and clearly saw my future in the stillness. Walls that echoed with silence were all I had in store for me. I couldn't face that loneliness yet, so I trudged upstairs to my room. *One more day. God…please…just give me one more day.*

I didn't bother turning on any lights as I walked through the house; I wanted to be bathed in darkness, it matched my mood. Entering my room, I closed the door, turned on some music, then lay down on my bed and stared at my ceiling. I ran through everything that had happened since Denny and Kiera had moved in, mentally catalogued every mistake I'd made. There were so many. I tried numbering them, but around seventy-two, I gave up.

Denny and Kiera came home later, after Kiera's shift. I glanced at my door when I heard them walk past. Had they talked yet? Did Denny know? They headed to their room together, so I figured he didn't. He probably wouldn't sleep in the same room with her if he knew she'd recently been with me. God…was that only last night? It felt like a lifetime ago.

Someone was in the bathroom for an eternity, but eventually that person stumbled to bed, closing the door behind them. I lay there, willing myself to pass out, but it wasn't happening. I was wide awake.

With a small sigh, I got up, opened my dresser, and pulled out Kiera's necklace. When would be a good time to give it to her? I wasn't sure. Sitting down on the far side of my bed, I examined the piece in the moonlight. It was stunning, just like her. Putting aside thoughts of our final, painful goodbye, I let myself imagine an alternate reality, one where I could give her the necklace on a joyous occasion, and we were together, happy. I blinked in surprise when I heard a voice whisper my name. As I turned, I saw Kiera on the inside of my door. I hadn't heard her come in. She shouldn't be in here.

Clenching my hand around the necklace, I shoved it under the bed; I wasn't ready to give it to her yet. "What are you doing here? We talked about this. You shouldn't be here."

"How could you do that?" she asked, her eyes glistening.

451

"What?" I had done so much, I wasn't sure what she was referring to anymore.

"Sing that song to me…in front of everyone. You killed me." Her voice broke as she dropped onto the bed.

My emotional night rolled over me, churning my conflicting desires. "It's what needs to happen, Kiera."

"You wrote that days ago…when you were gone?"

I couldn't answer her right away. I knew she wouldn't understand. She'd argue, she'd disagree with every word I spoke, but I knew where this was heading. I'd always known. "Yes. I know where this is going, Kiera. I know who you'll choose, who you've always chosen."

She surprised me by not arguing. Another sign that she was beginning to accept the truth. Denny had her heart, not me. "Sleep with me tonight," she blurted out in a trembling voice.

I felt like she'd just punched me in the gut. "Kiera, we can't…"

Her voice was soft when she answered me. "No…literally. Just hold me, please."

Hold her…one last time? Yes, I could do that. Lying back on the bed, I held my arms open for her. Regardless of our hazy future and complicated past, my arms would always be open for her. She snuggled into my side, her arm over me, her legs tangled with mine, her head nuzzled in my shoulder. My chest pounded with pain. *I'll have to give this up soon…*

Kiera sniffled and I squeezed my eyes shut and held her tighter. *I don't want to let her go…* A wavering sigh escaped me as I tried to hold in my grief. *I wish this wasn't happening…*

In the silence building with painful restraint, Kiera spoke the words that were crashing through my heart. "Don't leave me."

A near sob escaped me, but I choked it back. "Kiera…" I whispered, kissing her head and clutching her tight. *I have to.*

She looked up at me with wet cheeks and grieved eyes. "Please stay…stay with me. Don't go."

I closed my eyes to block out her pain and felt my own tears rolling down my cheeks. "It's the right thing to do, Kiera."

"Baby, we're finally together, don't end this."

Opening my eyes, I ran a finger down her cheek. Her words sounded so right, but I knew they weren't. "That's just it. We're not together..."

"Don't say that. We are. I just need time...and I need you to stay. I can't bear the thought of you leaving." Her hands cupped my cheeks as she brought her lips to mine.

It took a lot of willpower, but I pulled away. "You won't leave him, Kiera, and I can't share you. Where does that leave us? He's going to figure it out if I stay. That leaves us with one option...I go." Agony wrenched my throat shut, and I swallowed through the harshness so I could finish speaking. "I wish things were different. I wish I'd known you first. I wish I was your first. I wish you would choose me—"

"I do!" she exclaimed, cutting me off.

I couldn't breathe. I couldn't move. I was terrified that if I did anything or said anything, Kiera would take back the words she'd just said. And I didn't want her to take them back. I'd been waiting my entire life to hear those words, to hear that someone wanted me more than anyone else. I hadn't realized, until this very moment, just how badly I'd wanted to be chosen. And now I was scared to death that that was going to be taken away from me.

Kiera stared at me for achingly long seconds. My heart thudded against my rib cage while I waited for her to speak, to take it back, to rip everything I'd ever wanted away from me. *Kill me, Kiera...or save me.*

A slow smile spread over Kiera's face. It did nothing to calm the anxiety building inside me. "I do choose you, Kellan." Her brows drew together as she searched my face. "Do you understand me?"

Did I? She was choosing me. She wanted me. She was...mine? She was really mine? *I get...to keep her. I get to love her. I get to have this?* It all felt so wrong, so unbelievable, so temporary... but...what if it wasn't?

Rolling her onto her back, I pressed my body against hers, grabbed her face, and lowered my mouth to hers. *Finally.* We were panting, frantic and eager. She ran her hands through my hair, igniting me. I ripped off her tank top. Nothing would be between us now. I pulled off my shirt, then her pants. I was working on my jeans when Kiera breathlessly pulled away from me.

"What happened to your...rules?" she asked, surprised by my sudden intensity.

"I never was good at following rules. And I never could say no to your begging anyway..." Leaning in, I kissed her neck. *My* neck. I would never share her again.

I kicked off my jeans, then sought her lips. "Wait..." She gently pushed me back. "I thought you didn't want to do this...here."

She glanced at my closed bedroom door, but I didn't follow her line of sight. I wasn't concerned about Denny anymore. She was *my* girlfriend now, *my* lover, my... *everything*. The outside world no longer existed. She had chosen *me*, and I wanted to make love to her. Now. So that was exactly what I was going to do.

Slipping my fingers into her underwear, feeling how ready she was for me, I growled in her ear, "If I'm yours, and you're mine... then I will take you, wherever and whenever I can."

My words, my fingers, made her moan. Grabbing my face, she made me look at her again. "I love you, Kellan."

Her words softened my face, my voice, my heart, and my soul. "I love you too, Kiera." *So much.* "I will make you so happy." *You won't regret leaving him for me. I promise.*

Biting her lip, desire in her eyes, she started tugging off my boxers. "Yes, I know you will."

I knew what she meant by the look in her eye and the throatiness to her voice. While that wasn't exactly what I'd meant by my promise, it worked too. In every way possible, I would make her *very* happy.

Chapter 30

How to Hurt Someone

Covering myself more completely with my blankets, I smiled in the stillness of the dark. She chose me. She was mine.

I had a girlfriend.

I'd never had a real one before…I liked how it felt. I reached over to give her a hug, but the other side of the bed was empty. I sat up with a frown, then looked over at the clock. It was morning…Kiera had slipped out sometime last night and was probably with Denny. Bile started filling my mouth. We needed to tell him it was over.

I fell back to my pillows with a thud. Fuck. He was going to be devastated.

With a sigh, I got out of bed and started my morning exercises. Kiera and I would come up with a way to let him know things had changed. I'd even let him continue to stay here, if he wanted, although…I didn't see how he'd be able to stomach that.

When I got downstairs, I started the coffee and waited for Kiera. She joined me before the pot was completely done brewing. She was incredibly alluring in her pajamas, and the smile on her lips was breathtaking. "Morn—"

Her mouth was on mine before I could even finish greeting her. I loved how eager she was. "I missed you," she muttered.

455

"I missed you too. I hated waking up with you gone," I whispered back.

We spent several moments kissing. There was so much passion and intensity between us, you would think we hadn't seen each other in weeks. She brought that out of me though. Desire and love, as bottomless as a black hole and as tangled as untamed vines. I tried to ignore the fact that both of those comparisons were potentially disastrous.

Recalling that Kiera and I had something important to discuss, I gently pushed her away from me. Needing space to resist the draw of her lips, I took a step toward the table. "We should talk about Denny, Kiera…"

Just then, Denny stepped into the kitchen. "What about me?" he asked in a gruff voice.

Jesus fucking-H Christ. My heart leaped into my throat, but years of schooling my expression let me hold on to my composure. *If he'd walked in ten seconds earlier…*

Racking my brain for a reasonable response, I popped out the first lie that sounded like it could be the truth. "I was just asking Kiera if you would be interested in hangin' with me and the guys today. There's this thing at EMP—"

Denny cut me off. "No, *we'll* stay here." I risked a glance at Kiera. She was staring at me like I'd just told Denny I'd grown wings last night and flown around the city.

I didn't miss the way Denny had stressed "we'll." *Kiera's not going anywhere with* you. *Got it?* "Okay…come by if you change your mind. We'll be there all day."

Tension built up in the room, and I considered telling the truth. But Kiera and I hadn't had a chance to talk about the best way to do it yet. We were a team now; we should come at this with a united front. Not that that would matter much to Denny. In fact, maybe I should let Kiera handle this on her own. He might take it better from her. If I was there, he would just get angry. Yes, Kiera should tell him first, and then I would talk to him.

When the awkwardness got to be too much, I told them both,

"I'd better go...pick up the guys." I gave Kiera a meaningful glance when Denny's back was to me: *Please talk to him.* Her face was forlorn, and I knew she wasn't looking forward to this. Me either.

The house was silent as I gathered my things and left. Too silent. I wished Kiera well, kicked myself for not having the guts to make a stand *with* her, then headed to Evan's.

He wasn't surprised when he cracked open his door, but he did seem irritated. "I should just give you a key. Then I wouldn't have to get up every time you need to run away from something."

I was pretty sure I knew why he was mad. "I'm sorry I was a dick last night."

Evan leaned on his door frame, not letting me in. "Dick doesn't really cover it. I was thinking more along the lines of...self-absorbed diva."

That brought a small smile to my lips. "Yeah...maybe...but I really am sorry. I was out of line, and I shouldn't have said what I did. It's not my band. It's *our* band. You and I formed it together, and we wouldn't be where we are now without you."

Evan lifted an eyebrow, clearly waiting for more.

"And I'm a self-absorbed diva, an asshole, a dog of a human being, and unworthy of any sort of praise, kudos, acclaim, or love." I shut my mouth with a snap. I hadn't meant to go that far with my apology. I was just freaking out about what was going on at home without me. *I should be there. I should turn around and go home...*

Frowning, Evan shoved his door open. "That shit's not true, Kell. Well, yeah, you're an asshole sometimes, but you're not... unworthy of anything." At the moment, I wasn't sure if I agreed.

It was after dinnertime when I finally went home. Denny's car was there, and I didn't know what that meant. My stomach lurched as I walked into the house. I understood Kiera's anxiety over telling him about us. Denny meant a lot to me; I didn't want to hurt him either.

The light was on in the kitchen. Fortifying my stomach, I headed that way. Denny and Kiera were at the table, finishing up dinner. I thought that was odd. It didn't seem to me that Denny would want to sit down and have a meal with Kiera if she'd told him about us...which meant she hadn't told him a thing. I looked over to Kiera for confirmation, and she shook her head no. She hadn't said a damn word. We were still at square one.

From the look on her face, I could tell Kiera was wrestling with demons just as torturous as mine; she was probably beating herself up over her lack of courage. Knowing I was just as cowardly as her, I sympathized with her inability to break his heart. We'd have to do it together. By the dark look in Denny's eyes as he watched Kiera's every move, he had to know anyway. Needing a minute to gather my thoughts and go over my options, I opened the fridge and grabbed a beer.

I'd just popped it open when Denny disturbed the eerie quiet. "Hey, mate. I think we should all go out. How about the Shack? We could go dancing again."

The way he said "dancing" was odd. Did he know what Kiera and I had done at the Shack? Or more accurately, in the espresso stand in the parking lot. He couldn't possibly know specifics about that night, but he knew something wasn't right between us. Maybe we should go out though. One last hurrah before everything tumbled to the ground.

"Yeah...sure," I told him.

Denny was still staring at Kiera, who was studying her food like her life depended on it. I wished I could comfort her, but I couldn't go near her right now. All I could do was go upstairs with my beer and wait for everyone else to be ready for our last roommates' night out.

Denny and Kiera left the house while I was still in my bedroom. With a heavy sigh, I stood up to leave. I glanced back at my mattress, remembering that Kiera's necklace was under it. Not sure why I was grabbing it, I walked around to the other side of the bed and pulled it free. It felt cool in my palm as I curled my fingers around it. I supposed I didn't need the necklace as a parting gift anymore, but something inside me, some lingering doubt or insecurity, was whispering at me to take it. So I did.

Denny's car was in the parking lot when I arrived at the Shack, and I parked next to him. I couldn't help but glance at the espresso stand as I walked past it. That was where everything had changed, where Kiera's and my relationship had truly begun. A part of me wanted to break in one more time, and a part of me never wanted to see it again.

It was warm in the busy bar, but a quick sweep of the area showed me Denny and Kiera weren't in there. Frowning, I wondered if they were out back. Why would Denny want to sit out there? It was frigid outside.

A half dozen outdoor heaters were spaced around the beer garden, taking the edge off the air, so it was actually kind of pleasant. I spotted Denny and Kiera over by the gate in the fence. Oddly, it was the exact same place that we'd sat the first time we came here. Did Denny do that on purpose too? Was he trying to fluster us into confessing? No need. When the time was right, we would tell him everything. God, I wasn't ready to lose him, but I supposed I already had.

Keeping a casual, carefree smile on my face, I sauntered over to the table and sat down where an untouched beer was waiting for me at an open seat next to Kiera. I smiled at Denny as I sat down, and then did my best to ignore Kiera. Now wasn't the time, even I knew that.

Hidden speakers pumped music into the garden, and drunk people were up on the dance floor, warming their bodies with almost-rhythmic movements. Kiera shivered while she quietly sat beside me. I wanted to throw my arm around her, warm her up some, since she wasn't handling the nip in the air as well as me, but Denny had his eyes glued on her, so I left her alone.

We sat in awkward silence for an eternity, and I began to wonder what the point of this was. It was clear we couldn't hang out as a group together anymore, not like we used to. Honestly, we hadn't been able to for a while now. As I was running through appropriate ways to irrevocably shatter the bond between the three of us, Denny's work phone rang. *Just like last time.*

Kiera and I both turned to look over at Denny. Nonchalant, he answered it and brought it to his ear. After speaking a few words to the person on the other line, he put the phone away. Letting out a regretful sigh, he looked over at Kiera. "I'm sorry. They need me to come in." His gaze switched to me. "Can you take her home? I have to go."

I was so surprised, all I could do was nod. Kiera looked shocked too. Out of all the possible events that could have gone down tonight, Denny getting called away to work wasn't one either of us had anticipated.

Denny stood, then leaned down to Kiera. "Will you think about what I asked?" Kiera mumbled okay, and I instantly wondered what he'd asked her. Then Denny grabbed both of Kiera's cheeks and kissed her so passionately, I had to clench the sides of my chair to stay seated.

I looked away before I did something stupid. When Denny straightened, I heard Kiera breathing heavier. Quite a kiss they'd shared. Hating every second of this, I cleared my throat and shifted in my seat.

Kiera watched Denny until he disappeared into the bar, while I struggled with controlling the sudden jealous rage I felt. By the time Kiera swung her head around to look at me, I was more or less in control of myself. I would pretend it hadn't happened. *If I ignore it, then it isn't real.* A change of subject was what we both needed.

Smiling, I grabbed her hand, now that I could. "I was wondering…since you probably don't want to take me home to your parents yet…which I completely understand…maybe you'd like to spend winter break with me here? Or we could go up to Whistler? Canada is beautiful and…do you ski? Well, if not…we don't have to leave our room." Pausing, I gave her a wicked grin. I knew I was rambling, but I wanted her to focus on what she was gaining, not what she was losing. I would be the greatest boyfriend in the world to her. I'd give her everything I had, and then some.

She was staring at me, but I got the feeling she wasn't really listening. Her mind was somewhere else, with someone else. Not knowing what else to do, I kept talking. "We could get a room with a Jacuzzi tub, order some wine, maybe get some of those fancy chocolate-covered strawberries. Then we could walk around town, check out the shops. It will be great, you'll see."

She swallowed, but she didn't respond. Bunching my brows, I said, "That's just one idea. We could go somewhere else if you like. I just…I want to spend some time with you. Alone. We really haven't been able to do that. What would you like to do?" Her eyes had a faraway look, and she didn't answer me. "Did I lose you?" She was still staring right through me, so I shifted my head to get her attention, and again asked, "Kiera…did I lose you?"

Her cheeks filled with color, and she glanced down at our hands, like she was surprised we were still touching. Concerned, I asked her, "Are you all right? Do you want to go home?" I knew this was hard for her, but I wanted her to see the hope I was offering. She wouldn't be alone. I would be with her, every step of the way.

Nodding at my suggestion, she stood. I led her to the side exit gate with a hand on the small of her back. She scanned the parking lot when we stepped into it, and her eyes paused on the espresso stand. I smiled, wondering if she was thinking about our time there—the torture and the bliss. It was a night I'd never forget.

For the first time ever, I was actually really excited about my future. It was a strange but welcome feeling. It was certainly a lot better than endless despair. "After high school, I hitchhiked down the Oregon coast. That's actually how I met Evan. Anyway, we should go, you would love it. There are these caves you can walk through, with all these crazy-shaped stalagmites, stalactites, whatever you call 'em. And sea lions are everywhere along the beach. You can talk to them, and they'll talk back. They're cool, in a loud, obnoxious sort of way. Kind of like Griffin." I laughed, but Kiera didn't laugh with me. She was staring straight ahead while we walked to my car. I wondered if she'd noticed that Denny's car was gone. Probably.

"Anyway, we could keep going if you wanted. Down to L.A.? I could show you where I met the rest of the guys. Well...I won't show you where I met Matt and Griffin...but I can show you where our first gig was. And the place I stayed while I was there, where I bought the Chevelle. You know, the important places." I laughed again, but still Kiera remained silent.

Fear began racing up my spine and wrapping its icy tentacles around my heart. She wasn't listening to me at all...she was a million miles away. And she was with Denny. I knew it. Her eyes were shining more than they should be, and I knew her forming tears weren't for me. She was replaying their entire relationship. *She was changing her mind.*

When she suddenly stopped walking and yanked her hand away from me, I knew I was right. She *was* changing her mind. She was going to choose him after all. I felt like I should be surprised, but I wasn't. Something in the back of my mind was shouting at me that I'd been living in a fantasy. She was never going to be mine.

I turned to face her, and I knew...this would be the last time we talked. This was it. This was goodbye.

Kiera turned her eyes from me, but I saw the guilt. She was letting me go. Words seemed unnecessary, but I asked her anyway. "I did lose you...didn't I?"

She seemed surprised that I'd figured it out when she peeked up at me. She shouldn't be. It was written all over her face. "Kellan, I...I can't do this...not yet. I can't leave him. I need more time..."

"Time?" I was so sick of that word. "Kiera...nothing is going to change here. What good is time to you?" Angry, I pointed toward home, where more pain awaited us all if something didn't change. "Now that he knows you lied, time will only hurt him more." *It will hurt me more.*

"Kellan, I'm so sorry...please don't hate me." Her eyes were filled with tears now. Mine too. I'd almost had it all. Or maybe I'd never even been close.

Frustrated, I tangled my hands in my hair. I wanted to yank the long strands out by the roots. I needed this roller coaster to stop. I needed life to calm down, level out. I needed to feel safe again. "No, Kiera...no."

Her eyes widened with fear and her voice trembled when she spoke. "What do you mean? No, you don't hate me or no...you do?"

She looked so scared. I hated seeing that look on her face, but she was going to have to let one of us go. She was going to have to let me go. Bringing a hand up to her face in comfort, I softly told her, "No, I can't give you any more time. I can't do this. It's killing me..."

Kiera shook her head as tears rolled down her cheeks. "Please, Kellan, don't make me—"

"Ugh...Kiera." Grabbing her other cheek, I held her face tight in my hands and stared her down. *This isn't as hard as you're making it. Stop thinking, and listen to your heart. Be brave...cut the rope...and let one of us fall.* "Choose right now. Don't even think, just choose. Me...or him? Me or him, Kiera?"

Eyes locked on mine, she whispered, "Him."

In the back of my head, I heard a heavy iron cell door slamming closed, and I knew my heart was forever locked inside it. I'd never open up again. I'd never love again. I would never risk this pain again. I felt like an elephant was sitting on my chest, crushing me. I couldn't breathe, stars danced in my vision, and I thought I heard my father laughing in the distance. *She chose him...*

A hot tear splashed on my cheek, and I knew it was only the beginning. There would be many tears tonight. "Oh," I muttered. Was the light getting dimmer? Was I about to pass out? I would almost welcome that. I wanted to pass out and never wake up.

Releasing her face, I willed darkness to overwhelm me. My chest was being cracked open, my brain was being liquefied. *Please... someone take me away from this torture.*

Kiera clutched my jacket and pulled me toward her. "No, Kellan...wait. I didn't mean—"

Anger momentarily dimmed the agony. "Yes, you did. That was your instinct. That was your first thought...and first thoughts are usually the correct ones." Closing my eyes, I swallowed and pushed the anger aside. What good was getting mad at her? It wasn't her

463

fault. Denny was a good man, the better man…She was being smart by choosing him over me. *Why would anyone choose you?* my father's voice asked. "That's what's really in your heart. He's what's in your heart…" *And he should be.*

Kiera grabbed my hands and held them tight while I took a few calming deep breaths. I didn't want our last parting to be a screaming match. I wanted to say goodbye like I'd planned. Stoically. Opening my eyes, I said in a surprisingly calm voice, "I told you I would walk away, if that was your choice…and I will. I won't make trouble for you. I always knew where your heart really was anyway. I never should have asked you to make a choice…there never was a choice to make. Last night, I did hope that…" Sighing, I stared at the pavement. *No point in dwelling on what was never actually going to happen.* "I should have left ages ago. I was just…being selfish."

Kiera made a noise that sounded like a scoff. "I think I give new meaning to the word, Kellan."

Smiling, I looked up at her. Yeah, perhaps she did. We both did. "You were scared, Kiera. I understand that. You're scared to let go…I am too. But everything will be fine." *It has to be.* "We will be fine." *How am I going to live without her?*

We wrapped our arms around each other and squeezed as tight as we could. I never wanted to let her go, but I knew I had to. One of us had to. "Don't ever tell Denny about us. He won't leave you. You can stay at my place for as long as you like. You can even rent out my room if you want. I don't care."

She pulled back to look at me, and I could see the fearful question in her eyes. Was I leaving? Yes. I was. For good this time. "I have to leave now, Kiera…while I can." Tears were falling down her cheeks, one after another. Feeling that my own cheeks were wet as well, I dried hers as best I could. "I'll call Jenny and have her come get you. She'll take you to him. She'll help you." *You won't be alone.*

"Who will help you?" she asked, her voice soft with compassion.

No one. Swallowing down that painful truth, I ignored her question and continued providing her with happy thoughts to think about when I was gone. "You and Denny can go to Australia and be married. You can have a long, happy life together, the way it was supposed to be. I promise I won't interfere." My voice cracked. *I'm going to miss you...so much.*

Kiera didn't want to hear about her life, she wanted to know about mine. She wanted to know I would be okay. "What about you? You'll be alone..."

I know. With a sad smile, I told her, "Kiera...it was always supposed to be that way too."

She put a hand on my cheek in pain and understanding. "I told you you were a good man."

Was I? I didn't feel like one. "I think Denny would disagree."

She threw her arms around my neck again and we rested our foreheads together as a sad, slow beat drifted over the fence to us. It felt wholly appropriate that a melancholy song was playing right now. Would my life ever be anything but melancholy now? "God, I'm going to miss you..." *I don't want to go...*

Kiera clenched me tighter, and her words were frantic when she spoke. "Kellan, please don't—"

I knew what she was going to say, and I quickly cut her off. "Don't, Kiera. Don't ask me that. It has to happen this way. We need to stop this cycle, and we both seem incapable of staying away from each other...so one of us needs to leave." Feeling my willpower fading, I rocked my head against hers and spoke faster. "This is the way Denny doesn't get hurt. If I'm gone, he may not question your lie. But if you ask me to stay...I will, and he'll eventually find out, and we'll destroy him. I know you don't want that. I don't either, baby." *I want to stay. I want to stay. I want to stay.*

A sob escaped her, and it broke my broken heart. "But it hurts so much..."

Wishing it would somehow ease the ache, I kissed her. "I know, baby...I know. We have to let it hurt. I need to leave, for good this time. If he's what you want, then we need to end this. It's the only way." *Please, change your mind again. I want to stay with you.*

I kissed her again, then pulled back and searched her watery eyes. Now was the time. Reaching into my pocket, I grabbed the necklace. I held it enclosed in my fist, then opened one of her hands and gently placed it inside her palm. She looked down at the keep-sake in her fingers, at the diamond sparkling in the moonlight, and inhaled a sharp breath. This was why I'd brought it...some part of me had known this was going to happen.

As I spoke, Kiera's hand started to shake. "You don't have to wear it...I'll understand. I just wanted you to have something to remem-ber me by. I didn't want you to forget me. I'll never forget you." *You'll be in my mind every second of every day. I can promise you that.*

She looked up at me, and disbelief was as clear as the grief on her face. Tears falling like rain, she warbled, "Forget you? I could never..." The necklace laced in her fingers, she grabbed my face. Her voice intense and clear, she said, "I love you...forever."

I crashed my lips down to hers. *And I love you too...forever. There will never be another for me. Ever. You're the one I'll compare everyone to, and no one will measure up.*

We poured our souls into that kiss. Our last kiss. I knew it was. I knew the second we pulled apart, I would leave and she would stay with Denny. It was what fate had been trying to tell me all along. I didn't get to have her, because I didn't deserve her. But selfishly, I didn't want to let her go either. As the minutes ticked by, as our mouths moved together, as a sob escaped Kiera's lips, then mine, I doubted I could go. I needed a minute...or ten, or twenty...or a thousand.

I wasn't going to get that many though, because fate wasn't done fucking with me yet.

Behind Kiera, the gate to the bar had just slammed shut. My eyes snapped open and I watched, helpless, as my world crumbled around me. Someone was striding toward me, someone who wasn't supposed to be here, someone Kiera and I had foolishly been trying to shelter from this pain, but who was now getting smacked in the face with it. Denny. *No...*

Kiera broke off contact with me, but I couldn't look at her. I couldn't pull my eyes away from Denny. His hands were clenched into fists, and his dark eyes were drilling lethal holes into me. He wanted me dead right now, that much was certain.

"I'm so sorry, Kiera," I whispered. *This is going to be ugly. I never wanted it to happen like this... I never wanted him to see. In all honesty, I never wanted him to know.*

Nothing was ever going to be the same now.

Chapter 31

Just End My Pain Already

Kiera and I stepped away from each other while Denny said our
names. I couldn't help but notice that my name was said a lot more
harshly than Kiera's. Denny looked shocked, like he hadn't really
expected to catch us like this, but more than being surprised, he
was outraged. And I had to imagine he was hurt too.

Kiera put her hands up, trying to shield us from the storm that
was coming. "Denny..." She had no other words, nothing to por-
tray this in an innocent light, nothing to hide what we'd done.
There was no hiding it. The lies were over.

Denny's fiery eyes turned to me. "What the hell is going on?"

Almost relieved that the game was over, I told Denny the truth.
Well, the truth in its simplest form. "I kissed her. I was saying
goodbye...I'm leaving."

From the corner of my eye, I watched Kiera press her hands into
her stomach. Either the nightmare we were in now was causing her
grief, or my statement that I was still leaving was. As wrong as it
was to worry about it now, I kind of hoped it was the latter.

Denny's eyes sparked with hatred, and all of it was aimed at me.
Good. He should hate me, and only me. This was all my fault. "You
kissed her? Did you fuck her?"

My mind rewound to my childhood. Things were so much sim-

468

pler back then, although they had felt complicated at the time. I recalled blood trickling down Denny's lip while he sat on the ground, collecting his senses; my dad fleeing from the room like he was terrified of what Denny might do; and me, sitting on the ground beside Denny, dazed and in awe that someone would do what he'd just done for me. Denny deserved the truth.

"Yes." I cringed as I drove in the knife. The damage was done now. Our friendship was over.

Denny's mouth dropped open in shock. He must have been hoping he was wrong. I sort of wished he were. "When?"

"The first time was the night you broke up." I knew I was leading him to a horrible conclusion with my statement, but it was what it was.

He grasped what I was hinting at right away. "The first time? How many *times* were there?"

"Only twice…"

Kiera snapped her eyes to mine, and I saw a question in the hazel depths. *We've been together more than twice. Why did you tell him that?* Because he asked how many times we fucked. And once we told each other we loved each other, what we'd done was so much more than fucking. I never wanted to fuck again. Kiera's lips lifted into a ghost of a smile, and I knew she understood.

Returning my eyes to Denny, I told him what was in my heart. "But I wanted her…every day." *There's no point in holding back now. He should know everything I feel for her, everything she means to me.*

Denny's cheeks reddened, just like my dad's used to when he got really angry. I knew what he was going to do before he even moved to do it. Cocking his arm back, he twisted his body and threw his weight into a hit that landed on my jaw. Denny was strong, and the blow knocked me back a step. My jaw throbbed, my head started to pound, and I tasted blood in my mouth. Good. I deserved this.

When my vision stabilized, I straightened and faced him. I could feel warmth dribbling down my cheek as I spoke. "I won't fight you, Denny. I'm so sorry, but we never wanted to hurt you. We fought against…We tried so hard to resist this…pull…we feel toward each other." I hated the words coming out of my mouth. I hated the look on Denny's face. *I never wanted it to happen like this.*

Denny clenched his fists. "You tried? You tried to not fuck her?" he yelled. He hit me again, on the cheek this time. My ears started ringing, but I still clearly heard him when he screamed, "I gave up everything for her!"

He pummeled me again and again. I let him. I did nothing to block his blows, did nothing to protect my body. After each hit, I faced him again, giving him another perfect target for his rage. I deserved every strike. I deserved the full force of his anger. And…if Denny was kicking my ass, then he was leaving Kiera alone. *Better me than her.*

"You promised me you wouldn't touch her!"

He was right, I had. And I had shattered that promise like I had so many others before it. I'd wanted her, so I'd taken her. I was no friend to him, to anyone. And the really sad part was, it was all for nothing. She chose *him.* "I'm sorry, Denny," I whispered, but I doubt he heard me. And what good was an apology from me anyway? It was a tiny patch on a gaping wound. Worthless.

I felt my strength fading, my vision dulling. I wasn't sure how much longer I could take Denny's rage. But what did it matter anymore? What did anything matter anymore? I'd lost the only thing I'd ever wanted. I'd tasted love, then had it snatched away from me. I couldn't go on living my empty, meaningless life. If I was destined to be alone, then it might as well end right here. I fell to my knees while Denny shouted, "I trusted you!" His knee connected with my chin, knocking me to my back.

Everything went black, and for a second, I thought I'd passed out. But I couldn't be unconscious, because everything hurt—my head, my body, my heart. All of me was throbbing. *Just kill me and get it over with.*

Heavy blows from Denny's boots met my exposed abdomen. I left my body open to him. Made it as easy as possible for him to hurt me. Every hit sent shock waves of pain throughout my body, but I welcomed it. *I deserve this. I deserve worse than this.*

A solid strike to my arm resulted in a sickening snap as Denny broke the bone, and acidlike pain radiated up my forearm and across my chest. Unable to contain the agony, I cried out and held my arm close to my body. Denny didn't notice what he'd done. He only screamed, "You said you were my brother!"

Underneath the flood of pain, I felt nausea rising. Now, every kick Denny gave me jolted my arm, reigniting the painful break. *I deserve this. I deserve more than this. Just finish me.* I felt a rib break, maybe two, I had no idea. All I knew was pain. I really wasn't going to survive this. Good. I didn't want to go on without her. I wanted the pain to end.

Spitting out blood, I muttered, "I won't fight you…I won't hurt you…I'm sorry, Denny…" *I deserve your rage. My life is yours… take it.* In my daze of pain, I started repeating my words like a chant. Denny beat me the entire time I whimpered them. "I'm sorry…I won't fight you…I'm sorry…I won't hurt you."

"You fucking piece of shit! You fucking pathetic, fucking selfish bastard! Your word is worthless! *You* are worthless!"

I turned my head away from him then. *I know. I know I'm worthless. That's why I'm not fighting you. I deserve this.* "I'm sorry, Denny." *Don't feel bad when this is over. You did the right thing.*

"She is *not* one of your whores!" he screamed, ignoring my apology.

Denny paused in his attack, and I raised myself up onto my elbow. I was a little surprised I still could. My vision had only partly returned, and it wavered with darkness. My head throbbed, my arm was on fire, and I was bloody everywhere. It hurt to breathe, it hurt to move. All I had left was pain. And the truth. And what Denny had just yelled wasn't true. That wasn't how it was at all. *She was never a whore to me.*

"I'm sorry I hurt you, Denny, but I love her." Every breath was agony, but telling Denny what I'd held in for so long filled me with joy. It felt good to confess. I might not make it through this, I might have lost her, but for one second, I had loved and been loved in return. My life was complete. Peace filled me as I shifted my eyes to Kiera. She was frozen in shock with tears streaming down her cheeks. She'd never been more beautiful. Maybe what we'd done was wrong, but we'd loved with all our hearts, and no one could take that away from us. Not Denny, not fate, not life. Nothing mattered from here on out, because I had already reached the pinnacle of bliss. *Someone had loved me.* "And she loves me too." *We'll be together forever in my dreams…*

I tuned Denny out. It didn't matter what he did to me. I wanted to memorize every line on Kiera's face, every expression in her color-shifting eyes. If tonight was my last night on earth, I wanted to spend it staring at her. *It's okay, Denny. Do what you will…I'm ready.*

Kiera's gaze shifted from me to Denny, then back to me. She looked terrified. I wanted to tell her everything was okay, I was at peace, but she moved before I could focus long enough to say the words. My mind couldn't keep up with what she was doing. She screamed, "No!" then tackled me. I looked up at Denny just in time to see his boot connect with Kiera's temple.

No! It was supposed to be me…

"Kiera!" My mouth felt full of marbles, and my vision hazed in and out, but that was nothing compared to the sight of Kiera slumped on the ground beside me, motionless.

The blow she'd taken in my place had flung her away from me, and her hair was covering her face. I had no idea if she was okay or not. Adrenaline gave me strength, and I scrambled to get closer to her. *Please be okay.* I was scared to touch her, scared to move her. What was the rule about head injuries? I had no fucking clue.

By the time I had pulled myself around to where I could look at her more closely, Denny was on his knees at her side. "Kiera?" he said, shaking her shoulders.

"Don't," I muttered, "you could make it worse."

He looked up at me, his eyes wide. "Is she okay? Please tell me she's okay. Jesus, she's bleeding…there's so much blood. Kellan, is she okay? Did I…? What did I do to her?"

By the paleness of his cheeks and the frantic look in his eye, I knew he was losing it. Ignoring him, I focused on Kiera. "Baby?" I whispered, moving her hair away from her eyes so I could see her. "Tell me you're okay…please." She still didn't respond, and I could see that Denny was right about the blood. The ground beneath her head was so sickly red it looked black. Fuck. Cringing in pain, I held my cheek next to her mouth. *Let me feel a breath…don't let her be dead. I can't handle a world where she's dead. It was supposed to be me. Why did she do that?*

I felt like I waited an eternity to feel…something…and when I finally did, I exhaled in relief. "She's breathing," I told Denny. "It's faint, but it's there."

"We have to call for help. She needs a doctor, a hospital…we need to call an ambulance." He ran his hands back through his hair. His knuckles were torn and bloody from repeatedly hitting my face.

I knew time was of the essence, but I also knew that Denny would be in serious shit for this…especially if she died. *Fuck, please don't let her die.* "You need to leave. Now," I told him. Caring more about stopping the bleeding than any potential damage I could do to her head, I pulled Kiera into my lap the best I could with one good arm, and then held the bottom part of my shirt against the sticky section of her skull. My shirt instantly darkened.

Denny's eyes went wide as he watched me. "No…I'm staying with her." There was a trace amount of jealousy in his voice, but we didn't have time for that right now. This wasn't about us at the moment.

Irritated and scared, I snapped out, "Aren't you supposed to be a genius or something? Your stupid ass will go to jail if you stay here. Do you fucking understand me? You beat the living shit out of me, and…your girlfriend is…"

I couldn't finish, and Denny didn't let me. "I'm not leaving her side."

Seeing the blood stain growing on my shirt, I yelled, "Yes, you fucking are! You will get hauled off and locked away, and your career will be over! Is that what you fucking want? Is that what you think Kiera would fucking want?" I spat a wad of blood from my mouth to emphasize my point. "Now quit arguing with me and get the fuck out of here!"

Denny seemed to notice for the first time that he'd beaten me to a bloody pulp. He stared at me, then looked at his hands. "Jesus... what did I do...?"

I let out a calming breath. I needed to keep my cool if I was going to get him to leave. "You didn't do anything. You weren't even here. You understand me?" I raised my eyebrows. It hurt. Everything hurt. Carefully reaching into my back pocket with my good hand, I grabbed my wallet and tossed it at Denny. He seemed confused by that, so I quickly explained as I returned my hand to Kiera's makeshift compress. "Run. I'll tell them we got mugged and things turned nasty. I'll tell them Kiera tried to protect me...and...and she..." I sighed, then implored, "Get out of here, Denny, before it's too late!"

His gaze never leaving Kiera, Denny slowly stood up. "You'll get her help...you'll stay with her?"

I nodded, then indicated the road. "Yes. Now, please... leave...before someone comes out here."

Denny looked back at me. He seemed torn, like he wanted to go, but he also wanted to stay and confess. Fuck that. I wasn't letting him throw his life away because *I* had pushed him to the breaking point. This was my fault, not his. "Kiera would want you to go," I said, my voice firm. "She wouldn't want you punished for this. Not like that." My voice softened. "We punished you enough."

Denny glanced back down at Kiera on my lap, then nodded. Tears running down his cheeks, he looked up at me and whispered, "I'm sorry. Tell her I'm sorry." With one final pained expression, he ran off.

Relieved that he wouldn't be tied up in some legal mess because of this, I closed my eyes. Then I gathered my strength and yelled, "Somebody help me!" I kept screaming it, until finally a group of people opened the gate to the beer garden and peeked their heads out to see what all the fuss was about. When they spotted my

474

bloody, beat-up ass and Kiera's stone-still body, they sprang into action. A half dozen men and women ran toward me, three of them pulling out cell phones as they did. I nearly sobbed with relief. They would help her. They would fix her. They had to.

"What happened?" was the first thing they asked when they reached me.

The lie rolled effortlessly off my tongue. Someone brought a wet towel for her head, and I removed my ruined shirt from her scalp. Someone else asked me if I was all right. I heard myself murmuring that I thought my arm was broken, but I felt numb inside. Hollow. What if she didn't make it? What if she didn't survive this? I couldn't...No...it couldn't end this way. It just couldn't.

When the ambulances arrived, a group of paramedics descended on us. They tried to remove Kiera from my arms and I stubbornly held on to her. *She is alive right now. If I let her go...who knows what could happen?*

An older man with a kind face knelt beside me. "Sir, you need to let go of her so we can help her. We're here to *help* her."

Woodenly, I nodded. *Yes, help her.* "Will she be okay?" I asked, knowing they couldn't possibly know the answer.

A younger man started looking over my wounds while Kiera was pulled away. "She's in good hands. Let's just see how you're doing."

Kiera was put on a stretcher, and a mask was put over her mouth. I watched the mask fog with her breath. *Thank God...she's still alive.* She was shoved into an ambulance, and the doors were slammed shut behind her. I tried to stand. "Wait, I want to go with her. Let me go with her."

A firm hand held me down. "Stay still, sir. You're injured too. We're going to get you on a stretcher and put you in the other ambulance. But you'll be right behind her, I promise."

I suddenly felt extremely tired. I nodded, but there was no strength behind it, just a dead sort of flopping up and down. Dropping my heavy head, I stared at the smeared pool of blood Kiera had left behind. Lying near the edge of it was the necklace I had given her as a goodbye. It was touching the blood, and the pool was starting to creep around the sides of the pendant, surrounding it. With my good hand, I weakly scraped my fingers against the rough concrete.

The silver strand holding the guitar caught on my chilled fingers, and I grabbed the cool metal. When it was in my palm, I stared at the guitar tinged with Kiera's blood. The diamond in the center had once reminded me of my undying love for her, but now all I saw was a crystallized tear.

Please don't let her die.

I was moved to a stretcher, shoved into an ambulance, hooked up to complicated equipment, and driven away. My mind faded into oblivion at some point, and only bits and pieces of my "rescue" broke through my awareness. I recalled arriving at the hospital, remembered the jarring sensation of being removed from the van, heard some person tell a nurse all the things they'd found wrong with me so far, and heard myself asking about Kiera. My questions weren't answered, and my consciousness slipped away.

When I woke up, I was in a hospital bed, wearing a hospital gown. My arm was in a cast, my ribs were wrapped, and I had bandages on my face. A dull ache permeated my senses, and my head felt slow, like I was waking from delirium. Looking over to my good arm, I saw where an IV was attached to me, dripping clear liquid into my body. I wasn't sure what it was, but I knew it was probably the reason I wasn't in overwhelming pain right now.

I heard whispering across the room, and I looked over to see three nurses in the doorway, talking to one another. Two of them were giggling. "Excuse me." They all looked my way. One of them turned beet red in a way that reminded me of Kiera. How long had I been out? Was she okay? "I was brought in with a girl. Is she all right?"

A bubbly blonde walked my way. "The head injury? She's still in recovery. Her fiancé is with her now."

My words caught in my throat. Fiancé? I knew she meant Denny. He must have cleaned up and driven out here. Of course he would. I would have too. Nodding, I removed the sheet covering me. Just doing that was a challenge; I was so weak. All three nurses

476

immediately headed my way, palms raised like they were going to restrain me. "No, no, no. You need to rest."

"I need to see her."

The blonde put a hand on my shoulder, while the other two tucked me back into bed. "She's not going anywhere. And she's not awake yet. You can see her in the morning, and she won't know the difference."

I'll know the difference.

They all had jobs to do, and wouldn't be able to watch me twenty-four/seven, so I lay back and prepared myself to wait. I *was* getting out of this bed. I *was* going to see Kiera. I wouldn't be able to rest until I saw with my own eyes that she was okay. If the nurses knew anything about me, then they would have realized that *my* recovery depended on hers.

Once they did finally leave, I struggled to my feet. My arm burned, my chest ached, and every movement made something hurt, but I kept going. It took me an achingly long time, but I managed to dress myself. Once I looked semi-normal again, I made my way to the door and peered into the hallway. Feeling like I was sneaking out of prison, I waited until the coast was clear, then walked as quickly as my shuffling feet would take me.

When I was away from my area, I found a nurses' station and asked for Kiera. The guy on duty looked at me funny, but told me what room to find her in. The lights were off and her door was ajar when I found the room where she was recovering. I felt like I had run a marathon just getting this far, but anxious to see her, I hurried inside. When I saw her lying on the bed, her body softly lit by a nightlight across the room, I almost wished I hadn't come. She looked like a little girl in the massive bed, but with her head wrapped in thick bandages, and a sickly black-and-blue bruise along the right side of her face from her eyebrow to her cheekbone, she seemed like a very, very sick little girl.

While tears clouded my vision, a soft voice said, "What are you doing here? Shouldn't you be lying down somewhere?"

Steadying myself on a rolling tray near the foot of Kiera's bed, I looked over at Denny, sitting in a chair near the window. "I had to know she was okay. Is she?" My throat closed up. If she wasn't...I didn't know what I would do.

Denny frowned. "I don't...I don't know. They've got her on drugs to reduce the swelling, but if that doesn't work, they'll have to...operate."

I felt my legs start to give out, and Denny shot to his feet. With quick steps, he hurried over to me and helped me stay on my feet. His dark eyes took in all of my injuries. Well, the ones he could see, anyway. "Are you...okay?" he asked.

Staring at Kiera, her fate still unknown, and feeling the pins and needles of pain racing around my body, I shrugged him off me. *He did this to us.* "No...I'm not. My arm's broken, my ribs are broken, my insides are black and blue, and I feel like living shit."

Denny frowned as he backed away. "I'm sorry. I never meant..." His fists clenched and he closed his eyes. "You slept with my girl-friend, Kellan." His eyes reopened and heat crept into his voice. "You *slept* with her."

Scared that Kiera wouldn't make it, I unintentionally bit out, "No, actually, we didn't do much sleeping."

Denny pulled his arm back, like he was going to slug me again, then he glanced over at Kiera and let it drop. "You should go. I'm with her now. I'll let you know if anything changes."

Walking over to Kiera's bed, I gingerly sat down near her feet. "I'm not going anywhere until she wakes up."

"Kellan..."

I snapped my gaze to him; it made my head hurt, but I ignored it. "If you hate me, fine, I understand, but I'm not leaving...so deal with it."

"Fine, but sit in the chair, not by her." He pointed over to the seat he'd been sitting in. I wanted to tell him to go to hell, that I'd sit wherever I damn well pleased, but I really did feel like shit, and re-laxing back in the chair sounded a hell of a lot better than sitting at the end of a stiff bed. Although there was a certain appeal to the thought of being as close to Kiera as possible...

Pushing that thought from my mind, I stood up and moved to the chair. Kiera and I were many things, but still together wasn't one of them. If she woke up...*when* she woke up...I'd have to tell her we were over. Regardless of what Denny's plans with her were now, I was done. I couldn't do this anymore.

I sat in the plush chair while Denny sat on the bed. I think I fell asleep, because the next thing I knew, bands of sunlight were blinding my eyes. Blinking, I looked over at Kiera. She was stone-still on the bed, asleep or unconscious. The bruise on her face looked atrocious in the sunlight. Nurses were in the room checking on her, but Denny was nowhere to be found. "How is she?" I croaked.

A nurse looked over at me and was about to answer when a trio of nurses burst through the door. I frowned as I recognized them as *my* nurses. The blond one wasn't so bubbly anymore. "There you are. You can't just leave like that. You need to come back to your room so the doctor can check on you, and so we can check your bandages..."

Very carefully, I crossed my arms over my chest. "You can do whatever you want to me, but unless you plan on knocking me out and dragging me back to my room, I'm staying here."

The girl behind the blonde frowned; she looked extremely disappointed that I wouldn't be returning with them. "Well, you at least need to fill out the paperwork..."

I lifted my good hand. "Gladly. You know where to find me."

The nurse taking Kiera's vitals gave me an amused smile while the other nurses left in a huff. "And I thought I was stubborn," Kiera's nurse said. Standing straight, she gave me appraising eyes. "How is your pain? Do you need anything?"

I shook my head. The only pain I had was from the uncertainty revolving around Kiera. "How is she?" I asked again.

The nurse frowned. "Better than before, but not out of the woods. I'm sorry. I wish I had better news."

Swallowing, I nodded. It wasn't her fault. Denny reentered the room with a steaming cup of something that I had to assume was tea. My gaze swung his way. It was his fault...and my fault. We'd both done this.

Denny asked the nurse the same thing I had, and she gave him the same answer. After she left, Denny sat back down on Kiera's bed with a sigh. He glanced over at me with irritation in his eyes. "You should go home and change..."

I looked down at the shirt streaked in red. I probably should, but I couldn't leave Kiera. "I'll change later."

Denny's eyes narrowed. "Do you think she's going to want to see you like that? Covered in her blood? Do you think that will help her recover?"

I leaned forward in my chair. "Do you think it matters what the fuck my shirt looks like when my face looks like this?" I pointed at the eye that was so swollen I could barely see out of it.

Denny sighed and dropped his eyes back to Kiera. A tense silence built up in the room and I gritted my jaw and closed my eyes. Denny and I snapping at each other wasn't going to solve anything. "I'm sorry. You're right. Evan knows where my house keys are hidden. I'll call him and have him bring some clothes over." I opened my eyes to see Denny staring at me. "But I'm not leaving, so stop trying to get rid of me."

"I know," he quipped. "You just can't leave her alone, can you?"

Holding his gaze, I calmly said, "No. I can't. And I'm sorry."

"You're sorry? Well, that makes everything okay, doesn't it?" He lifted his free hand in the air and spoke to the room like it was full of people. "No need to worry, everyone, Kellan's sorry, so everything is fucking perfect again."

I lifted my arm to show him the cast covering me from wrist to elbow. "Sometimes you screw up so badly that apologizing is the only thing left that you can do, Denny. I figured you, of all people, would understand that." Denny sighed and looked away from me. I sighed too. I was so tired of this. "Look, I know you're mad. I know I fucked up, okay? But all I'm worried about right now is Kiera...and whether or not she's going to be okay. So maybe we could...hold off on trying to kill each other until she's better?"

Denny's eyes returned to mine. The anger had faded, and all I saw was sadness. "I don't want to kill you. I just…don't want to ever see you again."

His words stung, but I deserved them. Nodding, I whispered, "I know. And as soon as she's okay, you won't have to. But until then, maybe we could…sort of get along?"

Denny gave me a curt nod. "Yeah. All right. For her sake, we'll play nice."

Closing my eyes again, I laid my head back on the chair. *Good. Now let's just hope she wakes up soon.*

My nurses came back a little while later with paperwork and steri-strips. I let them do whatever they wanted while I signed myself out of the hospital's care. Denny excused himself to make some phone calls once my nurses were gone, so I picked up the phone and called Evan. He was naturally quite concerned when I told him where I was and what I needed.

"The hospital? Why are you at the hospital? Are you okay?" With a sigh, I told him the highlights of my night from hell. When I was finished, he was silent for a really long time. "You were leaving? Without saying goodbye? What about the band? Were you going to tell us, or would we just be wondering where the hell you were next rehearsal?"

I could hear the anger and hurt in his voice. "I was…I would have called when I got wherever…I'm sorry, Evan." My band hadn't entered my mind, just escaping Kiera. God, I was a selfish bastard.

"I'll be there as soon as I can." Evan hung up before I could apologize again, and I stared at the receiver. So I'd messed up in more than one way. My assholishness knew no bounds.

About an hour or so later, Evan walked into Kiera's room. He looked at her still body on the bed, then over at me. His eyes widened as his mouth opened in shock. "Jesus," he whispered.

His eyes flashed to Denny then, and I stood up. "Let's go in the hallway," I told him, "so Kiera can rest." And so he wouldn't start something with Denny.

481

Evan clenched his jaw and his fists started curling. One of them was holding a plastic bag full of fresh clothes for me. With my good hand, I pushed on his shoulder to get him out the door. I closed it once we were in the hallway.

Evan eyed me again in the bright fluorescents. "Denny did all this?" he whispered.

I shook my head. "No, Kiera and I were mugged. The *robbers* did all this." My voice was slow and deliberate. *This is our lie, and we need you to follow it. Please. Let this go. This was as much my fault as his.*

Evan looked away, muttering, "Yeah...robbers." With a sigh, he returned his gaze to me. Sticking out his hand, he passed me the grocery bag. "Here. Clean clothes. And I'll go get your car too, if you give me your keys."

"Thank you," I replied, digging into my jeans for my car keys.

When I handed them over, Evan frowned. "Don't thank me yet. You haven't heard what I'm about to say."

I tensed my muscles in anticipation. This was probably going to hurt. "Okay, hit me." I cringed at my own comment. *Bad choice of words.*

Evan crossed his arms. "You're a selfish son of a bitch, you know that?"

Yes, I'm aware. My eyes drifted back to Kiera's door. "Evan..."

"No." His finger dug into my shoulder. "You seem to think you're all alone in this world, but you keep forgetting the fact that the three of us followed your ass up here when you ran back to Seattle." Eyes boring into me, he shrugged. "Do you think we did that because we were bored?" I opened my mouth to speak, and he shoved me in the shoulder again. "No, you stupid asshole. We did that because we love you, and we believe in you. Your real parents may have been shit, but the three of us, we're your family now. Get that through your damn skull!" His voice was low but intense, and his words sliced me open like razors. I felt raw all over.

"I'm sorry...I didn't think..."

He recrossed his arms. "No, you didn't. How could you ditch us

482

like that? How could you abandon us? What the fuck were we supposed to do without you?" He lifted a hand into the air, like he was dumbfounded by my actions.

I felt like the biggest jackass on the planet. I'd been so stupid, so selfish. I needed to stop that. I needed to grow up. "I don't know. I didn't think of it that way. I just…I guess I thought you'd replace me and move on. I didn't think it would be a big deal…"

Evan's mouth dropped wide open. "Are you high? It *is* a big deal. We can't just *replace* you. You're not something that we can run down to the store and get another one of on a whim. There *are* no D-Bags without you." Careful not to hurt me, he placed his hand on my shoulder. "You say this is our band, but I'm not an idiot. It's not *ours*. This is *your* band, because you're the only one of us who truly is irreplaceable. And we will follow you to the ends of the earth, Kellan, because we believe in you. Don't you get that?"

With a disgruntled noise, he shoved my shoulder away from him. I took a step back as his words sank in. *Irreplaceable? Me?* That didn't sound right. I felt extremely…replaceable. My bandmates had never been anything but honest, patient, accepting, and incredibly loyal though. *We're your family now. Get that through your damn skull!* I was an idiot. Evan was right. We were family.

Thinking about my new family brought to mind a startling statement that Evan had made about my old one. *Your real parents may have been shit…* Shoving aside my lingering insecurities, I asked, "How do you know about my parents?"

Evan's expression softened as he answered me. "You told me, Kellan." I tilted my head in confusion. I never talked about them to anyone. Denny only knew because he'd witnessed the abuse. Evan understood my bewilderment and explained. "You were completely shit-faced at the time, so you probably don't remember. It was after you saw the house they left you…after you saw that all your stuff was gone. You told me that they'd moved and hadn't let you know. I was pretty surprised by that, but…then you told me what they used to do to you."

By the horrified look on his face, I was guessing I'd been pretty graphic. *Shit*. I'd told him. He knew. Did that mean...everyone else did too? "Did you...Did you tell...?"

He shook his head. "No, I didn't tell anybody else. It's not my story to tell," he said with a shrug.

I closed my eyes as relief washed over me. I didn't want to be looked at like a victim. I didn't want to see the sympathy on people's faces. I didn't want to answer questions. I didn't want to think about it. I thought about it enough. "Thank you. I don't...I don't talk about it..."

"Maybe you should?" Evan quietly asked.

I peeked up at him. His brown eyes were soft with compassion. "Maybe..." I whispered. *Someday. When it doesn't hurt so much.* Although, it had been easier than I'd thought it would be to talk to Kiera. That was different though. She was different.

After Evan left to get my car, I stepped into the bathroom and changed. I examined my face in the mirror when I was dressed again. *Damn, Denny did a number on me.* Dad had usually stayed away from my face; he preferred bruising me in places that weren't so obvious. Denny hadn't cared about being discreet, and my face was a detailed map of his fury.

A gash in my lip split it in two, which made smiling, talking, doing just about anything with my mouth painful. My cheek was cut, bruising, and being held together by surgical tape. One eye was near swollen shut, and would be completely black and blue in a few days. The other had a cut above it that was also taped together. Add that to my broken arm, broken ribs, and more bruises and scrapes than I could count, and I was a complete and total mess.

Shoving my dirty clothes into the bag, I stepped back into the room. Denny looked over at me; he seemed a little relieved that I wasn't covered in blood anymore. "Evan left?" he asked.

I nodded as I sat back down in my chair. "Yeah. He's bringing my car back here."

Denny looked thoughtful for a moment, then said, "I should have gone with him. I could have driven him out there..."

"No offense, but I don't think he wants to be around you right now." I tried to put that as politely as possible, but I was pretty sure Evan was still shocked by my appearance. And Kiera's.

Denny sighed and studied his hands. After a moment of silence, I said, "I know I don't have the right to ask, but...what are your plans now?"

He kept his eyes on his hands, and several seconds passed before he answered me. "I'm going to take the job in Australia. I'm going to go home."

I swallowed the lump in my throat, the pain in my chest. Even after everything, I would miss him when he left. I knew I couldn't ask him to reconsider though. "Oh...And Kiera? Are you going to take her with you? Once she's...better." It hurt even worse to ask him that, but I couldn't stop the words from exiting my mouth. I needed to know what her future held.

Denny looked up at Kiera, then looked over at me. "No. I'm going home alone."

My eyes drifted over to Kiera; her bandaged skull did nothing to diminish her beauty. This would shatter her, when she woke up. *She has to wake up.* "You're going to break up with her?"

Denny scoffed. "I don't think we ever truly got back together after she broke up with me when I was in Tucson, but...yes, I'm going to end it. She's all yours," he muttered under his breath.

I wasn't sure if he'd meant for me to hear that, but I had, and it brought up some conflicting emotions. With Denny out of the way, I probably could have her...but did I want her? Yes, I did. But not like this. I wanted her to choose me because I was the one she wanted. That wasn't going to happen though. We were over too.

Time ticked on. Kiera occasionally moved, occasionally groaned, but she never opened her eyes. Late that night, she finally spoke though. Eyelids flickering like she was having a nightmare, she muttered, "No..." followed by "Kellan...don't go..."

My eyes were wide as I stared at her in shock. I was thrilled she'd spoken, and amazed that she was thinking about me in her medicated daze. Feeling hopeful that she really was getting better, I looked over at Denny. I was about to ask him if he'd heard her, but his expression made it clear he had. He didn't look as happy as me.

Meeting my eyes, he stood from the bed. "Why don't you come over here and sit by her?"

I started to bunch my brows together, but it hurt, so I stopped. "Are you sure?"

Denny nodded, then looked out the window. "It's getting late. She seems to be getting better, so I think I'm... yeah, I'm gonna go home. Maybe pack up some stuff."

That got me out of the chair. "Where are you gonna go?"

From the sudden glint in his eye, I thought he might tell me it was none of my business, and really, it wasn't, but he let out a sigh and told me anyway. "I think I'll see if I can crash with Sam for a while."

Not knowing what to say to that, I simply nodded. In the silence, Denny gathered his jacket, gave Kiera a soft kiss on her forehead, and started to leave. Before he was all the way out the door, I called out, "Denny... I'm sorry."

He stopped in the doorway, then nodded. His back still turned to me, he said, "I'll be back in the morning. Call me... if anything changes." He left without waiting for an answer.

Once he was gone, I sat beside Kiera on the bed. Grabbing her hand, I whispered, "I'm here, baby. I'm not going anywhere."

Chapter 32

Permanent

When Denny returned the next morning, he was smiling. I thought that was kind of strange, considering the circumstances. "You seem...chipper," I told him, keeping my eyes on Kiera.

Denny sighed as he stood by Kiera's head. "I'm not. Not really. I just...I took the job. I'm starting in a couple weeks."

"Oh...congratulations." Peeking up at him, I asked, "Did Sam take you in?"

Denny glanced at me from the corner of his eye. "Yeah. I didn't go into a lot of detail, just said Kiera and I broke up."

After he said that, Kiera moved, and her eyelids fluttered open. We both leaned forward. "Kiera?" I said, grabbing her hand.

"Kellan?" she whispered, then her eyes drifted shut again.

Denny's gaze shifted between the two of us. "I'm gonna...get something to eat. Want anything?" I shook my head. All I wanted was for Kiera to open her eyes, look at me, and smile in a way that would let me know everything was okay.

The doctors came in, removed her bandages, and said the swelling was down and she should wake up anytime, but it wasn't until the following morning that she finally did.

I was talking to a nurse in the hallway when Denny approached. He'd spent the night at Sam's again last night, while I'd stayed at the hospital. I thanked the nurse for all her helpful information, which really wasn't that much. All they kept telling me was *Wait and see. Time will tell. It's up to Kiera now.* I was really sick of those kinds of answers. I wanted to know the exact minute she was going to wake up and be herself again. It was beyond frustrating that no one could tell me that.

The nurse flushed as she touched my elbow. "No problem, Kellan. Anything I can do to help. If you have any more questions, you just come and find me, okay?" She winked as she left.

Denny shook his head. "Even looking like that, women still hit on you." His eyes clouded and his smile faltered, like he suddenly remembered why he hated me. "How is she?" he asked.

"Same."

We walked back into her room and Denny's expression shifted again as he took in the slight form of Kiera's still body. Now he looked like he was remembering why he hated himself. "I talked to Anna last night. She's going to tell Kiera's parents for me. She sounded pretty worried...and mad..." His voice trailed off as he stared at his comatose girlfriend. Well, ex-girlfriend.

Watching him closely, I asked, "When are you going to tell Kiera about...?"

He looked over at me. "About the job, or about the breakup?"

"Both." I shrugged and looked back at Kiera on the bed. When was *I* going to tell her?

"I don't know. Sooner is probably better than later. If I tell her now, then leave...yeah, she'll be hurt, but I think she'll get through it." He gave me a meaningful glance, and I understood right away. *I would help her through the pain, just like before...*

As he studied me, his face changed again. "I am sorry, Kellan... for what I did to you. To her."

Looking down, I shook my head. *It wasn't your fault...*

He didn't give me a chance to shift the blame though. Turning to face me, he said, "I want you to take care of her when I'm gone. And...if you hurt her...I'll kill you. You know that, right?"

I laughed at the humor in his voice; it had been a while since

I'd heard it. I considered telling him that I wasn't going to date her...that I was breaking up with her too, but right at that moment, Kiera sat up straight on the bed and screamed, "No!" She immediately clutched her head and fell back to the pillows, gasping in pain.

Denny was closest to the bed. He stroked her face to calm her down, then twisted to me behind him. "Go get a nurse."

She's awake. Relief washed through me, and I didn't even hesitate. "I'll be right back."

Spinning on my heel, I darted out the door. Spotting Kiera's nurse, I sprinted over to her. "She's awake! And she's hurting. She needs you to do...something."

Grabbing her arm, I tried pulling her to Kiera's door, but she swatted me away. "Calm down. Let me finish up what I'm doing, then I'll be right there."

I inhaled a deep breath as excitement and anxiety coursed through me. *She's awake.*

After the nurse was finished jotting down notes, she made her way to Kiera's room. I waited in the open doorway while she stepped inside. "Good...she's awake. Probably in a good dose of pain too." Kiera tried to smile, but it was clearly forced. "My name is Susie and I'll be taking good care of you today."

She made Denny get off the bed, then added something to Kiera's IV. Kiera looked a little nauseous when she noticed she was attached to one. After checking her vitals, Susie asked, "Do you need anything, sweetie?"

"Water..." she whispered.

"Of course. I'll be right back."

When Susie turned to leave, Kiera's eyes drifted over to me. Her lips parted and her breath picked up. The machine tracking her heartbeat even started beeping faster. It warmed me that I still affected her. It also broke my heart a little. *She made her choice, now I need to let her go...*

Denny had moved around to sit on the other side of the bed. He looked my way when he noticed Kiera staring. He raised his eyebrows at me, then shifted his gaze to the hallway. I understood his silent message. *Could you give us some privacy? Because I'm about to break her heart.* A part of me wondered if maybe he should wait until she'd been awake for longer than twenty minutes, but I suppose it didn't matter.

I moved into the hallway and found a spot by the door to lean against the wall and wait. It was time.

Denny and Kiera were talking softly, but I could hear a phrase every now and again. "Yes…I'm angry." "I wish you'd just told me…" "I should have talked to you…" "I never thought you'd hurt me…" "Where do we go from here?"

That last one had been Kiera's voice. Knowing what Denny's answer was going to be made me slump against the wall. I almost walked farther away so I couldn't hear his answer, but my heart stubbornly wouldn't let me leave. "We go nowhere." "But I was leaving him. I love you…"

Kiera's response to Denny's decree stung, and I forced myself to step away. She *was* leaving me, she *had* chosen him.

As I walked down the hall, I contemplated Kiera's options. Where would she go when she was released? Denny had moved out, so it would be the two of us alone in the house, and I already knew that wouldn't work. I wouldn't be able to stay away from her in that situation. And I needed to stay away. I was stopping the cycle we were stuck in, which meant…I had to ask her to leave. But where would she go? Kiera's words spoken an eon ago echoed through my brain—*I managed just fine without you.* Yeah…she had, and she would again. She would be fine without me. Just fine.

When I returned to Kiera's door, I heard the light sounds of two people crying. Respectfully, I stayed away until I finally heard Denny say, "I'll be back to check on you tomorrow, okay?"

Denny came out of the room a few moments later. He stopped just on the other side of the doorway; his eyes were red and still a little watery. "You okay?" I asked him. Regardless of what Kiera had done to him, I knew what he'd just done hadn't been easy.

"Yeah…I'm gonna take off. I'm really tired. That was…" He

looked back at Kiera on her bed, then back to me, next to the wall. "…More difficult than I thought it would be."

I stared at the ground for a moment, hating what I was about to do. "Yeah…"

Denny's hand came into my field of vision. "Good luck, with everything…and again…I'm really sorry about what I did to you."

I clasped his hand and shook it. "Not half as sorry as I am, for what I did to you."

Denny gave me a brief smile, looked back at Kiera, then left. I watched him go for a moment, gathering my courage with each step he took, and then I made myself walk into Kiera's room. I needed to do this now.

Kiera was lying on the bed with her eyes closed, looking like she was trying to keep it together. Even with the bruise on her face, she was so beautiful against the crisp white linens.

Quietly stepping up to her bed, I stroked her cheek with my finger. Her eyes flashed open, and she seemed surprised to see me. Maybe she hadn't expected me to come back.

I sat down on the bed beside her, my smile warm and comforting. I wanted to savor our last few moments together. "Are you okay?"

"I guess. The pain meds kicked in, and I feel like I weigh a thousand pounds, but I guess I'm going to be fine."

Her eyes were still wet and her cheeks had drying trails of shiny tears on them. Her head might be fine, but her heart was a mess. "That's not what I meant. Believe me, I've talked to about every nurse in here, I know your situation…but are you okay?" I glanced at the door so she'd know I knew about the breakup.

A fresh tear rolled down her cheek as she stared up at me. "Ask me again in a couple days."

Nodding, I bent down to kiss her. How could I not? The heartbeat monitor started beeping faster as our lips moved together. I looked over at it with a laugh. "I suppose I shouldn't do that." I still made her heart race; she made mine pound too. I was going to miss her.

When I pulled away, Kiera grabbed my cheek and ran a finger along my bruise. "Are you okay?"

491

No. I don't think I'll ever be okay again.

I pulled her hand away from my face. "I'll be fine, Kiera. Don't worry about that right now. I'm just so glad that you're...that you're not..." I stopped myself from saying my biggest fear out loud.

Distracting myself from that thought, I held her hand in both of mine. Her fingers stroked my wrist, and I loved every single second of the contact. Would touching anyone else ever feel this good?

"You and Denny were both here?" she asked, surprised.

"Of course. We both care about you, Kiera."

She gently shook her head. "No, I mean, you were both here in the same room, talking calmly when I woke up. You weren't trying to kill each other?"

"Once was enough," I said with a wry smile. "You've been out of it for a couple days. Denny and I...have had several talks." I paused as I remembered our spats. "Those first few talks weren't so...calm." Reaching up, I pushed some hair out of her face. "Our concern for you eventually tempered those conversations, and we talked about what to do, instead of what was done."

Kiera opened her mouth to speak, but I confessed what I knew she must be wondering about. "He told me he took the job in Australia, and when I asked if he'd take you with him...he told me no."

More tears flowed down her cheeks, and I carefully stroked them away. She looked like she might lose it at any second. I hated that we were piling this on her now, when she was still weak and recovering, but it had to happen, and sooner was better than later. "You knew he was going to break up with me today?" she asked.

I nodded. "I knew he was going to do it soon. When you woke up and he looked at me...I figured he wanted to do it as soon as possible." The weight of what needed to be done crushed me, and I looked away. "Rip off the Band-Aid..." I murmured. *Do it now. Then walk away. It will only sting for a second.*

No. It won't. This sting will last for the rest of my life.

I stared at the ground as I willed myself to let her go. Denny was right. It was harder than I imagined. I had to though. This limbo

492

wasn't good for us. When I noticed Kiera's hand reaching out for me, I forced the words from my lips. "What are your plans now, Kiera?"

Her hand dropped as she stuttered for an answer. "My plans? I don't…I don't know. School…work…" *You.*

She didn't say that last option out loud, but I heard it plain as day. *He left me, so I guess I'll stay with you. Since you'll always be here waiting for me.*

Not this time, Kiera.

Heat was in my eyes when I returned my gaze to hers. If I could hold in the anger, I could hold back the pain. "And me? Do we just pick up where we left off? Before you left me…again… for him?"

Kiera's eyes fluttered closed. "Kellan…"

Tears stung my eyes as despair battered against my crumbling wall of rage; I couldn't keep holding it back. "I can't do this anymore, Kiera."

She opened her eyes, and I could see the agony in them, but I couldn't stop now. *Rip off the Band-Aid.* "I was going to let you walk away that night. I told you I'd let you go, if that was what you wanted, and when you said…" I closed my eyes with a sigh. "After that, I couldn't even find it in me to lie to Denny when he found us." Reopening my eyes, I focused on our hands. "I knew he'd attack me when he heard the truth…but I couldn't fight him back. I'd hurt him so badly, I couldn't find it in me to hurt him physically. What we did to him…He's the nicest guy I've ever known, the closest thing to real family I've ever had, and we turned him into my…"

I closed my eyes as the memory of my father merged with my image of Denny when he was attacking me. I'd done that. I'd made him snap. I'd created a monster. "I think a part of me wanted him to hurt me…" I lifted my eyes to Kiera's. "Because of you, because you always chose him. You never really wanted me, and you're all I've ever…" *I'd do anything for you. Why won't you do the same?*

493

Looking away, I swallowed a lump in my throat. "So...now that he's left *you*, now that the choice isn't yours, do I get you?" The heat returned to my voice as I pulled my anger around me like a shield. "Am I your consolation prize?" *Is that all I've ever been?*

Her mouth dropped open like she was shocked I'd come to that conclusion. *What other conclusion have you left me, Kiera?* She opened and shut her mouth, but no words came out. Truth was hard to argue with. "That's what I thought."

Releasing some of the anger, since it was pointless to hold on to it, I let out a long sigh. "Kiera...I wish..." *I wish we'd run away when we'd had the chance. I wish Denny had never returned from Tucson. I wish you'd come out here without him, and I'd fallen in love with you in an honest way, with no regret, no guilt...no pain.*

Knowing wishes were just as pointless as anger, I shifted what I'd been about to say. "I've decided to stay in Seattle. You wouldn't believe how much crap Evan gave me for almost leaving the band." I searched her face as I recalled Evan's disbelief and his odd-sounding words. *You're irreplaceable.* My gaze stopped on Kiera's wounds, and I felt like I was in a daze as I studied her. "I never even thought about my band in this whole mess. I hurt them when they figured out I was planning on ditching town." I hadn't spoken to the others yet, but I could easily picture Matt's shock and Griffin's disgust. I was such an idiot. And it was time to be smart.

I exhaled in preparation. "I'm sorry," I whispered. Leaning down, I placed a soft kiss on her lips, then trailed kisses across her cheek to the soft spot below her ear. I cherished the taste of her, the smell of her, the sound of her. This was probably the last time I'd be close to her. It was quite possibly the last time I would ever see her. The thought filled me with pain, dread, and a hollow ache that burned my insides. *What will I do without her?*

Resting my head against hers, I made myself say the words I never thought I would say to her. "I'm so sorry, Kiera. I love you...but I can't do this. I need you to move out."

Before she could react, I stood and left the room. Any reaction from her would spark a reaction in me, and my reaction to her pain would most likely end with me staying. And I couldn't. Not when her heart wasn't really in it.

I made it halfway down the hall before the tears came. Near the waiting room packed with magazines and vending machines, there was a dimly lit chapel. I headed in there to find some solace so I could fall apart in peace. It was done. I'd ripped off the Band-Aid, but the wound beneath it hadn't healed yet, and I was bleeding out. *How do I go on now?*

Hours later, when I came to grips with my new reality, I headed downstairs. Feeling more than a little lost, I walked the halls of the hospital. Eventually, I bumped into my band when I was coming out of the bathroom near the emergency room. Seeing them here shocked the hell out of me.

"Hey, what are you guys doing here?"

Griffin sniffed. "We came to see you and your chick. Well, your roommate chick." Matt nodded in agreement, and I scrunched my brows as I studied them. What exactly had Evan told them? While I contemplated that, Griffin added, "You look like shit, man. How many guys jumped you?" With a smirk he leaned in and said, "It was one, right? Some tiny five-foot-nothing teenager, huh?" He shook his head with a chuckle. "Wuss."

I looked over at Evan while Matt smacked Griffin in the chest. "They could have killed him, asswipe."

Griffin looked affronted. "Well, they obviously didn't. Lighten the fuck up, dude. You knew I was kidding…right, Kell?"

I managed to nod, but I was still a little dumbfounded. Evan told them the lie? Evan was remaining silent, but on his face was a knowing smile. "I…uh…Kiera's fine, but she's really not up for visitors…maybe tomorrow."

I looked away as I imagined her sobbing into her pillows. Evan put his hand on my shoulder. "Why don't we get out of here? We'll go to Pete's…relax."

"I don't want to relax," I murmured. Looking up at him, I added, "I want to stay here."

Griffin clapped his hands together. "Sweet! Let's go to the cafeteria and see if we can score free food from the desperate chicks."

Matt cocked an eyebrow at him. "Desperate chicks?"

Griffin shrugged. "You know, the fuglies with hairnets, moles, broken dreams, and crusty vaginas who work in cafeterias. It's part of the job description."

Matt could only shake his head at his cousin. "That's so... How is it that no one has murdered you yet?"

Snorting in answer, Griffin started walking down the hall. "Because you can't kill a god, dimwit."

As the pair of them strolled away, I turned to Evan. "You didn't tell them what happened? With me leaving... with Denny."

Evan shrugged. "Not my story, Kellan."

I smiled, then started following my bandmates. "Thank you. I'd rather they didn't know."

"Yeah, I figured as much," Evan replied.

I thought the guys might pester me about the "mugging" once we got to the cafeteria, but Griffin was beside himself once he learned that his stereotype about cafeteria workers was dead wrong. He was in hog heaven, surrounded by cute women offering him a wide assortment of food. But, almost as if they'd heard his derogatory comment in the hallway, none of them gave him the time of day, and he had to pay for every single item he consumed. Most of the staff hit on me while we were there, which led to a different sort of pestering from Griffin, but it was a distraction I gladly accepted. And for a moment, my grief wasn't overpowering and all-encompassing, and my "family" was the reason. I was tremendously grateful for that.

After the guys left, I went back to the quiet chapel. I ended up spending the night there, spread out on a row of chairs. It wasn't the best place to sleep, but it was the closest to Kiera I could get without actually being in the room with her. I was stiff, sore, and tired as hell when I woke up, but I threw on a smile so I could go talk to the nurses and make sure Kiera was fine.

After one of the nurses told me Kiera was up and walking

around, I wandered downstairs to watch people coming and going. Every face had a story—some happy, some sad. After a while, a face I recognized walked through the doors, and it was a face I hadn't been expecting to see.

Standing, I called out, "Anna?"

She turned to me at hearing her name. Her eyes brightened for a second, then darkened. She scanned me from head to foot as I walked over to her. "Oh my God, Kellan...are you okay?"

I forced a smile to my lips. I was getting really good at that lately. "I'm fine. It's good to see you." I wrapped my arms around her, and she gingerly held me back. It was obvious she didn't want to hurt me.

"Denny told me what happened," she whispered. Her eyes were quickly watering as she examined my face. "That son of a bitch. I can't believe he did this to you."

Holding her shoulders, I looked her in the eye. "Don't be mad at him. I did this. I betrayed him, I pushed him over the edge. It's not his fault."

Her jaw tightened, and I knew she didn't really care whose fault it was. "He could have killed her. He could have killed you. I don't care what you did to him, neither one of you deserved...this." Her hand indicated my body.

"Kiera would want you to play nice with him." I gave her a pointed look, then released her. She made some sort of noise that kind of sounded like "Whatever," and I figured that was the best I was going to get from her. Changing subjects, I said, "Kiera will be happy to see you, and she could probably use a dose of happiness right now."

A playful grin on her lips, she poked me in the shoulder. "She could probably use a dose of *you* right now. Coming?" She tilted her head, and her long, dark ponytail danced around her shoulders.

"No...I can't go back in there." Her mouth dropped open as surprise filled her. Her resemblance to Kiera was so striking, my heart constricted. Breathing hurt. Moving hurt. Everything hurt. "I broke things off with her...and...I asked her to move out. It's over. We're over." A knot formed in my throat, and I had to swallow three times to loosen it.

Anna's expression changed to one of sympathy. "Oh...I'm sorry."

I shifted my gaze to the floor so I wouldn't have to see Kiera in her eyes. "Yeah...so, I'm staying away from her. It's just...too hard. I need space." I peeked up at her face. "I need a minute."

She seemed confused by that phrase, and I almost smiled. That was Kiera's and my inside joke. Only, it wasn't funny. Not funny at all. "When you see her...don't let her know I'm here. It's better if she thinks I left."

Her brows bunched as she looked over my clothes. "How long have you been here?"

I kept my expression as even as possible. "Since the accident. I'm not leaving until I know she's okay. As long as she's here...I'm here. But...she doesn't need to know that, okay?" She frowned and I made my gaze as stern as I could with my swollen eye. "I'm serious, Anna. I don't want her to know I'm here."

Anna slowly shook her head, a sad smile on her face. "Okay, Kellan...if that's the way you want it, I won't tell her."

I nodded. "If anything changes with her...please let me know."

It was a couple of hours later when Anna came back down. I perked up when she walked over to where I was sitting in the cafeteria. "How is she?" I asked, hoping I didn't sound desperate for information but knowing I did.

Anna eyed me thoughtfully before she answered. I wasn't sure what that meant. "She's all right. Tired and teary-eyed, but all right." Changing her expression to an exuberant smile, she added, "I'm gonna stay in Seattle with her. Find a job, and a place for us to live." Her features softened into compassion. "I'm going to take care of her, Kellan, so you don't need to worry."

I exhaled in relief. *Good. She'll be taken care of.* "Did you tell her I was here?" I asked, watching her carefully for signs of guilt.

She averted her eyes. *Bingo.* She'd told on me. "It...may have come up." I was about to scold her for her lack of promise-keeping when she suddenly reached out and poked a finger into my chest. "But you can't complain about that, because you, sir, are on my shit list. The second you're healed, I'm smacking your ass. And not in a good way."

I frowned, confused. "What did I...?"

Anna raised an eyebrow. "You told her we slept together? Really?"

I snapped my mouth closed. *Oh yeah...that.* "It was more...I didn't deny it when she made the assumption that we had."

Anna leaned over me. "I don't like guys taking credit for shit they didn't do. And trust me, if you and I *had* screwed that night, you wouldn't have been able to deny it if you wanted to. You'd still be telling your friends about us..." She leaned in even closer, giving me a pretty decent shot of her cleavage. "...All the damn time."

With a huff, she straightened and stalked away from me. I watched her hips swaying as she walked, and thought she was probably right. Griffin sure as hell couldn't shut up about her. He was going to flip his lid once he found out she was back.

Once Anna was gone, I opened my palm and stared at the guitar pendant I'd been hiding in my fingers. I'd cleaned off the blood the last time I'd gone to the bathroom, and it glistened in the lights. I wasn't sure what I wanted to do with it, but staring at it was oddly soothing, and I found myself doing it all the time.

Now that Anna was here, it seemed like things were falling into place for Kiera. That made me feel better. Anna would take care of her. I could let her go now. Maybe that was what I should do with the necklace—toss it in the trash and let it go.

I stuffed it back into my pocket instead. I couldn't completely let Kiera go.

Anna was true to her word, and quickly found a place for her and Kiera. Once Kiera got out of the hospital, she'd be all set for her new life...without me. I wouldn't even see her at Pete's anymore; Jenny told me she quit. My world felt like it was crashing down around me, but I guess that was how breakups felt. I wouldn't know; I'd never had one before.

Everyone was helping Anna and Kiera get situated in their new place, so I helped too. I thought it would be cathartic, but really, it was just painful. I didn't have much to offer, but I gave Anna the only decent thing I owned—my comfortable chair. Kiera should have it. Maybe she'd think of me whenever she sat on it.

Leaving the hospital with Kiera still inside it had been difficult, but walking through her new apartment was so much worse. She'd build a life here, and I wouldn't be a part of it. Walking past a box of things in the hallway, I paused and reached into my jacket. Making sure no one was around, I pulled out Kiera's necklace. I stared at it a moment in the dark hallway, debating, then I turned my palm around and dumped it into the box. It wasn't mine to keep. I had given it to Kiera and, much like my plush chair, I wanted her to have it. I would remember Kiera in my own way.

Later, when I was walking through my home, the enormity of its emptiness settled over me. Everything of Kiera's was gone; all I had left were memories…but even those would fade with enough time. If I still had her necklace, I could stare at it, or wear it, and have something with me all the time that would remind me of her, but I didn't. All I had was an elastic hair band in my pocket, and that would eventually fray and snap as it aged. It wasn't enough. I wanted something more…permanent…to remind me of her.

A thought struck me as I headed back to my car. It overwhelmed me so fast, I had to lean against the door as I processed what I'd just imagined. *Permanent.* There was only one thing I could think of that wouldn't fade, break, or shatter. I could have her with me every second of every day. I could carry her, on my skin, seared into my flesh…permanently.

An ancient conversation floated through my brain…*Do you have one? Tattoo? No, I can't think of anything I'd want permanently etched on my skin.* Only now, I could. *Her.* I wanted Kiera's name branded on me for all time, because *she* was permanent. I would always love her. Always.

Chapter 33

Missing You

Kiera was released from the hospital the following day. The news was bittersweet for me. She was healed enough to go home, which was great, but that meant I had to go home too. We'd be so much farther apart now. But that was what needed to happen.

I left the hospital before Kiera was cleared. I didn't want her to accidentally see me downstairs and read too much into it. We were done, and that fact wasn't changing. My house was frigid when I stepped inside it. As I trudged up the stairs, I wondered if it would always be chilly here now, if that was my new reality—bone-numbing cold. When I got to the top of the stairs, I saw that Kiera and Denny's door was open. In slow motion, I walked over to it and peeked inside. All I saw was the bleakness of Joey's worn furniture. Pained, I gently closed the door. I wasn't going in there ever again, so there was no point in having it open. I wouldn't be renting that room anymore either. I couldn't. Even though she would never be returning to it, the room belonged to Kiera. I may as well board the door shut.

Feeling worn to the bone, I headed to my room and crashed on my bed. That was when I noticed that the Ramones poster Kiera had given me was still hanging on my wall. Even though I should take it down, I left it up. No matter what I did, Kiera would always be with me. Ripping down her memento wouldn't change that fact.

I spent a lot of time alone that week. Well, not entirely alone. My band started meeting for rehearsals again, and when we weren't playing, we were either at Pete's or my house. Like they'd all gotten together and decided on a Kellan-watching schedule, someone showed up at my place almost every day. It was usually Evan, but Matt popped over from time to time, and so did Griffin. Of course, Griffin mainly showed up to watch TV, but that was fine.

So, while I wasn't physically alone that much, mentally I'd checked out. I stared off into space a lot and spoke to others only when absolutely necessary. Left to my own devices, I probably would have become a recluse, but my friends wouldn't let me. Everyone kept trying to pull me out of my funk, but I didn't want to be pulled out.

The only thing I cared about was Denny and Kiera. I thought about both of them all the time, and they were each hurtful to think about, for vastly different reasons. I felt myself falling deeper into depression every day.

I was staring at the bubbles in my beer one night at Pete's when I felt someone sit beside me. Expecting a forward fan, I was a little startled to see Sam in the next chair. Running a hand over his buzz-cut hair, he sighed and said, "Look, I don't want to get in the middle of whatever is going on with you and Denny, but...he's leaving tomorrow. Like, *leaving*, leaving. I thought you might want to know, in case...you know, there was something you wanted to say to him."

He gave me a pointed glance, then stood up. As I watched him leave, I felt some of my haze start to lift. Denny was heading home, but he wasn't gone yet. I had one last chance to set things right between us. If that was even possible.

Finishing my beer, I laid down some money for my tab, then headed toward the door. Thinking about saying goodbye to Denny naturally brought Kiera to my mind. I missed her so much that every second was almost unbearable. I went to bed staring at the poster on my wall, and woke up every morning still facing the same direction, as if even in my sleep, I couldn't turn away from her.

Realizing that now was the perfect time to create my inked memorial of her, I turned around and found Matt over by the pool tables. "Hey, can you show me that tattoo place you like? I want to get something."

Matt looked shocked. I'd resisted getting anything on my body for a really long time now. The guys didn't even ask me to get one with them anymore, because they knew I'd say no. Except today. Today I was saying yes. "Uh...yeah, sure. When do you want to go?"

Reaching over to a nearby stool, I handed him his jacket. I wanted to do this while the idea was still fresh in my head. And the odds were good that Kiera would be with Denny tomorrow. If I was going to see her, I wanted to have her armor upon me. "Now," I told him. It was getting late, but I was betting the parlor was still open. Late hours were kind of good for them. Matt finished his beer with a shrug, then followed me out the door.

Forty-five minutes later, I was sitting back in a chair, being prepped for a tattoo of Kiera's name right above my heart. Matt looked unsettled by my choice. "Are you sure about this, Kellan? Removing tattoos is a bitch, and there's always a little bit left behind that you can see..."

I shook my head. "I don't want this removed. And yes, I'm sure." I wasn't doing this for Kiera. I wasn't doing this for show. This was purely for me, so I could have Kiera next to me for all time. I'd never been surer about anything in my life.

Once the design was in place and the tattoo was ready, the needle hummed to life. Matt cringed, but I didn't. I'd experienced more pain in my life than most. This was nothing. I didn't even flinch when the man started digging into my body. The sting brought me one step closer to Kiera, and I cherished the burn.

When the artist was done, he showed me the jet-black swirls, edged in raw, irritated skin. Kiera's name was backward to me in the mirror, but it was still obvious what it said. In awe, I tenderly traced my finger around the loop of the *A*. "It's perfect. Thank you."

He put some ointment on it, bandaged it up, then started giving me instructions on how to care for it. I only halfheartedly listened to him. My chest felt different where Kiera's tattoo was. I was conscious of her name above my heart, even if I could no longer see it. It felt like she was with me, forever by my side, like a piece of her soul had been infused into the ink and now it was embedded into my body. Ridiculous, yes, but that was how it felt. The actual girl might be out of my hands, but this was something I could hold on to.

I couldn't sleep that night. I tried for a while, but when it was clear it wasn't happening, I headed down to the airport. Searching the departures board, I found Denny's flight. It was hours from now, so I figured I had some time before he showed up. I found a spot, then began the tiresome act of waiting.

While I waited, I ran through a list of things that I could say to him. But really, the only thing left to say was goodbye. And maybe that was all that needed to be said.

As dawn approached, the airport grew busier and busier. I was sitting in my chair, staring at my cast, when I felt eyes on me. Either airport security was finally going to ask me to buy a ticket somewhere or leave, or Denny was here. When I raised my eyes, it was Kiera who was staring at me though. Seeing her after all this time was like a sledgehammer to the stomach, and I instinctually avoided looking directly at her face. Looking at her would be like staring into the sun; I'd be burned, blinded by her beauty.

Standing, I kept my gaze focused solely on Denny. He was the one I was here for anyway. Out of the corner of my eye, I still noticed Kiera though. Even though I couldn't see her well, she filled my mind, and my head was screaming at me to fully look at her. *A glimpse is not enough.*

Silencing the desperate voice in my head, I bored holes into Denny instead. I wasn't here for her. I didn't need to see how green her eyes were today, how plump her lips were. I didn't need to look at the curve of her jeans as they hugged her body, or the cut of her sweater. I didn't need to see any of it. And I didn't have to. My brain could easily supply the missing information. She was picture-

504

perfect in my head, and my chest burned around my new tattoo. My armor, my homage...my shout of devotion to the only person I would ever love.

Denny's dark eyes were wide with surprise. I was clearly the last person he'd expected to see here. I noticed him clench Kiera's hand tight, in an almost possessive way, before completely dropping it. Kiera didn't belong to either of us.

Not sure what he would do, I stuck my hand out when he was standing in front of me. Would he accept my token of friendship, or completely reject me? I honestly had no idea. After a moment of careful consideration, Denny grasped my hand. I was shocked, and I felt like a small bridge had been put in place between us with that one gesture. Maybe there was hope for our friendship after all.

I couldn't contain my happiness, and a brief smile lit my face. "Denny...man, I'm..." The joy faded as an apology faltered on my lips. I was so sick of saying "sorry." That word wasn't big enough for what I'd done.

Denny dropped my hand. "Yeah...I know, Kellan. That doesn't mean we're okay...but I know."

His voice was tight, and I knew he was still upset, but he was being a bigger man. That was Denny. Always willing to turn the other cheek. "If you ever need anything...I'm...I'm here." Even as I said the words, they sounded stupid to me. *What could I possibly do for him?* But I meant it, and I needed to say it.

Denny's jaw tightened. Anger, jealousy, and sadness rushed over his face, all at the same time. With a sigh, he looked away from me. "You've done enough, Kellan."

I couldn't tell where his emotions had ended up, and his statement could be construed in a few different ways, but knowing what I knew about him, I chose to believe that he'd meant that in a positive way. That he was thanking me, in the only way he could, since saying the actual words would be too much of an absolution of my sins.

With emotion threatening to tighten my throat and cloud my eyes, I clapped Denny on the shoulder. "Take care...mate." I wasn't sure if that's what I was to him anymore, but he would always be that to me. He would always have my friendship.

Surprising me again, Denny returned my gesture and my sentiment. His ability to forgive astounded me. "You too... mate."

Feeling good about coming here and saying goodbye to Denny, I pulled him in for a quick hug, then swiftly turned and left. I didn't want to cave and acknowledge Kiera. I didn't want to open that wound, and I didn't want to deviate from the point of this moment. Denny was the one I'd needed to talk to today. Kiera... well, I'd already said everything I needed to at the hospital. There was nothing left to say there. We were done.

Even still, I couldn't stop myself from one last look at her before the crowd completely separated us. She was watching me too, and for a few brief seconds, our eyes locked. It had been a long time since I'd looked her directly in the eye. It made a surge of pain rip through me, like I was holding on to an electric fence. It made me feel weak, and I was certain I would fall to the floor any second. Or, more accurately, I was going to run over and scoop her into my arms. I couldn't though, so even though my soul protested leaving, I turned away from her and let the crowd swallow me whole.

I stopped a ways down the hall and looked back. I could see Denny and Kiera through the breaks in the people. They were turned away from me. Denny had his arm around Kiera, and she had her head on his shoulder. Even from this distance, they seemed more like friends giving each other comfort than two people in love saying goodbye.

After a moment, Denny leaned down and gave her a kiss. It was clearly a goodbye kiss, probably the last one they would ever share. Feeling intrusive, I looked down. They should have their moment to end things without me looking on.

When curiosity compelled me to know what was happening, I looked up. Denny was gone, and Kiera was staring down a hallway. I had to assume that's where he had disappeared to. He was finally gone, and Kiera looked like she might throw up or pass out.

Maybe both. My feet were moving toward her before my brain even registered it. Without consciously meaning to be there, I was close beside her when her legs gave out.

I didn't make it in time to completely catch her as she fell, but I at least saved her head from smacking into one of the seats bolted into the floor. Huddling close to her, I lowered her head to my knees and waited for her to come around. "Kiera?" I said, stroking her back and feeling her flushed face.

She lifted her head slowly, like it was suddenly much heavier than normal. There were still traces of a yellowing bruise near her eye, but it was almost gone, and she was nearly perfect again. No…even with the bruise, she was perfect; always had been, always would be.

We stared at each other in silence for a moment, then she sat up and tossed her arms around my neck. Straddling my knees, she gripped me tight with everything she had. For a brief moment happiness filled me, but then I remembered our distance, remembered that we were through, and the joy turned to acid. I stiffened with the intensity of the pain burning through me…then I relaxed and held her back. I could push the agony away for a moment and enjoy the feel of her in my arms again. Just for a minute.

Rocking us back and forth, I murmured that everything was going to be okay. Kiera cried in my arms while I tenderly rubbed her back and kissed her hair. She was still hiccupping and struggling for breath, but the tears had stopped when I pulled away. Wanting to hold her tighter, I instead pushed her away. It felt wrong to do it, but it was time to end this. Kiera clutched me, not wanting to let me go. It took a lot of willpower, but I eventually released myself from her grasp and stood up.

Kiera peeked up at me, saw the resolution on my face, then shifted her gaze to the floor.

Leaning down, I gently touched the top of her head. When she looked up at me again, I gave her a soft smile. She was so beautiful. "Can you drive?" I asked, remembering how distraught she had been the last time Denny had left on a plane.

I thought she'd say no, but her face shifted from despair to deter-mination, and she gave me a stiff nod. She wanted to get through this on her own. Proud of her, I extended a hand and helped her stand up.

She stumbled as she stood, and braced herself with a hand on my chest, right over my tattoo. I hadn't removed the bandage yet, and the area was still a smidge on the sore side. I flinched before I could stop myself. Holding my breath, I hoped she didn't ask what was wrong. But there was so much wrong with this situation that she didn't ask, and I relaxed.

Removing her hand from my chest, I held her fingers in mine. A part of me never wanted to let go.

Staring into my eyes, her own a heartbroken shade of jade, she murmured, "I'm so sorry, Kellan—I was wrong."

I wasn't sure what she meant by that, but I didn't have it in me to ask. Holding her, being next to her, it felt too nice. I needed to get away. My head lowered to hers, hers lifted to mine, and our lips met in a warm, soft kiss. It would be so easy to ask her to take me back, to ask her if we could try again. But I needed more, and all I could hear on a never-ending loop was "*Him.*"

I made myself break away from the multiple tiny, hungry kisses I was giving her. Not caving in to a full, lengthy kiss made my heart spike, my breath quicken. I wanted her, but that was nothing new. I still couldn't have her. Dropping her hands, I forced myself to take a step back. "I'm sorry too, Kiera. I'll see you... around."

Turning, I got out of there as quickly as I could before my willpower evaporated. I knew I'd just lied to her when I said I'd see her around. The only way Kiera and I would get through this was if we remained apart. She would live her life, I would live mine, and Denny would live his. It was time for all three of us to move on.

If only I could.

Days passed. Then weeks. Then months. My cast was removed, my bruises faded, my cuts vanished. By the look of me, you'd never know I'd had my ass thoroughly kicked. No, there were no more physical reminders of that night's carnage. But the wound on my heart? That one was still seeping, oozing, and infecting the rest of my body with poisonous toxins that would surely kill me one day. I had become a bitch to be around. Even I knew it.

It may as well have been *Groundhog Day* over and over, because my life never changed. I woke up, exercised, had coffee, worked on lyrics, met with the guys, then spent the night either drinking or playing, or both. I was alive, but I wouldn't call what I was doing living. I drank a lot, cursed a lot, and generally gave people curt, sullen answers to their questions. My patience was all but gone. I hated every day that went by that I didn't get to see her face, hear her voice, touch her skin.

I even lunged at Griffin a time or two. The first incident was after he'd said, "Dude, why don't you go find a nice toy store downtown and buy yourself a strap-on, since it's obvious your dick has been sawed off." Matt had spared Griffin from a broken nose by about two seconds.

The next time I'd gone after Griffin, he'd purchased a "friend" for me, like he had for Matt a while back. After I'd politely turned the aggressive girl down, I'd found Griffin and asked him if that was his doing. "I'm just trying to help you out, man. You need to fuck something before you explode." I'd "exploded" on Griffin. Matt hadn't been fast enough that time, and Griffin sported a black eye for weeks, Of course, he wore it as a badge of honor and used it to pick up women.

He was still seeing Anna though, and every time they got together, my mood darkened. She looked so much like Kiera, it was painful. I wanted them to break up so I could stop being around the constant reminder of what I'd lost, but the two of them were still going at it. All I could do was suck it up and deal with it.

"Hey, Kellan," Anna said to me one night. She was dressed in her work uniform—bright orange shorts and a tight white tank top with the word "Hooters" right over her chest. Every guy in the bar was eyeing her, except me. I was trying to avoid looking at her.

"Hey," I said, studying the bottle in my hands.

Out of the corner of my eye, I saw her hand start to reach out for me, but she stopped herself and laced her fingers on the table. "How are things?" she asked.

"Fine."

She leaned forward, her dark hair brushing against the table. It was clear from her posture that she wanted me to look at her, but I didn't. "Do you need anything?" she asked.

Beer. Peace and quiet. More beer. And your sister . . .

"No."

I took a long swig of my drink, but Anna didn't leave. After I set it down again, she leaned toward me and whispered, "Matt told me about your tattoo. Did you really . . . ?"

I peeked up at her with cold eyes and she stopped talking. I wanted to ask her if Kiera knew about the tattoo, but I didn't. It didn't matter if she did know. I sullenly returned my eyes to my bottle, and Anna sighed in defeat. Standing, she put a hand on my shoulder and gave me a friendly squeeze. She started to walk away, then paused, like she was debating what to do. Leaning down, she whispered into my ear, "She misses you too."

I closed my eyes as they instantly filled with tears. I heard Anna leaving, but I couldn't watch her, couldn't tell her goodbye. All I could do was inhale and exhale in slow, controlled breaths and pray to God that I didn't break down.

She misses you too.

She misses you too.

I wasn't sure why my subconscious kept replaying Anna's message, but I wanted it to stop. I spotted Emily, Kiera's replacement, helping a table of frat boys halfway across the bar. She wouldn't be helping me anytime soon. Irritated, I looked up at Rita. She was busy too. *Damn it.* What did a guy have to do to get drunk around here?

Determined to satisfy my own needs, I stood up. I would hop over the bar and grab my own beer if I needed to. My vision swam as the change in position made the alcohol rush to my head. I put my hand on the edge of the table to steady myself. The dizziness would pass in a minute, and then I could finally get another fucking drink. Maybe if I had enough of them, I would black out tonight, and then maybe I wouldn't dream about Kiera.

She didn't choose me.

My dark thoughts made it hard to stand upright, and both of my hands dropped to the table as I leaned over it. Griffin stopped his conversation with Matt to glare at me. "Dude, are you gonna hurl? Hold that shit in until you get outside."

Matt's eyes were as sympathetic as Evan's. "You okay, Kell?"

Sniffling, I shoved myself away from the table. I stumbled, but managed to stay upright. I guess I'd had more than I realized. Oh well, a couple more wouldn't hurt then. When I moved to head toward the bar, Evan stood and grabbed my elbow.

"Let me go, Evan," I snapped.

His mouth compressed into a firm line. "You've had enough; I'm taking you home."

Scoffing, I jerked my arm away and pointed at the table. "I had two." My words were slightly slurred, but I didn't care.

Matt skewed his lips as he looked up at the ceiling. He counted something out on his fingers, then lowered his eyes to mine. "Uh, more like nine, Kell."

Annoyed, I grabbed my jacket. "Whatever, I don't need you guys babying me. I'm tired of being babied...I can take care of myself." If I couldn't drink in peace here, then I would drink in peace somewhere else. Scowling at Matt and Evan, I slipped my jacket on. Or tried to anyway. I couldn't seem to find the right holes.

Matt stood up when he figured out I was leaving. "You're not driving."

Irritated at my guitarist, irritated at my drummer, and irritated at my life, I jerked my head from one band member to the other; the room spun a little. "I'll do whatever the fuck I want! All of you can leave me the hell alone!" Finally successful, I slipped my jacket over my shoulders. Inexplicably, the leather smelled like Kiera.

Matt rolled his eyes and looked over to Evan. He sighed, then started rifling through my jacket pockets. I batted his hands away,

511

but he was way more coordinated than me at the moment. After fishing my keys out of my pocket, he tossed them down the table, out of my reach. They landed in front of Griffin; he stared at them blankly, then returned his attention to a girl at the next table.

I dove across the table to snatch my keys back, but Matt was quicker and nabbed them first. All I ended up doing was falling onto the table and knocking over Griffin's beer. That got his attention. Saving his bottle from rolling off the table, he snapped, "Dude! What the fuck?"

Wishing I was anywhere but here, I laid my cheek on the cool surface and stared up at Evan. He was even more concerned than he had been before, if that was possible. Conversations battled in my brain. Some with Kiera, some with Denny. Some of them were good, some really, really bad. All of them made electric pain rocket throughout my body; I felt my chest sizzle, like someone was holding a hot iron to my heart...right over Kiera's tattoo.

Not wanting to look like an idiot anymore tonight, I carefully stood up. Feeling weak, defeated, and utterly alone, I muttered, "All right...take me home."

Evan not only took me home, he walked me to my door and unlocked it for me. I scowled at him, but he wasn't intimidated by my anger. "Hey, if you don't want to be babied, then stop acting like a baby." Crossing his arms over his chest, he added, "Now, do I need to tuck you in?"

Grabbing my keys away, I shook my head. The world started spinning, so I stopped. I took a step inside, then looked back at Evan. "I'm sorry about tonight. I just wanted...I wanted to stop feeling like shit."

Evan sighed, then clapped me on the shoulder. "I know. Get some sleep, okay?"

I nodded and went into the house, but I really wasn't tired yet. At least, not tired in a lack-of-sleep kind of way. I was sick and tired of a lot of things. Stumbling my way into the kitchen, I poured a glass of water and started drinking it. As the soothing liquid went down, sobering me, I stared at my phone. Making a quick decision,

I picked up the receiver and entered a number I knew by heart, since I dialed it almost every single day. The phone picked up on the third ring. "Denny? Hey…it's Kellan. How are…things?"

I'd started calling Denny right after he left Seattle. At first, only his parents would pick up, and they'd always very nicely tell me to go to hell. I'd kept calling though, and eventually Denny had taken the phone from them and talked to me. He'd seemed mystified by my persistence, but…he was family to me. I'd wronged him, but I'd never stopped caring about him. He was my brother. I didn't want to give that up.

Our initial conversations hadn't been much. Denny didn't want to talk, and I understood. I talked though. I told him how wrong I was, how sorry I was, and that I wished I could do everything over again. If I could, I would have told him about my feelings for Kiera before I acted on them. I would have told him everything from the beginning.

Talking to him every day, while therapeutic for me, wasn't really getting our relationship anywhere. It wasn't until I confessed to him that Kiera and I weren't a couple that he really started talking back to me. He was shocked that we weren't together. He'd assumed we'd hooked up after the airport. I told him we hadn't, that I'd said goodbye to her there and hadn't seen or heard from her since. Surprising me, he'd actually told me that I was an idiot for letting her get away. That had made me laugh. I'd told him that it was for the best that we were apart, but only a part of me agreed with that. The rest of me agreed with him.

Denny's laughter on the line returned my thoughts to the present. "Have you been drinking, mate?"

A small, queasy laugh escaped me. "Drinking? Yeah…maybe… a little. So…what's up with you? How did your date go with that girl? Abby, was it?"

With a laugh, he started telling me about it. Things had loosened up between us even more once Denny had become interested in dating again. Now that he was seeing somebody, his entire mood had changed. Even though I didn't know much about this girl, I was grateful that Denny had met her. He needed somebody to love to help him get over Kiera.

Aside from the one time he'd chided me about not dating her, Kiera was one topic that Denny and I never discussed. Without actually verbalizing it, we'd both decided Kiera was off-limits. We had plenty of other things to talk about though, and my phone bill was a bitch now. But we were beginning to repair our damaged friendship, so it was worth it.

Chapter 34

Emotional Release

After that dark moment at Pete's, I toned it down with the alcohol. Instead of drinking away my problems, I shifted my need for emotional release into my work. I'd been writing ever since Kiera and I parted ways, and I finished a song that I'd written about her. Once it was done, I found I was reluctant to share my painful memory of Kiera with the world. Evan was the one who convinced me I should. He said it would be healing to sing about my pain. And unlike the last time I'd written a song for Kiera, Evan was okay with putting this one in the lineup, since this time around, the only person the song would hurt was me.

We debuted the song at Pete's. I was a little worried that I wouldn't be able to make it through the whole piece; I lost it once or twice during rehearsal, which was almost unheard of for me. I'd sung gut-wrenching songs countless times before and hadn't had any problems. But this one...it got to me.

It was probably the most emotional song I'd ever written, even more than the song I'd said goodbye to Kiera with. This one was about that last moment with Kiera in the parking lot, right before our lives had changed forever. I wrote down every damn detail of our parting. Then I shifted focus to where I was now...struggling to get through the days, scared I would never find love again, lonely, but never really alone, because Kiera was always with me wherever I went.

Evan and Matt had created a slow, haunting rhythm to accompany the song. It was different from our typical stuff, and I noticed that the crowd listened in a way they hadn't before. Even my looks took the backseat for this one song. It was intimidating, having the entire bar so focused on something that wasn't superficial, something real. It deepened my appreciation and respect for the art form that had ultimately saved my life. If I hadn't had music... I didn't even want to think about where I might be.

The bar was deathly quiet while I sang my grief. When I sang, *"Your face is my light. Without you, I'm drenched in darkness,"* some of the girls in the front started brushing away stray tears. With the words, *"I'm forever with you, even if you can't see me, hear me, feel me,"* they started to openly weep. I closed my eyes to block them out and finished the song as perfectly as I could. Evan was right. This was much better therapy than drinking my problems away night after night. We started playing the song at every performance.

I wasn't fully healed yet, not even close. Everything still reminded me of Kiera. My soul ached for her, and there was a void in me that would probably never be filled, but, slowly, I was starting to smile again, starting to talk again. Although, I still wasn't sleeping with anyone. Every night, I went home alone to my empty house and faced the ghosts of regret lurking around every corner. It was hard, but I was dealing.

Sometimes I pretended that Kiera was in the crowd when I sang that song for her. Closing my eyes, I pictured her crying right along with the girls in the front row. She never came in though, and as soon as the song ended and I opened my eyes, my fantasy evaporated. Her sister showed up a couple of times, but that was the closest I ever got to Kiera. It ate at me that she never came in to the bar, but at the same time, I knew it was for the best.

"Ready for tonight?" Evan asked one Friday evening, as he eyed me for any sign of a meltdown. Since I hadn't had one in a while, his inspection didn't last long.

"I'm always ready," I answered. Glancing over my shoulder, I looked at Jenny, then back at him. "Are you ready to admit defeat? I think you're being ridiculously stubborn about this."

Evan's brows bunched. "What the hell are you talking about?" He noticed where I'd been looking, then rolled his eyes. "Quit playing matchmaker, Kellan. You suck at it." With a laugh, he slapped me on the shoulder, then hopped up onstage to thunderous applause.

I shook my head at my friend. He flirted with Jenny like they were honeymooners, and she flirted right back, but neither one of them had taken a step toward a relationship. It baffled me. I might have to stage an intervention soon.

I was about to follow Evan up onto the stage, but I saw Anna in the crowd. She was desperately flagging me over. I glanced at Griffin, wondering if she meant him, but when my eyes returned to Anna, she was definitely signaling for me to wait for her. Frowning, I paused at my table and waited for Anna to fight her way through the crowds. She had a group of girls with her, and they quickly melded into the front row.

"What's up?" I asked her, wishing for the millionth time that she was blond and blue-eyed, so she wouldn't remind me of Kiera.

"Are you...singing that song tonight?" She bit her lip, like she was debating something.

She didn't have to explain which song. I knew exactly what she meant. Nodding, I told her, "Yeah, it's in the middle of the lineup, just like usual."

She gave me a quick smile. "Okay. Good."

I narrowed my eyes at her. "Why?"

She swished her hand at me in a dismissive gesture. "My girlfriend wanted to hear it." Before I could reply, she started elbowing her way through the crowd to rejoin her friends. *Okay. That was kind of weird.*

Putting Anna out of my mind, I climbed up onstage and acknowledged the fans with a small wave. The corresponding shriek made my ears ring. It made me smile that at least some things in my life hadn't changed. The people who came to see our shows were still noisy, dedicated, passionate, and hard-core devotees, and I appreciated each and every one of them.

Evan started the intro to our first song on the set list, and just like that, we were off and running. The fans danced, the lights blazed down on us, and the music blasted. I let myself get lost in it, allowed just a moment of pain-free reprieve. When Kiera's song approached, some of my levity faded. The beginning was always the hardest. In preparation for singing it, I had to allow any walls I might have built up to come tumbling down so the emotion could rush out in an honest way. The anticipation was draining, but the release afterward made it all worth it. Like wringing out a sponge to remove every drop of water, finishing the song made me feel fresh again. I could go on another day.

A bit before Kiera's song, I noticed Anna was gone. Guess her friend had gotten tired of waiting. Strange.

There was a commotion near the front of the bar as the song ended, but I blocked it out and concentrated on the fans right in front of me. Kiera's song was next; I needed to shut everything off and focus on making it perfect. I liked to think that every time I played it, Kiera somehow heard it, and I wanted it to be flawless.

The song began and I closed my eyes. Absorbing the words into my body, I let all of my defenses drop. This was me. Laid bare for all the world to see. I felt naked, but I felt free too. No more secrets, no more lies, no more guilt. Just me, sorrowful music, and haunting words of devotion to a lover I would never truly let go of.

I sang about my love and loss, about needing Kiera and feeling ashamed for it. About trying to say goodbye. About taking her spirit with me every day. When I got to a long instrumental section, I swayed to the beat and imagined Kiera was watching me, imagined she was listening to my heart bleeding through the speakers. In my mind, she always cried. The grief meant she cared... she still cared.

Highlights of our love affair flickered through my mind while I waited for my cue. That first awkward handshake. Our first comforting hug. Our first drunken kiss. Making love. Lying in each other's arms. Hearing her say, "I love you." It all replayed in my head in a microsecond.

Ready to wake from my fantasy, I slowly opened my eyes. That was when I saw something that couldn't possibly be real. Icy shock froze me in place as Kiera's eyes bored into me. Was I delirious? Had I imagined this so many times that I'd somehow made it real? Or was she an illusion? A trick of the lights? A by-product of my emotional cleansing? Would she vanish the instant I blinked?

Mesmerized, I watched the tears spilling from her eyes; it was just like how I'd always pictured her during this song. This hallucination of her was different from the visions of her I'd been having though. She was ten times more beautiful right now than she had ever been in all of my countless dreams. *She looks so real...*

Certain this mirage would evaporate into a wisp of smoke any second, I sang the last few lines of the song directly to her. When my voice drifted away along with the last strains of music, I waited for my vision to end. It didn't. Kiera was still in front of me, watching me with tears streaming down her cheeks. Was she really here?

Usually, after this song ended, I signaled Evan to start the next one. This song was so emotional for me that on rare occasions, I needed a minute to collect myself. Evan knew to wait for my signal. I couldn't turn away though. I couldn't do anything but stare at Kiera. Was this real? Would she vanish if I moved?

An uneasy silence filled the bar as Kiera and I stared at each other. I heard people start to shift, cough, and whisper, but I still couldn't move. From the corner of my eye, I saw Matt approaching me. With a light tap on my arm, he whispered, "Kellan, snap out of it. We need to start the next song." I still couldn't move. Every molecule in my body was attuned to Kiera. *God, she's so beautiful.*

Evan's voice disrupted the quiet. "Hey, everybody. We're gonna take a breather. Until then...Griffin's buying a round for everyone!"

Cheers broke out, as well as laughter. I didn't care about either response from the bar, because I was finally beginning to accept the fact that the Kiera in front of me wasn't a mirage, hallucination, or figment of my imagination. She *really* was here.

The crowd around Kiera started to thin out, but I stayed where I was on the stage. I felt safe up there. Jumping down to Kiera's level…could kill me. *Why is she here?*

Kiera stepped forward, momentarily breaking her hold on me. Now that I was able to move, I looked away from her, out over the thinning crowds. I could turn around and leave the bar right now. But…what was she doing here? And why now, after all this time? I was just starting to…well, I wasn't sure if I was feeling any better, but at least I wasn't getting any worse. If I went down there and talked to her…what would happen to me? What would happen if I didn't though? Nothing. Nothing would happen, and we would both continue on, and I would never really heal, never really let go. I'd just continue…getting by.

My decision made, I looked down, sniffed in a quick breath, then lowered myself to the floor. I had to at least know why she was here. Leaving without knowing would tear me apart.

I stepped as close to her as I dared. Our fingers touched and I inhaled a sharp breath; the fire was still there. Being near her was still as electrifying as it had always been. She had tears in her eyes and tears down her cheeks. Unable to resist, I reached up and stroked a bead of moisture away with my knuckle. Her skin was just as soft as I remembered.

Kiera closed her eyes and a sob escaped her. With her puffy, tired eyes, unruly hair, and worn expression, it was clear that she'd been battling the same depression as me; she was a wreck too. It gave me a small amount of comfort that she was. I wasn't the only one having a hard time with this. How much of her sadness was for me though, and how much was for Denny? After all, she'd picked him in the end, and he'd left her too.

Cupping her cheek, I stepped into her until our bodies were touching. I hadn't meant to, but somehow, my body shifted into autopilot around Kiera; being as close as possible was a subconscious action.

Her hand came up to rest upon my chest, and I wondered if she could feel my pounding heart. *I have missed you so much.*

The dispersing crowd had started re-forming once I'd dropped down into the mix. Kiera was jostled by a couple of the more eager girls, and I put an arm around her. Thinking we needed to be somewhere a little more private, I started leading her away. One of the drunker fans rushed right up to me and grabbed my face like she was going to plant a big one on me. I didn't let my fans molest me anymore, so, leaning back, I removed her hands from my skin. Then I shoved her away from me. I generally was a bit more polite when I disengaged from aggressive fans, but I was in the middle of something potentially life-changing here, and I wasn't in the mood to be subtle.

Kiera looked up at me with shock clear on her face. I'd never done anything like that around her before. *I did that for you, because I still love you, and honestly, I still want to be with you.*

Kiera's hand snaked out. For a second, I thought she was going to hit me, but her fingers closed around the wrist of the woman I'd just pushed. Kiera had just saved me from being smacked. That was new.

The fan's face went from shocked to embarrassed, and she scuttled off without a comment. I laughed as I met eyes with Kiera. "No one gets to smack me but you?" I asked, feeling lighter than I had in a long time.

"Damn straight," she said, smiling and blushing at the same time. I had to shake my head at her. She was still so damn adorable. Her expression changed as she watched me, and in a serious voice, she asked, "Can we go somewhere without so many...admirers?"

My good feelings hardened some as I grabbed her hand. Things weren't back to normal here. It was still awkward and awful. There were still too many unanswered questions. I pulled her into the hallway leading to the restrooms. For a minute, I considered pulling her into the back room, but...I couldn't. The memories were too thick in there. And besides, I didn't want to be completely alone with her. I didn't want to cave in to lust because she was next to me. I needed to be level-headed right now.

Kiera looked relieved when I stopped us well before the back room. Closing her eyes, she leaned against the wall. I guess she didn't want to be alone with me either. Were her reasons the same as mine? Or was she just not interested in me like that anymore? No. I was positive that a part of her still wanted me. But a part of her wasn't enough anymore. I wanted it all.

A flash of light around her neck caught my attention. When I recognized the guitar pendant I'd unceremoniously dumped into a box for her to find, my heart almost stopped. I hadn't even been sure she would keep it, much less wear it. The silver necklace seemed to glow against her skin. The diamond in the center shimmered in the lights. It was stunning on her, and with shaking fingers, I reached out to touch it. The metal was cool, but her skin beneath it was so warm... "You're wearing it. I didn't think you would."

She opened her eyes and stared up into mine. *God, she has beautiful eyes.* "Of course, Kellan." She put her hand over mine; it warmed me from the inside out. "Of course," she repeated.

She started to lace our fingers together, but I pulled away and averted my eyes. It was too wonderful, too comfortable. It would be so easy to cave, to give myself over to her. But I didn't want to fall again. I didn't want to get hurt again. Distance was good.

"Why are you here, Kiera?" I asked, returning my eyes to hers.

She flinched under my words, like she was hurt by them, and she seemed uncertain what to say. "My sister" was what she ended up saying. *Right. Anna dragged her to a show.* That was the only reason she'd shown up. She wasn't here for me...

I turned to leave and she grabbed my arm and yanked me back to her. "You... for you." Her voice was brimming with panic.

I searched her face, looking for the truth. "For me? You chose him, Kiera. Push come to shove... you chose him."

She pulled me closer to her as she shook her head. "No... I didn't. Not at the end, I didn't."

Denial? Really? That's her game plan? "I heard you, Kiera. I was there, I heard you clearly—"

"No...I was just scared." She put a hand on my chest, and her ever-changing emerald eyes searched mine. "I was scared, Kellan. You're...you're so..."

"I'm what?" I stepped into her so our hips were touching. Sparks began igniting around us, as they always did.

Kiera stared into my eyes and began to speak; I could tell from her expression and the tremor in her voice that she was speaking straight from her heart. "I've never felt such passion, like I feel when I'm with you. I've never felt this heat." She lifted her hand from my chest to my face. "You were right, I was scared to let go...but I was scared to let go of *him* to be with you, not the other way around. He was comfortable and safe and you...I got scared that the heat would burn out...and you'd leave me for someone better...and then I'd have nothing. That I'd throw Denny away for a hot romance that would be over before I knew it, and I'd be alone. Flash fire."

Understanding crashed over me. She was insecure, and insecurity was certainly something I could understand, but after everything I'd told her about me and my past, with everything that she knew she meant to me...how could she think that I would do anything other than cherish her?

I lowered my head to hers, and our chests pressed together. "Is that what you think we had? Flash fire? Did you think I'd just throw you away if that fire died?" *As if it ever would. Not for me, at any rate.* I shifted my leg between hers and her breath sped up. We were so close; she smelled so good. "You're...the only woman I've ever loved...ever. You thought I'd toss that out? Do you really think anyone in the world compares to you in my eyes?"

"I get that now," she murmured, "but I panicked. I was scared..." Her chin lifted and our lips brushed together.

It was too much. I took a step back. She clenched my arm to stop me from leaving. I gazed at the floor before looking back up at her. Why did I have to love her so much? Why couldn't I walk away?

"You don't think this scares me, Kiera? Do you think loving you has ever been easy for me…or even sometimes pleasant?" *It was a nightmare and a fantasy all rolled up in one.* Kiera looked down, my words stabbing through her like daggers. I didn't want to hurt her, but now wasn't the time to hold back. She needed to know just what she'd done to me. What she continued to do to me. "You have put me through hell so many times that I almost think I'm crazy for even talking to you right now."

A tear rolled down her cheek, and she started to move away like she was leaving. Grabbing her shoulders, I held her against the wall. I didn't want her to leave yet. I wasn't ready. When she looked up at me, another tear rolled down her skin. I brushed it away with my thumb, then I cupped her face and made her look at me.

"I know what we have is intense. I know it's terrifying. I feel that too, believe me. But it's real, Kiera." My hand drifted from my chest to hers. "This is real and it's deep, and it wouldn't have just…burned out. I'm done with meaningless encounters. You're everything I want. I'd never have strayed from you."

Her hands came up to reach me, and I stepped away. I wasn't ready for that either. Sadness filled me as I gazed at her standing a foot away from me. She'd said goodbye to me in that parking lot because of fear, and now I had to do the same to her. And it broke my heart. Again. "I still can't be with you, though. How can I ever trust that…?" My gaze fell to the floor, my voice faded to a whisper. "That you won't leave me one day? As much as I miss you, that thought keeps me away."

She was worried about me straying…but she was the one who'd slept with Denny after telling me she loved me. Right after I'd told her I couldn't stomach the thought of sharing her, she'd lain with him. While I understood how confusing the situation had been, I couldn't quite get over the fact that she had, in an odd way, cheated on me.

Kiera took a step toward me, her voice apologetic. "Kellan, I'm so—"

My eyes snapped to hers. "You left me for him, Kiera, even if it

524

was just some knee-jerk reaction, because the thought of us terrified you... You still were going to leave me for him. How do I know that won't happen again?"

Her answer was oddly calm, determined even. "It won't... I won't ever leave you. I'm done being apart from you. I'm done denying what we have. I'm done being scared."

For the first time ever, I envied her for her courage. "I'm not, Kiera. I still need that minute..."

Her hand drifted to my stomach; her fingertips burned like fire. "Do you still love me?" she asked, hope in her eyes.

A sigh escaped me as I looked over her face. "You would never believe how much."

She stepped closer and her hand ran up my chest. I closed my eyes as tendrils of electricity excited my flesh. Her fingers reached my heart, and I stopped them. Holding her hand over my tattoo, I whispered, "I never left you... I kept you with me, here."

Almost like she knew what I'd done to my body, she pulled my shirt aside. I dropped my hand and let her see. Honesty was all we could do for each other now. The minute she spotted her name upon my skin, her mouth dropped open and her eyes watered. She began to trace the swirling letters with her finger, and my skin pricked with joyous pain wherever she touched me.

"Kellan..."

Her voice cracked on my name. I pulled her searing fingers away, but laced them with mine instead of dropping them completely. Holding our hands against my chest, I rested our heads together again. "So... yes, yes I do still love you. I never stopped. But... Kiera..."

"Have you been with anyone else?" she whispered.

Surprised, I pulled back to look at her. "No... I haven't wanted..." *There is no one else for me but you.* Wondering if she'd been as faithful to a lost cause as I had been, I asked her, "Have you?"

Even though she was quick to answer, I thought I'd be sick waiting for it. "No. I just... I just want you." Relief washed through me, cleansing me. "We're meant to be, Kellan. We need each other," she added in a whisper.

I know. I need you so much, Kiera. No one will do...but you.

Without considering what I was doing, I stepped into her. Her hand slipped around my waist, mine went to her hip. We pulled each other closer, like we couldn't bear to be apart anymore. And I couldn't. I felt like I'd been waiting for this my whole life, and I didn't want to stop it...but...pain and doubt were still waging war within me.

We kept staring at each other's mouths, and the tension between us was mounting. I wanted to kiss her so badly. I wet my lip, dragging my teeth over the tender skin, but it was Kiera I wanted to feel touching me.

I angled my head down to hers; we were just inches apart now, and her fast breath washed over my face. "Kiera, I thought I could leave you. I thought distance would make this go away, and it'd get easier, but it hasn't." I paused to shake my head. "Being apart from you is killing me. I feel lost without you."

"I do too," she murmured.

Our fingers separated. Kiera ran hers up my shoulder, mine trailed down her necklace again. "I've thought about you every day." My fingers kept going, ghosting over her chest, her bra. "I've dreamt about you every night." My fingers trailed along her ribs, hers tangled in my hair. It was intoxicating, and confusing. "But...I don't know how to let you back in."

I pulled back a little to take in her expression; all I saw looking back at me was confident love. I wished I felt the same. I wanted so much to just push all of my fears aside and say yes to whatever this might be, because holding her felt so right. But it had gone so horribly wrong before...I wouldn't survive another heartbreak like that. She was so hard to resist though. My lips lowered to hover just above hers. "I don't know how to keep you out either."

That's when I was shoved from behind. Someone laughed, but I couldn't concentrate on it for long. That small push had closed the distance between Kiera's lips and mine, and now that we were

touching, all thought of walking away fled my mind. I simply...
couldn't.

We froze in shock for a few seconds, then we melted into a long-
desired kiss. It felt different than before, guilt-free, careless, and
about ten times as intense. I wasn't sure if I was going to start letting out tears of joy, curl into a ball of misery, or throw her down
on the ground and take her.

"Oh, God, I've missed..." I couldn't even complete my thought.
Our kiss heated, and still my stupid body tried to speak my conflicting emotions. "I can't..." *do this again.* "I don't..." *want to be
hurt again.* "I want..." *you.* A deep groan escaped me, and Kiera
matched the sound. "Oh, God...Kiera."

Breath intense, I pulled back to grip her face. Her tears were
streaming again, but her breath was just as quick as mine. I wanted
her...so much. "You wreck me," I growled before crashing my lips
down to hers.

I pushed her into the wall as our eager kiss revved up my body.
Her hands tangled into my hair. She wanted me, I wanted her, and
this was really happening. Just as I was running my fingers along
the amazing indentation along her lower back, contemplating how
many steps away from the back room we were, Kiera gently pushed
me away. Confused, I offered no resistance. Was she saying no
again? I shouldn't be surprised, this happened all the time, but
yeah, I was. Hurt immediately started filling my body, freezing my
chest with a bone-numbing ache.

Kiera seemed to understand what I was thinking. Seeing the
pain in my eyes, she immediately said, "I want you. I choose you.
It will be different this time, everything will be different. I want to
make this work with you."

The ache started fading as her words lessened my fears. She
wasn't saying no, she was saying, *Not like this.* I could accept that.
Still fighting the desire within me, I gazed at her lips, her eyes,
then back to her lips again. "How do we do that? This is what we
do...back and forth, back and forth. You want me, you want him.
You love me, you love him. You like me, you hate me, you want me,

you don't want me, you love me…you leave me. There's so much that went wrong before…"

The ever-cycling pain of our relationship overwhelmed me. Even if she did want me, I wasn't sure I could do it again. Being in love was so hard. But not being in love was even worse. I didn't know what to do anymore. Stay, go, love her, leave her.

Kiera brought a hand to my cheek, and I looked up to her eyes. "Kellan, I'm naïve and insecure. You're a…moody artist." My lip twitched at our inside joke that wasn't really a joke, but I contained my laugh. Kiera continued with a smile that warmed and relaxed me. "Our history is a mess of twisted emotions, jealousies, and complications, and we've both tormented and hurt each other…and others. We've both made mistakes…so many mistakes." Leaning back, her smile widened. "So how about we slow down? How about we just…date…and see how it goes?"

It seemed so simple, I was momentarily stunned. Everything about us had been so intense for so long, it was hard to picture it being any other way. But maybe…if we took a step back, went a little slower, we could ease into this, and maybe then we wouldn't both be so scared.

It was the perfect solution, and I was surprised it hadn't occurred to me earlier. I thought an all-or-nothing approach was it for us, but that wasn't necessarily true. I definitely wanted to do this, to see where this could go, but first…I had to tease Kiera a little for her choice of words. I tossed on a devilish smile, and Kiera instantly understood. She'd asked to date me, and in my past, dating had meant sex. Pointless, meaningless sex. I knew that wasn't what she meant now, but making her blush was fun.

Embarrassed, she looked down. "I meant…actual dating, Kellan. The old-fashioned kind."

I started laughing and she looked up. With a peaceful smile that actually felt genuine for once, I told her, "You really are the most adorable person. You have no idea how much I've missed that."

Her smile seemed equally untroubled. Stroking the rough stubble on my unshaven face, she asked me, "So…will you date me?"

She said it suggestively, and my grin grew. "I'd love to…date you." The playfulness of the moment died down, and seriousness blanketed my voice. "We'll try…we'll try to stop hurting each other. We'll take this easy. We'll go slowly."

It was the only way we could truly recover from what we'd done to each other.

Chapter 35

Dating

For the first time in my life, I was dating. Real, old-school dating. And Kiera had said she wanted it traditional, so that was exactly what I did. I opened doors for her when I took her out to dinner, I only held her hand, and I gave her a brief kiss on the cheek at the end of the night. And, surprisingly, I was happy that the evening hadn't ended with sex. It made me feel like we were building something, or rebuilding something. We were forming connections that went deeper than physical intimacy, and as frightening as that was, it was also ten times as euphoric.

When we were together, I couldn't stop looking at her. The fact that she was with me, and only me, was something that blew my mind. My cheeks hurt from smiling so much, and my band constantly asked me if everything was okay. *Yes, it is. Finally.* Or at least, it was getting that way. There were a lot of scars between Kiera and me, and scars took time to heal.

Wanting to prove to myself that I could touch Kiera without it getting overly sexual, I took her dancing next. Everyone came with us, and it turned into a group date. My hands, while desperately wanting to run over every inch of her seductive skin, stayed on her hips. We would have made seventh graders proud. Well, maybe fifth graders.

When we were all gathering together for our date night, Anna greeted me in her typical fashion. With a smack across the head, she muttered, "Ass." I only smiled at her in response. Someday she would get over the fact that I'd pretended that we'd slept together. And even if she didn't, Kiera's smile whenever Anna reprimanded me was glorious. I'd let Anna hit me every day to see Kiera's face light up like that.

Anna wrapped her arms around Griffin, and we didn't see much more of them for the remainder of the evening. Let me rephrase that. During the night, they disappeared for long stretches at a time, but when they *were* around us, we all saw *way* too much of them. Kiera turned green on several occasions.

Jenny came out with us too, and she brought along her roommate, Rachel. Rachel and Kiera worked together at Kiera's new job. I'd met her a time or two before. She was a cute blend of Latin and Asian, and she was quiet as a mouse. Jenny said that made her the best roommate in the world, but it was Matt who looked captivated. The two of them found a corner of the club that wasn't too noisy and spent most of the night talking instead of dancing. I'd never seen Matt really date anyone before—the band took up way too much of his time—but I thought he might actually give it a go with the laid-back girl. Assuming she was into music, of course. If she was ambivalent or uninterested, they'd never work out. I wished them the best.

With all the rest of us paired off, that just left Evan and Jenny. I cornered him in the club hallway. "Are you gonna man up and make a move?" I asked.

He actually had the gall to act clueless. "What are you talking about?"

I smacked his shoulder. "Jenny. You guys are here, dancing together, half-drunk and making moony eyes at each other. Kiss her already."

Evan pursed his lips. "You need to get off that kick."

This time *I* poked *his* shoulder. "And you need to get *on* that. Kiss her. That's an order."

He crossed his arms over his chest. "You can't order me."

I matched his posture. "Yes, I can. You said it was *my* band, remember? So if you want to stay in it, I'm commanding you to lay one on that little fireball. Got it?"

Not intimidated, he raised an eyebrow. "Really? You're gonna kick me out of the band if I don't kiss a girl?"

I shook my head. "No, not 'a girl.' Jenny. The person who you're supposed to be with, but you're too damn stubborn to see it." When he still didn't look impressed, I added, "And no, I won't kick you out…" Smiling, I leaned in and said, "I'll make you wear Griffin's bike shorts. After he's done using them. In the sauna."

Kiera and Jenny emerged from the bathrooms then, so I grabbed my girl and left Evan to chew on that. As we were walking away, I heard him shout, "You are one sick individual, Kyle!"

I raised my fist into the air in response. Kiera peeked up at me with curious eyes. "Do I want to know what that was about?"

"No, probably not." I gave her a wink, which made her bite her lip in such a sensual way that I instantly forgot all about Evan and Jenny. Squeezing Kiera's hand, I leaned down and whispered in her ear, "Come dance with me, beautiful."

Her cheeks turned a gorgeous shade of rose as she nodded. Leading the way, I pushed us back out to the dance floor and wrapped my arms around her waist again. The song was quicker paced than how we were dancing, but I didn't care. I wanted to slow dance with my girl. The DJ could kiss my ass.

I watched Kiera while she watched the crowd. She was so attractive with her hair pulled up into a ponytail, and a tight tank top on under a cream-colored see-through shirt. I wanted to be doing much more than dancing, but the restraint only added to the anticipation. This was technically only our second date, so I wasn't even going to kiss her tonight. A proper gentleman waited for the third date. Or at least, that sounded good in my head.

A look of surprise crossed over Kiera's emerald eyes, and I scanned the crowd to try to see what she'd seen. When she nudged my shoulder and flicked her head toward Evan and Jenny, I looked over at them. Was he finally kissing her? No, but they had their foreheads resting together, and Evan was playing with her hair while she gazed at him like he was the only person left on earth. He might still be resisting, but it wouldn't be much longer now. Good. I shouldn't be the only one feeling this amazing.

I was nervous for Kiera's and my next date. This was the one…lucky number three. I was going to kiss her, but I didn't want it to go too far. Just a kiss. That was it. I didn't want to get swept away—and at the same time, I really *did* want to get swept away. Not yet though. We still needed to keep this slow and steady.

After I walked her to her door, I asked if I could kiss her. With a smile bright enough to light the whole city, she murmured, "Yes."

My heart was racing as we leaned into each other, and all I kept thinking was *Keep it short, keep it simple.* Our lips briefly pressed together, and I instantly pulled away. There. Gentlemanly. Kiera wasn't as gentlemanly though. Reaching out, she grabbed my neck and pulled me into her again. As our mouths moved together, my thoughts shifted to *Yes…God, yes.* It took a lot of willpower, but we left it as a long, passionate kiss, and I was breathless when I walked away. *Damn.* Going slow was going to be harder than I thought.

Once we started kissing again, we both practiced a lot of restraint every time we saw each other, whether we were at her school, at the park, at her place, mine, or eventually, back at Pete's. Thankfully, it didn't take long for Kiera to quit her job at a diner in Pioneer Square and come back to the bar.

When Kiera returned to Pete's, I made damn sure everyone knew there was nothing hidden about our relationship: I gave her a heart-stopping kiss right in the middle of the bar. She was mine. And if anyone tried to take her from me, I would have their head. Maybe I was a bit too possessive now, but I'd tried sharing once, and I didn't care for it. Not one tiny little bit.

Kiera was breathless and red-faced when we pulled apart, but she didn't chide me for the very public display of affection. I'd wanted this from the beginning, and she knew that. With a nod and a smile, she gave me a brief kiss before walking to the back room. My eyes swept the crowd, looking for a challenge. I didn't find one.

Evan clapped me on the shoulder once I joined the band at our table. "You've developed a flair for the dramatic. I'm not sure if that's a good thing or a bad thing."

I smiled at him as I sat down. "And you've become the biggest procrastinator I know." I leaned forward so I could shout at Griffin at the end of the table. "Hey, you've still got those spandex shorts, right?" Griffin gave me a thumbs-up.

Matt's expression turned horrified, like I'd just asked Griffin for his jock strap. "What the hell do you want with those things, Kellan?"

He put his hand on my forehead, like he was taking my temperature. Evan tossed a crumpled napkin in my face. "Jerk. I think I liked you better when you were sprawled across the table, piss-ass drunk."

My eyes drifted over to Kiera as she reemerged from the back room in her red Pete's T-shirt. "Don't count on that happening again anytime soon," I told Evan. *All is right with the world again.*

But everything being right didn't mean that everything was perfect. Kiera and I had issues. We had insecurities. We even occasionally had doubts. But we did our best to talk them out, to work through them instead of burying them.

The universe made that challenging at times. A half-naked woman showing up on my doorstep brought a hefty dose of tension into the relationship. I asked her to leave and never come back, but after shutting the door on the disappointed woman, I turned to Kiera with a knot of dread in my stomach.

Her eyes were dark with suspicion, and I clearly knew what she was thinking—*What would you have done if I hadn't been here?* I answered the question in her eyes before she could even verbalize it. "In case you're wondering, yes, I would have done exactly what I just did if you weren't here. I only want you."

Impressing the hell out of me, Kiera let it go. If the situation were reversed, I think I would have reacted differently. In fact, sometimes *I* was the one who lost it. She came across me one day while I was staring at the closed door leading into the bedroom she'd once shared with Denny and thinking dark thoughts that I shouldn't have been thinking.

Maybe seeing my troubled expression, Kiera wrapped her arms around me and asked, "Everything okay?"

Not wanting to fight about things that didn't matter anymore, I turned from the door and started heading downstairs. "Yeah, fine."

She followed me, and at the bottom of the stairs, she grabbed my elbow. Searching my face, she said, "You're not okay. What's wrong?"

With a harsh swallow, I considered telling her that nothing was wrong, but swallowing my pain wouldn't help it go away, so I instead said, "It's just...I have to look at that damn door every day, and remember...that's where you had sex with another man. And sometimes, it's just too much."

I pulled away from her, but she held on tight. "I know. Trust me, when I look at that door—"

I didn't want to be angry with her, but her words stung. "It's not the same for you as it is for me!"

She bristled at my tone of voice. "Maybe *that* room isn't the same for me as it is for you...but I have to deal with the ghosts of all of your women every time I go in *your* room. Do you think that's easy for me?"

I understood where she was coming from, but I was in a dark place, and in no mood to be understanding. "I didn't take a woman to my bed after I told you I loved you. I stayed faithful to you...but you...you fucked him. You fucked him right after our perfect afternoon together. Well, it was perfect for me, but it must not have meant shit to you, because you fucked him, Kiera!"

Every time I swore, my voice got angrier and more intense. Kiera's cheeks flushed and her eyes watered. "Don't do this, Kellan. Don't open that door. I've already apologized, and you said you understood. I was...confused."

"I do understand! That's what makes it so fucked up. I under-

535

stand, but that doesn't make it any easier." A tear rolled down her cheek and regret washed over me. I hadn't meant to bring it up…I wanted to let the past go, I really did. Sinking my head into my hands, I muttered, "I'm sorry. I'm not trying to be a dick, it just…it hurts, Kiera. It really fucking hurts."

I felt the darkness and anger shifting into pain. I wished that had gone away the second Kiera and I had become a couple, but every once in a while, agony reared its ugly head. Kiera made multiple quiet apologies in my ear as she tried to put her arms around me. For a second, I didn't let her, but then I caved, because I knew I had to let this go if we were going to move forward. And I wanted to move forward with her…so much.

Letting go wasn't something that happened all at once though. It was a gradual process, with giant steps forward, and then a few steps back. We'd be happy and content, doting on each other, stealing soft kisses at Pete's, then all of a sudden, something would happen to disturb our peace…like a couple of girls inviting me out right in front of Kiera.

I knew by the look on Kiera's face that trouble was brewing, so I turned the girls down and hopped onstage as fast as I could. For the remainder of her shift, Kiera acted like everything was fine, but afterward, in the parking lot, she made a snide comment that I had almost been expecting. "Should we stop by the store on the way home? I think we're out of whipped cream."

Stopping in my tracks, I stared at her watery eyes. I knew she was upset, and I knew exactly what her comment was referencing. "I turned them down, Kiera. I always turn all of them down. You don't have anything to worry about."

She looked back at the bar, and a tear rolled down her cheek. "You didn't that night…"

I closed my eyes and a sigh escaped me. I'd known that night would eventually come back to bite me in the ass. "Kiera…"

Her eyes flashed back to mine. "I had to listen to you have an orgy, Kellan. That…hurt."

Guilt made me say something stupid. Stepping closer to her, I snapped out, "And I had to watch you leave the club with Denny. You left to go screw him while pretending he was me! If you want to discuss being hurt…then let's talk about how much *that* hurt!"

And we did. For hours, we discussed the myriad ways we'd tortured each other. And then, when the angry fire between us was doused, we went over to Kiera's place and cuddled on her couch until we fell asleep in each other's arms. Kissing her hair before I dozed off, I told her how sorry I was, and how much I loved her, and she repeated the feelings back to me. And that was how we healed, how we found balance. We allowed ourselves to get angry, to bring up things that had hurt us, over and over again if we needed to. We talked them out instead of brushing them aside, until eventually, the painful conversations became fewer and farther between, and the good parts of our new relationship became larger and more important.

Kiera and I still weren't having sex, but we weren't exactly keeping our hands off each other either. We were frequently in some stage of undress—my shirt, her shirt, something always seemed to be missing when we were alone. And while I loved bringing Kiera to the breaking point, then playfully pulling back and telling her we needed to slow down, I was ready to be with her again, and the painful need of wanting her was only growing every time we touched.

A part of me wanted to push us both past the point of no return, but a larger part wanted it to be something we talked about and were ready for, both emotionally and physically. And I didn't want to be the one to bring it up. It might seem like coercion if it came from me. I wanted Kiera to approach me. I wanted her to be bold enough, and confident enough, to tell me that she was ready to make love to me.

Evan thought it was odd we were waiting, but seeing as he hadn't even kissed Jenny yet, he didn't have room to talk. I was just about to put that intervention together when Kiera approached me at Pete's one night with red cheeks and a stunned expression. "You are not going to believe who I just walked in on in the back room."

I had a pretty good idea who it might be, since their flirting had ramped up recently, but I played dumb so I could tease Kiera. "Um...Anna and Griffin?" I raised an eyebrow. "Do you need me to scrub your eyes for you?" My gaze drifted down her body. "Or I could scrub somewhere else, if you prefer?"

Her cheeks turned a darker shade as she rapped my shoulder. "No..." Her face brightened again. "Evan and Jenny! They've been flirting a lot lately, but they were totally kissing and...stuff..."

She looked away and I wondered what all they'd been doing back there. Good for them. And about freaking time. With a laugh, I told her, "I've been waiting for that one."

Evan rejoined the table before it was time to go onstage. I simply smiled as I stared at him. He ignored me for a long time, then with a sigh, he looked my way and asked in a flat voice, "What?"

Putting my elbows on the table, I leaned forward. "Anything you want to say to me?"

With a sniff, he looked down at my shirt. "I don't think brown is your color." My smile not diminishing, I patiently waited until his eyes returned to mine. He sighed again. "Kiera told you she saw us, didn't she?" Grinning wider, I nodded. Evan rolled his eyes, then muttered, "Okay...you were right."

Putting a finger against my ear, I tilted my head and said, "What was that?"

He narrowed his dark eyes at me. "You were right. Fucker." He broke into a goofy, love-struck smile. "I like her."

Laughing, I leaned back in my chair. "Yeah, I know." As he was shaking his head, I added, "Hey, Evan...Told you so." He flipped me off.

I still played the emotional song that I'd written for Kiera at every show. Like always, I tuned out the world and sang it directly to Kiera. She cried every single time, which warmed my heart. A part of me had thought she'd been fine during our breakup, but she'd moped, cried, and thrown herself into schoolwork. She'd been just as torn up inside. It gave me peace that it had been just as hard on her as it had been on me.

One night, when her song ended, I hopped off the stage and rushed over to her. I had to wade through a sea of wandering fingers and eager mouths to do it, but I eventually reached her more or less unscathed. With a smile, she shook her head at my antics, but then my lips were on hers, and she didn't have time to do anything other than kiss me back. The crowd erupted into screams and whistles while I held her face against mine. I think a large chunk of the audience thought it was part of the act, and that they might get a shot with me later, but that absolutely wasn't happening.

"Your place tonight?" I asked after I finally pulled away from her.

Biting her lip, she nodded. Then she swatted my bottom and pushed me back toward the stage. Tease. I finished out the rest of the performance imagining her legs wrapped around me, her fingers in my hair, and her breathless moans in my ear. I couldn't wait to be alone with her.

It was hours later, but eventually we stepped through the door of the apartment Kiera shared with Anna. I wondered how long she'd stay here with her sister, but like sex, moving in together was something I didn't want to rush. When the time felt right, it would happen.

Walking into their small living space, I ran my fingers over the back of the comfortable chair I'd given Kiera. Coming up behind me, she wrapped her arms around my waist. "I was so surprised you gave that to me. And happy. And sad." I twisted to look at her and she shrugged. "It reminded me of you."

I nodded. "Everything reminded me of you, but that still wasn't enough. I needed something permanent." I patted the tattoo over my heart and stared into her eyes. She was my everything.

Kiera's eyes misted. "You astound me," she said, slipping off my jacket.

"There's nothing special about me," I said, helping her with my coat.

With a smirk, she pulled on the bottom of my shirt, leading us to the hallway. "I know about fifty thousand girls who would disagree with that assessment."

I raised an eyebrow at her. "Fifty thousand? My, my, I've been busy."

When her back was to her bedroom door, she yanked me into her. "Not everything revolves around sex, Kellan."

Stepping forward, I pressed my body along the length of hers. "I know."

Her mouth parted and she tilted her head up, like she wanted me to kiss her. I bent down like I was going to, but then I opened the door to her room and we both stumbled inside. Giggling, Kiera called me a brat while I kicked the door closed with my foot. My mouth went to her neck and my arms wrapped around her waist. She stopped laughing with a small, satisfied sigh. God, I loved holding her, touching her... being with her.

My lips worked their way up to her mouth. Her touch was so soft, so sweet. I had never kissed anyone else with lips quite like hers. They made my head spin, left me breathless. They filled my every waking moment, began my every fantasy, and ended my every dream. Those wonderful, erotic lips...

While our mouths moved together, our bodies began shuffling toward the futon that she was using as a bed. When her legs hit the edge of it, I leaned over, forcing her to sit on it. We broke apart just long enough for her to kick off her shoes and scoot onto the middle of the bed. She gave me a minute to take off my boots, then her hand snaked out for my shirt and pulled me back to her. I laughed as our mouths reconnected. "So aggressive today... I like it."

She laughed in my mouth as her fingers darted under my shirt. "I just missed you."

That made me laugh. We'd spent a good chunk of the day and night together. We'd been apart for maybe a few hours in the middle, when she went to work and I'd met with the guys, but it hadn't lasted very long. Rolling her onto her back, I hovered over the top of her. "I missed you too." I was getting harder and harder by the second.

Kiera started pulling on my shirt, so I reached back and removed it one-handed. As I twisted to toss it on her floor, she began tracing my tattoo. Smiling, I studied the serenity on her face. When I got the tattoo, I never imagined Kiera would see it. And I definitely never thought her fingers would be stroking the swirling letters of her name. I liked it. A lot.

With peaceful, loving eyes, Kiera looked up at me. My heart squeezed as I looked down at her. *She's mine. I can't believe she's really mine.* I tenderly stroked my knuckle down her cheek, then leaned down to kiss her again.

"Kellan," she whispered, right before our lips touched. I pulled back to gaze at her, and she swallowed. "I want to...be with you," she whispered.

My body reacted to her words, but I couldn't help teasing her for her vagueness. Placing a tender kiss on the corner of her mouth, I murmured, "You're with me all the time."

I ran my fingers across her shoulder, down her ribs. She shivered, then squirmed. "You know that's not what I meant," she whispered.

I shifted our position so I was more firmly on top of her, and her leg wrapped around mine, holding me in place. I felt fire surging throughout my body. I wanted so much more, but I held back, teasing her and myself. Running my tongue up the side of her neck, I murmured, "I have no idea what you're talking about. What is it that you want?"

My hand drifted up her shirt, my thumb circled her nipple; it was fully erect under her thin bra. Her breath was heavier when she answered me. "I want you."

My lips ghosted over hers. "You have me."

She gasped when our mouths almost touched but didn't. I pressed my hips into her, momentarily satisfying the ache building between us. Or maybe I was making it worse. Sometimes it was hard to tell. Kiera moaned and clutched my neck. Her fingers tangled into the back of my hair, sending jolts of electricity down my back. "Kellan...I want you...now."

My hand slid down her stomach to the waistband of her shorts as I moved to her side. With one hand, I unbuttoned them and tucked my fingers inside. Her other hand reached up to my shoulder, and her nails dug into my flesh so deep I was sure I had marks. *God, I loved that.*

She was panting as my fingers inched lower and lower. "You have me, now and always," I whispered in her ear.

She squirmed under my touch. "Yes, please, yes."

God, I loved it when she begged. Praying I could keep it together long enough to tease her, I let my fingers slide against her. She cried out when I touched her. She was so fucking wet. For me. All for me. "You already have me, so what is it you really want, baby?" I wanted this, but I needed her to be specific. I needed her to be sure she was ready. I certainly was.

I stroked against her in slow, teasing circles. She gripped me harder, squirming against me. "You...I want..."

I contained a groan as her words, her sounds, and the look on her face nearly undid me. Dipping a finger inside her, I softly asked, "You want this?"

She answered with incoherent groans and murmurings that sort of sounded like yes. Smiling, I kissed her throat. Kiera turned her head and found my mouth. She attacked me with eager, hungry kisses that made me want to rip her clothes off and plunge inside her.

Instead, I asked again, "What do you want to do to me, Kiera?"

She started groaning and moving in a rhythm that let me know she was close. I wanted her to say it before she came though, so I begged her, "Please tell me...please."

She made a noise laced with frustration, then she reached down and pulled my hand away from her. She was breathing hard as she stared at me. Surprisingly, my breath was fast too. "Why did you stop me?" I asked her.

Gazing at me, she took a deep inhale before settling into a peaceful smile. "Because I want to make love to you. I want to have a glorious release *with* you, not separate from you."

I gave her a lingering kiss. *That's exactly what I've been waiting to hear.* "I love you so much, Kiera. I'm so happy you're with me."

542

She kissed my forehead. "I feel the same, Kellan. I feel *exactly* the same. I don't want to ever go back to being without you. I love you too much to go back."

I smiled wider as the warmth of the moment washed over me. "You never have to. I'm yours as long as you want me."

She giggled. "Well, you already know how much I want you."

I laughed, then kissed her jaw. Then the moment turned more serious, and I knew it was time. We were ready. Recalling everything we'd gone through, everything she meant to me, I softly sang the emotional song I had written about her while I finished undressing us. Her eyes were wet with unshed tears, and my heart was in my throat as my fingers ran over her exposed, silky skin. There was nothing between us now but love. *This* was how it should have been, from the very beginning.

With one arm around her waist, I laid her back on the bed. Before joining her, I stopped and stared, awed at what I was seeing. This beautiful creature was mine, heart and soul. She wasn't a dream, she wasn't a fantasy, and she wouldn't evaporate the minute this was over. She was ready to love me, ready to be loved by me, and only me. And although she had her flaws, just as I did, she was perfect in my eyes—a goddess.

My mouth trailed slow kisses over her body. Every soft gasp, light moan, and gentle scrape of her fingernails over my skin ignited me. But knowing I no longer had to share this intimate moment with anyone else inflamed me. I wanted her, always.

As her soft hands explored my skin, mine traveled over her curves. When we could both take no more teasing, I shifted my body over hers. Her name washed over my lips as I slid myself into her, and the absolute euphoria of reconnecting was nothing compared to the emotional bond strengthening between us. We were free, no more barriers.

Gently, I pulled back, then sank into her again; we both cried out in unison. *Heaven.* As we began to effortlessly move together, I told her how beautiful she was, how much I'd missed her, how much I needed her, how empty I'd been without her. Every phrase that left my lips grew more impassioned as the fire between us spiked. But then the words "Don't leave…I don't want to be alone" slipped out of my mouth. It was embarrassing, but I couldn't stop myself from saying it. Not being with her was my greatest fear. My *only* fear.

The memory of who I was before she came into my life, exactly a year ago, pounded through my brain—the loneliness, the desperation to connect—I couldn't go back to that emptiness. I wouldn't survive it. "I don't want to be alone anymore," I muttered, barely conscious of saying it. *I don't want to be without you anymore. Ever.*

Her expression full of confidence and compassion, Kiera grabbed my face and told me she wouldn't ever leave me. Then she kissed me as fiercely as she could, pouring her heart into the action. I twisted our bodies so we were facing each other as we continued making love. And even though we were as close as two people could get, I pulled her tighter. "I don't want to be without you," I whispered.

"I'm right here, Kellan." Grabbing my hand, she placed it over her heart. "I'm with you…I'm right here."

Having everything I'd ever wanted laid out in front of me was too much, too powerful. I didn't know how to handle the vast amount of love and joy churning within me, and I was momentarily struck with terror that it would all crumble to dust in an instant. But I knew her words were honest and true, and I found some comfort in them.

My hand over Kiera's heart seared her hope and love into me, relaxing me. She placed her fingers over my heart, and I hoped she felt my love pouring into her too. I got lost in the rhythm of our bodies, the smell of her wrapped around me, the softness of where our skin touched. And, above it all, the rising tide of bliss that was quickly overtaking me. I knew I was getting close, but I didn't want to feel this life-altering moment on my own, so cupping her cheek, I begged her to finish *with* me. Still teetering on an emotional cliff, I also told her that I didn't want to be alone again.

She told me I wasn't alone anymore, then she completely fell apart. Experiencing her response, both verbal and physical, pushed me over the edge. At the peak of the moment, we locked eyes, and the entire world seemed to come to a stop. And in that moment, all of my lingering fears vanished. I wasn't alone. We were in this *together* now—100 percent.

Our first time together as a genuine couple was one of those pebble-in-the-pond moments that I knew I would remember for the rest of my life. And it was only the first of many, many moments that we were going to share together. Hopefully, it was the beginning of a lifetime together. Because that was what I wanted with her. Forever.

And a lifetime together actually seemed possible now. Several things were seeming possible lately. Matt had gotten confirmation about Bumbershoot. We were gonna rock the festival this summer, and who knew where that might lead. Denny and I continued to be on speaking terms. He even knew that Kiera and I were officially together, and he was still cordial with me. The other D-Bags were doing well. Rachel and Matt were still together, and so were Evan and Jenny. Griffin and Anna were…well, they were happy with whatever they were doing with each other. And Kiera and I…we were progressing at a steady pace, and I'd never been happier in all my life. Yes. Things were definitely looking up.

I'd never really given much thought to my future before now. I guess I'd never really believed I would have one, or one with any true significance or meaning. But now, so many things seemed possible to me, and those possibilities gave my life new meaning and purpose. I was actually excited to see what might happen next. I just prayed to God that I didn't do anything stupid to screw it all up. I supposed only time would tell, but with Kiera by my side I felt good about my odds. I felt good about *our* odds. And for the first time, I was beginning to believe that my parents had been wrong about me. Sure, I might make mistakes, I might do things I shouldn't, I might stumble and fall, and I might even hurt people in the process, but I was going to be just fine. We all were.

Acknowledgements

This book would not exist without the support of my fans, so my first thank-you goes to you! And much love goes out to my core readers from the very first place I ever published anything— Fictionpress.com. The group of you cheering me on in the beginning of my hobby-that-turned-into-a-career was what kept me going! The numerous books that followed *Thoughtless* would not have happened without your daily encouragement.

I want to thank all the authors who have supported and inspired me, especially: K.A. Linde, Nicky Charles, J. Sterling, Rebecca Donovan, Jillian Dodd, C.J. Roberts, Kristen Proby, Tara Sivec, Nicole Williams, Tarryn Fisher, A.L. Jackson, Tina Reber, Laura Dunaway, Katie Ashley, Karina Halle, Christina Lauren, Alice Clayton, Colleen Hoover, Abbi Glines, Jamie McGuire, Tammara Webber, Jessica Park, Emma Chase, Katy Evans, K. Bromberg, Kim Karr, Jessica Sorensen, Jodi Ellen Malpas, Lisa Renee Jones, T. Gephart, Gail McHugh, and many, many more! And I want to thank all the authors who loved my characters enough to ask me if they could invite them into their worlds. It always makes me smile to see the D-Bags roaming throughout other stories.

To my lovely, devoted, and hardworking group of beta readers—THANK YOU!!!!! Your help over the years has been invaluable to me, as has your willingness to fit me into your lives on really short notice! You're amazing! And I appreciate all of you so much!

I want to thank the bloggers who have passionately shouted their love of my stories: *Totally Booked, Maryse's Book Blog, Flirty and Dirty Book Blog, Tough Critic Book Reviews, The Autumn Review, SubClub Books, Martini Times Romance, Brandee's Book Endings, Crazies R Us Book Blog, Shh Mom's Reading, Kayla the Bibliophile, Nose Stuck in a Book, Chicks Controlled by Books, Fictional Men's Page, Fictional Boyfriends, A Literary Perusal, Sizzling Pages Romance Reviews, My Secret Romance Book Reviews, Madison Says, The Rock Stars of Romance, Literati Literature Lovers, Aestas Book Blog, The Book Bar, Schmexy Girl Book Blog, Angie's Dreamy Reads, Bookslapped, Three Chicks and Their Books, We Like It Big Book Blog, The Little Black Book Blog, Natasha Is a Book Junkie, Love N. Books, Ana's Attic Book Blog, Bibliophile Productions, Sammie's Book Club*, and countless more! You are all one of the major reasons why anyone even knows who I am!

I'd like to extend a special thank-you to all the various members of Team Kellan aka #SexyKK, for always being up to the challenge of campaigning Kellan for whatever he's been nominated for. The craziness is so much fun to watch, and the fan art is so creative and beautiful. Since I can't Photoshop to save my life, I'm constantly impressed by the artwork you all create. And what can I say...the #BeggingSC campaign worked! Hope you love this book as much as I loved writing it!

Thank you to my incredible, fantastic—patient—superagent, Kristyn Keene of ICM Partners. Your advice, support, and encouragement are greatly appreciated! And a heartfelt thank-you to Beth deGuzman at Forever, for being such a huge supporter of my work, and Megha Parekh, editor extraordinaire, for polishing *Thoughtful* into the beautiful story it is today. I would also like to thank Lalone Marketing, The Occasionalist, JT Formatting, Debra Stang, Okay Creations, Toski Covey Photography, and Tara Ellis

Photography, for all their help in designing and/or promoting me and my books.

On a personal note, I want to thank my family and friends for their endless support and for their patience and understanding of my wacky schedule, especially my children, who sometimes struggle with Mommy being home but unavailable. I love you all very much!

And lastly, I need to thank Kellan Kyle. You may be fictional, but you completely changed my life, and for that, I owe you everything.